THE
CURSE
WORKERS

THE CURSE WORKERS

HOLLY BLACK

MARGARET K. McELDERRY BOOKS

NEW YORK   LONDON   TORONTO   SYDNEY   NEW DELHI

MARGARET K. McELDERRY BOOKS
An imprint of Simon & Schuster Children's Publishing Division
1230 Avenue of the Americas, New York, New York 10020
For information about special discounts for bulk purchases, please contact Simon & Schuster Special Sales at 1-866-506-1949 or business@simonandschuster.com.
The Simon & Schuster Speakers Bureau can bring authors to your live event. For more information or to book an event, contact the Simon & Schuster Speakers Bureau at 1-866-248-3049 or visit our website at www.simonspeakers.com.
The text for this book is set in Cambria.
Manufactured in the United States of America
First Margaret K. McElderry Books edition November 2021
10 9 8 7 6 5 4 3 2 1
CIP data for this book is available from the Library of Congress.
ISBN 9781534488199 (hc)
ISBN 9781534488182 (pbk)
ISBN 9781534488205 (ebook)
These titles were previously published individually.

CONTENTS

WHITE CAT

For all the fictional cats
I've killed in other books.

I'M DREAMING OF A

cat with bone white fur. It's leaning over me, inhaling as if it's trying to suck the breath from my lungs. It bites out my tongue instead. There's no pain, only a sense of over-whelming, suffocating panic. In the dream, my tongue is a wriggling red thing, mouse-size and wet. I want it back. But the cat is carrying it away in her mouth, padding toward a partially ajar door. I spring up out of my bed and grab for her, but she's too lean and too quick. She runs. I give chase.

I wake barefoot, teetering on the cold tiles of a slate roof. Looking dizzily down, I suck in a breath of icy air. The dream still clings to me, like cobwebs of memory. My heart thunders.

Being a sleepwalker is being at war with your unconscious. It wants you to do things you did not consent to do. It wants to take you places you never agreed to go. For instance, my unconscious appears to be steering me straight to an early grave.

Above me are stars. Below me, the bronze statue of Colonel Wallingford makes me realize I'm seeing the quad from the peak of Smythe Hall, my dorm.

I have no memory of climbing the stairs up to the roof. I don't even know *how* to get where I am, which is a problem since I'm going to have to get down, ideally in a way that doesn't involve dying.

Teetering, I will myself to be as still as possible. Not to inhale too sharply. To grip the slate with my toes. To fight down the rising tide of panic.

The night is quiet, the kind of hushed middle-of-the-night quiet that makes every shuffle or nervous panting breath sound loud. When the black outlines of trees overhead rustle, I jerk in surprise. My foot slides on something slick. Moss.

I try to steady myself, but my legs go out from under me.

I scrabble for something to hold on to as my bare chest slams down on the slate. My palm comes down hard on a sharp bit of copper flashing, but I hardly feel the pain. Kicking out, my foot finds a snow guard, and I press my toes against it, halting my fall. I laugh with relief, even though I am shaking so badly that climbing is out of the question.

Cold makes my fingers numb. The adrenaline rush makes my brain sing.

"Help," I say softly, and feel crazy nervous laughter bubble up my throat as the ridiculousness of this moment commingles with terror. I bite the inside of my cheek to tamp it down.

I don't want to shout for help. I'm in my boxers. It will be embarrassing.

Looking across the roof in the dim light, I try to make out the pattern of snow guards, tiny triangular pieces of clear plastic that keep ice from falling in a sheet, tiny triangular pieces that were never meant to hold my weight. If I can get closer to a window, maybe I can climb down.

I edge my foot out, shifting as slowly as I can and worming toward the nearest snow guard. My stomach scrapes against the slate, some of the tiles chipped and uneven beneath me. I step onto the first guard, then down to another and across to one at the edge of the roof. There, panting, with the windows too far beneath me, nowhere left to go, and no plan, I decide I am not willing to die from embarrassment.

I suck in three deep breaths of cold air and yell.

"Hey! Hey! Help!" The night absorbs my voice. I hear the distant swell of engines along the highway, but nothing from the windows below me.

"HEY!" I scream it this time, guttural, as loudly as I can, loud enough that the words scrape my throat raw. *"Help!"*

A light flickers on in one of the rooms and I see the press of palms against a glass pane. A moment later the window slides open. "Hello?" someone calls sleepily from below. For a moment her voice reminds me of another girl. A dead girl.

I hang my head off the side and try to give my most chagrined smile. Like she shouldn't freak out. "Up here," I say. "On the roof."

"Oh, my God," Justine Moore gasps.

Willow Davis comes to the window. "I'm getting the hall master."

I press my cheek against the cold tile and try to convince myself that everything's okay, that no one worked me, I haven't been cursed, and that if I just hang on a little longer, things are going to be fine.

A crowd gathers below me, spilling out of the dorms.

"Jump," some jerk shouts. "Do it!"

"Mr. Sharpe?" Dean Wharton calls. "Come down from there at once, Mr. Sharpe!" His silver hair sticks up like he's been electrocuted, and his robe is inside out and badly tied. The whole school can see his tighty-whities.

Of course, he's not the only one in his underwear. If he looks ridiculous, I look worse.

"Only one way down," I call back. "That's the problem."

"Cassel!" Ms. Noyes yells. "Cassel, don't jump! I know things have been hard..." She stops there, like she isn't quite sure what to say next. She's probably trying to remember what's so hard. I have good grades. Play well with others. Maybe she figures anyone with a mother in prison and a brother in the mob has to have problems.

I look down again. Camera phones flash. Freshmen hang

out of windows next door in Strong House, and juniors and seniors stand around on the grass in their pajamas and nightgowns, even though teachers are desperately trying to herd them back inside.

I give my best grin and wave, like this is all some enormous prank. "Cheese," I say softly.

I wish my unconscious mind had thought to bring spray paint. If it had, I would have been a legend.

"Get down, Mr. Sharpe," yells Dean Wharton. "I'm warning you!"

"I'm okay, Ms. Noyes," I call, ignoring Wharton. "I don't know how I got up here. I think I was sleepwalking."

A siren wails in the distance, drawing closer. My cheeks hurt from smiling.

———⟡———

The last time I was in the headmistress's office, my grandfather was there with me to enroll me at the school. I remember watching him empty a crystal dish of peppermints into the pocket of his coat while Dean Wharton talked about what a fine young man I would be turned into. The crystal dish went into the opposite pocket.

Wrapped in a blanket, I sit in the same green leather chair and pick at the gauze covering my palm. A fine young man indeed.

"Sleepwalking?" Dean Wharton says. He's dressed in a brown tweed suit, but his hair is still wild. He stands near a shelf of outdated encyclopedias and strokes a gloved finger over their crumbling leather spines.

I notice there's a new cheap glass dish of mints on the

desk. My head is pounding. I wish the mints were aspirin.

"I used to sleepwalk," I say. "I haven't done it in a long time."

Somnambulism isn't all that uncommon in kids, boys especially. I looked it up online after waking in the driveway when I was thirteen, my lips blue with cold, unable to shake the eerie feeling that I'd just returned from somewhere I couldn't quite recall.

Outside the leaded glass windows the rising sun limns the trees with gold. The headmistress, Ms. Northcutt, looks puffy and red-eyed. She's drinking coffee out of a mug with the Wallingford logo on it and gripping it so tightly the leather of her gloves over her knuckles is pulled taut.

"I heard you've been having some problems with your girlfriend," Headmistress Northcutt says.

"No," I say. "Not at all." Audrey broke up with me after the winter holiday, exhausted by my secretiveness. It's impossible to have problems with a girlfriend who's no longer mine.

The headmistress clears her throat. "Some students think you are running a betting pool. Are you in some kind of trouble? Owe someone money?"

I look down and try not to smile at the mention of my tiny criminal empire. It's just a little forgery and some bookmaking. I'm not running a single con; I haven't even taken up my brother Philip's suggestion that we could be the school's main supplier for underage booze. I'm pretty sure the headmistress doesn't care about betting, but I'm glad she doesn't know that the most popular odds are on which teachers are hooking up. Northcutt and Wharton are a long shot, but that doesn't stop people laying cash on them. I shake my head.

"Have you experienced mood swings lately?" Dean Wharton asks.

"*No,*" I say.

"What about changes in appetite or sleep patterns?" He sounds like he's reciting the words from a book.

"The problem is my sleep patterns," I say.

"What do you mean?" asks Headmistress Northcutt, suddenly intent.

"Nothing! Just that I was *sleepwalking*, not trying to kill myself. And if I wanted to kill myself, I wouldn't throw myself off a roof. And if I *was* going to throw myself off a roof, I would put on some pants before I did it."

The headmistress takes a sip from her cup. She's relaxed her grip. "Our lawyer advised me that until a doctor can assure us that nothing like this will happen again, we can't allow you to stay in the dorms. You're too much of an insurance liability."

I thought that people would give me a lot of crap, but I never thought there would be any real consequences. I thought I was going to get a scolding. Maybe even a couple of demerits. I'm too stunned to say anything for a long moment. "But I didn't do anything wrong."

Which is stupid, of course. Things don't happen to people because they deserve them. Besides, I've done plenty wrong.

"Your brother Philip is coming to pick you up," Dean Wharton says. He and the headmistress exchange looks, and Wharton's hand goes unconsciously to his neck, where I see the colored cord and the outline of the amulet under his white shirt.

I get it. They're wondering if I've been worked. Cursed. It's not that big a secret that my grandfather was a death worker for the Zacharov family. He's got the blackened stubs where his fingers used to be to prove it. And if they read the paper, they know about my mother. It's not a big leap for Wharton and Northcutt to blame any and all strangeness concerning me on curse work.

"You can't kick me out for sleepwalking," I say, getting to my feet. "That can't be legal. Some kind of discrimination against—" I stop speaking as cold dread settles in my stomach. I seriously contemplate the possibility that I *was* cursed. I try to think back to whether someone brushed me with a hand, but I can't recall anyone touching me who wasn't clearly gloved.

"We haven't come to any determination about your future here at Wallingford yet." The headmistress leafs through some of the papers on her desk. The dean pours himself a coffee.

"I can still be a day student." I don't want to sleep in an empty house or crash with either of my brothers, but I will. I'll do whatever lets me keep my life the way it is.

"Go to your dorm and pack some things. Consider yourself on medical leave."

"Just until I get a doctor's note," I say.

Neither of them replies, and after a few moments of standing awkwardly, I head for the door.

Don't be too sympathetic. Here's the essential truth about me: I killed a girl when I was fourteen. Her name was Lila, she was my best friend, and I loved her. I killed her anyway. There's a lot of the murder that seems like a blur, but my brothers found me standing over her body with blood on my hands and a weird smile tugging at my mouth. What I remember most is the feeling I had looking down at Lila—the giddy glee of having gotten away with something.

No one knows I'm a murderer except my family. And me, of course.

I don't want to be that person, so I spend most of my time at school faking and lying. It takes a lot of effort to pretend you're something you're not. I don't think about what music I like; I think about what music I should like. When I had a girlfriend, I tried to convince her I was the guy she wanted me to be. When I'm in a crowd, I hang back until I can figure out how to make them laugh. Luckily, if there's one thing I'm good at, it's faking and lying.

I told you I'd done plenty wrong.

I pad, still barefoot, still wrapped in the scratchy fireman's blanket, across the sunlit quad and up to my dorm room. Sam Yu, my roommate, is looping a skinny tie around the collar of a wrinkled dress shirt when I walk through the door. He looks up, startled.

"I'm fine," I say wearily. "In case you were going to ask."

Sam's a horror film enthusiast who has covered our dorm room with bug-eyed alien masks and gore-spattered posters. His parents want him to go to MIT and from there to some profitable pharmaceuticals gig. He wants to do special effects for movies. Despite the facts that he's built like a bear and is obsessed with fake blood, he is too kind-hearted to inform them there's a disagreement about his future. I like to think we're sort of friends.

We don't hang out with many of the same people, which makes being sort of friends easier.

"I wasn't doing . . . whatever you think I was doing," I tell him. "I don't want to die or anything."

Sam smiles and pulls on his Wallingford gloves. "I was just going to say that it's a good thing you don't sleep commando."

I snort and drop onto my cot. The frame squeaks in protest. On the pillow next to my head rests a new envelope, marked with a code telling me a freshman wants to put fifty dollars on Victoria Quaroni to win the talent show. The odds are astronomical, but the money reminds me that someone's going to have to keep the books and pay out while I'm away.

Sam kicks the base of the footboard lightly. "You sure you're okay?"

I nod. I know I should tell him that I'm going home, that he's about to become one of those lucky guys with a single, but I don't want to disturb my own fragile sense of normalcy. "Just tired."

Sam picks up his backpack. "See you in class, crazy-man."

I raise my bandaged hand in farewell, then stop myself. "Hey, wait a sec."

Hand on the doorknob, he turns.

"I was just thinking . . . if I'm gone. Do you think you could let people keep dropping off the money here?" It bothers me to ask, simultaneously putting me in his debt and making the whole kicked-out thing real, but I'm not ready to give up the one thing I've got going for me at Wallingford.

He hesitates.

"Forget it," I say. "Pretend I never—"

He interrupts me. "Do I get a percentage?"

"Twenty-five," I say. "Twenty-five percent. But you're going to have to do more than just collect the money for that."

He nods slowly. "Yeah, okay."

I grin. "You're the most trustworthy guy I know."

"Flattery will get you everywhere," Sam says. "Except, apparently, off a roof."

"Nice," I say with a groan. I push myself off the bed and take a clean pair of itchy black uniform pants out of the dresser.

"So why would you be *gone*? They're not kicking you out, right? You could sue."

Pulling on the pants, I turn my face away, but I can't keep the unease out of my voice. Being from a family of criminals and con artists, legal action is the only kind of action I can't take. Northcutt and Wharton know it too. "No. I don't know. Let me set you up."

He nods. "Okay. What do I do?"

"I'll give you my notebook on point spreads, tallies, everything, and you just fill in whatever bets you get." I stand, pulling my desk chair over to the closet and hopping up on the seat. "Here." My fingers close on the notebook I taped above the door. I rip it down. Another one from sophomore year is still up there, from when business got big enough I could no longer rely on my pretty-good-but-not-photographic memory.

Sam half-smiles. I can tell he's amazed that he never noticed my hiding spot. "I think I can manage that."

The pages he's flipping through are records of all the bets made since the beginning of our junior year at Wallingford, and the odds on each. Bets on whether the mouse loose in Stanton Hall will be killed by Kevin Brown with his mallet, or by Dr. Milton with his bacon-baited traps, or be caught by Chaiyawat Terweil with his lettuce-filled and totally humane trap. (The odds favor the mallet.) On whether Amanda, Sharone, or Courtney would be cast as the female lead in *Pippin* and whether the lead would be taken down by her understudy. (Courtney got it; they're still in rehearsals.) On how many times a week "nut brownies with no nuts" will be served in the cafeteria.

Real bookies take a percentage, relying on a balanced book to guarantee a profit. Like, if someone puts down five bucks on a fight, they're really putting down four fifty, and the other fifty cents is going to the bookie. The bookie doesn't care who wins; he only cares that the odds work so he can use the money from the losers to pay the winners. I'm not a real bookie. Kids at Wallingford want to bet on silly stuff, stuff that might never come true. They have money to burn. So some of the time I calculate the odds the right way—the real bookie way—and some of the time I calculate the odds my way and just hope I get to pocket everything instead of paying out what I can't afford. You could say that I'm gambling too.

"Remember," I say, "cash only. No credit cards; no watches."

He rolls his eyes. "Are you seriously telling me someone thinks you have a credit card machine up in here?"

"No," I say. "They want you to take their card and buy something that costs what they owe. Don't do it; it looks like you stole their card, and believe me, that's what they'll tell their parents."

Sam hesitates. "Yeah," he says finally.

"Okay," I say. "There's a new envelope on the desk. Don't forget to mark down *everything*." I know I'm nagging, but I can't tell him that I need the money I make. It's not easy to go to a school like this without money for all the extras no one talks about, like clothes and books and off-campus pizza. Not to mention that I'm the only seventeen-year-old at Wallingford without a car.

I motion to him to hand me the book.

Just as I'm taping it into place, someone raps loudly on the door, causing me to nearly topple over. Before I can say anything, it opens, and our hall master walks in. He looks like he's half-expecting to find me threading a noose out of my bedclothes.

I hop down from the chair. "I was just—"

"Thanks for getting down my bag," Sam says.

"Samuel Yu," says Mr. Valerio. "I'm fairly sure that breakfast is over and classes have started."

"I *bet* you're right," Sam says, with a smirk in my direction.

I could con Sam if I wanted to. I'd do it just this way, asking for his help, offering him a little profit at the same time. Take him for a chunk of his parents' cash. I could con Sam, but I won't.

Really, I won't.

As the door clicks shut behind Sam, Valerio turns to me. "Your brother can't come until tomorrow morning, so you're going to have to attend classes with the rest of the students. We're still discussing where you'll be spending the night."

"You can always tie my wrists to the bedposts," I say, but Valerio doesn't find that very funny.

My mother explained the basics of the con around the same time she explained about curse work. For her the curse was how she got what she wanted and the con was how she got away with it. I can't make people love or hate instantly, like she can, turn their bodies against them like Philip can, or take their luck away like my other brother, Barron, but you don't need to be a worker to be a con artist.

For me the curse is a crutch, but the con is everything.

It was my mother who taught me that if you're going to screw someone over—with magic and wit, or wit alone—you have to know the mark better than he knows himself.

The first thing you have to do is gain his confidence. Charm him. Just be sure he thinks he's smarter than you. Then you—or, ideally, your partner—suggest the score.

Let your mark get something right up front the first time. In the business that's called the "convincer." When he knows he's already got money in his pocket and can walk away, that's when he relaxes his guard.

The second go is when you introduce bigger stakes. The big score. This is the part my mother never has to worry about. As an emotion worker, she can make anyone trust her. But she still needs to go through the steps, so that later, when they think back on it, they don't figure out she worked them.

After that there's only the blow-off and the getaway.

Being a con artist means thinking that you're smarter than everyone else and that you've thought of everything. That you can get away with anything. That you can con anyone.

I wish I could say that I don't think about the con when I deal with people, but the difference between me and my mother is that I don't con myself.

I ONLY HAVE ENOUGH

time to pull on my uniform and run to French class; breakfast is long over. Wallingford television crackles to life as I dump my books onto my desk. Sadie Flores announces from the screen that during activities period the Latin club will be having a bake sale to support their building a small outdoor grotto, and that the rugby team will meet inside the gymnasium. I manage to stumble through my classes until I actually fall asleep during history. I wake abruptly with drool wetting the sleeve of my shirt and Mr. Lewis asking, "What year was the ban put into effect, Mr. Sharpe?"

"Nineteen twenty-nine," I mumble. "Nine years after Prohibition started. Right before the stock market crashed."

"Very good," he says unhappily. "And can you tell me why the ban hasn't been repealed like Prohibition?"

I wipe my mouth. My headache hasn't gotten any better. "Uh, because the black market supplies people with curse work anyway?"

A couple of people laugh, but Mr. Lewis isn't one of them. He points toward the board, where a jumble of chalk reasons are written. Something about economic initiatives and a trade agreement with the European Union. "Apparently you can do lots of things very nimbly while asleep, Mr. Sharpe, but attending my class does not seem to be one of them."

He gets the bigger laugh. I stay awake for the rest of the period, although several times I have to jab myself with a pen to do it.

I go back to my dorm and sleep through the period when I should be getting help from teachers in classes where I'm struggling, through track practice, and through the debate team meeting. Waking up halfway through dinner, I feel the rhythm of my normal life receding, and I have no idea how to get it back.

Wallingford Preparatory is a lot like how I pictured it when my brother Barron brought home the brochure. The lawns are less green and the buildings are smaller, but the library is impressive enough and everyone wears jackets to dinner. Kids come to Wallingford for two very different reasons. Either private school is their ticket to a fancy university, or they got kicked out of public school and are using their

parents' money to avoid the school for juvenile delinquents that's their only other option.

Wallingford isn't exactly Choate or Deerfield Academy, but it was willing to take me, even with my ties to the Zacharovs. Barron thought the school would give me structure. No messy house. No chaos. I've done well too. Here, my inability to do curse work is actually an advantage—the first time that it's been good for anything. And yet I see in myself a disturbing tendency to seek out all the trouble this new life should be missing. Like running the betting pool when I need money. I can't seem to stop working the angles.

The dining hall is wood-paneled with a high, arched ceiling that makes our noise echo. The walls are hung with paintings of important heads-of-school and, of course, Wallingford himself. Colonel Wallingford, the founder of Wallingford Preparatory, killed by the bare-handed touch of a death worker a year before the ban went into effect, sneers down at me from his gold frame.

My shoes clack on the worn marble tiles, and I frown as the voices around me merge into a single buzzing that rings in my ears. Walking through to the kitchen, my hands feel damp, sweat soaking the cotton of my gloves as I push open the door.

I look around automatically to see if Audrey's here. She's not, but I shouldn't have looked. I've got to ignore her just enough that she doesn't think I care, but not too much. Too much will give me away as well.

Especially today, when I'm so disoriented.

"You're late," one of the food service ladies says without looking up from wiping the counter. She looks past retirement age—at least as old as my grandfather—and a few of her permed curls have tumbled out the side of her plastic cap. "Dinner's over."

"Yeah." And then I mumble, "Sorry."

"The food's put away." She looks up at me. She holds up her plastic-covered hands. "It's going to be cold."

"I like cold food." I give her my best sheepish half smile.

She shakes her head. "I like boys with a good appetite. All of you look so skinny, and in the magazines they talk about you starving yourselves like girls."

"Not me," I say, and my stomach growls, which makes her laugh.

"Go outside and I'll bring you a plate. Take a few cookies off the tray here too." Now that she's decided I'm a poor child in need of feeding, she seems happy to fuss.

Unlike in most school cafeterias, the food at Wallingford is good. The cookies are dark with molasses and spicy with ginger. The spaghetti, when she brings it, is lukewarm, but I can taste chorizo in the red sauce. As I sop up some of it with bread, Daneca Wasserman comes over to the table.

"Can I sit down?" she asks.

I glance up at the clock. "Study hall's going to start soon." Her tangle of brown curls looks unbrushed, pulled back with a sandalwood headband. I drop my gaze to the hemp bag at her hip, studded with buttons that read POWERED BY TOFU, DOWN ON PROP 2, and WORKER RIGHTS.

"You weren't at debate club," she says.

"Yeah." I feel bad about avoiding Daneca or giving her rude half answers, but I've been doing it since I started at Wallingford. Even though she's one of Sam's friends and living with him makes avoiding Daneca more difficult.

"My mother wants to talk with you. She says that what you did was a cry for help."

"It was," I say. "That's why I was yelling 'Heeeelp!' I don't really go in for subtlety."

She makes an impatient noise. Daneca's family are cofounders of HEX, the advocacy group that wants to make working legal again—basically so laws against more serious works can be better enforced. I've seen her mother on television, filmed sitting in the office of her brick house in Princeton, a blooming garden visible through the window behind her. Mrs. Wasserman talked about how, despite the laws, no one wanted to be without a luck worker at a wedding or a baptism, and that those kinds of works were beneficial. She talked about how it benefited crime families to prevent workers from finding ways to use their talents legally. She admitted to being a worker herself. It was an impressive speech. A dangerous speech.

"Mom deals with worker families all the time," Daneca says. "The issues worker kids face."

"I know that, Daneca. Look, I didn't want to join your junior HEX club last year, and I don't want to mess with that kind of stuff now. I'm not a worker, and I don't care if you are. Find someone else to recruit or save or whatever it is you are trying to do. And I don't want to meet your mother."

She hesitates. "I'm not a worker. I'm not. Just because I want to—"

"Whatever. I said I don't care."

"You don't care that workers are being rounded up and shot in North Korea? And here in the U.S. they're being forced into what's basically indentured servitude for crime families? You don't care about any of it?"

"No, I don't care."

Across the hall Valerio is headed toward me. That's enough to make Daneca decide she doesn't want to risk a demerit for not being where she's supposed to be. Hand on her bag, she walks off with a single glance back at me. The combination of disappointment and contempt in that last look hurts.

I put a big chunk of sauce-soaked bread in my mouth and stand.

"Congratulations. You're going to be sleeping in your room tonight, Mr. Sharpe."

I nod, chewing. Maybe if I make it through tonight, they'll consider letting me stay.

"But I want you to know that I have Dean Wharton's dog and she's going to be sleeping in the hallway. That dog is going to bark like hell if you go on one of your midnight strolls. I better not see you out of your room, not even to go to the bathroom. Do you understand?"

I swallow. "Yes, sir."

"Better get back and start on your homework."

"Right," I say. "Absolutely. Thank you, sir."

I seldom walk back from the dining hall alone. Above

the trees, their leaves the pale green of new buds, bats weave through the still-bright sky. The air is heavy with the smell of crushed grass, threaded through with smoke. Somewhere someone's burning the wet, half-decomposed foliage of winter.

Sam sits at his desk, earbuds in, huge back to the door and head down as he doodles in the pages of his physics textbook. He barely looks up when I flop down on the bed. We have about three hours of homework a night, and our evening study period is only two hours, so if you want to spend the break at half-past-nine not freaking out, you have to cram. I'm not sure that the picture of the wide-eyed zombie girl biting out the brains of senior douchebag James Page is part of Sam's homework, but if it is, his physics teacher is awesome.

I pull out books from my backpack and start on trig problems, but as my pencil scrapes across the page of my notebook, I realize I don't really remember class well enough to solve anything. Pushing those books toward my pillow, I decide to read the chapter we were assigned in mythology. It's some more messed-up Olympian family stuff, starring Zeus. His pregnant girlfriend, Semele, gets tricked by his wife, Hera, into demanding to see Zeus in all his godly glory. Despite knowing this is going to kill Semele, he shows her the goods. A few minutes later he's cutting baby Dionysus out of burned-up Semele's womb and *sewing him into his own leg*. No wonder Dionysus drank all the time. I just get to the part where Dionysus is being raised as a girl (to keep him hidden from Hera, of course), when Kyle bangs against the door frame.

"What?" Sam says, pulling off one of his buds and turning in his chair.

"Phone for you," Kyle says, looking in my direction.

I guess before everyone had a cell phone, the only way students could call home was to save up their quarters and feed them into the ancient pay phone at the end of every dorm hall. Despite the occasional midnight crank call, Wallingford has left those old phones where they were. People occasionally still use them; mostly parents calling someone whose cell battery died or who wasn't returning messages. Or my mother, calling from jail.

I pick up the familiar heavy black receiver. "Hello?"

"I am very disappointed in you," Mom says. "That school is making you soft in the head. What were you doing up on a roof?" Theoretically Mom shouldn't be able to call another pay phone from the pay phone in prison, but she found a way around that. First she gets my sister-in-law to accept the charges, then Maura can three-way call me, or anyone else Mom needs. Lawyers. Philip. Barron.

Of course, Mom could three-way call my cell phone, but she's sure that all cell phone conversations are being listened to by some shady peeping-Tom branch of the government, so she tries to avoid using them.

"I'm okay," I say. "Thanks for checking in on me." Her voice reminds me that Philip's coming to pick me up in the morning. I have a brief fantasy of him never bothering to show up and the whole thing blowing over.

27

"Checking up on you? I'm your mother! I should be there! It is so unfair that I have to be cooped up like this while you're gallivanting around on rooftops, getting into the kind of trouble you never would have if you had a stable family—a mother at home. That's what I told the judge. I told him that if he put me away, this would happen. Well, not this specifically, but no one can say I didn't warn him."

Mom likes to talk. She likes to talk so much that you can mmm-hmm along with her and have a whole conversation in which you don't say a word. Especially now, when she's far enough away that even if she's pissed off she can't put her hand to your bare skin and make you sob with remorse.

Emotion work is powerful stuff.

"Listen," she says. "You are going home with Philip. You'll be among our kind of people, at least. Safe."

Our kind of people. Workers. Only I'm not one. The only nonworker in my whole family. I cup my hand over the receiver. "Am I in some kind of danger?"

"Of course not. Don't be ridiculous. You know I got the nicest letter from that count. He wants to take me on a cruise with him when I get out of here. What do you think of that? You should come along. I'll tell him you're my assistant."

I smile. Sure she can be scary and manipulative, but she loves me. "Okay, Mom."

"Really? Oh, that'll be great, honey. You know this whole thing is so unfair. I can't believe they would take me away from my babies when you need me the most. I've spoken to my lawyers, and they are going to get this whole thing straightened out. I told them you need me. But if you could write a letter, that would help."

I know I won't. "I have to go, Mom. It's study period. I'm not supposed to be on the phone."

"Oh, let me talk to that hall master of yours. What's his name. Valerie?"

"Valerio."

"You just get him for me. I'll explain everything. I'm sure he's a nice man."

"I've really got to go. I've got homework."

I hear her laugh, and then a sound that I know is her lighting a cigarette. I hear the deep inhalation, the slight crackle of burning paper. "Why? You're done with that place."

"If I don't do my homework, I will be."

"Sweetheart, you know what your problem is? You take everything too seriously. It's because you're the baby of the family—" I can imagine her getting into that line of theorizing, stabbing the air for emphasis, standing against the painted cinder block wall of the jail.

"Bye, Mom."

"You stay with your brothers," she says softly. "Stay safe."

"Bye, Mom," I say again, and hang up. My chest feels tight.

I stand in the hallway a few moments longer, until the break starts and everyone files down to the common lounge on the first floor.

Rahul Pathak and Jeremy Fletcher-Fiske, the other two junior-year soccer players in the house, wave me over

to the striped couch they've settled on. I take a hot chocolate packet, and mix it into a large cup of coffee. I think
technically the coffee is supposed to be for staff, but we all
drink it and no one says anything.

When I sit down, Jeremy makes a face. "You got the heebeegeebies?"

"Yeah, from your mother," I say, without any real heat.
HBG is the abbreviation for some long medical term that
means "worker," hence "the heebeegeebies."

"Oh, come on," he says. "Seriously, I have a proposition for you. I need you to hook me up with somebody who
can work my girlfriend and make her really hot for me. At
prom. We can pay."

"I don't know anyone like that."

"Sure you do," Jeremy says, looking at me steadily, like
I'm so far beneath him he can't figure out why he has to
even try to persuade me. I should be delighted to help.
That's what I'm for. "She's going to take off her charms and
everything. She wants to do it."

I wonder how much he'd pay for it. Not enough to keep
me out of trouble. "Sorry. I can't help you."

Rahul takes an envelope out of the inside pocket of his
jacket and pushes it in my direction.

"Look, I said I can't do it," I say again. "I can't, okay?"

"No, no," he says. "I saw the mouse. I am completely
sure it was heading toward one of those glue traps. Dead
before tomorrow." He mimes his hand slashing across his
throat with a grin. "Fifty dollars on glue."

Jeremy frowns, like he's not sure he's ready to give up

says, pointing to the papers. "Unofficially. I brought some articles from the library. Some guy was even driving in his sleep. I was thinking you could just say—"

"That I was medicating myself for insomnia?" I ask, rolling over and pressing my face against her shoulder, breathing in the smell of her, filtered through sweater fabric.

She doesn't push me away. I consider kissing her right there on the dirty couch, but some instinct of self-preservation stops me. Once someone's hurt you, it's harder to relax around them, harder to think of them as safe to love. But it doesn't stop you from wanting them. Sometimes I actually think it makes the wanting worse.

"It doesn't have to be true. You can just *say* you were taking sleeping pills," she says, like I don't understand lying, which is sort of sweet and sort of humiliating.

It's not a bad plan, really. If I had been smarter and had thought of it myself earlier, I'd probably still be at school. "I already told them I had a history of sleepwalking as a kid."

"Crap," she says. "Too bad. There's this other pill in Australia that's made people binge eat and paint their front doors while asleep." She tilts her head, and I see six tiny protective amulets slide across her collarbone. Luck. Dreams. Emotion. Body. Memory. Death. The seventh one—transformation—is caught on the edge of her sweater.

I imagine crushing her throat in my hands and am relieved to be horrified. I feel guilty when I think of killing girls, but it's the only way I know to test myself, to make sure that whatever terrible thing is inside of me isn't about to get out.

I reach out and unhook the little stone pendant, letting it fall against her neck. Hematite. Probably a fake. There aren't enough transformation workers around for there to be many real amulets. One worker every generation or two. That charm makes me wonder if the rest are fake too. "Thanks. For trying. It was a good idea."

She bites her lip. "Do you think this has something to do with your dad dying?"

I shift abruptly, so that my back's against the armrest. Real smooth. "Do I think what has to do with it? He was in a car accident in the middle of the day."

"Sleepwalking can be triggered by stress. What about your mom being in jail? That's got to be stressful."

My voice rises. "Dad's been dead for almost three years and mom's been locked up practically as long. Don't you think—"

"Don't get mad."

"I'm not mad!" I rub my hand over my face. "Okay, look. I almost fall off a roof, I'm getting kicked out of school, and you think I'm a head case. I've got reasons to be pissed." I take a deep breath and try to give her my most apologetic smile. "But not at you."

"That's right," she says, shoving me. "Not at me."

I catch her gloved hand in mine. "I can handle Northcutt. I'll be back at Wallingford in no time." I hate having her here in the middle of my messy house, already knowing more about me than is comfortable. I feel turned inside out, the raw parts of me exposed.

I don't want her to leave, either.

"Look," she whispers with a glance in the direction of the kitchen. "I don't want to set you off again, but do you think you could have been touched? You know, heebeegeebies?"

Touched. Worked. Cursed. "To sleepwalk?"

"To throw yourself off a roof," she says. "It would have looked like suicide."

"That's a pretty expensive work." I don't want to tell her I've thought about it, that my whole family thought about it so much they even had a secret meeting to discuss the possibility. "Plus, I lived. That makes it less likely."

"You should ask your granddad," she says softly.

If you're so smart, you tell me what's going on.

I nod, barely noticing as she puts the papers back into her purse. Then she hugs me lightly. My hands rest on the small of her back and I can feel her warm breath against my neck. With her, I could learn to be normal. Every time she touches me, I feel the heady promise of becoming an average guy.

"You better go," I say, before I do something stupid.

At the door, as she leaves, I turn to look at my grandfather's face. He's twisting a screwdriver into the stove to pop off a crusted burner, without any apparent concern that the entire Zacharov family might be after me. He's worked for them, so it's not like he doesn't know what they're capable of—he knows better than I do.

Maybe that's why he's here.

To protect me.

The thought makes me need to lean against the sink from a combination of horror, guilt, and gratitude.

That night, in my old room with the ratty Magritte posters taped to the ceiling and bookshelves stuffed with robots and Hardy Boys novels, I dream of being lost in a rainstorm.

Even though it's a dream, and I'm pretty sure it's a dream, the rain feels cold against my skin and I can barely see with the water in my eyes. I hunch over and run for the only visible light, shading my face with one hand.

I come to the worn door of the barn behind the house. Ducking through the doorway, however, I decide I was mistaken about it being our barn. Instead of the old tools and discarded furniture, there's only a long hallway, lit by torches. As I get closer, I realize that the torches are held by hands too real to be plaster. One hand shifts its grip on a metal shaft, and I leap back from it. Then, stepping closer, I see how the wrist of each has been severed and stuck on the wall. I can see the uneven slice of the flesh.

"Hello," I call, like I did from the roof. This time, no one answers.

I glance back. The barn door is still open, sheets of rain forming puddles on the wooden planks. Because it's a dream, I don't bother to go back and close the door. I just head down the hall. After what seems like a disproportionately long time walking, I come to a shabby door with a handle made from the foot of a stag. The coarse fur tickles my palm as I pull it.

Inside sits a futon from Barron's dorm room and a dresser I'm sure I recall Mom buying off of eBay, intending to paint it apple green for the guest room. I open the drawers and find several pairs of Philip's old jeans. They're dry, and the top pair fits me perfectly when I pull them on. There's a white shirt that was Dad's hanging on the back of the door; I remember the cigarillo burn just below the elbow and the smell of my father's aftershave.

Since I know I'm dreaming, I'm not frightened, just puzzled, when I walk back into the hall and this time find steps going up to a painted white door with a hanging crystal pull. The pull looks like the kind that summons servants in grand houses on PBS shows, but this one is made from glittering parts of an old chandelier. When I pull it, a series of bells rings loudly, echoing through the space. The door opens.

An old picnic table and two lawn chairs rest in the middle of a large gray room. Maybe I'm still in the barn after all, because the spaces between the planks in the walls are wide enough that I can see rain against a storm-bright sky.

The table is draped with some kind of embroidered silk cloth and topped with silver candlesticks, two silver chargers, and gilt-edged plates, the center of each covered by a silver dome. Cut glass goblets stand at each place setting.

Out of the gloom, cats come, tabbies and calicos, marmalade cats and butterscotch cats and cats so black I can barely tell them from their shadows. They creep toward me, hundreds of them, swarming over one another to get close.

I jump up onto one of the chairs, snatching a candle-stick, not sure what sick thing my brain is about to conjure next when a small, veiled creature walks into the room. It's wearing a tiny gown, like the kind that expensive dolls wear. Lila had a whole row of dolls in dresses like that; her mother would yell at her if she touched them. We played with the dolls anyway when her mother wasn't looking. We dragged the princess one through Grandad's backyard pretending she was being held captive by one of my Power Rangers, with a broken Tamagotchi as an interstellar map—until its dress was streaked with grass stains and torn along the hem. This dress is torn too.

The veil slips and falls. Underneath is a cat's face. A cat, standing on two legs, her triangle head tilted to one side, almost like her neck's been broken, her body cov-ered in the dress.

I can't help it, I laugh.

"I need your help," says the tiny figure. Her voice is sad and soft and sounds like Lila's, but with an odd accent that might just be how cats sound when they talk.

"Okay," I say. What else can I say?

"A curse was placed on me," the Lila cat says. "A curse that only you can break."

The other cats watch us, tails flicking, whiskers twitch-ing. Still silent.

"Who cursed you?" I ask, trying to smother my laughter.

"You did," says the white cat.

At that my smile becomes more of a grimace. Lila's

dead and cats shouldn't stand, shouldn't press their paws together in supplication, shouldn't talk.

"Only you can undo the curse," she says, and I try to watch the movement of her mouth, the flash of her fangs, to see how she can speak without lips. "The clues are every-where. We don't have much time."

This is a dream, I remind myself. A deeply messed-up dream, but a dream just the same. I've even dreamed about a cat before. "Did you bite out my tongue?"

"You seem to have it back," the white cat says, her shad-owed eyes unblinking.

I open my mouth to speak, but I feel claws on my back, nails sinking into my skin and I yelp instead.

Yelp and sit up. Wake up.

I hear the steady patter of rain against my window and realize that I'm soaked, blankets wet and clinging. I've been outside. I might be back in my room, in my old bed, but my hands are shaking so hard that I have to press them under-neath my body to make them stop.

WHEN I STAGGER DOWN

to the kitchen in the morning, I find Grandad boiling coffee and frying eggs in bacon grease. I have on jeans and a faded Wallingford T-shirt. I don't miss my itchy gloves or strangling tie; comfort's the consolation prize for getting booted, I guess, but I don't want to get too used to it.

I found a leaf stuck to my leg while I was getting dressed, and that was enough to make me remember waking, drenched with rain. I've been sleepwalking again, but the more I think about the dream, the more confused I get. Nothing lethal happened, which takes the Zacharov revenge scenario off the table. So maybe it's just guilt that makes me dream of Lila. Guilt makes you crazy, right? It festers inside of you.

Like in Poe's "The Tell-tale Heart," which Ms. Noyes made us read out loud, where the narrator hears the heart of his victim beating beneath the floorboards, louder and louder until he confesses, *"I admit the deed! Here, here! It is the beating of his hideous heart!"*

"I need to talk to you," I say, taking out a mug and pouring milk into it first, then adding the coffee. The milk billows up from the bottom, along with flecks of dust I should have probably checked for. "I had a weird dream."

"Let me guess. You got tied up by lady ninjas. With big hooters."

"Uh, no." I take a sip of the coffee and wince. Grandad made it ridiculously strong.

My grandfather shoves a strip of bacon in his mouth with a grin. "Guess it would have been kind of weird if we'd had the same dream."

I roll my eyes. "Well, you'd better not tell me anything else. Don't ruin the surprise in case I have it tonight."

Grandad chuckles, but it turns into a wheeze.

I look out the window. There are no cats on the grass. As I watch Grandad pour ketchup onto his eggs, the red liquid spreading, I think, *There's too much blood, and I don't remember stabbing her, but a wet knife is in my hand and the blood is smeared over the floorboards like a thick glaze.*

"So are you going to tell me about the dream you did have?" My grandfather sits down at the table, smacking his lips.

"Yeah," I say, blinking as I remember where I am. Mom

said those sudden, sickening flashes of the murder would get better over time, but they just got less frequent. Maybe some small decent part of me didn't want to forget.

"You waiting for an engraved invitation?" Grandad asks.

"The dream started with me outside in the rain. I walked out to the barn, and then I woke up in my bed, with mud all over my feet. Sleepwalking again, I guess."

"You guess?" he asks.

"Lila was in my dream." I force the words out. We never talk about Lila or the way the whole family protected me, after. How my mother wept into the fur collar of her sweater and hugged me and told me that even if I had done it, then she was sure that little Zacharov bitch deserved it, and she didn't care what anyone said, I was still her baby. How there was something dark under my fingernails and I couldn't seem to get it out. I tried with my own nails and then with a butter knife, pressing until I started to bleed. Until my blood washed away the other darkness.

So my own conscience is finally doing me in. It's about time.

Grandad raises an eyebrow. "Maybe it would help if you talk about her. Talk about killing her. Get it off your chest. I've done bad things, kid. I'm not going to judge you."

Mom got arrested not long after Lila's murder. Not because of me, not exactly, but she was off her game. She wanted a big score and she wanted it fast.

"What do you want me to say? I killed her? I know I did,

even if I don't remember it. I always wondered if Mom paid someone to make me forget the details. Maybe she thought if I didn't remember how it felt, I wouldn't do it again." There's got to be something dead inside me, because normal people don't stand over the corpse of someone they love and feel nothing but a distant, horrible joy. "Lila was a dream worker, and so I guess the sleepwalking and the nightmares seem ironic. I'm not saying I don't deserve them; I just want to understand why they're happening."

"Maybe you should come down to Carney. See your uncle Armen. He can still do some memory work. Maybe he can help you remember."

"Uncle Armen has Alzheimer's," I say. He's a friend of Grandad's from when they were kids, and not really even my uncle.

Grandad snorts. "Nah. Blowback. But let's see what that fancy doctor thinks first."

I pour more coffee into my cup. A week after Lila died and Barron and Philip hid her body wherever bodies get hidden, I went to a pay phone and called Lila's mother. I'd promised I wouldn't, had listened to my grandfather explain that if anyone found out what I'd done, the whole family would pay. I knew that the Zacharovs were unlikely to forget who had dug the grave and mopped up the blood and failed to turn me in, but I couldn't stop thinking about Lila's mother alone in that house.

Alone and waiting for her daughter to come home.

The ringing seemed too harsh. I felt light-headed. When her mother answered, I hung up. Then I walked around to the back of the convenience store and puked my guts out.

Grandad stands up. "How about you start on the upstairs bathroom? I'm going out for supplies."

"Don't forget the milk," I say.

"*My* memory's fine," he shoots back at me as he reaches for his jacket.

The floor tiles of the bathroom are cracked and torn in places, and there's a cheap white cabinet shoved against one wall. Inside are dozens and dozens of mismatched towels, some full of holes, and amber-colored plastic bottles with a few pills in each. On the shelf beneath that there are jars crusted with dark liquids and tins of powder.

As I clean silken balls full of baby spiders from the corners of the shower and toss out sticky, mostly empty shampoo bottles, I force myself to think about Lila.

We were nine when we met. Her parents' marriage was coming apart and she and her mother went to live with her grandmother in the Pine Barrens. She had wooly blond hair, one blue eye and one green one, and all I knew about her was that Grandad said her father was someone important.

Lila was what anybody might expect from a girl who could give you nightmares with a bare-handed touch, from the head of the Zacharov family's daughter. She was spoiled rotten.

At nine she beat me mercilessly at video games, raced up hills and trees so fast I was always three steps behind her long legs, and bit me when I tried to steal her dolls and hide them. I couldn't tell if she hated me half the time, even when we spent weeks hiding under the branches of a willow tree, drawing civilizations in the dirt and then crushing them like callous gods. But I was used to brothers who were fast and cruel. I didn't mind that. I worshipped her.

Then her parents divorced. I didn't see her again until we were both thirteen.

Grandad comes back with several shopping bags around the time it starts to rain again, most of them full of Windex, beer, or paper towels. He's also brought back traps.

"For raccoons, but they'll work," he says. "And they're humane—says so on the package—so don't get your panties in a twist. There's no guillotine attachment."

"Nice," I say, lifting them out of the trunk.

He leaves me alone to carry them to the barn. The cats are in there; I can see their eyes gleaming as I set up the first metal cage with its swinging door. I pop the tab on a can of wet food, sliding it inside the trap. Something thumps softly to the ground behind me and I turn.

The white cat stands not three feet from me, pink tongue licking her sharp teeth. In the afternoon light I can see that her ear's torn. Crusts of garnet scabs—fresh—run along the back of her neck.

"Here, kitty kitty," I say, nonsense words coming automatically from my mouth. I open another can. The cat jumps when the lid cracks open, and I realize how tense I've been. Like she's going to stand up and speak. But the cat's just a cat. Just an underfed stray living in a barn and about to be trapped.

I reach out a gloved hand, and she shies back. Smart animal.

"Here, kitty kitty," I say.

The cat approaches me slowly. She sniffs my fingers, and as I hold my breath, she rubs her cheek against my hand; soft fur and twitching whiskers and the edge of her teeth digging into my skin.

I put down the can of cat food, watching as she laps at it. I reach out to stroke her again, but she hisses, back arching and fur lifting. She looks like a snake.

"That's more like it," I say, petting her anyway.

She follows me back to the house. Her shoulder blades jut out of her back, and her white coat's streaked with mud. I let her into the kitchen anyway and give her water in a martini glass.

"You're not bringing that dirty animal in here, are you?" my grandfather says.

"She's a cat, Grandad, not a cockroach."

He regards her skeptically. His T-shirt's covered in dust and he's pouring bourbon into one of those big plastic soft drink cups that come with their own straws. "What do you want with a cat?"

"Nothing. I don't know. She looks hungry."

"You going to let all of them in here?" Grandad asks. "I bet they're all hungry."

I grin. "I promise no more than one at a time."

"This is not why I bought those traps."

"I know," I say. "You bought the traps so we can catch all

the cats, drop them off in a field ten miles from here, and take bets on which one comes back first."

He shakes his head. "You better get back to cleaning, smart-ass."

"I have that doctor's appointment with—," I say.

"I remember. Let's see how much you can get done before you have to leave."

Shrugging, I go into the living room with a bunch of flat boxes and packing tape. I build the boxes and drag in the trash can from out back. Then I start going through the piles.

The cat watches me with shining eyes.

Circulars advertising charms and an old fur muff that looks like it has mange go in the trash can. Paperbacks go back onto shelves unless they look like something I want to read or the pages look too crumbly. A basket of leather gloves, some of them stuck together from being too close to a heating vent, goes into the trash as well.

No matter how much I throw away, there's always more. Piles slide into one another and confuse me about where I was clearing last. There are dozens of wadded-up plastic bags, one with a pair of earrings and the receipt still attached, others holding a random swatch of cloth or the crust of a sandwich.

There are screwdrivers, nuts and bolts, my fifth-grade report card, the caboose from a toy train, rolls of PAID stickers, magnets from Ohio, three vases with dried flowers in them and one vase overstuffed with plastic flowers, a cardboard box of broken ornaments, a sticky mess of something dark and melted covering an ancient radio.

As I pick up a dust-covered dehumidifier, a box full of photographs spills across the floor.

They're black-and-white pinups. The woman in them is wearing wrist-length summer gloves, a vintage corset, and nylon panties. Her hair's styled like Bettie Page's and she's kneeling on a couch, smiling at the person taking the pictures, a man whose fingers show up in one of the pictures wearing an expensive-looking wedding ring over his black gloves. I know the woman in the pictures.

Mom looks pretty good.

The first time I realized I had a talent for crime was after Mom took me out—just me—for a cherry slushy. It was a scorching summer day and the leather seat in her car was hot from the sun, burning the backs of my legs just slightly unpleasantly. My mouth had turned bright red when we pulled into a gas station and then around back, like Mom was going to put air in the tires.

"See that house?" she asked me. She was pointing to a ranch-style place with white aluminum siding and black shutters.

"I want you to go through that window in the back by the stairs. Just shimmy on in and grab the manila envelope off the desk."

I must have stared at Mom like I didn't understand her.

"It's a game, Cassel. Do it as fast as you can and I'll time you. Here, give me your drink."

I guess I knew it wasn't a game, but I ran anyway and I

boosted myself up on the water spigot and poured through the window with the boneless grace of little kids. The manila envelope was right where Mom'd said it would be. Nearby, piles of paper rested under coffee cups stuffed with pens and rulers and spoons. There was a little glass cat on the desk with what looked like glittering gold inside it. The air-conditioning made the sweat dry on my arms and back as I held the sculpture up to the light. I tucked the cat into my pocket.

When I brought the envelope back to her, she was sucking on my slushy.

"Here," I said.

She smiled. Her mouth was bright red too. "Good work, sweetie." And I realized that the reason she had taken me instead of my brothers was just that I was the smallest, but it didn't bother me, because I also realized that I could be useful. That I didn't need to be a worker to be useful. That I could be good at things, better than they were, even.

That knowledge sang through my veins like adrenaline.

Maybe I was seven. I'm not sure. It was before Lila.

I never told anyone about the cat.

I stack the photographs, with a few more of Grandad and Lila's dad in Atlantic City in front of a bar. They're standing with an older man that I don't know, arms draped over each others' shoulders.

I sweep layers of dust from under the couches and chairs until it billows up and chokes me.

When I flop down to rest, I find a notebook shoved

under one of the cushions, filled with Mom's writing. No more racy photos, just boring stuff. "Oil tank removal—buried" is scrawled on one side of the page, while the other side reads, "get carrots, chicken (whole), bleach, matches, motor oil." Two pages later there are some addresses, with one circled. Then a script for calling a car dealership and talking them out of a rental car for a week. There are a few more scripts for different scams, with notes on the side. I read them over, smiling despite myself.

In a couple of hours I'm going to run my own scam, so I better study up.

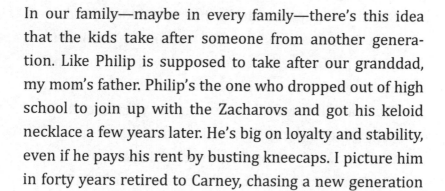

In our family—maybe in every family—there's this idea that the kids take after someone from another generation. Like Philip is supposed to take after our granddad, my mom's father. Philip's the one who dropped out of high school to join up with the Zacharovs and got his keloid necklace a few years later. He's big on loyalty and stability, even if he pays his rent by busting kneecaps. I picture him in forty years retired to Carney, chasing a new generation of worker kids off his lawn.

The family legend says that Barron is just like Mom, even though he works luck and she works emotion. Mom can make anyone her friend, can strike up a conversation anywhere because she genuinely believes that the con is a game. And all she cares about is winning every single time.

That leaves me to be like my luck worker dad. He was the person that held things together. When he was alive, Mom acted normal most of the time. It was only when he was gone that she started chasing around millionaires with her gloves off. The second time a guy woke up at the end of a cruise a hundred grand lighter and head over heels in love, his lawyer called the cops.

She can't help it. She loves the con.

I love it too, just not that much.

I flip through the notebook, looking for I don't know what—maybe something familiar, maybe just some secret that will make me laugh. As I turn more pages, I find an envelope taped to a divider. Written beside it are the words "Give this to Remember!" I rip it open and find a memory charm, silver, with the word "remember" stamped on it and an uncracked blue stone set off center. It looks old, the silver tarnished black in the grooves and the whole piece heavy in my hand.

Charms to throw off curse work, charms like the ones Audrey has hanging around her neck, are as old as curses themselves. Workers make them by cursing stone—the only material that absorbs a whole curse, including the blowback. Then that stone is primed and will swallow up a curse of the same type. So if a luck worker curses a piece of jade and wears it against her skin, and then someone tries to curse her with bad luck, the jade breaks and she's not affected. You have to get another charm each time you're worked, and you have to have one for each type of magic, but you're safe. Only rock is effective, not silver or gold, leather or wood. Certain people prefer one type to another; there are charms made out of everything from gravel to granite. If what I'm holding is a charm, the blue stone is what powers it.

I wonder if Mom grifted some ancestral heirloom or if it actually belongs to her. It's kind of funny to think of forgetting a memory charm. I tuck it into my pocket.

While cleaning the living room, I find a button-making machine, two plastic bags of bubble wrap, a sword with rust staining the blade, three broken dolls I don't remember anyone owning, an overturned chair that creeped me out as a kid because I swore it looked identical to one I'd seen on television the night before Barron and Philip dragged it home, a hockey stick, and a collection of medals for various different military accomplishments. It's almost noon by the time I finish, and my hands and the cuffs of my pants are black with filth. I throw away stacks of newspapers and catalogs, bills that probably went unpaid for years, plastic bags of hangers and wires, and the hockey stick.

The sword I lean against the wall.

The outside of the house is already piled with garbage bags from the morning's work. There's enough stuff that we're going to have to take a trip to the dump before long. I look over at the neighbors' tidy houses with their manicured lawns and brightly painted doors, and then back at my own. The shutters hang off-kilter on either side of a row of front-facing windows, and one of the panes is broken. The paint is so worn that the cedar shingles look gray. The house is rotting from the inside.

I'm in the process of dragging the chair out to the side

of the road when Grandad comes downstairs and dangles the keys in front of me.

"Be back in time for dinner," he says.

I take the keys, gripping them hard enough for the teeth to dig into my palm. Leaving the chair where it is, I head out the driveway as if I really have an appointment to be late for.

THE ADDRESS I GOT OFF

the Internet for Dr. Churchill's office is on the corner of Vandeventer Avenue in the center of Princeton. I park next to a fondue restaurant and check myself in the rearview mirror, finger-combing my hair flat in the hopes of making myself look more like a good kid, reliable. Even though I washed my hands three times in the bathroom of a convenience store when I stopped for coffee, I can still feel the oily grit of dirt on my skin. I try not to rub my fingers against my jeans as I walk into the reception area and up to the desk.

The woman answering the phone has dyed red curls and glasses hanging around her neck on a beaded chain. I wonder if she made the chain herself; irrationally I associate crafting with friendliness. She looks like she might be in her fifties from the lines on her face and all the silver at her roots. "Hi," I say. "I have an appointment at two."

She looks at me without smiling and taps the keyboard in front of her. I know there's not going to be anything on her screen about me, but that's okay. It's part of my plan.

"What's your name?" she asks.

"Cassel Sharpe." I try to stick to the truth as much as possible, in case there's a need for elaboration or photo identification. As she clicks around to figure out who made a mistake, I take stock of the office. There's a young woman behind the desk, wearing light purple scrubs, and I think she might be a nurse, since there's only one doctor's name—Dr. Eric Churchill, MD—on the door. The few files on top of the cabinets in the back are in dark green folders, and a note about the holiday hours is taped to the front of the desk. On stationery. I reach for it.

"I don't see anything here, Mr. Sharpe," she says.

"Oh," I say, my hand freezing. I can't rip the tape without her noticing the movement. "Oh." I try to seem worried and hope that she'll take pity on me and do some more fruitless searching or, better yet, go ask someone.

She doesn't seem to notice my fake distress and seems, in fact, more irritated than sympathetic. "Who made the appointment?"

"My mom. Do you think it might be under her name?" The nurse in the scrubs takes out a file and sets it on the counter, close to where I'm standing.

"There's no Sharpe here," the receptionist says, her gaze steady. "Maybe your mother made a mistake?"

I take a deep breath and concentrate on minimizing tells. Liars will touch their faces, obscuring themselves. They'll stiffen up. They'll do any of dozens of nonverbal things—breathe quickly, talk fast, blush—that could give them away. "Her last name's Singer. Could you check?"

As she turns her face toward the screen, I slide the file off the counter and under my coat.

"No. No Singer," she says, with profound annoyance. "Would you like to call your mother, maybe?"

"Yeah, I better," I say contritely. As I turn, I pull the stationery sign off the front of the desk. I have no idea if she sees me. I force myself not to look back, just to keep walking with one arm crossed over my coat to keep the file in place, and the other sliding the sheet of paper into the file, everything perfectly natural.

I hear a door close and a woman—maybe the patient that goes with the file—say, "I don't understand. If I'm cursed, then what good is this amulet? I mean, look at it, it's covered in emeralds; are you telling me it's no better than a dime-store—"

I don't pause to hear the rest. I just walk toward the doors.

"Mr. Sharpe," a male voice says.

The doors are right in front of me. Just a few more steps will take me through them, but I stop. After all, my plan won't work if they remember me, and they'll remember a patient they have to chase down. "Uh, yeah?"

Dr. Churchill is a tan, thin man with thick glasses and close-cropped curling hair as white as eggshells. He pushes his glasses back up onto the bridge of his nose absently. "I don't know what happened to your appointment, but I've got some time right now. Come on back."

"What?" I say, turning toward the receptionist, hand still holding my coat closed. "I thought you said—"

She frowns. "Do you want to see the doctor or not?"

I can't think of anything to do but follow.

A nurse leads me to a room with an examining table covered in crinkly paper. She gives me a clipboard with a form that asks for an address and insurance information. Then she leaves me alone to stare at a chart showing the different stages of sleep and their waveforms. I rip the lining of my coat enough to drop the file inside it. Then I sit on the end of the table and write down facts about myself that are mostly true.

There are several brochures on the counter: "The Four Types of Insomnia," "Symptoms of HBG Assault," "Dangers of Sleep Apnea," and "All About Narcolepsy."

I pick up the one on HBG assault. That's the legal term for what my mother did to that rich guy. Assault. There are bullet points with a list of symptoms, and the caution that the diagnostic differential (whatever that means) on each is pretty broad:

- Vertigo
- Auditory Hallucinations
- Visual Hallucinations

- Headaches
- Fatigue
- Increased Anxiety

I think of Maura's music and wonder just how weird the hallucinations can get.

My phone buzzes and I take it out of my pocket automatically, still staring at the pamphlet. I'm not surprised by any of the information—like, I know I get headaches a lot because my mother gave an emotional working the way other parents give a time-out—but it's still strange to see it printed in black and white.

I flip open my phone and let the pamphlet fall to the floor. *Get over here*, the message reads. *We've got a big problem.* It's the only text message I've ever gotten where everything is spelled right. It's from Sam.

I push the buttons to call him back immediately, but the call goes to voice mail and I realize he must be in class. I check the time on my phone. A half hour more until lunch. I text quickly—*wht did u do?*—which might not be the most sensitive message, but I'm imagining disaster.

I'm imagining him caught with my book, ratting me out. I'm imagining being doomed to sifting through my parents' detritus until Grandad finds some other odd job for me.

The reply comes fast. *Payout.*

I breathe. Someone must have won a bet and, of course, he doesn't have the cash to cover it. *B ovr soon*, I text back as the door opens and the doctor walks in.

Dr. Churchill takes the clipboard and looks at it

instead of at me. "Dolores says there was some kind of mix-up?"

I assume that Dolores is the unfriendly reception desk lady. "Mom told me that I had an appointment with you today." The lie comes out easily; I even sound a little resentful. There's a tipping point with lies, a point where you've said something so many times that it feels truer than the truth.

He looks at me then, and I feel like he sees more than I want him to. I think about the file sitting in my coat, so close that he could reach down and grab it before I could stop him. I hope he doesn't have a stethoscope, because my heart is trying to beat its way out of my chest. "So why'd she make you an appointment with a sleep specialist? What kind of problems are you having?" he asks.

I hesitate. I want to tell him about waking up on the roof, about my sleepwalking and the dreams, but if I do, he might remember me. I know he's not going to write the note I need—no doctor in his right mind would—but I can't risk him writing Wallingford any other kind of letter.

"Let me guess," he says, surprising me, because how could anyone *guess* why a patient came to a sleep clinic? "You're here for the test." I have no idea what he's talking about.

"Right," I say. "The test."

"So, who canceled the appointment? Your father?"

I'm in over my head, with nothing to do but play along. "Probably my father."

He nods like that makes sense, fishing around in a drawer until his gloved hand emerges holding a fistful of electrodes. He begins attaching them to my forehead, their sticky sides pulling at my skin. "Now we're going to measure your gamma waves." He switches on a machine and it jumps to life, needles skittering across paper in the pattern that's mirrored on a screen to my left.

"Gamma waves," I repeat. I'm not even asleep, so I don't see the point in measuring my gamma waves. "Is this going to hurt?"

"Quick and painless." The doctor peers down at the paper. "Any reason why you think you're hyperbathygammic?"

Hyperbathygammic. That long medical term for worker. HBG. Heebeegeebies.

"Wh-what?" I stammer.

His eyes narrow. "I thought—"

I think of the woman I heard in the reception area. She was complaining about getting worked, and she sounded like they'd done a test on her to prove it. But he's not asking me if I think I've been worked. He's asking if I think I'm a *worker*.

This is the new test, the one that they keep talking about on the news, the one that conservative politicians want to make mandatory. Theoretically, compulsory testing will keep HBG kids from breaking the law by accident when using their powers for the first time. Theoretically, the results are supposed to stay private, so there's no harm, right? But no one really thinks those results are going to stay private.

They'll wind up with the government, which loves to draft workers for counterterrorism and other odd jobs. Or—legally or not—those results wind up in the hands of local authorities. If mandatory testing happens, the rest will be hard on its heels. Yeah, I know the slippery slope argument is a logical fallacy, but occasionally a slope feels particularly greased.

Supporters of the proposition have urged nonworkers to go get tested. The idea is simple. Even if workers don't get the test, they'll be the only ones to refuse it. That way, even if compulsory testing doesn't pass, it'll still be easier to figure out who's hyperbathygammic.

I hop off the table, ripping the electrodes off my skin. I might not get along with my family, but being part of some database of nonworkers used like a net to trap Philip and Barron and Grandad is horrible. "I have to go. I'm sorry."

"Sit back down. We'll be done in just a moment," he says, grabbing for the wires. "Mr. Sharpe!"

This time when I head for the doors, I don't stop until I'm through them. Keeping my head down, I ignore the nurse calling after me and the people in the waiting room staring. I ignore everything but my need to be somewhere other than here.

I keep telling myself to breathe as I drive. My foot pushes harder and harder on the gas pedal and my fingers fiddle with the radio just to have some sound to drown out the single thought: *I screwed up.*

I was supposed to be inconspicuous, but I'd become

memorable. Plus, I used my own name. I know where I went wrong: when the doctor said he knew what I was there for. I have this problem. Sometimes I'm too in love with the con; even when it goes wrong, I'd rather let it turn on me than walk. I should have stopped the doctor and corrected him, but I was too curious, too eager to play along and see what he would say next.

I still have the stationery. I can still make the plan happen. With recrimination pounding in my ears louder than the music, I pull into the Target parking lot. The front displays are all pastel baskets with chocolate eggs in them, even though it seems like they'd get stale before Easter. I walk to electronics and pick up a disposable cell phone. My second stop is a copy shop, where I rent computer time. The steady hum of the copiers and the smell of printer ink remind me of school and calm, but when I take the file out of my bag, my heart starts racing all over again.

The other mistake I made. Stealing a file. Because I was memorable enough now that they might think of me when they consider all the ways the file could have gone missing.

All I need is the sleep center's logo—the resolution on the one from the Internet is so bad I can't use it for anything but a fax. I don't need a file. A file could get me in real trouble. But when I saw the folder on that counter, I just grabbed.

And now, letting it fall open on this counter, I feel even more stupid. It's just some woman's name, her health insurance, a bunch of numbers and charts with jagged lines. None of it means anything to me. The only good thing is that Dr. Churchill signed one of the pages; at least I can copy his scrawl.

I flip though a few more pages, until I see a graph labeled "gamma waves" with red circles around the spikes in the jagged line. Gamma waves. A little Googling explains what I'm looking at. Apparently dream work puts someone into a sleep state that's like deep sleep, except with gamma waves. Gamma waves—according to the article—are usually present only during waking or light REM sleep. On the chart, gamma waves are present during the deepest sleep stages, when there's no eye movement and when both sleepwalking and night terrors occur. That's what proves she was sleep worked.

Apparently, according to the same site, gamma waves are the key to determining if you're a worker too. Worker gammas are higher than normal people's, asleep or awake. Much higher.

Hyperbathygammic.

I stare at the screen. This information has always been available to me with only a few clicks of a mouse, and yet I never really thought about it. Sitting here, I try to figure out why I handled the situation in the doctor's office so badly. I wasn't cunning. I panicked. My mother instructed me over and over again not to tell anyone anything about the family—not what I knew and not what I guessed—so it's awful to realize that nothing needs to be said. They could know through your skin.

And yet. And yet there's a pathetic part of me that wants to call the doctor and say, *You almost finished the test.*

Did you get a result? And he'd go, *Cassel, everyone's wrong about you. You're the awesomest worker on Awesome Street. We don't know why you didn't figure it out. Congratulations. Welcome to the life you're supposed to have.*

I have to push those thoughts out of my head. I can't afford to get any more distracted. Sam's waiting for me at Wallingford, and if I want to do more than visit the campus over and over again to sort out his messes, I have to fix a letter.

First I scan in the stationery. Then I find the font that the address is in, use the photo editing program to get rid of the old information, and type in the phone number of my new prepaid cell. I erase all the text about the office's holiday hours and type my own words in their place. "Cassel Sharpe has been my patient for several years. Against the strict orders of this office, he discontinued his medication, which resulted in an episode of somnambulism."

I'm not sure what to type next.

Another quick Google turns up a bit of likely doctor-ish mumbo jumbo. "The patient indicated a stimulant-dependant sleep disorder that induced bouts of insomnia. He has been prescribed medication and is sleeping through the night with no more incidents. As insomnia is often causal for sleepwalking, I believe there is no medical reason for Cassel to be restricted from classes or to be monitored at night."

I smile at the screen, wishing to grab hold of one of the businessmen getting pie charts printed and show him how smart I am. I feel like bragging. I wonder what else fake Dr. Churchill could convince Wallingford to believe.

"Furthermore," I write, "I have eliminated any outside assault as a cause for the patient's sleepwalking."

No point in them worrying about something that's probably just my crazy self-immolating guilt. No point in my worrying about it either.

I print my letter out on the fake stationery and print myself a fake envelope. Then I lick it and pay my bill at the copy shop. As I drop the letter into the mailbox, I realize that my plan better have a second prong if I'm going to stay unsuspended.

Stop sleepwalking.

I get to Wallingford around four, which means Sam's at play practice. It's easy to slip into the Carter Thompson Memorial Auditorium and sit in one of the seats in the back. The lights are dim there, all of them flooding the stage, where the cast are blocking Pippin murdering his dad.

"Stand closer to one other," Ms. Stavrakis, the drama teacher, says, clearly bored. "And lift that knife high, Pippin. It's got to catch the light so we can see it."

I see Audrey standing next to Greg Harmsford. She's smiling. Even though I can't see her face clearly, memory tells me that the blue sweater she's wearing is the color of her eyes.

"Please try to stay dead," Ms. Stavrakis calls to the kid playing Charles, James Page. "You only have a few moments of lying there before we bring you back to life."

Sam walks out on the stage and clears his throat. "Um, excuse me, but before we do this again, can we at least try out the effect? It looks lame without the blood packet and we need the practice. Uh, and don't you think it would be awesome if Pippin *shot* Charles instead of stabbing him? Then we could use the caps and it would really splatter."

"We're talking about the eighth century here," Ms. Stavrakis says. "No guns."

"But at the beginning of the musical they're in different historical costumes from different time periods," he says. "Doesn't that imply—"

"No guns," says Ms. Stavrakis.

"Okay, how about we use one of the packets? Or I could attach a blood capsule to the end of the retractable blade."

"We have to run through the rest of the scene, Sam. See me before rehearsal tomorrow and we'll talk about this. Okay?"

"Fine," he says, and stalks backstage. I get up and follow him.

I find him standing by a table. Bottles of red liquid rest on it next to scattered condom wrappers. I can hear Audrey's voice somewhere on the other side, yelling something about a party on Saturday night.

"What the hell goes on back here?" I ask him. "Drama club parties hard."

Sam turns around suddenly. I don't think he had any idea I was there. Then he looks down at what's in front of him and laughs nervously.

"They're for the blood," he says, but I can see red creeping up his neck. "You fill them up. They're pretty sturdy, but they pop easy too."

I pick one up. "Whatever you say, man."

"No, look." He takes it from me. "You rig a small explosive charge onto a foam-covered metal plate, and then you cover the charge with the blood pack. It's powered by a battery, so you just have to tape it and thread the trigger down the actor's body to somewhere out of sight. Like, with gaffer tape. If it's for a video or something, seeing wires doesn't matter so much. You can just edit them out. But onstage it's got to look neat."

"Right," I say. "It's a shame they won't let you do it."

"They're not big on my prosthetics either. I wanted to give James a beard. I mean, has Ms. Stavrakis even seen paintings of Charlemagne? Totally bearded." He looks at me for a long moment. "Are you okay?"

"Sure. Of course. So who won what?"

"Oh, yeah, sorry." He goes back to putting his equipment away. "Two teachers were spotted hooking up—practically no one bet on it, but three people did. Your payout is, like, six hundred bucks." He corrects himself. "Our payout."

"I guess the house doesn't always win." I miscalculated my odds in a big way, but I don't want him to know how big a hit I'm going to take. I rely on people making bad bets. "Who?"

He grins. "Ramirez and Carter."

I shake my head. Music teacher and the freshman English teacher. Both married to other people. "Evidence? You better not be handing out any winnings without—"

He flips open his laptop and shows me the picture. Ms. Carter's got her hand on the back of Ms. Ramirez's neck and her mouth on the front of it.

"Doctored?" I ask hopefully.

He shakes his head. "You know, people have been acting really weird since I took over your operation. Asking my friends about me."

"People don't like to think of their bookies as having friends. Makes them nervous."

"I'm not going to give up my friends."

"Of course you're not," I say automatically. "I'll go get the cash. Look," I say, and sigh. "I'm sorry if I seem like a hard-ass or whatever, asking you for evidence." My skin itches with discomfort. I've been acting like Sam's a fellow criminal.

"You aren't being weird," he says, looking puzzled. "No weirder than usual, anyway. You seem fine, man."

I guess he's used to suspicious people with crappy tempers. Or maybe I've never seemed as normal as I thought. Trudging down the path to the library, I keep my head down. I'm pretty sure that if Northcutt or any of her lackeys see me, they'll consider my roaming around campus a violation of my "medical leave." I manage to avoid looking anyone in the eye or walking into anyone on the way to the library.

Lainhart Library is the ugliest building on campus, constructed with a musician's donated funds in the eighties, when apparently people thought that a round building tilted at a weird angle was just the thing to update all the grand old brick edifices surrounding it. But as ugly as it is on the outside, the inside is couch-filled and comfortable. Bookshelves fan out from a central parlor with lots of seating and a massive globe that seniors try to steal year after year (a popular bet).

The librarian waves from behind her big oak desk. She's just out of library school and has cat's-eye glasses in every color of the rainbow. Several losers put down money on hooking up with her themselves. I felt bad when I told them the odds I'd assigned.

"Good to have you back, Cassel," she says.

"Good to be back, Ms. Fiske." Once spotted, I figure the best I can manage is not being conspicuous. Hopefully by the time she figures out I'm not back for real, I will be.

My working money—a total of three thousand dollars— is hidden between the pages of a big leather-bound onomasticon. I've kept it there for the last two years without incident. No one ever touches it but me. My only fear is that the book will be culled, since no one ever uses an onomasticon, but I think Wallingford keeps it because it looks expensive and obscure enough to reassure visiting parents that their kids are learning genius-type stuff.

I open the book and slide out six hundred dollars, poke around for a couple of minutes acting like I'm considering reading some Renaissance poetry, and then slink back to the dorm, where Sam's supposed to meet me. As I step off the stairs and into the hall, Valerio walks out of his room. I dodge to the side, into the bathroom, and then close myself in a stall. Leaning against the wall while waiting for my heart to start beating normally, I try to remind myself that so long as no one sees you doing something embarrassing, there's no reason to be humiliated. Valerio doesn't follow. I text Sam.

He walks into the bathroom moments later, laughing. "What a clandestine spot for a meeting."

I push open the stall door. "Laugh it up." There's no rancor in my voice, though. Just relief.

"The coast is clear," he says. "The eagle has flown the coop. The cow stands alone."

I can't help smiling as I dig out the money from my pocket. "You are a master of deception."

"Hey," he says. "Can you teach me to calculate odds? Like, if there was something I wanted to take bets on? And what's the deal with the point spreads on the games? How do you figure those? You aren't doing it the way they say online."

"It's complicated," I say, stalling. What I mean is: It's fixed.

He leans against the sink. "Didn't you hear? We Asians are all math geniuses."

"Okay, genius. Maybe another time, though?"

"Sure," he says, and I wonder if he's already planning to cut me loose from my own business. I figure I can probably screw him somehow if he does, but the thought of having to plan it just makes me tired.

Sam counts the money carefully. I watch him in the mirror. "You know what I wish?" he asks when he's done.

"What?"

"That someone would convert my bed into a robot that would fight other bed robots to the death for me."

That startles a laugh out of me. "That would be pretty awesome."

A slow, shy smile spreads across his mouth. "And we could take bets on them. And be filthy rich."

I lean my head against the frame of the stall, looking at the tile wall and the pattern of yellowed cracks there, and grin. "I take back anything I might have implied to the contrary. Sam, you *are* a genius."

I'm not good at having friends. I mean, I can make myself useful to people. I can fit in. I get invited to parties and I can sit at any table I want in the cafeteria.

But actually trusting someone when they have nothing to gain from me just doesn't make sense.

All friendships are negotiations of power.

Like, okay, Philip has this best friend, Anton. Anton is Lila's cousin; he came down to Carney with her in the summers. Anton and Philip spent three heat-soaked months drinking whatever liquor they could get out of the locals and working on their cars.

Anton's mother is Zacharov's sister Eva, making him Zacharov's closest living male relative. Anton made sure that Philip knew that if Philip wanted to work for the family, that meant he was going to be working for Anton. Their friendship was—and is—based on Philip's acknowledgment that Anton's in charge and Philip's ready to follow his lead.

Anton didn't like me because my friendship with Lila seemed to come without acknowledgment of his status.

One time, when we were thirteen, he walked into Lila's grandmother's kitchen. Lila and I were wrestling over some dumb thing, banging into the cabinets and laughing. He pulled me off her and knocked me to the floor.

"Apologize, you little pervert," he said.

It was true that all the pushing and shoving was mostly an excuse to touch Lila, but I'd rather get kicked around than admit it.

"Stop it!" she screamed at Anton, grabbing for his gloved hands.

"Your father sent me down here to keep an eye on you," he said. "He wouldn't want you spending all your time with this deviant. He's not even one of us."

"You don't tell me what to do," Lila told him. "Ever."

He looked back down at me. "How about I tell *you* what to do, Cassel? Get down on your knees. That's how you're supposed to act in front of a laborer princess."

"Don't listen to him," Lila said stiffly. "Stand up."

I was starting to rise when he kicked me in my shoulder. I fell back onto my knees.

"Stop it!" she yelled.

"Good," he said. "Now why don't you kiss her foot? You know you want to."

"I said leave him alone, Anton," said Lila. "Why do you have to be such a jerk?"

"Kiss her foot," he said, "and I'll let you up." He was nineteen and huge. My shoulder hurt and my cheeks were already burning. I leaned forward and pressed my mouth to the top of Lila's sandaled foot. We'd been swimming earlier that day; her skin tasted like salt.

She jerked her leg back. Anton laughed.

"You think you're in charge already," she said, her voice trembling. "You think Dad's going to make you his heir, but I'm his daughter. Me. I'm his heir. And when I am the head of the Zacharov family, I won't forget this."

I stood up slowly and walked back to Grandad's house.

She wouldn't talk to me for weeks after, probably because I'd done what Anton told me instead of what she'd said. And Philip went on like nothing had happened. Like he'd already chosen who he cared more about, already chosen power over me.

I can't trust the people I care about not to hurt me. And I'm not sure I can trust myself not to hurt them, either.

Friendships suck.

I look at the clock on my phone on my way to the car and figure that I better head home if I want my grandfather not to notice how long I've been gone. But I have one more stop to make. On my way out to the car, I call Maura. She's the final ingredient in my plan: someone to answer the prepaid phone if it rings.

"Hello?" she says softly. I hear the baby crying in the background.

"Hey," I say, and let out my breath. I was worried Philip would answer. "It's Cassel. You busy?"

"Just trying to clean some peaches off the wall. You looking for your brother? He's—"

"*No,*" I say, maybe a little too fast. "I have to ask for a favor. From you. It would really help me out."

"Okay," she says.

"All you have to do is answer a cell phone I'm going to give you and pretend that you're the receptionist at a sleep center. I'll write down exactly what you have to say."

"Let me guess. I have to say that you can go back to school."

"Nothing like that. Just confirm the office sent over a letter and that the doctor is with a patient but he'll call them back. Then call me and I'll handle the rest. I don't think it will even come to that. They might want to verify the office really sent out the letter, but that's probably it."

"Aren't you too young to be living a life of crime?"

I smile. "Then you'll do it?"

"Sure. Bring over the phone. Philip isn't going to be back for an hour. I'm assuming that you don't want him to know about this."

I grin. She sounds so normal that it's hard to recall a sunken-eyed Maura perched at the top of the stairs, talking about angels. "Maura, you are a goddess. I will carve your likeness in mashed potatoes so all can worship you like I do. When you leave Philip, will you marry me?"

She laughs. "You better not let Philip hear you say that."

"Yeah," I say. "Are you still? I mean, does he know?"

"Know about what?"

"Oh," I say awkwardly. "The other night. You were talking about leaving—but, hey, I guess you guys worked things out. That's great."

"I never said that," Maura says, her voice flat. "Why would I say that when Philip and I are so happy?"

"I don't know. I probably misunderstood. I gotta go. I'll be over with the phone." I hang up, my hands slippery with sweat. I have no idea what just happened. Maybe she doesn't want to say anything over the phone, in case people are listening. Or maybe someone's there—someone she couldn't talk in front of.

I think of Grandad saying Philip was working her, and I wonder if *I* misunderstood. Maybe she really doesn't remember what she said, because he hired someone to take those memories from her. Maybe she doesn't remember lots of things.

Maura opens the door when I ring the bell, but only partway. She doesn't invite me in either. Unease roils in my stomach.

I look at her eyes, trying to read *something* from them, but she just looks blank, drained. "Thanks again for doing this." I hold out the phone, wrapped in a slip of paper with directions on it.

"It's fine." Her leather gloves brush mine as she picks up the cell, and I realize she's about to close the door. I stick my foot in the gap to stop her.

"Wait," I say. "Hold on a second."

She frowns.

"Do you remember the music?" I ask her.

She lets the door fall open, staring at me. "You hear it too? It started just this morning and it's so beautiful. Don't you think it's beautiful?"

"I've never heard anything like it," I say warily. She honestly doesn't remember. I can think of only one person who'd benefit from her forgetting to leave her husband.

I dig around in my pocket and take out the memory charm. *Give this to remember.* It looks like an heirloom, something that might be passed on to a favored daughter-in-law to welcome her to the family. "My mother wanted you to have this," I lie.

She shrinks back, and I remember that not everyone likes my mother. "Philip doesn't like me to wear charms," she says. "He says a worker's wife shouldn't look afraid."

"You can hide it," I say quickly, but the door's already closing.

"Take care of yourself," Maura says through the sliver of space that remains. "Good-bye, Cassel."

I stand on the steps for a few moments with the charm still in my hand, trying to think. Trying to remember.

Memory is slippery. It bends to our understanding of the world, twists to accommodate our prejudices. It is unreliable. Witnesses seldom remember the same things. They identify the wrong people. They give us the details of events that never happened. Memory is slippery, but my memories suddenly feel slipperier.

After Lila's parents divorced, she got dragged around Europe for a while, then spent several summers in New York with her father. I only knew where she was because her grandmother told my grandmother, so I was surprised to walk into the kitchen one day and see Lila there, sitting on the counter and talking to Barron like she'd never been gone.

"Hey," she said, cracking her gum. She'd cut her hair chin length and dyed it bright pink. That and thick eyeliner made her look older than thirteen. Older than me.

"Scram," said Barron. "We're talking business."

My throat felt tight, like swallowing might hurt. "Whatever." I picked up my Heinlein book and an apple and went back to the basement.

I sat staring at the television for a while as an anime guy with a very large sword hacked up a satisfying amount of monsters. I thought about how much I didn't care that Lila was back. After a while she came down the stairs and flopped onto the worn leather couch next to me. Her thumbs were stuck through holes in her mouse gray sweater, and I noticed a Band-Aid along the curve of her cheek.

"What do you want?" I asked.

"To see you. What do you think?" She gestured to my book. "Is that good?"

"If you like hot cloned assassins. And who doesn't?"

"Only crazy people," she said, and I couldn't help smiling. She told me a little about Paris, about the diamond her father had bid on and won at Sotheby's, which was supposed to have belonged to Rasputin and given him eternal life. About the way she'd had her breakfast on a balcony, drinking milky cups of coffee and eating bread slathered with sweet butter. She didn't sound like she'd missed south Jersey very much, and I couldn't blame her.

"So, what did Barron want?" I asked her.

"Nothing." She bit her lip as she pulled all that pink hair into a sleek, tight ponytail.

"Secret worker stuff," I said, waving my hands around to show how impressed I was. "Ooooh. Don't tell me. I might run to the cops."

She studied the warped yarn around her thumb. "He says it's simple. Just a couple of hours. And he promised me eternal devotion."

"That spends well," I said.

Worker stuff. I still don't know where they went or what she did, but when she got back, her hair was messed up and her lipstick was gone. We didn't talk about that, but we did watch a lot of black-and-white caper movies in the basement, and she let me smoke some of the unfiltered Gitanes she'd picked up in Paris.

Poisonous jealousy thrummed through my veins. I wanted to kill Barron.

I guess I settled for Lila.

I GET BACK TO THE OLD

house in time for dinner, which turns out to be goulash of some kind, thick with noodles and dotted with slivers of carrot and pearl onions. I eat three plates and wash it all down with black coffee as the cat winds around my ankles. I hand her down all the beef I can nonchalantly pick out.

"How'd the doctor's visit go?" Grandad is drinking coffee too, and his hand shakes a little as he brings the cup to his lips. I wonder what else is in the cup.

"Fine," I say slowly. I don't want to tell him about the test or about Maura and her missing memories, but that leaves me with very little to say. "They hooked me up to a machine and wanted me to try and sleep."

"Right there in the office?"

That did sound pretty unlikely, but there's no backing down now. "I managed to doze a little. They were just trying to get some basic results. A baseline, he said."

"Hu-uh," Grandad says, and gets up to clear the dishes. "That must be why you were so late."

I pick up my plate and walk to the sink, saying nothing.

Later that night, when I'm covered with dust but most of the upstairs is clean, we watch *Band of the Banned*. On it, curse workers who belong to a secret FBI team use their powers to stop other workers, mostly drug dealers and serial killers.

"You want to know how to tell if someone's a worker?" Grandad asks with a grunt. He's saved the chair I hate and is sitting in it, his face lit with blue from the screen. The hero of the show, MacEldern, has just kicked down a door while an emotion worker makes the bad guys weep with remorse and begin a rambling confession. It's pretty lame, but Grandad won't let me change the station.

I look at the blackened stumps of my grandfather's fingers. "How?"

"He's the only one gonna deny he's got powers. Everyone else thinks they got something. They got some story about the one time they wished for a bad thing to happen to someone and it did, or wished for some moron to love them and got loved. Like every goddamn coincidence in the world is a working."

"Maybe they do have a little power," I say. "Maybe everyone does."

Grandad snorts. "Don't go believing that crap. You might not be a worker, but you come from a proud worker family. You're too smart to sound like—wasshisname—who said that if kids took enough LSD, they'd unlock their powers."

One in a thousand people is a worker, and of all of them, 60 percent are luck workers. People just want to game the odds. Grandad should understand that.

"Timothy Leary," I say.

"Yeah, well, see how that turned out. All those kids trying to give each other the touch, winding up half out of their heads, imagining they'd worked and been worked, imagining they were dying from blowback, clawing each other apart. The sixties and seventies were stupid decades, full of misinformation and crazy rock stars trying to be prophets, pretending to be workers. You know how many workers were hired just to do the work Fabulous Freddie said he did alone?"

There's no point in trying to distract Grandad from his rants once he's gotten started. He loves them way too much to bother realizing I've heard them about a million times before. The best I can hope for is to push him toward some new rant. "You ever get hired by one of them? You would have been, what, twenty-, thirtysomething back then?"

"I did what old man Zacharov said, didn't I? No freelancing. Know some people who did, though." He laughs. "Like a guy who toured with Black Hole Band. Physical worker. Really good. Someone pissed off the band, that someone'd be in traction."

"I would have thought emotion work would be more popular." Despite myself I'm drawn in. Usually when he delivers this speech, I feel like he's giving it to the rest of the family and I'm just overhearing it. This time we're alone. And I think of all the stuff I've seen photos of on the Internet or on VH1 specials from back then. Performers with goat heads, mermaids who danced in tanks until they drowned because the transformer hadn't known what she was doing when she'd cursed them, people remade like cartoons with big heads and huge eyes. All turning out to be the work of a single transformation worker who died of an overdose in her hotel room, surrounded by worked animals that stood on two legs and spoke gibberish.

There aren't any transformation workers for bands to hire to do any of that today, even if it was legal. There might be one in China, but no one's heard about him for a long time.

"Well, no one can work a crowd. Too many people. There was this one kid who tried. He figured what the heck; he'd ride out the blowback. He'd let a whole crowd of people touch him, one after another, and make them feel euphoric. Like he was a drug."

"So the blowback would be euphoric too, right? Where's the harm in that?"

The white cat jumps onto the couch next to me and starts shredding the cushions with her claws.

"See, that's the problem with kids—that's how you all think. Like you're immortal. Like all the stupid things you're doing, no one ever thought of before. He went crazy. Sure, drooling, grinning, happy crazy, but crazy all the same. He's the son of one of the bigwigs in the Brennan family, so at least they can afford to take care of him."

Grandad goes off again on his rant about the dumbness of kids in general and worker kids in specific. I reach over to pet the cat and it quiets under my hand, not purring, just going still as stone.

Before I go to bed that night, I root through the medicine cabinet. I take two sleeping pills and fall asleep with the cat at my elbow.

I don't dream.

Someone's shaking me. "Hey, sleepyhead, get up."

Grandad hands me a cup of too strong coffee, but this morning I'm grateful for it. My head feels like it's packed with sand.

I reach for my pants and pull them on. My hands automatically tuck in the pockets, but halfway through the gesture I realize something's missing. The amulet. Mom's amulet. The one I tried to give Maura.

Remember.

I go down on my knees and crawl under the bed. Dust, paperback novels I haven't seen in years, and twenty-three cents.

"What are you looking for?" Grandad asks me.

"Nothing," I say.

When we were little, Mom would stand Philip and Barron and me next to each other and tell us that family was everything, that we were the only people we could really rely on. Then she would touch our shoulders with her bare hands, each in turn, and we would be suffused with love for one another, suffocated by love.

"Promise your brothers that you will love one another forever and ever and that you will do whatever you have to to protect one another. You will never hurt one another. You will never steal from one another. Family is the most important thing. There is no one who will love you like your family."

We would hug and cry and promise.

Emotion work fades over months and months, until a year later you feel silly about the stuff you did and said when you were worked, but you don't forget what it was like to be glutted with those emotions.

Those were the only times I've ever felt safe.

Still holding the coffee, I walk outside to clear my head. One foot in front of the other. The air is cold and clean, and I suck in lungfuls like a drowning man.

Things fall out of pockets, I tell myself, and figure that before I melt down completely, I should check the car. If it's there, wedged down in the seat or glittering on one of the floor mats, I am going to feel pretty stupid. I hope I get to feel stupid.

Impulsively I flip open my cell. There are a couple of missed calls from my mother—she must hate not being able to call me on a landline—but I ignore them and call Barron. I need someone to answer questions, someone I can trust not to protect me. The call goes right to voice mail. I stand there, hitting redial again and again, listening to the ringing. I don't know who else to phone. Finally it occurs to me that there might be a way to call his dorm room directly.

I phone the main number for Princeton. They can't seem to find his room, but I remember his roommate's name.

A girl picks up, her voice throaty and soft, like the phone woke her.

"Oh, hey," I say. "I'm looking for my brother Barron?"

"Barron doesn't go to school here anymore," she says.

"What?"

"He dropped out a couple of months into the year." She sounds impatient, no longer sleepy. "You're his brother? He left a bunch of his stuff, you know."

"He's forgetful." Barron *has* always been forgetful, but right now forgetting seems ominous. "I can pick up whatever he left."

"I already mailed it." She stops speaking abruptly, and I wonder what went on between the two of them. I can't imagine Barron dropping out of school because of a girl, but I can't imagine Barron dropping out of Princeton for any reason. "I got tired of him promising to come get it and never showing up. He never even gave me money for the postage."

My mind races. "The address you mailed all that stuff to—do you still have it?"

"Yeah. You sure you're his brother?"

"It's my fault I don't know where he is," I lie quickly.

"After dad died I was a real brat. We had a fight at the funeral and I wouldn't take any of his calls." I'm amazed when my voice hitches in the right place automatically.

"Oh," she says.

"Look, I just want to tell him how sorry I am," I say, further embroidering my tale. I don't know if I sound sorry. What I feel is a cold sort of dread.

I hear the rustling of papers along the line. "Do you have a pen?"

I write the address on my hand, thank her, and hang up as I walk back to the house. There I find my grandfather stacking up dozens of holiday cards he's pulling out from behind a dresser. Glitter dusts his gloves. It's odd how empty the rooms look stripped of junk. My footsteps echo.

"Hey," I say. "I need the car again."

"We still got the bedroom upstairs to do," he says. "Besides the porch and the parlor. And even the rooms that are done we got to box up."

I lift the phone and wave it slightly, like it's to blame. "The doctor needs me to go back for some more tests." Lie until even you believe it—that's the real secret of lying. The only way to have absolutely no tells.

Too bad I'm not quite there yet.

"I thought it might be something like that," he says with a deep sigh. I wait for him to call me out, to say that he's already talked to the doctor or that it's been clear to him from the start that I'm full of it. He doesn't say any of those things; he reaches into the pocket of his jacket and tosses me the keys.

My amulet isn't on the floor of Grandad's Buick or

stuck in the crease of the driver's seat, although I do find a crumpled-up take-out bag. I stop for gas and buy more coffee and three chocolate bars. While I wait for the guy to come back with my change, I program Barron's new address into the GPS on my phone. The place is in Trenton, on a street I've never been.

I don't have much more to go on than a hunch that all the weird things—my sleepwalking, Maura's contradictory memories, Barron's dropping out of school without telling anyone, even the missing amulet—are related.

But as my foot presses on the gas and the car speeds faster, I feel like for the first time in a long while I'm heading in the right direction.

Lila had her fourteenth birthday party at some big hotel of her father's in the city. It was the kind of thing where lots of workers got together, passed around envelopes that only theoretically had to do with the party, and talked about things that were better not overheard by the likes of me. Lila pulled me into her hotel room an hour before it was supposed to start. She had on a ton of glittery black makeup and an oversize shirt with a cartoon cat face on it. Her hair wasn't pink anymore; it was white blond and spiky.

"I hate this," she said, sitting down on the bed. Her hands were bare. "I hate parties."

"Maybe you could drown yourself in a bucket of champagne," I said amiably.

She ignored me. "Let's pierce each other's ears. I want to pierce your ears."

Her ears were already hung with tiny pearls. I know if I scratched them against my teeth, they'd turn out to be real. She touched an earring self-consciously, like she could hear my thoughts. "I got these done with an ear gun when I was seven," she said. "My mom told me that she would give me ice cream if I didn't cry, but I cried anyway."

"And you want more holes because you think pain will distract you from all the annoying celebrating? Or because stabbing me will make you feel better?"

"Something like that." She smiled enigmatically, went into the bathroom, and came out with a wad of cotton balls and a safety pin. After setting them down on top of the minibar, she pulled out one of the tiny bottles of vodka. "Go get ice from the machine."

"Don't you have friends—I mean, not that we're not friends, but—"

"It's complicated," she said. "Jennifer hates me because of something Lorraine and Margot told her. They're always making up stuff. I don't want to talk about them. I want ice."

"You are kind of a bully," I said.

"I have to be able to order people around someday," she said, her gaze steady. "Like Dad does. Besides, you already knew I was a bully. You know me."

"What makes you think I even want my ears pierced?"

"Girls think pierced ears are hot. Besides, *I* know *you*, too. You like to be bullied."

"Maybe I did when I was nine," I said, but I took the bucket into the hall and brought it back full of ice.

She walked over to the dresser, hopped up, and pushed

a pile of CDs, underwear, and folded-up notes onto the floor.

"Come here," she said, her voice hushed, dramatic. "First you light the match, and then you run the pin through the flame. See?" Lila struck the match and twirled the pin in its fire. Her eyes shone. "It goes black and iridescent. Now it's sterile."

I pushed up the shaggy black mop of my hair and tilted my head like a willing sacrifice. The press of the ice made me shiver. Her legs were slightly apart and I had to stand between her knees to get close enough.

"Hold still," she said, her fingers cold on my skin. I watched melting ice running down her wrist to drip off her elbow. We both waited, quietly, as though this was a ceremonial rite. After a minute or so she dropped the cube and pressed the pin against my ear, slowly stabbing through.

"Ow!" I pulled away at the last moment.

She laughed. "Cassel! The pin's sticking half out of your ear."

"It *hurt*," I said, half in astonishment. But it wasn't that. It was too much sensation—the feel of her thighs holding me in place mixing with the sharp pain.

"You can hurt me worse if you want," she said, and pushed the pin through with a sudden, savage thrust. I sucked in my breath.

She slid off the dresser to fetch new ice for her own ear from the bucket. Her eyes were glittering. "Do mine up high. You're going to have to really press to get through the cartilage."

I ran a safety pin above a match and lined it up above the ear holes she already had. Lila bit her lip, but she didn't cry out, even though I saw her eyes water. She just dug her fingers into the corduroy striping of my pants as I pressed. The metal pin bent a little, and I wondered if I was going to be able to get it all the way through, when it suddenly went with an audible pop. She made a strangled sound, and I carefully closed the safety pin so that it hung like a fancy formal earring at the very top of her ear.

Then she dipped the cotton swabs in vodka to wipe away the blood and poured us a gagging shot apiece. Her hands were shaking.

"Happy birthday," I said.

I heard steps outside the door, but Lila didn't seem to notice them. Instead she leaned in. Her tongue was as hot as a match on my ear, and it made my body jerk in surprise. I was still trying to convince myself that it had really happened when she stuck out her tongue and showed me my own blood.

That was when the door opened and Lila's mother walked in. She cleared her throat, but Lila didn't step back. "What's going on in here? Why aren't you ready for your party?"

"I'll be fashionably late," Lila said, a smile threatening at the corners of her mouth.

"Have you been drinking?" Mrs. Zacharov looked at me like I was a stranger. "Get out."

I walked past Lila's mother and out the door.

The party was in full swing when I got there, full of

people I didn't know. I felt out of place as I stalked to my seat, and my ear throbbed like a second heart. Overcompensating, I tried to be funny in front of Lila's friends and wound up being so obnoxious that some boy she went to school with threw a punch at me in the men's room. I pushed him, and he gashed his head on one of the sinks.

The next day Barron told me he had asked Lila out. They'd started dating around the time I was being escorted from the hotel.

According to my GPS, Barron's new place is a row house on a street with cracked sidewalks and a few boarded-up apartment buildings. One of his front windows is missing most of its glass and is partially covered with duct tape. I open the screen door and knock on the cheap hollow-core door beyond. Paint flakes off on my hands.

I knock, wait, and knock again. There's no answer and no motorcycle parked nearby either. I don't see any lights on through the newspaper taped up in place of blinds.

There's a basic lock and a dead bolt on the door. Easy to get around. My driver's license slid through the gap unlocks the first. The dead bolt is trickier, but I get a wire from the trunk of the car, thread it through the keyhole, and rake it over the pins until they all stick at the right height. Luckily Barron hasn't upgraded to anything fancy. I turn the knob, pick up my license, and walk into the kitchen.

For a moment, looking at the laminate countertops, I think I've broken into the wrong house. Covering the white cabinets are sticky notes: "Notebook will tell you what you forgot," "Keys on hook," "Pay bills in cash," "You are Barron Sharpe," "Phone in jacket." A carton of milk sits open on the counter, its curdled contents gray with cigarette ash. Butts float on the surface. There's a pile of bills—mostly student loans—all of them unopened.

"You are Barron Sharpe" doesn't leave a lot of room for doubt.

His laptop and a pile of manila folders cover the card table in the center of the kitchen. I slump down on one of the chairs and glance over the files—legal briefs from my mother's appeal. He's made notes in ketchup-red marker, and it finally occurs to me that this could be the reason he dropped out of school. He must be managing the case. That makes some sense, but not enough.

There's a composition notebook sitting under one of the folders, marked February to April. I flip it open, expecting to see more notes on the case, but it looks a lot like a diary. At the top of each page is a date, and beneath it is an obsessively detailed list of what Barron ate, who he talked to, how he was feeling—and then at the bottom, a bulleted list of things to be sure to remember. Today started:

March 19

Breakfast: Protein shake
Ran 1 mile
Upon waking, experienced slight lethargy and
soreness in muscles.

Wore: light green buttoned shirt, black cargo
pants, black shoes (Prada)

Mom continues to complain about the other inmates, how much she's suffering without us, and her fear that, basically, we're out of her control. She needs to realize that we're grown up, but I don't know if she's ready for that. As we get closer and closer to the trial, I worry more about what life's going to be like when she comes home.

She says that she's enticed some millionaire and is pinning a lot of her hopes on him. I have sent her clippings about him. I'm worried about her getting herself in trouble again and I honestly can't believe that this man has no idea who she is—or that if he doesn't, that he's going to remain ignorant. When she does get out of jail, she is going to have to be more circumspect, something I'm sure she's not going to be willing to do.

I can't remember faces from high school. I ran into someone on the street who said he knew me. I told him that I was Barron's twin and that I went to another school. I must study the yearbook.

Philip is as tedious as ever. He acts as though he is resolved to do what is necessary, but he isn't. It's not just weakness but a continual romantic need to believe himself manipulated against his will instead of admitting he wants power and privilege. He sickens me more each day, but Anton trusts him in a way that Anton will never really trust me. But Anton believes I can deliver, and I doubt he can say that about Philip.

Maybe the money we get will be enough to control Mom for a while. By the time this is over, Anton'll owe us everything.

The notes for today stop there, but glancing back over the past few weeks, I can see that he recorded random details, conversations, and feelings as though he expected to forget them. I open the laptop gingerly, not sure what other weirdness I'm going to discover, but it's set to sleep, with the page showing my YouTube debut.

The raw footage was taken with a cell phone, so the quality is grainy and I don't look like much more than a pale, shirtless blob, but I wince when I look like I'm losing my balance. I hear someone yell "jump" in the background, and the angle swings toward the crowd. In that moment I see her. A white shape near the scrubby bushes. The cat, licking her paw. The cat I was chasing in my dream. I stare at the video and stare at her, trying to make some sense of how a cat from my dream—a cat that looks a lot like the cat that has been sleeping at the foot of my bed—could have really been there that night.

I take the notebook off the table and flip to the day the video was uploaded.

March 15th

Breakfast: Egg whites
Ran 1 mile
Upon waking, felt fine. Clipped nose hair.

Wore: dark blue jeans (Monarchy), coat, blue
dress shirt (HUGO)

Logged into C's email and found video. Clearly shows L.
but no clues as to where she is now. C is at the old house,
but G there and keeping an eye on everything. P says he's
going to take care of it. This is all his fault.

Beware the ides of March. Some joke. I found her collar,
but no clue as to how she got out of it. P must have not
clipped it on correctly. I have to find a way to use this to
wedge P and A further apart.

I have to control the situation.

"Control" is underlined twice, the second line so heavy that
it ripped through the page.

I stare at the entry until the words blur in front of
me. C is Cassel—the video must have been of me up on
the roof. P must be Philip. A could be Anton, since Barron
mentioned him before. I blink at G for a moment and then
realize it's for our grandfather. But L? I immediately think
of Lila, even though it makes no sense.

I grab the laptop and play the video of me again,
frame by frame. We barely see any of the crowd; the
camera pans over people too fast to catch anything but
blurs. The only faces I can pick out belong to students.
No Lila. No dead girls. No one that doesn't belong. No
one wearing a collar.

The only thing in that video that could be wearing a collar is the cat.

Only you can undo the curse.

The thought is so absurd that it actually makes me grin.

I walk toward the bathroom to splash water on my face, but as I pass a door, the strong smell of ammonia stops me. It opens into a room, empty except for a metal cage that sits near the window. The hinged wire door is open. The newspaper stuffed into the cage and the wooden floor around it is stained with what, given the sharp smell and the yellowing, is probably cat piss. Thick crusted layers of it, like something was kept locked up for a long time and not cleaned up after.

I hold my breath and lean closer. Caught in a wire joint are a few short white hairs. I back out of the room.

Barron's losing his memories. So's Maura, and maybe me too. I don't remember the details of Lila's murder. I don't remember how I got onto the roof. I don't remember what happened to my memory charm.

Let's say someone is taking those memories. I don't think that's too much of a stretch.

Let's also say someone gave me that dream, the one where the cat was begging for help. If I were cursed to have it, that would mean someone had to touch me, hand to skin. The cat—the one that slept on my bed, the one near my dorm room in the video—did touch me.

So maybe the cat gave me the dream.

Of course, that's ridiculous. Cats are animals. They can no more perform curse work than they can perform a sonata or compose a villanelle.

Unless the cat was once a girl. A transformed girl. A dream worker. Lila.

Which would mean something so monumental that I almost can't contemplate it. It would mean *she's not dead.*

IN BARRON'S BATHROOM

the beige tile walls look too familiar, but like I'm seeing them from the wrong angle.

It's crazy, the idea of Lila being a cat. The idea that Barron had her locked up in his house all this time is even crazier. And the idea that I might not have killed Lila throws me so off balance that I don't know how to right myself.

I look in the mirror—staring at my face. Looking at the scraggly black hair curling around my jaw and my ink-blot eyes, looking to see if I should be afraid. If I'm still a murderer. If I'm cracking up.

There's a dizzy sense of déjà vu as I glance at the reflection of the tub behind me. I stumble and barely catch myself.

I thrashed in the water and my hands turned to arms turned to starfish curling like snakes. Everything went wrong and I was coming apart and water closed over my head and—

More things I half-remember.

I turn and crouch on the floor, touching the tile near the tub faucet. I can almost recall my fingers reaching for the same handle, but then the memory goes surreal and dreamlike and my fingers become scrabbling black claws.

Animal fear, instinctual and horrible, overwhelms me. I have to get out of here—that's the only thing I can think. I head for the front door, barely smart enough to twist the knob so that the door locks behind me when it closes. I get into Grandad's car and sit for a moment, waiting to feel like a stupid kid running from some pretend ghost. I eat one of the candy bars while I wait. The chocolate tastes like dust, but I swallow it anyway.

I have to sort things out.

My memories are full of shadows, and no amount of chasing them around my head seems to make them any more substantial.

What I need is a worker. One that's going to give me answers without asking a lot of questions. One that can help me make these puzzle pieces fit together and show me the picture. I turn the ignition and head south.

The dirt mall on Route 9 is less a mall and more one big warehouse with aisles of individual shops separated by counters or curtains. Barron and I would get Philip or Grandad to drive us, and then we'd spend the day eating hot dogs and buying cheap knives to hide in our boots. Barron would complain about being stuck with me, but as soon as we got there, he'd disappear to chat up the girl who worked selling pickles out of vats.

The place doesn't look all that different from how it did then. Out front a woman stands by a barrel of pastel-colored baskets while a guy is trying to hawk a bunch of rabbit pelts. Three for five bucks.

Inside, the smells of fried food make my stomach growl. I head toward the back, past the eel-skin wallet stall and the place with the heavy silver rings and pewter dragons, toward the fortune-tellers with their velvet skirts and marked cards. They charge five dollars to say "You sometimes feel lonely, even in the company of others" or "You once experienced a tragic loss that has given you an unusual perceptiveness" or even "You are usually shy, but in the future you are going to find yourself the center of attention."

There are lots of little malls like these in Jersey, but this one's only twenty minutes from Carney. The fortune-tellers' real business is selling charms made by retired residents; a few workers even freelance their services out of the back. It's the best place to go for a little cheap curse work that's not directly related to the crime families. And the charms are a lot more reliable and varied than the kind you get from a regular mall or the gas station.

I walk up to a scarf-draped table. "Crooked Annie," I say, and the old woman smiles. One of her teeth is black with rot. She's wearing plastic and glass rings over her purple satin gloves, and she's got on several layers of dresses with tiny bells along the hem.

"I know you, Cassel Sharpe. How's your mother?"

Annie's been selling magic for longer than I've been alive. She's old school. Discreet. And with as little knowledge as I have, the one thing I'm sure of is that I can't afford to share it.

"Jail. Got caught working some rich guy."

Annie sighs. She's in the life, so she's not surprised or embarrassed for me, like people at school would be. She shifts her weight forward. "Out soon?"

I nod, although I'm not sure. Mom keeps saying she didn't do it (which I don't believe), that the evidence against her is prejudice and hand waving (which I sort of do believe), and that it will be overturned on the appeal that's been dragging on. "You miss your mother, don't you?"

I nod again, although I'm not sure about that, either. It's easier with her slightly removed, unable to upturn our lives at a moment's notice. From jail she's a benevolent, slightly crazy matriarch. At home she'd go back to being a despot.

"I need to buy a couple of charms. For memory. Good ones."

"What? You think I sell ones that are no good?"

I smile. "I know you do."

That turns her grin wicked. She pats my face with a satin-covered hand. I remember that I haven't shaved and that my cheeks are probably rough enough to catch the fabric, but she doesn't seem to mind. "Just like your brothers.

You know what they used to say about boys like you? Clever as the devil and twice as pretty."

It's kind of a ridiculous compliment, but it embarrasses me into looking at the floor. "I have some questions, too. About memory magic. Look, I know I'm not a worker, but I really need to know."

Annie pushes aside a worn pack of tarot cards. "Sit," she says, and rummages under the table, pulling out a large plastic toolbox. Inside it is an array of rocks. She pulls out a shining piece of onyx with a hole bored through the middle, and a chunk of cloudy pink crystal. "First things first. Here are the charms you're asking for."

Lots of really good amulets look like junk. These don't look so bad.

"I hate to ask," I say, sitting down backward on the hard metal folding chair. "But—"

"You want something fancier?"

I shake my head. "Just smaller."

She mutters under her breath and turns back to her stock. "Here, I've got this." She holds up a pebble, maybe a piece of driveway gravel.

"I'll take these," I say, pointing to the pebble and the onyx circle. "In fact, give me three of the little ones if you've got them. Plus the onyx."

Annie raises her eyebrows but says only, "Forty. Each."

Normally I would dicker with her, but I figure she's inflating the cost so she can justify giving me the information. I pull out the bills and slide them over.

She grins her black-toothed grin. "So, what do you want to know?"

"How can you tell if your memories have been changed? Is there just a black hole in your thoughts? Can memories be replaced with other memories?"

She lights a hand-rolled cigarette that stinks of green tea leaves. "I'm not admitting to knowing anybody when I answer this. I'm just speculating, you understand? All I do is I make some of these amulets and I sell a few that my friends make, and the government hasn't managed to make that illegal yet."

"Sure," I say, affronted. "Just because I'm not—"

"Don't get your nose in a twist. I'm not explaining for you. I'm explaining it for the edification of anyone who happens to be listening in on this conversation. And they do."

"Who does?"

She gives me a long look, like I'm slow, and sucks on her cigarette, blowing herbal smoke into the air. "The government."

"Oh," I say. Even though I'm pretty sure she's just paranoid, possibly with a touch of dementia, I feel an intense urge to look behind me.

"On to your questions. How it feels depends on who did the working. The best workers make it seamless. They'll remove a memory and replace it with a new one. The worst ones are slobs. They might be able to make you remember you owe them money, but if there's no money in your pocket and you don't remember spending any either, you're going to start asking questions.

"Most memory workers fall somewhere in the middle in terms of skill. They leave behind pieces, threads. A blue sky without the rest of a day. Aching sorrow with no cause."

"Clues," I say.

"Sure, if you want to call them that." She takes another long drag on her tea cigarette. "There's four different kinds of memory curses. A memory worker can rip memories right out of your head, leaving that big hole you're talking about, or they can give you new memories of things that never happened. They can sift through your memories and learn stuff, or they can simply block your access to your own memories."

"Why would they do that last one? The blocking access one?" I touch the smooth black circle of the memory stone. It glides against the pad of my gloved finger.

"Because it's easier to block access than to remove a memory entirely, which makes it cheaper. Just like changing a single piece of a memory is easier than creating a whole new one. And if you remove the block, then the memory comes back, which is nice if you want to be able to reverse the process."

I nod my head, although I'm not sure I'm following.

"A shady memory worker will charge for ripping a memory but just put a block in. Then he'll go and charge the victim to take the block back out again. That's bad business, but what do these kids know? They've got no respect anymore." She looks at me intently. "Your family never told you any of this?"

"I'm not a worker," I remind her, but shame heats my

face. I should know; my family should have trusted me enough. That they didn't speaks volumes about what they think of me.

"But your brother—," she says.

"Can it be reversed?" I ask, interrupting her. I really don't want to talk about my family right now.

She looks at me so intently that I drop my gaze. Then she clears her throat and starts talking like I wasn't just incredibly rude. "Memory magic's permanent. But that doesn't mean people can't change their minds. You can make someone remember that you're the hottest thing out there, but they can take a good look at you and decide otherwise."

I force a smile, but my stomach feels like I've swallowed lead. "What about transformation work?"

She shrugs her shoulders. The bells on her skirts jingle. "What about it?"

"Is it permanent too?"

"Another transformation worker can undo it, so long as the person was turned into a living thing. A changer can turn a boy into a boat and then back to a boy, but the kid won't live through the transformation. Once a living thing becomes a nonliving thing, that's that."

That's that. I want to ask her about a girl changed into a cat, but I can't risk being that specific. I've risked enough.

"Thanks," I say, standing. I'm not sure what I learned, except that the answers I need aren't going to be easy to get.

She winks. "You tell that grandfather of yours that Crooked Annie was asking after him."

"I will," I say, although I know I won't. If I told him I was down near Carney, he'd want to know why.

I start down the aisle when I remember something and turn back. "Hey, is Mrs. Z still living in town?"

Lila's mother. I think of how I hung up the pay phone at the sound of her voice, about the way she looked at me when she found me in the hotel room at Lila's birthday party.

How for years I thought she saw some secret darkness in me that even I hadn't seen.

"Sure is," Annie says. "Can't leave Carney, or that husband of hers is going to come after her."

"Come after her?"

"He thinks she knows where that daughter of theirs got to and won't tell him. I told her not to worry. She'll outlast him. Even the Resurrection Diamond can't work forever."

"That stone he got in Paris with Lila?" I remembered the diamond had something to do with Rasputin, but I didn't remember that it had a name.

"Supposed to hold a curse so that the wearer never dies. Sounds like a load of crap, right? That would mean a stone could do more than deflect curses. But it seems to work. No one's killed him yet, and plenty of people have tried. I'd love to have a look at it." She tilts her head to the side. "You were in love with his girl Lila, huh? Now that I think of it, I remember you mooning after her. You and that brother of yours."

"That was a long time ago."

She leans up to kiss my cheek, which startles me into flinching. "Two brothers in love with the same woman never goes well."

Barron dated lots of other girls while he dated Lila. Girls his age, girls that went to his school and had their own cars. Lila would call and ask for Barron, and I would tell some obvious sloppy lie that I hoped she saw through, but she always believed. Then we'd talk until either Barron came home in time to say good night to her or she fell asleep.

The worst times, though, were when he was home and he talked to her in a bored voice while he watched television.

"She's just a kid," he told me when I asked about her. "She's not my real girlfriend. Besides, she lives, like, two hours away."

"Why don't you dump her, then?" I thought about the sound of her breath on the phone, evening out into sleep. I didn't understand how he could want anyone more than her.

He grinned. "I don't want to hurt her feelings."

I slammed my hand down on the breakfast table. Stacks of plates and junk quivered. "You're just dating her because she's Zacharov's daughter."

His grin widened. "You don't know that. Maybe I'm dating her just to mess with you."

I wanted to tell her the truth about him, but then she'd have stopped calling.

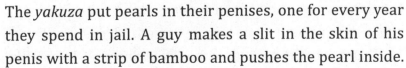

The *yakuza* put pearls in their penises, one for every year they spend in jail. A guy makes a slit in the skin of his penis with a strip of bamboo and pushes the pearl inside. It must be spectacularly painful. I figured it couldn't be nearly as bad to shove three tiny pebbles under the skin of my leg.

In the backseat of Grandad's car I fold up the left leg of my jeans to my knee. I bought what I thought were the necessary supplies at the nearby mart, and now, in the parking lot, I dump them out of the plastic bag and onto the seat. First I shave a three-inch spot on my calf with a disposable razor and splash it clean with bottled water. It's slow going. The razor's cheap, and by the time I'm done, my skin is red and bleeding from tiny cuts.

I realize I don't have anything to mop up what's likely to be more blood than I expected. I take off my shirt and press it to the skin, ignoring the sting. I have a bottle of hydrogen peroxide to sterilize with, but I don't. Maybe I'll have the balls to use it at the end, but right now my leg is hurting enough.

Sliding a razor blade out of a box of them, I look guiltily out the window of the car. Families are walking through the lot, children pushed in the baskets of carts, men carrying trays of coffees. *Don't look*, I tell them silently, and slide the sharp edge over my leg.

It goes in so easily and with so little pain that it frightens me. I feel only a sharp sting and a cold strangeness move through my limbs. It even seems to trick my skin, because for a moment there's only a line on my leg where the flesh parts. Then blood blooms along the cut, first in spots, then welling up in a long strip of red.

Pushing in the pebbles is the agonizing part. It feels like I'm ripping off my own skin as I slide in the three pebbles, one for every year I thought I was a murderer. Each one hurts so much that I have to choke down nausea as I thread the needle, bend it, and give myself two terrible, sloppy, agonizing stitches.

I'm going to go home and get Lila and we're getting as far away as we can. Maybe we'll go to China and find someone to turn her back into a girl, maybe I'll take her to her father and try to explain. But we're going tonight.

I'm no further along in figuring out who the memory worker is than I was before the visit to Crooked Annie, but I'm more sure than ever that I've been worked. I'm guessing it's Anton, since obviously he and Philip and Barron are conspiring together. I thought Anton worked luck, but he might have messed up my head to think that. If he is the memory worker, he sure messed up Barron's.

And Philip just let it happen.

As I watch the hydrogen peroxide froth, I tell myself that it's okay to be light-headed now, okay for my hands to shake, because it's done. It's over. Nobody is going to be able to make me forget one single thing. Not ever again.

When I get out of the car in the driveway of the house, I notice the doors of the barn are open. I walk over and look inside. No traps. No cats. No eyes shining from the shadows.

I stand there, looking for a long moment, trying to understand what happened. Then I run to the house and yank open the door.

"Where are the cats?" I yell.

"Your brother called the animal shelter," Grandad says,

looking up from a pile of moth-eaten linens. "They came this afternoon."

"What about the white cat? My cat?"

"You know you couldn't keep her," he says. "Let her go to people that can take care of her."

"How could you do that? How could you let them take her?"

He reaches out his hand, but I step back.

"Which brother? Who called the shelter?" My voice is shaking with rage.

"You can't blame him," he says. "He was just trying to do right by this place. They were making a mess of the barn."

"Who was it?" I ask.

"Philip," he says with a defeated shrug of his shoulders. He's still talking, explaining something about how the cats being gone is a good thing, but I'm not listening.

I'm thinking about Barron and Maura and my stolen memories and the missing cat and how I'm going to make Philip pay for it. All of it. With interest.

I HATE WALKING INTO

shelters. I hate the smell of urine, feces, food, and wet newsprint all tangled up together. I hate the desperate whining sound of animals, the endless crying from the cages, and the guilt at not being able to do anything for them. I'm already feeling a little crazy when I walk into the first shelter, and it takes me until the third to find her. The white cat.

She looks at me from the back of the cage. She's not howling or rubbing her face against the bars, like some of the other animals. She looks like a snake, ready to strike.

But she doesn't look like anything that was ever human.

"What are you?" I say. "Lila?"

That makes her stand up and come to the front of the bars. She meows once, plaintively. A shudder runs through me that's part terror and part revulsion.

A girl can't be a cat.

Unbidden the memory of the last time I saw Lila rises. I can smell the blood. I can feel the smile pulling at my mouth when I look down at her body. Even if that memory's false, it feels real. This—the idea that she's alive, that I can still save her—feels like playing pretend. Like lying to myself. Like losing my mind.

Her mismatched green and blue eyes are very like Lila's, though. And she's looking up at me. And even though I might be going crazy, even though it feels impossible, I'm certain it's her.

I turn, and she yowls again and again, but I make myself ignore her and walk out of the animal housing area. I go up to the desk, where a heavyset woman in a schnauzer-print sweatshirt is telling some guy where to hang flyers promising a reward for his missing ball python.

"I'd like to adopt the white cat," I tell her.

She slides me a form. It asks me for the name and address of my veterinarian, how long I've lived at my current address, and whether I approve of declawing. I put down the answers that I think they want to hear and I leave the vet part blank. My hands are shaking and I feel the way I did after my father's car accident, when time seemed to move differently for me than for other people. It's too fast and too slow, and all I can think is that if I walk out of here with the cat, then I'll be able to sit and wait for time to catch up with itself again.

"This is your birthday?" she asks me, tapping the paper.

I nod.

"You're only seventeen." She points to where it says in bold print at the top of the page: *Must be 18 to adopt.* I just stare at the words. Normally I pay attention to things like that. I prepare. Map out the variables. But instead I'm sucking air like a fish.

"You don't understand," I say, and I watch a frown pinch her brows. "That didn't come out right. That's my cat—I mean, the one I wanted to adopt. Someone must have brought her here, but she's really mine."

"She didn't come in with a collar," she says. "Or tags."

I laugh uneasily, caught. "She's always catching it on something."

"Kid, that cat was a stray living in a barn. It came in only a couple of hours ago, and if someone was feeding it, they weren't feeding it much or for long."

"She was living in a barn," I say. "But now she lives with me."

The woman shakes her head. "I don't know what happened, but I can guess. You didn't get permission to bring that cat home and your parents sent it to a shelter. Irresponsible—"

"That's not what happened." I wonder what she'd do if I told her what I thought *had* happened. I almost laugh.

The bell in the front jingles as a couple with a kid walk in the door. The schnauzer-shirted woman turns toward them with a smile.

"We're here to get a puppy!" shouts the little girl. All around her mouth looks sticky. Her gloves are smeared with brown stains.

"Wait," I say desperately. "Please."

The woman gives me a quick, pitying look. "Come back when you convince one of your parents to give you permission. Like this kid."

I take a deep breath. "Are you working here tomorrow?" I ask her.

She puts a hand on her hip, annoyed now, probably more angry because she briefly felt sorry for me, but I don't care. "No, but the guy on tomorrow is gonna tell you the same thing. Get a parent."

I nod, but I'm not really listening anymore, because my head is full of the sound of Lila shrieking from behind bars. Crying and crying with no one coming.

My dad taught me this trick to calm down. Like, before I was going into a house to steal something or if the police were questioning me. He said to imagine that I was on a beach and concentrate on the sounds of clear blue water lapping at my feet. The feel of the sand beneath toes. Take deep breaths of sea air.

It doesn't work.

Sam picks up on the second ring. "I'm at play practice," he says in a near-whisper. "Stavrakis is giving me the stink eye. Talk fast."

I have very little to offer Sam. I'm trusting him despite

myself, and I know trust isn't worth much. I don't even know if he'll want it. "I really need your help."

"Are you okay? You sound serious."

I make myself laugh. "I have to spring a cat out of the Rumelt Animal Shelter. Think of it as a prison break."

It does the trick. He laughs. "Whose cat?"

"My cat. What do you think? That I break out the cats of strangers?"

"Let me guess, she was framed. She's innocent."

"Just like everybody else in prison." I think of Mom. The laugh bubbles up my throat all wrong: sarcastic, harsh. "Good, so tomorrow?" I say, once I've managed to stop.

"Yeah, it's him," I hear Sam say, but his voice is smothered, like maybe his hand is over the phone. "You want to come?" He says something else, too, but I can't hear it.

"Sam!" I say, hitting my hand on the dashboard.

"Hey, Cassel." It's Daneca, talking softly. Daneca with her hemp and her causes and her never noticing that I avoid her. "What's all this about a cat? Sam says you need some help."

"I just need one person," I tell her. The last thing I want is to have to pull this off with Daneca looking over my shoulder.

"Sam says he could use a ride."

"What's wrong with his car?" Sam drives a hearse, which apparently are gas guzzlers, so to be environmentally responsible, he's converted it to run on grease. The inside of it always smells pleasantly of fried food.

"Not sure," she says.

I guess I don't have a lot of choices. I bite the inside of

my cheek and grate out the words. "That would be great, then. You're a real pal, Daneca."

I hang up the phone before I can be more obnoxious, my mind occupied with imagining how I can possibly pay the debt I am going to owe them. If all friendships are negotiations of power, I need some new leverage.

Grandad is furious when I get home. He starts yelling at me when I walk through the door. Stupid crap about taking the car without permission and how this is my house and I should be the one taking care of it. He has a lot to say about how old and infirm he is, which just makes me laugh, and me laughing makes him yell louder.

"Just *shut up!*" I shout, and walk up to my room.

He doesn't say a thing.

Let's go with the cat being Lila. Just for another minute, even if you think I've lost it. Just to try and figure some things out.

Someone made her that way.

And that someone is working with my brothers.

And that someone must be a transformation worker, which makes him (or her) one of the most powerful workers in America.

Which means I'm screwed. I can't fight that.

The Magritte poster taped above me shows the back of a well-groomed nineteenth-century man looking into the mirror on his mantle, but the reflection in the mirror is the well-groomed back of his head. When I bought it, I liked that you could never see the man's face, but now when I look at it, I wonder if he has one.

My phone rings at around ten that night. It's Sam, and when I pick it up, I can hear he's drunk.

"Come out," he says, manic and slurring. "I'm at a party."

"I'm tired," I say. I have been staring at the same cracked patch of plaster for hours. I don't feel like getting up.

"Come on," he says. "I wouldn't even be here if it wasn't for you."

I roll onto my side. "What do you mean?"

"These guys love me now that I'm their bookie." He laughs. "Gavin Perry just offered me a beer! You did this for me, man, and I'm not going to forget it. Tomorrow we're going to get back your cat, and then—"

"Okay. Where are you?" It's kind of funny that he thinks he owes me anything when he's been doing stuff for me left and right. I push myself off the bed.

After all, there's no point in staying here. All I'm doing is thinking of Lila as a cat, stuck in a cage and crying until her throat is raw, or wearing my own memories thin with scrutinizing.

He gives me an address. It's Zoe Papadopoulos's place. I've been there before. Her parents travel for their jobs, meaning that she hosts a lot of parties.

Grandad is asleep in front of the television. On the news I see Governor Patton, who has been a big proponent of Proposition 2, the thing that's supposed to force everybody to get tested to ascertain who's a worker and who's not. Patton is going on and on about how he believes that workers should come forward in support of his proposition so that they can let the world know that they are the good, law-abiding citizens they claim to be. He says no one ever needs to know what's on the paper, except the individual. At this time he has no plans to propose any legislation that gives the government access to those private medical records. Right.

Grandad snores.

I pick up the keys and go.

Zoe's house is in one of the new developments in Neshanic Station, on a stretch of several acres with woods attached. It's huge, and when I get there, the driveway is clogged with cars. The massive double doors are flung wide open, and there's a girl I don't know laughing hysterically on the front porch, leaning against a fat Corinthian column with a bottle of red wine in her hand.

"What are you celebrating?" I ask her.

"Celebrating," she repeats, like she doesn't understand the word. Then a slow smile lifts the corners of her mouth. "Life!"

I can't even force a smile in return. My skin itches to be elsewhere. To be breaking into the animal shelter. To be *doing something*. The wait is the worst part of the con, the long stretch of hours before things start to happen. That's when nerves get the best of people.

I walk inside, willing my nerves not to get the best of me.

The living room is lit with candles that have burned down, so that melting wax pools on furniture. Only a few kids are there, sitting on the floor and drinking beer. A sophomore says something, and they all look over at me.

It took two and a half years to get people to forget what was different about me, and only fifteen minutes to get them to remember.

I give them a nod and wonder if Sam's at least taking bets on the rumors about me. He'd better.

In the kitchen a bunch of seniors are gathered around Harvey Silverman, who's downing a pyramid of shots. Outside, by the pool, I see most of the rest of the partygoers. It's too cold to swim, but a couple of fully clothed people are anyway, their lips blue in the patio lights.

"Cassel Sharpe," Audrey says, looping her arm through mine. "Look what the cat dragged in."

Audrey's eyes are glassy, her smile vague. She still looks lovely. She glances toward Greg Harmsford leaning against a bookshelf, talking with two girls from the field hockey team. I wonder if they came to the party together.

"Just like always," she says, looking back at me. "Watching from the shadows. Observing everybody. Judging us."

"That's not what I'm doing," I say. I don't know how to explain how afraid I am of being judged.

"I liked when you were my boyfriend," she says, and leans her head against my shoulder, maybe out of habit, maybe because she's drunk. It's enough like tenderness for me to pretend. "I liked you watching me."

I resist the urge to promise her that if she tells me all the things I did right, I'll do them again.

"Didn't you like it when I was your girlfriend?" she

asks, her voice gone so soft that it's mostly breath.

"You're the one who broke it off," I tell her, but my voice has dropped low, and the words come out like a caress. I don't care about what I'm saying. I only care about keeping her here, talking with me. She makes me feel like it's possible to slip out of my old life and into hers, where everything is easy and honest.

"I'm not over you," she says. "I don't think."

"Oh," I say, and then I lean in and kiss her. *I don't think. Don't think.* I just mash my mouth against hers. She tastes like tequila. It's an awful kiss, too full of grief and frustration and the knowledge that I am screwing everything up and don't know how to do anything but screw things up worse.

She reaches up her hands and touches my shoulders gently. She doesn't push me away. Her fingers curl against the nape of my neck, which tickles a little and makes me smile against her lips. I slow down. Better. She sighs into my mouth.

I let my fingers trace her collarbone, dip into the hollow of her neck. I want to kiss her there. I want to let my mouth and tongue follow the road map of freckles across her milky skin.

"Hey," Greg says. "Get off her."

Audrey stumbles back, nearly into Greg. I feel like I've come up out of such deep water that I have the bends. I forgot that we're at a party.

"You're drunk," Greg tells her, and grabs hold of her upper arm. Audrey sways a little unsteadily.

My fingers curl into fists. I want to shove him against the wall. I want to break open my knuckles on his face. I look at Audrey for a signal. I tell myself that if she looks scared or even angry, I am going to hurt him.

She's looking down, though, her face turned away from me. All that rage curdles into self-loathing.

"What are you even doing here?" Greg says. "I thought the dean finally figured out that you're a criminal and kicked you out."

"I didn't think this was an official school-sponsored event," I say.

"Nobody wants you around, working their girlfriends." His smile is smug. "You and I both know that's the only way you can get a date."

I think of Maura, and my sight narrows. It's like I'm looking at Greg through a tunnel of blackness. My fists clench so tightly that I can feel my nails through the leather of my gloves. I hit him, hard, sending him sprawling on the wooden floor. My foot is digging into his ribs before Rahul Pathak grabs me around the waist and pulls me away from him.

"Chill out, Sharpe," Rahul says, but I struggle against his hold. All I want to do is kick Greg again. Someone I can't see grabs my wrist and twists it behind me.

Audrey's gone.

Greg stands up, wiping his mouth. "I saw your mother's trial in the paper, Sharpe. I know you're just like her."

"If I was, I would make you beg to blow me," I sneer.

"Get him outside," someone says, and Rahul steers me

toward the door. The swimmers look up when we march through. Several people sitting on chaises rise, like they're hoping for a fight.

I try to pull my way out of the guys' grip, and when they let me go, I don't expect it. I drop onto the grass.

"What got into you?" Rahul says. He's breathing hard.

I look up at the stars. "Sorry," I say.

The other person holding me turned out to be Kevin Ford. He's short but built. A wrestler. He's watching me like he hopes I try something.

"Be chill," Rahul says. "This isn't like you, man."

"I guess I forgot myself," I say. I forgot that I didn't belong, that I would never belong. That I had charmed my way into being their bookie but that I was never their friend. I forgot the delicate foundation my excuse for a social life was built on.

Kevin and Rahul walk back to the house. Kevin says something, too low for me to hear, and Rahul snickers.

I look up at the stars again. No one ever taught me the constellations, so to me they are all just bright dots. Chaos. No pattern at all. When I was a kid, I made up a constellation, but I couldn't find it a second time.

Someone shuffles through the grass to loom over me, blotting out the chaotic stars. For a moment I think it might be Audrey. It's Sam. "There you are," he says.

I get up slowly as Sam turns, stumbles, and pukes in the hydrangea bush near the kitchen window. Some girls on lounge chairs start to laugh.

"I'm glad you're here," Sam says when he's done, "but I think you better drive me home."

I get him coffee at a drive-through fast-food place and mix in a lot of sugar. I figure it will help him sober up, but he vomits most of it onto the asphalt of the parking lot. He washes his mouth out with the rest.

I turn on the radio and we sit there listening to it as his stomach gurgles. Another song about being worked by love. Like it's romantic to be brainwashed.

"I used to pretend I was a worker when I was a kid," he says.

"Everyone does," I tell him.

"Even you?"

"Especially me." I offer him the other cup of coffee. It's mine and I've left it black, but there might be more packets of sugar somewhere. He shakes his head.

"How does anyone find out they're a worker? When did you know you weren't?"

"I'm sure it was the same with you. Our parents told us not to mess around with working. My mom went so far as to tell us that kids who did work before they were grown-up could die from the blowback."

"That's not true?"

I shrug. "Only way it kills you outright is if you're a very unlucky-with-blowback death worker, and even then it doesn't matter how old you are. But my brothers knew when they were pretty young. Barron won stuff by other people losing, you know? And Philip was always doing too well in a fight." I remember Mom getting called into the junior high when Philip had broken the legs of three guys much bigger than he was. The blowback made him sick for a month, but no one ever messed with him again. I don't know how she managed it, but no one reported him to the law, either. I try to think of an example with Barron in it, but nothing comes to mind. That's one good thing about working luck, I guess. "Once you find out you're a worker, you learn secret stuff from other workers. I can't tell you that part because I don't know it."

"Are you supposed to tell me *any* of that?"

"Nope," I say, turning on the car. "But you're so drunk that I'm pretty sure you won't remember anyway."

Somewhere between apologizing to Mrs. Yu for bringing Sam home so late, dumping him onto his bed, and backing out of the driveway of his huge brick colonial, I realize something.

I've been so focused on the possibility that Lila might be a cat that I've glossed over the ramification of there being a transformation worker, here in the United States. Working with Anton—or maybe Anton himself. Either way, that's a big secret. The government would fall all over itself to hire that person. The crime families would be desperate to recruit them. That's what Anton and Philip are conspiring about. That's why they needed to scramble my memories.

They've got a real transformation worker.

That's something worth making me forget.

SAM AND DANECA MEET

me outside the coffeehouse. They're sitting on the hood of his 1978 vintage Cadillac Superior side-loading hearse in the parking lot, and Sam looks awful, taking tons of tiny sips from his cup like he's got the shakes. The car is perfectly polished; its waxed metallic black paint is marred only by the sticker reading POWERED BY 100% VEGETABLE OIL pasted just above the chrome bumper. Sam's wearing a suit jacket over a white shirt with a tie, but the jacket is too short in the arms, as if maybe it's been in the back of his closet for a long time.

Daneca looks strange out of uniform. Her jeans are

worn along the bottom, above her thin flip-flops, but her white shirt is perfectly ironed.

"I see your car is out of the shop," I say to Sam.

He looks confused. "My car's—"

Daneca talks over him. "I thought I'd come along anyway, since I already said I would."

I take a deep breath and wipe my damp palms against my pants. I'm too nervous to care that they lied. "I really appreciate you guys giving up your Saturday to help me," I say, turning over a new leaf of gentlemanly behavior.

"So, what's the deal with this cat?" Daneca asks.

"It's a family friend," I say, hoping they'll laugh.

Sam looks up from his cup. I can see the shimmer of sweat on his face. He looks massively hungover. "I thought you said the cat was yours."

"Well, it is. It was. It was mine." I am confusing myself. I am forgetting the basics of lying. Keep it simple. The truth is complicated, which is why no one ever believes it over a halfway decent lie. "Here's what I need you to do—I guess you didn't get my text?"

"Am I not dressed rich enough?" Sam asks, leaning back so that we can appreciate the full glory of his suit. "Don't be drinking the Haterade."

"You look crazy," I say, shaking my head. "Like a crazy valet. Or a waiter."

He looks over at Daneca, and she bursts out laughing. "Is that why you're dressed like that?"

Sam flops back on the car. "This is so not good for my ego."

"Daneca can do it," I say. "Daneca looks the part."

"Humiliation on top of humiliation," Sam groans. "Daneca looks rich because she is rich."

"So are you," she tells him, which makes him put his sunglasses over his eyes and groan again. Sam's parents own a string of car dealerships, which makes it ironic that he both drives a hearse and opposes big oil.

"It won't be hard," I tell her, trying to push out of my head all the times I blew her off. "You're going to be a nice well-to-do girl who was supposed to be taking care of her grandmother's long-haired white cat. Its name is Coconut, but it has a longer show name that you don't know. The cat also had a Swarovski crystal collar worth thousands."

Sam sits up. "Your cat is a Persian? I love their little pushed-in faces. They always look so angry."

"No," I say as calmly as I can, even though I want to knock Sam in the head. "Not my cat. Her cat. Just let me finish."

"But she doesn't have a cat." He holds up his hands at my look. "Fine."

"First you go in looking for Coconut, but then you ask if they have *any* fluffy white cats. You're desperate. Your grandmother is going to be home on Monday and she's going to kill you. You'll pay the person behind the desk five hundred bucks for any all-white fluffy cat—no questions asked." They're staring at me strangely. "There aren't any monitors on the desk, I checked."

"So then they give me the cat and I give them the money?" Daneca asks.

I shake my head. "No. They don't have a fluffy white cat. Our cat is a shorthair."

"Dude, I think your plan has a flaw," Sam says slowly.

"Trust me," I tell them, and smile my biggest, charmingest smile.

Daneca goes over to the Rumelt Animal Shelter and comes back, looking a little shaken.

"How did it go?" I ask.

"I don't know," she says, and for a moment I'm furious that I couldn't have played her part too. I am furious that her parents haven't taught her how to lie and cheat properly, so that now I am betrayed by her inexperience.

"Was there a woman there?" I ask, biting the inside of my mouth.

"No, it was a skinny guy. In his twenties, I'd guess."

"What did he say when you talked about the money? Or the collar?"

"Nothing," she said. "He didn't have any fluffy white cats. I don't know if I did it right. I was just so freaked out."

"It's okay." I take her hand. "Freaked out is good. You just lost Granny's Coconut. Anyone would be freaked out. Just tell me you gave him your number."

"That was the only time he seemed interested in what I was saying." She laughs. "Now what?"

I shrug my shoulders. "Now we wait. Next part can't happen for an hour—at least." I look over at Daneca, and she gives me the same look she gave me when I refused to sign up for any of her causes. The look that said I'd betrayed who she thought I should be. But she doesn't take her gloved hand out of mine.

"Is that when I get to do my part?" Sam asks. I'm sick with nerves. This part is delicate and if it doesn't work, my only backup plan is recruiting homeless guys to try and adopt the cat.

"I can handle it," I say.

He gives me a hurt look. "I want to come watch you work your magic."

I feel bad for dragging him out here on a Saturday for no reason. "Okay," I say finally. "Just follow my lead."

We wait an hour and a half, drinking coffee and hot chocolate until my skin feels jumpy. Finally I take a bracelet out of a Claire's bag, put it in my pocket, and pull out a bunch of flyers from my bag. Daneca's eating a package of chocolate-covered coffee beans and looking at me strangely. I wonder if I can ever go back to Wallingford or if I've already revealed too much of myself.

I wonder if I should tell her that her part's over and she can go home, but if I was going to tell her that, I should have told her more than an hour ago, so I decide that I better not do it now.

"What are those for?" Sam asks, pointing to the flyers.

"You'll see," I say. We cross the highway, which involves running across two lanes of traffic when the light changes, and then walk down a side street until we get to the shelter. There's a lot of people there on a Saturday, most of them in a cat room where giant carpet-covered trees are perched upon by dozens and dozens of hissing, dozing, and clawing felines. I feel my heart drop when I see that Lila is not in there. The possibility that she's been taken home with a family already stutters my heart.

Lila.

I'm not pretending or considering anymore when I think it.

The white cat is Lila.

Sam looks at me like he's just realized that I have no idea what I'm doing. I clear my throat. The guy at the desk looks up. His face is a mess of pimples.

"Hey, can I hang this here?" I say, and hold up a flyer.

It's on bright white paper, and there's a photograph I downloaded off the Internet of the cutest fluffy white Persian cat I could find without a collar. A dead ringer for our description of Coconut. Above it is the word "FOUND" and then a phone number. I put the flyer on the desk in front of the guy.

"Sure," he says.

He's a perfect mark. Young enough to want the money and the glory of helping out a pretty girl. I'm suddenly very glad Daneca decided to be part of the plan.

I start tacking another copy to the board, praying that in the chaos the desk guy looks at the flyer I left for him. An older woman starts asking him about a pit bull mix, distracting him. Sam is fidgeting next to me like he has no idea what's going on. I drop the copy as if it's an accident and pick it up again.

Finally the woman leaves.

"Thanks for letting me post this," I say to get the guy's attention, and he finally looks down at the flyer. I can see the gears move behind his eyes.

"Hey, you found this cat?" he says.

"Yeah," I say. "I'm hoping to keep her." People love to help. It makes them feel good. Greed is the icing on the cake. "My little sister is super excited. She's been wanting a cat for a while."

Sam gives me a look when I say "super." He's probably right; I need to tone it down.

I slip my hand into my pocket and take out the bracelet. It shines in the fluorescent lights. "Look at this gaudy collar." I laugh. "Who puts a cat in something like this?"

"I think I might know the owner," the guy says slowly. His eyes sparkle like the stones.

As convincers go, I've seen worse.

"Man, my sister's going to be disappointed." I take a breath, let it out again. "Well, tell your friend to call me."

This is the moment of truth, and when I look into the face of the mark at the counter, I can tell that I've got him. He's probably not a bad guy, but that five hundred dollars is quite a lure. Plus the collar.

Plus, he'd have an excuse to call Daneca.

"Wait," he says. "Maybe you could bring the cat here. I'm sure I know the owner. The cat's name is Coconut."

I turn toward the door and then back to him. "I was stupid to tell my sister, but now she's all excited and—well, I don't suppose you have a white cat here? All I told her about it was the color."

He looks eager. "We do. Sure."

I let out my breath. I'm not faking the relief that I know floods my face. "Oh, great. I'd love to have a white cat to take home to her."

He grins. Like I said, people love to help, especially when they can help themselves in doing so.

"Cool," I say. "Let me fill out the paperwork and we'll take the cat. Your friend's fluffy kitty is at this guy's house, so we'll go get her and bring her right to you." I gesture toward Sam.

"The thing's probably giving fleas to my mother's couch," Sam says, which is perfect. I wish I could tell him that, but all I can do is give him a grateful glance.

The mark hands me the form, and this time I know what to do. I write down my age as nineteen, specify a veterinarian, and make up a name that's not even close to my own.

"Do you have any ID?" he asks.

"Sure," I say, and reach into my back pocket for my wallet. I flip it open and touch the place where driver's licenses go. Mine's not there.

"Oh, *man*," I say. "This isn't my day."

"Where'd you leave it?" the guy asks.

I shake my head. "No idea. Look, I totally understand if that breaks the rules or whatever. I have one other place to hang up fliers, then I'll go look for my license. Maybe your friend can give me a call and I can just drop the cat with her. My sister will understand."

The guy gives me a long evaluating look.

"You have the adoption fee?" he asks.

I look down at the paper, but I already know what it says. "Fifty bucks, sure."

The door rings, and some people walk through it, but the man behind the desk keeps his eyes on me. He licks his lips.

I take out the cash and set it down on the counter in

front of him. I've blown through a chunk of my savings in the last few days, between bad bets and spending. I'm going to have to be careful if Lila and I wind up having to get out of town on the rest.

"Okay, I'll hook you up," the mark says, taking the money.

"Oh," I say. "Cool. Thanks." I know better than to over-play it.

"So, this long-haired cat," Sam says, and I freeze, willing him not to stick his foot in it. He's looking at the guy behind the counter. "Do you need to call your friend or anything?"

"I will," he says, and I can see the red creeping up his neck. "I want to surprise her."

A woman walks up to the desk, a filled out form clutched in her hand. She looks impatient. I have to push.

"Can we take the cat now?" I ask. I put the bracelet down on the counter. "Oh, your friend will probably want her collar back too."

He looks at the woman and then at me. Then his hand closes over the bracelet and he heads into the back and comes back a few minutes later swinging a cardboard pet carrier.

My hand shakes when I take it. Sam grins at me in amazement, but all I can think of is that I have her. I did it. She's right here in my hands. I look through the air holes and I can see her, prowling back and forth. Lila. A cold jolt of terror runs through me at the wrongness of her impris-oned in that tiny body.

"Be back in an hour," I tell the guy, hoping I never see him again.

I hate this part.

I always hate the part where I know they are going to wait, their hope souring into shame at their own gullibility.

But I clench my jaw, take the cat carrier with Lila in it, and walk out the door.

When I open it up in the parking lot of the coffeehouse, the first thing she does is bite me hard on the heel of my hand. The next thing she does is purr.

Mom says that because she can make people feel what she wants, she's learned how to see into their hearts. She says that if I was like her, I'd have the instinct too. Maybe being a worker tempts you to be all mystical, but I think mom knows about people because she watches faces very closely. There're these looks people get that last less than a second—micro-expressions, fleeting clues that reveal a lot more than we wish they did. I think my mother pays attention to those without being aware of what she's doing. Me, I had to practice.

Like, walking back toward the coffee shop with the cat in my arms, I can tell that Sam is freaked out by the con, by his part in it, by my planning it. I can tell. No matter how much he smiles.

I'm not my mother, though. I'm no emotion worker. Knowing that he's freaked out doesn't help me. I can't make him feel any different.

I dump the cat onto one of the café tables and grab some napkins to wipe the blood off my wrist. My hand's throbbing. Daneca is smiling down at the cat like she's a full set of Gorham silver recently fallen off a truck.

This whole thing might be a delusion, the fantasy of a guilty conscience. But I am going with it.

Lila cries, and the barista looks over from behind the espresso machine. The cat cries again, then takes a lick of the foam on the edge of Daneca's paper cup.

I just stare at Lila the cat, utterly incapable of doing more than smothering the strange keening sound that's crawling up the back of my throat.

"Don't," Daneca says, waving the cat off. The cat hisses and then slumps down on the tabletop. She starts licking her leg.

"You won't believe how he did it," Sam tells Daneca, leaning forward eagerly.

I look at the barista, at the other customers, and then back at him. Everyone's already paying us too much attention. The cat starts chewing on the end of a claw.

"Sam," I say, cautioning.

"You know, Sharpe," he says, looking at me and then around. "You've got some interesting skills. And some interesting paranoia."

I smile in acknowledgment of his words, but it hurts. I've been so careful not to let anyone at school see the other side of me, to see what I am, and now I've blown that in a half hour.

Daneca tilts her head. "It's sweet. All this trouble for a kitty." She brushes the top of the cat's head, rubbing behind her ears.

My cell rings in my pocket, vibrating. I stand up, dropping the bloody napkins into the trash can, and answer the phone. "Hey."

"You better get over here with my car," Grandad says. "Before I call the cops and tell them you stole it."

"Sorry," I say contritely. Then the rest of what he said sinks in and I laugh. "Wait, did you just threaten me with calling the police? Because that I'd like to see."

Grandad grunts, and I think maybe he's laughing too. "Drive on over to Philip's—he wants to have some kind of dinner with us. He says Maura's going to cook. You think she's a good cook?"

"How about I pick up a pizza?" I say, looking at the cat. She's rubbing against Daneca's hand. "Let's just chill out at the house." I don't think I'm ready to see Philip and not spit in his face.

"Too late, you little slacker. He already picked me up and you're my ride home, so get your ass over to your brother's apartment."

I start to say something back, but the line goes dead.

"You in trouble?" Sam asks. The way he says it, I wonder if he's thinking about how to get out of here if I am.

I shake my head. "Family dinner. I'm late." I want to tell them how grateful I am, how sorry I feel that they had to get dragged into my mess, but none of it's true. I'm just sorry for myself. Sorry that now they know something I didn't want them to. I wish I could make them forget. For a moment I understand that memory working impulse right down to my bones.

"Uh," I say. "Can either one of you hold on to the cat for a few hours?"

Sam groans. "Come on, Sharpe. What's really going on here?"

"I'll take her," Daneca volunteers. "On one condition."

"Maybe I could keep her in the car," I say. Mostly I want to stare into her strange cat eyes and look at her tiny paws and ask her if she's Lila. Even though I've already decided. I want to decide again.

"You can't keep a *cat* in a *car*," she says. "She'll get too hot."

"Of course. You're right." I smile, but it feels like a rictus. Then I shake my head, like I'm trying to shake off my expression. I'm way off my stride. I'm rattled. "Could you hold on to her overnight?"

The cat growls deep in her throat.

"Trust me," I say to the cat. "I have a plan." Daneca and Sam look at me like I've lost my mind.

I don't want to be away from her, but I'm going to need a little time to get the rest of my money out of the library and get a hold of a car. Then we can go somewhere far from here, lay low. I'll keep her safe until I can figure out who I have to bribe or con to turn her back into herself.

Daneca shrugs. "I guess, but I'm going to the dorm tonight. My parents have some conference, so they're driving up to Vermont after dinner. My roommate's not allergic or anything, though, and I'm pretty sure we'll be able to hide her. I think it will be okay."

Lila hisses, but I get up anyway. I wonder what kind of dreams Daneca is going to have.

"Thanks," I say mechanically. My mind is racing with plans.

"Wait," she says. "I told you there was a condition."

"Oh," I say. "Sure."

"I want you to give me a ride home."

"I can—," Sam starts.

Daneca interrupts him. "No, I need Cassel to take me. And to agree to come in the house for a minute."

I sigh. I know her mother wants to talk to me, probably because she thinks that I'm a worker refusing to join the cause. "I don't have time. I have to get to my brother's place."

"You have time," Daneca says. "I said just a minute."

I sigh again. "Okay, fine."

Daneca's house is just off the main street in Princeton, an elegant old brick Colonial with green and amber hydrangeas framing the front walk. It stinks of old money, overwhelming privilege, and the kind of education that ensures the elite will continue looking down on everyone else. I have never even broken into a house like that.

Daneca, of course, goes inside like it's nothing. She drops her book bag in the entryway, sets down the cat carrier on the polished wood floor, and heads down a hallway filled with old etchings of the human brain.

The cat cries softly from her cage.

"Mom," Daneca calls. *"Mom."*

I stop in the dining room, where a blue and white vase filled with only slightly wilted flowers rests on a polished table, between silver candlesticks.

My fingers itch to shove those candlesticks in my bag.

I look back toward the hall, instinctively, and see a blond boy—he looks like he's around twelve—standing on the stairs. He's watching me like he knows I'm a thief.

"Uh, hi," I say. "You must be Daneca's brother."

"Screw you," the kid says, and walks back up the stairs.

"In here," Daneca's mom calls, and I head in that direction. Daneca's waiting for me near a half-open door to a room filled to its high ceilings with books. Mrs. Wasserman sits on a small sofa near a desk.

"Get lost?" Daneca asks me.

"It's a big house," I say.

"Well, bring him in," Mrs. Wasserman says, and Daneca ushers me inside. She flops down onto her mother's wooden desk chair and spins it a little with her foot.

I am left to perch on the edge of a brown leather ottoman.

"It's nice to meet you," I say.

"Really?" Mrs. Wasserman has a whole mess of light brown curly hair that she doesn't seem interested in corralling. Her bare feet are tucked up under a soft-looking oatmeal throw. "I'm glad. I heard that you were a little bit wary of us."

"I don't want to disappoint you, but I'm not a worker," I tell her. "I thought maybe there was some misunderstanding."

"Do you know where the term 'worker' comes from?" she asks, leaning forward, ignoring my floundering.

"*Working* magic?" I ask.

"It's much more modern than that," she says. "Long, long ago, we were called theurgists. But from about the seventeenth century until the 1930s, we were called dab hands. The term 'worker' comes from the work camps. When the ban was passed, no one knew how to actually enforce it, so people waited for prosecution in labor camps. It took the government a long time to figure out how to conduct a trial. Some people waited years. That's where the crime families started—in those camps. They started recruiting. The ban created organized crime as we know it.

"In Australia, for instance, where working has never been illegal, there is no real syndicate with the kind of power our crime families have. And in Europe the families are so entrenched that they are practically a second royalty."

"Some people think workers are royalty," I say, thinking of my mother. "And Australia never made curse work illegal because it was founded by curse workers—or dab hands or whatever—who'd been sent to a penal colony."

"You do know your history, but I want you to look at something." Mrs. Wasserman places a stack of large black-and-white photos in front of me. Men and women with their hands cut off, balancing bowls on their heads. "This is what used to happen to workers all over the world—and still does in some places. People talk about how workers abused their power, about how they were the real power behind thrones, kingmakers, but you have to understand that most workers were in small villages. Many still are. And violence against them isn't taken seriously."

She's right about that. Hard to take violence seriously when workers are the ones with all the advantages. I look at the pictures again. My eyes keep stopping on the brutal, jagged flesh, healed dark and probably burned.

She sees me staring.

"The surprising thing," she says, "is that some of them have learned to work with their feet."

"Really?" I look up at her.

She smiles. "If more people knew that, I don't know if gloves would be as popular. Wearing gloves goes back as far as the Byzantine Empire. Back then people wore them to protect themselves from what they called *the touch*. They believed that demons walked among people and their touch brought chaos and terror. Back then workers were thought to be demons who could be bargained with for great rewards. If you had a worker baby, it was because a demon had gotten inside of it. Justinian the first—the emperor—took all those babies and raised them in an enormous tower to be an unstoppable demon army."

"Why are you telling me this? I know workers have been thought of lots of different idiotic ways."

"Because Zacharov and those other heads of crime families are doing the same thing. Their people hang around bus stations in the big cities waiting for the runaways. They give them a place to stay and a few little jobs, and before they know it, they're like the Byzantine child-demons, in so much debt that they might as well be prisoners or prostitutes."

"We have a boy staying with us," Daneca says. "Chris. His parents threw him out."

I think of the blond boy on the stairs.

Mrs. Wasserman gives Daneca a stern look. "That's Chris's story to tell."

"I have to get going," I say, standing. I'm uncomfortable; I feel like my skin is too tight. I have to get out of this conversation.

"I want you to know that when you're ready, I can help you," she says. "You could save a lot of boys from towers."

"I'm not who you think I am," I say. "I'm not a worker."

"You don't have to be," Mrs. Wasserman says. "You know things, Cassel. Things that could help people like Chris."

"I'll walk you out," says Daneca.

I head toward the door quickly. I have to get away. I feel like I can't breathe. "That's okay. I'll see you tomorrow," I mumble.

THE RICH ODOR OF

garlicky lamb hits me when I open the door to Philip and Maura's apartment. Despite giving me all that crap about getting right over, Grandad is asleep in a recliner with a glass of red wine resting on his stomach, cradled in the loose grip of his left hand and tipping slightly toward his chest. On the television in front of him some fundie preacher is talking about workers coming forward and volunteering to get tested, so people can touch hands in friendship, ungloved. He says that all people are sinners and power is too tempting. Workers will give in eventually if they're not kept in check.

I'm not sure he's wrong, except about all that hand touching with strangers, which sounds gross.

I hear the clink of plates as Philip walks out of the kitchen. I flinch at the sight of him. It's like having some kind of surreal double vision. Philip my brother. Philip who's probably stealing Barron's and my memories.

"You're late," he says.

"What's the occasion?" I ask. "Maura's going all out."

Barron comes out behind Philip, holding two more glasses of wine. He looks thinner than the last time I saw him. His eyes are bloodshot and his lawyer-short hair looks grown out, shaggy, curling. "She's freaking. Keeps saying she's never thrown a dinner party before. You better get back in there, Philip."

I want to feel sorry for him, thinking of all those crazy notes to himself, but all I can see is the small steel cage on a floor made sticky with layers of piss. All I can imagine is him turning up his music to drown out the cat's crying.

Philip throws up his hands. "Maura always makes a big deal out of nothing." He heads back toward the kitchen.

"So why are we doing this?" I ask Barron.

He smiles. "Mom's appeal is almost over. We're just waiting for a verdict. It's happening."

"Mom's getting out?" I take the glass from his hand and drink the wine in a gulp. It's wrong that the first feeling I have is panic. Mom getting out of jail means her back in our lives, meddling. It means chaos.

Then I remember I'm not going to be here. On the drive over I gave up on the idea of getting a car. Tomorrow I'm going to use one of the school computers to book a train headed south.

Barron looks over at Grandad and then back at me. "Depends on the verdict, but I'm pretty optimistic. I asked a couple of my professors, and they thought there was no way she wouldn't win. They said she had one of the best cases they'd ever seen. I've been doing work on the case as an independent study, so my professors have been involved too."

"Great," I say, half-listening. I'm wondering if I can afford a sleeper car.

Grandad opens his eyes, and I realize he wasn't passed out after all. "Stop with all that crap, Barron. Cassel's too smart to believe you. Anyway, your mother's getting out and—God willing—should be happy to come home to someplace clean. Kid's been doing nice work."

Maura ducks her head out from the other room. "Oh, you're here," she says. She's got on a pink tracksuit. I can see her collarbones jutting out just above the zipper on her hoodie. "Good. Sit down. I think we're ready to eat."

Barron heads into the kitchen, and when I start to follow, Grandad grabs my arm. "What's going on?"

"What do you mean?" I ask.

"I know something's going on with you boys, and I want to know what it is." I can smell the wine on his breath, but he looks perfectly lucid.

I want to tell him, but I can't. He's a loyal guy, and it's hard for me to picture him having a hand in the kidnapping of his boss's daughter, but my lack of imagination isn't a good enough reason for trust.

"Nothing," I say, roll my eyes, and go sit down for dinner.

Maura spread a white tablecloth over the kitchen table and added a couple of folding chairs. On it are the silver candlesticks that a guy that goes by Uncle Monopoly gave Philip at his wedding, ones I'm pretty sure were stolen. The lit tapers make everything look better, mostly by throwing the rest of the kitchen into shadows. A lamb roast with slivers of garlic sticking out from the meat like bits of bone rests on a platter beside a bowl of roasted carrots and parsnips. Grandad drinks most of the wine out of a glass that Barron keeps refilling, but there's enough for me to feel pleasantly tipsy. Even the baby seems happy to bang a silver rattle against his tray and smear his face with mashed potatoes.

I recognize the plates we're eating off too. I helped Mom steal those.

Looking at the mirror in the hall, it's like I'm watching us all in a fun house glass, a parody of a family gathering. Look at us celebrating our criminal enterprises. Look at us laugh. Look at us lie.

Maura is just bringing out coffee when the phone rings. Philip gets up and comes back a few minutes later, holding it out to me.

"Mom," he says.

I take it from him and walk back into the living room. "Congratulations," I say into the receiver.

"You've been avoiding my calls." Mom sounds amused rather than annoyed. "Your grandfather said you were feeling better. He says that boys who feel better don't call their mothers. That true?"

"I'm tip top," I tell her. "The peak of health."

"Mmm-hmm. And you've been sleeping well?"

"In my own bed, even," I say cheerfully.

"Funny," she says. I can hear the long exhalation that tells me she's smoking. "That's good, I suppose, that you can still be funny."

"Sorry," I say again. "I've got a lot on my mind."

"Your grandfather said that, too. He said you were thinking a lot about a certain someone. Thinking leads to talking, Cassel. Other people were there for you back then. Be there for them and forget about her."

"What if I can't?" I ask. I don't know what she knows or whose side she's on, but some childish part of me wants to believe she'd help me if she could.

There is a moment's hesitation. "She's gone, baby. You've got to stop letting her have power over—"

"Mom," I say, interrupting her. I'm walking farther from the kitchen, until I stand near the picture window in the living room, close to the front door. "What kind of worker is Anton?"

Her voice drops low. "Anton is Zacharov's nephew, his heir. You stay away from him and let your brothers look out for you."

"Is he a memory worker? Just tell me that. Say yes or no."

"Put Philip back on the phone."

"Mom," I say again, "please. Tell me. I might not be a worker, but I'm still your son. Please."

"Put your brother back on the phone, Cassel. *Right now.*"

For a moment I consider hanging up. Then I consider

chucking the phone against the floor until it breaks. Neither option will give me anything but satisfaction.

I walk through the house and put the phone down next to Philip's plate of pie.

"In my day," Grandad says. He's in the middle of one of his speeches. "In my day workers were still respected. We kept the peace in neighborhoods. It was illegal, sure, but the cops looked the other way if they knew what was good for them."

He's clearly drunk.

Barron and Grandad go into the living room to watch television, while Philip talks to Mom on the extension in the loft. Maura stands at the sink, scraping food into the whirring garbage disposal. She scrubs a pot, and her lips draw back from her gums like a dog before it bites.

I want to tell her about the missing memories, but I don't know how to do it without pissing her off.

"Dinner was good," I say finally.

She spins around, relaxing her features into some pleasant and vague expression. "I burned the carrots."

I put my hands in my pockets, fidgeting. "Tasty."

She frowns. "Do you need something, Cassel?"

"I wanted to thank you. For helping me out the other day."

"And lying to your school?" she asks with a sly smile, drying the pot. "They haven't called yet."

"They will." I pick up another dish towel and start mopping the water off a knife. "Don't you have a dishwasher?"

"It dulls the blade," she says, taking it from me and sliding it into a drawer. "And the pot had too much gunk stuck on the bottom. Some things you still have to do by hand."

I set the rag down on the counter with sudden decision. "I have something for you." I walk out to where my jacket is hanging and reach into the inside pocket.

"Hey, come sit down," Barron calls.

"In a second," I say, walking quickly back to the kitchen.

"Look," I say to Maura, holding out my hand to show her the onyx charm. "I know what you said about a worker's wife and being—"

"Very thoughtful of you," she says. The stone shines under the recessed lights like a spilled droplet of tar. "Just like your brother. You don't understand favors, just exchanges."

"Get a needle and sew it into your bra," I tell her. "Promise?"

"Charming." She tilts her head. "You look like him, you know. My husband."

"I guess," I say. "We're brothers."

"You're handsome with all that messy black hair. And your crooked smile." They're compliments, but she doesn't sound complimentary. "Do you practice smiling like that?"

Sometimes in intense situations I can't help grinning a little. "My smile's naturally crooked."

"You're not as charming as you think you are," she says, walking up to me, so close that her breath is warm and sour on my face. I take a step back, and my legs bang against the edge of her counter. "You're not as charming as him."

"Okay," I say. "Just promise me that you'll wear it."

"Why?" she asks. "What kind of amulet is so important?"

I glance at the doorway. I can hear the television in the other room, some game show Grandad likes.

"A memory charm," I say softly. "It's better than it looks. Say that you'll wear it."

"Okay."

I try a smile, as non-crooked as I can make it. "We non-workers have got to stick together."

"What do you mean?" She narrows her eyes. "Do you think I'm stupid? You're one of them. I remember *that*."

I shake my head, but don't know what to say. Maybe it's better if I wait for the charm to show her the truth before I try to argue with her over things that don't matter anyway.

"Grandad's passed out," Barron says when I walk into the living room. "Looks like you're going to have to stay over. I don't think I'm going anywhere either." He yawns.

"I can drive him," I say. I feel suffocated by all the things I can't say, about all the things I suspect my brothers of doing. I want to get home and start packing.

"What did you tell Mom?" he asks. He's drinking black coffee from one of Maura's good cups, the kind with a saucer. "It's taking him a while to calm her down."

"Just that she knows something she's not telling me," I say.

"Come on, if we had a dollar for everything Mom never told us, we'd have a million bucks."

"I'd have a lot more money than you would." I sit down on the couch. I can't just leave without at least trying to warn him. "Can I ask you something?"

Barron turns toward me. "Sure. Shoot."

"Do you remember when we were kids and we went to the beach down by Carney? There were toads in the scrub brush. You caught a really tiny one that jumped out of your hands. I squeezed mine until it puked up its guts. I thought it was dead, but then when we left it alone for a moment, it disappeared. Like it sucked in its guts and hopped away. Do you remember that?"

"Yeah," Barron says, with a shrug of his shoulders. "Why?"

"How about when you and Philip got all those *Playboy* magazines out of the Dumpster and you cut out all the breasts and covered a lamp shade with them. And then it caught on fire and you gave me five dollars to lie to Mom and Dad about it?

He laughs. "Who could forget that?"

"Okay. How about when you smoked all that weed that you thought was laced with something? You fell in the tub, but you refused to get out because you were convinced the back of your head was going to fall off. The only thing that would calm you down was reading out loud, so I read the only book in the bathroom—one of Mom's romances, called *The Windflower*, cover to cover."

"Why are you asking me about this?"

"Do you remember?"

"Sure, yeah, I remember. You read the whole book. It

was easy to clean up the blood once I got out. Now, what's with the interrogation?"

"None of those things happened," I tell him. "Not to you. You weren't there for the toad thing. My roommate told me the story about the boob lamp fire. *He* paid *his* little sister to lie. The third story happened to a guy, Jace, in my dorm. Sadly, no one had *The Windflower* on hand. Me and Sam and another guy on our hall took turns reading *Paradise Lost* through the locked door. I think it actually made him more paranoid, though."

"That's not true," he says.

"Well, he *seemed* more paranoid to me," I say. "And he still gets a little weird at the mention of angels."

"You think you're so funny." Barron sits up straighter. "I was just playing along, trying to figure out what your game was. You can't play me, Cassel."

"I did play you," I say. "You're losing your memories and you're trying to cover it up. I've lost memories too."

He gives me a strange look. "You mean about Lila."

"That's ancient history," I say.

He looks over at Grandad again. "I remember you were obviously jealous that I was dating her. You had a crush or something and you were always trying to get me to dump her. One day I walk into Grandad's basement and she's lying on the floor. You're standing over her with this stunned expression on your face." I suspect he's telling this story just to needle me, just to get me back for embarrassing him.

"And a knife," I say. It bothers me that the thing I most remember—my horrible smile—is absent from his telling.

"Right. A knife. You said you didn't remember anything, but it was obvious what happened." He shakes his head. "Philip was terrified that Zacharov would find out, but blood's thicker than water. We covered up for you—hid her body. Lied."

There's something wrong with the way he's describing the memory. It's like he's remembering a few lines from a textbook about a battle instead of actually remembering a battle. No one would really say blood's thicker than water when their memory should be full of smeared, clotted redness.

"You loved her, right?" I ask him.

He makes a gesture—a wave of his hands—that I can't interpret. "She was really special." A grin lifts a side of his mouth. "You certainly thought so."

He must have known what was in the cage in his spare room, what was crying and eating whatever he gave her and soiling his floor. "I guess it's true what they say—I have loved too much not to hate."

Barron tilts his head. "What do you mean?"

"It's a quote. From Racine. Also, you may have heard, there's a thin line between love and hate."

"So you killed her because you loved her too much? Or aren't we talking about you and her anymore?"

"I don't know," I say. "I'm just talking. I want you to be careful—"

I stop as Philip comes into the doorway.

"I just got off the phone with Mom," he says. "I need to talk to Cassel. Alone."

Barron glances at Philip and then back at me. "So, what is it you suspect is going on? You know, that I should be careful about."

I shrug my shoulders. "I'd be the last to know."

Philip leads me back to the kitchen and sits down at the table, folding his hands on the stained white cloth. Around him are a few remaining plates and several mostly empty wineglasses. He picks up a bottle of Maker's Mark and fills one of the used coffee cups with amber liquor. "Sit down."

I sit, and he regards me silently.

"What's with all the grimness?" I say, but my fingers reach down unconsciously to rub the spot where the pebbles rest under my skin. The soreness is reassuring and as addictive as touching the tip of my tongue to the raw socket of a recently lost tooth. "I must have really upset Mom."

"I have no idea what you think you know," Philip says. "But you have to understand that all I've been trying to do—all I've ever tried to do is protect you. I want you to be safe."

What a line. I shake my head, but don't contradict him. "Okay, then. What are you protecting me from?"

"Yourself," he says and now he looks me in the eye. For a moment I see the thug that people are afraid of—jaw clenched, hair shadowing his face. But after all these years, at least he's finally looking at me.

"Get over *your*self," I say. "I'm a big kid."

"Things are tough without Dad," he says. "Law school

isn't cheap. Wallingford isn't cheap. Mom's legal bills alone are staggering. Grandad had some savings, but we burned through that. I've had to step up. And I'm doing the best I can. I want us to have things, Cassel. I want my son to have things." He takes another slug from the cup and then laughs to himself. His eyes shine when he looks over at me, and I wonder just how much liquor he's already had. Enough to get him pretty unwound.

"Okay," I say.

"That means taking some risks. What if I told you there was something I needed you for?" Philip says. "Something Barron and I both need your help with." I think of Lila in my dream, asking for help. The overlay of the memories is dizzying.

"Do you need my help?" I ask.

"I need you to trust us," Philip says, tilting his head to one side and giving me that superior older brother smile. He thinks he's teaching me a lesson.

"I should be able to trust my own brothers, right?" I ask. I think I manage to say it without sarcasm.

"Good," he says. There's something sad and tired in the sag of his shoulders, something that seems less like cruelty and more like resignation. It makes me unsure of my conclusions. I think of us being kids all together and how much I loved it when Philip paid me any attention—even the kind of attention that came in the form of an order. I loved to scramble to get a beer out of the fridge for him and pop the top like a bartender, then grin at him, waiting for the offhanded nod of acknowledgment.

And here I am, trying to find a way where he isn't the villain. Looking for the nod. All because he finally met my eyes.

"Things are going to be different for us real soon. Vastly different. We're not going to have to struggle." He makes a sweeping gesture that knocks over one of the wineglasses that Maura didn't clear. There's only a little bit of liquid in it, but it rushes over the white cloth in a tide of pink wetness. He doesn't seem to notice.

"What's going to be different?" I ask him.

"I can't tell you details," he says, and looks toward the living room. Then he stands up unsteadily. "For now, just don't rock the boat. And don't mess with Mom. Give me your word."

I sigh. The conversation is circular, pointless. He wants me to trust him, but he doesn't trust me. He wants me to obey him. "Yeah," I lie. "You've got my word. Family looks out for family. I get it."

As I stand up, I notice the wineglass he knocked over isn't as empty as I thought. Some kind of sediment remains at the bottom. I lean over and drag my finger through the sludge of sugarlike granules, trying to remember who was seated where.

Over Maura's protests and Barron's annoyed insistence, I half-carry Grandad out to the car. My heart beats like I'm in a fight as I turn down the offers to sleep in the study or on the sofa. I say I'm not tired. I invent an appointment Grandad has with a bingo-playing widow in the morning.

Grandad is heavy and so drugged and drunk that he barely responds.

Philip drugged him. The reason eludes me, but I think of the sludge and I know Philip must have done it.

"You should just stay," Barron says for the millionth time.

"You're going to drop him," Philip says. "Careful."

"Then help me," I say, grunting.

Philip puts out his cigarette on the aluminum siding and slips his shoulder under Grandad's arm to lift him up.

"Just bring him back into the house," Barron says, and a look passes between them. Barron's frown deepens. "Cassel, how are you going to get him into the house on the other end if you need Philip's help getting him into the car?"

"He'll have sobered up some by then," I say.

"What if he doesn't?" Barron calls, but Philip walks toward the car door.

For a moment I think he's going to block my way, and I have no idea what I'll do if he does. He opens the door, though, and holds it while I heave Grandad inside and belt him in.

As I pull out of the driveway, I look back at Philip, Barron, and Maura. Relief floods me. I'm free. I'm nearly gone.

My phone rings, startling me. Grandad doesn't stir, even though it's loud; the sound is turned all the way up. I watch for the rise and fall of his chest to make sure he's still breathing.

"Hello?" I say, not even bothering to check who's calling. I wonder how far the hospital is and whether I should go.

Philip and Barron wouldn't kill Grandad. And if they were planning on killing him, Philip wouldn't poison him in his own kitchen. And if he did, he sure as hell wouldn't try and get me to put the body to bed in his guest room.

I repeat that thought to myself over and over.

"Can you hear me? It's Daneca," she says, whispering. "And Sam."

I don't know how long she's been speaking.

I look at the clock on the dashboard. "What's wrong? It's, like, three in the morning."

She tells me but I'm barely listening to her answer. My mind is going through all the possible things you can give someone to knock them out. Sleeping pills are the most obvious. They go great with booze too.

I realize the other end of the line is expectantly silent. "What?" I ask. "Can you say that again?"

"I said *your cat's disgusting*," she says slowly, clearly annoyed.

"Is she okay? Is the cat okay?"

Sam starts laughing. "The cat's fine, but there's a little brown mouse on Daneca's floor with its head ripped off. Your cat killed our mouse."

"Its tail looks like a piece of string," Daneca says.

"*The* mouse?" I ask. "The mouse of legend? The one everyone's been betting on for six months?"

"What happens if everybody loses a bet?" Sam asks. "Nobody got it right. Who the hell do we pay?"

The way I calculate odds isn't like a normal bookie for just such situations as this. If no one wins, I get a windfall.

Well, *we* get a windfall. "Get a picture for documentation," I tell him.

"Who cares about that? What do *I* do?" Daneca says. "The cat is just staring at me, and I think there's blood on her mouth. I look at her and see the deaths of hundreds of mice and birds. I see them just lining up to march into her mouth along an unfurling carpet of tongue like in an old cartoon. I think she wants to eat me next."

"Pet the cat, dude," says Sam. "She brought you a present. She wants you to tell her how badass she is."

"You are a tiny, tiny killing machine," Daneca coos.

"What's she doing?" I ask.

"Purring!" says Daneca. She sounds delighted. "Good kitty. Who's an amazing killing machine? That's right! You are! You are a brutal, brutal tiny lion! Yes, you are."

Sam laughs so hard he chokes. "What is wrong with you? Seriously."

"She likes it," Daneca says.

"I hate to be the one to have to point this out to you," he says, "but she doesn't understand what you're saying."

"Maybe she does," I say. "Who can tell, right? She's purring."

"Whatever, dude. So, do we keep the money?"

"It's either that or release another mouse into the walls."

"Right, then," Sam says. "We keep the money."

I drive the rest of the way home, unbuckle Grandad, and shake him. When that doesn't work, I slap him in the face hard enough that he grunts and opens his eyes a little.

"Mary?" he says, which freaks me out because that's my grandmother's name and she's been gone a long time.

"Hold on to me," I say, but his legs are rubbery and he's not much help. We go slowly. I bring him right into the bathroom and let him slouch on the tiles while I mix up a cocktail of hydrogen peroxide and water.

When he starts puking, I figure that my Wallingford's AP chemistry class was good for something. I wonder if this would be a good argument to give Dean Wharton in favor of letting me back in.

"HEY, GET UP," SOMEONE

is saying. I blink in confusion. I am lying on the downstairs couch and Philip's standing over me. "You sleep like the dead."

"If the dead snored," says Barron. "Hey, good job in here. The living room looks great. Cleaner than I've ever seen it."

Dread coils around my throat, choking me.

I look over at Grandad. He's still passed out in the reclining chair with a bucket next to him. Grandad was sick for hours, but he seemed fine by the time he fell asleep. Coherent. I would have thought all the noise would have woken him. "What did you give him?" I ask, throwing a leg out from under the afghan.

"He's fine," says Philip. "I promise. It will wear off by morning."

I am reassured by the rise and fall of Grandad's chest. As I watch him sleep for a moment I think I see his eyelids flicker.

"You always worry," Barron mumbles. "And we always tell you he's fine. They're always fine. Why do you worry so much?"

Philip shoots him a look. "Leave Cassel alone. Family looks out for family."

Barron laughs. "That's why he shouldn't worry. We're here to look after them both." He turns to me. "Better get ready fast, though, worrywart. You know how much Anton hates to wait."

I don't know what else to do, so I pull on my jeans and zip a hoodie over the T-shirt I slept in.

They seem totally comfortable waiting for me, so comfortable that, thinking over what Barron said, I come to the groggy conclusion that this has all happened before. They've gotten me out of this house—maybe my dorm—and I don't remember a thing. Have I ever panicked? I'm panicking now.

I grab my gloves and slide on a pair of work boots. My hands are trembling with adrenaline and fear—enough that I can barely get the gloves on.

"Let me see your pockets," Philip says.

"What?" I stop tying the laces to look up at him.

He sighs. "Turn them inside out."

I do, thinking of the stinging cut in my calf, the charms healing inside my skin. He rubs the pocket cloth, checking for something hidden in it, then pats down my clothes. My hands fist, and I want to take a swing at Philip so much that my arms ache from the strain of not hitting him. "Looking for a mint?"

"We need to know what you're bringing, is all," Philip says mildly.

Adrenaline has pushed back exhaustion. I'm wide awake and starting to get angry.

He looks at Barron, who reaches over for my arm. He's not wearing a glove.

I pull back. "Don't touch me!"

It's funny how instinct is; I keep my voice low when I say it. Because in some ridiculous part of my head this is still family business. It doesn't even occur to me to go for help.

Barron holds up both his hands. "Hey, okay. But this is important. It takes a few minutes for the old memories to settle. Think back. We're in this together. We're on the same side."

That's when I realize they've already worked me. Before they woke me up. My skin crawls with horror and I have to take quick, shallow breaths to keep from running away from them, from the house. This is my chance to find out what's really going on. I nod, buying myself what time I can. I have no idea what memories they expect me to have.

I watch Barron pull his glove back on and flex his hand, stretching the leather.

I realize what a bare hand means.

Philip isn't the one behind the stolen memories. Anton's not the memory worker.

Barron is—he must be. He didn't lose his memories because he was worked; he's not absentminded. Every time he takes a memory from me or Maura or all the other people he must be stealing them from, he loses one of his own. Blowback. I search my memories for an occasion when he worked for luck, but there's nothing, just a dim sense that I know he's a luck worker. I can't even recall when I started "knowing" that.

Now that I focus on it, the memory doesn't even seem real. It slips away from me, like the blurred copy of a copy.

"You ready?" Philip asks.

I stand, but my legs are shaky. It's one thing to suspect my brother was working me, another to stand next to him once I know he's done it. *I am a better con artist than any of you,* I tell myself, trying to believe it, *needing* to believe it. *I had to do everything without magic, so you won't catch me. I can pretend to be calm until I am calm.*

But another part of my mind is howling, rattling around and scraping for other false memories. I know it's impossible to look for what's not there, and yet I do, running through the last few days—weeks, years—in my mind, as though I will stumble in the gaps.

How much of my life has been reimagined by Barron? Panic chills my skin like a sickness.

We walk down the stairs of the house quietly, out to a Mercedes parked on the street with the headlights turned down and the engine humming. Anton's in the driver's seat. He looks older than the last time I saw him, and there's a scar that runs over the edge of his upper lip. It matches the keloid scar stretching across his neck.

"What took you so long?" Anton says, lighting a cigarette and throwing the match out the window.

Barron slides into the backseat next to me. "What's the rush? We've got all night. This one here doesn't have school in the morning." He musses my hair.

I shove away his gloved hand. The annoyance feels surreally familiar. It's like Barron thinks we're on a family car trip.

Philip gets into the passenger seat, looks back at us and grins.

I have to figure out what they think I know. I have to be smart. It sounds like they might believe some disorientation but not complete cluelessness. "What are we doing tonight?"

"We're going to rehearse for this Wednesday," Anton says. "For the assassination."

I'm sure I flinch. My heart hammers. Assassination?

"And then you're going to block the memory," I say, fighting to keep my voice steady. I remember what Crooked Annie said about blocking access to memories so that the block can be removed later and the memory loss reversed. I wonder if we've rehearsed before. If so, I'm screwed. "Why do you have to keep making me forget?"

"We're protecting you," Philip says automatically.

Right.

I lean forward in the seat. "So my job is the same?" I say, which seems vague enough not to show my ignorance, but encourages an answer.

Barron nods. "All you do is walk up to Zacharov and put

your bare hand on his wrist. Then you change his heart to stone."

I swallow, concentrating on keeping my breathing even. They can't mean what they're saying. "Wouldn't shooting him be easier?" I ask, because the whole thing is ridiculous.

Anton looks at me with hard eyes. "You sure he can do this? All this memory magic—he's unstable. This is my future we're talking about."

My future. Right. He's Zacharov's nephew. Anything happens to the man in charge, the mantle slips onto his shoulders.

"Don't punk out on us," Philip says to me in his I'm-being-patient voice. "It's going to be a piece of cake. We've been planning this for a long time."

"What do you know about the Resurrection Diamond?" Barron asks.

"Gave Rasputin immortality or something," I say, deliberately vague. "Zacharov won it at an auction in Paris."

Barron frowns, like he didn't expect me to know even that much. "The Resurrection Diamond is thirty-seven carats—the size of a grown man's thumbnail," he says. "It's colored a faint red, as though a single bead of blood dropped into a pool of water."

I wonder if he's quoting someone. The Christie's catalog. Something. If I just concentrate on the details like it's a puzzle, then maybe I won't completely freak out.

"Not only did it protect Rasputin from multiple assassination attempts, but after him it went to other people. There have been reports of assassin's guns turning out not to be loaded at the critical moment, or poison somehow finding its way into the poisoner's cup. Zacharov was shot at on three separate occasions and the bullets didn't hit him. Whoever has the Resurrection Diamond can't be killed."

"I thought that thing was a myth or something?" I say. "A legend."

"Oh, so now he's an expert on working," Anton says.

But Barron's eyes are shining. "I've been researching the Resurrection Diamond a long time."

I wonder how much of that research he even remembers or if it has been winnowed down to just a few phrases. Maybe he wasn't quoting an auction catalog; maybe he was quoting one of his notebooks.

"How long have you been researching it?" I ask.

He's really angry now. "Seven years."

In the front seat Philip snorts.

"So you started *before* Zacharov got the diamond?"

"I'm the one who told him about it." Barron's expression is firm, certain, but I think I can see the fear in his face. He's lying, but he will never admit he's lying. There is no evidence in the world that will make him back off a claim once he's made it. If he did, he would have to admit how much of his memory is already gone.

Philip and Anton snicker to each other. They know he's lying too. It's like going to the movies with them in the summers when we all stayed in Carney with our grandparents. The familiarity makes me relax despite myself.

"So I actually agreed to do this?" I say.

They laugh more.

I have to proceed very carefully. "If the Resurrection Diamond is supposed to prevent assassination, are you sure I'm going to be able to get around it?"

It seems to be within the bounds of believable ignorance or hesitation. Anton grins at me in the rearview mirror. "You're not doing death work. Whatever that stone is, it won't stop your kind of magic."

My kind of magic.

Heart to stone.

Me? I'm the transformation worker?

Who cursed you? I asked the cat in my dream.

You did.

I think that I'm going to be sick. No, I'm really going to be sick. I press my eyes shut, turn my head against the cold window, and concentrate on holding down my gorge.

He's lying. He's got to be lying.

"I'm—," I start.

I'm a worker. I'm a worker. I'm a worker.

The thought repeats in my head like one of those tiny ricocheting rubber balls that just won't stop banging into everything. I can't think past it.

I thought I'd give anything to be a worker, but somehow this feels like a hideous violation of my childhood fantasy.

What's the point of pretending to be anything less than the most talented practitioner of the very rarest curses? Except, I guess I'm not pretending anymore.

"You okay over there?" Barron asks.

"Sure," I say slowly. "I'm fine. Just tired. It's really late. And my head is killing me."

"We'll stop for coffee," says Anton.

We do. I manage to spill half of mine down my shirt, and the burn of the scalding liquid is the first thing that makes me feel halfway normal.

The entrance to the restaurant—Koshchey's—is so ornate that it looks like something out of another time. The front door is a brass so bright it looks like gold. Stone fire birds flank it, their feathers painted pale blue, orange, and red.

"Oh, tasteful," Barron says.

"Hey," says Anton, "it belongs to the family. Respect."

Barron shrugs. Philip shakes his head.

The sidewalk outside has the kind of stillness that comes only very early in the morning, and in that stillness I think the restaurant looks oddly majestic. Maybe I have bad taste.

Anton twists a key in the lock and opens the door. We walk into the dark room.

"You sure no one's here?" Philip asks.

"It's the middle of the night," says Anton. "Who's going to be here? This key wasn't easy to come by."

"Okay," Barron says, "so this place is going to be full of tables and political people. Rich bored folks that don't mind kicking it with gangsters. Maybe some workers from the Volpe and Nonomura families—we're currently allying ourselves with them." He walks across the room to point to a spot underneath a massive chandelier hung with a few huge blue crystals among the clear ones. It glitters, even in the dim light. "There will be a podium and loud, boring speeches."

I look around. "What is this?"

"Fund-raiser for 'Vote No on Proposition 2.' Zacharov is hosting it." Barron looks at me strangely. I wonder if I was supposed to know that.

"And I'm going to just walk up to him?" I ask. "In front of everyone?"

"Chill," Philip says. "For the millionth time, we've got a plan. We've been waiting too long for this to be idiots, okay?"

"My uncle has some very specific habits," says Anton. "He's not going to have his bodyguards close to him, because he can't have his society folks or the other families thinking he's afraid. So instead of guards he gets high-up laborers to take turns as his entourage. Philip and I are scheduled to be up his ass for two hours, starting at ten thirty."

I nod my head, but my gaze strays to the walls, to oil paintings of houses with chicken legs scampering beside women riding cauldrons through the skies, all reflected in massive mirrors. All our movements shimmer in them too, so that I keep thinking I see someone else moving when it's only myself.

"Your job is to keep an eye on us after that and wait for Zacharov to head to the bathroom. He wants it cleared when he uses it, so we'll be alone. That's where you're going to give him the touch."

"Where is it?" I ask.

"There are two men's bathrooms," Anton says, pointing. "One has a window. He'll pick the other one. I'll show it to you."

Barron and Philip head toward a glossy black door

stenciled in gold with the image of a man on horseback. I follow.

"We go in with Zacharov," Philip says. "You wait a few minutes and then go in yourself."

"I won't be in the room," Barron says. "I'll be outside— with you—to make sure everything goes smoothly."

I push the door and walk into a large bathroom. A mural of tiles takes up the whole far wall, an enormous bird of red and orange and gold flies in front of a tree covered in what look like cabbages but I assume are just really stylized leaves. The hand dryer is attached to that wall, but someone has painted it almost the same gold as the tiles. Stalls are along one side, urinals on the other, and a stretch of marble countertop filled with shining brass sinks.

"I'll play Zacharov," Anton says, and goes to stand at the sink. Then he looks at me, and I think he realizes he's about to be mock-assassinated. "No, wait. I'll play me. Barron, you be my uncle." They change places.

"Okay, go ahead," Anton says to me.

"What do I say?" I ask.

"Pretend you're drunk," says Barron. "Too drunk to notice you're not supposed to be there."

I stagger from near the doorway up to Barron.

"Get him out of here," Barron says in a fake accent that I think is supposed to be Russian.

I extend my gloved hand and try to slur my voice. "It's a real honor, sir."

Barron just looks at me. "I don't know if he'd shake."

"Sure he will," says Anton. "Philip here will say that Cassel's his little brother. Try again, Cassel."

"Sir, it's a real honor to be here. I really appreciate the way that you're doing your part to make workers safe so that we can exploit all the little people." I hold out my hand again.

"Stop being a comedian," Philip says, but not like he really means it. "Concentrate on the money and how you're going to get your fingers on his skin."

"I'm going to shove my hand under the cuff of his sleeve. Precut a hole in my glove. I just need my longest finger to touch skin."

Barron laughs. "Mom's old trick. The way she did that guy at the racetrack. You remembered."

I bite back a comment about remembering and just nod, looking down.

"Go ahead," Anton says. "Show me."

I extend my right hand, and when Barron takes it, I wrap my left hand around his wrist and shake. The left hand holds Barron's arm in place so that even if he struggles it'll take him a moment to get away. Anton's eyes widen a little. He's afraid. I can read his tells.

And just like that I'm sure he hates me. Hates being afraid and hates me for making him feel that way.

"A real honor, sir," I say.

Anton nods. "So, then you turn his heart to stone. That should look like—"

"Very poetic," I say.

"What?"

"Very poetic, turning his heart to stone. Was that your idea?"

"It'll look like a heart attack—at least until the autopsy," Anton says, ignoring my question. "And that's what we're going to let them think it was. You're going to ride out the blowback in here, and then we're going to call for a doctor."

"You didn't seem drunk enough," says Barron.

"I'll seem drunker," I say.

Barron's looking at himself in the mirror. He smoothes out one of his eyebrows, then turns his head to admire his profile. His shave is so close that it might have come from a straight razor. Handsome. A real snake-oil salesman. "You should throw up."

"What? You want me to stick my finger down my throat?"

"Why not?"

"Why?" I lean against the wall, studying Philip and Barron. Their faces are the two I know best in all the world, and right now they're unguarded. Philip shifts back and forth, grim-faced. He crosses and uncrosses his arms over his chest. He's a loyal laborer and he's got to be a little uncomfortable at the idea of taking out the head of the family, even if it means becoming rich and powerful overnight. Even if it means putting his childhood friend in charge and making himself indispensable.

Barron, however, appears to be having fun. I don't know what he's getting out of this, except that he loves to be in control. And it's obvious that he's managed to make Anton and Philip need him. He might be burning through his own memories to do it, but he's got power over all of us.

Of course, maybe he's in it for the money too. We're talking about a lot of money, being the head of a crime family.

"Afraid you won't be able to do it?" Barron asks, and I remember we're talking about vomiting. "But think— the hardest thing is getting in the door. This way you can burst in the door with your hand over your mouth, push into the stall, close it behind you, and toss your cookies. He'll be laughing at you when you come out. Easy mark."

"It's not a bad idea," Philip says, nodding.

"I've never made myself throw up before," I say. "I have no idea how long it will take."

"How about this," says Barron. "Go in the kitchen. Hurl in a bowl. We'll bottle up the puke and tape it behind the toilet in the first stall. If someone finds it, then you're on your own, but otherwise you can take whatever time you need now and not worry about it then."

"That's disgusting," I say.

"Just do it," says Anton.

"No," I say. "I can act drunk off my ass. I can pull it off." I don't intend to pull any of this off on Wednesday, although I don't quite know what I am going to do instead. But I can scheme in the morning; right now I need to observe.

"Throw up, or I am going to make you wish you did," Anton says.

I turn my neck to the side, so he can see the length of unmarked skin. "No scars," I say. "I'm not in your family, and you're not my boss."

"You better believe I'm your boss," Anton says, walking

up to me and grabbing the collar of my shirt, stretching it toward him.

"Enough." Philip gets between us, and Anton lets go of me. "You, get in the kitchen and stick your finger down your throat," he says to me. "Don't be so squeamish." He turns to Anton. "Lay off my brother. We're putting enough pressure on him."

It doesn't escape my notice that as Anton turns away and punches the door of a stall, Barron is smirking.

The more we fight, the more Barron is in control.

I push past Anton and keep going on through the big double doors to where I figure the kitchen is, pitch black and filled with the smells of paprika and cinnamon.

I reach around on the wall and flip the switch. Battered stainless and copper pots reflect the fluorescent lights. I could keep going out the back door, but there's no point. I need them to keep thinking that I'm clueless. I don't need them chasing me through the streets and then searching me until they find the amulets in my leg, even if staying here means the degrading and unpleasant duty of puking into a bowl. I open one of the industrial refrigerators and drink a few swallows of milk out of the carton. I hope it will coat my stomach.

The liners of my gloves are damp with sweat when I strip them off. My hands look pale in the lights.

I think of the hydrogen peroxide I fed to Grandad and wonder if this is some kind of karmic punishment. I put my finger on my tongue, testing how awful it's going to be. My skin tastes like salt.

"Hey," someone says.

When I turn, I see that it isn't Anton or Philip or Barron. It's a guy I don't know with a long coat and a gun pointed right at me.

The milk slides out of my hands and falls to the floor, splashing out of the carton.

"What are you doing here?" the man says.

"Oh," I say, thinking fast. "My friend has a key. He works for one of the owners."

"Are you talking to someone?" comes a voice from the back, and another man with a shaved head walks into the room. His T-shirt has a deep V, revealing his necklace of scars. He looks over at me. "Who's that?"

"Hey, man," I say, holding up my hands. I'm making up a story in my head about who I am, falling into the role. I am a worker kid, just off the bus, looking for a job and a place to crash—someone told me about this place because of its connection to Zacharov. "I was just stealing food. I'm sorry. I'll wash the dishes or whatever to pay for it."

Then the door on the other side opens and Anton and Philip step through.

"What the hell?" the man with the shaved head says.

"Get away from him," says Philip.

The guy with the long coat swings his gun toward my brother.

I reach out my hand instinctively, to push the barrel away from Philip. The metal is warmer than I thought it would be. I have spent my whole life listening to workers talk about the mechanics of magic, about focusing and unfocusing your thoughts at the same time. I have even practiced, hoping for luck, for death, for *something* to channel itself through my skin. All that goes through my head as I close my fingers around the barrel and *change* the gun.

It's like I can see the metal all the way down to the particles, but instead of being solid, it's liquid, flowing into endless shapes. All I have to do is choose one.

I look up, and the man is holding what I imagined, a snake coiling around his fingers, its green scales as bright as the wings of the phoenix out in front.

The man screams, shaking his arm like it's on fire.

The snake ripples, tightening its coils, its mouth opening and closing like it's choking. A moment later a bullet drops from its mouth, bouncing against the stainless steel counter and rolling.

Two shots ring out.

Something's wrong with me—with my body.

My chest constricts painfully and my shoulder jerks. For a moment I think that I'm the one that's shot, until I look down and see my fingers becoming gnarled roots. I take a step forward, and my legs buckle. One of them is covered in fur and bends backward. I blink, and I am seeing everything out of dozens of eyes. I can even see behind me, like I have eyes there, too, but all there is to see is cracked tile floor. I turn my head and see the two men lying on the ground. Blood is mixing with the milk, and the gun is slithering toward me, its tongue flicking out to taste the air.

I am hallucinating. I'm dying. Terror rises up in my throat, but I can't scream.

"What the hell were they doing here? Killing our people

isn't part of the plan," Anton is shouting. "This wasn't supposed to happen!"

My arms are the trunk of a tree, the arms of a sofa, they are twisting into coils of rope.

Someone help me. Please help me. Help me.

Anton points at me. "All this is his fault!"

I try to stand, but my bottom half is like a fish's. My eyes are moving in my head. I try to speak, but gurgling sounds come from whatever I have in place of lips.

"We have to get rid of the bodies," Barron says.

There are other sounds then, snapping bone and a wet thunk. I try to roll my head so I can see, but I no longer know how.

"Keep him quiet," Anton shouts.

Was I making a sound? I can't even hear myself.

I feel hands clasp on me and lift me up, hauling me through the restaurant. My head falls back, and I notice that the ceiling is painted with a mural of an old naked man, his scimitar held high, riding a brown horse down a hill. The mane of the horse and the man's long hair are blowing in the wind. It makes me laugh, which comes out like a teakettle whistle.

"It's just blowback," Philip says softly. "You'll be okay soon."

He puts me in the trunk of Anton's car and slams down the top. It stinks of oil and something else, but I'm so out of it I barely notice. I twist around in the dark as the engine starts, my body not my own.

We're on a highway when I come back to myself. Headlights of following cars stream erratically through the outline of the trunk. My head is banging uncomfortably against the carpeted tire well with each bump of the road, and I can feel the shaking of the frame underneath me. I push myself into a different position and touch plastic filled with something soft and still warm.

For a moment I think of laying my head against it, until I touch a patch of sticky wetness and realize what I'm touching.

Garbage bags.

I gag in the dark and try to crawl as far away from them as I can. I press myself against the far back of the car until I can't go any farther. The metal presses into my back and I can only support my neck awkwardly with my arm, but I stay like that for the whole ride.

When the car lurches to a stop, I am sore and lightheaded. I hear the doors slam, gravel crunch, and then the trunk opens. Anton is standing over me. We're in the driveway of my house.

"What did you have to go and do that for?" he shouts.

I shake my head. I don't know why I changed the gun, or even how I did it. I look at my hand and see that it's smeared with a dull, dark red.

My bare hand.

"This is supposed to be a secret. *You* are supposed to be a secret." Then he notices my hands too. They must have left my gloves in the restaurant.

His jaw clenches.

"I'm sorry," I say, climbing woozily to my feet. I am sorry.

"How do you feel?" Barron asks me.

"Seasick," I tell him, but it isn't the recent car ride that is making me want to puke. I know I'm shaking, and there's nothing I can do to control it.

"I killed those men because of you," Anton says. "Their deaths are on your hands. All I want to do is bring back the old days when it meant something to be a worker. When it was good, not a thing to be ashamed about. When we owned all the politicians, all the cops. We were like princes in this city back then, and we can be again.

"Dab hands, they used to call us," he says. I think of Daneca's mother and her not entirely, yet wholly dissimilar lecture. "Dab hands. Experts. *Skilled*. When I'm in charge, I'm going to bring back the old days and make this city tremble. That's a good goal, a worthy goal."

"And just how are you going to do that?" I ask. "You think the government is going to roll over because you've murdered your way to the top of a crime family? You think Zacharov could have the world by the balls, but he's all 'No, thanks'?"

Anton hits me square in the jaw. Pain explodes in my head and I stumble backward, barely keeping my balance.

"Hey," Philip says, pushing Anton back. "He's just a big-mouthed kid."

I take two steps toward Anton, and Barron grabs my arm.

"Don't be stupid," he says, and pulls my sleeves down over my hands.

"Hold him," Anton tells Barron. He looks at me. "I'm not done with you, kid."

Barron's grip on me tightens.

"What are you doing, Anton?" Philip asks, trying to sound reasonable. "We don't have time for this. Plus, he's going to wake up with those bruises. Think."

Anton shakes his head. "Get out of my way, Philip. I shouldn't have to remind you that I'm your boss."

Philip looks back and forth between me and Anton, weighing Anton's rage and my stupidity.

"Hey," I say, struggling against Barron's hold. I'm exhausted, and I don't struggle hard, but that doesn't stop my mouth. "What are you going to do? Murder me, too? Like those men? Like Lila. Come on, what did she really do? Did she get in your way? Insult you? Not grovel?"

Sometimes I am very stupid. I guess I deserve the punch that Barron holds me in place for. The one that catches me just under my cheekbone and makes my vision go white. I can feel the blow all the way to my teeth.

"Shut up!" Anton shouts.

My mouth floods with the taste of old pennies. My cheeks and tongue feel like they're made of raw hamburger, and blood dribbles over my lips.

"Enough," says Philip. "Enough already."

"I decide when it's enough," Anton says.

"Okay, I'm sorry," I say, spitting a mouthful of blood onto the ground. "Lesson learned. You can not beat the crap out of me now. I didn't mean it."

I look up in time to see Philip light a cigarette and turn away, blowing smoke into the air. And to see Anton bring his fist down on my gut.

I try to twist out of the way, but I'm already too hurt to be fast, and there's nowhere to go with Barron's hands clamped on me. Bright pain makes me sag forward, moaning. I'm grateful when I feel him drop my arms so I can slide to the ground and curl my body around itself. I don't want to move. I want to lie very still until everything stops hurting.

"Kick him," Anton says. His voice is shaking. "I want to know you're loyal to me. Do it or this whole thing is called off."

I force myself to sit up and try to push myself upright. The three of them are looking down at me like I'm something they found on the bottom of their shoes. The word "please" repeats in my mind. "Not in the face," I say instead.

Barron's foot knocks me to the ground. It only takes a few more kicks for me to lose consciousness.

I DON'T WANT TO MOVE

because even breathing hurts my ribs. The bruises hurt more in the morning than they had the night before. Lying on the bed in my old room, I test my memory for blank spots. It reminds me of being a kid, sticking my tongue into my gums after a tooth fell out. But I remember last night very clearly: my brothers standing above me, Barron kicking my stomach over and over. I remember the gun changing, coiling around the man's wrist. The only thing I don't remember is how I got to bed, but I think that's because I blacked out.

"Oh, God," I say, rubbing my hand over my face, then looking at my hand to make sure it's still mine. Make sure it hasn't twisted into some other shape.

I reach my arm down slowly and carefully to touch the wound in my leg where the worked stones are. I feel the hardness of a whole one under my fingers and the outline of shards where two broke. My skin jumps, alight with pain, at the pressure. I wasn't crazy. A stone cracked last night, under my skin, each time Barron tried to work me.

Barron.

He's the memory worker. He's the one who changed Maura's memories. And mine.

My stomach clenches and I roll gingerly to one side, afraid that I'm going to throw up and then choke on it. Dizzily I see the white cat sitting on a pile of laundry, her eyes slitted.

"What are you doing here?" I whisper. My voice sounds like shards of glass are stuck in my throat.

She stands up, stretching her paws to knead the sweater she was lying on. Her nails sink into the fabric like little needles. Then her back arches.

"Did you see them bring me back here?" I croak.

Her pink tongue swipes her nose.

"Stop screwing with me," I say.

She hunkers down and then jumps onto the bed, startling me. I groan with fresh pain. "I know what you are," I say. "I know what I did to you."

Only you can undo the curse. Of course.

Her fur is soft against my arm, and I reach out a hand toward her. She lets me stroke down her back. I'm lying. I don't know what she is. I think I know who she was, but I'm not sure what she is anymore.

"I don't know how to turn you back," I say. "I figured out that it was me who changed you. I figured out that part. But I don't know how I do it."

She stiffens, and I turn to bury my face in her fur. I feel the rough pads of her paws. Her tiny claws are sharp against my skin.

"I don't have a dream amulet," I say. "I don't have anything to stop you from working me. You can make me dream, can't you? Like the rainstorm and the roof. Like before you were a cat."

Her purr is a rumble, like distant thunder.

I close my eyes.

I wake up still hurting. I am lying in a pool of blood, slipping as I try to rise. Leaning over me are Philip, Barron, Anton, and Lila.

"He doesn't remember anything," Lila the girl says. When she smiles, her canine teeth come to sharp points. She looks older than fourteen. She looks beautiful and terrible. I cower back from her.

She laughs.

"Who got hurt?" I ask.

"Me," she says. "Don't you remember? I died."

I push myself up onto my knees and find myself on the stage of the theater at Wallingford. Alone. The heavy blue curtain is closed in front of me, and I think that I can hear the sounds of a crowd beyond it. When I look down, the blood is no longer there, but a trapdoor is open. I scramble to my feet, slip, and nearly fall into the pit.

"You need makeup," someone says. I turn my head. It's Daneca, in shining plate mail, approaching me with a powder puff. She hits my face with it. There's a cloud of dust.

"I'm dreaming," I say out loud, which doesn't help nearly as much as it should. I open my eyes and find myself no longer on the Wallingford stage but in the aisle of a majestic theater. The wood-paneled walls are grooved with dust above a scarlet rug. Lights drip crystals, and the plaster ceilings are painted in frescoes of gold. In the rows of seats on the terraces in front of the stage, cats in clothes fan one another, wave programs, and mew. I turn around and around, and a few of them glance in my direction, their eyes shining with reflected light.

I stumble into one of the empty rows and take a seat as a dark red curtain opens.

Lila walks onto the stage, wearing a long white Victorian dress with pearl buttons. She's followed by Anton, then Philip and Barron. Each of the guys is in a costume from a different period. Anton's got on a purple zoot suit with an enormous feathered hat, Philip is dressed like an Elizabethan lord with a doublet and ruff, and Barron's wearing a long black robe. I can't decide if he's supposed to be a priest or a judge.

"Lo," Lila says, pressing the back of her wrist against her forehead. "I am a young girl and very much given to amusement."

Barron bows deeply. "It just so happens that I can be amusing."

"It just so happens," says Anton, "that Philip and I have

a little side thing going where I get rid of people for money. I can't have her father know. I'm going to take over the business someday."

"Alas, alack," says Lila. "Woe."

Barron smiles and rubs his hands together. "It just so happens that I like money."

Philip looks right at me, as though I was the one he was speaking to. "Anton's going to be our ticket out of being small time. And I think my girlfriend is pregnant. You understand, right? I'm doing this for all of us."

I shake my head. I don't understand.

On the stage Lila gives a small scream and starts shrinking, changing shape until she's the size of a mouse. Then the white cat springs down from one of the balconies, her dress tearing on the jagged splinters of the floorboards and pulling free from her furry body. Pouncing, she catches the Lila-mouse in her teeth and bites off the tiny head. Blood spatters across the stage.

"Lila," I say. "Stop it. Stop with all the games."

The cat gulps down the remains and looks out at me. And then the stage lights are turning toward me, the brightness making me blink in confusion. I stand up. The white cat stalks toward me. Her eyes—those blue and green eyes—are so clearly Lila's that I stumble back and into the aisle.

"You have to cut off my head," she says.

"No," I tell her.

"Do you love me?" she asks.

Her teeth are like ivory knives. "I don't know," I say.

"If you love me, you'll have to cut off my head."

Somehow I have a sword in my hand and am swinging it. The cat is changing like Lila did, but she's getting larger, growing into something monstrous. The audience's applause is deafening.

My ribs are throbbing, but I force myself to swing my legs off the bed. I walk into the bathroom, piss, and then chew up a handful of aspirin. Staring at myself in the mirror, taking in my bloodshot eyes and the mass of bruises near my ribs, I think over the dream, about the cat looming over me.

It's ridiculous, but I'm not laughing.

"Is that you?" Grandad's voice comes from down the stairs.

"Yeah," I call back.

"You slept late," he says, and I can hear him muttering, probably about how lazy I am.

"I'm not feeling good," I tell him from the stairwell. "I don't think I can clean today."

"I'm not that great myself," he says. "Rough night last night, huh? I drank so much I don't remember most of it."

I walk downstairs, cradling my ribs half-unconsciously. I stumble. Nothing feels right. My skin doesn't fit. I am Humpty Dumpty. All the king's horses and all the king's men have failed to put me back together again.

"Did anything happen you want to tell me about?" Grandad asks. I think of his eyes seeming to blink in the dark. I wonder what he heard. What he suspects.

"Nothing," I say, and pour myself a cup of coffee. I drink it black, and the warmth in my belly is the first comforting thing I remember feeling in a while.

Grandad tilts his head in my direction. "You look like crap."

"I told you I didn't feel good."

The phone rings in the other room, a shrill sound that jangles my nerves. "You tell me lots of things," Grandad says, and walks off to answer it.

I see the cat on the stairs, her white body ghostly in a beam of sunlight. She blurs in my vision. My brothers were uncomfortable, but not for the reasons I thought. Not because I was a murderer or an outsider. I was such an insider that I never even knew it. I was inside of the insiders. I was hidden inside my insides. For a moment I want to dash all the crockery to the floor. I want to scream and shout. I want to take this newfound power and change everything that I can touch.

Lead to gold.

Flesh to stone.

Sticks to snakes.

I hold up the coffee cup, and I think about the muzzle of the gun melting and shifting in my hand, but no matter how I try to summon that moment, the cup stays. The slogan keeps reading AMHERST TRUCKING: WE LIFT STUFF on a glossy maroon background.

"What are you doing?" Grandad asks me, and my hand jerks, sloshing coffee onto my shirt. He's holding out the phone. "Philip. For you. Says you left something over there."

I shake my head.

"Take it," Grandad says, sounding exasperated, and I can't think of an excuse not to, so I do.

"Yeah?" I say.

"What did you do to her?" His voice sounds thick with anger and something else. Panic.

"Who?" I ask.

"Maura. She's gone, and she took my son. You have to tell me where she is, Cassel."

"Me?" I ask him. Last night he watched Barron kick me in the stomach until I blacked out, and today he's accusing me of masterminding Maura's escape? Anger makes my vision blur. I grip the phone so tightly that I'm afraid the plastic case is going to crack.

He should be apologizing to me. He should be begging.

"I know you've been talking to her. What did you tell her? What did you do to her?"

"Oh, sorry," I say automatically, cold fury in every word. *"I don't remember."* I click the off button on the phone, feeling so vindictively pleased that it takes me a moment to realize how incredibly stupid I've just been.

Then I remember I'm not Cassel Sharpe, kid brother and general disappointment, anymore. I'm one of the most powerful practitioners of one of the rarest curses.

I'm not taking Lila and leaving town. I'm not going anywhere.

They should be afraid of me.

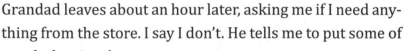

Grandad leaves about an hour later, asking me if I need anything from the store. I say I don't. He tells me to put some of my clothes in a bag.

"What's going on?" I ask.

"We're taking a road trip down to Carney," he says.

I nod my head, cradle my ribs, and watch him go.

Lila stares at me from the center of the mounds of papers, clothes and platters on the dining room table. She's eating something. I get closer and see a piece of bacon, the grease soaking into a scarf.

"Grandad give you that?" I ask.

She sits on her hind legs and licks her mouth.

My cell phone is ringing. The caller ID says Daneca.

"You gave her the slip," I say. "Did you really walk all the way here?"

Lila yawns, showing her fangs.

I know I have to change her, now before Grandad returns. Before my ribs start to hurt again and I can't concentrate.

If only I knew how.

Her eyes are shining as I walk toward her.

A curse was placed on me. A curse that only you can break.

I reach out my hand and touch her fur. Her bones feel light, fragile, like the bones of a bird. I think of the moment when the barrel of the gun began to turn to scales, try to summon the impulse that made it transform.

Nothing.

I imagine Lila, imagine the cat elongating, growing into a girl. As I picture it, I am aware that I don't know what Lila would look like now. I push that out of my head and let myself make up some combination of the girl I knew and the girl from my dream. Close enough is close enough. I imagine her changing, imagine it until I'm shaking with concentration, but she still doesn't change.

The cat growls deep in her throat.

I push out one of the dining room chairs and flop down on it, resting my forehead against the wood of the back.

I think about the ant Barron told me I never turned into a stick, but I don't remember how I did it. He stripped that memory out so cleanly, there's not even a trace.

It can't be triggered by strong emotion. I've been angry lots of times and I've never accidentally turned my gloves into squirrels or anyone into anything. Besides, I am feeling plenty of strong emotion right at the moment.

When I changed the gun, Philip was about to get shot. Maybe it was like some kind of muscle memory or a part of my brain that I could access only when someone I cared about was in danger.

I look around the room. The sword I found when I was cleaning out the living room is right where I left it, leaning against the wall. I pick it up, feel the weight, as though I am distant from my body. I note the rust running down the blade. The sword feels heavy in my hands, not like the light fencing foils at school.

If you love me, cut off my head.

"Lila," I said. "I don't know how to change you."

She pads to the edge of the table and jumps onto the floor. Surreal. Everything is surreal. None of this is happening.

"I am thinking of doing something to force myself. Something crazy. Something you maybe suggested. To force the magic."

This is stupid. Someone has to stop me. She has to stop me.

She rubs her cheek against the blade, closing her eyes, and then rubs her whole body against it. Back and forth. Back and forth.

"You really think this is a good idea?"

She yowls and hops back up onto the table. Then she sits, waiting.

I reach out and place one hand on the fur of her back. "I'm going to swing this sword at your head, okay? But I'm not going to hit you."

Stop me.

"Stay still."

She's just watching me, just waiting. She doesn't move, except for her twitching tail.

I pull back the sword and swing it toward her tiny body. I swing it with all my weight behind it.

Oh, God, I'm going to kill her again.

And then I see it. Everything goes fluid. I know I can shift the sword in my hand into a coil of rope, a sheet of water, a dusting of dirt. And the cat is no longer a collection of fragile bird bones and fur. I can see the badly woven curse on her, obscuring the girl underneath. A simple mental tug and it pulls apart.

I'm suddenly bringing the sword down on the naked form of a crouching girl. I pull back, but my weight is way off balance.

I topple to the floor and the sword flies out of my hands. It crashes into a water-stained Venetian chest at the other end of the dining room.

She is a tangled mass of dredded curls the color of hay

and sunburned skin. She tries to stand up and can't. Maybe she's forgotten how.

This time when the blowback hits, it's like my body is trying to rip itself apart.

"Cassel," she says. She's bent over me, in a too big shirt. I can see almost the entire length of her bare legs when I turn my head. "Cassel, someone's coming. Wake up."

My ribs are hurting again. I don't know if that's a good thing or a bad thing. I just need to sleep. If I sleep long enough, when I wake up, I'll be back in Wallingford and Sam will be spraying himself with too much cologne and everything will go back to the way things are supposed to be.

She slaps me, hard.

I suck in a deep breath and open my eyes. My cheek is stinging. When I turn my head, I can see the hilt of the sword and a shattered vase that must have fallen off the chest. The whole floor is freshly strewn with books and papers.

"Someone's coming," she says. Her voice sounds different from how I remember. Scratchy. Hoarse.

"My grandfather," I say. "He went to the store."

"There are two people out there." Her face is both familiar and strange. Looking at her makes my stomach hurt. I reach out a hand.

She flinches back. Of course she doesn't want me to touch her. Look what I can do.

"Hurry," she says.

I stumble up. "Oh," I say out loud, because I remember the stupid thing I told Philip. I can't believe I ever thought that I was good at deception.

"The closet," I say.

The coat closet is choked with fur and moth-eaten wool. We kick out the boxes at the bottom and squeeze ourselves inside. The only way to fit without pressing against the door is to duck under the bar holding up the hangers and let that wedge me in. The rod bangs into my arm, and Lila comes in after me, closing the door. Then she's pressed against my sore ribs, breathing in short rapid gasps. Her breath is warm against my throat.

I can't see her, just slivers of lights along the outline of the door. One of my mother's mink collars brushes my chin, and there's a faint trace of perfume.

I hear the front door open and then Philip's voice call, "Cassel? Grandad?"

Automatically I make a sudden movement. It's just a reflex, not much but it makes Lila grab my arms and dig her fingers into my biceps.

"Shhhhh," she says.

"*You* be quiet," I whisper back. I've grabbed hold of her shoulders without consciously deciding to, a mirror of her gesture. In the dark she's a phantom. Not real. Her shoulders are trembling slightly, vibrating under my hands.

Both our hands are bare. It's shocking.

She's leaning forward.

Then her mouth is sliding against mine. Her lips open, soft and yielding. Our teeth click together, and this is the kiss I fantasized about when I was fourteen, and even later than that, when I knew it was sick and wrong and horrible to desire the girl I murdered. Every kiss I ever gave or took was shadowed by her presence, so the real thing catches me wholly off guard. My shoulders press against the wall. I reach out with one hand to steady myself, gripping the wool shoulder of a coat so hard I can feel the ancient cloth rip.

She bites my tongue.

"He's not here," Barron says. "The car's gone."

Lila turns away from me abruptly, tilting her neck so that her hair is in my face.

"What do you think he said to Grandad?" Philip asks.

"Nothing," Barron says. "You're overreacting."

"You didn't hear him on the phone," says Philip. "He remembered—I don't know what. Enough to know some-one had been working him."

Something crunches under one of their feet. Considering all the stuff scattered on the floor, it could be anything. "He's a smart-ass. You're just being paranoid."

Lila's breath is hot on my neck.

Footfalls on the stairs tell me they're going to look for me up there.

We're so close that it's impossible not to touch her. And that makes me recall that she must have been touching me to make me dream.

"That night, at Wallingford—were you in the room with me?" I whisper.

"They needed me to get you," she says. "To make you

sleepwalk out to them. I made lots of people sleepwalk right into their hands."

I picture a white shape on the steps, the hall master's dog starting to bark before she made the dog dream too.

"Why did you kiss me?" I ask her, keeping my voice low.

"To shut you up," she says. "Why do you think?"

We're silent for a moment. Above us I can hear my brothers walking across the creaking boards. I wonder if they're in their old bedrooms. I wonder if they're in my bedroom, going through my things like I went through Barron's.

"Thanks," I say, finally, sarcastically. My heart is beating like a rattle.

"You don't remember any of it, do you? I figured that part out. Barron told me that you laughed when he told you I was in a cage, but you didn't laugh, did you?"

"Of course I didn't," I say. "No one told me you were alive."

She gives a weird short, gurgling laugh. "How did you think I died?" I think of the cage and of her being there for the last three years. How that could drive anyone crazy. Not that she seems crazier than anyone else. Me, for instance.

"I stabbed you." My voice breaks on the words, even though I know the memory's not true.

She's quiet. All I can hear is the hammering of my own heart.

"I *remember* it," I say. "The blood. Slipping on the blood. And feeling gleeful, like I'd gotten away with it. Looking down at your body and feeling the way I did—the memory still seems so real. Like something that no one could make up, because it was so awful. And how I was—It's worse than feeling nothing, like you're just psycho. It's much worse to think you enjoyed it." I'm glad we're in the dark. It is impossible to imagine saying all this to her face.

"They were supposed to kill me," Lila says. "Barron and I were in your grandfather's house in the basement, and he grabbed my arms. At first I thought he was kidding around, that he wanted to wrestle, until you and Philip walked in. Philip was saying something to you, and you just kept shaking your head."

I want to say that it isn't true, that it didn't happen, but of course I really have no idea.

"I kept asking Barron to let me get up, but he wouldn't even look at me. Philip took out a knife, and that's when you seemed to change your mind. You walked over to me and looked down, but it was like you weren't really looking at me. Like you didn't even know who I was. Barron started to get up, and I was relieved, until you took my wrists and pressed them down on the shag rug. You pressed them down harder than he did."

I swallow hard and close my eyes, dreading what she'll say next.

Steps on the stairs make her clam up.

"Tell me," I whisper. My voice comes out louder than I planned. Probably not loud enough to get their attention. "Tell me the rest."

She presses her bare hand against my mouth. "Shut up." She's whispering, but she sounds fierce.

If I struggle, I really am going to make noise.

"I don't want you to tell Anton," Philip says. He sounds close, and Lila's body jolts. I try to slide my hand against her upper arms to gentle her, but that only seems to make her shake worse.

"Tell him what?" asks Barron. "That you think Cassel's going to flake? Do you want this whole thing to come apart?"

"I don't want it to blow up in our faces. And Anton's acting more unstable."

"We can take care of Anton when this is over. Cassel's fine. You baby him too much."

"I just think that this is risky. It's a risky plan and Cassel needs to be on board. I think you forgot to make him forget."

"You know what I think?" Barron says. "I think that bitch wife of yours is the problem. I told you to cut her loose."

"Shut up." I hear the growl under Philip's seeming calm.

"Fine, but he was hanging around her last night after dinner. She obviously figured out enough to leave."

"But Cassel—"

"Cassel nothing. She told him what she suspected. And he did a little fishing to find out if it was true. See how you'd react. He doesn't know anything yet, unless you freak out. Simple. Case closed. Now let's go."

"What about Lila?"

"We'll find her," he says. "She's a cat. What can she do?"

I hear the front door slam. We wait what feels like ten minutes and then slide under the pole to open the closet door. I look around the room. It's trashed, but no more than it was before.

Lila steps out behind me, and when I look back at her,

her mouth curves up at one corner. She turns toward the bathroom.

I catch her wrist. "They're gone and I still want to hear the rest. Tell me. Please. How you got away from Barron. Why you lured me up to the roof of Smythe Hall with that crazy dream."

"I wanted to kill you," she says, that slight smile widening.

I drop her wrist like it's burning me. "You what?"

Here I was, eating my whole heart over her, forgetting what she was actually like back then.

"I couldn't do it," she says. "I hated you even more than I hated them, but I still couldn't do it. That's something, right?"

I feel like she knocked the air out of my lungs.

"No," I say. "It's nothing. Less than nothing."

The kitchen door opens with a creak. Lila presses herself against the wall, shooting me a warning glance. There's no time to dash for the closet, so I step into the kitchen to take whatever's coming.

Philip smiles from the doorway. "I knew you were here."

"I just walked in," I say, even though he knows I'm lying.

He takes a step toward me, and I take a step back. I wonder if he's going to try to kill me. I hold up my hands, still bare. He doesn't seem to even notice.

"I need you to tell her," Philip says, and for a moment I don't know who he's talking about. "Tell Maura I was weak. Tell her I'm sorry. Tell her I didn't know how to stop."

"I told you I don't know where Maura is."

"Fine," he says tightly. "See you Wednesday night. And, Cassel, maybe you're pissed off or you have questions, but it's going to be worth it in the end. Trust us just a little bit longer and you're going to have everything you ever wanted."

He walks out and down the hill to Barron's idling car. Lila walks into the room and puts her hand on my shoulder. I shrug it off.

"We have to get out of here," she says.

I turn to agree, but she's already pulling out gloves and a coat from the closet.

LATE AFTERNOON SUNLIGHT

streams through the window, and I wake up with my head pillowed against blond curls and warm skin. At first I'm so disoriented that I can't understand who could be next to me and why she doesn't have many clothes on.

Sam's closing the door to the room. "Hey, dude," he says in a whisper.

Lila makes a small gesture of complaint and rolls against the wall, her body sliding against mine, her shirt rucking up. She mashes the pillow over her head.

I dimly recall walking to the convenience store three blocks from my house, calling a cab, and then sitting on the sidewalk to wait, Lila leaning against me. I figured my dorm room was going to be empty for a couple of hours. There was no other place I could think of to go.

"Don't worry," Sam says. "I haven't seen Valerio. But next time put a sock on the door."

"A sock?"

"My brother says that's the universal signal for getting some—the nice way to alert your roommate so that he can make other plans for the evening. As opposed to letting your roommate walk in on you."

"Uh, yeah," I say, yawning. "Sorry. Sock. I'll remember."

"Who is she?" he whispers, indicating her with his chin. "Does she even go to school here?" He drops his voice even lower. "And are you crazy?"

Lila rolls over again and smiles sleepily at Sam. "The uniform's cute," she says in her new, rough voice.

Sam flushes.

"I'm Lila, and yes, he's crazy. But you must have noticed that before now. He was crazy back when I knew him, and he's obviously gotten crazier over time." Her gloved fingers tousle my hair.

I grimace. "She's an old friend. A family friend."

"Everyone's coming back," Sam says, raising his eyebrows. "You and your buddy better get out."

Lila pushes herself up on her elbow. "You feeling better?" It doesn't seem to bother her to be half dressed with one leg pressed against me. Maybe she got used to being naked when she was a cat, but I am completely unused to it.

"Yeah," I say. My ribs are sore, but the pain is duller.

She yawns and stretches up her arms, canting her body to one side and making her spine crack audibly.

It feels like the whole world has turned upside down. There aren't any more rules.

"Hey," I say to Sam, because if the world's gone crazy, then I guess I can do whatever I want. "Guess what? I'm a worker."

He stares at me, openmouthed. Lila jerks to her feet.

"You can't tell him that," she says.

"Why not?" I ask, then turn to him. "I didn't have any idea until yesterday. Wacky, right?"

"What kind?" he manages to squeak out.

"If you tell him *that*," Lila says, "I'm going to kill you, but first I'm going to kill him."

"Consider the question retracted," Sam says, holding his hands out in a peace offering.

Some of my clothes are still in the drawers and in the closet. I grab what I need, then head for the library to take out a loan from my business.

We walk down to the corner store where all the Wallingford students go to shoplift gum. Lila picks out a bottle of shampoo, some soap, an enormous cup of coffee, and three bars of chocolate. I pay.

The owner, Mr. Gazonas, smiles at me. "He's a good kid," he tells Lila. "Polite. No stealing. Not like the other kids who come in here. Hang on to this one."

That makes me laugh.

I lean against the wall outside. "Do you want to call your mom?"

Lila shakes her head. "With all the gossip down in Carney? No way. I don't want anyone but my father to know I'm back."

I nod slowly. "So we call him, then."

"I need to take a shower first," Lila says, winding the plastic handle of the bag around her wrist. She has rolled up a pair of my dress slacks and looks homeless in them, the baggy shirt, and some lace-up boots she found in the back of my closet.

I dial the same cab company that gave us a lift over here. "We don't have any place to clean up," I say.

"Hotel room," she tells me.

There's a hotel not too far a walk from where we're standing, a nice basic place that parents stay at sometimes, but it's not going to work. "Believe me, they are not going to let the two of us get a room. Kids try all the time."

She shrugs.

I hang up on the dispatcher. "Fine," I say. I'm thinking of how when the rooms get cleaned, the doors are open. We're never going to be able to get a room, but we might be able to steal one for a shower if we get lucky.

As we start across the parking lot, I see Audrey with two of her friends, Stacey and Jenna. Stacey gives me the finger. Jenna nudges Audrey with her elbow. I know I should look away, but I don't. Audrey lifts her head. Her eyes are shadowed.

"Do you know her?" Lila asks.

"Yeah," I say, and finally turn toward the hotel.

"She's pretty," says Lila.

"Yeah," I say again, and jam my hands in my pockets, deep—gloved fingers against the crease.

Lila keeps looking back. "I bet she's got a shower."

Here's another thing Mom told me over and over about scams. The first thing you have to get is the mark's confidence, but it's always more convincing when someone other than you suggests the score to the mark. That's why most confidence schemes demand a partner.

"Cassel told me all about you," Lila tells Audrey. Her smile changes her from homeless vagabond to regular girl, even with her matted hair.

Audrey looks from me to Lila and then back at me, as if she's trying to decide whether this is part of some game.

"What did he say?" asks Jenna, taking a long swig of her Diet Coke.

"My cousin just got back from India," I say, and nod in Lila's direction. "Her parents were living in some ashram. I was telling her about Wallingford."

Audrey's hands go to her hips. "She's your cousin?"

Lila scrunches her eyebrows for a moment, then a wide grin splits her face. "Oh! Because I'm so pale, right?"

Stacey flinches. Audrey looks at me like she's trying to see if I'm offended. Wallingford's idea of political correctness is never to mention anything about race. Ever. Brown skin, especially ambiguously light brown skin like mine, is supposed to be as invisible as red hair or blond hair or skin so white it's marbled with blue veins.

"No, it's all good," says Lila. "We're stepcousins. My mother married his mother's brother."

My mother doesn't even have a brother.

I don't lift an eyebrow.

I don't smile.

I don't admit to myself that scamming the girl I might still be in love with is making my pulse race.

"Audrey," I say, because I know this script pretty well, "can we talk for a minute?"

"*Cassel*," says Lila. "I have to cut my hair. I have to take a shower. Come on." She grins at Audrey and grabs my arm. "It was nice meeting you."

I keep my gaze on Audrey, waiting for her to answer.

"I guess you can talk when you get back to school," says Jenna.

"She could use the shower at the dorm," Audrey says hesitantly.

I am a very bad person.

"So we can talk?" I ask her. "That would be great."

"Sure," she says, not looking at me.

As we all walk back to Wallingford, Lila flashes me a grin. "Smooth," she mouths.

Audrey and I sit on the cement steps in front of the arts building. Her neck is blotchy, the way it gets when she's nervous. She keeps pushing her red hair out of her face, hooking it over one ear, but it tumbles loose with every breeze.

"I'm sorry about what happened at the party," I say. I want to touch her hair, smooth it back, but I don't.

"I'm an independent woman. I make my own deci-sions," she says. Her gloved hands pull at the weave of her gray tights.

"I just meant that I—"

"I know what you mean," she says. "I was drunk, and you shouldn't kiss drunk girls, certainly not in front of their boyfriends. It's not chivalrous."

"Greg's your boyfriend?" That certainly explains his reaction.

She bites her lower lip and shrugs.

"And then I hit him!" I say quickly, to make her laugh. "You must be so disappointed in me. Chivalry is truly dead."

She grins, clearly relieved I'm not going to interrogate her. "I *am* disappointed."

"I'm funnier than Greg," I say. It's easy to talk to her today, knowing I didn't kill the last girl I was in love with. I had no idea how heavy a burden that was until I set it down.

"But he likes me better than you ever did," she says.

"He must like you a whole lot, then." I look into her eyes as I say it, and am rewarded by the blotchy blush spreading across her cheeks.

She punches me in the arm. "Oooh. You are funny."

"Does that mean you're not quite over me?"

She leans back and stretches. "I'm not sure. Are you coming back to school?"

I nod. "I'll be back."

"Tick tock," she says. "I might forget all about you."

I grin. "Absence diminishes little passions and increases great ones."

"You've got a good memory," she says, but her gaze is focused somewhere behind me.

"Did I mention that I was smarter than Greg too?" When she doesn't react, I turn to see what she's staring at.

Lila is heading across the quad toward us in a long skirt and a sweater that she obviously talked someone out of. She cut off so much of her hair that it's shorter than mine: a pale silvery cap on her head. She's still wearing my boots, and her lips are shining with pink gloss. For a moment I don't breathe.

"Big difference," Audrey says.

Lila's smile widens. She walks up and links her arm with mine. "Thank you so much for letting me use the shower."

"No problem," says Audrey. She's watching us, like she suddenly thinks that there's something off about what occurred. Maybe it's just how different Lila looks.

"We have to catch a train, Cassel," says Lila.

"Yeah," I say. "I'll call you."

Audrey nods her head, still looking bewildered.

Lila and I head toward the sidewalk, and I know what this is. The blow-off and the getaway. High stakes or low stakes, the steps are the same.

Turns out I'm not like my dad at all. I really am just like my mother.

The train station is practically empty without the weekday commuter traffic. A guy about my age sits on one of the painted wooden benches, arguing with a girl whose eyes look red and puffy. An old woman leans over a pull cart of groceries. Standing in the far corner two girls with slender mohawks dyed a deep pink giggle together over a Game Boy.

"We should call your dad." I fish my cell phone out of my pocket. "Make sure he's going to be in his office when we get there."

Lila stares into the glass of a vending machine, her expression unreadable. Her reflection wavers a little, like maybe she's trembling. "We're not going to New York. We have to get him to meet me somewhere else."

"Why?"

"Because I don't want anyone but him to know I'm back. Anyone. We have no idea who's working with Anton."

"Okay," I say, nodding. After all she's been through, a little paranoia is probably not misplaced.

"I overheard a lot," she says. "I know their plan."

"Okay," I say again. I never thought she didn't.

"Promise me you won't tell him what happened to me," she says and lowers her voice. "I don't want him to know I was a cat."

"Okay," I say again. "I'm not going to say anything you don't want, but he's going to expect me to say *something*." I'm ashamed at my own relief. I wasn't sure what would happen next. As angry as I am at Barron and Philip, as much as I hate them right now, if Zacharov knew what they did, he'd kill them. I'm not sure I want them dead.

Lila reaches out her hand for my phone. "You won't be there. I'll go by myself."

I open my mouth, and she gives me a warning look that lets me know I better think carefully before I talk. "Look, just let me come with you on the train. I'll take off once you're wherever. Safe."

"I can take care of myself," she says, and there is a burr in her voice that sounds like a growl.

"I know that." I hand her the phone.

"Good," she says, flipping it open.

I frown as she punches in the numbers. Not telling Zacharov, even if it delays my need to make decisions, isn't a solution. His life is in danger. We need a strategy. "You can't think your dad is going to blame you? That's crazy."

"I think my father is going to feel sorry for me," she says. I can hear the ringing on the other end.

"He's going to think you were brave."

"Maybe," she says, "but he's not going to think I can take care of myself."

I hear a woman's voice, and Lila puts the phone to her ear. "I'd like to talk with Mr. Ivan Zacharov."

There is a long pause. Her lips press together into a thin line. "No, this is not a joke. He'll want to talk to me."

She kicks the wall with one too large boot. "Put him on the line!"

I raise my eyebrows. She covers the receiver with her hand. "They're getting him," she mouths.

"Hello, Daddy," she says, closing her eyes.

A few moments later she says, "No, I can't prove I'm me. How could I prove that?" I can hear his voice like a distant buzz, growing louder.

"I don't know. I don't remember," she says tightly. "Don't call me a liar. I *am* Lillian!"

She bites her lip and, after a few more moments, thrusts the phone in my direction. "Talk to him."

"What do you want me to say?" I keep my voice low, but the prospect of talking to Mr. Zacharov makes my palms sweat.

She reaches over to a tray of brochures and shoves one at me. "Tell him to meet us there."

I look down at it.

"He's got a room at the Taj Mahal," Lila hisses.

I take the phone. "Um, hello, sir," I say into the receiver, but he's still yelling. Finally it seems to register that she's no longer on the line.

His voice is that of someone used to his commands being obeyed. "Where is she? Where are you now? Just tell me that."

"She wants us to meet you in Atlantic City. She says you have a place there. At the Taj Mahal."

The phone goes so silent that for a moment I think he hung up on me.

"What kind of setup am I walking into?" he says finally, slowly.

"She just wants you to meet her. Alone. Be there at nine tonight. And don't tell anyone." I don't know how else to keep him from arguing, so I close the phone.

I look at Lila. "Can we actually get there by nine?"

She spreads open the schedule. "Yeah, plenty of time. That was perfect."

"See? I came in useful. Maybe I'll come in useful again."
She sighs. Nods.

I carefully feed a twenty into the machine out by the steps and punch in our destination. The change comes in coins, silver dollars ringing against the tray like bells.

You can't take a train from the middle of Jersey directly to Atlantic City. You have to ride all the way to Philadelphia and change trains at Thirtieth Street Station for the Atlantic City line. As soon as we settle into our seats, Lila rips open the bag and eats the three convenience store chocolate bars in quick greedy bites. Then she wipes her face with a fist, knuckles down over her cheek to her nose. It isn't a human gesture, or at least it isn't how humans make the same gesture.

Uncomfortable, I look out the cracked grimy glass at the sea of houses blurring past. Each one, full of secrets.

"Tell me what happened that night," I say. "The rest of it. When I changed you."

"Okay," she says. "But first I need you to understand why my father can't know what happened to me. I'm his only child and I'm a girl. Families like mine—they're really traditional. Women might be powerful workers, but they're seldom leaders. Get it?"

I nod my head.

"If Dad found out what happened, he'd bring down vengeance on Anton and your brothers—maybe even on you. But afterward I'd be the daughter who needed to be protected. I could never be the head of the family."

"I'm going to get my own vengeance and I'm going to save my father from Anton. Then he's going to see that I deserve to be his heir." She crosses her legs, propping her feet next to me. My boots are huge on her, and one of the laces has come undone.

It's hard to picture her as the head of the Zacharov family.

I nod again. I think of Barron kicking me in the ribs. I think of Philip looking down at me as I writhed. Anger rises up in me, white hot and dangerous. "You're going to need me to do that."

Her eyes narrow. "Is that a problem?"

I loathe them, but they're my family. "I want you to leave my brothers out of your plans."

I can see her jaw clench as she brings her teeth together abruptly. "I deserve revenge," she says.

"You want to deal with your family your way. Fine. Let me deal with *my* family."

"You don't even know what they did to you."

I flinch from the surge of dread I feel. Swallow it down. "Okay, tell me."

She licks her lips. "You want to know what happened that night? I told you that they were arguing. Anton told Barron to get rid of me. You were supposed to turn me into . . . into something. Something glass so he could smash me. Something dead so I'd be dead. That's what they kept saying while you were pinning me to the floor.

"Philip said that if you didn't do it, they were going to have to hurt me and it would make a mess. Barron kept saying something about remembering what I did to you and I kept shouting that I didn't do anything." Her gaze drops for a moment.

Tells. Everyone has them. "Why did Anton want you dead?"

"He wants to take over my family. He was afraid Dad would never tap him as his heir with me around. So he always wanted me dead. He just needed a way to make it happen that wouldn't implicate him.

"The excuse for getting rid of me was that Barron had asked me to make some people sleepwalk out of their houses. I would brush against them during the day, and then that night they'd have a dream and they'd get up and go stand on their lawns. Sometimes they woke up on the way out and the curse faded, sometimes not. I didn't know what it was for. Barron said they were people who owed my father money and that Barron would be able to talk to them, keep them from getting hurt. Anton found out that Barron had used me to help and told him that I had to be killed or else."

"Or else what? What's the big deal about making people sleepwalk?" I lean back. The vinyl seat squeaks.

"Um, your brothers? They make people disappear. That's what they do."

"They kill people?" My voice comes out too loud. I don't know why I'm shocked. I know criminals do bad things, and I get that my brothers are criminals. I had just assumed that whatever Philip did for Anton was small time. Leg-breaking stuff.

Lila frowns at me and looks around the train, but even after my outburst no one seems interested in us. Her voice goes low, to practically a whisper, like she can make up for my mistake through overcompensation. "*They* don't kill anyone. They get their little brother to do it for them. He turns people into objects. Then they dump the objects."

"What?" I heard her; I just can't believe I heard her right.

"They've been using you as a human garbage disposal." She makes a frame with her hands and looks at me through it. "Portrait of a teenage assassin."

I stand up, even though we're on a train and there's nowhere for me to go.

"Cassel?" She reaches out for me, and I step back.

There's a roaring in my ears. I'm grateful. I don't think I can listen to much more.

"I'm sorry. But you had to suspect—"

I push my way through the heavy doors and onto the platform between the cars. The joining between the two cars swings back and forth beneath my feet. I am standing right above the hooks and chains that connect the train into its snaking shape. Cold air blows back my hair, then hot air from the engine hits my face.

I stand there, hands against the sliding metal, until I start to calm down.

I think I understand why all those workers got rounded up and shot. Why people were so scared of us that they wanted us dead. Even I'm scared of me right now.

We are, largely, who we remember ourselves to be.

That's why habits are so hard to break. If we know ourselves to be liars, we expect not to tell the truth. If we think of ourselves as honest, we try harder.

For three whole days I wasn't a killer. Lila had come back from the dead, and with her, the abatement of my self-loathing. But now the pile of corpses teeters above me, threatening to crash down and suffocate me with guilt.

All my life I wanted my brothers to trust me. To let me in on their secrets. I wanted them, Philip especially, to think of me as a worthy accomplice.

Even after they kicked the crap out of me, my instinct was to try and save them.

Now I just want revenge.

After all, I'm already a murderer. No one really expects a murderer to stop killing. I grip the metal bar on the rolling train, my fingers clenching around it like it's Philip's throat. I don't want to be a monster, but maybe it's too late to be anything else.

The door swings open and the conductor steps onto the platform and past me. "You can't ride out here," he says, looking back.

"Okay," I say, and he opens the door to the next car, ready to collect more tickets. He doesn't really care. I could probably stay where I am for a long while before he comes back through again.

I suck in another couple breaths of fetid air and then go back to Lila.

"Very dramatic," she says when I sit down. "Storming off and all." Her eyes look bruised around the edges. She'd found a pen somewhere and started doodling in ink on her leg, below the knee.

I feel awful, but I don't apologize.

"Yeah," I say, "I'm a dramatic guy. High-strung."

That makes her smile, but it fades fast. "I hated you, lying in your comfortable bed at your school, caring about grades and girls and not about what you did to me."

I grit my teeth. "You slept in my bed. You really think it's that comfortable?"

She laughs, but it sounds more like a sob.

I look out the window. We're in woods now. "I shouldn't have said that. You were sleeping in a cage. I'm not a good person, Lila." I hesitate. "But I did—I do care what I've done to you. I thought about you every single day. And I am sorry. I'm grovelingly, pathetically sorry."

"I don't want your pity," she says, but her voice sounds gentler.

"Too bad," I say.

She gives me a wry lopsided grin and kicks me with my own boot.

"I'd like it if you'd tell me the rest of what happened. How I transformed you. How you got away. I'm not going to freak out anymore. I'll listen to whatever you want to tell me."

She nods and goes back to drawing on her leg. Swirls that spiral out from an ink blue center. "Right. So. There you are, pressing me down to the carpet.

"You look crazy, angry. But then you get this weird smile on your face. I'm scared, really scared, because I think you're going to do it. You lean down and whisper in my ear. '*Run.*' That's what you say."

"Run?" I ask.

"I know. Crazy, right? You're still on top of me—how am I supposed to do anything? But then I start to change." The pen presses against her skin, hard now. It's scratching her leg. "It felt like my skin was getting tight and itchy. My bones twisted and I grew hunched, small. My vision blurred, and then I could crawl away from you. I didn't know how to run on four legs, but I ran anyway.

"I heard you scream, but I didn't look back. There was a lot of shouting.

"They caught me under some bushes. I made it out of the house, but I just couldn't run fast enough."

She stops drawing lines and starts punching the point of the pen against her leg.

"Hey," I say, putting my gloved hand on top of hers.

She blinks quickly, like she forgot where she was. "Barron put me in a cage and he put a shock collar around my neck—the kind they use on little dogs. He said that it was better than if I was dead. I was out of the way, but he could still use me. I made people sleepwalk right out to you guys; it's easy for a cat to slip into a house and to touch someone. I even made you sleepwalk out of the dorms to where your brothers were waiting.

"You looked at me like I was nothing. An animal." Her nostrils flare. "I thought you'd been trying to save me. But you never tried to save me again."

I don't know what to say. I feel a deep, aching sorrow

that hurts more than I know how to express. I don't have the words. I want to touch her, but I don't deserve it.

She shakes her head. "I know Barron worked you. I'm here now because of you. I shouldn't say that."

"It's okay." I take a deep breath. "I have a lot to be sorry for."

"I should have guessed that they'd changed your memories. Barron's so busy trying to make people remember what he wants them to and make them forget everything else that he doesn't notice that he's strip-mining his own brain. He can't pull the strings because he's forgotten where they are.

"It's just that you go so crazy being alone like that. Sometimes he'd forget my water or food and I'd cry and cry and cry." She stops talking and looks out the window. "I would try to tell myself stories to pass the time. Fairy tales. Parts of books. But they got used up.

"In the beginning I tried to escape, but I guess after a while I just used up all my hope like I used up the stories." Lila lowers her voice and leans into me, so close that the hairs on the back of my neck rise with her breath. "When I found out you were going to hurt my dad, when I overheard them, I realized escaping didn't matter. I knew I had to kill you."

"I'm glad you didn't," I say. I think of my bare feet sliding on slate.

She smiles. "It turned out Barron wasn't watching me as closely as he had before. I wore down the nylon part of the collar enough. It was still hard to get it the rest of the way off, but I did it."

I think of the blood crusted on her fur when I saw her that first time.

"Do you still hate me?" I ask.

"I don't know," she says. "A little."

My ribs ache. I want to close my eyes. Somewhere on the train a baby starts to cry. The businessman two seats in front of us is on the phone. "I don't want sorbet," he says. "I don't like sorbet. Just give me some damn ice cream."

I think maybe I deserve for my ribs to hurt more.

THE LIGHTS OF ATLANTIC

City glitter along the boardwalk, as bright as day. We finally get out of the taxi in front of the Taj Mahal hotel, both of us sleepy and stretching from the long trip.

I look at my watch. It's about fifteen minutes after nine. She's late.

"I guess I can take it from here," Lila says.

Yawning, I take out a pen, her pen. The one she was writing on her leg with. I write my number on her arm, right above the top of her glove.

She's watching with half-lidded eyes as ink marks stretch across her skin. I wonder what it would be like to kiss her now, under the streetlight, with my eyes open.

"Let me know when you're okay," I say softly instead.

She looks at the number. "Are you going back?"

I shake my head. "I'll stretch my legs and get something to eat. I'm not going anywhere until you call."

She nods. "Wish me luck."

"Luck," I say.

I watch her walk off, a swagger in her stride, toward the hotel entrance. I wait a couple of minutes, then I start through the doors into the casino.

Inside I inhale the familiar smell of stale cigarillos and whisky. The machines sing and clank. Coins clatter in the distance. People hunker over the slots, big plastic cups in one hand and tokens in the other. Some of them look like they've been there a long time.

Two security guys peel away from the wall and start in my direction.

"Hey, kid," one of them calls. "Wait a sec." They probably figure I'm underage.

"Just leaving," I say, and push through the back door. The sea air stings my face.

I stalk down the worn gray planks, hands in my pockets, thinking of Lila upstairs with her father. When I was a kid, Zacharov was a shadowy figure, a legend, the boogeyman. I met him maybe three times, and one of those times was while I was being thrown out of his daughter's birthday party.

He laughed, I remember that.

At the back of the Taj Mahal a few old women lean over a railing, throwing something onto the sand. Some guys in tracksuits smoke near the entrance, calling to women as they pass. And a man in a long cashmere coat and silvery white hair looks out at the sea.

I touch my pocket with my phone in it. I should call Grandad, but I'm not ready to make excuses.

The white-haired man turns toward me. Glancing around, I notice two huge guys trying to look inconspicuous near a taffy shop window.

"Cassel Sharpe," Mr. Zacharov says, slight accent making my name sound exotic. Even though it's already dark, sunglasses cover his eyes. A fat, pale red stone glitters in the pin on his tie. "I believe a phone call was made to me from your cell phone."

Turns out Mom was right about landlines after all.

"Okay," I say, trying to act casual.

He looks around as if he'll be able to pick her out of the crowd. "Where is she?"

"Up in the room," I tell him. "Where she said she was going to be."

There's a deep-throated yowl, and I turn suddenly, my body jerking. My muscles hurt. I forgot how sore they already were.

Mr. Zacharov laughs. "Cats," he says. "Dozens of feral cats under the boardwalk. Lila always loved cats. You remember."

I don't say anything.

"If she was in the room, my people would have called." He tilts his head and slips a gloved hand into his pocket. "I think you are playing a game. Who did you get to pretend to be my daughter on the phone? Were you going to ask me for money? This seems like a very stupid game."

"She said to meet her alone." I lean toward him, and he holds out a gloved hand to stop me from getting too close. One of his goons heads toward us. I lower my voice. "She probably saw one of *your people* and split."

He laughs. "You are a pathetic villain, Cassel Sharpe. A real disappointment."

"No," I say. "She really is—" The big guy jerks my arms back and up, hard.

"Please," I gasp. "My ribs."

"Thanks for telling me where to hit," the guy says. His nose is permanently bent to one side.

Mr. Zacharov pats my cheek. I can smell the leather of his glove. "I thought you might turn out more like your grandfather, but your mother spoiled all you boys."

That makes me laugh.

The guy jerks my arms up again. They make a sound like they're popping out of their sockets, and I make a different kind of sound.

"Daddy." Lila's voice, pitched low and oddly menacing, cuts through the noise of the boardwalk. "Leave Cassel alone."

Lila steps up from the beach. For a moment I see her as he must, half ghost and half stranger. She's a woman, not the child that he lost, but her cruel mouth is identical to his own.

Besides, there can't be that many people with a single blue eye and a single green one.

He blinks. Then he takes off his sunglasses slowly. "Lila?" He sounds as brittle as glass.

The guy relaxes his grip, and I jerk away from him. I try to rub some feeling back into my arms.

"I hope you trust your men," she says. Her voice breaks. "Because this is secret. I am a secret."

"I'm sorry," says Mr. Zacharov. "I didn't think you were real—" He reaches out gloved hands toward her.

She just stands there, bristling, like she's fighting something wild inside her. She doesn't go to him.

"Let's get out of here," I say, touching her arm. "We'll get this sorted out in private."

Zacharov looks at me like he can't quite remember who I am.

"Inside," I say.

The two big guys in long coats seem relieved to have something to do.

"People are looking," one of them says, putting his hand on Mr. Zacharov's back and steering him into the casino.

The other glances at me warily. Lila takes my gloved hand and gives him a cold look that I'm grateful for. He backs off, hanging behind us as we head into Taj Mahal.

I raise my eyebrows at Lila.

"You have a real talent for getting your ass kicked," she says.

No one questions us as we walk across the casino floor and get into the elevator.

The raw emotion on Zacharov's face is something private—something I know he wouldn't want me to see. I wonder if I should try to leave, but Lila's gloved hand is clutching mine hard enough to hurt. I try to keep my gaze trained above the elevator doors, watching the numbers go up and up and up.

In the suite there's a wood-paneled wall with a single flat screen, a leather divan, and a bowl of fresh hydrangeas on a low table. The place is enormous, cavernous, with massive windows open to show the expanse of ink black ocean beyond. One of the big guys throws his coat over a chair and lets me see the guns strapped underneath his arms and across his back. More guns than he's got hands.

Zacharov pours pale liquid into cut glass and throws it back. "You two want a drink?" he says to us. "Minibar is full of Cokes."

I get up.

"No," he says. "I am your host." He nods to one of his men. The man grunts and moves to the refrigerator.

"Just water," Lila says.

"Some aspirin," I say.

"Oh, come on," the guy says as he hands over the glasses and the pills. "I didn't hurt you that bad."

"Nope," I say. "You didn't." I chew three aspirins and try to lean back against the pillows in a way that doesn't make me want to scream.

"You go down to the casino," Zacharov tells the guys. "Win some money."

"Sure thing," one says. He gets his coat again and they head slowly for the door. Zacharov looks at me like he wants to ask me to join them.

"Cassel," he says, "how long have you known the location of my daughter?"

"About three days," I say.

Lila narrows her eyes, but I figure there's no point in hiding that.

He pours himself another drink. "Why didn't you call me sooner?"

"Lila just showed up out of nowhere," I say, which is basically true. "I thought she was dead. I haven't seen her since we were both fourteen. I was just following her lead."

Zacharov takes a sip from his glass and winces. "Lila, are you going to tell me where you've been?"

She shrugs slim shoulders and avoids his gaze.

"You're protecting someone. Your mother? I always thought she'd taken you away from me. Tell me you got fed up with the old—"

"No!" Lila says.

He's still lost in the thought. "She practically accused me of having you murdered. She told the FBI that I said you were better off dead than with her. The FBI!"

"I wasn't with Mom," Lila says. "Dad, Mom had nothing to do with this."

He stops and stares at her. "Then what? Did someone do . . ." He leaves the sentence unfinished and turns toward me. "Did you? Did you hurt my daughter?"

I hesitate.

"He didn't do anything to me," Lila says.

Zacharov touches a gloved hand to my shoulder. "Your mother's appeal is coming up, isn't it, Cassel?"

"Yes, sir," I say.

"I'd hate to see anything go wrong with that. If I find out—"

"Leave him alone," says Lila. "Listen to me, Dad. Just listen for a minute. I'm not ready to talk about what happened. Stop trying to find someone to blame. Stop with the interrogation. I'm home now. Aren't you glad I'm home?"

"Of course I'm glad," he says, clearly stricken.

I touch my sore ribs without thinking. I want another aspirin, but I don't know where the guy put the bottle.

"I'm trusting you for her sake," he says to me, and then his voice softens. "My daughter and I need to talk. We need to be alone—you understand that, right?"

I nod my head. Lila is looking out at the black water. She doesn't turn.

Zacharov takes his wallet from inside his jacket and counts out five hundred dollars. "Here," he says.

"I can't take that," I say.

"I'd feel better if you did," he says.

I stand up and try not to wince while doing it. I shake my head. "I hope you didn't have your heart set on feeling better."

He snorts. "One of the boys will see you home."

"I can go? Really?"

"Don't kid yourself. I can pick you up like a dime off the sidewalk anytime I want."

I want to say something to Lila, but her back is still to me. I can't guess her thoughts.

"I'm having a little party on Wednesday at a place called

Koshchey's. A fund-raiser. You should come," Zacharov says. "Do you know why I like Koshchey's?"

I shake my head.

"Do you know who Koshchey the Deathless is?"

"No," I say, thinking of the strange mural on the ceiling of the restaurant.

"In Russian folklore Koshchey is a sorcerer who can become a whirlwind and destroy his enemies." Zacharov touches the glittering pin on his chest. "He can't be killed. Don't cross me, Cassel. I am not a safe man to make your enemy."

"I understand," I say, and open the door. What I understand is that Lila and I are on our own and we don't even have a plan.

"And, Cassel?"

I turn.

"Thank you for bringing my daughter back."

I walk out the door. As I wait for the elevator to come, my phone rings. I am so tired that it seems a huge effort to take it out of my pocket.

"Hello?" I say.

"Cassel?" says Dean Wharton. He doesn't sound happy. "I'm sorry to be calling so late, but we just got the final call from one of our board members on the West Coast. Welcome back to Wallingford. We got the report from your doctor and spoke to our lawyers. We'd like you to remain a day student on a probationary basis, but so long as you don't have any more episodes, we may consider letting you return to the dorms for your senior year."

I smother the ironic laughter that threatens to crawl up my throat. My con worked. I can go back to school. But I can't go back to being the person I thought I was. "Thank you, sir," I manage to say.

"We'll expect to see you tomorrow morning, Mr. Sharpe. Since you've paid through the end of the year, please feel free to eat breakfast and dinner in the cafeteria."

"Monday morning?" I echo.

"Yes, tomorrow, in the morning. Unless you have other plans," he says dryly.

"No," I say. "Of course not. See you tomorrow, Dean. Thank you, Dean."

One of Zacharov's guys drives me home. His name turns out to be Stanley. He's from Iowa and doesn't know practically any Russian. He's not good with languages, he says.

He tells me all that when he lets me out in front of my house. Even though he made me sit in the back of the town car with the tinted privacy divider up, I guess he could see more than I thought. I guess he watched me unbutton my shirt and brush my fingers over the bruises purpling the skin over my ribs, testing each bone for give. I'm not guessing that just because he was so friendly when we got to the house—he also gave me his entire bottle of aspirin.

MY GRANDFATHER'S NOT

at home when I get there, but there's a note scratched in pen on the back of a receipt and stuck to the fridge with an I ♥ CHIHUAHUAS magnet.

Gone to Carney for a few days.
Call me when you get in.

I stare at the note, trying to decipher what it means, but I can't quite think beyond the fact that there won't be a car for me to borrow tomorrow. I stumble upstairs, set the alarm on my phone, push a chair up against the door, and chew up another handful of aspirin. I don't even bother kicking off my shoes or getting under the covers; I just smother my face in the pillow and drop down into sleep like a dead man finally returning to his grave.

For a moment after my alarm goes off and I'm jolted awake, I don't know where I am. I look around the bedroom that I slept in when I was a kid and it seems that it must have belonged to someone else.

I lean over and switch off my phone, blink a few times.

My head feels clearer than it has in days.

The pain has abated some—maybe because I finally got some sleep—but the reality of what's happened and what's about to happen seems to finally be sinking in. I don't have a lot of time—three days—to plan.

And I need to stay away from my brothers long enough to do it. Wallingford will be good for that. They don't know I've been let back in, and even if they figure it out, at least being at school isn't obviously hiding. At least I can continue to act like I'm a killer robot waiting for them to utter a command word.

I fumble in my closet for my scratchy shirt and uniform pants. I didn't bring my jacket or shoes with me when I packed up the stuff in my dorm, but I have a bigger problem than that. I don't have a ride to school.

I put on sneakers and call Sam.

"Do you have any idea what time it is?" he says groggily.

"I need you to pick me up," I tell him.

"Dude, where are you?"

I give him the address and he hangs up. I hope he doesn't just roll over and go back to sleep.

In the bathroom, as I brush my teeth, I see that my cheek is purpled with bruising above the thin beard that's grown in. My hair was getting too long before and it's even shaggier now, but I wet it down and try to comb it into shape.

I don't shave, even though it's against the rules to be anything but as smooth as a baby's bottom, because I can just guess how bad that bruise would look if they could see the rest of it.

Downstairs, as I brew the coffee and watch the black liquid drip down, I think of Lila looking out at the sea. I think of her with her back to me as I'm walking out the door.

Mom says that when you're scamming someone, there needs to be something at stake, something so big that they're not going to walk away, even if things get sketchy. They have to go all in. Once they're all in, you win.

Lila's at stake. She's not walking away, which means I can't walk away either.

I'm all in.

They're winning.

All the teachers are really nice to me. They mostly—with the exception of Dr. Stewart, who gives me a whole bunch of zeros, enunciating the numbers carefully as he puts each one in the grade book—understand that I failed to keep up with the homework, even though they emailed me assignments daily. They tell me they're happy I'm back. Ms. Noyes even hugs me.

My fellow students look at me like I'm a dangerous lunatic with two heads and a nasty communicable disease. I keep my head down, eat my Tater Tots at lunch, and try to look interested in my classes.

All the while I'm daydreaming schemes.

Daneca sits down next to me in the lunchroom and pushes her civics notebook in my direction. "You want to copy my notes?"

"Copy your notes?" I say slowly, looking at the book.

She rolls her eyes. Her hair is in two braids, each one tied with rough string. "You don't have to if you don't want to."

"No," I say. "I do. I definitely do." I look at the notebook in front of me, flipping the pages, seeing her looping handwriting. I outline the marks with my gloved finger, an idea starting to form in my mind.

I start to grin.

Sam sets down a tray on the other side. It's piled with a gooey lump of delicious-smelling mac-n-cheese.

"Hey," he says. "Prepare to be very happy."

That's the last thing I expect him to say. "What?" I ask. My fingers are tracing new words in the margin of Daneca's notebook. Plans. I'm writing in a familiar style, but not my own.

"Nobody thought you were coming back. Nobody. Noooooobody."

"Thanks. Yeah, I can see how you'd think I'd find that thrilling."

"Dude," he says. "A lot of people just lost a lot of money. We made up for that bad bet. We're kings of finance!"

I shake my head in amazement. "I always said you were a genius."

We punch each other in the shoulder and punch fists and just keep smiling like morons.

Daneca wrinkles her brow, and Sam stops. "Uh," Sam says. "There were some other things we wanted to talk to you about."

"Less fun things, I'm guessing," I say.

"I'm sorry about losing your cat," she says to me after a few moments.

"Oh," I say, looking up. "No. The cat's fine. The cat's back where she belongs."

"What do you mean?"

I shake my head. "Too complicated."

"Are you in some kind of trouble?" Sam asks. "Because if you were in some kind of trouble, maybe you could tell us. Dude, no offense, but you seem like you're losing it."

Daneca clears her throat. "He told me what you told him when he found you in bed with that girl. About being a—"

I look around the cafeteria, but no one seems close enough to hear. "You told her I was a worker?"

Sam looks down quickly. "We've been hanging out a lot, what with the play and all. I'm sorry. Sorry. I know that wasn't cool."

Of course. Normal people gossip. Normal people tell each other things, especially when they're trying to impress each other. I guess I should feel betrayed, but all I feel is relief.

I'm tired of pretending.

"Are you guys a thing?" I ask. "A boyfriendly-girlfriendly thing?"

"Yeah," Daneca says, her expression some combination of pleasure and embarrassment.

Sam looks like he's going to pass out.

"That's great," I say. "I didn't mean to lie to your mother, Daneca. I didn't know." But I know I wouldn't have told her. I would have lied; I just didn't get a chance.

"Are you going out with that girl?" she asks. "The one you were sleeping with?"

That startles a laugh out of me. "No."

"So, what, you were just—"

"We weren't," I say quickly. "Believe me, we weren't. For one thing, she's probably insane. And for another, she hates me."

"Okay, so who is she?" Daneca asks.

"I thought you'd want to know what I am."

"I want you to believe you can trust me. And Sam. You can trust us." She pauses. "You have to trust somebody."

I bow my head. She's right that if I want any plan to succeed, I'll need help. "Her name is Lila Zacharov."

Daneca gapes at me. "The girl that disappeared back, like, when we were in middle school?"

"You heard of her?"

"Sure," Daneca says, picking up one of my Tater Tots. Oil soaks her glove. "Everyone heard about it. A crime family princess. Her case was on the news a lot. My mom got weird about letting me go anywhere by myself after it happened." She puts the tot into her mouth. "So, what really happened to her?"

I hesitate, but it's all or nothing now. "She was turned into a cat," I say. I can feel my face twisting into an awkward grimace. It feels so unnatural to tell the truth.

Daneca chokes, spitting the food into her hand.

"A transformation worker?" Daneca says. Then, after a moment, she whispers. "*The* cat?"

"That's *crazy*," says Sam.

"I know you think that I'm making this up," I say, rubbing my face.

"We don't," she says, and she shifts a little.

Sam winces. I think she kicked him under the table. "I didn't mean crazy like 'You're crazy,'" he says. "I meant it like 'Whoa.'"

"Sure. Okay." I'm not sure if they believe me, but I feel a dizzy sense of hope.

It occurs to me that I've done exactly what I need to in order to set up Daneca and Sam for a con job. They're already invested. They trust me. They've seen me pull a scam before. This is bigger stakes; I just have to promise them a bigger score.

My phone buzzes and I look down. It's a number I don't know. I flip it open and bring it to my ear.

"Hello?"

"This is what I want you to do," says Lila. "You're going to go to the party on Wednesday and pretend to work my dad—the same way you were supposed to. I'm trusting you to fake it. I think Dad's smart enough to go along with you."

"That's the plan?"

"That's your part. I can't talk for long, so you have to listen.

A few minutes later I'm going to come through the door with a gun, shoot Anton and save Dad. My part. Simple."

There is so much that can go wrong with that plan that I don't even know where to start. "Lila—"

"I even got your brother Philip out of it—just like you wanted," she says.

"How?" I ask, startled.

"I told my bodyguard he was poking around the penthouse and saw me. They let me lock him up here. That means we just have Barron and Anton to worry about."

Just Barron and Anton. I rub the bridge of my nose. "You said you were going to keep *both* my brothers out of it."

"Our arrangement has changed," she says. "There's just one problem."

"What's that?"

"No one here is supposed to carry a gun at the party. They won't let me have one."

"I don't have a—" I stop myself. Really not a good idea to talk about me and guns in school—especially not in the same sentence. "I don't have one."

"There's going to be a metal detector," she says. "Get one and think of a way to get it in."

"That's impossible," I say.

"You owe me," says Lila. Her voice is as soft as ash.

"I know," I say, defeated. "I know that."

The line goes dead.

I am left staring at the cafeteria wall, trying to convince myself that she isn't setting me up.

"Did something happen?" Sam asks.

"I've got to go," I say. "Class is going to start."

"We'll skip class," says Daneca.

I shake my head. "Not on my first day back."

"We'll meet up at activities period," Sam says. "Outside the theater. And then you're going to tell us what's going on."

On the way to class, I call back the number Lila called from.

A man answers; not Zacharov. "Is she there?" I ask.

"I don't know who you're talking about," he says gruffly.

"Just tell her I need two more tickets for Wednesday."

"There's no one here—"

"Just tell her," I say.

I have to believe he does.

Leaning against the brick wall of the building, I start talking. Telling Sam and Daneca feels like peeling off my own skin to expose everything underneath. It hurts.

I don't play them. I don't even try. I just start at the beginning and tell them about being the only nonworker in a family of workers. I tell them about Lila and thinking that I'd killed her, about finding myself on the roof.

"How could all of you be curse workers?" Sam asks.

"Working is like green eyes," Daneca says. "Sometimes it just shows up in families, but if the parents are both workers, worker kids are more likely. Like, look at how almost one percent of Australians are workers, because the country was founded as a worker penal colony, but only, like, one one-hundredth of a percent of people in the U.S. are workers."

"Oh," says Sam. I don't think that he was expecting such a comprehensive answer. I know I wasn't.

Daneca shrugs.

He turns to me. "So, what kind of worker are you?"

"He's probably a luck worker," says Daneca. "Everyone's a luck worker."

"He's not," Sam says. "He'd tell us that."

"What I am . . . doesn't matter. The point is that my brothers want me to kill this guy and I don't want to do it."

"So you're a death worker," Sam says.

Daneca punches him in the arm, and despite being huge, he flinches. "Ow."

I groan. "Look, it really doesn't matter because I'm not going to work anyone, okay?"

"Can you just bail?" Sam asks. "Skip town?"

I nod for a moment, then shake my head. "Not going to."

"Let me try to understand," Sam says. "You believe your brothers can potentially make you kill someone, but you're going to stick around and let them try. What the hell?"

"I *believe*," I say, "that I am a very clever young man with two fantastically clever friends. And I further believe that one of those friends has been looking for an opportunity to display his expertise in fake firearms."

At that, Sam's eyes take on an acquisitive gleam. "Really? The guy who's getting shot has to put the wires through his pants, put the trigger in his pocket or something. And it would have to be timed so it happens at the exact moment as the gunshot. Unless you're talking about faking death work. That's a whole lot easier, really."

"Gunshots only," I say.

"Wait," Daneca says. "What is it—exactly—that you're planning on doing?"

"I have a couple of ideas," I say, as innocently as possible. "Mostly bad ones."

We talk through the plan a dozen times at least. We refine it down from the ridiculous to the unlikely to something that might work. Then, instead of going to dinner in the cafeteria, they drive me over to Barron's house and I show them how to pick a lock.

Without Grandad the house feels empty and enormous. I miss the teetering piles as I brew a pot of coffee. This house feels unfamiliar and disturbingly full of possibilities. I spread out the new notebooks in a fan in front of me, crack my knuckles, and get ready for a long night.

When I wake up Tuesday morning with drool darkening the cuff of my shirt and Sam hitting the horn in the driveway, I barely manage to brush my teeth before I stumble out the door.

He hands me a cup of coffee. "Did you sleep in those clothes?" he asks.

I almost can't stand the thought of drinking more coffee, but I do. "Sleep?" I ask.

"You have blue ink on your cheek," he says.

I flip down the visor and look in the tiny mirror. My face scruff is looking scruffier and my eyes are bloodshot. I look terrible. The smear of ink across my jawline is the least of my problems.

At school I am so out of it that Ms. Noyes takes me aside and asks if everything is okay at home. Then she checks to see if my pupils are dilated. Dr. Stewart tells me to shave.

I fall asleep in the back of the debate team meeting. I wake up in the middle of a debate about whether or not to wake me. Then I drag myself over to the drama department for a tutorial from Sam on weapons.

I wolf down dinner and then head out to the parking lot with Sam.

"Mr. Sharpe," Valerio calls, walking toward us. "Mr. Yu. I hope you weren't thinking of going off campus."

"I'm just going to drive Cassel home," Sam says.

"You have a half hour to get back before study hall starts," he says, pointing to his watch.

I go back to the table and the notebooks and wind up sleeping on the downstairs couch with all the lights on. There's so much work to do. I don't remember half of what I write and when I look at the words in the morning, they don't look like I wrote them at all.

Sam arrives right on time.

"Can I borrow your car?" I say. "I don't think I'm going to school today. I've got a big night."

He hands over the keys. "You'll want a hearse of your own when you feel how this thing hugs the road."

I drive him to school, then I break back into Barron's house. I'm the best kind of thief, the kind that leaves behind items equal in value to those he's stolen.

Then I go home and shave until my skin is as slick as any slickster's.

I'm so exhausted that I fall asleep at four and don't wake up until Barron shakes my arm.

"Hey, sleepyhead," says Barron, sitting in the chair I've never liked, with his arms folded. He rocks back, pushing the front legs off the floor with his weight.

Anton leans against the door frame leading into the dining room. A toothpick rests on the swell of his bottom lip. "Better get dressed, kid."

"What are you doing here?" I ask, trying to sound sincere. I walk past them into the kitchen and pour myself some of the day-old coffee. It tastes a little bit like battery acid, but in a good way.

"We're going to a party," Barron says, making a face when he sees what I'm doing. "In the city. It's going to be pretty swank. Lots of hoodlums."

"Philip's stuck," says Anton. "Zacharov sent him on an errand at the last minute." I know that's not true, but I can't tell if Anton is worried. I can imagine Lila sending him a message with Philip's phone.

I rub my hand over my eyes. "You want me to come?"

Anton and Barron exchange glances. "Yeah," Barron says. "I thought we told you about it."

"No—look, you guys go ahead. I've got a lot of homework."

Anton takes the cup out of my hand and spits his toothpick into it. "Don't be stupid. No kid your age wants to sit home doing homework instead of partying. Now get upstairs and get in the shower."

I go. The shower feels like hot needles on my back,

relaxing my muscles. There's a spider—one I missed—hunched in a corner of the ceiling, tending a knot of eggs. I shampoo my hair and watch the beads of water catch in her web.

When I step out into the foggy bathroom, the door is open and Barron's there to hand me a towel. He gives me a quick glance before I wrap it around me. I try to turn to one side, but I'm not fast enough.

"What's that on your leg?"

I realize that naked means easy to check for amulets.

"Hey," I say, "there's this thing called privacy. You might have heard of it."

He grabs my shoulder. "Let me see your leg."

I clutch the towel tighter. "It's just a cut."

He lets me push past him into the hall, but Anton's waiting in my bedroom.

"Grab him," Barron says, and Anton kicks my leg, knocking me off balance. I fall onto the bed, which isn't bad except that Barron locks his arm under my jaw and pulls me up on the mattress.

"Get off me!" I yell. The towel is gone and I struggle, embarrassed and scared, while Anton reaches into his back pocket.

A knife blade springs up out of the ebonized hilt in his hands. "What have we here?" Anton says, poking my calf where the stones are sewn up in my skin. The whole area throbs when he presses on it. Infected.

When he cuts me, I can't help it. I scream.

17

"SLICK," BARRON SAYS, looking at my bloody leg. He places the remains of three wet, red pebbles into his pocket. "How long have you been using that trick?"

Even the best plans go wrong. The universe doesn't like anyone thinking it can be controlled. All plans require some degree of improvisation, but they usually don't go wrong *right away*.

"Shove it up your ass," I say, which is pretty juvenile, but he's my brother and he brings that out of me. "Come on, hit me so hard that you knock a couple of my teeth out. That will be a great party look."

"He remembers," says Anton, shaking his head.

"We're screwed to the wall, Barron. Nice work."

Barron curses under his breath. "Who did you tell?"

I turn to him. "I know I'm a worker. A *transformation worker*. Let's start with *you* telling *me* why you made me think I wasn't one."

They exchange a maddening glance, like somehow they're going to be able to call a time-out, go into the other room, and discuss what to tell me.

Barron sits on the end of my bed and composes himself. "Mom wanted us to lie to you. What you are—it's dangerous. She thought you'd be better off if you didn't know until you were older. When you figured it out as a little kid, she asked me to make you forget. That's how it started."

I look down at the gory sheets and the sluggishly bleeding hole in my leg. "So she knows? About all of this?"

Barron shakes his head, ignoring the dark look Anton sends in his direction. "No. We didn't want her to worry. Jail's been tough on her and the blowback from her work makes her emotions unstable. But money's been tight, even before she went inside. You know that."

I nod slowly.

"Philip came up with a plan. Assassination is the biggest, quickest money there is. And the crazy money goes to killers who are reliable—who can get rid of bodies permanently. With you, we could do that." He says all this like I'm going to be thrilled with my brother's cleverness. "Anton made sure that no one knew who was really responsible for the murders."

"And I don't get a say? In being a killer?"

He shrugs his shoulders. "You were just a kid. It didn't seem fair for you to go through a bunch of trauma. So we made you forget everything you did. We were trying to protect—"

"How about kicking me in the stomach? Was that the right amount of trauma? Or how about that?" I point to my leg. "You still protecting me, Barron?"

Barron opens his mouth, but no clever lie comes out.

"Philip tried to protect you," Anton says. "You wouldn't shut your mouth. You've had it easy. Time to toughen up." He hesitates, his tone becoming less sure. "When I was your age, I knew enough not to talk back to worker royalty. My mother cut these marks in my throat when I turned thirteen and reopened them to pack them with ash every year until I turned twenty. To remind me who I was." He touches the scars pearling his neck. "To remind me pain is the best teacher."

"Just tell us if you talked to anyone," Barron says.

You can't con an honest man. Only the greedy or the desperate are willing to put aside their reservations to get something they don't deserve. I've heard lots of people— my dad included—use that to justify grifting.

"Cut me in on the money," I say to Anton. "If I'm earning it, I decide how to spend it."

"Done," Anton says.

"I told my roommate Sam that I was a worker. But when I did, I thought it was a lie."

Anton lets out a long breath. "That's it?" He starts to laugh.

Barron joins in. Soon we're laughing like I told the best joke anyone ever heard.

A joke they're greedy and desperate enough to believe.

"Good, good," Anton says. "Put on a nice suit, okay? This isn't some school dance we're going to."

I limp to my closet. Leaning down, I sort through my rucksack as if for something appropriate. Pushing aside my uniform and a few pairs of jeans, I find a dress shirt and straighten up.

"So Philip had an idea and you went along with it? That doesn't sound like you," I say, walking awkwardly back to the doorway. Something catches my foot accidentally-on-purpose and I fake-stumble into Barron. My fingers are quick and nimble. "Whoa, sorry."

"Careful," he says.

I lean against the door frame and then yawn, covering my mouth with my hand. "Come on. Tell me why you really didn't say anything."

A weird half smile grows on Barron's face. "It's so unfair. You, of all people, get the holy grail of curse work. And me stuck with changing memories like I'm some kind of cleanup crew. Sure, it's useful when you want to make some mundane thing easier. I could cheat at school or I could keep someone from remembering what I did to them, but what does that mean? Not much. Do you know how many transformation workers are even born in the world in a given decade? Maybe one. Maybe. You were born with real power and you didn't even appreciate it."

"I didn't *know* it," I say.

"It's wasted on you," he says, placing his ungloved hand on my shoulder. The hair on the back of my neck rises.

I try to react like I haven't palmed the last unbroken stone charm he cut out of me and then swallowed it. Maybe transformation work is wasted on me, but sleight of hand isn't.

I end up taking one of Dad's old suits out of my parents' room. Mom, predictably, didn't throw out any of Dad's belongings, so all the suits still hang in the back of his closet, slightly out of date and smelling of mothballs, as though they're waiting for him to return from a long vacation. A double-breasted jacket fits me surprisingly well, and when I stick my hands in the pockets of the pin-striped pants, I find a crumpled tissue that still smells like his cologne.

I make a fist around it as I follow Anton and my brother out to Anton's Mercedes.

In the car Anton smokes cigarette after nervous cigarette, watching me in the rearview mirror. "You remember what you're supposed to do?" he asks as we head into the tunnel to Manhattan.

"Yeah," I say.

"You're going to be okay. After this, if you want, we'll cut you a necklace. Barron, too."

"Yeah," I say again. In Dad's suit I feel strangely dangerous.

The brass front door of Koshchey's is wide open when we pull up in front, and there are two enormous men in sunglasses and long wool coats checking a list. A woman in a glittering gold dress pouts on the arm of a white-haired man as they wait behind a trio of men smoking cigars. Two valets come and open the doors of the Mercedes. One of them looks about my age, and I grin at him, but he doesn't smile back.

We're waved right through. No list for us. Just a quick check for guns.

The inside is packed with people. Lots of them crowding the bar, passing drinks back for people to carry to tables. A bunch of young guys are pouring shots of vodka.

"To Zacharov!" one toasts.

"To open hearts and open bars!" calls another.

"And open legs," says Anton.

"Anton!" A slim young man leans over with a grin, holding out a shot glass. "You're late. Better catch up."

Anton gives me a long look, and he and the other man move away from Barron and me. I push on into the large ballroom, past laughing laborers from who knows how many families. I wonder how many of them are runaways, how many of them slipped out of some normal life in Kansas or one of the Carolinas to come to the big city and be recruited by Zacharov. Barron follows me, his hand pressing against my shoulder blades. It feels like a threat.

Up on the little stage on the other side of the ballroom, a woman in a pale pink suit is speaking into the podium microphone. "You might ask yourselves why we here in New York need to give funds to stop a proposition that's going to affect New Jersey. Shouldn't we save our money in case we need to fight that same fight here, in our own state? Let me tell you, ladies and gentlemen, if Proposition 2 passes in one place, especially in a place where so many of us have relatives and family, then it will spread. We need to defend the rights of our neighbors to privacy, so that there will be someone left to defend ours."

A girl in a black dress, her brown curls pulled back with rhinestone clips and her smile a little too wide, brushes against me. She looks great, and I have to stop myself from telling her so.

"Hi," Daneca says languorously. "Remember me?"

I somehow manage not to roll my eyes at her over-the-top performance. "This is my brother Barron. Barron, this is Dani."

Barron looks between us. "Hey, Dani."

"I beat him at chess when his school came up to play my school," she says, embellishing on the simpler cover story we came up with yesterday.

"Oh, yeah?" He relaxes a little and grins. "So you're a very smart girl."

She blanches. Barron looks sharp in his suit, with his cold eyes and angelic curls. I don't think that Daneca's used to slick sociopaths like him flirting with her; she stumbles over her words. "Smart enough to—smart enough."

"Can I talk to her for a minute?" I ask him. "Alone."

He nods. "I'll get some food. Just watch the time, player."

"Right," I say.

He grips my shoulder. His fingers dig into the knotted muscles in a way that feels good. Brotherly. "You're ready, right?"

"I will be," I say, but I have to look away. I don't want him to know how much it hurts for him to act kind now, when none of it's true.

"Tough guy," he says, and walks off toward the samovars of tea, and the trays heaped with dilled herring, with fish glistening in the ruby glaze of pomegranate sauce, and with about a million different kinds of piroshki.

Daneca leans into me, presses a blood packet wrapped with wires under my jacket, and whispers, "We got the stuff to Lila."

I look up involuntarily. The knots in my stomach pull tighter. "Did you talk to her?"

Daneca shakes her head. "Sam's with her now. She's really not happy that all we could get in is a pretend gun that Sam is still gluing together."

I picture Lila's sharp-edged smile. "She knows what she's got to do?"

Daneca nods. "Knowing Sam, he's overexplaining it. He wanted me to make sure you were okay with reattaching your wires to the trigger mechanism."

"I think so. I—"

"Cassel Sharpe," someone says, and I turn. Grandad is wearing a brown suit and a hat turned at a rakish angle, feather pin through the band. "The hell are you doing here? You better have some peach of an explanation."

Yesterday when we went over the plan again and again, I never thought about Grandad showing up. Because I'm an idiot, basically—an idiot with poor planning skills. Of course he's here. Where else would he be?

Seriously, what else could go wrong?

"Barron brought me," I say. "Aren't I allowed out on a school night? Come on, this is practically a family event."

He looks around the room, like he's looking for his own shadow. "You should go on home. Right now."

"Okay," I say, placatingly, holding up my hands. "Just let me get something to eat and I'll go."

Daneca backs away from us, heading in the direction of the bar. She gives me a wink that seems to indicate she thinks I have things under control. That's an outrageous assumption and I am outraged by it.

"No," he says. "You are going to get your ass out on the sidewalk, and I am going to drive you home."

"What's wrong? I'm not getting in any trouble."

"You should have called me after I left you a message, that's what's wrong. This isn't a good place for you, understand?"

A man in a dark suit with a gold tooth looks in our direction with a laugh at the familiar story we're playing out. Bratty kid. Old man. Except that Grandad's acting like he knows something.

"Okay," I say, looking up at the clock. Ten after ten. "Just tell me what's going on."

"I'll tell you on the way," he says, wrapping his hand around my upper arm. I want to pull away from him, but my arm's been wrenched out of its socket too many times in the last few days. I let him lead me toward the door until I come close enough to the bar to be able to get Anton's attention.

"Look who I found," I say. "You know my grandfather."

From the way Anton's eyes narrow I'm guessing Grandad isn't his favorite person. The zinc bar top is littered with shot glasses and at least one empty bottle of Pshenichnaya.

"I just stopped in to see some old friends," Grandad says. "We're going."

"Not Cassel," Anton says. "He hasn't had a drink yet." He pours one for me, which gets the attention of some of the other young laborers. They turn their evaluating gazes in my direction.

There is a burning intensity in Anton's face, belied by his half smile and the languid way he's leaning against the bar. If he wants to lead the family, he's going to have to lead guys like Grandad. He can't afford to be shown up by an old man. He's got something to prove, and he's happy to use me to prove it.

"Take the drink," Anton says.

"He's underage," says Grandad.

That makes the guys at the bar laugh. I throw back the vodka in a single swallow. Warmth floods my stomach and sears my throat. I cough. Everyone laughs harder.

"It's like everything," one of the guys says. "The first one's the worst."

Anton pours me another shot. "You're wrong," he says. "The second one's the worst because you know what's coming."

"Go ahead," Grandad says to me. "Take your drink, and then we're going."

I look up at the clock. Ten twenty.

The second shot burns all the way down.

One of the guys claps me on the back. "Come on," he says to my grandfather. "Let the kid stay. We'll take good care of him."

"Cassel," Grandad says firmly, making my name into a reprimand. "You don't want to be tired for that fancy school of yours."

"I came with Barron," I say. I reach across the bar and pour myself a third shot. The guys love that.

"You're leaving with me," Grandad says under his breath.

This time the vodka goes down my throat like water. I step away from the bar and make myself stumble a little. I feel heady with confidence. *I'm Cassel Sharpe.* My mouth wants to shape the words. *I'm smarter than everybody else and I've thought of everything.*

"You okay?" Anton asks, looking at me like he's trying to figure if I'm drunk. His plans depend on me. I look as blank as possible and hope that it freaks him out. No point in my being the only miserable one.

Grandad tugs me toward the double doors, against the tide of people. "He'll sleep it off in the car."

"Let me just run to the bathroom," I tell Grandad. "I'll be right back."

He looks furious.

"Come on," I say. "It's a long ride." On the wall the clock reads ten thirty. Anton's going to be heading into position, guarding Zacharov. Barron's probably already looking for me. But how long before Zacharov will show is anyone's guess. His bladder could be made of iron.

"I'll go with you," Grandad says.

"I think you can trust me to piss without getting in any trouble."

"Yeah," he says, "but I don't."

We head toward the bathrooms, which are near enough to the kitchen that we have to head into the shadowy, windowless area behind the bar. I look over and see Zacharov and a beautiful woman with long honey-colored hair hanging on his arm. The pale red gem on his tie is overmatched by the rubies hanging from her ears. People are declaring their support and shaking his hand, leather glove against leather glove.

There in the crowd I think I see her. Lila. Her hair white under the lights. Her mouth painted blood bright.

She's not supposed to be here yet. She's going to ruin everything.

I veer off toward the buffet. Toward her. By the time I get there, she's gone.

"What now?" Grandad asks.

I pop a rose-flavored *syrniki* in my mouth.

"I'm trying to sneak food," I say, "since you're so crazy that you won't let me eat."

"I know what you're trying to do," he says. "I see you looking at the clock. No more bull, Cassel. Piss or don't."

"Okay," I say, and walk into the bathroom. Ten forty. I don't know how much longer I can drag my feet.

There are a few other guys in here, combing their hair in the mirrors. A skinny puffy-eyed blond is doing a line of coke off the counter. He doesn't even look up when the door opens.

I go into the first stall and sit down on the lid of the toilet seat, trying to calm myself.

My watch reads ten forty-three.

I wonder if Lila wants everything ruined. I wonder if I really saw her in the crowd or if I just conjured her out of my fears.

I take off my suit jacket, unbutton my shirt, and tape the packet of fake blood directly onto my skin, resigning myself to the gluey hair removal I am going to get later when I rip it off. I tug the wire through the inside of my pants pocket, ripping the seam and adding more tape so the trigger's easy to grab.

Ten forty-seven.

I check for the bottle of puke taped behind the toilet bowl. It's there, but I have no idea which one of them finally gave in and threw up. I smile at the thought.

Ten forty-eight. I attach the wire to the trigger.

"You okay in there?" Grandad calls. Someone snickers.

"Just a second," I say.

I make a choking noise and pour out half the contents of the puke bottle. The room fills with the vinegary three-day-old smell of sick. I gag again, this time for real.

I pour out the other half and carefully return the empty bottle to the tape. Leaning down is the worst. I gag again.

"You okay?" Grandad doesn't sound impatient anymore. "Cassel?"

"Fine," I say, and spit.

I flush the toilet and button up my shirt carefully, then pull on the suit jacket but don't button that.

The door opens and I hear Anton's voice. "Everyone out. We need the bathroom clear."

My legs feel unsteady with relief. I open the door of the stall and lean against the frame. Almost everyone has already been chased out by my fake vomiting, but the stragglers and the cokehead are filing past Anton. Zacharov stands at the sinks.

"Desi Singer," he says, rubbing the side of his mouth. "It's been a long time."

"This is a very nice party," my grandfather says gravely, nodding toward Zacharov, his nod almost a bow. "I hadn't figured you for politics."

"We who break laws should care the most about them. We deal with them more than other people, after all."

"They say that all really great crooks eventually go into politics," Grandad says.

Zacharov smiles at that, but when he sees me, his smile fades. "No one's supposed to be in here," he tells Anton.

"Sorry," I say, sticking out my hand. "I'm a little drunk. This is a great party, sir."

My heart speeds with fear. So much can go wrong.

Grandad grabs for my arm to pull it away, but Anton stops him.

"This is Philip's little brother." Anton's grinning, like this is all a hilarious joke. "Give the kid a thrill."

Zacharov extends his hand slowly, looking me in the eye. "Cassel, right?"

Our eyes meet and I am suddenly not sure I can go through with this. "It's okay, sir. If you don't want to shake."

He holds my gaze. "Go ahead."

No way out.

I take his hand in mine and cover his wrist with my other hand, pushing my gloved fingers up his sleeve, worming my finger through the small opening in the leather so I can brush the skin of his wrist. His eyes open wide when I touch him, like I've given him an electric shock. He jerks back.

I pull him sharply toward me. "Your heart just turned to stone," I whisper against his ear. "Take a dive."

Zacharov staggers away from me, stricken. He looks toward Anton, and for a moment I think he's going to ask something that will doom me. Then he lurches against the outer panel of the stalls and, stumbling, bangs his head against the hand dryer. Gasping soundlessly, he slides down the wall beneath it, hand knotting in his shirt like he was trying to grasp his chest.

We watch him as his eyes close. His mouth gapes once more, like he's trying for a last gasp of air.

It's a hell of a performance.

"What did you do?" Grandad shouts. "Undo it, Cassel. Whatever you've done—" My grandfather looks at me like he doesn't know me.

"Shut up, old man," Anton says, punching the stall behind Grandad's head.

I want to snap at Anton, but there's no time. Lack of blowback's going to give me away.

I concentrate on transforming myself. I picture a blade coming toward my own head, try to feel the impulse to work the work that danger feeds.

I have to freak myself out. I think of Lila, and me with a knife standing over her. I imagine raising the blade and feel the full weight of horror and self-loathing. The false memory still has the power to terrify me.

I actually jerk my hand a tiny bit in response, and then I feel my flesh go malleable. I imagine my father's hand in place of my own. I picture his blunt fingers and rough calluses.

My father's hand to go with his suit.

A small transformation. A little change. One that I hope will have minimal blowback.

A ripple runs through my flesh. I concentrate on taking a step toward the wall, but my foot feels like it's spreading out, melting.

Anton reaches into his coat and flips open a butterfly knife. It twirls in his fingers, as bright as the scales of a fish. He leans over Zacharov and carefully cuts the pin from his tie. "Everything's going to be different now," he says, slipping the Resurrection diamond into his pocket.

Anton turns toward me, still holding the knife, and suddenly this seems like a terrible, terrible plan.

"I'm sure you don't remember," Anton says, his voice low. "But you made me an amulet. Don't even think about trying to work *me*."

As if I could do anything but fall to my knees as my body twists and contorts.

Through blurry, changing vision, I see my grandfather crouching near Zacharov.

My limbs change, fins rising on my skin, and fifth and sixth arms banging into the wall. My head thrashes back and forth. My tongue forks. Everything cramps as the bones wrench themselves out of their sockets. My eyes become a thousand eyes, blinking together at the painted ceiling. I tell myself it will be over soon, but it goes on and on and on.

Anton walks toward Grandad. "You're a loyal worker, so it makes me sad to have to do this."

"Stop right there," Grandad says.

Anton shakes his head. "I'm glad Philip doesn't have to watch. He wouldn't understand, but I think you do, old man. A leader's got to be careful who gets to tell stories about him."

I try to turn over, but my legs are hooves and they clatter against the tiles. I don't know how to work them. I try to shout, but my voice isn't my own—there's a birdlike whistle in it, probably from the beak hardening on my face.

"Good-bye," Anton says to my grandfather. "I'm about to become a legend."

Someone bangs on the door. The knife stops, hovering in front of Grandad's throat.

"It's me," Barron says from the other side. "Open up."

"Let me open the door," says Grandad. "Put away the knife. If I'm loyal to anyone, it's this boy here. And if you want him loyal to you, you'll be careful."

"Anton," I say from the floor. It's hard to form the words with my curling tongue. "Door!"

Anton looks at me, slings the knife back into its sheath, and opens the door.

I concentrate on moving my transformed hand into the pocket of my pants.

Barron takes a few stiff steps into the room, then staggers forward, like he was pushed from behind.

"Keep your hands where I can see them," a girl's voice calls. Lila is wearing a red dress as tight as it is short. Her only accessory is the huge silver gun gleaming in the fluorescent lights. The door swings shut behind her.

The gun sure looks real. And she's pointing it straight at Anton.

Anton's lips part, like he's going to say her name, but no words come out.

"You heard me," she says.

"He killed your father," Anton says, pointing the closed knife at me. "It wasn't me. It was him."

Her gaze shifts to where Zacharov's body is resting, and the barrel of the gun wavers.

I reach under my jacket, hoping that my fingers stay fingerlike long enough to be usable. My tongue is working again. "You don't understand. I never meant—"

"I'm tired of your excuses," she says, leveling the gun at me. Her hand is shaking. "You didn't know what you were doing. You don't remember. You didn't mean to hurt anyone."

She doesn't sound like she's pretending.

I try to stand. "Lila—"

"Shut up, Cassel," she says, and shoots me.

Blood spatters cover my shirt.

I gasp like a fish.

As my eyes close, I hear Grandad choke out my name.

There's nothing like a gunshot to make you the life of the party.

IT HURTS. I EXPECTED THAT,

but it still knocks the breath out of me. Wetness seeps through my shirt, making it stick to my skin.

I try to still my breathing as much as possible. My body's shifting has slowed; the blowback's wearing off. I want to keep my eyes open, but I need Anton to really believe I was shot, so I listen instead of looking.

"Both of you, against the sinks," Lila says. "Put your hands where I can see them."

People are moving around me. I hear a grunt from my grandfather's direction, but I can't afford to look.

"How can you be here?" Anton asks her.

"Oh, come now," Lila says, low and dangerous. "You

know how I got here. I walked. From Wallingford. On my little paws."

I try to shift, just a little, so it will be easier to stand later.

Like a stage magician, the con artist misdirects suspicion. While everyone's watching for him to pull a rabbit out of a hat, he's actually sawing a girl in half. You think he's doing one trick when he's actually doing another.

You think that I'm dying, but I'm laughing at you.

I hate that I love this. I hate that the adrenaline pumping through the roots of my body is filling me with giddy glee. I'm not a good person.

But deceiving Anton and Barron feels fantastic.

I can hear footsteps echoing around me, moving toward her. "I'm sorry, Lila," says Anton. "I know that—"

"You should have killed me when you had the chance," she says.

Someone touches my shoulder, and I almost flinch. Rough bare fingers on my neck, looking for a pulse. The one thing I can't fake. He pulls open my jacket. If he unbuttons my shirt, he's going to see wires.

"You're a little devil, Cassel Sharpe," Grandad says under his breath.

Clever as the devil and twice as pretty. I force myself not to smile.

"Give me the gun," Anton says, and this time I do open my eyes a sliver. He's got the knife in one hand. "You know you don't want to do this."

"Get against the sinks!" she says.

He drops his knife and swipes his hand toward her, knocking the gun out of her grip. It skitters across the floor.

She lunges for it at the same time he does, but he gets to it first. I try to get up, but Grandad presses me back down.

Lifting the gun, Anton fires three times into her chest.

She staggers back, but she isn't wired up so there's no bang, no blood. The pellets hit her harmlessly, bouncing to the floor.

We're made.

Anton stares at her, then at the gun in his hand. Then he looks at me. My eyes are wide open.

"I'll kill you," he growls, throwing aside the fake gun. It hits the tiles so hard a piece of it chips off.

This is bad.

My grandfather gets between us, and I try to shove him out of the way, as a voice comes from the other side of the room.

"Enough," Zacharov says, into a sudden pocket of silence. He climbs unsteadily to his feet and stretches his neck, as though it's stiff.

Anton stumbles back, like Zacharov's a ghost. We all freeze.

Barron points an accusing finger in my direction. "You played me." He sounds unsteady.

"You're all playing," Zacharov says in his accented voice. "You were like this with water pistols when you were children. Waving them around and soaking everything."

"Why did— What did you know?" Anton asks. "Why did you pretend—"

Zacharov grimaces. "I would never have believed that you, Anton, would betray our family. I would never have believed that you would plot to kill me. You, of all people, who I would have made my heir." Zacharov looks at my grandfather. "Family means nothing anymore, does it?"

Grandad looks from Barron to me, like he's not sure how to answer.

Anton takes two steps toward Zacharov, his mouth twisting in an ugly way. Barron picks up the knife that Anton dropped and flips it around in his hand. Flips it closed, then open again.

I roll over and push myself up, skittering across the floor on fake blood. I manage to get up onto my knees.

"You're never going to leave here alive," Anton tells Zacharov, gesturing to Barron and the knife.

I have only one card left to play, but it's a good one. I stand. This is like being on the roof of Smythe Hall all over again; if I slip, I die.

"I'm not afraid," Zacharov says, still looking at Anton. "It takes guts to kill a man with your hands. You don't have the balls."

"Shut up," says Anton. He turns to Barron. "Give me the knife. I'll show him scared."

Lila rushes Anton, but her father grabs hold of her arms and pushes her behind him.

Her lip curls. Her eyes smolder with banked fire as she stares at her cousin. "I'll kill you," she says.

Barron doesn't hand over the knife, but he does start to smile. He raises the tip to Anton's throat.

"Don't point that thing at me," Anton says, shoving at Barron's hand. "What are you waiting for? Give it here."

"I'm pointing the right way," Barron says. "Sorry."

I take a deep breath and spring my trap. "We've been meeting with Zacharov for months, Barron and me. Right, sir?"

Zacharov gives me a hard look. I imagine he's fed up with my shenanigans, but he's got to realize that keeping the knife at Anton's neck is the most important thing. Zacharov's fingers tighten on Lila's arms. "That's right."

Barron nods.

"No, you haven't," Anton says to Barron. "Why? Even if you'd screw me over, there's no way you'd screw Philip."

"He's in this too," says Barron. He twists the knife in his hand, letting the fluorescent lights reflect off the blade.

"Philip would never turn on me. That's impossible. We planned this together. We planned it for years."

Barron shrugs his shoulders. "If that's true, then where is he? If he was so loyal, wouldn't he be here?"

Then Anton looks at me. "This doesn't make any sense."

"What doesn't make sense?" Lila asks. She cuts her eyes toward me for a moment. "You think you're the only one who can betray people, Anton? You think you're the only liar?"

I can see the conflict in Anton's face. He's still trying to figure out his next move.

"We had to be sure you were serious about killing the head of our family," Barron says. He doesn't look confused; he doesn't even flinch.

"But he's going to kill you, idiot," Anton says. He sounds lost. "You threw everything away for nothing. You kidnapped his daughter. You're dead men. He's going to execute us all."

"He forgave us," Barron says. "He made a deal with Philip and me to let that slide. It was more important to prove that you planned to kill him. We're nobodies. You're his nephew."

Zacharov snorts softly, shaking his head. Then he extends his hand toward Barron, who gently drops the knife into Zacharov's hand.

I let out my breath.

"Anton," Zacharov says, letting go of Lila as though he suddenly realizes that he should. "You're outnumbered. Time to pack it in. Get down on the floor. Lila, you go get Stanley. Tell him there's something in here we've got to deal with."

Lila wipes her hands on her dress and doesn't look any of us in the face. I try to catch her eye, but it's impossible. She heads toward the door.

Zacharov is the one who meets my gaze. He knows that I played him, even if he doesn't know how. He gives me a slight nod of his head.

I guess I proved myself after all.

"Thank you, Barron. And Cassel, of course." I can hear the grind of his teeth as he thanks my brother and me for a lie. "Why don't you both go with Lila and wait for me in the kitchen? We're not done here. Desi, you make sure they don't wander off."

"You," Anton says, looking at me. "You did this. You made this happen."

"I didn't make you into a moron," I say, which maybe isn't the smartest thing, but I'm dumb and giddy with relief.

Plus, you know I'm terrible at keeping my mouth shut.

Anton lunges at me, closing the distance before I can react. We crash backward into one of the stalls, and my head slams into the tile beside one of the toilets. I see Grandad grabbing for Anton's neck like he's going to pull him off me, but Anton is way too huge and hardened for that.

His knuckles slam against my cheekbone. I lean up, cracking my forehead against his skull hard enough to make me dizzy with pain. He arches, like he's going to punch me again, when his eyes lose focus. He falls heavily on top of me and just lies there, heavy as a blanket.

I scrabble backward, not caring about the filthy floor, just trying to get out from under his weight. He looks pale, his lips already going blue.

He's dead.

Anton is dead.

I'm still staring at him when Lila leans down and touches a wad of toilet paper to my mouth. I didn't even realize I was bleeding.

"Lila," Zacharov says. "Come on. I need you out of here."

"You ever think you're too clever for your own good?" she asks me softly, before going back over to her father.

Grandad is holding his own wrist, hunched over it protectively.

"Are you okay?" I ask him, pushing myself up and leaning heavily against the wall.

"I'll be okay when we get out of this bathroom," Grandad says. Then I notice that his right hand is bare and his ring finger is darkening, blackness spreading down from the nail.

"Oh," I say. He saved my life.

He laughs. "What? You didn't think I still had it in me?"

I'm embarrassed to admit that I forgot he's *still* a death worker. I've always thought of his being a worker in the past tense, but he killed Anton with a single touch, a press of fingers against a vulnerable neck.

"You should have let me help you," Grandad says. "I overheard them talking after dinner that night when they dosed me."

"Lila, Barron," Zacharov says, "you two come with me. We'll leave Cassel and Desi alone for a moment to clean themselves up." He looks at us. "Don't go anywhere."

I nod as they go.

"You've got a lot of explaining to do," Grandad says.

I'm still pressing the wad of paper to my cheek. Real blood drooling from my mouth drops onto my shirt next to the fake blood. I look down at Anton's body. "You thought I was still memory worked—that's why you were trying to drag me out of here."

"What was I supposed to think?" Grandad says. "That you three had some ridiculously complicated plan? That Zacharov was in on it too?"

I grin in the mirror. "We're not in on anything. I forged

Barron's notebooks. Barron believes everything in those books. He has to, what with his memory loss."

That's what I did that last day and a half. What I stayed up all night doing. Rewriting pages and pages of notes in handwriting easy to forge because I already knew it so well. I constructed an entirely different life for Barron; the kind of life where he'd want to save the head of a crime family because Zacharov is Lila's dad. The kind of life where my brothers and I worked together for noble purposes.

The easiest lies to tell are the ones you want to be true.

Grandad frowns, and then understanding smoothes his features out into shock. "You mean he never met with Zacharov?"

I shake my head. "Nope. He just thinks he did."

"Did *you* meet with Zacharov?"

"Lila wanted us to take care of things ourselves," I say. "So, also no."

He groans. "This is trouble heaped on top of trouble."

I give Anton's body a last look. Something glitters in the light. Zacharov's diamond tie tack near Anton's left hand. He must have taken it from his pocket.

I reach down and pick up the pin.

Zacharov is leaning against the doorway when I stand. I didn't hear him come in. "Cassel Sharpe." He sounds tired. "My daughter tells me that this was her idea."

I nod my head. "It would have worked better with a real gun."

He snorts. "Since it was her idea, I am not going to

cut off your hand for touching my skin. Just tell me one thing—how long have you known you are a transformation worker?"

For a moment I open my mouth to protest. I didn't work him; how can he be sure that I wasn't faking? Then I remember the blowback, and me twisting on the tile floor. "Not long," I say.

"And you knew?" Zacharov turns to Grandad.

"His mother wanted to keep it a secret until he was old enough. She was going to tell him after her release." Grandad looks over at me. "Cassel, what you can do is very valuable to some people. I'm not saying your mother was right, but she's a smart lady and—"

I cut him off. "I know, Grandad."

Zacharov is watching us, like he's weighing something in his mind. "I want to make this clear: I never agreed to let your brothers live. Either of them."

I nod, because I can hear that he's not done talking.

"Your grandfather's right. You're valuable. And now you're mine. So long as you keep working for me, your brothers stay alive. Understand?"

I nod again.

I should tell him I don't care. That it doesn't matter to me if they're dead. But I don't. I guess it's true; no one will ever love you like your family.

"We're settled here," he says. "For now. Go into the kitchen and see if someone can scare you up a clean shirt."

Grandad pulls back on his right-hand glove. Now one of its fingers hangs as floppily as those on his left hand.

"Oh. I found—," I say to Zacharov, holding out the Resurrection Diamond before I notice something strange. A corner of the huge rock is chipped.

Zacharov takes it from me with a tight smile. "Thank you once more, Cassel."

I nod, trying not to let it show that I know the Resurrection Diamond can't protect anyone. It's worthless. It's made of glass.

Outside the bathroom the party is still going full swing. The noise crashes over me like a surreal wave, music and laughing and speeches loud enough to cover gunshots. None of what's happened—definitely not Anton being dead—seems real in the dancing light of the chandeliers or reflected in thousands of champagne bubbles.

"Cassel!" Daneca yells, running up to me. "Are you all right?"

"We were worried," Sam says. "You were in there for too long."

"I'm fine," I say. "Don't I seem fine?"

"You're covered in blood standing in the middle of a party," Sam says. "No, you don't seem fine."

"This way," Zacharov says, pointing toward the kitchens.

"We're coming with you," says Daneca.

I feel drained, and my cheek is throbbing. My ribs still hurt. And I don't see Lila anywhere.

"Yeah," I say. "Okay."

People nearly trip over themselves getting out of my way as I walk. I guess I really do look bad.

The kitchen looks smaller with people running around in it, carrying out trays of blini slathered in caviar, golden pastries leaking garlic butter, and tiny cakes topped with crystallized lemon.

My stomach growls, surprising me. I shouldn't be hungry after watching Anton be killed, but I'm starving.

Philip is standing in the back flanked by two burly men who appear to be restraining him. I don't know if Lila brought him to the party or if Zacharov sent to have him escorted over from wherever she was keeping him.

When he sees me, his eyes narrow.

"You took everything from me," he shouts. "Maura. My son. My future. My friend. You took *everything*."

I guess I did.

I could tell him that I didn't mean for it to happen.

"Sucks, doesn't it?" I say.

He struggles against the bodyguards holding him. I'm not worried. I let Daneca steer me to the area by the pantry and sinks.

"I'm going to make you regret the day you were born," Philip shouts to my back. I ignore him.

Lila is waiting with a bottle of vodka in one hand and a rag in the other. "Get up on the counter," she says.

I do, pushing aside a bowl of flour and a spatula. Philip's still yelling, but his voice seems to come from far away. I smile. "Lila, this is Daneca. I think you met Sam. They're my friends from school."

"Did he actually admit we're his friends?" Sam asks, and Daneca laughs.

Lila pours some vodka onto the napkin.

"I'm sorry I didn't tell you about the rest of my plan," I say to Lila. "About Barron."

"The notebooks, right? You fixed them somehow."

When I look surprised, she smiles. "I lived with him for years, remember? I saw the notebooks. Clever." She presses the cloth against my cheek, and I hiss. It stings like crazy.

"Ow," I say. "You ever think you're kind of a bully?"

Her smile goes wide. If it could, I think it would curl up at the corners. She leans close to me. "Oh, I know I am. And I know you like it."

Sam snickers. I don't care.

I do like it.

I SPEND THE NEXT TWO

weeks slammed, making up all the homework I missed.
Daneca and Sam help me, sitting with me in the library until
in-room curfew, when I have to head home and they have to
go back to the dorms. I spend so much time at school that
Grandad gets me my own car. He takes me to some friend
of his who hooks me up with a 1980 Mercedes-Benz Turbo
for two grand.

It runs like crap, but Sam promises to help convert it
to grease. He won some kind of state science fair with the
conversion of his hearse, and he thinks we can make it all
the way to an international science fair with the tinkering

he's got planned for my ride. Until then, I keep my fingers crossed that the engine keeps turning over.

When I go out to my car to drive myself home that Tuesday, I find Barron leaning against it, twirling keys around one black-gloved finger. His motorcycle is parked next to my car in the lot.

"What do you want?" I ask.

"Pizza night," he says.

I look at him like he's lost his mind.

He returns the look. "It's Tuesday."

The problem with forging an entire year of someone's life very quickly is that your fantasies creep in. Maybe you meant to just get in the stuff that you needed, but that leaves a lot of space to fill. I filled the space with the relationship I wished we had.

It's a little embarrassing now that Barron is standing here, really believing we go out for pizza every other Tuesday and talk about our feelings.

"I'll drive," I say finally.

We order a pizza heaped with cheese and sauce and sausage and pepperoni at a little place with booths, and miniature jukeboxes above each linoleum tabletop. I cover my slice with hot pepper flakes.

"I'm going back to Princeton to finish school," he says, biting into a chunk of garlic bread. "Now that Mom's getting out. Something tells me she's going to need a lawyer again soon." I wonder if he can go back, if he can fill the holes in his brain with law books and remember them as long as he doesn't work anymore. That's a big "as long as."

"Do you know when her actual release happens?"

"They say Friday," he says. "But they've already changed the date twice, so I don't know how seriously to take it. I guess we should get a cake or something, in case. Worst case scenario: We eat the cake anyway."

Memory is funny. Barron seems relaxed, like he really likes me, because he doesn't remember hating me. Or maybe he remembers the feeling of dislike but he assumes that he liked me more than he hated me. But I'm not relaxed. I can't stop remembering. I want to leap up out of the chair and choke him.

"What do you think is the first thing she's going to do when she gets out?" I ask.

"Meddle," he says, and laughs. "What do you think? She's going to start trying to get everything to go the way she wants it to go. And we all better pray that's the way we want it to go too."

I suck soda through my straw, lick grease off my glove, and contemplate transforming Barron into a slice of pizza and then feeding him to the kids at the next table.

Still, it's nice to have a brother I can talk to.

Keep your friends close and your enemies closer.

That's what Zacharov says when he explains that he's keeping Philip working for the family, where he can keep an eye on him. People don't usually leave crime families alive, so I guess I shouldn't be surprised.

I ask Grandad if he's seen Philip, but all he does is grunt.

Lila calls me on Wednesday.

"Hey," I say, not recognizing the number.

"Hey, yourself." She sounds happy. "You want to hang out?"

"I do," I say, my heart slamming. I switch my messenger bag over to the other shoulder with suddenly clumsy hands.

"Come up to the city. We can get hot chocolate, and maybe I'll let you beat me at a video game. I'm four years out of practice. I might be a little rusty."

"I'll beat you so bad your own avatar will laugh at you."

"Jerk. Come up on Saturday," she says, and hangs up.

I smile all the way through dinner.

On Friday at lunch I head out onto the quad. It's warm out and lots of kids have brought their food to eat on the grass. Sam and Daneca are sitting with Johan Schwartz, Jill Pearson-White, and Chaiyawat Terweil. They wave me over.

I hold up my hand and turn toward a small copse of trees. I've been thinking through everything that happened, and there's one thing still bothering me.

I take out my phone and punch in a number. I don't expect anyone to pick up, but she does.

"Dr. Churchill's office," says Maura.

"It's Cassel."

"Cassel!" she says. "I was wondering when you'd call. You know what the best feeling in the world is? Just driving down the road with the music blasting, the wind in your hair, and your baby gurgling happily in his car seat."

I smile. "You know where you are headed?"

"Not yet," she says. "I guess I'll know when we get there."

"I'm glad for you," I say. "I just wanted to call and tell you that."

"You know what I miss most?" she says.

I shake my head, and then realize she can't see me. "No."

"The music." Her voice drops, low and soft. "It was just so beautiful. I wish I could hear it again, but it's gone. Philip took the music with him."

I can't help shuddering.

Daneca is walking toward me when I hang up the phone. She looks annoyed.

"Hey," she says. "Come on. We're going to be late."

I must look shell-shocked or something, because she hesitates. "You don't have to do this if you don't want to."

"It's not that. I want to," I say. I'm not sure I mean it, but I am sure that Daneca and Sam were there for me when I really needed them. Maybe the point of real friendship isn't that you have to repay kindness, but whatever. At least I should try.

As Daneca, Sam, and I cross the quad, I see Audrey eating an apple near the entrance to the arts center.

She's smiling at me the way she used to. "Where are you guys going?"

I take a deep breath. "HEX meeting. Learning about worker rights."

"For real?" She looks toward Daneca.

"What can I say?" I shrug. "I'm trying new things."

"Can I come?" She doesn't stand up, like she's expecting me to say no.

"Of course you can," Daneca says, before I can get past the idea that she *wants* to come. "HEX meetings are for us all to better understand one another."

"They have free coffee," Sam says.

Audrey chucks her apple toward the shrubs by the entrance. "Count me in."

The meeting is being held in Ms. Ramirez's music room; she's the adviser. A piano sits in one corner, and a few drum toms rest near the back wall, against a bookshelf filled with thin folders of sheet music. A cymbal balances on the low shelf near a wall of windows, near a gurgling coffeemaker.

Ms. Ramirez is sitting the opposite way on the piano bench in a circle of students. I come in and pull up four more chairs. Everyone scoots politely aside, but the girl who's standing doesn't stop talking.

"The thing is that it's really hard to stop discrimination when something's illegal," the girl says. "I mean, everybody thinks of workers as being criminals. Like, people use the word 'worker' to mean criminals. And, well, if we work a work, even once, we are criminals. So most of us are, because we had to figure it out somehow and that was usually by making something happen."

I don't know her name, just that she's a freshman. She doesn't look at anyone when she speaks, and her voice is affectless. I am a little awed by her bravery.

"And there are lots of workers who never do anything bad. They go to weddings and hospitals and give people good luck. Or there's people who work at shelters and they give people hope and make them feel confident and positive. And that word—'cursing.' Like all we can do is bad magic. I mean, why would you even want to do the bad stuff? The blowback's awful. Like, if all a luck worker ever does is make people have good luck, then all he has is good luck too. It doesn't have to be bad."

She pauses and raises her gaze to look at us. At me.

"Magic," the girl says. "It's just all magic."

When I get home that night, Grandad is making a cup of tea in the kitchen. We've cleaned up a lot. The counters are mostly clear and the stove is no longer crusted with old food. There's a bottle of bourbon on the table, but the cap's still on it.

"Your mother called," he says. "She's out."

"Out?" I repeat dumbly. "Out of prison? Is she here?"

"No. But you do have a guest," he says, turning back to wipe the faucet. "That Zacharov girl is in your room."

I look up, like I can see through the ceiling, surprised and happy. I wonder what she thinks of the house, and then I remember she's been here before, lots of times. She's even been in my room before—just as a cat. Then the rest of what Grandad said hits me. "Why are you calling Lila 'that Zacharov girl'? And where's Mom? She can't have gotten far. Jail has to slow you down a little."

"Shandra rented a hotel room. She says she doesn't want us to see her the way she is. Last I heard, she was ordering champagne and french fries drenched in ranch dressing up to her bubble bath."

"Really?"

He laughs, but it sounds hollow. "You know your mother."

I walk past him and the remaining boxes of unsorted stuff in the dining room, up the stairs, taking them two at a time. I don't understand his mood, but my need to see Lila overwhelms other concerns.

"Cassel," he calls, and I turn, leaning over the banister. "Go up there and bring her down. Lila. There's something I need to tell you both."

"Okay," I say automatically, but I don't really want to hear whatever it is. Two quick steps down the hall and I open the door to my bedroom.

Lila is sitting on the bed, reading one of the old collections of ghost stories I never returned to the library. She turns to give me a sly smile. "I really missed you," she says, reaching out a hand.

"Yeah?" I can't stop looking at her, at the way the sunlight from the dirty window catches on her lashes, making them gleam like gold, the way her mouth parts slightly. She looks like the girl I remember climbing trees with, the one who pierced my ear and licked my blood, but she looks unlike that girl too. Time has hollowed her cheeks and made her eyes feverishly bright.

I've thought of her so many times in this room that it seems like those thoughts conjured her, a fantasy Lila, spread out on my bed. The unreality makes it easier to walk over to her, although my heart is beating like a hammer in my chest.

"Did you miss me?" she asks, stretching her body like a cat might. She drops the book without marking her place.

"For years," I say, helplessly honest for once. I want to press bare fingers against the line of her cheek and trace the dusting of freckles on her pale skin, but she still doesn't seem real enough to touch.

She leans in close, and everything about her is dizzyingly warm and soft.

"I missed you, too," she says.

I laugh, which helps me clear my head a little. "You wanted to kill me."

She shakes her head. "I always liked you. I always wanted you. Always."

"Oh," I say stupidly. And then I kiss her.

Her mouth opens under mine and she lies back, drawing me down onto the bed with her. Her arms twine around my neck and she sighs against my mouth. My skin feels pricklingly hot. My muscles tense, like I'm ready for a fight, everything clenched so hard that I'm shaking.

I take a single shuddering breath.

I am full of happiness. So much happiness that I can barely contain it.

Now that I've started touching her, I can't seem to stop. Like somehow the language of my hands will tell her all the things I don't know how to say out loud. My gloved fingers slide under the waistband of her jeans, over her skin. She shimmies a little, to shove her pants down, and reaches for mine. I am breathing her breath, my thoughts spiraling into incoherence.

Someone bangs on the door to the room.

For a moment I don't care. I don't stop.

"Cassel," Grandad calls from the other side of the door.

I roll off the bed and onto my feet. Lila is flushed, breathing hard. Her lips are red and wet, her eyes dark. I am still reeling.

"What?" I yell.

The door opens and my grandfather is there, holding the phone. "I need you to come and talk to your mother," he says.

I look over at Lila apologetically. Her cheeks are stained pink and she's fumbling with her jeans, trying to get them buttoned.

"I'll call her back." I'm glaring at him, but he barely seems to notice.

"No," he says. "You take this phone and you listen to what she has to say."

"Grandad," I say.

"Talk to your mother, Cassel." His voice is harder than I've ever heard it.

"Fine!" I grab the phone and walk into the hall, ushering Grandad out with me.

"Congrats on getting out of jail, Mom," I say.

"Cassel!" She sounds ecstatic to talk to me, like I'm the prince of some foreign country. "I'm sorry about not coming right home. I want to see my babies, but you don't know what it's like to live with a bunch of women for all these years and never have a moment alone. And none of my clothes fit. I lost so much weight from that awful food. I need a lot of new things."

"Great," I say. "So you're at a hotel?"

"In New York. I know we have a lot to talk about, baby. I'm sorry I didn't tell you about being a worker sooner, but I knew people would try to take advantage of you. And look at what they did. Of course, if the judge had just listened to me and realized that a mother needs to be with her children, none of this would have happened. You boys needed me."

"It happened before you went to jail," I say.

"What?"

"Lila. They tried to get me to kill her before you went to jail. They locked her in a cage before you went to jail. It had nothing to do with you."

She falters a little. "Oh, honey, I'm sure that's not true. You're just not remembering right."

"Don't—talk—to me—about—memories." I practically spit out the words. Each one falls from my tongue like a drop of poison.

She goes silent, which is so unusual that I can't remember it ever happening before. "Baby—," she says finally.

"What's this call about? What's so important that Grandad made me talk to you right this second?"

"Oh, it's nothing really. Your grandfather is just upset. You see, I got you a present. Something you always wanted. Oh, honey, you don't understand how happy I am that you managed to get your brothers out of a bad situation. Your *older* brothers too—and you, the baby, taking care of them. You deserve something just for you."

Cold dread uncoils in my stomach. "What?"

"Just a little—"

"What did you do?"

"Well, I went to see Zacharov yesterday. Did I ever tell you that we know each other? We do. Anyway, I ran into that adorable daughter of his on the way out. You always liked her, didn't you?"

"No," I say. I'm shaking my head.

"You didn't like her? I thought—"

"No. No. Mom, please tell me that you didn't touch her. Say you didn't work her."

She sounds uncertain, but also unrepentant, like she's trying to cajole me into liking a sweater she bought on sale. "I thought you'd be happy. And she grew up very pretty, don't you think? Not as handsome as you, of course, but prettier than that redhead you were spending all your time with."

I step back against the wall, slamming my shoulders against it like I no longer remember how to move my legs. "Mom," I moan.

"Baby, what's wrong?"

"Just tell me what you did. Just say it." It is a terrible desperate thing to plead with someone to crush your hope.

"This really isn't the kind of thing you just say over the phone," she says reprovingly.

"Say it!" I shout.

"Okay, okay. I worked her so that she loves you," Mom

says. "She'll do absolutely anything for you. Anything you want. Isn't that nice?"

"Fix it," I say. "You have to undo it. Put her back the way she was. I'll take her to you and you can work her again so she's back to normal."

"Cassel," she says, "you know I can't do that. I can make her hate you. I can even make her feel nothing at all for you, but I can't take away what I've already done. If it bothers you so much, just wait it out. The way she feels will fade eventually. I mean, she won't be exactly the same as she was before—"

I hang up the phone. It rings over and over again. I watch it light up, watch the hotel's name scroll across the caller ID.

Lila finds me sitting in the hall, in the dark, holding a still-ringing phone when she comes out to see what's taking so long. "Cassel?" she whispers.

I can barely look at her.

The most important thing for any con artist is never to think like a mark. Marks figure they're going to get a deal on a stolen handbag, then they get upset when the lining falls out. They think they're going to get front row tickets for next to nothing off a guy standing out in the rain, then they're surprised when the tickets are just pieces of wet paper.

Marks think they can get something for nothing.

Marks think they can get what they don't deserve and could never deserve.

Marks are stupid and pathetic and sad.

Marks think they're going to go home one night and have the girl they've loved since they were a kid suddenly love them back.

Marks forget that whenever something's too good to be true, that's because it's a con.

ACKNOWLEDGMENTS

Several books were really helpful in creating the world of the curse workers. In particular, David R. Maurer's *The Big Con*, Sam Lovell's *How to Cheat at Everything*, Kent Walker and Mark Schone's *Son of a Grifter*, and Karl Taro Greenfeld's *Speed Tribes*.

I am deeply indebted to many people for their insight into this book. I want to thank everyone at Sycamore Hill 2007 for looking at the first few chapters and giving me the confidence to keep going. I am grateful to Justine Larbalestier for talking with me about liars and Scott Westerfeld for his detailed notes. Thanks to Sarah Rees Brennan for helping me with the feeeelings. Thanks to Joe Monti for his enthusiasm and book recommendations. Thanks to Elka Cloke for her medical expertise. Thanks to Kathleen Duey for pushing me to think about the larger world issues. Thanks to Kelly Link for making the beginning far better and also for driving me around in the trunk of her car. Thanks to Ellen Kushner, Delia Sherman, Gavin Grant, Sarah Smith, Cassandra Clare, and Joshua Lewis for looking at very rough drafts. Thanks to Steve Berman for his help working out the details of the magic.

Most of all, I have to thank my agent, Barry Goldblatt, for his encouragement; my editor, Karen Wojtyla, who pushed me to make the book far better than I thought it could be; and my husband, Theo, who not only put up with me during the writing, but also gave me lots of advice about demerits, scams, private school, and how to talk animal shelters out of things.

RED GLOVE

For the little white cat
that appeared on our doorstep
just after I started this series.
She lived only a short while
and she is much missed.

I DON'T KNOW WHETHER

it's day or night when the girl gets up to leave. Her minnow silver dress swishes against the tops of her thighs like Christmas tinsel as she opens the hotel door.

I struggle to remember her name.

"So you'll tell your father at the consulate about me?" Her lipstick is smeared across her cheek. I should tell her to fix it, but my self-loathing is so great that I hate her along with myself.

"Sure," I say.

My father never worked at any consulate. He's not paying girls a hundred grand a pop to go on a goodwill tour of Europe. I'm not a talent scout for *America's Next Top Model*.

My uncle doesn't manage U2. I haven't inherited a chain of hotels. There are no diamond mines on my family land in Tanzania. I have never been to Tanzania. These are just a few of the stories my mother has spent the summer spinning for a string of blond girls in the hope that they'll make me forget Lila.

They don't.

I look up at the ceiling. I keep on staring at it until I hear my mother start to move in the adjoining room.

Mom got out of jail a couple months back. After school let out she relocated us both to Atlantic City, where we've been grifting rooms and charging up whatever food and drink we want to them. If the staff gets too demanding about payment, we simply move down the strip. Being an emotion worker means that Mom never leaves a credit card at the desk.

As I think that, she opens the door between our rooms.

"Honey," Mom says, as though it's not at all weird to find me lying on the floor in my boxers. Her black hair is up in clips and wrapped in one of her silk scarves, the way she always wears it when she sleeps. She's got on the hotel robe from the last hotel, tied tightly around her ample waist. "You ready for some breakfast?"

"Just coffee, I think. I'll make it." I push myself up and pad over to the complimentary pot. There's a bag of grounds, sugar, and some powdered creamer sitting on a plastic tray.

"Cassel, how many times do I have to tell you that it isn't safe to drink out of those things? Someone could have been brewing meth in it." Mom frowns. She always worries about the weirdest things. Hotel coffeepots. Cell phones. Never normal stuff, like the police. "I'll order us both up coffee from the kitchen."

"They could be brewing meth there, too," I say, but she ignores me.

She goes into her room and I can hear her make the call. Then she comes back to the doorway. "I ordered you some egg whites and toast. And juice. I know you said you weren't hungry, but you need to keep your strength up for today. I found us a new mark." Her smile is big enough that I almost want to smile along with her.

That's my mom.

Believe it or not, there are magazines out there called, like, *Millionaire Living* or *New Jersey Millionaires* or whatever, that feature profiles of old guys in their homes, showing off their stuff. I have no idea who else buys them, but they're perfect for my mother. I think she sees them as gold digger shopping catalogs.

That's where she found Clyde Austin. He's on the page after a feature with curse-worker-hating Governor Patton at his mansion, Drumthwacket. Despite a recent divorce, according to the article, Austin still manages to enjoy a lifestyle that includes a private plane, a heated infinity pool, and two borzois that travel with him everywhere. He has a home in Atlantic City, where he likes to go out to dinner at Morton's and play a little blackjack when he can get away from the office. The picture of him shows a short, squat dude with hair plugs.

"Put on something dirty," Mom says. She's at her desk, altering a new pair of bright blue gloves. She's seeding them with tiny holes at the fingertips: small enough to go unnoticed, big enough for her skin to touch the mark's.

"Dirty?" I say from the couch I'm slumped on in her suite. I'm on my third cup of coffee, all three choked with cream. I ate the toast, too.

"Wrinkled. Something that makes you look homeless and desperate." She begins to take down her curls, one by one. Soon she'll start rubbing gunk into her skin and curling her eyelashes. It takes her hours to get ready.

"What's the plan?" I ask.

"I posed as his secretary and pretended I forgot when his reservation was for," Mom says. "At Morton's. Wasn't it great how the magazine comes right out and says where to find him? It absolutely worked. He's going to eat there at eight o'clock tonight."

"How long have you known that for?" I ask her.

"A couple days." She shrugs, making a careful line of black above her eyes. There's no telling how long she really knew. "Oh—and grab the plastic bag over by my suitcase."

I slug down the last of the coffee and get up. The bag contains panty hose. I put them on her desk.

"They're for you."

"You want me to look homeless, desperate, but also kind of fabulous?" I ask.

"Over your head," she says, turning in her chair and miming the gesture like I'm a moron. "If Clyde works out, I want him to be able to meet you as my son."

"It sounds like you've really got some plan cooked up," I say.

"Oh, come on," she demands. "School starts in less than a week. Don't you want to have a little fun?"

Several hours later Mom clops along the boardwalk behind me in platform heels. Her white dress blows in the late summer wind. The neckline is low enough that I'm worried her boobs are going to actually fall out if she moves too fast. I know it's disturbing that I notice, but I'm not *blind*.

"You know what you're supposed to do, right?" she says.

I wait for her to catch up. She has on gold lamé gloves and is carrying a gold clutch purse. I guess she decided against the blue. Altogether it's quite an outfit. "No, why don't you tell me for the millionth time?"

I see the fury pass over her face like a storm. Her eyes go hard.

"I've got it, Mom," I say in what I hope is a conciliatory way. "Go on ahead. We shouldn't be talking."

She totters off toward the restaurant, and I walk to the railing, looking at the sea. It's the same view I had from Zacharov's Atlantic City penthouse. I think of Lila with her back to me, staring out at black water.

I should have told her I loved her back then. Back when it would have meant something.

Waiting is the hardest thing about any con job. The moments slip by and your hands start to sweat, anticipating what's coming. Your mind wanders. You're all keyed up from adrenaline, but there's nothing to do.

Distraction leads to disaster. Mom's rule.

I turn back toward the restaurant and slip my gloved hand into my pocket, touching the wadded-up piece of panty hose. I hacked off the foot with a room service knife.

I keep focused, eyeing the crowd, watching my mother vamp up her incredibly slow stroll. We could be here awhile. And, honestly, this plan might not even work. That's another thing about cons; you have to go after a bunch of marks before you find the perfect one. The one you can really take for all he's worth.

We wait for twenty minutes, almost a block apart from each other. Mom has done all the innocent things someone does on a nighttime stroll: smoked a cigarette, checked her lipstick, made fake calls on the cell phone she borrowed from me. I, on the other hand, have taken to begging for change. I've made about $3.50 and am about to land another quarter when Clyde Austin lurches out of Morton's.

Mom starts to move.

I jump up and take off toward her, yanking the panty hose down over my face. That slows me down some, because there is no way in hell these things are sheer. I can barely see.

People start yelling. Yeah, because a guy with hose over his head is never the good guy. He's a robber from central casting.

I keep running, flying past my mother and yanking the gold clutch out of her hand.

She adds her screams to the chorus.

"Thief!" my mother screams. "Help! Heeeeelp!"

Now, this is the tricky part. I have to keep running, but I have to run just slowly enough that a drunk and out-of-shape guy with a couple of martinis rolling around in his belly actually thinks he can catch me.

"Please—someone!" Mom shrieks. "He has all my money!"

It's really hard not to laugh.

I practically run into Clyde, making sure he's got a shot at me. But I've got to give it to Mom. She's right when she says that guys want to be knights in shining armor. He grabs for my arm.

I let myself fall.

It's a bad one. Maybe it's the panty hose over my face, or maybe I'm just off balance, but I go down hard on the asphalt, scraping one hand so roughly, I can feel my glove shred. I'm pretty sure I scrape my knees, too, but all they feel is numb.

I drop the purse.

Clyde clocks me in the back of the head before I can push myself to my feet. It hurts. She better appreciate this. Then I'm up and running. Full out. Pulling that crap off my face and hurling myself through the night as fast as I can.

Leaving Clyde Austin to be a hero, bringing a damsel in distress her golden clutch purse.

Leaving him to notice how charming she is when her eyes well up with gratitude.

Leaving him to check out her rack.

Mom is exultant. She breaks out the bottle of Prosecco from the minibar while I pour frothing hydrogen peroxide over my hand. It stings like crazy.

"He wants to meet for drinks tomorrow night. I told him it was the least I could do to take him out. He said that, after what I'd been through, he was going to pay, and that was that. Now, doesn't that sound promising?"

"Sure," I tell her.

"He's going to pick me up here. At six. Do you think I should be ready when he gets here or do you think I should invite him in for a drink while I do a few last little things? Maybe be in my robe?"

I make a face. "I don't know."

"Stop thinking of it that way. This is a job. We need someone to provide for us. Pay for your fancy school—and Barron's loans. Especially now that Philip can't be sure how long he's going to stay employed." She cuts me a dark look, like I somehow forgot that I'm the one that got him in trouble with the boss of a crime family. Like I am going to start caring. They've done much worse to me.

"So long as you don't work Clyde," I say quietly. "You don't need to. You're plenty charming on your own."

She laughs and pours her Prosecco into a water glass. It fizzes like the peroxide. "Like mother, like son. We're both charming when we want something. Right, Cassel?"

"So I want you to stay out of jail," I say. "So what? Is that supposed to be a secret?"

The doorbell of her room buzzes. "What did you order?" I ask her, and head over to open it.

Mom makes a sound of alarm, but she's too late.

Clyde Austin is standing in the hallway, a bottle of Jack Daniel's swinging from one hand. "Oh," he says, embarrassed. "I must have the wrong room. I thought—"

Then he gets a good look at me—at the blood on my jeans, the scrape on my bare hand. And he sees my mother sitting on the bed. And he knows. His face goes ugly.

"You set me up," he says. "You and her." The way he says "her" tells me everything he's thinking about us.

I start to explain, when he swings the bottle at my head. I see it moving, but I am too clumsy, too slow. It makes a hollow, horrible thunk against my temple.

I hit the carpet, dizzy. Dull pain makes me nauseous. That's what I get for underestimating the guy. I roll onto my back just in time to see him over me, raising the Jack Daniel's to strike again.

With a shriek Mom rakes her nails against his neck.

He whirls around, wild, swinging. His elbow connects. She flies back against the desk. Her magnifying mirror cracks against the wall, the shards falling like glittering confetti.

I reach up my bare hand. I could stop him with a single touch.

I could change him into a cockroach.

I could transform him into a puddle of grease.

I really want to.

Clyde has gone still, though, looking around like he suddenly doesn't know where he is. "Shandra?" he says gently, reaching for my mother. "I'm so sorry. Did I hurt you?"

"That's okay," Mom says in a soothing voice, getting up slowly. She winces. There's blood on her lip. "You just came by to bring me a little liquor, didn't you? And you saw my son. Maybe you mistook him for someone else."

"I guess," he says. "We got along so well that I figured why wait until tomorrow night? And then . . . He does look like the mugger, you have to admit."

Mom's an emotion worker. She can't change his memories; my brother Barron could do that, but he's not here. What Mom can do with a single bare-handed touch is make Clyde Austin like her so much that he's willing to give her the benefit of the doubt. About anything. Everything. Even this.

A wave of dizziness overwhelms me.

"That's true, baby," she says. "He does look a little like the mugger. It was an honest mistake. I'm just going to walk you to the door now." Her fingers go to his neck, which should make anybody flinch—bare fingers, no glove—but it doesn't bother him at all. He lets himself be steered.

"I'm really sorry for what happened," he says. "I don't know what came over me."

"I understand," Mom tells him. "And I forgive you, but I don't think that we can see each other tomorrow night. You get that, right?"

Shame heats his face. "Of course."

My vision blurs. She says something else soothing, but not to me.

We check out in the morning. Sunlight makes my brain feel like it's throbbing inside my skull. Sweat slicks my skin—the kind of unnatural sweat that comes along with injury. Each movement makes me as dizzy as riding a thousand roller coasters all at once. While we wait for the valet to get my car, I fumble through my backpack for sunglasses and try to avoid looking at the dark bruise on Mom's shoulder.

She's been totally silent since she told me we were leaving—all through packing and even the ride down in the elevator. I can tell she's seething.

I feel too sick to know what to do about it.

Finally my ancient and rusted Benz drives up to the front of the hotel. Mom hands something to the driver and gets the keys while I slide in on the other side. The seat is hot on the backs of my legs, even through jeans.

"How could you answer the door like that?" she shouts as soon as we pull away from the curb. "Not looking through the peephole. Not calling out to ask who was there?"

I flinch at her voice.

"Are you stupid, Cassel? Didn't I teach you better than that?"

She's right. It was thoughtless. Stupid. Private school has made me careless. It's exactly the kind of dumb mistake that separates a decent con man from an amateur. Plus the blowback from the emotion work makes her unstable. Not that she isn't normally pretty unstable. But working magnifies it. So does anger. There's nothing for me to do but ride it out.

I was used to her being like this when I was a kid. But she's been in jail long enough for me to forget how bad she can get.

"Are you stupid?" she screeches. "Answer me!"

"Stop," I say, and lean my head against the window, shutting my eyes. "Please stop. I'm sorry, okay?"

"No," she says, her voice vicious and certain. "No one's that pathetic. You did it on purpose! You wanted to ruin things for me."

"Oh, come on," I say. "I wasn't thinking. I said I was sorry. Look, I'm the one with the goose egg to show for it. So we have to leave Atlantic City? We'd have to leave in a week anyway when I went back to school."

"You did this to me because of Lila." Her gaze is on the road, but her eyes glitter with fury. "Because you're still angry."

Lila. My best friend, who I thought I killed.

"I'm not talking about her," I snap. "Not with you."

I think about Lila's wide, expressive mouth turning up at the corners. I think about her spread out on my bed, reaching for me.

With one touch of her hand, Mom made Lila love me. And made sure I could never, ever have her.

"Hit a nerve?" Mom says, gleefully cruel. "It's amazing you actually thought you were good enough for Zacharov's daughter."

"Shut up," I say.

"She was *using* you, you stupid little moron. When everything was said and done, she wouldn't have given you the time of day, Cassel. You would have been a reminder of Barron and misery and nothing more."

"I don't care," I say. My hands are shaking. "It would still have been better than—" Better than having to avoid her until the curse fades. Better than the way she'll look at me once it does.

Lila's desire for me is a perversion of love. A mockery.

And I almost didn't care, I wanted her so much.

"I did you a favor," my mother says. "You should be grateful. You should be thanking me. I got you Lila on a silver platter—something you could have never in your life had otherwise."

I laugh abruptly. "I should be thanking you? How about you hold your breath until I do?"

"Don't talk that way to me," Mom roars, and slaps me, hard.

Hard enough that my battered head hits the window. I see stars. Little explosions of light behind the dark glasses. Behind my eyelids.

"Pull over," I say. Nausea overwhelms me.

"I'm sorry," she says, her voice seesawing back to sweet. "I didn't mean to hurt you. Are you okay?"

The world is starting to tilt. "You have to pull over."

"Maybe right now you'd rather walk than deal with me, but if you're really hurt, then you better—"

"Pull over!" I shout, and something about the urgency of my tone finally convinces her. She steers the car abruptly onto the shoulder of the road and brakes hard. I stumble out while we're still moving.

Just in time to heave my guts up in the grass.

I really hope no one at Wallingford wants me to write an essay on how I spent my summer vacation.

I PARK MY BENZ IN THE

seniors' lot, which is much closer to the dorms than where underclassmen are forced to leave their cars. I feel a little smug until I shut off the engine and it makes an odd metallic cough, like maybe it just gave up the ghost. I get out and kick the front tire halfheartedly. I had a plan to fix up the car, but with Mom home I never quite got around to it.

Leaving my bags in the trunk, I walk across campus toward the Finke Academic Center.

Over the doorway of the large brick building hangs a hand-lettered sign: WELCOME FRESHMEN. The trees rustle with a light wind, and I am overcome with a feeling of nostalgia for something I haven't yet lost.

At a table inside, Ms. Noyes is looking through a box of cards and giving out orientation packets. A few sophomores I don't know too well are shrieking and hugging one another. When they see me, they quiet down and start whispering instead. I overhear "kill himself" and "in his underwear" and "cute." I walk faster.

At the desk a blotchy, trembling girl and her father are picking up dorm keys. She clings to his hand like she'd be lost without it. This is clearly the first time the girl has spent any time away from home. I feel sorry for her and envy her all at once.

"Hey, Ms. Noyes," I say when it's my turn. "How's it going?"

She looks up and smiles. "Cassel Sharpe! I am so pleased you'll be living on campus again." She gets me my manila folder and room assignment. In addition to the exclusive parking lot and, bizarrely, a stretch of grass—no, really, it's called "senior grass"—seniors also get the best dorm rooms. It looks like mine is on the ground level. I guess they're a little leery of me on a high floor after that whole almost-falling-off-a-roof thing.

"Me too." And I am glad to be back. I really, really am. "Has Sam Yu checked in yet?"

She flips through the cards. "No, you beat him."

Sam has been my roommate since we were sophomores, but it wasn't until the end of last year that we got to be friends. I'm still not really good at friendship, but I'm trying.

"Thanks. See you later," I say. There's always an assembly on the first night before classes start. Headmistress Northcutt and Dean Wharton tell us that we're intelligent, capable young men and women, and then proceed to lecture us about how only the school rules keep us safe from ourselves. It's a good time.

"Try to stay out of trouble," she says with a grin. Her voice is teasing, but there's a firmness there that makes me think she doesn't say this to all incoming students.

"Absolutely," I say.

Back in the parking lot I start unloading the car. There's a bunch of stuff. Mom spent Labor Day weekend pretending we'd never had a fight and buying me extravagant presents to make up for that fight we never had. I am now the owner of a new iPod, a leather bomber jacket, and a laptop. I'm pretty sure I saw her paying for the laptop with Clyde Austin's credit card, but I pretended not to notice. Mom packed my bags for me too, on her working theory that no matter what I say I want, she knows what I'll actually need. I repacked them as soon as she was out of the room.

"You know I love you, right, baby?" Mom asked this morning as I was leaving.

The weird thing is, I do know.

When I get to my new dorm room—bigger than the one we had last year, plus the ground floor means I don't have to haul all my crap up a million flights of stairs—I dump everything on the floor and sigh.

I wonder where Lila is right now. I wonder if her father shipped her off to some Swiss Boarding School for worker crime family kids, some place with armed guards and high gates. I wonder if she likes it. Maybe the curse has already worn off and she's just sitting around, sipping hot chocolate and chatting up ski instructors. Maybe it would be safe to call her, just to talk for a few minutes. Just to hear her voice.

I want to, so badly that I force myself to call my brother Barron instead, just to remind me what's real. He told me to call once I settled in, anyway. I figure this is settled enough.

"Hey," he says, picking up after only one ring. "How's my favorite brother?" Every time I hear his voice, I get the same knot in my stomach. He made me into a killer. He used me, but he doesn't remember that. He thinks that we're thick as thieves, hand in glove. All the things I made him think.

Blowback ate away so many of his memories that he believes the fake ones I carefully forged into his notebooks— the ones of us being close. And that makes him the only person I'm sure I can trust.

Pathetic, right?

"I'm worried about Mom. She's getting worse," I say. "Reckless. She can't get caught again, or she's going to jail forever."

I'm not sure what he can do. It's not like I did such a good job of keeping her out of trouble in Atlantic City.

"Oh, come on." He sounds bored and a little drunk. I hear soft music in the background. It's not even noon. "Juries love her."

I'm pretty sure he's missing the point. "Just, please— she's not careful. Maybe she'll listen to you. You were going to be the lawyer—"

"She's an old lady," Barron says. "And she's been locked up for years. Let her have some fun. She needs to blow off steam. Seduce old dudes. Lose money at canasta."

I laugh, despite myself. "Just keep an eye on her before she takes those old dudes for everything they've got."

"Roger dodger. Mission heard and accepted," he says, and I find myself relaxing. Then he sighs. "Have you talked to Philip recently?"

"You know I haven't," I say. "Every time I call, he hangs up on me, and there's nothing I can—"

The doorknob starts to turn.

"Let me call you later," I say quickly. It's too weird to be talking to Barron and pretending everything is normal in front of my roommate, who knows what Barron's done. Who'd wonder *why* I would call Philip. Who doesn't understand what it means to have a family as messed up as mine.

"Peace out, little brother," Barron says, and hangs up.

Sam walks in, duffel bag over his shoulder. "Hey," he says with a shy smile. "Long time, no see. How was Toronto?"

"There was supposed to be an ice castle," I say. "But it melted."

Yeah, I lied to him about where I spent the summer. I didn't have to—there was no really good reason not to tell him I went to Atlantic City, except it didn't seem like a place normal people go with a parent. I told you I'm no good at this friends thing.

"That's too bad." Sam turns to put an aluminum toolbox on the rickety wooden dresser. He's a big guy, tall and round. He always seems to move carefully, like someone who is uncomfortable with taking up too much space. "Hey, I got some new stuff you're going to love."

"Oh, yeah?" I unpack the way I usually do—by shoving everything under my bed until room inspection. That's what happens when you grow up in a garbage house; you feel more comfortable with a little squalor.

"I have a kit to make molds of teeth and craft really perfect fangs. Like, *perfect*. They fit over your teeth as if they were tiny little gloves." He looks happier than I remember him. "Daneca and I went into New York—to this special effects warehouse, and cleaned the place out. Resins. Elastomer. Poly foams. I could probably fake setting someone on fire."

I raise my eyebrows.

"Hey," he says. "After last year I figured I'd better be prepared."

Carter Thompson Memorial Auditorium is the place where, every year, all the students gather to listen while the rules are repeated for anyone too lazy to read the handbook. "Boys must wear the Wallingford jacket and tie, black dress pants, and a white shirt. Girls must wear the Wallingford jacket, a black skirt or black dress pants, and a white shirt. Both boys and girls should wear black dress shoes. No sneakers. No jeans." Fascinating stuff like that.

Sam and I try to grab a seat in the back, but Ms. Logan, the school secretary, spots us and points out an empty row in the front.

"Boys," she says. "We're trying to be an example to all the new students, now that we're seniors, aren't we?"

"Can't we be bad examples?" Sam asks, and I snort.

"Mr. Yu," says Ms. Logan, pressing her lips together. "Senioritis is a serious condition this early in the year. Lethal. Mr. Sharpe, I would appreciate it if you didn't encourage him."

We move to the new seats.

Dean Wharton and Headmistress Northcutt are already up at the lectern. Northcutt starts off with lots of rah-rahing about how we're all one big family here at Wallingford, how we support one another through the hard times, and how we'll look back on our years here as among the best of our lives.

I turn to Sam to make some crack and notice him scanning the auditorium. He looks nervous.

The problem with being a con artist is that it's hard to turn off the part of your brain that's always assessing the situation, looking for a mark, a sucker you can sucker out of stuff. Trying to figure out what that mark wants, what's going to convince him to part with his money.

Not that Sam's a mark. But my brain still supplies me with the answer to what he's looking for, in case it comes in useful.

"Everything okay with you and Daneca?" I ask.

He shrugs his shoulders. "She hates horror movies," he says finally.

"Oh," I say as neutrally as I can.

"I mean, she cares about really important stuff. About

political stuff. About global warming and worker rights and gay rights, and I think she thinks the stuff I care about is for kids."

"Not everyone's like Daneca," I say.

"No one is like Daneca." Sam has that slightly dazed look of a man in love. "I think it's hard for her, you know. Because she cares so much, and most people barely care at all. Including me, I guess."

Daneca used to annoy me with all her bleeding-heart crap. I figured there was no point in changing a world that didn't want to be changed. But I don't think that Sam would appreciate me saying that out loud. And I don't even know if I believe it anymore.

"Maybe you could change her mind about the horror genre," I say instead. "You know, show her some classic stuff. Rent *Frankenstein*. Do a dramatic reading of 'The Raven.' Ladies love 'Get thee back into the tempest and the Night's Plutonian shore! Leave no black plume as a token of that lie thy soul has spoken!' Who can resist that?"

Sam doesn't even smile.

"Okay," I say, holding up my hands in the universal sign of surrender. "I'll stop."

"No, it's funny," he says. "It's not you. I just can't—"

"Mr. Yu! Mr. Sharpe," Ms. Logan says, coming up the center aisle to sit right behind us. She puts her finger to her lips. "Don't make me separate you."

That thought is humiliating enough that we're quiet through Dean Wharton's long list of things we will be punished for—a list that ranges from drinking, drugs, and being caught in the dorm room of someone of the opposite sex, to skipping class, sneaking out after hours, and wearing black lipstick. The sad truth is that there is probably at least one person in each graduating class who's managed to break all the rules in a single wild night. I am really hoping that, this year, that person is not going to be me.

I don't look all that good in lipstick.

Daneca finds us on the way to dinner. She's got her curly brown hair divided into seven thick braids, each one ending in a wooden bead. The collar of her white dress shirt is open, to show seven jade amulets—protection against the seven types of curse work. Luck. Dreams. Physical. Emotion. Memory. Death. Transformation. I gave her the stones for her last birthday, just before the end of junior year.

Amulets are made by curse workers of the type the amulet is supposed to protect against. Only stone seems able to absorb magic, and even then it will work only once. A used stone—one that has kept a curse from its wearer—cracks instantly. Since there are very few transformation workers in the world—perhaps one a decade—real transformation amulets are rare. But Daneca's transformation amulet is the real thing. I know; I made it myself.

She has no idea.

"Hey," she says, bumping her shoulder against Sam's arm. He puts his arm around her.

We walk into the cafeteria like that.

It's our first night back, so there are tablecloths and a rose with some baby's breath in little vases on all the tables. A few parents of new students hang around marveling at the high paneled ceiling, the stern portrait of Colonel Wallingford presiding over us, and our ability to eat food without smearing it all over ourselves.

Tonight's entree is salmon teriyaki with brown rice and carrots. For dessert, cherry crumble. I poke at my carrots. Daneca starts with dessert.

"Not bad," she pronounces. And with absolutely no segue she launches into an explanation of how this year it's going to be really important for HEX to get out the word about Proposition 2. About some rally happening next week. How prop two augurs a more invasive government, and some other stuff I tune out.

I look over at Sam, ready to exchange a conspiratorial glance, but he is hanging on her every word.

"Cassel," she says. "I know you're not listening. The vote is in November. This November. If Proposition 2 passes, then workers are going to be tested. Everyone will be. And no matter how much the government of New Jersey says it is going to keep that information anonymous, it's not. Soon workers are going to be refused jobs, denied housing, and locked up for the crime of being born with a power they didn't ask for."

"I know," I say. "I know all that. Could you try to be a little less condescending? *I know*."

She looks, if possible, even more annoyed. "This is your life we're talking about."

I think of my mother and Clyde Austin. I think of Barron. I think of me and all the harm I've done. "Maybe workers *should* all be locked up," I say. "Maybe Governor Patton is right."

Sam frowns.

I shove a big hunk of salmon into my mouth so I can't say anything else.

"That's ridiculous," Daneca says after she recovers from her shocked silence.

I chew.

She's right, of course. Daneca's always right. I think of her mother—a tireless advocate and one of the founders of the worker-rights youth group, HEX—and of Chris, that poor kid staying at her house, with nowhere else to go and maybe no legal reason to be allowed to stay. His parents kicked him out because they thought workers were all like me. There are workers who aren't con artists, workers who don't want anything to do with organized crime. But when Daneca thinks of workers, she thinks of her mother. When I think of workers, I think of mine.

"Anyway," Daneca says, "there's a rally next Thursday, and I want the whole HEX club to go. I got Ms. Ramirez, acting as our adviser, to apply for buses and everything. It's going to be a school trip."

"Really?" Sam says. "That's great."

"Well." She sighs. "It's not *exactly* a go. Ramirez said that Wharton or Northcutt would have to approve her request. And we'd have to get enough HEX members to sign up. So, can I count on you guys?"

"Of course we'll go," says Sam, and I level a glare in his direction.

"Whoa," I say, holding up my hand. "I want more details. Like does this mean we have to make our own signs? How about 'Worker Rights for Everyone Except People Who Don't Need Them' or 'Legalize Death Work Today. Solve Overpopulation Tomorrow!'"

The corner of Sam's mouth lifts. I can't seem to stop myself from being a jerk, but at least I'm amusing someone.

Daneca starts to say something else, when Kevin LaCroix comes up to the table. I look at him with undisguised relief. Kevin drops an envelope into my messenger bag.

"That stoner dude, Jace, says he hooked up with someone over the summer," Kevin whispers. "But I hear all the pictures he's showing around are really pictures of his half sister. Fifty bucks says there's no girlfriend."

"Find someone to bet that he *did* hook up or does have a girlfriend, and I'll give you odds," I say. "The house doesn't bet."

He nods and heads back to his table, looking disappointed.

I started being the school bookie back when Mom was in jail and there was no way I could afford all the little stuff that doesn't come with the price of tuition. A second uniform so that the one you had could get washed more than once a week, pizza with your friends when they wanted to go out, plus sneakers and books and music that didn't fall off a truck somewhere or get shoplifted out of a store. It isn't cheap to live near the rich.

After Kevin LaCroix leaves, Emmanuel Domenech drops

by. I get enough traffic to keep Sam and Daneca from being able to point out how obnoxious I've been. They spend their time writing notes back and forth in Daneca's notebook as other students casually turn over envelope after envelope— each one, a brick rebuilding my tiny criminal empire.

"I bet Sharone Nagel will get stuck wearing the mascot fur suit to football games."

"I bet the Latin club will sacrifice one of its members at the spring formal."

"I bet Chaiyawat Terweil will be the first person to get called into Headmistress Northcutt's office."

"I bet the new girl just got out of a loony bin."

"I bet the new girl just broke out of a prison in Moscow."

"I bet Mr. Lewis will have a nervous breakdown before winter break."

I note down each bet for and against these in a code I created, and tonight Sam and I will calculate the first master list of odds. They'll change as we get more bets, of course, but it gives us something to tell people at breakfast if they want to know where to throw their cash. It's amazing how rich kids get itchy when they can't spend money fast enough.

Just like criminals get itchy when we're not working all the angles.

As we get up to go back to our rooms, Daneca punches my arm. "So," she says. "Are you going to tell us why you're such a moody bastard tonight?"

I shrug. "I'm sorry. I guess I'm just tired. And an idiot."

She reaches up to put her gloved hands around my

neck and mock-chokes me. I play along, falling to the floor and pretending to die, until she finally laughs.

I'm forgiven.

"I knew I should have brought a blood packet," Sam says, shaking his head like we're humiliating him.

It is at that moment that Audrey walks by, hand in hand with Greg Harmsford. Audrey, who was once my girlfriend. Who dumped me. Who, when we were dating, made me feel like a normal person. Who I could have, maybe, once, convinced to take me back. Who now doesn't even look at me as she passes.

Greg, however, narrows his eyes and smiles down at me like he's daring me to start something.

I'd love to wipe that smug expression off his face. First, though, I'd have to get up off my knees.

I don't get to spend the rest of the night putting away my stuff or joking around in the common lounge like I planned, because our new hall master, Mr. Pascoli, announces that all seniors have to meet with their guidance counselors.

I have seen Ms. Vanderveer exactly once a year for all the time I have been at Wallingford. She seems nice enough, always prepared with a list of which classes and activities are most likely to get me into a good college, always full of suggestions for volunteer work that admission committees love. I don't really feel the need to see more of her than I already have, but Sam and I, along with a group of other upperclassmen, trudge across the grounds to Lainhart Library.

There, we listen to another speech—this one on how

senior year is no time to slack off, and if we think things are hard now, just wait until we get to college. Seriously, this guy—one of the counselors, I guess—makes it sound like in college they make you write all your essays in blood, your lab partners might shank you if you bring down their grade point averages, and evening classes last all night long. He clearly misses it.

Finally they assign us an order for the meetings. I go sit in Vanderveer's section, in front of the screen that's separating her from the rest of us.

"Oh, man," Sam says. He sits at the very edge of his chair, leaning over to whisper to me. "What am I going to do? They're going to want to talk about colleges."

"Probably," I say, scooting closer. "They're guidance counselors. They're into colleges. They probably *dream* of colleges"

"Yeah, well, they think I want to go to MIT and major in chemistry." He says this in a tragic whisper.

"You can just tell them that you don't. If you don't."

He groans. "They'll tell my parents."

"Well, what *is* your plan?" I ask.

"Going to one of the schools that specializes in visual effects. Gnomon or Academy of Art University in San Francisco. Look, I love doing the makeup and practical effects, but most stuff today is done on a computer. I need more practice on the digital end. I already started working on my applications." Sam runs his hand through his short hair, over his damp forehead, like he's making a confession. "I guess I better ask about loans too."

"Cassel Sharpe," Ms. Vanderveer says, and I stand.

"You'll be fine," I say to him, and head behind the screen. His nervousness seems to be contagious, though. I can feel my palms sweat.

Vanderveer has short black hair and wrinkly skin covered in age spots. There are two chairs arranged in front of a little table where my folder is sitting. She plops herself into one. "So, Cassel," she says with false cheerfulness. "What do you want to do with your life?"

"Uh," I say. "Not really sure." The only things I am good at are the kinds of things colleges don't let you major in. Con artistry. Forgery. Assassination. A little bit of lock-picking.

"Let's consider universities, then. Last year I talked about you choosing some schools you'd really like to try for, and then some safety schools. Have you made that list?"

"Not a formal, written-down one," I say.

She frowns. "Did you manage to visit any of the campuses you are considering?"

I shake my head. She sighs. "Wallingford Preparatory takes great pride in seeing our students placed into the world's top schools. Our students go on to Harvard, Oxford, Yale, Caltech, Johns Hopkins. Now, your grades aren't all we might hope for, but your SAT scores were very promising."

I nod my head. I think of Barron dropping out of Princeton, about Philip dropping out of high school to take his marks and work for the Zacharovs. I don't want to wind up like them. "I'll start that list," I promise her.

"You do that," she says. "I want to see you again in a week. No more excuses. The future's going to be here sooner than you think."

When I walk out from behind the divider, Sam isn't there. I guess that he's having his conference. I wait a few minutes and eat three butterscotch cookies they have put out as refreshments. When Sam still doesn't emerge, I stroll back across campus.

The first night in the dorms is always strange. The cots are uncomfortable. My legs are too long for them and I keep falling asleep curled up, then straightening in the night and waking myself when my feet kick the frame.

One door over, someone is snoring.

Outside our window the grass of the quad shines in the moonlight, like it's made of metal blades. That's the last thing I think before I wake up to my phone shrilling the morning alarm. From a look at the time, it seems like the alarm has been ringing for a while.

I grunt and throw my pillow at my sleeping roommate. He raises his head groggily.

Sam and I shuffle to the shared bathroom, where the rest of the hall are brushing their teeth or finishing their showers. Sam splashes his face with water.

Chaiyawat Terweil wraps a towel around himself and grabs a pair of disposable plastic gloves from the dispenser. Above it, the sign reads: PROTECT YOUR CLASSMATES: COVER YOUR HANDS.

"Another day at Wallingford," Sam announces. "Every

dorm room a palace, every sloppy joe a feast, every morning shower—"

"You enjoy your showers a lot, do you?" Kyle Henderson asks. He's already dressed, smoothing gel into his hair. "Think about me while you're in there?"

"It does make a shower go faster," Sam says, undaunted. "God, I love the Wall!"

I laugh. Someone whips a towel at Sam.

By the time I'm clean and dressed, I don't really have enough time for breakfast. I drink some of the coffee our hall master has brewed for himself in the common room, and eat raw one of the Pop Tarts Sam's mother sent.

Sam gives me a dark look and eats the other.

"We're off to a good start," I say. "Fashionably late."

"Just doing our part to keep their expectations low," says Sam.

Despite having spent the whole summer going to bed around this time in the morning, I feel pretty good.

My schedule says that my first class today is Probability & Statistics. This semester I also have Developing World Ethics (I thought Daneca would be pleased I chose that for my history requirement, which is why I haven't told her), English, Physics, Ceramics 2 (laugh if you must), French 4, and Photoshop.

I am studying the slip of paper as I head out of Smythe House and walk into the Finke Academic Center. Probability & Statistics is on the third floor, so I make for the stairs.

Lila Zacharov is walking through the hallway in the Wallingford girl's uniform: jacket, pleated skirt, and white oxford shirt. Her short blond hair shines like the woven gold of the crest. When she sees me, the expression on her face is some kind of mingled hope and horror.

I can't even imagine my own face. "Lila?" I say.

She turns away, head down.

In a few quick steps I've grabbed hold of her arm, like I'm afraid she's not real. She freezes at the touch of my gloved hand.

"What are you doing here?" I ask, turning her roughly toward me, which is maybe not an okay way to behave, but I'm too astonished to think straight.

She looks like I slapped her.

Good job, me. I'm a real charmer.

"I knew you'd be mad," she says. Her face is pale and drawn, all her usual ruthlessness washed from it.

"It's not about that," I say. But for the life of me, in that moment, I have no idea what it *is* about. I know she's not supposed to be here. And I know I don't want her to leave.

"I can't help—," she says, and her voice breaks. Her face is full of despair. "I tried to stop thinking about you, Cassel. I tried all summer long. I almost came to see you a hundred times. I would sink my nails into my skin until I could stay away."

I remember sitting on the steps in my mother's house last March, begging Lila to believe she'd been worked. I remember the slow way the horror spread over her features. I remember her denials, her final defeated agreement that we shouldn't see each other until the curse ended. I remember everything.

Lila's a dream worker. I hope that means she's sleeping better than I am.

"But if you're here—," I start, not sure how I can finish.

"It hurts not to be near you," she says quietly, carefully, like the words cost her something. "You have no idea how much."

I want to tell her that I have some idea what it feels like to love someone I can't have. But maybe I don't. Maybe being in love with me really is worse than I can imagine.

"I couldn't keep—I wasn't strong enough." Her eyes are wet and her mouth is slightly parted.

"It's been almost six months. Don't you feel any different?" The curse should have begun to fade, surely.

"Worse," she says. *"I feel worse.* What if this never stops?"

"It will. Soon. We have to wait this thing out, and it's better if—," I start, but it's hard to concentrate on the words with her looking at me like that.

"You liked me before," she says. "And I liked you. I *loved* you, Cassel. Before the curse. I always loved you. And I don't mind—"

There is nothing I want more than to believe her. But I can't. I don't.

I knew this conversation would happen, eventually. No matter how much I tried to avoid it. And I know what I have to say. I even planned it out, knowing that otherwise I couldn't say the words. "I didn't love you, though. And I still don't."

The change is immediate and terrible. She pulls back from me. Her face looks pale and shuttered. "But that night in your room. You told me that you missed me and that you—"

"I'm not *crazy*," I say, trying to keep my tells to a minimum. She's known a lot of liars. "I said whatever I thought would make you sleep with me."

She takes a quick, sharp breath of air. "That hurts," she says. "You're just saying it to hurt me."

It's not supposed to hurt. It's supposed to disgust her. "Believe what you want, but it's the truth."

"So why didn't you?" she asks. "Why don't you? If all you wanted was some ass, it's not like I'm going to say no. I can't say no to you."

The bell rings somewhere, distantly.

"I'm sorry," I say, which isn't part of the script. It slips out. I don't know how to deal with this. I know how to be the witness to her grief. I don't know how to be this kind of villain.

"I don't need your pity." Dots of hectic color have appeared on her cheeks, like she's running a fever. "I'm waiting the curse out at Wallingford. If I'd told my dad what your mother did, she'd be dead by now. Don't forget it."

"And me with her," I say.

"Yeah," she says. "And you with her. So get used to the idea that I'm staying."

"I can't stop you," I say quietly as she turns away from me and heads for the stairs. I watch the way the shadows move down her back. Then I slump against the wall.

I'm late for class, of course, but Dr. Kellerman only raises his bushy eyebrows as I slink in. I missed the morning announcements on the television suspended over the blackboard. Members of the AV club would have explained what lunch was going to be and when after-school clubs were meeting. Not exactly thrilling stuff.

Still, I'm glad Kellerman decides not to give me a hard time. I'm not sure I could take it.

He resumes explaining how to calculate odds—something I am pretty good at, being a bookie and all—while I concentrate on trying to stop my hands from shaking.

When the intercom on the wall crackles to life, I barely notice it. That is, until I hear Ms. Logan's voice: "Please send Cassel Sharpe to the headmistress's office. Please send Cassel Sharpe to the headmistress's office."

Dr. Kellerman frowns at me as I stand up and gather my books.

"Oh, *come on*," I say ineffectually to the room.

A girl giggles.

One thing's in my favor, though. Someone just lost the first bet of the year.

HEADMISTRESS NORTHCUTT'S

office looks like a library in a baronial hunting lodge. The walls and built-in bookcases are polished dark wood and lit by brass lamps. Her desk is the size of a bed and is made of the same wood as the walls, with green leather chairs resting in front of it, and degrees hanging behind it. The whole thing is designed to be intimidating to students and reassuring to parents.

When I'm shown in, I see Northcutt is the one that looks uncomfortable. Two men in suits are standing beside her, clearly waiting for me. One has dark sunglasses on.

I check for bulges under their arms or against their calves. Doesn't matter how custom the suit is, the fabric pulls a little over most guns. Yeah, they're carrying. Then I look at their shoes.

Black and shiny as fresh-poured tar, with rubbery flexible soles. Made for running after people like me.

Cops. They're cops.

Man, I am so screwed.

"Mr. Sharpe," Northcutt says. "These men would like to have a conversation with you."

"Okay," I say slowly. "About what?"

"Mr. Sharpe," says the white cop, echoing Northcutt. "I'm Agent Jones, and this is Agent Hunt."

The guy in sunglasses nods once in my direction.

Feds, eh? Well, federal agents are still cops to me.

"We understand that we're interrupting your school day, but I'm afraid what we have to talk about is sensitive enough that we can't discuss it here, so—"

"Wait a moment," Northcutt interrupts. "You cannot take this student off campus. He's underage."

"We can," says Agent Hunt. He's got a slight accent. Southern.

Northcutt flushes when she realizes he's not going to say more than that. "If you walk out of here with that boy, I will contact our lawyer immediately."

"Please do," Agent Hunt says. "I'd be happy to talk with him."

"You haven't even told me what this is about," she says in an exasperated tone.

"I'm afraid that's classified," says Agent Jones. "But it has to do with an ongoing investigation."

"I don't suppose *I* have a choice?" I ask.

Neither agent even bothers to answer. With a slight pressure against my back, Agent Jones steers me out of the room, while Agent Hunt gives Northcutt his card, just in case she wants to follow up with that lawyer.

I see her face as we leave. Northcutt's not calling anyone.

Someone should warn her never to play poker.

They bundle me into the backseat of a black Buick with dark tinted windows. My mind is running through all the bad things this could be about. Clyde Austin's credit card and my hot laptop come to mind. Plus there's all the hotel employees who let us slide. And God only knows what else Mom has done.

I wonder if the Feds would believe that Austin assaulted me, although the bump on my head is nearly gone. I wonder if there's a way to convince them I'm the one who's responsible for whatever crimes we're talking about. I'm still underage. At seventeen I'd probably get sentenced like a kid. Most of all, I wonder what I can give up that will make them leave my mother alone.

"So," I say experimentally. "Where are we going?"

Agent Hunt turns to me, but with his sunglasses on it's impossible to read his expression. "We have some confidential materials to share with you, so we're taking you to our resident agency in Trenton."

"Am I under arrest?"

He laughs. "No. We're just having a little chat. That's all."

I glance at the doors. It's hard to tell if I could flip the lock myself and jump. Trenton's a big enough city for traffic. Stop and go. Red lights. They can't take the highway straight to the building. If I could get the door open, I could probably run for it. Use my phone. Warn someone. Grandad, probably. He'd know what to do.

I shift closer to the door and snake my fingers toward the lock. I press the window button instead. Nothing happens.

"Do you want the air turned up?" Agent Jones asks, amusement in his voice.

"It's stuffy in here," I say, defeated. If the window controls don't work, there's no way a lock will.

I watch the scrubby landscape slide by until we come to the bridge. TRENTON MAKES, THE WORLD TAKES, it says in big block letters. Then we go over it. We take a couple of turns and park behind an innocuous office building. We go in the back way, one of agents standing on either side of me.

The hallway is tan-carpeted and sterile. All the doors have keypads above the locks. Otherwise it looks like a dentist might rent space here. I don't know what I was expecting, but not this.

We go into an elevator and come out on the fourth floor. The carpet is the same.

Agent Jones punches in a code and twists the doorknob. The con artist part of my brain thinks that I should be memorizing numbers, but I'm not that good. His finger is a blur of movement, and all I get is that he might have hit the number seven once.

We go into a windowless room with a cheap table and

five chairs. There's an empty coffeepot on a sideboard and a mirror—probably two-way—on the wall.

"You've got to be kidding," I say, nodding toward the mirror. "I watch television, you know."

"Hold on," says Agent Hunt. He goes out, and a moment later the lights go on in the other room, turning the mirror to tinted glass. The room beyond the mirror is empty.

Agent Hunt comes back. "See?" he says. "It's just the three of us."

I wonder if he's counting anyone listening to us via whatever recording devices are in the room, but I decide not to push my luck. I want to know what's going on.

"Okay," I say. "You got me out of class. I appreciate that. What can I do in return?"

"You're a character," Agent Jones says, shaking his head.

I study him as best I can, while trying to look bored. Jones is built like a barrel—short and solid, with thinning light brown hair the color of bread. There's a scar at the edge of his narrow upper lip. He smells like aftershave and stale coffee.

Agent Hunt leans in. "You know, most innocent people get upset when they get picked up by the Feds. They demand to see their lawyer, tell us that we're violating their civil liberties. Only criminals are calm like you."

Hunt is longer and leaner than Jones. He's older, too, his short-cropped hair dusted with gray. When he speaks, his voice has the cadences of someone used to speaking to a congregation. I'd bet there's a preacher somewhere in his family.

"Psychologists say that's because subconsciously criminals want to get caught," Agent Jones says. "What do you think about that, Cassel? Do you want to get caught?"

"Sounds like someone's been reading too much Dostoyevsky." I shrug.

Agent Hunt's lip curls a little. "Is that what they teach you at that private school of yours?"

"Yeah," I say. "That's what they teach me." Hunt's contempt is so obvious that I add a mental note about him to my imaginary profile: *He thinks I have it easy, which means he thinks he had it hard.*

"Look, kid," Agent Jones says, clearing his throat. "It's no picnic, leading a double life. We know about your family. And we know you're a worker."

I freeze, my whole body going stiff and still. I feel like my blood just turned to ice.

"I'm not a worker," I say. I have no idea how convincing I sound. I can feel my speeding heartbeat all the way to my skull.

Agent Hunt opens the folder on the table and pulls out a couple of sheets of paper. They look familiar. It takes me a moment to realize they're exactly like the papers I swiped from the sleep clinic, except these have my name across the top. I am looking at my own test results.

"Dr. Churchill sent these to one of our contacts after you ran out of his office," Agent Jones says. "You tested positive. You're hyperbathygammic, kid. But don't tell me you didn't know that already."

"There wasn't enough time," I say numbly. I think of

how I ripped all of the electrodes off my skin after I figured out what the test was for, how I ran out of the office.

"Apparently," says Agent Hunt, understanding me perfectly, "there was."

Mercifully, after that they offer to get me some food. They leave me alone in a locked room with a piece of paper charting my gamma waves. It means nothing to me, except that I am well and truly screwed.

I take out my cell phone and flip it open before I realize that this is probably exactly what they hope I will do. Call someone. Reveal something. The room is definitely wired; it's set up for interrogation, whether they're using the two-way mirror or not.

There are probably hidden cameras, too, now that I think of it.

I flip through the functions on my phone until I get to the one that lets me take pictures. I turn on the flash, aim at the walls and ceiling, and take picture after picture until I get it. A reflection. Pretty invisible when I was just looking at the frame of the mirror, but the tiny lens glows brightly with reflected light, captured in the photo.

I grin and pop a stick of gum into my mouth.

Three chews and it's soft enough to stick over the camera.

Agent Hunt comes in about five seconds later. He's holding two cups of coffee, and he's obviously been rushing. The cuff of his shirt is wet and stained with sloshed liquid. I bet he burned his hand too.

I wonder what he thought I was going to do, once I

was hidden from the camera. Try to escape? I have no idea how to get out of the locked room; I was just showing off. Letting them know I wasn't going to fall for the really obvious stuff.

"Do you think this is a joke, Mr. Sharpe?" he demands.

His panic doesn't make any sense. "Let me out of here," I say. "You said I'm not under arrest, and I'm missing ceramics class."

"You're going to need a parent or guardian to pick you up," he says, placing the coffees on the table. He's no longer flustered, which means they planned for me to ask to be let go. He's back to a script he knows. "We can certainly get your mother to come down and get you, if that's really what you want."

"No," I say, realizing I've been outmaneuvered. "That's okay."

Now Agent Hunt just looks smug, wiping his sleeve with a napkin. "I thought you'd see it my way."

I pick up one of the coffees and take a sip. "And you didn't even have to spell your threat out. Honestly, I must be some kind of model prisoner."

"Listen, smart-ass—"

"What do you want?" I ask. "What is all of this for? Fine, okay, I'm a worker. So what? You've got no proof that I've ever worked anyone. I'm not a criminal until I do, and I'm not gonna." It's a relief to tell a lie this big; I feel like I'm daring them to contradict it.

Agent Hunt doesn't look happy, but he doesn't seem suspicious, either. "We need your help, Cassel."

I choke on the coffee.

Agent Hunt is about to say something else when the door opens and Agent Jones comes in. I have no idea what he's been doing all this time, but the lunch they promised is nowhere in sight.

"I hear you've been a handful," Agent Jones says. Either he was watching the camera feed or someone told him about my little trick, because he glances over at the gum.

I try to stop coughing. It's hard. I think some of the coffee went down the wrong pipe.

"Listen, Cassel, there's lots of kids like you," Agent Hunt says. "Worker kids who fall in with the wrong element. But your abilities don't have to lead you in that direction. The government has a program to train young workers to control their talents and to use them in the cause of justice. We'd be happy to recommend you."

"You don't even know what my talents are," I say. I really, really hope that's true.

"We employ all different types of workers, Cassel," says Agent Jones.

"Even death workers?" I ask.

Agent Jones regards me closely. "Is that what you are? Because it would be very serious if it were true. That's a dangerous ability."

"I didn't say that," I say, hoping that I sound unconvincing. I don't care if they think I'm a death worker like my grandfather. I don't care if they think I'm a luck worker like Zacharov, a dream worker like Lila, a physical worker like Philip, a memory worker like Barron, or an emotion worker like Mom. So long as they don't guess that I'm a transformation worker. There hasn't been one in the United States since the 1960s, and I am sure that if the government happened to stumble on one now, they wouldn't just let him go back to high school.

"This program," Agent Jones goes on. "It's run by a woman—Agent Yulikova. We'd like you to meet her."

"What does that have to do with you needing my help?" I ask.

This whole setup feels like a con. The way they're acting, the grim glances they share when they think I don't notice. I'm sure their generous offer to let me be part of some secret government training program is part of the shakedown, what I'm not sure about is why they're shaking *me* down.

"I know you have some familiarity with the Zacharov crime family, so there's no point in denying it," Agent Jones begins, holding up his hand when I start to speak. "You don't need to confirm it either. But you should know that over the past three years, Zacharov's been stepping up assassinations both in and out of his organization. Mostly we don't get too worked up about mobsters killing one another, but one of our informants was the most recent target."

A creeping dread chills my skin as he puts a black-and-white photograph down on the table in front of me.

The man in the photo has been shot several times in the chest, and his shirt is a mess of black. He's lying on his side. Blood has soaked into the carpet underneath him, and his loose hair partially obscures his face. Still, it's a face I would know anywhere.

"He was shot sometime last night," says Agent Hunt. "The first bullet penetrated between the seventh and eight ribs and entered his right atrium. He died instantly."

I feel like someone punched me in the gut.

I push the picture back toward Agent Jones. "What are you showing me this for?" My voice shakes. "That's not Philip. That's not my brother."

I'm standing, but I don't even remember getting up.

"Calm down," Agent Hunt says.

There is a roaring in my ears like a tide coming in. "This is some kind of trick," I shout. "Admit it. Admit that this is a trick."

"Cassel, you have to listen to us," Agent Jones says. "The person who did this is still out there. You can help us find your brother's killer."

"You've just been sitting here chatting with me, and my brother's *dead*? You knew my brother was dead and you just let me—you let me . . . ," I stammer. "No. No. Why would you do that?"

"We knew it would be hard to talk with you after you found out," Agent Jones says.

"Hard to talk to me?" I echo, because the words don't make sense. And then something else strikes me, something that doesn't make sense either. "Philip was your informant? He would never do that. He hates snitches."

Hated. Hated snitches.

In my family going to the cops is cowardly, despicable.

Cops already can do whatever they want to workers—
we're criminals, after all—so going to the cops is kissing
the ass of the enemy. If you turn someone in, you're not
just betraying the people around you. You're betraying
what you are. I remember Philip talking about someone in
Carney who'd reported on somebody else for some petty
reason—old guys I didn't know. He spat on the floor whenever he said the man's name.

"Your brother came to us about five months ago,"
Agent Hunt says. "April of this year. Said he wanted to
change his life."

I shake my head, denying what has to be true. Philip
must have gone to the Feds because he had nowhere else
to go. Because of me. Because I thwarted his plan to assas-
sinate Zacharov, a plan that would have resulted in Philip's
closest friend leading the crime family. A plan that would
have gotten my brother riches and glory. Instead I got him
killed; if Philip is dead, Zacharov must be behind it. I can't
think of anyone else with a reason. And what would Zacharov care about his promise to leave my family alone, especially if he was faced with the discovery that Philip made a
deal with the Feds? I was an idiot for believing Zacharov's
word was worth anything.

"Does my mother know about Philip?" I finally manage,
throwing myself back down into a chair. I feel like I could
suffocate on guilt.

"We've managed to keep it quiet," Agent Jones says. "As
soon as you leave here, she'll get the call. And we won't be
much longer. Try to hang in there."

"There's a kitten poster like that." My voice doesn't sound like my own.

They both look at me oddly.

I feel suddenly so overwhelmingly tired that I want to put my head down right there on the table.

Agent Jones goes on. "Your brother wanted to get out of organized crime. All he needed from us was to get a hold of his wife so he could apologize for what he put her through. We were going to send them into witness protection together. As soon as we got them into the program, he said that he'd give up everything he had on Zacharov's hatchet man. Maybe bring down Zacharov along with him. The guy's real bad news. Philip gave us the names of six workers this sicko killed. We didn't even know for sure they were dead, but Philip was going to lead us to the bodies. Your brother really was trying to turn over a new leaf, and he died for it."

I feel like they're talking about a stranger.

"You find Maura?" I ask.

Maura lit out of town last spring, their kid in tow, once she discovered that Barron had been changing her memories. He'd made her forget every fight she'd had with Philip and remember only some kind of sweet dreamlike relationship. But not remembering their problems didn't stop those problems from cropping up again and again. Plus, being worked that often results in bad side effects, like hearing music that's not there.

Philip was devastated when she left. He blamed me more than Barron, which I don't think is entirely fair, although I guess in the end I gave her the charm that let her realize what was going on. Still, I refuse to feel guilty about breaking up his marriage.

I've got enough to feel guilty about already.

Agent Jones nods. "We talked to her today. She's in Arkansas. We contacted her for the first time about a week ago, and she agreed to hear your brother out; first step was gonna be getting them on the phone together. Now she says she won't come back, not even to claim the body."

"What do you want me to do?" I ask. I just want this to be over.

"Philip told us enough that we think you have access to information. Information we need," says Agent Hunt. "You know some of the same people that he did—and you have connections to the Zacharov family that he never had."

He means Lila. I'm almost sure of it.

"That's not—," I start, but Jones cuts me off.

"We've been hearing about Zacharov making people disappear for years. Just poof! Nothing. No body. No evidence. We still don't know how he—or his wetworks guy—did it. Please, just look at some of the cases. See if there's something familiar. Ask around. Your brother was our first big break. Now he's dead." Jones shakes his head with regret.

I grit my teeth, and after a moment he looks away, like maybe he realizes that was a jackass thing to say. Like maybe, to me, my brother was a human being.

Like maybe if I start looking around, I'll wind up dead too.

"Are you even trying to find who killed Philip?" I ask, since they seem fixated on Zacharov.

"Of course we are," says Agent Jones. "Finding your brother's murderer is our number one priority."

"Any leads on this case are going to point us directly at his killer," Agent Hunt says, standing. "Just to show you we're on the level, I want you to see what we've already got." Reluctantly I follow him out into the hall and then through a door into the observation room behind the mirror. He presses a button on some video equipment.

"This is sensitive material," says Agent Jones, looking at me like he expects me to be impressed. "We're going to need you to be a smart kid and keep this information under wraps."

On a small screen my brother's condo complex comes to life in full color. It's evening, the sun glowing from the edge of the building as it slips below the tops of the trees. I can see the heat shimmer on the asphalt of the driveway. I can't quite see his unit, but I know it's just to the right of the frame.

"The complex put in these surveillance cams recently," Agent Hunt says quietly. "There was a break-in or something. The angle's terrible, but we were able to get this footage from last night."

A figure in a dark coat passes in front of the camera, too close and too fast for the film to register much. There's no glimpse of the face, but a few thin fingers of a leather glove are visible at the hem of a billowing black coat sleeve. The glove is as red as newly spilled blood.

"That's all we have," Agent Hunt says. "Nobody else in or out. It looks like a woman's coat and a woman's glove. If she's Zacharov's regular hatchet guy, shooting isn't her usual method of killing. But lots of death workers turn to nonworker techniques after they lose too many body parts to blowback. That's usually how they trip themselves up. Of course, she could be a new recruit Zacharov sent out blind, just someone to get a job done with no obvious connection to the organization."

"So you've basically got no idea," I say.

"We believe that the person responsible for the murders found out that Philip was going to finger him. Or *her*. When Philip came to us, asking to make a deal, we asked other informants about him. We know he had a falling-out with Zacharov and we know it had something to do with Zacharov's daughter, Lila."

"Lila didn't do this," I say automatically. "Lila's not a death worker."

Jones sits up straighter. "What kind of worker is she?"

"I don't know!" I say, which comes out sounding like the obvious lie that it is. Lila is a dream worker, a really powerful one. Powerful enough to make dreamers sleepwalk out of their own houses. Or dorm rooms.

Hunt shakes his head. "All we know is that the last person to enter Philip's apartment was a woman with red gloves. We need to find her. Let us focus on that. You can help by getting us the information that Philip died trying to impart. Don't let your brother's death be in vain. We are certain those disappearances and your brother's death are linked."

It's very moving, the speech. Like I'm really supposed to believe that Philip's last wish was for me to square him with the Feds. But the vision of the woman entering his apartment haunts me.

Agent Jones holds out some folders. "These are the names your brother gave us—the men he swore were killed and disposed of by Zacharov's guy. Just look the pages over and see if anything jumps out at you. Something you might have overheard, someone you might have seen. Anything. And we'd appreciate it if you didn't show these files to anyone else. It serves both our interests if this meeting never happened."

I stare at the tape where he's paused it, like somehow I should recognize the person. But she's just a blur of cloth and leather.

"The school already knows I went for a ride with you," I say. "Northcutt knows."

Agent Hunt smiles. "We don't think that your headmistress will be a problem."

A terrible thought occurs to me, but I quash it before I can even articulate it to myself. I would never hurt Philip.

"Does this mean I'm working for you?" I ask, forcing myself to smirk.

"Something like that," Agent Jones says. "Do a good job, and we'll recommend you to come aboard with Agent Yulikova. You'll like her."

I doubt that. "What if I don't want to go to this training program?"

"We're not like the Mafia," Agent Hunt says. "You can get out any time you want."

I think of the locked door of the room, the locked car doors. "Yeah, sure."

They drive me to Wallingford, but by the time I am back on campus, classes are half over. I don't bother going to lunch. I head to my room, tuck the folders under my mattress, and wait for the inevitable summons from the hall master.

We're so sorry, he's going to say. *We're so sorry.*

But I'm sorriest of all.

PHILIP'S FACE LOOKS LIKE

it's made of wax. Whatever they did to preserve it for the viewing gives his skin an odd sheen. When I go up to the casket to say my final good-byes, I realize they have painted the visible parts of him with some flesh-colored cosmetic. If I look closely, I can see traces of bloodless skin they missed—behind his ears, and in a stripe above his gloves but below the cuff of his sleeves. He's wearing a suit Mom picked out, along with a black silk tie. I don't recall him wearing either one in life, but they must have come from his closet. His hair has been pulled back into a sleek ponytail. The high collar of his shirt mostly obscures the necklace of keloid scars that mark him as a gangster. Not that there's anyone in this room who doesn't know what his job was.

I kneel in front of his body, but I have no words for Philip. I don't want his forgiveness. I don't forgive him.

"Did they take out his eyes?" I ask Sam when I get back to my seat. The room is filling up fast. Men in dark suits, sipping from breast-pocket flasks; women in black dresses, their shoes as pointed as knives.

Sam looks at me, surprised by the question. "Probably, yeah. They probably use glass." He blanches a little. "And fill the body with disinfecting fluid."

"Oh," I say.

"Dude, I'm sorry. I shouldn't have told you that."

I shake my head. "I asked."

Sam is dressed a lot like Philip. I'm wearing my father's suit, the one that had to be dry-cleaned to get rid of Anton's blood. Morbid, I know. It was that or my school uniform.

Daneca comes up to us, looking like she's masquerading as her mother in a navy sheath and pearls.

"Do I know you?" I ask.

"Oh, shut up," she says automatically. Then, "Sorry, I didn't—"

"Everyone has to stop saying they're sorry," I say, maybe a tiny bit too loudly.

Sam looks around the room in a slightly panicked way. "Uh, I don't know how to tell you this, but *all* these people are going to tell you that. That's, like, pretty much the point of funerals."

The corner of my mouth lifts. Having them around makes everything a little better, even this.

The funeral director comes in with another mountain of flowers, Mom trailing him. She's crying, mascara bleeding down her face theatrically as she points to the spot where he's allowed to put the arrangement. Then, seeing Philip's body for about the tenth time, she lets out a small shriek and half-collapses into a chair, sobbing into her handkerchief. A small group of women rushes over to comfort her.

"Is that your *mother*?" Daneca asks, fascinated.

I'm not sure what to say. Mom's putting on a show, but that doesn't mean she's not actually sad. It's just that she isn't letting her grief get in the way of her performance.

"That's our mom over there, all right," a slightly bored voice says from behind me. "It's kind of a miracle we weren't knocking over drugstores in our diapers."

Daneca jumps like she's been caught shoplifting.

I don't have to turn around. "Hello, Barron."

"Dani, right?" he says, giving Daneca a predatory smile as he takes a seat next to me. I find it a hopeful sign that he actually remembers her—maybe he's been staying away from doing much memory work—but I also am suddenly conscious of the danger I have put Daneca and Sam in just by letting them come here. These people are not safe to be around.

"I'm Sam Yu." Sam extends his hand, leaning over so that he's in front of Daneca.

Barron shakes it. His suit is a lot nicer than mine, and his dark hair is clipped, short and tidy. He looks like the good boy he's never been. "Any friends of my baby brother's are friends of mine."

A minister walks up to the lectern off to one side and

then says a couple of words to my mother. I don't recognize him. Mom's not exactly the religious type, but she hugs him like she's ready to be baptized with the next bowl of water she comes across.

A few moments later she yells loudly enough to be heard clearly above the pumped-in elevator music. I have no idea what set her off. "He was murdered! You tell them that! You put that in your sermon. You tell them there's no justice in the world."

On cue, Zacharov sweeps into the room. He's wearing another of his long black coats, this one draped over the shoulders of his suit. His fake Resurrection Diamond glints at his throat, the pin stabbed into the loop of his tie. His eyes are as hard and cold as the chip of glass.

"I can't believe he had the nerve to come here," I say softly, standing. Barron touches my arm in warning.

Beside Zacharov is Lila. It's the first time I've seen her since our disastrous conversation in the hallway at Wallingford. Her hair is damp with rain and she's all in black except for red lipstick so bright that the rest of her fades away. She's all mouth.

She sees me, and then her gaze goes to Barron. Stone-faced, she takes a seat.

"Someone better tell that daughter of mine to pipe down," Grandad says, pointing at my mother as if we might think he had some other daughter here. "I could hear her all the way to the street." I didn't notice him come in, but he's here, shaking out his umbrella and frowning at Mom. I let out my breath all at once, I'm so relieved.

He tousles my hair like I'm a little kid.

The minister clears his throat at the lectern and every-one slowly moves to sit down. Mom is still moaning. As soon as the minister starts speaking, she begins to wail so loudly that I can't hear most of his sermon.

I wonder what Philip would think of his own funeral. He'd be sad that Maura couldn't even bother to bring his son to see him for the last time. He'd be embarrassed by Mom and probably pissed that I'm even here.

"Philip Sharpe was a soldier in God's army," says the minister. "Now he marches with the angels."

The words echo in my head unpleasantly.

"Philip's brother, Barron, will join me at the lectern and say a few words about his beloved departed sibling."

Barron walks to the front and begins telling a story about him and Philip climbing a mountain together and the various meaningful things they learned about each other along the way. It's touching. It's also completely plagiarized from a book we had when we were kids.

I decide it's time I swipe someone's flask and go sit outside.

I find a good spot on the stairs. Across the hall a different viewing is going on. I can just hear the blur of voices in the room, not quite as loud as Barron's voice. I lean back and look up at the ceiling, at the twinkling lights of the crystal chandelier.

This is the same funeral home where we had my dad's viewing. I remember the mothball smell of it, the overly heavy brocade of the curtains, and the flocked wallpaper. I remember the funeral director who looked the other way when envelopes of ill-gotten cash were quietly passed to the grieving widow. The place is outside of the town of Carney—it's the one that a lot of workers use. After we're done here, we'll go over to the Carney cemetery, where Dad and Grandma Singer are already resting. We'll put some of the flowers on their graves. Maybe we'll see whoever's in the next room there too; curse working has a high mortality rate.

My most vivid memory from Dad's funeral is seeing Aunt Rose for the first time in years. As I stood in front of Dad's casket, I answered her "How are you doing?" with "Good" before I even realized what she meant. It was just what you said to that question, automatic. I remember how her lip curled, though, like I was a terrible son.

I felt like one.

But I was a much better son than I was a brother.

Zacharov walks out of the viewing, carefully closing the door behind him. For a moment Barron's voice swells and I hear the words "we will always remember Philip's unusual balloon animals and his skill with the longbow."

Zacharov has a small smile on his face, and his thick silver eyebrows are raised. "I am learning some very interesting things about your brother."

I stand. Maybe I have nothing good to say about Philip, maybe I have no apologies for him, but there is one thing I can do. The least I can do. I can hit the guy who killed him.

Zacharov must notice the look on my face, because he

holds up both his gloved hands in a gesture of peace. I don't care. I keep coming.

"We had a deal," I say, lifting my fisted hand.

"I didn't murder your brother," he says, stepping back, out of my range. "I came here to pay my respects to your family and to tell you I had nothing to do with this."

I walk toward him. It gives me dark pleasure to watch him flinch.

"Don't," he says. "I had nothing to do with Philip's death, and you'd realize it if you thought about it for more than a minute. You're much more valuable to me than revenge on some underling. And you're not stupid. You are well aware how valuable you are."

"You sure about that?" I ask.

I hear the echo of Philip's words from months back. *You obviously didn't grow out of stupid.*

"Tell me, how is it that your mother isn't accusing me? Not even Barron. Not even your grandfather. Would they let me walk in here if they really thought I was responsible for Philip's death?" I can see a muscle in his jaw jump, he's clenching his teeth so hard. If I hit him right now, his stiffness would make the blow hurt worse. He obviously hasn't been in a fistfight in a long time.

My hand's shaking with violence. I slam it into a vase sitting near the doorway. The vase shatters; thick chunks of pottery, water, and flowers rain on the carpet.

"You're not sorry Philip's dead," I say finally, breathing heavily with raw fury that's only starting to abate. I don't know what to think.

"Neither are you," Zacharov says, his voice steely. "Don't tell me you're not sleeping better at night with him gone."

In that moment I hate Zacharov more than I ever have. "You're doing a really bad job of convincing me not to punch you."

"I want you to come work for me. Really work for me," says Zacharov.

"No deal," I say, but it makes me realize that by losing Philip, Zacharov has lost half his hold over me. More, even, because if I can't trust him to keep his promises, then all his future threats become hollow. If he tells me I've got to do something "or else" and the "or else" happens even if I go along with him, there's not much motivation for me to do what he says. Philip's death cost him leverage, and as I realize that, I start to believe he's actually not responsible. I'm valuable to him; it's not often that a crime lord gets a transformation worker practically dumped into his lap.

Zacharov inclines his head toward a curtained alcove, one where people are supposed to go to hide their weeping. I follow him uncertainly. He sits down on the long bench. I stay standing.

"You're ruthless, and I don't frighten you," he says quietly. "Both these things I like, though I would like it more if the latter was tempered with a little respect. You are the best kind of killer, Cassel Sharpe, the kind that never has blood on his hands. The kind that never has to sicken at the sight of what he's done, or come to like it too much."

I am chilled to the bone.

"Come work for me, Cassel, and you'll have my protection. For your brother. For your mother. For your grand-father, although I consider him one of mine already. My protection and a very comfortable life."

"So you want me to—," I start, but he cuts me off.

"Philip's death shouldn't have happened. If I'd had people in place, watching over him, it wouldn't have happened. Let me look out for you. Let your enemies become mine."

"Yeah, and vice versa. No, thanks." I shake my head. "I don't want to be a killer."

He smiles. "You may turn our colleagues into living things, if that helps you sleep at night. They will be just as effectively removed."

"That's not going to happen," I say, thinking of the white cat watching me with shining eyes.

"It has happened. Maybe Barron made you forget what you did, but now you remember. You proved that when you undid one of your own curses."

"That was *your daughter* whose curse I undid," I say.

Zacharov takes a sharp breath, and then lets it out slow. "It happened, Cassel. You know how to work. And one of these days, you're going to find yourself in a position where it's going to be tempting. And then more than tempting; there's going to be no other way out. Wake up. You're one of us."

"Not yet," I say. "Not quite." Which is about all I can cling to.

"You will think about my offer," he says. "You'll think about it when you realize there are people close to you that you will have to deal with eventually."

"You mean Barron," I say, amazed. "You're a son of a

bitch to imply at one brother's funeral that I would think about killing the other."

Zacharov rises and dusts off his pants. "I'm not the one who thought of him." Then he smiles. "But you're right—I'm a son of a bitch. And someday soon you're going to need me."

Then he goes back in to the service.

Lila finds me. I'm staring at the fabric of the bench, wondering how many people have wept on it. I'm wondering about whether the inside is crusted with salt, like a blanket that's been soaking in seawater. I'm going a little crazy.

"Hey," she says, holding out a cup of coffee, her mouth still bright as blood. "One of Philip's friends is giving the eulogy now. I think he's telling the story of the first time they held up a liquor store."

I take the cup. I think the only thing I've eaten in the past three days has been coffee. I should be bouncing off the walls. Maybe that explains my nearly attacking her father. "You should go back to the viewing. I'm not—I *can't*—" I shake my head to indicate the enormity of the things I can't do. For one, I can't tell her the truth about my feelings for her. For another, I'm not sure I can keep lying.

I want you so much that I would do almost anything to have you.

Please let me not be willing to do what's unforgivable.

"We used to be friends," she says. "Even if there was nothing else."

"We're still friends," I say automatically, because I really want it to be true.

"Well, good, then." She sits down next to me on the bench. "I don't want you to be mad that I'm here. I'm not going to jump you or anything."

I snort. "My virtue is safe, eh? Well, thank goodness for that."

She rolls her eyes.

"No—I understand why you came. It must be good to see him dead." I think of Zacharov's words about sleeping better at night, even if I steadfastly refuse to apply them to myself. "You must feel safer."

She gapes at me like she can't believe I just said those words. "Death doesn't erase someone's flaws." I look at the wall to avoid looking at her. There's a photo of the funeral parlor, tinted sepia. I can't make out the date. I wonder how many generations of workers have been wept over here. "If it did, it would erase him. I don't want that. I want to remember Philip the way he was. I loved him, and he was my brother, and he did terrible things, and sometimes tried to make things better, and all of it matters, and maybe none of it matters too."

"All of it matters," she says, like she's sure.

"I don't know," I say. "But I'm glad you're here. I worried, after everything . . ." *Everything I did to you. Everything my family did.*

She laughs, but not like what I said was funny. "It's hard to be a girl again—a human girl with hands and feet and clothes and school. Hard to talk when I'm out of practice. And sometimes I feel—" She stops herself.

"Yeah?"

"Like—I don't know. This is your brother's funeral. We should be talking about *your* feelings."

I take a long, grateful swallow of the coffee. "Honestly, that's the last thing I want to do."

"I can be very comforting," she says with a small, wicked smile.

"Hey—my virtue, remember? Come on, tell me what you were going to say."

She kicks the wall lightly with one of her shiny black pumps. I can see her big toe through the opening in the front. The nail is painted a deep shining blue. "Okay. Do you ever feel so angry that you think you could devour the whole world and still not be satisfied? Like you don't know how to stop feeling that way and it scares you, but that just makes you angry too?"

"I thought we weren't going to talk about my feelings," I say, trying for lightness, because I know exactly what she means. It's like she was speaking my own thoughts aloud.

She looks at the floor, the corner of her lip tilted up. "I'm not."

"Yeah," I say slowly. "Yeah."

"Some days I just hate everything." She looks at me earnestly.

"Me too," I say. "Especially today. I have all of these questions that will never be answered. Like, was Philip ashamed of using me like he did? Was that why he couldn't look me in the face all those years? But then, when the whole con was over and Anton was dead, it was him who couldn't forgive me. We could have called it even—okay, not really even, but even enough, but it was like he couldn't face anything he'd done and somehow I was the enemy. Like I wasn't even human to him anymore. Like I wasn't his brother. Why?"

I should shut up, but I don't. I guess I wanted to talk about my feelings after all. "And now you. You were the only real friend I had for years. I mean, I had friends at school, but then Mom would mess things up or pull us out of school for some con she was running, or those friends would find out about me being from a family of workers, and that would be that. But you. There was a time when I could tell you anything—and then I thought I killed you, and now when I have you back, I can't—You're—She took—"

Lila leans forward swiftly. Her lips are soft on my cheek.

I close my eyes. Her breath is warm and it would only take the smallest shift of my mouth, just a slight acquiescence, for us to be kissing. Kissing Lila would wash away my grief and pain and guilt. It's all I want in the world.

"You're going to get all the things you think you can't have," she says quietly, reaching out to rub red lipstick from my cheek. "You just don't know it yet."

I sigh at the touch of her glove.

After the eulogies are finished, Grandad steers me toward a black limousine. I slide in, next to my mother, who is already drinking from the minibar. Something brown, out of a heavy-bottomed glass. Barron slides in after me.

We're quiet, riding. I hear the clink of ice cubes, the exhalation of a single ragged breath. I close my eyes.

"I don't know what to do with all of Philip's things,"

Mom says suddenly. "Maura's not coming to get them. We'll have to put it all in his old room at the house."

Grandad groans. "I just cleaned that place out."

"You two better box everything up after the police are finished," Mom says, ignoring Grandad, her voice threatening hysteria. "His son might want them someday."

"His son's not going to want them," Barron says wearily.

"You don't know that." She goes to pour herself more booze from the bar, but the limo hits a bump and the liquor splashes her dress. She starts to cry, not the loud keening from before but quiet sobs that shake her whole body.

I grab some napkins and try to blot the spill. She pushes my hand away.

"You don't know," she says to Barron through her tears. "Look at Cassel. That's his father's suit."

"Yeah, and it's a million years out of style," says Barron. I shrug, playing along.

Grandad grins. "It's going to be all right, Shandra," he says. Mom shakes her head.

"Save the kid from looking like Cassel there," says Barron. "Throw the stuff out. Besides, I got a line on a guy in Princeton looking to buy a painting. I need a roper. We'll buy a dozen silk suits."

Mom sniffs and slugs back the rest of her drink.

The burial takes place in the rain. Barron and I share an umbrella, which means that water constantly streams down the back of my neck. Barron puts his arm over my shoulders and I lean against him for a moment, like he really is my older brother who wants to protect me. The ceremony is subdued, since all the eulogies have been given. My mother's tears appear to be wrung out.

Or maybe even she can't compete with the weather.

After it's over, Lila and her father get into the back of a car, and his bodyguards drive them away. She throws me a small wave as she goes.

The rest of us go to my grandfather's house for the wake. The old women of Carney are out in force, and Grandad's dining room table is groaning under the weight of casseroles, pies, and cold cuts trays.

A middle-aged woman in a black tweed suit is whispering to her friend. The other woman laughs and says, "Oh, no, Pearl! I've been married three times, and I never let any of them see me without *my* gloves, no less take off theirs."

I head for the kitchen.

Mom stops me on the way out of the room. Her eyes are outlined in the gray remainder of her makeup, making them look sunken. Haunted.

"Baby," she says.

"Mom," I say, trying to slide past. I want her away from me. I already feel too much. I can't bear feeling anything more.

"I know that you always looked up to Philip," she says, as though the last six months never happened. As though the last three years never happened. The smell of liquor is strong on her breath. "But we've both got to be strong."

I say nothing. I don't trust myself to speak.

"Barron says I should move in with him. He says he worries about me being alone."

"That's great," I say, and mean it. Maybe he can distract her.

One of the casserole-makers comes in and wants to console Mom. I get out while the getting's good. Sam follows me, looking a little shaken. I don't think he's used to so many criminals displaying their scarred throats in one place. Daneca stays in the dining room, clearly in awe of being in the center of a worker party in one of the best-known worker towns.

I prepare to get blind drunk in the most efficient way possible. Taking a bottle of vodka out of Grandad's liquor cabinet, I grab three shot glasses from the kitchen and automatically head to the basement.

The basement is just like I remember it from all the summers I spent here. Cool and damp, with a slight smell of mildew. I flop down onto the leather couch in front of the television.

I set up the glasses on the coffee table, pour a shot into each one, and grimly down the whole line.

I feel better, but also worse here. Better because the memories are so close. Worse because of the memories themselves.

"Oh," I say, looking over at Sam. "I should have gotten another glass for you."

He lifts his eyebrow and picks up one of mine. "How about I just take this one at the end."

"Lila and I used to come down here a lot. Watch movies," I say, waving vaguely toward the set.

Philip and Barron and I spent a lot of time in this room too. I remember lying on the floor and playing Battleship with Philip, laughing so hard I was afraid I was going to piss my pants. I remember a teenage Anton and Philip forbidding us to come into the room while they had on a horror movie. Barron and I sat on the stairs instead, not technically in the room, watching from the dark so we wouldn't get in trouble, utterly terrified.

I pour myself two more shots. Grudgingly I pour one for Sam, too.

"What's going on with you and Lila?" he asks. "I thought you liked her—you know, last year, when we pulled the thing. But you've been avoiding her since she started at Wallingford."

Self-revulsion lets me gulp down the booze without wincing.

"I don't want to talk about that," I say, shaking my head. "Not here. Not tonight."

"Okay," says Sam, with a false reasonableness in his voice. "What do you want to talk about?"

"My new career," I say. "I am going to help the Feds catch my brother's killer. It's going to be just like *Band of the Banned*."

"No one watches that show," Sam says. "No one under fifty."

Someone is coming down the stairs. I pour another round of drinks in case the newcomer is planning on stealing my booze. In this crowd one can't be too safe.

"A wonderful piece of cinema verité," I declare. "It is going to be my new life. And I am going to get a badge and a gun and hunt down evildoers." I am flooded with a sense of well-being. Everything sounds perfect. Like a dream I don't want to wake from.

"Did you just say 'evildoers'?" Daneca asks, flopping onto the couch next to us. "Did you know Betty the Butcher is upstairs? And she's wearing a gold mask. That means it's got to be true! Killing her last husband must have rotted her nose off."

I point to the shots I have lined up. She takes one. I feel quite magnanimous. Also kind of light-headed. "That's what I plan on calling them when I apprehend them. Evil-doers, that is, not Betty. I would call only Betty by the name Betty. Well, I call her Aunt Betty, but still."

"I'm not really sure," Sam tells Daneca, "but I believe our drunk friend here is claiming that he was approached by federal agents."

"They gave me files," I say delightedly.

"You really do have all the luck," says Daneca.

We sit in the basement, drinking steadily until I pass out on the old leather couch in front of the television. The last thing I remember is blurrily noticing Sam and Daneca kissing on the floor. I want to get a glass of water, but I don't want to disturb them, so I stay where I am and close my eyes as tightly as they will go.

When I wake up, Sam and Daneca are curled up together on the rug under an afghan. I go to the kitchen, sticking my head under the sink and guzzling as much water as I can get down.

Out the window I can see by the light cast from the kitchen that it has stopped raining. I can also see Grandad sitting on a lawn chair, a beer in hand, looking at the dark expanse of his muddy backyard and ramshackle shed. I still feel a little tipsy.

I let the screen door slam behind me as I join him. He barely even looks up.

"Hey," I say as I fumble to unfold another chair.

"You look a little worse for wear," Grandad says, pulling out a pipe from his pocket and packing it with tobacco. "Better sit down before you fall down."

I sit unsteadily. The chair creaks. "Since when do you smoke a pipe?"

"I don't," he says, lighting a match and touching it to the tobacco. "Quit years ago, after Shandra was born."

"Right," I say. "Silly me."

"We couldn't have kids, me and your grandmother. Mary kept having miscarriages. She really took it hard—went on bed rest as soon as she thought she might be pregnant. The doctors said we had the Rh factor, but I kept thinking that it was really because of my death work. I thought maybe the blowback made it so I couldn't make healthy babies. Could be superstition, but when I stopped killing people with curses, your mother got born."

"I didn't think you were allowed to quit that kind of job," I say.

"The Zacharovs wouldn't have let me stop being a killer, but no one gets to tell me how to kill." Sweet smoke rises from his pipe. "A man's got to be an expert at his own trade."

"Ah," I say. Even though I saw him kill Anton, it's still hard to think of my grandfather as really dangerous. But I have to remember that he was already an assassin when Lila's scary dad was still a boy.

"Magic gives you a lot of choices," Grandad says. "Most of them are bad."

He takes another sip of his beer.

393

I wonder if that's my future. Bad choices. It certainly feels a lot like my present.

"If I'd done things different," Grandad goes on, "maybe your brother would be alive right now. Me and Mary spoiled your mother rotten, but I didn't keep her out of the life the way I should've. We thought that because she never officially joined up with one of the families, that meant you kids would have a chance at another kind of life, but then I let you all come down here in the summers. I wanted to see my grandkids."

"We wanted to see you, too," I say. My voice sounds a little slurred. For a moment, I miss being a kid with a painful intensity. I miss my dad being alive. I miss running around on Grandad's lawn under the sprinkler.

"I know." He claps his hand against my shoulder. "But I didn't keep you three out of the life either. I guess I thought that even though I was leading the horse directly to the water, it didn't mean I was making it drink."

I shake my head. "We were *born* into the life. Just like every other curse worker kid in the world. You couldn't have kept us out if you tried."

"Philip's dead at twenty-three. And I'm still around. That's not right." He shakes his head.

I have nothing to say to that, except that if I had to pick him or Philip, the choice would be easy. I'd take him any day. Since I know he doesn't want to hear that, I take a sip of Grandad's beer and join him in contemplating the muddy lawn and fading stars.

I WAKE UP SUNDAY MORNING

with a pounding headache and a mouth that tastes of death.
I get up out of the lawn chair in the chill sunlight. Grandad's
not there. When I head to the basement, I see that Daneca
and Sam are gone too, but at least they've left a note:

SEE YOU BACK AT WALLINGFORD.
—S & D

I stumble back upstairs and realize that for some people
the wake is still going on. The dining table is in bad shape,
hunks of macaroni and cheese oozing onto the tablecloth,
mingling hideously with blueberry pie filling. Bottles and

cans litter all surfaces. I see Barron in the living room, his arm around an elderly lady I don't know. She's telling him about how back in her day, if you really wanted to make money, you went into opium. Clearly she doesn't know that today all you need for meth is a hotel coffeepot, but I'm not going to be the one to tell her.

Grandad is asleep in his recliner, the steady rise and fall of his chest an indicator that he's okay.

A few other people are sitting around, mostly young mobsters still in their rumpled suits, collars loose enough to show their neck scars. When I pass, I hear them talking about a big job involving a bank, thirty feet of rope, and a lot of WD-40. They are red-eyed and laughing.

I go into the guest bedroom and find my mother sitting in front of a television, watching the soap opera channel. "Oh, honey," she says when she sees me. "I never met those friends of yours. They seemed really nice."

"Yeah," I say.

She studies me for a long moment. "You look terrible. When's the last time you ate?"

I lean my head against the wall, arching my neck. "I have a hangover."

"There's aspirin in the bathroom, but it'll tear up your stomach if there's nothing in it. You should eat."

"I know," I say. She's right.

I get into my car and drive to a diner I remember from the summers when Philip, Barron, and I lived with Grandad. The waitress doesn't seem to be bothered by my wrinkled day-old suit or by the fact that I eat two breakfasts, one right after the other. I cut the eggs and watch the yolk run across my plate in a yellow tide. Then I pepper the mess and sop it up with rye toast. By the time I get through a pot of coffee, my head stops hurting.

I leave some bills on the table and head for school. The steering wheel of my car has been warmed by the sun, and as I cruise along the highway, I roll down my windows to drink in the last rain-soaked breath of summer.

What I don't expect is to walk into the dorm and find Daneca and Sam with a two-liter bottle of Mountain Dew and all of the files the Feds gave me spread out across various surfaces of my room. I freeze with my hand on the door frame.

For a moment all I can feel is blind, unreasoning rage. Those papers are *mine*.

"Oh, hey," Daneca says, looking up from the floor, where she's sitting with her back braced against my bed. She's looking pretty casual for someone who is courting a demerit just for being in here. She grins. "Nice look. I can't believe you were telling the truth about the Feds."

"That's because after Barron's eulogy, you have all new trust issues regarding my family," I say, as casually as I can manage. I take off my jacket and throw it onto the bed. Then I roll up my shirtsleeves. That's about as together as I can get myself without a shower and a change of clothes. "And now I have all new trust issues with you. What exactly do you think you're doing?"

"Wait, you're saying that thing Barron told us about

the Himalayas and saving that goat wasn't true?" Sam asks. He's got on a black T-shirt and jeans. His hair's still wet.

I am almost one hundred percent sure he's messing with me.

I roll my eyes. "Anyway, just because I said I had files—during a period, I will remind you, when I was severely compromised by drink and grief—doesn't mean I gave you permission to read them."

"Evildoers don't care about rules," Daneca says, and then has to snicker for a while.

"Oh, come on," Sam says. "You hid them under the mattress. That's like *begging* for someone to find them."

I have a bad feeling that Sam is quoting something I said back at me. I groan and slump into my desk chair, then realize I am sitting on a stack of papers. I pull them out from under me.

"So, what are we looking at?" I ask them, peering at what I'm holding. There are pictures clipped to the files, a bunch of tough-looking guys clearly getting their picture taken because they were busted for something. And then, candid shots of those same guys drinking coffee in cafés or reading the paper on the balcony of a hotel, a woman in a bathing suit beside them. Surveillance shots.

"There are six victims here," Daneca says. "All workers."

"All dudes," puts in Sam.

Daneca stretches, grabbing one of the pages. "Giovanni 'Scars' Basso. He's in the real—and fake—amulet trade. Was apparently shorting some people money. As far as the Feds know, he didn't work directly for Zacharov. Probably did deals with a bunch of the families. No body. No nothing. One night he was just gone."

"So we don't even know that he didn't just skip town," says Sam.

"Yeah," I say. "Maybe they *all* skipped town."

"Together?" Daneca asks Sam. "Like now all six of them are living in a villa in the south of France like in a wacky TV sitcom?"

Sam shakes his head sadly. "Okay. Admittedly, probably not."

Daneca shuffles. "Guy number two—James 'Jimmy' Greco. He ran an illegal gambling operation—Hey, kind of like you, Cassel."

I make a rude gesture halfheartedly. I am sure the federal agents don't want me sharing these files with civilians, especially ones they have no legal reason to harass. Even though I am still annoyed with Daneca and Sam, that knowledge gives me some measure of satisfaction. Anything that pisses off the Feds can't be all bad.

Daneca smiles. "Greco was a luck worker, so no surprises there on his choice of profession. No idea how he crossed Zacharov, since he was a big earner. Then, bam. Taken out. Last seen passed out in a bar in Philadelphia."

It seems easy to imagine that hit. Greco stumbling, carried out on the shoulder of someone claiming to be a friend. Maybe someone who *was* a friend. Tip to the bartender. Killed in the car.

Or the killer was a woman, pretending to be his girlfriend, his wife. Even better. Maybe even a last drink, with a little something to make him sleep. Flash of her red gloves.

Nothing the Feds haven't already considered, I'm sure.

"That brings us to Antanas Kalvis. Ran a pretty high-end call girl service out of Newark along with his wife." Daneca likes playing detective. It's just a game to both of them, a murder mystery with fancy props. At the end you guess it was the butler with the candlestick and turn over a card to find out if you're right.

"They ran it together?" Sam asks.

"When I picture pimps, I picture fur coats, wide lapels, and no fixed address," I say.

"Yeah, because all criminals are like in the movies," Daneca snaps. Maybe she's taking it more seriously than I thought. "Kalvis was an emotion worker. Ugh. That's just so gross. Anyway—"

"You said he was married, right?" I say, interrupting her. "How did he go missing without his wife knowing anything about it?"

She flips over a couple of pages. "Actually, it's really creepy. He disappeared from bed. Like, right next to her. So either that's true or Mrs. Kalvis was in on the hit."

I'm warming to the idea of a murderess. I imagine her posing as one of the call girls—maybe in distress—and arranging an emergency meeting with Kalvis. He slips out of bed without waking his wife.

Or maybe he was sleepwalking. Right into Philip and Anton's waiting arms. Then someone makes the body disappear.

Me.

When the thought comes, it feels so obvious that I can't believe it took me so long to put it together.

"It sounds like the wife was covering up," Daneca says speculatively. "We could start with her. Maybe you know someone who knows someone who could ask—!"

"Cassel? Is something wrong?" Sam scoots to the edge of his bed.

"No," I say, shaking my head. "Let's hear the rest."

"Okay," Daneca says slowly. "Henry 'Trigger' Janssen. Physical worker. Soldier in the Zacharov family. Apparently worked closely with an Anton Abramov. Anton? Is that the Anton who died—"

I nod. "His mother's maiden name was Zacharov."

"Could he have been the killer?" Sam asks. "I mean, not of your brother, obviously."

"So that we're talking about two different people? Yeah, I'm wondering about that too. The Feds think—" I pause, because I don't know if I should tell them that the Feds are looking for a woman with red gloves. And I am sure I shouldn't tell them the Feds probably should be looking for me. "They think the person got sloppy, but I don't know. These other people just disappeared."

"Maybe the FBI have evidence they're not telling you about," Daneca says.

Sam shrugs. "Or maybe they want you to help solve this case and they think if they tell you it had something to do with your brother, you will."

"That's really paranoid," I say admiringly. "I'm going with that."

"You can't seriously think that federal agents would lie in a way that would put you in danger." Daneca seems exasperated with both of us, which seems just as ridiculous to me.

"Yeah, because they are tireless advocates of worker rights," I say with plenty of sarcasm.

"Next up," she says, ignoring my point because she'd have to concede it. "Sean Gowen."

I hold up a hand. "Wait, how did Janssen die?"

"Going home from his mistress's house, apparently. She says he left in the middle of the night and she figured he went home to his wife, which pissed her off, until she found out he was dead. Or, well, *gone*. No body."

An involuntary shudder runs through me, like someone's walking over my grave.

Middle of the night again. No body.

Lila told me how Barron and Philip sent her into houses as a cat. She could make anyone she'd given the touch to sleepwalk right out into my waiting arms. Then, although I can't remember it, I transformed them. We must have been a hell of a team.

No bodies.

"Back to Sean Gowen," Daneca says. "Gowen was a loan shark and a luck worker. That's weird. He disappeared in the early afternoon. All the others—"

"He worked nights," I say.

"What?" Sam says. "Did you know him or something?"

I shake my head. "It's just a guess. Did he?" I want very badly to be wrong.

That prompts a hunt through the strewn files. Finally Sam holds one up. "Yeah, I guess so. Or at least he usually got home around four in the morning, which is pretty much the same thing."

He was asleep. The one thing they all had in common.

"Do you have a theory or something?" Daneca asks.

I shake my head. "Not yet," I say, lying through my teeth. I've told Daneca and Sam more about me than I've ever told anyone else, but I can't tell them this. I think I did it. I'm the killer. I grip my knees to keep my hands from shaking.

No wonder Zacharov wants to hire me. All those people, gone. Just gone. What was it Lila called me? *A human garbage disposal.*

Daneca flips pages relentlessly. "Well, let's look at the last one. Then we can hear your not-a-theory. This guy is Arthur Lee. Another luck worker and an informant for the FBI. Died out on a job for Zacharov."

A cold sweat breaks out at my temples. Now that I believe I did it, every piece of paper seems damning. Every detail, a flashing red arrow.

Anton and Barron in the front of the car, me and Philip in the back with Lee. No sleep magic needed. Just a touch from my bare hand.

"The thing I don't understand is—," Daneca begins.

Our new hall master, Mr. Pascoli, clears his throat outside the open door. Daneca's busted. At least it's a new year and we're all starting from zero demerits. I open my mouth and try to come up with some excuse for why she's in a guy's room, no matter how flimsy.

"I think this project of yours has taken long enough, don't you?" he asks, before I can speak.

"Sorry," Daneca says, gathering up some of the papers.

Pascoli smiles benevolently and walks away, like nothing happened.

"What was that?" I ask.

"I just told him that Sam and I had a project to do together and that the common room was too noisy. He said as long as we kept the door open and actually studied, he didn't mind."

"Nerds get away with everything," Sam says.

Daneca grins. "Don't we just."

I smile back, but if there's one thing I know, it's that eventually we all get caught.

Even though I'm exhausted, I can't sleep. I pored over the files once Daneca left, and I run through the details again and again in my mind, trying to remember some part of what happened. I keep twisting on my bed, making the springs squeak. My body feels wrong, hot and uncomfortable.

Finally I grab my phone and text Lila.

U awake? I type.

Then I actually look at the screen and realize it's three thirty in the morning. I punch my pillow and flop down onto it, face forward.

My phone chirrups. I roll over and snatch it up.

Bad dreams, it says. *Always awake.*

Sneak out, I text back, and pull on a pair of jeans.

The great thing about a room on the ground floor is that

you can just push open your window and hop right into the bushes. Sam moans at the creak of the wooden frame, kicks at his blankets, and goes back to snoring.

I'm not sure which dorm is hers, so I stand in the middle of the quad.

The night air is still and heavy. Nothing feels real. I wonder if this was what it was like when we waited outside someone's house for the victim to walk right into our arms. The whole world seems dead already.

After a few moments I see a rope dangle from a low window in Gilbert House. I pad over and realize Lila has somehow managed to jam a grappling hook into the sill. Which means she thought to bring a grappling hook to school and managed to hide it in her room. I am all admiration.

She spiders down and then drops, barefoot, still in her pajamas. She's grinning, but when she sees my face, her smile fades.

"What's wrong?" Lila asks.

"Come on," I say softly. "We have to get away from the dorms."

She nods and follows me without saying anything else. This, the language of deception, we both understand. We were born to it, along with the curses.

I go out to the track. Nearby are only tennis courts and the patch of woods that separates the Wallingford campus from a stretch of suburban homes.

"So, what do you think of it here?" I ask her.

"School's school," she says with a shrug. "A girl on my hall wanted me to go shopping with her and her friends. I didn't go. Now she's always on my case about being stuck up."

"How come you didn't—?"

Lila is looking at me uncertainly. I can see the hope in her face, along with the dread. "Who cares?" she asks finally. "Well, *what*? Why are we here?" Her pajamas are blue, covered in stars.

"Okay. I want to ask you about what we did—about what I did. The murders or whatever you want to call them." I don't look at her, so instead I look back at Wallingford. Just some old brick buildings. I have no idea how I thought they were going to shelter me from my own life.

"That's what you brought me all the way out here to talk about?" she says, her voice hard.

"This is definitely not where I would take someone for a romantic rendezvous." When she flinches, I keep going. "I saw some files. Some names. I want you to tell me if they're the ones."

"Fine," she says. "But it's not going to help you to know."

"Antanas Kalvis?"

"Yeah," she says. "You changed him."

"Jimmy Greco?"

"Yeah," she says again, softly. "Him, too."

"Arthur Lee."

"I don't know. If you did, I wasn't there. But since you knew the names of the first two, you're probably right about the third."

My hands are shaking again.

"Cassel, what's the difference? You knew about all of this before. They're just names."

I sink down to the grass. It's damp with dew. I feel sick, but self-loathing has become a familiar sickness. I was a monster before. A monster with the excuse that he didn't know details so he didn't really have to think about it. "I don't know. I guess there's no difference."

She sits next to me and pulls up a handful of weeds. She tries to throw it, but most of the blades stick to her bare fingers. Neither of us is wearing gloves.

"It's just—why? Why did I do it? Barron could make me remember anything, but what did I remember that let me change these people into *objects*?"

"I don't know," Lila says in a monotone.

I reach out for her shoulder without thinking, rubbing my fingers over the cotton. I no longer know how to say aloud what I feel. Sorry my brothers kept her in a cage, sorry that it took me so long to save her, sorry I changed her in the first place. Sorry I'm bringing up those memories now.

"Don't," she says.

My bare fingers still. "Right. I wasn't thinking."

"My father wants you to work for him, doesn't he?" she asks, scooting away from me. Her eyes are bright in the moonlight.

I nod. "He offered me a job at Philip's funeral."

Lila groans. "He's got some conflict going with the Brennan family. He does a lot of his business at funeral parlors these days." She pauses. "Are you going to do it?"

"You mean am I going to keep on murdering people? I don't know. I guess I'm good at it. It's good to be good at something, right?" There's bitterness in my voice, but not as much as there should be. The horror I felt earlier is fading, being replaced by a kind of resignation.

"Maybe they don't die when you change them into objects," Lila says. "Maybe they're just in suspended animation."

I shudder. "That sounds even worse."

She flops back in the grass, looking up at the night sky. "I like how you can see stars out here in the country."

"This isn't the country," I say, turning toward her. "We're close to two cities and—"

She smiles up at me, and all of a sudden we're in dangerous territory. I'm above her, looking down at the fall of her silvery hair on the grass, at the way her neck moves when she swallows nervously, at the way her fingers curl in the dirt.

I try to say something, but I can't remember what we were talking about. All my thoughts melt away as her lips part and her bare hand slides through my hair, pulling me down to her.

She makes a soft sound as my mouth presses against hers, hungry, desperate. Only a monster would do this, but I already know I'm a monster.

I roll toward her, not breaking the kiss, crushing her body against mine. My eyes close, so I don't have to see what I'm doing, but my hands find her easily enough. She moans into my mouth.

Her fingers are still knotted in my hair, gripping it hard, like she's afraid I am going to pull away.

"Please," I say breathlessly, but then we're kissing again

and it's hard to concentrate on anything but the feel of her body arching under mine, and I never get the rest of the words out.

Please stop me.

I drag my mouth away from hers, moving to kiss the hollow of her throat, my teeth gliding over her skin, my tongue tasting sweat and dirt.

"Cassel," she whispers. She's said my name a hundred times before, a thousand times, but never like this.

I pull back, abruptly, panting. Never like this.

She rises with me, but now at least we're both sitting up. That helps. She's breathing hard, her eyes black with pupil.

"I don't—," I start. "It's not—not real."

The words make no sense. I shake my head to clear it.

She looks at me with an expression I cannot name. Her lips are slightly apart and swollen.

"We have to go back," I say finally.

"Okay." I can barely hear the word. Her voice is all breath.

I nod, pushing myself to my feet. I reach out my hand, and she lets me pull her up. For a moment her hand is in mine, warm and bare.

At the window to my room, I catch my reflection in the glass. Shaggy black hair. Sneer. I look like a hungry ghost, glowering in at a world I am no longer fit to be part of.

The dream takes me by surprise. I'm standing at the edge of a lawn. Barron's beside me. I know, without any reason to know, that we're waiting for someone to come out of the big pillared white house in front of us.

"Join me in a cup of tea?" he asks, holding out a paper cup with a smirk. The amber liquid inside is boiling, bubbles rising along with steam. It's going to scald us both.

"Oh," I say. "Do you think we'll fit?"

I'M USELESS IN CLASSES

the next day. I fail a quiz in physics and conjugate my verbs completely weirdly in French. Luckily, I probably won't need French in my future assassination career, unless I'm one of those fancy movie assassins who travel the world and also steal jewels. Physics I might need—got to calculate the trajectory of bullets somehow.

I call Barron on my lunch break to avoid the cafeteria. I don't know how to say anything to Sam and Daneca that isn't all lies. And I don't know how to say anything to Lila that isn't the truth.

"Hey," he says. "We still on for Tuesday pizza?" His voice

is casual. Normal. It makes me almost believe that I can relax.

"I need to ask you something. In person. Where are you?" A teacher walks by and gives me a look. We're not supposed to be calling people during the school day, even between classes. I'm a senior, though, so she doesn't give me a hard time.

"Mom and I are having fun. We're staying at the Nassau Inn. It's pretty swank."

"That's in Princeton," I say. It's right downtown, minutes away from Daneca's house. I experience a frisson of horror at the thought of my mother and hers in the same pharmacy line.

Barron laughs. "Yeah. And? Mom says you two basically tore up Atlantic City, so we're looking for a fresh start."

I have no idea why I thought that Barron would do anything but amplify all of Mom's problems. A memory of him saying something about a painting nags at me; I should have seen this coming.

"Look, whatever," I say. "Can you meet me somewhere at six? I can skip dinner and some of study hall."

"We'll come over now. Mom can sign you out, remember? We'll get sushi."

"Sure, okay," I say.

It takes them an hour and a half to make the twenty-minute trip from Princeton to Wallingford. By the time they get there, I am in the "extra help" period, where I have to suffer through realizing that almost all my physics mistakes were dumb and obvious.

It's a relief to be called to the office.

Barron is lounging against the secretary desk in a sharkskin suit. Mom is next to him, her hair pulled back into a Hermès scarf with a massive black-and-white hat over it, black gloves, and a low-cut black dress. They're both wearing sunglasses. She's bent over, signing a sheet.

I think she's supposed to look like she's in mourning.

"Mom," I say.

"Oh, honey," she says. "The doctor wants to see you to make sure you don't have the same thing that killed your brother." She turns to Ms. Logan, who looks scandalized by the whole encounter. "These things can run in families," she confides.

"You're afraid I'm going to come down with a bad case of getting two in the chest?" I say. "'Cause you might be right about that running in families."

Mom purses her lips in disapproval.

Barron claps me on the back hard. "Come on, funnyman."

We walk toward the parking lot. I shove my gloved hands deep into the pockets of my uniform. Barron is keeping pace with me. He has left the top couple buttons of his crisp white shirt undone, enough so that I can see a new gold chain slide against his tan skin. I wonder if he's wearing charms against being worked.

"I thought you *wanted* us to come get you," Mom says as she lights a cigarette with a gilt lighter and takes a deep drag. "What's the matter?"

"All I want is for Barron to tell me where the bodies are," I say, keeping my voice down as I walk across the lawn.

Having them here is surreal. They don't belong at Walling-ford, with its manicured lawns and low voices. They're both larger than life.

They exchange a look brimming with discomfort.

"The people I transformed. Where are they? What did I turn them into?"

I don't know exactly what Barron remembers about the disappearances of Greco and Kalvis and all the rest. I have no idea how many of Barron's memories are missing, how extensively he's damaged himself with blowback, but if there's a record in his journals, then maybe he knows something. Yeah, sure, I changed his journals so that he forgot that he wanted to use me to kill Zacharov, forgot that he wasn't on my side against Philip and Philip's buddy, Anton. But I didn't change anything else.

"There's no reason why you need to know that," Barron says slowly. Which sounds promising.

"Let's just say that I do." I stop walking, forcing them to either stop too or go on without me. They stop.

"Don't argue, boys," Mom says, blowing out a cloud of smoke that hangs in the air. "Cassel, come on, baby. Let it go."

"One," I say. "Give me one body."

"Fine." Barron shrugs nonchalantly. "Remember that chair you hated?"

I open my mouth and then close it, like a fish. "What?" I say, but I know which chair he means. The one I almost threw out when Grandad and I cleaned the house, because the thing always creeped me out. It was a too-exact replica of one I'd seen on television.

He laughs and tilts up his sunglasses, so I can see him raise his eyebrows at me. "Yep."

I root my keys out of my bag. "Thanks for signing me out, Mom," I say, kissing her on her powdered cheek.

"I thought we were going to have lunch," she says. "Whatever you're thinking of doing—"

"I've got to go," I say. "I'm sorry."

"Sorry nothing," Mom says in a syrupy voice, grabbing hold of my upper arm. "You can come to lunch with us or I can call that nice lady at the desk and tell her that your appointment got canceled, I brought you back to school, and won't she be a dear and make sure you're where you're supposed to be?"

"Don't threaten me," I say, which makes Barron look at me like I've gone crazy. Telling Mom what to do is never a great idea.

Her hand clenches tighter around my arm, nails biting into my skin through the white dress shirt. I look down; somehow she got her glove off without my noticing. If she slides her fingers lower, she could touch my bare wrist. Or she could go higher and grab for my neck. "A mother shouldn't have to threaten her son into wanting to spend time together."

She's got me there.

Mom slides into the booth at Toriyama's and plunks down her purse next to her, leaving Barron and me to use the chairs. Her gloves are back in place. When I study them to figure out how she rigged things to remove one so fast, she gives me a pointed look. I study the framed kimonos hanging above us and the pale bamboo table instead.

The waitress comes, dressed all in black, and pours us tea. She's pretty, with supershort bangs and a nose ring that glitters like a single drop of absinthe. Her name tag says Jin-Sook.

Barron orders one of the big platters of sushi. "It comes on one of the boats, right?" he asks, pointing toward a shelf of lacquered wooden ships, some of them with two masts, that rests above where the chef carves fish. "Because one time I ordered it and it just came on a plate. But on the menu it says boat, so I just want to be sure."

"It comes on a boat," Jin-Sook says.

I take a sip of the tea. It's a jasmine, so hot it nearly scalds my throat.

"So," Barron says. "We've got a new mark we're looking at. Someone big. We could use a hand. And you could use the money. Besides, we're family."

"Family looks out for family," says Mom, a line I've heard her recite more times than I can count.

It's tempting to say yes, even after everything. I used to long to be asked to grift alongside my brother. To prove that even though I wasn't a worker, I could con along with the best of them. And my brother and mother are up there with the best of them.

But now I know I'm a worker and a con artist and maybe a murderer, too. And if there is one thing I want to prove to myself, it's that I can be different.

"Thanks, but no thanks," I say.

Barron shrugs philosophically.

Mom reaches for her teacup, and I see the flash of a fat blue topaz circled in diamonds sitting on her first finger, over her leather glove. The ring's new. I shudder to think where it came from. Then I spot the ring on the other hand. The stone is reddish, like a single droplet of blood spilled into water.

"Mom," I say hesitantly.

Something in my expression makes her look down at her hands.

"Oh," she gushes, clearly pleased. "I met the most fantastic man! He's absolutely perfect." She waggles the finger wearing the topaz. "And such good taste."

"He's the one I was telling you about," Barron says. At my blank look he lowers his voice and raises his eyebrows. "The *mark*."

"Oh," I say. "But what about that other ring?"

"This old thing?" Mom says, holding out her other hand. The pale red diamond flashes in the fluorescent restaurant lights. "Also a gift. One I haven't worn in years."

I think of the pictures I found when I was cleaning out the house. Photos of Mom in vintage lingerie, posing for a person I couldn't see. Someone with an expensive wedding ring. Someone who wasn't my dad. I wonder if the man from the photograph had something to do with the diamond.

"Who gave *that* to *you*?" I ask.

She gives me a look across the table like she's daring me to contradict her. "Your father, sweetheart. He had the best taste of any man."

"Well, I don't think you should wear it in public. That's all." I smile to let her know I'm not fooled. It feels like we're alone in the restaurant. "Someone might *steal* it."

That makes her laugh. Barron looks at us both like we're speaking a language he doesn't understand. For a change, I am the person with the insider information.

The food comes. I mix plenty of wasabi into my soy sauce and drag a piece of sashimi through it. The fish is salty on my tongue, and the green horseradish flares all the way up my nose.

"I'm glad you came to lunch," Barron says, leaning in to me. "You seemed a little freaked-out back at school."

I don't mention that by the time they picked me up it was way past time for lunch. We're surrounded by an early dinner crowd.

"What you're feeling is part of the grieving process," he goes on, with the total sincerity that makes him so convincing. "There's no making sense out of what happened to Philip, so you're trying to make sense out of something else instead."

"Maybe that's it," I say.

He ruffles my hair with a gloved hand. "Sure it is. You'll see."

Jin-Sook brings our check in a narrow black folder. Mom pays for it with one of a dozen stolen credit cards.

Unfortunately for her, the credit card is declined. The waitress brings it back with apologies.

"Your machine must be broken," my mother says, her voice rising.

"It's fine," I say, reaching for my wallet. "I've got it."

Barron turns to our waitress. "Thanks for such great service." His bare hand is on her wrist.

For a moment she looks disoriented. Then she smiles back, a big grin. "Thank *you*! Come back again."

Mom and Barron get up and start toward the door, leaving me there staring after Jin-Sook, trying to figure out how to tell her that her memories just got rearranged.

"What's done is done," Mom says from the front of the restaurant. The look she gives me is a warning.

Family looks after family.

The girl's memories are gone. I could get Barron in trouble, but I can't undo what's already done.

I push back my chair and follow my mother and brother out. Once we're on the street, though, I shove Barron's shoulder. "Are you crazy?"

"Come on!" he says, grinning like it's all a great joke. "Paying is for suckers."

"I get that you don't care about other people. But you're messing up your own head," I say. "You'll use up all your memories. There won't be anything of you left."

"Don't worry," Barron says. "If I forget anything important, you can just remind me."

Mom looks over at me, eyes glittering.

Yeah. Right. What's done is done.

They drop me off back at Wallingford, in front of my own car. I start to get out.

"Wait," Mom says and takes out a pen from her handbag. "I got a cute little phone! I want to give you the number."

Barron rolls his eyes.

"You hate cell phones," I say.

She ignores me as she scribbles. "Here, baby," she says. "You call me whenever. I'll call you back from the nearest pay phone or landline."

I take the slip of paper with a smile. After her three years in jail, I don't think she realizes just how rare pay phones are these days. "Thanks, Mom."

She leans in and kisses my cheek. I can smell her perfume, sweet and heavy, long after they pull away.

My car makes a horrible noise when I try to start it up. For a moment I think I am going to have to chase down Mom and Barron for a ride. Finally I put it in second gear and get it rolling. Somehow the engine turns over and the motor roars to life. I have no idea how long my car is going to stay running or whether I'm going to be able to get it started again when I want to return to Wallingford.

I drive to the big old house I grew up in. From the outside the unpainted shingles and off-kilter shutters give it the look of a building long abandoned. Grandad and I cleaned out most of the garbage, but inside I can smell the faint odor of mold under the Lysol. The place still looks tidy, but I can tell Mom's been here. There are a couple of shopping bags on the dining room table and there's a mug of tea rotting in the kitchen sink.

Good thing Grandad's down in Carney; he'd be annoyed.

I walk straight to the chair. It's covered in a kind of a mustardy cloth and is perfectly normal-looking for a club chair, except for the feet, which, now that I really look at them, are awful. I thought they were claw feet holding on to painted balls, and at a glance that's what they look like. But now that I am inspecting the chair closely, those claws are actually human hands, the knuckles bent under.

A shudder runs through me.

I sit down on the floor beside it, despite wanting nothing more than to get as far away from it as I can. I reach out a hand and concentrate. The power still feels strange, and my whole body is braced for what comes after, for the pain and helplessness of the blowback.

As my palm comes down on the chair, everything goes fluid. I can feel the curse here, feel the threads of it, and even feel the man underneath. I rip the magic with a push that's almost physical.

After a moment I open my eyes, not even realizing I had closed them.

A man stands before me, his skin pink with life, his eyes open. He's wearing a white sleeveless undershirt and underwear. I feel a wild hope.

"Henry Janssen," I say, my voice trembling. He looks just like the picture paper-clipped to his file.

Then he falls, his skin turning ashen. I remember how we tried to fake Zacharov's death. Seeing Janssen fall, I realize how wrong we had it. You can see the moment it happens, like a light burning out in a lamp.

"No," I yell, crawling over to him.

And the blowback hits me. My body cramps all over, limbs elongating like a spider, reaching toward the ceiling.

Then it's like I'm made of glass and each twist of my body creates cracks that turn to fissures until I am lying in pieces. I try to scream, but my mouth has turned to crumbling earth. My body is turning itself inside out. As agony grips me, I turn my head and stare into the glassy eyes of a dead man.

I wake up, drenched in sweat, next to Henry Janssen.

Every muscle in my body is sore, and when I look at the corpse, I feel nothing except a growing sense that I have to get rid of it. I no longer understand the urgency that sent me here. I no longer understand why I thought there could be any other outcome but this. What did I think was going to happen? I know nothing about transformation or its limits. I don't even know if it's *possible* to turn an inanimate object back into something alive.

I don't care, either. I'm tired of caring.

It's like the part of me that feels all that guilt has finally overloaded. I feel nothing.

Even though the most practical solution is to curse him back into being a chair, I can't face another round of blowback. I think of burying him, but I'm pretty sure the hole has to be deeper than I have time to dig.

I could dump him in deep water, but since I'm not even sure my car is going to start, that seems problematic too. Finally I remember the freezer in the basement.

It's harder to carry a dead person than someone who's alive. It's not that they're heavier; it's that they don't help you. They don't bend their body into your arms or hold on to your neck. They just lie there. On the plus side, you no longer have to worry about hurting them.

I drag Janssen down the stairs by his shoulders. His body makes a sickening thud with each step.

There's nothing in the freezer except half a pint of Cherry Garcia ice cream, rimed with frost. I take it out and set it on my father's old workbench. Then I put one hand under the dead man's clammy neck and hook the other around his knee. I lift and half-roll, half-toss him into the freezer. He sort of fits, but I have to bend his limbs so that I will be able to close the lid. It's pretty bad.

I'll come back, I tell myself. *In a day or two I'll come back and change him.*

Looking down at a freezer full of Henry Janssen, I think about Philip's corpse laid out in the funeral home. Someone—a woman—was caught on video walking into Philip's condo. And since I know I killed the rest of the people in the files, the FBI are on the entirely wrong track. They're looking to connect the killers. But whoever murdered Philip had nothing to do with all this, probably didn't know anything about it.

Maybe I should get back to thinking about suspects other than myself.

My car starts without a problem; the first good thing that's happened to me in a while. I drive back to Wallingford eating the Cherry Garcia ice cream and thinking about red gloves, gunshots, and guilt.

IT'S IMPOSSIBLE TO AVOID

the cafeteria forever.

When I walk in to dinner, I see Daneca and Sam sitting with Jill Pearson-White and a bunch of Sam's chess club friends. I start over to them, until I see Lila, her head bent toward Daneca's. I can only imagine the speech Lila is being given about worker rights and HEX meetings.

I veer abruptly toward another table and spot the flame of Audrey's red hair.

"Hi," I say as I sit down.

Greg Harmsford is there, along with Rahul Pathak and Jeremy Fletcher-Fiske. They all look surprised to see me. Greg's hand clenches around his fork in a way that suggests I better say something clever, fast. He might be dating Audrey now, but I dated her once, and clearly Greg worries there might still be something there. Probably because once, at a party, she arrived with him but made out with me.

Here's the thing about influencing a group to do what you want. It's a lot easier if what you want and what they want line up. Getting marks interested in easy money only works on the greedy. I hope I can interest Greg in the promise of easy revenge while I distract the rest of the table. I'm counting on his being threatened enough that he'll want to make me look like a fool. I just hope that he's not so threatened that he decides to punch me in the face.

"Get out of here," Greg says.

"I wanted to talk with you all about the senior prank," I improvise wildly.

Rahul frowns. "The school year just started."

I nod. "Look, last year the class left it until the end and they got the kind of lame prank that you'd expect. I want ours to make our graduating class infamous."

"You're totally taking bets on it," says Jeremy. "You just want an inside line."

"I want to get a horse into Northcutt's bedroom," I say. "Wearing an enormous thong. Now, please tell me how admitting that to you is going to make me any money."

Rahul and Jeremy laugh, Jeremy spitting a piece of salad out onto his plate. Now Greg can't just boot me from the table. He won't let me leave with Rahul and Jeremy well-disposed toward me.

"Can you picture her face?" Rahul says gleefully.

"Whatever," says Greg. "We can come up with something better than that."

"Like what?" asks Audrey. She doesn't sound like she's challenging him. She sounds like she's sure he's going to come up with an absolutely brilliant suggestion in just a moment and she's patiently waiting. She sounds kind. I'm sure she wouldn't mind if her new boyfriend made her old boyfriend look like a fool either.

By this point I'm sure I have somewhere to sit for dinner. I get my food and eat it, listening to them trade prank ideas back and forth. The more we talk about it, the more I warm to the idea of deciding the scheme early so we can focus for the rest of the year on the perfect execution. I let Greg get in a few digs.

And if I sometimes flash to the image of the body in the freezer, to the waxen face of my brother, or to the wide-eyed way Lila looked when I pulled away from her last night, well, then, I have had a lifetime of experience keeping what I'm thinking off my face.

"Hey, look at the new kid. Isn't she supposed to be some crime boss's daughter?" Jeremy says.

I swivel my head to see Lila standing. A junior girl I don't know is talking to her, gesturing grandly with blue-gloved hands. I can't hear what they're saying over the general dining hall noise, but the junior's expression is alight with malicious glee.

"Girl fight," Rahul says, grinning.

But when Lila takes a step toward the sophomore,

it's not to punch or pull hair. She starts removing a single black glove.

I see a flash of bare fingers and hear Greg's indrawn breath beside me. The junior girl stumbles back.

"She's crazy," says Jeremy. "That's *nuts*. She's going to—"

People are getting up, conversations are pausing. In that lull of sound I hear Lila's voice distinctly.

"You sure you want to cross me?" she says. In that moment she's her father's daughter.

The junior runs off toward the teacher's table, and Lila sits down, pulling her glove back on. I see Daneca gaping at her. After a few moments Dean Wharton comes over and escorts Lila out of the building.

I push around the Salisbury steak in front of me. After a while of doing that, I get up.

"Greg," Audrey says, rising with me. "Can you give me a minute with Cassel?"

"Whatever." He shrugs, but the look he shoots me is anything but casual. It's hard to picture a guy like Greg Harmsford loving anyone, but the way he watches Audrey is at least possessive.

"What's going on with you?" Audrey asks as we walk toward the dorms. The sun is just going down and the sky is dim. The leaves are turned over on their backs, waiting for rain. "You don't care about the senior prank. I know that because you never, ever say what you actually mean."

Six months ago we almost got back together. I'd thought that being with her would, through some power of alchemy, transmute me into being a normal guy with normal problems. When she looks at me, I see the reflection of a different self in her eyes. Someone I long to be.

I lean toward her. She puts a hand on my chest and pushes me back, hard.

"What are you doing?" she says.

"I don't know. I thought—" I thought I was supposed to kiss her.

"*Cassel*," she says, exasperated. "You're always like this. Hot or cold. Do you even know what you want?"

I look at the concrete path beneath me, at the desiccated bodies of earthworms who crawled out of the ground in the rain, only to get scorched by the sun.

"You're the one who wanted to talk," I say defensively.

"Do you even remember last year? I cried my eyes out after you came back to school and acted like nothing we'd said to each other while you were kicked out mattered."

I nod, not looking at her, because she's right. After my mother worked Lila, the only reason I didn't flunk out was because Sam did half of my homework for me. Everything felt hollow and unreal. I blew off Audrey without even making up excuses.

"Why? And why talk to me now like *that* never happened?" Her voice has a funny quality to it. I know that if I look up at her, her neck will be all blotchy, like it always gets when she's upset.

"I'm sorry," I say. "You're right. I'm not really good at relationships."

"No, you're not!" Audrey says, seeming relieved that I

have finally said something she can totally endorse. "You're not, and I don't know how to deal with you."

I consider and dismiss many variations of the suggestion that we be friends. Finally I look at her.

"I'm sorry," I say.

"Lila's not your cousin either, is she?" Audrey asks.

"No," I say. "I told you that because—"

She holds up her hand, and I gratefully stop talking. "You didn't tell me that. She did."

At that I just stare. I honestly don't remember who started that whole line of lies. We did it just to borrow her shower. Now it seems like the height of callousness.

"I've seen the way you look at her," Audrey says. "I know you, Cassel. So that brings me to asking you again—what are you *doing*?"

"Screwing up," I say.

"Good answer." She smiles a little, almost despite herself, and leans in to pat me on the cheek. "Stop it."

Then she walks off. I turn to go back to my dorm, but my gaze is caught by Lila, standing across the quad. She sees me and enters the Gilbert Hall dorms, leaving me to wonder how long she was standing there. Leaving me to wonder how in the world she talked her way out of all the trouble.

Sam is tapping away on his laptop when I come in. He looks up and goes back to what he's doing, for which I'm thankful. I get through my Probability & Statistics homework (possibly my favorite class *ever*), and start a proposal paper for the semester-long project in physics. Then I settle on my bed to do some of my *Madame Bovary* reading.

I don't get too far before Sam closes his computer. "Everything okay? Daneca said you got called to the office."

"Family stuff," I say. "My mom."

He nods sagely. "Get anywhere with those files?"

I shake my head. "There goes my career in law enforcement, I guess."

Sam snorts and starts hooking up his PlayStation to the tiny portable television he got for his birthday. "When you're done with that, you want to shoot some bad guys?"

"Evildoers," I say. "Yeah. Definitely."

It should bother me to point my controller at the screen and watch pixelated guys fall over. It should remind me of Janssen or Philip and my hand should hesitate or something. I get the high score instead. After all, it's just a game.

After dinner we have study hall in our rooms. This is the time of night when we're supposed to do homework. If we actually finish it in the two hours allotted, then we can spend half an hour in the common room. But it also means that once we're checked on by our hall master to make sure we're studying, we have almost three hours before we're likely to be checked on again.

"I think I am going to go out," I say to Sam.

He frowns at me. "Where?"

"There's someplace I've got to see." I push open the window. "For the investigation."

"Okay," says Sam. "I'll come too. Let's go."

"You know we're sneaking out of here. We could get busted." I hold up my hands. "It's your senior year. You don't have to do this."

"Well, you're our expert on getting away with things. It's your job to make sure we *don't* get caught, right?"

"No pressure. Thanks," I say. I open iTunes on my laptop and set a file to play. Then I turn up the volume a couple of notches.

"What's that?" he asks.

"I recorded this last year. Study hall. So things won't be too quiet. It's mostly just clicking on laptops and us joking around. I thought it might come in handy someday."

"That's creepy, dude," he says.

I point to my head with both hands. "Expert, remember?"

Then we go out the window and close it behind us. I think of the night before and Lila, her back pressed against the lawn. The smell of crushed grass underfoot is as heady as any perfume.

"Walk casually," I say.

We get into my car, which stalls twice before it starts, causing Sam to give me the wide-eyed expression of a man who's looking down the barrel of explaining a suspension to his parents. A moment later, though, we're pulling out of the lot with the headlights off. I click them on as we turn onto the highway.

Then I head toward the address in the file, the one where Janssen was last seen. Quarter of an hour later we're parking near Cyprus View apartment complex. I get out.

It's one of those modern places with a doorman in the lobby and probably a gym up near the penthouse. There are bright lamps burning on the manicured lawn, bushes cut into round balls near the stretch of concrete walkways, and a park across the street. A block over is a supermarket, and a block from that is a gas station, but when you look at it from the right angle, the place is nice. Expensive. Sprinkler system, but no cameras that I can see, and I walk twice around one of the lights to be sure.

"What are we looking at?" Sam asks, leaning against the side of the car. In his uniform jacket, with his tie loose, he could almost be a gangster. So long as you don't notice the Wallingford logo over his breast pocket.

"Janssen's mistress's condo. I wanted to see if it felt—I don't know—familiar."

Sam frowns. "Why would it be familiar? You didn't even know Janssen. Did you?"

I'm slipping up. I shake my head. "I don't know. I just wanted to see it. Look for clues."

"Okay," Sam says skeptically, glancing down at his watch. "But if this is a stakeout, I vote for us getting snacks."

"Yeah," I reply, distracted. "Just give me a second."

I walk across the grass and past the groomed bushes. I don't remember any of this. I must have stood on this grass and waited for Janssen, but I don't recall a single thing.

A woman in jogging clothes runs in the direction of the apartment building. She's got two of those big black standard poodles on a leash. Staring at her, I get a flash of memory, but it feels so distant that I can barely catch it. She looks in my direction, then turns abruptly, jerking the leashes. I get a really good look at her face just before she takes off down the street.

She must be an actress, because the memory I have of her is a scene from a movie. I'm sure it was the jogger, but she was wearing a short black dress, with her hair up, and a necklace with a single sparkling amulet dangling in the valley between her breasts. She had a bruise on her face and she'd been crying. A faceless actor in my brother's leather jacket took her by the shoulders. A man was lying on the grass, facedown.

I can't remember anything else. No plot. Not even whether I saw the film in a theater or on television late one night. The memory makes no sense.

If she's some actress, how come she started running when she saw me?

And how come one of the actors was wearing my brother's leather jacket?

Only one way to find out. I chase after her, my Wallingford dress shoes clacking like beetles on the pavement.

She veers off across the street, and I follow. A car's high beams catch me, and the grill of a Toyota nearly slams into me. I hit my hand against his hood and keep going.

She's almost made it to a small park. There are a couple of other people, walking under flickering streetlights, but she doesn't call out to them and they don't seem to want to involve themselves.

I pump my legs faster, pounding my feet against

the dirt. I'm gaining on her now. One of the dogs barks as I reach out and catch the hood of the woman's pink velour top.

She stumbles, and the dogs go crazy. I had no idea enormous poodles were so protective, but these things look like they want to rip my arms off.

"Wait," I say. "Please. I'm not going to hurt you."

She turns back toward me, the barking dogs between us. I hold up my hands in surrender. The park is quiet and dim, but if she starts running again, she could make it to the buildings beyond it, businesses that would probably not see my chasing her in a favorable light.

"What do you want?" she says, studying my face. "Our business is over. Done. I told Philip I didn't want to see any of you."

The creeping realization that there was no movie comes over me. *Of course*. Barron must have taken my memory and changed one small detail—the part where it happened in real life. That must have been easier for him than erasing the memory completely. And I'd forget it the same way I forget every other late-night cop show.

"I already paid you," she's saying, and I focus on memorizing her, shaking off all other thoughts. Her dark hair is pulled back into a ponytail, and her artificially plumped lips are painted a bubble-gum pink. Her eyes are tilted up at the corners, her eyebrows high enough to give her a perpetual expression of mild surprise. Between that and her wrinkled neck, I guess she's had some work done. She's beautiful and unreal; I can see why Barron changed her into a movie star in my head. "I'm not giving you anything else. You can't blackmail me."

I have no idea what she's talking about.

"He strung me along, you know. Told me he was going to marry me. Then, *bam,* starts knocking me around when I find out he's *already* married. But what do you care about that? Nothing. You probably have a girl back home that you treat no better. Get out of here, you piece of trash."

When I look at her, I still see the woman I mistook her for. I wonder what she sees when she looks at me. A drip of sweat runs over the curve of her cheek. Her breathing is rapid and shallow. She's scared.

An assassin, that's what she sees.

"You're the one who wanted the hit," I say, untangling what she's saying. "You paid Anton to take out Janssen."

"What are you, wearing a wire?" she asks, raising her voice and talking into my chest. "I never killed nobody. I never had nobody killed." She looks back toward her apartment building, like she's thinking about bolting.

"Okay," I say, holding up my hands again. "Okay. That was stupid."

"Yeah," she says. "Are we done?"

I nod my head, and then suddenly think of another question. "Where were you on Tuesday night?"

"Home with the dogs," she says. "I had a headache. Why?"

"My brother got shot."

She frowns. "Do I look like a killer?"

I don't point out that she hired a team of hit men to kill

her lover. My silence must make her feel like she scored a point, because with a final triumphant glare she takes off, dogs sprinting alongside her.

I walk back to my car, feeling each step. A blister has risen on my big toe. These shoes were never made for chase scenes.

The door of the Benz opens. "Cassel?" Sam calls from the driver's side. "She tell you anything good?"

"Yeah," I say. "That she was going to mace me."

"I was ready to fire up the getaway car." Sam grins. "Doesn't she know that muggers don't wear ties?"

I straighten my collar. "I'm a better class of criminal. A gentleman thief, if you will."

I let Sam drive. We head back to Wallingford, stopping for drive-through coffee and fries along the way. When we hop back through the dorm window, the smell of take-out clings to our clothes so strongly that it takes half a bottle of air freshener to disguise it.

"Stop smoking in your room," the hall master says at lights-out. "Don't think I can't tell what you've been doing in here."

We laugh so hard that, for a moment, it seems like we're never going to be able to stop.

The next morning I am walking to Developing World Ethics when Kevin Ford runs up to me. He stuffs an envelope into my hand.

"What are the odds that Greg Harmsford nailed Lila Zacharov?" he asks, breathless.

"What?" I say.

"Am I the first one to put down money? Dude!"

"Kevin, what are you talking about?" I resist grabbing his shoulders and shaking him, but I don't think I manage to keep the edge out of my voice. "I can't calculate odds on something when I have no idea what you're talking about."

"Last night I heard that they went into the sitting room and did it. Greg was bragging about it. His roommate, Kyle, had to totally distract their hall master."

"Okay," I say, nodding. My mouth feels dry. "I'll keep the money, but if no one else bets or no one bets against, I'm going to have to give it back." That's my standard line for things like this and I say it automatically.

He nods and races off. I stagger into class.

Greg Harmsford is sitting in his usual desk by the windows. I take a seat on the other side, staring at the back of his head, flexing my gloved hands.

While Mr. Lewis rattles on and on about trade agreements, I think about what it would be like to shove a sharpened pencil into Greg's ear. This is the kind of rumor that people start about new girls, I remind myself. They're never based on anything but wishful thinking.

Once we're dismissed, I head toward the door, passing Greg. He smirks, raising his eyebrows like he's daring me to start something.

Okay, that's weird.

"Hey, Cassel," he says, his smile getting wider.

I bite the inside of my cheek and continue into the

hallway. The copper taste of blood fills my mouth. I keep walking.

As I stalk toward Probability & Statistics, I see Daneca, her arms full of books.

"Hey, have you seen Lila?" I ask her, my voice strained.

"Not since yesterday," she says with a shrug.

I clamp my gloved hand on her shoulder. "Do you have any classes with her?"

Daneca stops and looks at me oddly. "She does a lot of remedial stuff."

Of course. Being a cat for three years might leave you a little behind on your schoolwork. But I've been too much in my own head to notice.

I get passed three more envelopes in statistics. Two of them are betting on Lila and Greg. I hand both of those back with such a dark look that no one asks me for an explanation.

She's not at lunch, either. Finally I walk into her building and head up the stairs, figuring that if I get caught, I'll come up with some explanation. I count over the number of doors, assuming that, like in my dorm, everyone gets one window to a room.

Then I knock. Nothing.

The locks are simple. I've been breaking into my own room for so long that I don't even carry my keys half the time. Just a quick pin twist and I'm inside.

She's got a single, which means her father must have made a pretty hefty donation. Her bed is jammed up against the window and there's a tangle of light green sheets dragging on the floor. An overstuffed bookcase that she must have brought with her sits against one wall. A totally forbidden electric kettle, and a tiny scarab-green iPod glittering in an expensive-looking speaker system, wires connecting it to headphones, all rest on top of a low trunk. She's also brought in a vanity with a mirror that sits against the wall where a roommate's desk usually goes. The walls are covered in black-and-white photos of old movie stars: Bette Davis, Greta Garbo, Katharine Hepburn, Marlene Dietrich, and Ingrid Bergman. And Lila's pasted-up quotes near them.

I walk up to the picture of Garbo, smoldering behind a Vaselined lens. The paper near her says, "I'm afraid of nothing except being bored."

It makes me smile.

I relock the door and turn to go down the steps, when I realize that the dull hum in the background—a sound I barely even registered—is a shower running in the hall bathroom.

I head toward it.

The bathroom is tiled in pink and smells like girls' shampoos, tropical and sugary. As I push open the door, I realize that there is no excuse that can explain my being in here.

"Lila?" I call.

I hear a soft sob. I stop caring about getting caught.

She's sitting in the middle shower stall, still in her uniform. Her hair is plastered to her head and her clothes are soaked through. The water is pounding down so relentlessly that I'm surprised she can breathe. It runs in rivulets over her closed eyes and half-open mouth. Her lips look blue with cold.

"Lila?" I say again, and her eyes open wide.

I did this to her. She was always the fearless one, the dangerous one.

Now she looks at me like she doesn't believe I'm really here. "Cassel? How did you know—" She bites off the question.

"What did he do to you?" I say. I am trembling with fury and powerlessness and sick jealousy.

"Nothing," she says, and I can see that familiar, cruel smile of hers, but all of its mockery is turned inward. "I mean, I wanted him to. I thought maybe it would break the curse. I've never really—I was just a kid when I changed— and I figured that maybe if I slept with someone, it would help. Obviously it didn't."

I swallow carefully. "Why don't you come out of there and dry off? It's cold." I put on a fake voice, like I'm one of the old ladies from Carney. "*You'll catch your death.*"

She looks a little less dire, her smile a little less like a rictus. "The water was hot before."

I hold out a towel that's lying on a bench nearby. It's a sickly shade of magenta, covered with purple fish. I'm pretty sure it's not hers.

She gets up slowly, stiffly, and comes out of the shower. I wrap her in the towel. For a moment my arms close around her. She leans into me and sighs.

We walk together across the hallway to her room. There

she pulls away to sit on the bed, dripping onto her sheets. She looks curled in on herself, arms crossed over her chest.

"Okay," I say. "I'm going to go stand in the stairway and you're going to get dressed, and then we're going to get out of here. I've got lots of untried schemes for walking out of Wallingford in the middle of the day; let's try one. We can get some hot chocolate. Or tequila. And then we can come back and kill Greg Harmsford, something I personally have wanted to do for a while."

Her fingers pull the towel tighter. She doesn't smile. Instead she says, "I'm sorry I haven't been handling this— the curse—very well."

"No," I rasp. Guilt is closing up my throat. "Don't. You shouldn't have to apologize. Not to me."

"At first I thought I could just ignore it, and now— well—it's like ignoring made the wound go septic. And then I said that if I came here and at least could see you, it would help. But it didn't. Everything that I think will help just makes it worse.

"So I want to ask you to do something," she says, looking at the floor, at a collection of textbooks that I'm pretty sure she's not actually seeing. "And I understand it's not fair, but it won't cost you much, and it would mean everything to me. I want you to be my boyfriend."

I start to say something, but she talks over me, already sure I'm going to say no.

"You don't have to really like me. And it will just be for a little while." She's looking up at me now, her eyes hard. "You can pretend. I know you're a good liar."

I don't even know how to protest. I'm scrambling. "You said that everything you think will help actually makes it worse. What if *this* makes it worse?"

"I don't know," she says, so low I can barely hear it.

It's not real or right or fair, but I no longer have any idea what is. "Okay," I say. "Okay. We can date. But we can't—I mean, that's all that can happen. I can't live with you sitting on the floor of a shower in six months, regretting being with me."

I am rewarded with her coming into my arms, her clothes damp and cold, her skin feverishly hot. I can see the relief in the sag of her shoulders, and when I put my arm around her, she leans against my chest, tucking her head under my chin.

"Hopefully . . . ," she says, a hitch in her voice like a swallowed sob. "Hopefully by then I won't be thinking about you at all."

She smiles up at me, and I am, for a long moment, unable to speak.

Boyfriends, even fake boyfriends, sit with their girlfriends at dinner. So I'm not surprised when Lila sets her tray down next to mine and touches me briefly on the shoulder. Daneca, however, bristles with curiosity. It's clearly costing her something not to speak.

When the first person walks over and tosses an envelope into my bag, Lila smiles into her paper napkin.

"You're a bookie? I thought you were the good brother," she says.

"I'm good at what I do," I say. "Virtue is its own revenge."

"Its own *reward*," says Daneca, rolling her eyes. "Virtue is its own reward."

I grin. "That's not the version I've heard."

Sam plunks down his tray and grabs for the apple about to roll off it. "You know how Mr. Knight is getting a little bit on the senile side? Like walking past the classroom and having to double back, or putting on his sweater over a winter coat?"

I nod, although I haven't had Mr. Knight for anything. I've just seen him in the halls. He looks like a typical ancient English professor—tweedy, with leather elbow pads and white nose hair.

"Well, today he came into class, and not only had he forgotten to zip up after a trip to the bathroom, he forgot to *tuck his junk back in.*"

"No way," I say.

Lila starts to laugh.

"That's the thing, right? It should be funny," Sam says. "It's funny now. But right then it was so awful that all we could do was sit there in shock. I was so embarrassed for him! And he just lectured the class on Hamlet like nothing was happening. I mean, he's quoting Shakespeare while we're all just trying not to look down."

"Didn't anyone say anything?" Daneca asks. "All those jokers?"

"Finally," says Sam, "Kim Hwangbo raises her hand."

I shake my head. Kim is quiet, nice, and will probably go to a better college than anyone else at Wallingford.

Even Daneca is laughing now. "What did she say?"

"'Mr. Knight, your pants are unzipped!'" says Sam. He laughs. "So Mr. Knight looks down, barely has a reaction, says 'Uneasy lies the head that wears a crown,' tucks himself in, and zips up. The end!"

"Are you going to tell anyone?" Daneca asks.

Sam shakes his head as he opens his milk. "No, and don't you, either. Mr. Knight is harmless—it's not like he did it on purpose—and he'd get in a lot of trouble if Northcutt found out. Or parents."

"They're going to find out," I say. I wonder how long it will take before bets start flooding in about him getting fired. "No one can hide anything for long around here."

Daneca frowns in my direction. "Oh, I don't know about that."

"What do you mean?" Lila asks, not entirely friendly.

Daneca ignores her question. "We're going to the movies this weekend," she says instead. "Do you guys want to come? We could double-date."

A flush creeps up Sam's neck.

Lila turns to me uncertainly. I smile.

"Sure," she says. "If you want to, Cassel?"

"What's the movie?" I ask. With Daneca, we could wind up going to some kind of documentary on the evils of baby seal clubbing.

"We're going to see *The Giant Spider Invasion*," Sam says. "They're playing it at the Friday Rewind. It's a classic Bill Rebane film—the special effects crew created the giant spider by covering a Volkswagen Beetle in fake fur and using the taillights as its red glowing eyes."

"What's better than that?" I ask.

No one can think of a thing.

That night I dream I'm in a room of corpses, all of them wearing dresses and lipstick, sitting stiffly on couches. It takes me a moment to realize they're all my ex-girlfriends, their dead eyes glittering, their mouths barely moving as they whisper a list of my flaws.

He kisses like a fish, says my kindergarten girlfriend, Michiko Ishii. We'd meet behind a fat oak tree on the playground, until we got caught by another girl who ratted us out. Her corpse is that of a very little girl; glassy eyes make her look like a doll.

He flirted with my friend, says the girl who ratted us out, Sofia Spiegel, who was technically also my girlfriend at the time.

He's a liar, says a girl from Atlantic City. The one in the silver dress.

Such a liar, says my eighth-grade girlfriend. I didn't tell her that I was going to Wallingford until after I left. I don't blame her for still being mad.

After the party he pretended not to know me, says Emily Rogers, who, to be fair, pretended just as hard that *I* didn't exist after we'd spent the night rolling around on a pile of coats at Harvey Silverman's freshman-year house party.

He borrowed my car and totaled it, says Stephanie Douglas, a worker girl I met in Carney over the summer after I was sure I'd killed Lila. She was two years older than me and could knot the stem of a cherry with her tongue.

He never really loved me, says Audrey. *He doesn't even know what love is.*

I wake up while it's still dark outside. Rather than go back to sleep, I start on some homework. I'm tired of the dead ganging up on me. There's got to be a problem somewhere that wants solving.

WALLINGFORD PREPARATORY

prides itself on getting its young men and women ready not just for college but for their place in society. To that end, students not only have to attend all their classes—they also have to participate in two enriching after-school activities. This year mine are track in the fall and debate club in the spring. I like the feeling of running, the rush of adrenaline and the pounding of my feet on the pavement. I like that it's just me deciding how far to push myself.

I also like thinking up ways to trick people into agreeing with me, but debate club doesn't start for many months.

I'm just finishing my last lap when I see two dark-suited men talking to Coach Marlin. He waves me over.

Agent Jones and Agent Hunt are wearing mirrored sunglasses along with their dark suits and darker gloves, even though the weather is still unseasonably warm. I'm not sure they could be more unsubtle if they tried.

"Hello, Officers," I say with a fake grin.

"Haven't heard from you in a while," Agent Jones says. "We got concerned."

"Well, I had this funeral to go to, and then I had all this extra grieving to do. Really filled up my social calendar." Although I think I'm managing to smirk like an innocent man, knowing that I'm the murderer they're looking for really adds an uncomfortable layer of terror to the whole interaction. "There's been loads going on since last Wednesday."

"Why don't you take a ride with us?" says Agent Hunt. "You can tell us all about it."

"I don't think so," I say. "I've got to take a shower and get changed. Like I said, really busy. But thanks for stopping by."

Coach Marlin has already started over toward other runners. He's shouting their times off his stopwatch. He's either forgotten about me or is trying to forget.

Agent Jones lowers his glasses. "Heard your mother was skipping out on some hotel bills in Princeton."

"You should probably just ask her about that," I say. "I'm sure it's a big misunderstanding."

"I don't think you really want us asking her about it, do you?" Agent Hunt asks.

"That's true, I don't, but I can't control what you decide

to do. I'm just an underage minor and you're big strong federal agents." I start walking away.

Agent Hunt grabs my arm. "Stop messing around. Come with us. Right now, Cassel. You don't want us making things hard on you."

I look over at my team, jogging toward the locker room, Coach Marlin in the lead. Some of them are jogging backward to see what's going to happen to me.

"The only way I am getting in a car with you is if you handcuff me," I say with resolve. There are some things a boy like me can't live down, and being too friendly with the law is definitely one of them. No one wants to make an illicit bet with someone unless they're sure that someone is actually a criminal.

They take the bait. I am pretty sure Agent Hunt has been wanting to do this since the moment we met. He catches my wrist, pulls it behind me and smacks a cuff down onto it. Then he grabs for my other wrist. I only struggle a little, but apparently it's enough to annoy him, since when he gets the other cuff on me, he gives me a little shove. I wind up on my stomach in the dirt.

I turn my head toward the locker room and see a couple of guys and the coach still watching the show. Enough people to pass on the rumor.

Agent Jones pulls me back to my feet. Not too gently either.

I don't say anything as they march me to the car and shove me into the back.

"Now," Agent Jones says from the front seat, "what do

you have for us?" He doesn't start the car but I hear the locks of all four doors engage.

"Nothing," I say.

"We heard Zacharov came to the memorial service," says Agent Hunt. "And he brought his daughter with him. A girl that no one has seen in public in a long time. Now she's back. Here at Wallingford, even."

"So what?" I say.

"We hear that you and her were pretty close. If that's even his daughter."

"What do you want?" I ask, giving an experimental tug on the cuffs. They're double-lock and plenty tight. "You want me to tell you whether that's really Lila Zacharov? It is. I used to play marbles with her down in Carney. She's got nothing to do with this."

"So what's she been doing all this time? If you know her so well, how about you tell me that."

"I don't know," I lie. I have no idea where this line of questioning is going, but I don't like it.

"You could have a life outside of all this," Agent Jones says. "You could be on the right side of the law. You don't have to protect these people, Cassel."

I am these people, I think, but his words make me fantasize for a moment about what it would be like to be a good guy, with a badge and a stainless reputation.

"We talked to your brother," Agent Hunt says. "He was very cooperative."

"Barron?" I say, and burst out laughing. I let myself flop down onto the leather seat with relief. "My brother is a *compulsive liar*. I'm sure he was cooperative. There is nothing he likes better than an audience."

Agent Jones looks embarrassed. Agent Hunt just seems pissed. "Your brother said that we might start looking at Lila Zacharov. And he said that you'd protect her."

"Did he?" I say, but I'm in control of this conversation now, and they both know it. "I looked over those files you gave me. Are you saying that Lila is a death worker who started killing people at the age of fourteen? Because that's how old she was when Basso disappeared. And not only that, but she would have to have hidden the death rot really well. Really well, because I can tell you that I've see her with not even a stitch of—"

"We're not saying anything." Agent Jones puts his hand down hard on the seat, interrupting my little speech. "We're coming to you for information. And if you don't give us something, then we're going to have to listen to other sources. Maybe even sources you don't consider to be as reliable. You understand me?"

"Yeah," I say.

"So what are you going to have next time we come to talk?" Agent Jones asks in a kind voice. He takes out a business card, reaches back, and tosses it into my lap.

I take a deep breath, let it out. "Information."

"Good," says Agent Hunt.

They exchange a look I can't interpret, and Agent Hunt gets out of the car. He opens my door. "Turn around so I can take those off."

I do. A twist, two clicks, and I'm rubbing my wrists, free.

"In case you get some idea that we can't pick you up whenever we want," Hunt says. "You're a worker. You know what that means?"

I shake my head. Finding the business card Jones tossed at me, I shove it into my pocket. Jones watches me from where he's standing.

Hunt grins. "It means you've already done something illegal. All workers have. Otherwise, how would you know what you are?"

I get out of the car and look him in the face. Then I spit on the hot black asphalt of the parking lot.

He starts toward me, but Agent Jones clears his throat, and Hunt stops.

"We'll be seeing you around," Agent Jones says, and they both get back into the car.

I walk back to Wallingford, hating both of them so much that I'm jittery with rage. The thing I hate most is that they're right about me.

I am called into Headmistress Northcutt's office almost immediately. She opens the door and waves me inside.

"Welcome, Mr. Sharpe. Please have a seat."

I sit in the green leather chair opposite her wide expanse of a desk. Several tidy folders are corralled in a wooden box on one side, and a well-used planner sits beside a golden pen in a stand. Everything is organized, elegant.

Except for the cheap glass bowl of mints. I take one and unwrap it slowly.

"I understand you had some visitors today?" Northcutt asks. Her eyebrows lift, like having any visitors at all is suspect.

"Yeah," I say.

She sighs deeply at my forcing her to ask the question directly. "Would you like to explain what two federal agents wanted with you this time?"

I lean back in the chair. "They offered to make me a narc, but I said that the workload here at Wallingford was too intensive for me to take on an after-school job."

"Excuse me?" I didn't think it was possible for her eyebrows to rise even higher on her forehead, but they do. It isn't a nice thing I'm doing—selling a story that's less ridiculous than my presentation of it. Worst thing she can do is give me a couple of detentions or a demerit for my smart mouth, though.

"A narc," I say excessively politely. "An informant who reports on observed narcotic violations. But don't worry, there is no way I would ever agree to rat out my fellow students. Even if they made the poor decision to use drugs, which I am sure no one here ever would."

She leans forward and picks up her golden pen, points it at me. "Do you seriously expect me to believe that, Mr. Sharpe?"

I widen my eyes. "Well, I guess there are some people here who do look like they're stoned all the time, I'll give you that. But I always figured they were just—"

"Mr. Sharpe!" She looks like she's ready to actually stab me with the pen. "It is my understanding that the agents handcuffed you. Would you like to change your story?"

I think of sitting in this same office last year, begging to be allowed to stay. Maybe I'm still angry about that.

"No, ma'am. They just wanted to give me a little demonstration of how safe I would be working with them, although I can see how someone observing it might have come to a different conclusion. You can call the agents yourself," I say, reaching into my pocket. I pull out the card Agent Jones gave me and set it down on Northcutt's desk.

"I will do that," she says. "You may go. For now."

The agents will back me up. They have to. They're not done with me yet. And Agent Hunt doesn't really want to explain why he was slamming around a seventeen-year-old with no criminal record. So I get the satisfaction of their having to agree to a silly story. And I get Northcutt's annoyance at having to accept a story she's pretty sure isn't true.

Everyone wants to get out of a situation with dignity.

The HEX meeting has already started by the time I get there. The desks in Ms. Ramirez's music room have been rearranged into an impromptu circle, and I see Lila and Daneca are sitting together. I pull up a seat next to Lila.

She smiles and reaches over to squeeze my hand. I wonder if this is her first meeting. I haven't attended enough to know.

On the blackboard, there's the address for the worker rights protest Sam promised we'd attend way back when school started. Turns out it's tomorrow. I guess that's what they were talking about before I got here. Rules are written below the protest information: stick together, no talking to strangers, stay in the park.

"I'm sure that many of you didn't see yesterday's speech, since it ran during study hall," Ramirez says. "I thought we could watch it together and discuss."

"I really hate Governor Patton," says one of the sophomore girls. "Do we have to see his face spewing more crap?"

"Like it or not," says Ms. Ramirez, "this is what America sees. And this is what New Jersey will be thinking about in November when we vote on Proposition 2. This or a speech very like it."

"He's ahead in the polls," Daneca says, biting the end of one of her braids. "People actually approve of his performance."

The sophomore gives Daneca a horrible look, like Daneca was suggesting people *should* approve of Patton.

"It's a stunt," says one of the boys. "He just acts like he cares about this because it's a popular issue. Back in 2001 he voted with worker rights. He goes where his bread is buttered."

They talk some back and forth, but I lose the thread of it. I'm just happy to be here, not getting yelled at or handcuffed. Lila's watching the discussion, gaze flashing to each of the speaker's faces, but her hand rests in mine and she seems more relaxed than I've seen her in a long time.

Everything seems possible.

If I just think hard enough, plan carefully enough, maybe

I can solve my problems—even the ones I was considering unsolvable. First off, I need to actually figure out who killed Philip. Once I know that, I can engineer the steps to get the Feds off my back. Then maybe I can figure out what to do about Lila.

Ms. Ramirez pushes a television in front of a chair on one side of the circle. "Enough! Let's leave some discussing until after watching, okay?"

She presses a button, and the screen flickers to life. She points the controller at it, and Governor Patton's pasty face fills the screen. He's at a lectern, with a blue stage curtain hanging behind him. The few white hairs he still has are slicked back, and his whole vibe screams benevolent tyrant.

The camera pulls back so that we can see the press pit in front of him. Lots of people in suits raising their hands like it's high school all over again, just waiting for the teacher to call on them. And at one side there's an aide standing on the narrow steps to the stage, like he's guarding them. Beside the aide is a woman in a severe black dress, her hair pulled into a chignon. There is something about her that makes me look again.

"You're hurting my hand," Lila whispers.

I let go of her, ashamed. My glove was pulled tight over my knuckles, like I was trying to make a fist.

"What?" she asks me.

"It's just hard to listen to," I say, which seems to be true, since I wasn't actually listening at all.

She nods her head, but there is a pin scratch line

between her brows. I wait interminable minutes until I think I can safely turn to her and say, "Be right back.

"Bathroom," I say to her frown of inquiry.

I head down the hallway the opposite way from the bathroom, lean against the wall, and take out my phone. As it rings, I think over and over about *Millionaires at Home* or whatever that stupid magazine was.

"Hello, sweetheart," my mother says. "Let me call you back on a landline."

I clear my throat. "First, would you explain what you were doing on television?"

She laughs girlishly. "You saw that? How did I look?"

"Like you were wearing a costume," I say. "What were you doing with Governor Patton? He hates workers, and you're a worker *ex-convict.*"

"He's a nice man once you get to know him," she says sweetly. "And he doesn't hate workers. He wants mandatory testing to save worker lives. Didn't you listen to the speech? Besides, I'm not an ex-convict. My case was overturned on appeal. That's different."

At that moment I hear shouting back where the HEX meeting is being held.

"I got you freaks," someone yells.

"I'll call you back," I say, folding the phone closed against my chest as I head back down the hall. Greg is watching as Jeremy holds a video camera in front of the doorway, swinging it back and forth, like he's trying to get everyone. Jeremy's moving so fast that I wonder if he's recording.

Ms. Ramirez steps into the hall, and the boys stumble

back, but they keep filming. Now they're just filming her.

"I am giving you both two demerits," she says. Her voice sounds odd, shaky. "And for every second that you don't turn off the camera, I am giving you another one."

Jeremy swings it down, right away, fumbling with the controls.

"You are both going to have detention with me for the rest of this week, and you are going to erase the recording, do you understand me? That was an invasion of privacy."

"Yes, Ms. Ramirez," Jeremy says.

"Good. Now you can go." She watches them lope off. I watch her watching them, a cold dread settling into my bones.

The website goes up that night. On Thursday morning I hear the rumor that Ramirez goes ballistic, but Northcutt doesn't know who to blame. Jeremy claims he was intending to delete the footage, that someone snuck into his room and stole his camera. He says he didn't upload the stills; Greg says that he never touched any of it.

The bets start flooding in. Are they or aren't they? It seems like everyone in the school wants to put down money on which of the people at that meeting were workers. A room that I would have been in too, if it wasn't for the barest coincidence.

"Do we take the money?" Sam asks me in the hallway between classes. He looks miserable. He's a clever guy and he's thought through this far enough to know that there are no easy answers.

"Yeah," I say. "We have to. If we don't, we won't be able to have any control."

We take their money.

On Thursday afternoon the website goes down without a trace.

BACK AT THE DORMS SAM

is stripping off his uniform and putting on a T-shirt with I'M
THE HONOR STUDENT YOU READ ABOUT across the front. He
sprays some cologne at his neck while I dump my books
onto the bed.

"Where are you going?" I ask.

"The protest." He rolls his eyes. "Don't try to weasel out
of it. Daneca will kill you. She will *skin* you."

"Oh, right," I say, combing my fingers through my hair.
It's getting shaggy again. "I guess I thought, with all the
craziness . . ."

He lets me trail off vaguely but doesn't say anything
helpful. He is probably used to me being an idiot. I sigh

and kick off my dress shoes and black dress pants, pulling on jeans. After unknotting my tie and tossing it onto my rickety desk, I'm pretty much ready to go. I'm not even bothering to change out of my white button-down.

We cross the quad together and find Daneca with Ramirez outside of Rawlings Fine Arts Center, home to Ramirez's music room, and the location of most HEX meetings. The day is warm for September. Daneca's dressed up in a long batik skirt with bells dangling from the hem. She's even dyed the tips of her braids a muddy purple.

"It's canceled," Daneca says, turning to us. She's practically shouting. "Can you believe it? All Northcutt cares about is placating alumni donors! This isn't fair! She already said okay."

"It's not just the administration," Ms. Ramirez says. "*Students* dropped out of the trip too. No one wants to be seen getting on the bus."

"That's ridiculous," Daneca mutters, then louder she says, "We could have done something. Met somewhere other than here."

"Some of them are actually workers, you know," I say. "It's not just a cause for them. It's their actual lives. So maybe they're worried about the actual consequences of people guessing their secret."

Daneca gives me a look of loathing. "How do *they* think anything's going to get better with that attitude?" She clearly thinks *they* means *me*.

"Maybe *they* don't," I say.

"I'm sorry," Ramirez says with a heavy sigh. "I know you had your heart set on this."

"What's going on?" a soft voice asks from behind us. I turn to see Lila, backpack over one shoulder. She's wearing a yellow sundress and big, clunky boots. I feel that same odd shock that I always feel when I see her, like an electric current passing through my body.

"Trip's canceled due to administrative cowardice," Sam says.

"Oh." Lila looks down at her boots and kicks a clump of dirt. Then she looks up. "Well, can the four of us still go?"

Daneca stares at her for a long moment, then turns to Ramirez. "Yes! She's right. We already turned in our permission slips, so our parents have already agreed to letting us out."

"On a school-supervised trip," Ramirez protests.

"We're *seniors*," Daneca says. "We've got our parents' permission. Northcutt can't stop us."

"I don't recall Mr. Sharpe turning in a permission slip."

"Oops," I say. "Left it in my room. Let me just run back and get it."

Ramirez sighs. "Fine. Give me that form, Cassel, and the four of you can sign out and go to the protest. But I want your word that you will be back in time for study hall."

"We will," Lila promises.

After a little bit of forgery on my part, we're heading to Sam's 1978 vintage Cadillac Superior side-loading hearse. Lila stops to read the bumper sticker.

"This thing really runs on vegetable oil?" she asks.

The afternoon sun bakes the asphalt of the parking lot, making heat radiate off it. I wipe my brow and try not to consider the sweat beading at Lila's collarbone.

Sam grins proudly and slaps the hood. "It wasn't easy to find a diesel hearse to convert, but I did."

"Smells like french fries," says Daneca, climbing in. "But you get used to it."

"French fries are delicious," says Sam.

Lila scrambles into the backseat, which is custom—scavenged from a regular Cadillac and installed by Sam—and I slide in after her.

"Thank you guys for coming," Daneca says. She looks in my direction. "I know you don't really want to go, so let me just say—I appreciate it."

"It's not that I don't want to," I say, and take a deep breath. I think of my mother at that other rally with Patton. "I'm just not that into politics."

Daneca turns around in her seat to look at me incredulously. "Oh?" She doesn't seem mad, more amused.

"Deathwërk's playing later," Sam says, steering the hearse out of the parking lot as he steers the conversation away from me. "We'll probably get there in time for Bare Knuckles."

"*Bands?* Really? I was imagining less fun, more marching with placards," I say.

Daneca grins. "Don't worry, there'll be plenty of placards. The march goes past city hall to Lincoln Park—that's where the bands are supposed to perform. There are going to be speeches, too."

"Well, good," I say. "I would hate to think we're giving

up valuable studying time for anything less than a—"

Lila laughs, leaning back against her headrest.

"What?" I say.

"I don't know," Lila says. "You have nice friends." She touches my shoulder lightly with the tips of her gloved fingers.

A shiver starts low on my spine. For a moment I remember the feel of her bare hands on my skin.

It's just the four of us in the car, and even though the plan is to go to the movies tomorrow, I have to try really hard to convince myself this isn't anything like a double date.

"That's *right*," says Sam. "You knew our man Cassel back when. Got the dirt for us?"

She looks at me slyly. "When he was a kid, he was a total shrimp. Then around thirteen, he shot up like a beanpole."

I grin. "And you stayed a shrimp."

"He loved cheap horror novels, and when he started one, he'd read it straight through until the end, no matter what. Sometimes his grandfather would come into his bedroom and switch off the lamp when it got really late, so Cassel would climb out the window and read by the streetlight. I'd come over in the morning and find him asleep on the lawn."

"Awwww," Daneca says.

I make a rude sound, accompanied by an equally rude gesture.

"One time, at a fair in Ocean City, he ate so much cotton candy that he threw up."

"Who hasn't?" I say.

"He had a black-and-white film marathon, after which

he wore a fedora." She raises her brows, daring me to contradict her. "For a *month*. In the middle of summer."

I laugh.

"A fedora?" Sam says.

I remember sitting in the basement for hours, watching movie after movie of rough-voiced women and men in dapper suits with drinks in their gloved hands. When Lila's parents got divorced, she went to Paris with her father and came back smoking Gitanes and outlining her eyes in smudgy black kohl. It was like she'd stepped out of the movie I wanted to be in.

I see her now, the stiffness of her body as she leans deliberately away from me, pressing her cheek against the window. She looks tired.

In Carney, back then, I didn't care about blending in. I wasn't constantly trying to bluff my way into seeming like a better guy. I had no secrets I was desperate to keep. And Lila was brave and sure and totally unstoppable.

I wonder what the kid I was then would think of the people we are now.

Cops are standing by blockades far from where the march is supposed to be. Traffic cones are set up, flares sparking with sizzling orange flames. There are people, too, more than I expected, and a distant roar that promises even more than that.

"There's no place to park," Sam complains, slowly circling the same block for the third time.

Daneca pokes at her phone as we inch along behind a

line of cars. "Turn left when you can," she says after a few minutes. "I have an app that says there's a garage a couple blocks from here."

The first two we pass are full, but then we find cars just parking on top of the median and along the sidewalks. Sam pulls the hearse onto a patch of green grass and kills the engine.

"Rebel," I say.

Daneca grins hugely and opens the door. "Look at all these people!"

Lila and I get out, and the four of us head in the direction most are going.

"It makes you feel like everything could change, you know?" Daneca says.

"Everything *is* going to change," says Sam, surprising me.

Daneca turns and gives him a look. I can tell he surprised her, too.

"Well, it is," he says. "One way or another."

I guess he's right. Either Proposition 2 will get voted down and workers will see that organizing works and do a whole lot more of it, or Proposition 2 will pass and other states will fall all over themselves to try the same trick.

"Changing is what people do when they have no options left," Lila says cryptically.

I try to catch her eye, but she's too busy watching the crowd.

We walk like that for a few more blocks and start to see signs.

WE ARE NOT A CURSE, one reads.

I wonder what kind of slogans they had at the press conference Mom attended.

A group of kids are sitting on the steps of a Fidelity bank. One throws a beer in the direction of the protesters. It shatters, glass and foam making everyone near its impact start shouting.

A man whose huge beard is long enough to overlap his T-shirt jumps up onto the hood of a car and yells louder than the others, "Down with Proposition 2! Flatten Patton!"

A policeman standing in front of a bodega picks up his radio and starts speaking rapidly into it. He looks flustered.

"I think the park is this way," Daneca says, pointing from the screen of her phone to a side street. I'm not sure she noticed anything else.

A couple more blocks and the crowd becomes so thick that it's more like a tide we have been swept up in. We're a vein rushing blood toward the heart, a furnace of sun-warmed body heat, a herd barreling toward a cliff.

I see more and more signs.

HANDS OFF OUR RIGHTS.

TESTING EVERYONE/TRUSTING NO ONE.

THIS ISN'T WORKING.

"How many people are they estimating will come out for this?" Lila shouts.

"Twenty, maybe fifty thousand maximum," Daneca shouts back.

Lila looks toward where our street intersects with Broad, where the main protest is. We can't see too far, but the wall of noise—of slogans being screamed through bull-horns, of drums, of sirens—is almost deafening. "I think that number was off—way off."

As we get closer, it's easy to see why. I no longer have to imagine what signs Patton's supporters might have been waving around. They are out in force, lining the street on either side of the march.

MURDERERS AND MANIPULATORS OUT OF MY STATE, says one sign.

NO MORE HEEBEEGEEBIES.

WHAT DO YOU HAVE TO HIDE?

And finally, simply, GOTCHA, with a circle drawn to look like the crosshairs of a gun. That one is held up by an old woman with frizzy red hair and bright pink lipstick.

She's standing on the steps of city hall, the golden dome glowing above her.

As I scan the crowd of Proposition 2 supporters, I see a familiar face far in the back. Janssen's mistress. She's got her dark hair pulled into a ponytail, sunglasses on top of her head. No poodles with her today.

I slow down, trying to make sure I'm seeing what I think I'm seeing.

She's taking bills from someone, both of them standing close to the glass window of a restaurant.

The crowd keeps moving around me, pushing me along with it. Someone's shoulder bangs into my arm. A guy a little older than me, snapping pictures.

"Who are you looking at?" Lila asks me, craning her neck.

"See that woman by the window?" I say, trying to shove

my way sideways through the crowd. "Ponytail. She hired the hit on Janssen."

"I know her. She used to work for him," Lila says, following me.

"What?" I stop so suddenly that the man behind me slams into my back. He grunts.

"Sorry," I tell him, but he just gives me a dirty look.

Daneca and Sam are ahead of us in the crowd. I want to call out to them to slow down, but there's no way they'd hear.

The woman is walking away from the march. As slowly as I'm moving, I am never going to get to her.

"I thought she was his girlfriend," I tell Lila.

"Maybe, but she was also his underling," she says. "She lines up buyers. High rollers. People who can afford to buy regular doses of ecstatic emotion—the kind of blissed-out happiness that'll send you spiraling into depression if you stop. Or they buy luck from half a dozen curse workers at a time. Use enough luck at once and it can change big things."

"Did she know Philip?" I ask.

"You said she ordered the hit."

Janssen's mistress disappears into the throng. We're not moving fast enough to follow. Daneca and Sam are gone too—somewhere ahead of us on Broad Street, I'm sure, but I can't spot them anymore.

I mop my brow with the tail of my white shirt. "This sucks."

Lila laughs and gestures to the large sign flapping in the wind above us. It's covered in glitter and reads BARE

HANDS; PURE HEARTS. "Before Wallingford, I'd never met many people who weren't workers—I never know what to make of them."

"Just me," I say. "I was the nonworker you knew."

She gives me a quick look, and I realize, of course, that she left out the most critical thing when she summarized my past in the car.

Back then I was beneath her.

Even if she never said it to me, even if she didn't act like what she could do mattered, everyone else said it enough that there was no chance I'd forget. She was a worker; I was part of the world of marks who existed to be manipulated.

I see another sign in the crowd, POWER CORRUPTS EVERYONE.

"Lila—," I start.

Then a girl walking just ahead of us takes off her gloves. She holds up her hands. They look pale and wrinkled from being inside leather in this heat.

I blink. In my life I haven't seen many bare female hands. It's hard not to stare.

"Bare hands, pure heart!" the girl yells.

Beside her I see a few other people pulling off gloves with wicked smiles. One throws a pair up into the sky.

My fingers itch for release. I imagine what it would be like to feel the breeze against my palms.

The combination of heat and rebellion spreads like a ripple through the crowd, and suddenly bare fingers are waving in the air. We are stepping over discarded gloves.

"Cassel!" someone calls, and I see Sam. He's managed to wedge himself and Daneca between two parked cars and out of foot traffic. He's red-faced from the heat. She's glove-less and beckoning us over.

Her hands are pale, with long fingers.

We push our way through the crowd to them. We're almost there when we hear the sound of a bullhorn from somewhere in front of us.

"Everyone must cover their hands immediately," a tinny voice booms. A siren wails. "This is the police. Cover your hands immediately."

Daneca looks as horrified as if they were talking personally to her.

There is technically nothing illegal about bare hands. Just like there is technically nothing illegal about a sharp kitchen knife. But when you wave one around, the police don't like it. And when you point it at something, that's when the cuffs really come out.

"Lift me up," Lila says.

"What?"

All around us people are jeering. But there is another sound, farther away, a roar of engines and cries that no longer contain words.

A news helicopter buzzes overhead.

"Up," she says with a smile, pointing in the air. "I want to see what's happening."

I put my arms around her waist and lift her. She's light. Her skin is soft against me, and she smells like sweat and crushed grass.

I set her down on the hood of the car, next to where Sam's standing.

"There's a bunch of cops," she says, hopping down. "Riot gear. We've got to get out of here."

I nod once. Criminals like us are good at running.

"We're not doing anything illegal," Daneca says, but she doesn't sound sure. Around us the crowd feels it too. They aren't moving in the same direction anymore. They're scattering.

"Inside," I say. "If we can get to one of the buildings, we can wait out whatever happens."

But as we move toward the doorway nearest to us, cops start streaming across the sidewalk, their faces covered by helmets.

"Get down on the ground!" comes the command. They spread out, shoving protestors if they hesitate. One girl tries to argue, and a cop swings a baton at her leg. Another girl gets sprayed in the face with some chemical. She falls to the ground, clawing at her skin.

Lila and I drop down onto the asphalt immediately.

"What's going on?" Sam says, kneeling down too. Daneca squats beside him.

"Under the car," Lila says, crawling forward on her elbows.

It's a pretty good plan. We still get arrested, but at least it takes a little longer.

The last time I was in a prison was to visit Mom. Prisons are places where people live. They're dehumanizing, but they have things like tables and cafeterias and exercise rooms.

This is different. This is a jail.

They take our wallets, cell phones, and bags. They don't even bother fingerprinting us. They just ask us our names and march us down to a holding cell. Girls in one, guys in the one next door. And so on, down a long noisy hallway.

There's a couple of benches, a sink, and a single disgusting toilet. All occupied.

Daneca tries to tell them that we're underage, but the cops don't pay any attention to her. They just lock us up.

Sam is standing near me, his head leaning against the bars and his eyes closed. Daneca found a spot on one of the benches and is sitting, her face streaked with tears. They made her cover her hands before they hauled us into their armored van—and when she couldn't find one of her gloves, they taped a bag all the way to her elbow. It's cradled against her body now.

Lila paces back and forth.

"Lila," I say, and she whirls, teeth bared, hand striking at me through the bars.

"Hey," I say, catching her wrist.

She looks so surprised that I wonder if, for a moment, she forgot she was human.

"We're going to be okay," I say. "We're going to get out of here."

She nods, embarrassed now, but her breaths are still coming too fast. "What time do you think it is?"

We got to the protest at about four thirty and we never even made it to the park. "Maybe around seven," I say.

"Still early. God, I am such a mess." She pulls away from me, rubbing her gloved hand through her hair.

"You're fine," I say.

She snorts.

I look around the room at all the desperate faces. I bet none of them have ever seen the inside of a jail before. I bet none of them have family who've been in prison.

"Ever think about the future?" I ask, trying to distract her.

"Like, the future in which we're not locked up?"

"After graduation. After Wallingford." It is much in my thoughts lately.

She shrugs, leaning her face against a metal bar. "I don't know. Dad took me to Vieques this past summer. We'd just lie on the beach or swim. Everything's brighter and bluer there, you know? I'd like to go back. Soak it all up. I'm tired of being shut in dark places."

I think of her trapped in that horrible wire cage by Barron for months at a time. During one of my bleaker moments the past summer, I looked up the effects of solitary confinement on prisoners. Depression, despair, crippling anxiety, hallucinations.

I can't imagine what it must be like to be in a cage again.

"Never been out of the country," I say.

"You could come," she says.

"If you still want me with you after we graduate, I'm yours," I say, trying to make my vow sound a little more casual. "So that's it? You're just going to lie around on a beach."

"Until Dad needs me," she says. Her breaths are more

even now, her eyes less wide and wild. "I've always known what I was going to be when I grew up."

"The family business," I say. "You ever think of doing something else?"

"No," she says, but there's something in her voice that makes me wonder. "It's all I'm good at. Besides, I'm a Zacharov."

I think about the things I'm good at. And I think about Ms. Vanderveer, my guidance counselor. *The future's going to be here sooner than you think.*

We're in the cells for what I estimate to be another hour before a cop walks in, one we haven't seen before. He's got a clipboard.

Everyone starts shouting at once. Demands to see lawyers. Protestations of innocence. Threats of lawsuits.

The policeman waits for the furor to die down, then speaks. "I need the following people to come to the front of your cell and press your hands together in front of you with your fingers laced. Samuel Yu, Daneca Wasserman, and Lila Zacharov."

The cells again erupt in shouts. Daneca gets up off the bench. Sam follows her to the front of the cell, turning back toward me and widening his eyes in an expression of bafflement. After a few moments, the shouting dies down.

I wait for him to call me next, but there appear to be no more names on the clipboard.

Lila steps forward, then hesitates.

"Go," I tell her.

"We have a friend with us," Lila tells the officer, looking back in my direction.

"Cassel Sharpe," Sam supplies. "That's his name. Maybe you missed it?"

"This is all my fault—," Daneca starts.

"Be quiet, look straight ahead, hands clasped in front," the cop yells. "Everyone else take three steps away from the door. Now!"

They're cuffed and marched away, all of them turning their heads back toward me as I try to come up with explanations for why they're gone and I'm not. Maybe their parents were called and mine couldn't be reached. Maybe it was just random groups of three that were being taken for fingerprinting. I'm still trying to convince myself when Agent Jones saunters up to the cell door.

"Oh," I say.

"Cassel Sharpe." A small smile lifts a corner of his mouth. "Please step to the front of the cell, hands clasped together in front of you."

I do.

Jones leads me grimly into another hallway, one he has to swipe a card to enter. One without cells, just white walls and windowless doors. "We put an alert on your name, Cassel. Imagine my surprise when it turned up that you were in custody in Newark."

I swallow nervously. My throat feels dry.

"You got that information for me yet?" His breath smells like sour coffee and cigarettes.

"Not quite yet," I say.

"Have a good march?" he asks. "Get lots of exercise running from the law? Growing boy has got to get his exercise."

"Ha, ha," I say.

He grins like we really did just share a joke. "Let me tell you how this is going to go. I'm going to give you two choices, and you're going to make the right one."

I nod my head to show I'm listening, although I'm sure I'm not going to like what comes next.

"A couple doors down I've got Lila Zacharov and the other two you were brought in with. You and I can go there, and I'll explain that any friend of Cassel's is free to go. Then I'll let them out. Maybe I'll even apologize."

My shoulders tense. "They'll think I'm working for you."

"Oh, yeah," he says. "Definitely."

"If Lila thinks I'm working for the Feds and tells her father, I'm not going to be able to find out anything for you. I'll be useless." I'm talking too fast. He can tell he's getting to me. If the rumor gets around that I'm working for the Feds, my own mother won't want to be seen with me.

"Maybe I don't consider you all that useful anymore." Jones shrugs. "Maybe if we're all the friends you've got, you'll see things a little differently."

I take a deep breath. "What's my second choice?"

"Tell me that by the end of next week you'll have that lead for me. You're going to find out something on this mysterious assassin. Something I can use. No more excuses."

I nod. "I will."

He claps my shoulder heavily with his gloved hand. "I told you you'd make the right choice."

Then he lets me into the room with the others.

Daneca scrambles up from where she's sitting on the floor and hugs me. She smells like patchouli. Her eyes look bloodshot.

"I'm sorry," she says. "You must be so mad at me. But we're not going to do it. Don't worry. We would never—"

"Nobody's mad," I say, then look over at Sam and Lila to see if they can explain the rest of what she was saying.

"They told us we could walk out of here," Sam starts, then pauses, "if we volunteered to be tested."

"Tested?" I want to kill Jones right then. Of course he's got some stupid extra angle going.

"The hyperbathygammic test," Lila says quietly. She looks tired.

I punch the concrete wall. It just hurts my hand.

"We're not going to take the test, Cassel," Daneca says.

"No," I say. "No. You should. Both of you. Then you can call someone for Lila and me when you get out."

I have no doubt that Zacharov's lawyers will have Lila out of jail within moments. Me? Well, it'll take Grandad a little longer, but if the Feds want me to hunt for their lead, they're going to have to help out.

"But they're going to know that you're both—," Sam starts.

"That's the beauty of the test," Lila says. "The only people afraid to take it are people with something to hide."

"It's not legal to force us," Daneca says, shaking her head. "We're being held unlawfully. We weren't properly booked or Mirandized. We didn't commit any crime. This is a clear case of the government exploiting its power for its own anti-worker agenda."

"You think?" I sit down next to Lila on the floor. But despite my flippant answer, it's impossible not to be impressed with Daneca. She's never been in trouble before, and even in *jail*, she cares about what's right.

"You're shaking," Lila says softly, putting her gloved hand on my arm.

I'm surprised. I look down at my hands like I no longer remember to whom they belong. The knuckles of my left glove are scuffed from throwing that punch. Scuffed and trembling.

"Sam," I say, trying to steady myself. "You, at least, don't have to stay."

Sam looks at me and turns to Daneca. "I know you want to do the right thing, but if we don't agree to get tested, what happens next?" He lowers his voice. "What if they stop asking?"

"What if they don't let us out, even after they test us?" Daneca says. "I'm not doing it. It's against absolutely every-thing I believe in."

"You think I don't know it's wrong?" Sam snaps. "You don't think I get that this is unfair? That it sucks?"

I don't want them to fight. Not over this.

"Forget it," I say loudly, trying to sound like I know what I'm talking about. "Let's just wait. They're going to let us out soon. They've got to. Like Daneca said, they didn't really book us. We're going to be fine."

We lapse into an uneasy silence.

An hour later, just as panic begins to gnaw my gut, just when I'm ready to admit that I'm wrong and they're going to let us rot in here, just as I'm about to bang on the door and beg to see Agent Jones, a cop comes in and tells us we're free to go. No explanation. We're just shown the door.

The car's as we left it, except for the driver-side mirror, which is cracked.

We get back to Wallingford by ten. As we cross the quad, I have the strange feeling that we've been gone for days instead of just a couple of hours. We're too late for study hall, but in time for in-room check.

"I heard Ramirez let you boys go to that protest," Mr. Pascoli says, giving me a suspicious look. "How was it?"

"We decided to drive down to the beach instead," says Sam. "Good thing too. I hear the march got really out of control." His cheeks color a little as he speaks, like he's ashamed of lying.

He doesn't say anything else about it.

By lights-out it's as if the whole thing never happened.

Friday afternoon I'm sitting in the back of physics class, staring at the quiz in front of me. I am concentrating on the problem of a girl increasing the amplitude of a swing's oscillations by moving her legs along with the motion. I am not sure if this is an example of resonance, wave transmission, or something else that I've forgotten. The only thing that I am sure of is that I am going to fail this quiz.

I'm filling in one of those multiple-choice bubbles, my pencil going around and around in a circle, when Megan

Tilman screams. My pencil streaks across the paper, making a line of graphite.

"Ms. Tilman," Dr. Jonahdab says, looking up from her desk. "What is the matter?"

Megan is clutching her chest and staring at Daneca, who's one desk over from her. "My luck amulet broke. It snapped in half."

Gasps run through the class.

"You worked me, didn't you?" Megan says.

"Me?" Daneca asks, blinking at her like she's gone crazy.

"When did you feel your amulet break?" Dr. Jonahdab asks. "Are you sure that it broke right at this moment?"

Megan shakes her head. "I don't know. I just—I grabbed for it and there was only half still on the chain. Then when I moved, the other piece fell onto my desk. It must have been stuck in my blouse."

Yes, she really says "blouse," like she's someone's grandmother.

"Sometimes stones just break," says Dr. Jonahdab. "They're fragile. No one *touched* you, Megan. Everyone here is wearing gloves."

"She's on the video at that worker meeting," Megan says, pointing to Daneca. "She sits right next to me. It must have been her."

I expect Daneca to lecture her. I really do. I figure Daneca's been waiting all the time I've known her for a chance to really let some idiot have it, especially after yesterday. Instead she sinks down in her chair, her face going bright red. Tears glisten in her eyes. "I'm not a worker," she says quietly.

"Then why do you go to those meetings?" one of the other girls asks.

"Heebeegeebies." Someone fake coughs.

I stare at Daneca, willing her to speak. To tell Megan that a decent person cares about people other than herself. To explain about the plight of workers and put everyone in their place. All the righteous stuff she says to me and Sam. All the stuff she said, even in jail. I open my mouth, but even in my mind the lecture gets garbled. I can't remember the slogans. I don't know how to talk about worker rights.

Besides, for some reason, that seems like the last thing Daneca wants me to do.

I turn to Dr. Jonahdab, but she's glancing between Daneca and Megan, like somehow she's going to be able to sense the truth if she just watches them a little longer. Something's got to wake her up. Leaning toward the guy at the desk next to mine—Harvey Silverman—I say, "Hey, what did you get for problem three?" I say it loud enough that my voice carries even to the front of the class.

Daneca turns toward me. She shakes her head narrowly in warning.

Harvey looks down at his paper, and Dr. Jonahdab finally seems to snap out of her trance. "All right, everyone, that is enough talking! We are in the middle of a quiz. Megan, you may bring up your paper and take the rest of the test at my desk. After that we will go to the office together."

"I can't concentrate," Megan says, standing up. "Not while she's here."

"Then you can go down to the office now." Dr. Jonahdab writes something on a piece of paper and rips it off a legal pad. Megan takes her bag and the paper, leaving all her books behind as she walks out.

As soon as the bell rings, Daneca races toward the door, but Dr. Jonahdab calls her back. "Ms. Wasserman, I know they'll want to talk to you."

Daneca reaches into her bag. "I'm calling my mother. I'm not—"

"Look, we know that you didn't do anything wrong—" She cuts herself off when she notices me loitering by the door. "Can I help you, Mr. Sharpe?"

"No," I say. "I was just—no."

Daneca gives me a tremulous smile as I go.

On my way to French class, I walk by one of the announcement boards. It's plastered with a bunch of those public service posters you see in magazines—the kind that say I'D RATHER GO NAKED THAN BE WITHOUT MY GLOVES. Or JUST BECAUSE EVERYONE ELSE IS DOING IT, DOESN'T MAKE IT OKAY. HIRING CURSE WORKERS IS A CRIME. Or simply NO GLOVE, NO LOVE—except that the faces of models have been replaced with grainy stills of students from the video. Photos that the school secretary is frantically trying to rip down.

By the time I get to my French class, the news of what happened to Megan is all over the school.

"Daneca cursed her with bad luck, so she'd fail the test," someone says as I pass. "That's how she keeps up her GPA. She's probably been doing it to all of us for years."

"And Ramirez knew about it. That's why she's leaving."

I spin around. "What?"

It turns out the speaker is Courtney Ramos. Her eyes go wide. She was in the middle of applying lip gloss, and the wand hovers in the air, like she's frozen.

"What did you say?" I shout. People in the hallway turn toward us.

"Ms. Ramirez resigned," Courtney says. "I heard it when I was in the office waiting for my guidance counselor."

Ramirez, who let us go to the protest. Who was the only one willing to sponsor HEX, so Daneca could organize the club on campus two years ago. Who doesn't deserve to get taken down for us. Mr. Knight flashes his class, but he stays. Ramirez goes.

I grab Courtney's shoulder. "That can't be true. Why would that be true?"

She pulls out of my grip. "Get off of me. There's something really wrong with you, man. You know that?"

I turn away from her and walk off toward Ramirez's music room. I get halfway across campus before I see her in the faculty parking lot, shoving a cardboard box into the trunk of her car. Ms. Carter is with her, a milk crate under her arm.

Ramirez looks over at me and then shuts the trunk with a finality that keeps me from walking toward her.

Everyone knows "resigned" is a fancy word for "fired."

It feels totally surreal to take Lila to the movies. We both have notes from our parents on file that let us leave on

Fridays for the weekend, so we can just get into my car and meet Daneca and Sam at the theater.

She slides into the passenger side. She's got on long silver earrings that dangle like daggers, and a white dress that rides up her thighs when she sits down. I try not to notice. Okay, I try not to *stare*, because that would make me crash the car and kill us both.

"So is this what kids at Wallingford do when they're going out?" Lila asks me.

"Oh, come on," I say, laughing. "You've been gone for three years; you're not a time traveler. You know what a date is."

She smacks my arm. It stings, and I smile. "No, I'm serious," she says. "It's just all very proper. Like maybe we're going to go parking later or you're going to give me your pin."

"How was it at your old school? Straight-up Roman orgies?"

I wonder if she's seen any of her friends from that fancy Manhattan school. I remember them from her fourteenth birthday, full of glittering superiority. Rich worker kids, about to rule the world.

"There were a lot of parties. People just hooked up sometimes. No one was exclusive." She shrugs her shoulders, and then looks up at me through her pale lashes. "But worry not. I am amused by your quaint customs."

"Thank goodness for that," I say, touching my heart in mock earnestness.

Sam and Daneca are waiting for us at the concessions

stand, having an argument about whether red licorice is or is not more disgusting than black licorice. Sam's cradling an enormous glistening tub of popcorn.

"So, uh, you want anything?" I ask Lila.

"Are you offering to buy me my movie snacks?" she asks delightedly.

Sam laughs, and I give him the filthiest look I can summon up.

"Cherry slushy," Lila says quickly, maybe feeling she's taken teasing me too far, and comes with me to the counter.

We watch as they color the ice red. Lila leans against my shoulder.

"I'm sorry if I'm horrible," she says, her mouth moving against my sleeve. "I'm really nervous."

"I thought we already established that I like it when you're horrible," I say under my breath, picking up the slushies.

Her smile is as bright as the marquee lights.

Then the four of us get our tickets ripped and go into a room that's already playing the opening credits. The theater isn't crowded or anything, so we get to sit in the back.

Through some unspoken decision, none of us mentions the previous day's events, not the protest or the jail. The cool of the movie theater seems solid and real, making everything else feel very far away.

The Giant Spider Invasion is awesome. Sam talks through the whole thing, explaining which spiders are puppets and what the webbing is constructed from. I have no idea what the plot is except that the giant spider crisis seems to be powered by some kind of outer space energy. Scientists make out. The spiders die.

Even Daneca has a good time.

Afterward we go to a diner and eat club sandwiches and fries, accompanied by endless cups of black coffee. Sam shows us how to use ketchup, sugar, and Worcestershire sauce to make pretty decent-looking fake blood. The waitress is not amused.

Lila tells me I can just drop her off at the train station, but I drive her into Manhattan instead. And as we stop in front of her father's Park Avenue apartment, surrounded by city lights, she leans over to kiss me good night.

Her lips and tongue are still stained cherry red.

I STAY AT THE GARBAGE

house, in my old room, tossing and turning on the bed. Try as I might to not think about the dead guy chilling in the freezer two floors below me, all I can imagine is Janssen's dead eyes staring up through the floorboards, begging silently to be discovered.

He deserves a better burial than being shut in an ice chest, no matter what he did in life. And God knows what I deserve for putting him there.

Since I can't sleep anyway, I open up the file the Feds gave me and spread the pages across my mattress. It gives me Janssen's girlfriend's name—Bethenny Thomas—and some sketchy details about her statement that night. Nothing all that interesting. I picture her, pressing an envelope of cash against Anton's chest. And then I picture myself, leaning over Janssen, my bare hand reaching for him, fingers curling.

I wonder if I'm the last thing he saw, a gawky kid with a bad haircut, fifteen years old at the time.

I flop onto my back, scattering papers. None of them matter. They don't add up to Philip's murderer. No wonder the Feds are confused. All they want to know is what this big secret is Philip had, but it isn't here. It must be maddening to get so close to solving something and then have a new mystery on top of the old one. What was Philip's big secret, and who killed him to protect it?

The first part is easy. I'm the secret.

Who would kill to protect me?

I think of the figure in the oversize coat and the red gloves. Then I think about her some more.

The next morning I pad downstairs and make coffee, never having managed more than a little fitful sleep. Somewhere in the night I determined that the only way I am going to be able to figure out anything is if I start looking.

I figure the best place to start is Philip's house. The cops might have already gone through it, and so might the Feds, but they don't know what they're looking for. Of course, I don't know what I'm looking for either, but I know Philip.

And I'm on a deadline.

I drink the coffee, take a shower, put on a black T-shirt

and dark gray jeans, and go out to my car. It doesn't start. I pop the hood and stare at the engine for a while, but diesel cars aren't really my area of expertise.

I kick the tires. Then I call Sam.

His hearse pulls into my driveway not long after.

"What did you do to her?" Sam asks, petting the hood of my car and looking at me accusingly. He's wearing his weekend attire: a shirt with Eddie Munster on it, a pair of black jeans, and mirrored aviator sunglasses. How his parents don't see that he wants to work on special effects for movies, I don't know.

I shrug.

He pokes around for a couple of minutes and tells me I need to replace one of the fuses and probably the battery, too.

"Great," I say, "but there's something else I need to do today."

"What's that?" Sam asks.

"Solve a crime," I say.

He tilts his head, like he's considering whether or not to believe me. "Really?"

I shrug. "Probably not. How about committing a crime instead?"

"Now, that sounds more like you," he says. "Any particular one you had in mind?"

I laugh. "Breaking and entering. But it's my brother's house. So it's not that bad, right?"

"Which brother?" he asks, pulling the sunglasses down his nose so he can peer over them and raise a single eyebrow. He looks like a cop in a bad TV show, which I think is what he's going for.

"The dead one."

He groans. "Oh, come on! Why don't we just get the key from your mother or something? Doesn't his place belong to you guys anyway? Next of kin and all that."

I get in on the passenger side. The fact that he's trying to think of an easier way to get in is close enough to assent for me. "I think it belongs to his wife, but I really doubt she's going to come back to claim it."

I give him directions. He drives, shaking his head the whole time.

Unlike Bethenny's fancy apartment building with the doorman, Philip lived in a condo complex that looks like it might have been built in the 1970s. When we pull up, I hear the distant sounds of jazz on a radio, and I smell frying garlic. Inside, I know, the condos are huge.

"I'm going to wait in the car," Sam says, looking around nervously. "Crime scenes creep me out."

"Fine. I won't be long." I can't really blame him.

I know there's a security camera, since I saw the pictures it took of the red-gloved woman. It's easy to disconnect on my way to the door.

Then, as I pull out a stiff piece of metal from my backpack and squat in front of the knob, my nerves get the best of me. I'm not sure I'm ready to confront my brother's empty home. I take a couple of deep breaths and concentrate on the lock. It's a Yale, which means I have to turn it clockwise and the pins will have beveled edges. The familiar work is a welcome distraction from my thoughts.

Picking locks isn't hard, although it can be annoying. Normally you stick a key in the keyway, it turns the pins, and bingo, the door opens. When you're picking a lock, the easiest thing to do is scrub over the pins until they set. There are more sophisticated techniques, but I'm not the expert my dad was.

A few minutes later, I'm inside.

Philip's apartment has a stale rotten-food smell when I open the door. There's still police tape up, but it comes away easily. Other than that, the place just looks messy. Take-out boxes, beer bottles. Stuff a depressed guy leaves out when he has no wife and kid around to object.

When Philip was alive, I was afraid of him. I resented him. I wanted him to suffer like he'd made me suffer. Looking around the living room, I realize for the first time how honestly miserable he must have been. He lost everything. Maura ran off with his son; his best friend, Anton, was killed by our grandfather; and the only reason a crime boss he'd worked for since he was a teenager didn't kill him was because of me.

I thought of how proud he was when he took the marks—cutting the skin of his throat in a long slash and then packing it with ashes until keloid scars rose up. He called it his second smile. It was a brand, marking Philip as belonging to the Zacharovs, marking him as an insider, a killer. He would walk around with his collar open, a swagger in his step, grinning when people crossed to the other side of the street. But I also remember him in the bathroom of the old house, tears in his eyes as he took a sharp razor to the swollen, infected skin so he could darken his scars with fresh ash.

It hurt. He felt pain, even if it's easier for me to pretend he didn't.

There's a chalk outline of his body on the carpet and deep brown stains around a chunk of rug that's been removed—I assume for forensics.

I walk through the familiar rooms, trying to see what's out of place. Everything and nothing. I have no idea what Philip moved around before he died—I was in the house enough to know where things were in general, but not enough to memorize details. I go up the stairs and into his office—basically a spare room with a converted crib and a desk. The computer is missing, but I figure the Feds took it. I open a few drawers, but there's nothing more interesting than a bunch of pens and a switchblade.

Philip's bedroom is strewn with clothes that he obviously just dropped onto the floor when he took them off, and maybe occasionally kicked into piles. There's broken glass chunks near the baseboard, including the jagged bottom of a highball glass with some brown fluid dried inside.

His closet is full of his remaining clean clothes and not much else. In one of his shoe boxes I find foam cut to accommodate a gun, but the gun's gone. There's a rattling assortment of bullets in another.

I try to think back to when we were kids, when Dad was

alive. I can't remember any of Philip's hiding spots. All I remember is Dad coming into my room to get—

Oh.

I walk into Philip's son's room. His bed is still pushed against one wall, covered in stuffed animals. The drawers of the dressers are open, although some of them still have clothes in them. I can't tell if Maura left the room like this or if this is the result of cops pawing through everything.

The closet door is standing ajar. I carry over a mushroom-shaped stool and hop up onto it, reaching up to where I keep my bookmaking operation in my own dorm room, up to the shadowy recesses of the closet above the door. My hand connects with a piece of cardboard. I rip it down.

It's painted the same light blue as the wall. Nearly impossible to find just by looking, even with flashlights. Taped to the back is a manila envelope.

I take the whole thing back out into the room, where my movements have made the sailboat mobile over the toddler bed dance. Glassy-eyed bears watch as I fold up the brass tab and slide out a bunch of papers. The first thing I see is what looks like a legal contract granting Philip Sharpe immunity for past crimes. It's detailed—there are a lot of pages—but I recognize the signatures in the back. Jones and Hunt.

Behind that, though, I see three pages in Philip's looping handwriting. It's an account of whose ribs he cracked to make sure that Mom's appeal went through. I don't know what it means to find this here—whether it's with these other papers because he never gave it to the Feds or if it's here because he did.

All I know is that this could get Mom sent back to prison.

All I know is that Mom would have never forgiven him.

I push that thought out of my head as I walk back toward the living room, tucking the envelope into the waistband of my jeans and pulling my T-shirt over it. On the coffee table is a big brass ashtray, empty of all cigarette butts but one. As I walk closer, I notice it's white with a gold band. I recognize it.

It's a Gitanes. The brand Lila smoked when she came back from France all those years ago. I pick it up and look at it, see the imprint of lipstick. The first thought that occurs to me is that I didn't know she still smoked.

The second thought is that I have already seen that the Feds took stuff from Philip's apartment. I assume the ashtray is empty because the forensics team already took all the butts, along with the chunk of rug, Philip's computer, and the gun. Which means Lila came later.

The door opens and I spin around, but it's only Sam.

"I got bored," he says. "Besides, you know what's creepier than walking around your dead brother's apartment? Sitting alone in a hearse in front of his apartment."

I grin. "Make yourself at home."

He nods toward my hand. "What's that?"

"I think Lila was here," I say, holding up the remains of her cigarette. "She used to smoke these. The lipstick looks right."

He looks a bit stunned. "You think Lila killed your brother?"

I shake my head, but what I mean is that I don't think

that the cigarette proves anything. It doesn't prove that she did and it doesn't prove that she didn't.

"She must have been here *after* the place got swept for evidence," I say. "She came in here, sat on this couch, and smoked a cigarette. Why?"

"Returning to the scene of the crime," Sam says, like he's a television detective.

"I thought you liked Lila," I say.

"I *do*," he says, and suddenly looks serious. "I do like Lila, Cassel. But it's weird that she was in your brother's house after he was murdered."

"*We're* in my brother's house after he was murdered."

Sam shrugs his massive shoulders. "You should just ask her about it."

Lila loves me. She has to; she's been worked to. I don't think she would do something that would hurt me, but I can't explain that to Sam without explaining the rest. And I won't tell him about the envelope.

I don't want to even think about those three pages and what they might mean. I don't want to imagine my mother being the woman in the red gloves. I want the murderer to be someone I have never met, a hired gun. So long as it's no one I know, I am free to hate them, at least as much as I hated my brother.

Back in the car I get Sam to drive me into the parking lot of a large supermarket I spot on the way to the highway. Behind the store is a sad stretch of trees and several large Dumpsters. He watches while I fumble through my backpack for matches and make a small fire as discreetly as I can, add-ing scraps of nearby debris, the immunity agreement, and Philip's scrawled confession. When it's hot enough, I drop the cigarette butt into it.

"You're destroying evidence," he says.

I look up at him. "Yeah?"

He smacks his hand into his forehead. "You can't do that! What do those papers even say?"

Sam, despite everything he's seen, is a good citizen.

I watch the edges of the paper curl and the filter smoke. I knew Philip had bargained away his own secrets—and mine—but I never thought he'd bargain away Mom's, too. "The papers say that my brother was a hypocrite. He was so pissed off that I'd dare betray our family. Turns out he was just mad I did it first."

"Cassel, do you know who killed him?" There's some-thing odd in Sam's voice.

I look at him and realize what he's thinking. I laugh. "They found video footage of a woman entering his apart-ment the night of his death. So *not me*."

"I didn't think it was you," he says too quickly.

"Whatever." I stand. I honestly don't blame him for being suspicious. "It'd be okay if you did. And thanks for being my wheelman."

He snorts as I disperse the blackened remains of my findings with one shoe. "Do you care if we go to Daneca's?" he asks. "I told her I was going to stop over."

"She's going to be disappointed if I tag along," I say with a smile.

He shakes his head. "She's going to want to know what you found. Remember how obsessed she was with those files?"

"You're going to tell her about this little bonfire, aren't you? Man, no wonder you want me to come along. You just want her yelling at the right person." I'm not really mad, though. I like that Sam doesn't lie to his girlfriend. I like that they are in love. I even like the way that Daneca gets on my case.

"If you tell me not to, I won't tell her," Sam says, "but I'm not sure you're really objective about this, uh, investigation."

I feel a rush of gratitude that makes me want to tell him everything, but the ashes behind us remind me not to trust anyone completely.

Sam flips on the car radio. It's set to some news program where the hosts are talking about the protest in Newark. The cops are claiming a riot broke out, but several YouTube videos show peaceful demonstrators being arrested. Some are still in custody—the numbers remain uncertain. The whole conversation deteriorates into jokes about girls with naked hands.

Sam changes the channel abruptly. I look out the window to avoid meeting his eyes. We stop at an auto parts store for a package of fuses and a new battery. Over the piped-in elevator music, he explains how to install them. I act even more incompetent with cars than I am, mostly to annoy Sam into laughing.

Minutes later, we pull into Daneca's family's fancy

Princeton driveway. A guy in a green uniform is dusting the lawn with a leaf blower. In the back I can see Mrs. Wasserman in her garden, cutting a dark orange sunflower. She's got a basket of them on her arm and waves when she sees us.

"Cassel, Sam," Mrs. Wasserman says, walking over to the gate. "What a pleasant surprise."

I thought people didn't say things like that in real life, although I guess there are exceptions for people who live in houses like hers. Mrs. Wasserman doesn't look as elegant as she sounds, though. Her cheek is smeared with dirt, her green Crocs are ragged, and her hair is pulled back into a messy ponytail. Somehow, though, her lack of effort is even more intimidating.

She doesn't look like a tireless campaigner for worker rights. You wouldn't figure her for the person who admitted on national television to being a worker. But she is.

"Oh, hi," says Sam. "Is Daneca home?"

"Inside," she says, and holds out the basket of flowers. "Can you two take these to the kitchen? I have to get the last of the zucchini. No matter how few you plant, somehow they always come in at once and then you have too many."

"Can I help?" I ask impulsively.

She gives me an odd look. "That would be great, Cassel."

Sam takes the basket of flowers and shakes his head at me, clearly guessing that I'm trying to delay answering Daneca's inevitable questions.

I follow Mrs. Wasserman into the backyard while Sam goes inside. She picks up another basket from a pile of them inside a shed. "So how are things? I heard about Ms. Ramirez's resignation. It's ridiculous what that school thinks it can get away with."

The garden is idyllic and huge, with lavender plants and blooming vines crawling up pyramids of woven sticks. Tiny red cherry tomatoes cover one raised bed, while another is bright with summer squash.

"Yeah," I say. "Ridiculous. I was wondering, though. There was something I was hoping to ask you."

"Of course." She gets down on her knees and starts to snap off striped green vegetables with a twist of her garden-gloved hands. The zucchini grow from the center of a large leafy plant with yellow flowers and seem to just sprawl heavily on the ground. After a moment I realize that offering to help her means I should be mimicking what she's doing.

"Um," I start, bending down. "I heard about this thing— this organization the federal government has. For worker kids. And I wondered if you'd heard about it too?"

Mrs. Wasserman nods, not bringing up the fact that the last time I saw her, I was insisting up, down and sideways that I wasn't a worker and wasn't interested in them either. "No one will confirm much about it, but anyone trying to legislate in favor of protections for worker kids runs into government push-back concerning their own program. I've heard it called the Licensed Minority Division."

I frown over the name for a moment. "So is it legit?"

"All I know," she says, "is that I used to correspond with a kid about your age before he got recruited by them. I never heard from him again. Worker teenagers are a valuable resource, until the blowback cripples them—and the LMD tries to recruit before the mob does. The LMD goes after other workers—sometimes for legitimately terrible crimes, sometimes for minor infractions. It can sour the soul. If someone told you about the Minority Division, then you need a lawyer, Cassel. You need someone to remind them you're still a citizen with choices."

I laugh, thinking of the holding cell, thinking of all the people who might still be in it. But even if I believed citizens had choices, the only person with any legal expertise I know is Barron, and all he managed was a couple years of pre-law at Princeton. Mom has a lawyer, but I can't pay him the way she does. Of course, there's Mrs. Wasserman. *She's* a lawyer, but she's not exactly volunteering. "Okay. I'll try to keep my nose clean."

She pushes back a lock of woolly brown hair and manages to paint her forehead with dirt. "I don't mean to say that they aren't a worthwhile organization. And I'm sure that some kids wind up with fine, upstanding government jobs. I just want us to live in a world where worker kids don't have to play cops or robbers."

"Yeah," I say. I can't imagine that world. I don't think I'd fit in there.

"You should go on into the house," she says, and then smiles. "I can manage the rest of the vegetable picking."

I stand up, understanding a dismissal when I hear one.

"I didn't know what I was," I say, swallowing hard. "Before. I didn't mean to lie to you."

Mrs. Wasserman looks up at me, shading her eyes with

one gloved hand. For the first time in this conversation, she looks rattled.

Daneca and Sam are sitting on stools at the massive island in her kitchen. Resting on the marble counter in front of him is a glass of iced tea with a sprig of actual mint stuffed into it.

"Hey, Cassel," Daneca says. She's wearing a white T-shirt and jeans with knee-high brown suede boots. One purple-tipped braid hangs in front of her face. "You want something to drink? Mom just went to the store."

"I'm good," I say, shaking my head. I always feel awkward in Daneca's house. I can't help casing the joint.

"Why did you go investigating without me?" Daneca demands, clearly done with being a hostess. "I thought we were in this together."

"It was on the way," I say. "Sam mostly waited in the car. Anyway, the police and the Feds were already through there. I just wanted to see if I noticed anything they wouldn't."

"Like the cigarette?"

"I see Sam told you about that. Yeah, like the cigarette. But that came later, I'm pretty sure."

"Cassel, I know this is hard to hear, but she has every reason to want to kill your brother. You said he kidnapped her."

I'm probably thinking about this the wrong way, but right now I regret telling them anything. The problem with starting to talk is that the parts you leave out become really obvious. Plus there's the temptation to just reveal everything.

And I can't do that. Now that I have friends, I don't want to lose them.

"I know," I say, "but I don't think she did it. She didn't seem guilty at his funeral."

"But she *went* to the funeral," Daneca says, insisting. Sam isn't saying anything, but I can see him nod along with her. "Why would she even go to the funeral of someone she hated? Murderers do that. I've read about it."

"Revisiting the scene—," Sam starts.

"Philip wasn't killed at a funeral parlor! Besides, she came there with Zacharov," I say. "He wanted to offer me a job."

"What kind of job?" Daneca asks.

"The kind you don't talk about," I say. "The kind that gets you a big fat keloid necklace and a new nickname."

"You didn't take it, right?" she says. I am pretty sure that, like the Feds, Daneca and Sam have come to the conclusion that I'm a death worker along the lines of Grandad.

I pull at the collar of my shirt. "You want to see my throat?"

"Oh, come on," she says. "Just answer the question."

"I didn't take the job," I say. "Honest. And I have no plans to. *And* I want some of the iced tea that Sam has. *With* a mint sprig, please."

Daneca smiles tightly and hops down from her stool. "Fine, but that doesn't mean we're done discussing Lila. I mean clearly you've got a crazy, epic thing for her—but that doesn't mean that she's not a suspect."

I try not to take it too hard that even though Lila has

been worked to love me, I'm the one whose feelings are obvious. "Okay. What if she did kill my brother? Will knowing that help anyone?"

"It'll help you protect her," Sam says. "If you want to."

I look at him in surprise, because it's not at all what I expected him to say. It's also absolutely true.

"Okay," I say. "Okay. Is it really that obvious I'm into her?" I think of Audrey, practically saying the same thing outside the cafeteria. I must be pathetic.

"We went to the movies together," Daneca says. "Last night. Remember?"

"Oh, yeah," I say. "That."

Sam frowns as Daneca pours my tea.

"Maybe you should just call and *ask* if she killed Philip," Sam says.

"No!" says Daneca. "If you do that, then she's going to put on an act. Hide evidence. We have to make a plan."

"Okay." I hold up my hand. "I don't think Lila did this. I really don't. It's not that I think she's not capable of killing someone. I'm sure she is. And I'm sure she hated Philip, although if she was going to kill one of my brothers, I'm pretty sure she would have started with Barron. But she—I know this isn't going to sound convincing—she really likes me. Like, likes me so much that I don't think she'd do something that would hurt me or make me hate her."

They both exchange a glance.

"You're a charming dude," Sam says carefully. "But no one is that charming."

I groan. "No, I'm not *bragging*. She's been cursed to love

me. Now do you get it? Her feelings are reliable because they're not real." My voice breaks on the last two words, and I look at the floor.

There is a long pause.

"How could you do that to her?" Daneca says finally. "That's like brain rape. That's like actual rape if you— How could you, Cassel?"

"I *didn't*," I say, biting off each word. She could have given me the benefit of the doubt for just one minute. She's supposed to be my friend. "I'm not the one who worked Lila. And I never wanted her to—I never wanted this."

"I'm going to tell her," Daneca says. "She has to be told."

"Daneca," I say, "just shut up for a minute. I already told her. What kind of person do you think I am?" Looking at Daneca's face, I can see exactly what kind of person she thinks I am, but I keep going anyway. "I told her and I've tried to stay away from her, but it's not easy, okay? Everything I do seems to be the wrong thing."

"So that's why—" Sam cuts himself off.

"Why I've been acting so weird about her?" I say. "Yeah."

"But you're not an emotion worker?" Daneca says cautiously, no longer quite so disgusted. I appreciate that she's at least trying to sort through what I've already said, but I can't help resenting that the one thing I actually didn't do is what she's accusing me of.

"No," I say. "I'm not. Of course not."

Sam looks over at the doorway, and I follow his gaze to see the blond worker kid that Mrs. Wasserman took in.

"So if you're not the one who cursed her . . . ?" Daneca asks me, whispering.

"That part's not important," I say.

The kid turns to us, his face pinched. "I already heard you. You don't have to whisper."

"Leave us alone, Chris," Daneca says.

"I'm just getting a soda." He opens the refrigerator.

"We have to do something," Daneca says. Her voice is still low. "There's some emotion worker going around hurting people. We can't just let—"

"Daneca," Sam says. "Maybe Cassel's not ready to—"

"Emotion workers are *dangerous*," Daneca says.

"Oh, shut up," says Chris suddenly. The refrigerator gapes open behind him. He has the soda in his gloved hand, and he seems ready to hurl it at one of us at any moment. "You always act like you're better than everybody else."

"This is none of your business," says Daneca. "If you don't get your soda and get out of here, I'm calling Mom."

Sam and I share the awkward look of outsiders in the middle of a family squabble.

"Oh, yeah?" Chris says. "Maybe you should tell your friends that *you're* an emotion worker instead of hiding it. Do you think they'll still listen to you then?"

For a moment everything stops.

I look at Daneca. She has the blank look of shock, eyes wide. Her hand is raised protectively as if words could be warded off. The kid isn't lying.

Which means that Daneca has been.

Sam falls off his stool. I think he was trying to stand up and wasn't really thinking about it, but he winds up stumbling back as the stool crashes to the floor. His back hits the cabinet. The expression on his face is awful. He doesn't know her anymore. It cuts me to the bone because that's exactly how I'm afraid he'll look at me.

I lean down and right the fallen stool, glad to have something to do.

"We've got to go," Sam says. "Cassel, come on. We're out of here."

"No, *wait*," Daneca says, walking toward him. She falters as if not sure what to say, then turns back to the kid. "How could you do this to me?" Her voice is a thin wail.

"It's not my fault you're a liar," Chris says haltingly. He looks terrified. I think if he could, he'd take the words back.

Sam stumbles toward the door.

"I'll talk to him," I say to Daneca.

"*You* lie," she says, grabbing my arm, desperate. I can feel her nails through the thin leather of her gloves. "You lie to him all the time. Why is it okay when you do it?"

I shrug off her hand, not letting her see how much the words hurt. Right now all my impulses are bad ones. I hadn't realized how little Daneca trusted me until this afternoon. And if she's anything like my mother—the only other emotion worker I know—maybe I shouldn't trust her, either. "I said I would talk to him. That's all I can do."

Outside, Sam's hearse is still in the driveway but I don't see him anywhere. Not in Daneca's mother's elegant garden, not over the hedge in the neighbor's backyard with an in-ground pool. Not walking down the side of the road. Then one of the doors of the hearse swings open. Sam is lying on his back inside.

"Get in," he says. "Also, girls suck."

"What are you doing?" I climb inside. It's creepy. The roof is lined in gathered gray satin and the windows are tinted very dark.

"I'm thinking," he says.

"About Daneca?" I ask, although I can't imagine the answer is anything other than yes.

"I guess now we know why she wouldn't get tested." He sounds bitter.

"She was scared," I say.

"Did you know she was a worker?" he asks. "Be honest."

"No," I say. "*No.* I mean, I guess I thought she might be—before I really knew her—because of her being so gung ho about HEX, but I figured she *wished* she was a worker. Like I used to. But you have to understand how frightening—"

"I don't," Sam says. "I don't have to understand."

It finally occurs to me what's bothering me about the hearse. Being in the back reminds me of being in the trunk of Anton's car, next to garbage bags of bodies. I remember vividly the smell of spilled guts. "She cares about you," I say, trying to force my mind back to the present. "When you care about someone it's harder to—"

"I never asked you what kind of worker you are," Sam says, flinging the words at me like a challenge.

"Yeah," I say carefully. "And I really appreciate that."

"If I did . . ." Sam pauses. "If I did, would you tell me?"

"I hope so," I say.

He's quiet then. We lie next to each other, twin corpses waiting for burial.

WE CAN'T STAY IN DANECA'S

driveway. Instead, we go to Sam's house, steal a six-pack
of his dad's beer, and drink it between us in his garage.
There's an old maroon couch out there near a drum set
from his older sister's band. I flop down on one side of the
sofa, and he flops on the other.

"Where is your sister now?" I ask, reaching for a handful of sesame-coated peanuts—we found a bag of them
near the beer. They crunch in my mouth like salted candy.

"Bryn Mawr," he says, belching loudly, "driving my
parents crazy because she has a girlfriend covered in
tattoos."

"Really?"

He grins. "Yeah, why? You didn't think anyone related to me could be a rebel?"

"How much of a rebel can she be in that fancy college?" I say.

He throws a musty pillow at me, but I manage to block it with my arm. It tumbles to the concrete floor.

"Didn't your brother go to Princeton?" he asks.

"Touché," I say, and gulp from the beer. It's warm. "Shall we duel for the dishonor of our siblings?"

Sam frowns at me, suddenly serious. "You know, I thought—for most of the first year we lived together—that you were going to kill me."

That makes me nearly spit out beer.

"No, look—living with you, it's like knowing there's a loaded gun on the other side of the room. You're like this leopard who's pretending to be a house cat."

I roll my eyes.

"Shut up," he says. "You might do normal stuff, but a leopard can drink milk or fall off things like a house cat. It's obvious you're not—not like the rest of us. I'll look over at you, and you'll be flexing your claws or, I don't know, eating a freshly killed antelope."

"Oh," I say. It's a ridiculous metaphor, but the hilarity has gone out of me. I thought I did a good job of fitting in—maybe not perfect, but not as bad as Sam makes it sound.

"It's like Audrey," he says, stabbing the air with a finger, clearly well on his way to inebriated and full of determination to make me understand his theory. "You acted like she went out with you because you did this good job of being a nice guy."

"I am a nice guy."

I try to be.

Sam snorts. "She liked you because you scared her. And then you scared her too much."

I groan. "Are you serious? Come on, I never did anything—"

"I'm as serious as a heart attack," he says. "You're a dangerous dude. Everyone knows this."

I take the remaining throw pillow and press it over my face, smothering myself. "*Stop,*" I say.

"Cassel?" Sam says.

I peek out from under the cushion. "Don't traumatize me any more than you already—"

"What kind of worker are you?" Sam's looking over at me with the benevolent curiosity of the drunk.

I bite off what I was going to say, hesitate. The moment drags on, suspended in amber.

"You don't have to tell me," he says. "It doesn't matter."

I know what he thinks my answer is going to be. He figures I'm a death worker. Maybe he even thinks I killed somebody. If he's really clever—and at this point I have to assume he's more clever than I am, since he's saying that he figured out I was dangerous long before I did—he's got a theory that I killed one of the men the Feds are looking for. If I say I'm a death worker, he'll swallow it. He'll think I'm a good friend. He'll think I'm honest.

My palms sweat.

I want to be that friend. "Transformation," I say. It comes out like a croak.

He sits up fast, staring at me. All traces of humor are gone. "What?"

"See? I'm getting better at being truthful," I say, trying to lighten the mood. My stomach hurts. Honesty freaks me right the hell out.

"Are you crazy?" he asks me. "You shouldn't have told me that! You shouldn't tell anyone! Wait, you're really—?"

I just nod.

It takes him a long moment before he can come up with anything else.

"Wow," he says finally, awe in his voice. "You could create the best special effects *in the world*. Monster masks. Horns. Fangs. Totally permanent."

I never thought of that, never considered using working for anything fun. The corner of my lip lifts in an unexpected smile.

He pauses. "The curses *are* permanent, right?"

"Yeah," I say, thinking of Lila, and Janssen. "I mean, I can change things back to the way they were. Mostly."

Sam gives me a considering look. "So you could stay young forever?"

"That *sounds* possible," I say with a shrug. "But it's not like the world is full of transformation workers, so it must not work." The sheer enormity of what I don't know about my limitations—the stuff I don't even want to deal with—is suddenly a lot more obvious.

"How about giving yourself a huge you-know-what?"

He leans back on the couch and points to his pants with both hands. "Like, unnaturally big."

I groan. "You've got to be kidding me. That's what you want to know?"

"I've got my priorities straight," he says. "You're the one who's not asking the right questions."

"Story of my life," I say.

Sam finds a dusty bottle of Bacardi in the back of his parents' pantry. We split it.

Late Sunday afternoon I wake up to someone ringing the doorbell. I don't remember how I got home; maybe I walked. My mouth still tastes like booze, and I am pretty sure my hair is sticking straight up. I try to smooth it out as I walk down the stairs.

I don't know what I expect, really. A package that I have to sign for, maybe. Missionaries, kids selling cookies, something like that. Even the Feds. Not Mr. Zacharov, looking as crisp as a fake hundred-dollar bill, at the door of my dingy kitchen.

I flip the locks. "Hey," I say, and then realize my breath must be awful.

"Are you busy this evening?" he asks, giving every appearance of not noticing that I just rolled out of bed. "I'd like you to come with me." Behind him is a goon in a long, dark coat. He's got a tattoo of a skull on his neck, above the keloid scars.

"Sure," I say. "Okay. Can you give me a minute?"

He nods. "Get dressed. You can have breakfast on the way."

I walk back upstairs, leaving the kitchen door open so that Zacharov can come in if he wants.

In the shower, as hot water pounds down like needles onto my back, I realize that it's really, really odd that Zacharov is waiting for me downstairs. The more awake I get, the more surreal it seems.

I come back into the kitchen fifteen minutes later, chewing aspirin, in black jeans and a sweater, with my leather jacket on. Zacharov is sitting at my kitchen table, looking relaxed, fingers tapping on the worn wood.

"So," I say. "Where are we going?"

He stands and raises both steel gray eyebrows. "To the car."

I follow him out to a sleek black Cadillac. It's already running, with Stanley—a bodyguard I met before—in the driver's seat. The guy with the skull tattoo is sitting beside him. Zacharov waves me in, and I scoot across the backseat.

"Hey, kid," Stanley says. There's a steaming cup of coffee in the cup holder and a fast-food bag over on my seat. I open it up and take out the bagel and egg sandwich inside.

"Stanley," I say, nodding to him. "How's the family?"

"Never better," he says.

Zacharov sits beside me as the tinted privacy divider grinds up.

"I understand that you and my daughter spent Friday together," he says as Stanley backs the Cadillac out of my driveway.

"I hope she had fun," I say between chews. I wonder suddenly if Zacharov found out about the curse. If so, it was nice for him to let me get cleaned up and fed before he killed me.

But Zacharov has an amused curl to his lip. "And I understand that you spent some time with some federal agents the day before that."

"Yeah," I say, trying not to look too relieved. Questions about the Feds from a mob boss should not *relax* anyone. "They came to see me at school. About Philip."

He narrows his eyes. "What about Philip?"

"He was making a deal with them," I say. There's no point in lying to Zacharov about this. Philip's dead. There's no real harm in his knowing. I feel a pang of guilt nonetheless. "They say he was an informant. And then someone murdered him."

"I see," Zacharov says.

"They want me to help them find the killer." I hesitate. "At least that's what they say they want."

"But you don't think so," he says.

"I don't know," I say, and take a long swig of the coffee. "All I know is that they're assholes."

He laughs at that. "What are their names?"

"Jones and Hunt." The combination of coffee and grease is soothing my stomach. I feel pretty good, leaning back against the leather seat. I'd feel better if I knew where we were going, but for the moment I am willing to wait.

"Huh," he says. "Luck workers, both of them."

I look over at him, surprised. "I thought they hated workers."

He smiles. "Maybe they do. I just know they *are* workers. Most of the agents in the division that deals with us folks are workers themselves." By "us folks," I'm guessing he means organized crime families on the East Coast. Families like his.

"Oh," I say.

"Didn't know that, eh?" He seems pleased.

I shake my head.

"They have been worrying you about your mother, too, yes? I know how these men operate." He nods his head, clearly indicating that I can answer if I want to, but it's not required. "I could get them off your back."

I shrug my shoulders.

"Yes, you're not sure. Maybe I pushed you too hard at Philip's funeral. Lila thinks so, anyway."

"Lila?" I say.

His smile smoothes out with something like pride. "Someday she will lead the Zacharov family. Men will die for her. Men will kill for her."

I nod my head, because, of course, that's what it means to be Zacharov's daughter. It's just that his saying it makes it uncomfortably real. Makes the future seem to come too soon.

"But some men might not like to follow a woman," Zacharov says as the car takes a sharp turn. We pull into the covered garage of a building, and park. "Especially a woman he knows too well."

"I really hope you're not talking about me," I say.

The locks pop up on the doors.

"Yes," he says. "As do I."

The garage is unfinished. Just rough concrete without signs or even lines painted to delineate one space from another. Someone must have run out of money partway through the build.

I'm guessing that means screaming for help is off the table.

We get out of the car. I follow Zacharov and Stanley into the building. The tattooed goon follows me, his gloved hand giving me a little push at the base of my spine when I look around too much.

If the parking lot is new and unfinished, the building it connects to is ancient, with a plaque that reads TALLINGTON STRING-MAKERS GUILD AND NEEDLE FACTORY. It has clearly been abandoned a long time, the windows covered with nailed-up boards, and the wooden planks covered in a thick layer of sticky black dirt. I'm guessing someone wanted to convert where I'm standing into lofts before the last recession hit.

The thought rises unbidden that I've been brought here to die. Grandad told me that's how they do it. Take a guy for a ride, real friendly. Then, *pow*. Back of the head.

I stick my right hand into the pocket of my jacket and start worming off that glove. My heart's racing.

We come to stairs, and Stanley hangs back. Zacharov holds out his hand, indicating I should go first.

"You lead, I follow," I say. "Since you know where we're going."

Zacharov laughs. "Someone is cautious."

He starts toward the stairs, and Stanley follows him,

then skull tattoo guy, leaving me last. I've managed to work off my glove. I cradle it in my palm.

The hallway we come to is lit by flickering overhead fluorescents. They look yellowed and, in a few cases, burned. I follow the skull tattoo guy's suit-jacketed back until we all come to a large steel door.

"Put this on," Zacharov says, reaching into his coat and taking out a black ski mask.

I pull it over my head somewhat haphazardly with my one gloved hand. Zacharov and his guys must notice I keep the other hand in my pocket, but no one says anything about it.

Stanley knocks three times.

I don't recognize the man who swings the door open. He's tall, maybe forty, wearing stained jeans and no shirt. He's so skinny that his chest looks concave. He's covered in tattoos. Naked women being beheaded by skeletons, demons with curling tongues, blocky words in Cyrillic. No color, just black ink and an unsteady hand. It's amateur work. Jailhouse, I'm guessing. The guy's hair hangs over his cheekbones in greasy strings. One of his ears is as blackened as Grandad's fingers. He's obviously been living for a while in the room that he ushers us into. There's a cot covered in a filthy blanket. A table made from sawhorses and a single sheet of plywood rests in the center of the room, piled with cardboard pizza boxes, a mostly empty bottle of vodka, and a take-out foil container of half-eaten pelmeni.

His gaze darts hungrily from me to Zacharov, then back again.

"Him?" the guy says, and spits on the floor.

"Hey," Stanley says, stepping between us. The other body-guard was leaning against the wall near the door. He stands up a little straighter, like he's expecting trouble.

I look over at Zacharov, waiting for his reaction.

"You are going to change his face," he tells me calmly, as if he was discussing the weather. "For old times' sake. For the debt you still owe me."

"Make me pretty," the man says, coming as close to me as he can with Stanley between us. He smells like stale sweat and vomit. "I want to look like a movie star."

"Yeah, okay," I say, taking my hand out of my pocket. Bare. The air feels cool on my skin. I rub my thumb against my fingers in an unfamiliar gesture.

The man dances away. Stanley turns to see what freaked the guy out, and backs off too. Ungloved hands get attention.

"You sure he's what you say he is?" the guy asks Zacharov. "This isn't your way of getting rid of a problem, right? Or making me forget my own name?"

"No need to bring a boy to do either of those things," Zacharov says.

That doesn't seem to reassure the guy. He looks at me and gestures to his neck. "Show me your marks."

"I don't have any," I say, pulling at the front of my sweater.

"We don't have time for these pointless questions," Zacharov says. "Emil, sit down now. I am a busy man and I do not oversee murders. I also do not take pointless risks."

That seems to settle him. He pulls up a folding metal chair and sits in it. Rust has eaten away at the joints, but he doesn't seem to notice. He's too busy watching my hand.

"What's this for?" I ask.

"I will answer all of your questions later," Zacharov says. "But for now, do as I ask."

Stanley eyes me coldly. Zacharov's not *asking*. There never were any good choices.

Emil's eyes go wide when I touch the pads of my fingers to his filthy cheek. I bet my heart is beating just as fast as his.

I've never done anything like this transformation, something requiring fine detail and finesse. I close my eyes and let myself see with that odd second sense, let every part of Emil become infinitely malleable. But then I panic. I can't think of a single movie star whose features I recall in detail. Not a guy, anyway. They're all blurs of eyes and noses and some vague sense of familiarity. The only actor that comes to mind at all is Steve Brodie as Dr. Vance in *The Giant Spider Invasion*.

I change Emil. I'm getting the hang of this. When I open my eyes, he looks like a passably hot dude from the 1970s. No more tattoos. No more scars. I fixed his ear, too.

Stanley sucks in his breath. Emil reaches up to touch his face, his eyes wide.

Zacharov is staring at me, one corner of his thin mouth lifted in a hungry smile.

Then my knees cramp and I go down hard. I can feel my body start to spread, my fingers branching out into dozens of iron nails. My back spasms and my skin feels like it's sloughing off me. I can hear a sound coming out of me, more a moan than a scream.

"What's wrong with him?" Emil yells.

"It's the blowback," Zacharov says. "Give him some space."

I hear the table being dragged back as I flop around on the floor.

"Is he going to bite his tongue?" That's Stanley's voice. "I don't think that looks right. He's going to give himself a concussion. We should at least put something under his head."

"Which one?" asks someone else. Emil? The guy by the door? I no longer know.

It hurts. It really, really hurts. Blackness rises up, looming and terrible, before breaking over me like a wave, dragging me down to the bottom of the dreamless sea.

When I wake, I'm on the cot, swaddled in Emil's stinking blanket, and only Zacharov and Stanley remain. They're sitting on the folding chairs, playing cards. The boarded-up windows have a halo of light around their edges. It's still daytime. I can't have been out for that long.

"Hey," says Stanley, spotting me shifting. "Kid's awake."

"You did good, Cassel," Zacharov says, turning his chair to face me. "You want to sleep some more?"

"No," I say, pushing myself up. It's a little awkward, like I've been sick or something. The mask is gone. They must have taken it off me while I was sleeping.

"You hungry?" he asks.

I shake my head again. I feel a little queasy after the change, like I'm not sure where my stomach is. The last thing I want is food.

"You will be hungry later," he says, with such certainty

that it seems impossible to contradict him. I'm too tired to bother, anyway.

I let Stanley help me up, and he half-carries me out to the car.

We ride for a while, with my head resting against the window. I think I fall asleep again. I drool on the glass.

"Time to wake up." Someone is shaking my shoulder. I groan. Everything is stiff, but otherwise I feel okay.

Zacharov is grinning at me from the other side of the car. His silver hair is bright against the blackness of his wool coat and the leather seats. "Give me your hands," he says.

I do. One is gloved; the other one isn't.

He takes off my remaining glove and holds my bare hands in his gloved ones, palms up. I feel uncomfortably vulnerable, even though he's the one who's in danger of being worked. "With these hands," he says, "you will make the future. Be sure it is a future in which you want to live."

I swallow. I have no idea what he means. He lets go, and I fish in my pocket for the other glove, avoiding his gaze.

A moment later the car door opens on my side. Stanley's there, holding it wide. We're in Manhattan, skyscrapers looming over us and traffic streaming past.

I shuffle out, breathing the car exhaust and roasting-peanut-scented air. I'm still blinking the sleep out of my eyes, but I realize that not being in New Jersey means that whatever I've been brought to do isn't over.

"Oh, *come on,*" I say to Zacharov. "I can't. Not again. Not today."

But he just laughs. "I only want to give you some dinner.

Lila would never forgive me if I sent you back on an empty stomach."

I'm surprised. I must have really looked in bad shape back at the warehouse, because I am sure he's got better things to do than feed me.

"This way," Zacharov says, and walks toward a large bronze door with a raised relief of a bear. There's no sign on the building; I have no idea what to expect when we go in. It doesn't look like a restaurant. I glance back at Stanley, but he's getting back into the driver's seat of the Cadillac.

Zacharov and I walk into a small mirrored entranceway with a polished brass elevator. There's no furniture other than a gilt and black bench and, from what I can see, no intercom or bell. Zacharov fishes around in his pocket and removes a set of keys. He puts one into a hole on an other-wise blank panel and twists. The doors open.

The inside of the elevator is richly burled wood. A video screen above the doors is showing a black-and-white movie without any sound. I don't recognize the film.

"What's this place?" I ask finally as the doors slide shut.

"A social club," Zacharov says, clasping his gloved hands in front of him. Neither of us has pushed any button. "Here, things are private."

I nod, as though I actually understand what he's talking about.

When the elevator opens, we're in a huge room—*huge* like, seriously, you can't figure this place is really in New York. The marble floor is mostly covered in an enormous carpet. Along it are islands of two or four club chairs with high backs. The ceiling far above our heads is decorated with intricate plaster moldings. Along the nearest wall is a massive bar, its marble top shining against dark wood paneling. Behind the bar, on a high shelf, are several hulking jars of clear liquor with fruits and spices floating in them: lemons, rose petals, whole cloves, ginger. Uniformed staff move through the room silently, carrying drinks and small trays to the occupants of the chairs.

"Wow," I say.

He gives me a half grin, one that I have seen on Lila's face before. It's unnerving.

An old man with sunken cheeks in a black suit walks up to us. "Welcome, Mr. Zacharov. May I take your coat?"

Zacharov shucks it off.

"Would you like to borrow a sport jacket for your friend?" the man asks him, barely glancing in my direction. I guess I'm breaking some kind of dress code.

"No," Zacharov says. "We will have drinks and then dinner. Please send someone to us in the blue room."

"Very good, sir," the man says, just like a butler in a movie.

"Come," says Zacharov.

We walk through double doors into a far smaller library. Three bearded men are sitting together, laughing. One smokes a pipe. Another has a girl in a very short red dress sitting on his knee doing a bump of cocaine off a sugar spoon.

Zacharov sees me staring. "Private club," he reminds me.

Right.

In the third room a fire is blazing. The room is smaller

than the other two, but there's only one set of doors—the ones we came through—and no one else inside. Zacharov motions that I should sit. I sink into the soft leather. There's a small, low table between us. A crystal chandelier swings gently above us, scattering bands of colored light across the room.

A uniformed attendant appears. He looks me over, obviously skeptical, then turns to Mr. Zacharov. "Would you care for a drink?"

"I will take Laphroaig with a single cube of ice to begin, and Mr. Sharpe will have—"

"A club soda," I say lamely.

"Very good," says the attendant.

"After that you will bring us three ounces of the Iranian osetra with blinis, chopped egg, and plenty of onion. We will both take a little Imperia vodka with that, very cold. Then a turbot with some of the chef's excellent mustard sauce. And finally two of your *pains d'amandes*. Any objections, Cassel? Anything you don't care for?"

I have never eaten most of the things he named, but I am unwilling to admit it. I shake my head. "Sounds great."

The attendant nods, not even looking at me now, and walks off.

"You are uncomfortable," Zacharov says, which is true but seems like an uncharitable observation. "I thought Wallingford prepared you to take your place in society."

"I don't think they expect my place to be anywhere near *this* place," I say, which makes him smile.

"But it could be, Cassel. Your gift is like this club—it makes you uncomfortable. It's a bit too much, isn't it?"

"What do you mean?"

"A man may daydream of how he would spend a million dollars, but playing the same game with a billion dollars sours the fantasy. There are too many possibilities. The house he once wished for with all his heart is suddenly too small. The travel, too cheap. He wanted to visit an island. Now he contemplates buying one. I remember you, Cassel. With all your heart you wanted to be one of us. Now you're the best of us."

I look into the fire, turning back only when I hear the clink of our drinks being set down on the table.

Zacharov picks up his Scotch and swirls the glass, making the amber liquor dance. He pauses another moment. "Do you recall being thrown out of Lila's birthday party because you had a fight with some kid from her school?" He laughs suddenly, a short bark of sound. "You really cracked his head on that sink. Blood everywhere."

I touch my ear self-consciously and force a grin. I stopped wearing an earring when I enrolled at Wallingford, and the hole has almost closed up, but I still have the memory of her with the ice and the needle that same night, her hot breath against my neck. I shift in the chair.

"Back then I should have seen you were worth watching," he says, which is flattering but pretty obviously not true. "You know I'd like you to come work for me. I know you have some reservations. Let me answer them."

The attendant returns with our first course. The tiny gray pearls of caviar pop on my tongue, leaving behind the briny taste of the sea.

Zacharov seems like a benevolent gentleman, loading his blini with chopped egg and crème fraîche. Just a distinguished guy in a perfectly tailored suit with a bulge under one arm where his gun rests. I'm thinking he's not the best person in whom to confide my moral quandaries. Still, I've got to say something. "What was it like for my grandfather? Did you know him when he was younger?"

Zacharov smiles. "Your grandad's from a different time. His parents' generation still thought of themselves as good people, thought of their powers as gifts. He was part of that first generation to be *born* criminals. Desi Singer came into the world—what?—not ten years after the ban was passed. He never had a chance."

"Dab hands," I say, thinking of Mrs. Wasserman's version of this story.

He nods. "Yes, that's what we used to be called, before the ban. Did you know that your grandfather was conceived in a worker camp? He grew up tough, like my father did. They had to. Their whole country had turned on them. My grandfather, Viktor, was in charge of the kitchens; it was his job to make sure everybody got fed. He did whatever he had to do to make the meager rations go around—made deals with the guards, made his own still and distilled his own booze to trade for supplies. That's how the families started. My grandfather used to say that it was our calling to protect one another. No matter how much money we had or how much power, we should never forget where we came from."

He stops speaking as the attendant returns, setting

the fish down before us. Zacharov calls for a glass of 2005 Pierre Morey Meursault, and it comes a moment later, lemon pale, the base of the glass cloudy with condensation.

"When I was a young man of twenty, I was in my second year at Columbia. It was the late seventies, and I thought the world had changed. The first Superman movie was on the big screen, Donna Summer was on the radio, and I was tired of my father being so old-fashioned. I met a girl in class. Her name was Jenny Talbot. She wasn't a worker, and I didn't care."

The fish is cooling in front of us as Zacharov strips off one of his gloves. His bare hand is striped with scars. They're a ruddy brown and pulled like taffy.

"Three boys cornered me at a party in the Village and pressed my hand against one of the burners on an electric coil stove. Seared through my glove, fused the cloth into my flesh. It felt like someone was flaying me to the bone. They said I should stay away from Jenny, that the thought of someone like me touching her made them sick."

He takes a long swallow of wine and pokes his fork into the turbot, one hand still bare.

"Desi came to the hospital after my father and mother left. He wanted my sister Eva to wait in the hall. When he asked me what happened, I was ashamed, but I told him. I knew he was loyal to my father. After I'd finished the story, he asked me what I wanted done to those boys."

"He killed them, didn't he?" I ask.

"I wanted him to," says Zacharov, taking a bite of the fish and pausing to swallow. "Every time the nurse changed the dressing on my hand, every time they dug tweezers into blistered skin to pull out cloth, I imagined those boys dead. I told him so. Then your grandfather asked me about the girl."

"The girl?" I echo.

"That's exactly what I said, in that exact incredulous tone. He laughed and said that someone put those boys up to what they did. Someone told them something to rile them up. Maybe she liked to have boys fighting over her. But he was willing to bet that that girl of mine wanted to end our relationship and had decided to throw me out like garbage. It was easier, after all, if she seemed like a victim rather than the kind of girl who liked messing around with workers.

"Your grandfather was right. She never came to the hospital to see me. When Desi finally paid a visit to the boys, he found Jenny in one of their beds."

Zacharov pauses to eat a few bites. I eat too. The fish is amazing, flaky and redolent of lemon and dill. But I don't know what to make of the story he's telling.

"What happened to her?" I ask.

He pauses, fork in hand. "What do you think?"

"Ah," I say. "Right."

He smiles. "When *my* grandfather said we had to protect one another, I thought he was a sentimental old man. It wasn't until *your* grandfather said it that I understood what it meant. They hate us. They might give us a smile. They might even let us into their beds, but they still hate us."

The door opens. Two attendants have arrived with coffee and pastries.

"They'd hate you most of all," says Zacharov.

The room's warm, but I feel very cold.

It's late when Stanley drops me back at the house. I've only got maybe twenty minutes to get my stuff and get back to Wallingford before room check.

"Stay out of trouble," Stanley says as I hop out of the back of the Cadillac.

I unlock the door and head for the back room, gather up my books and backpack. Then I look for my keys, which I thought were right with my bag but aren't. I stick my hands beneath the cushions of the couch. Then I kneel down to see if they fell underneath. I finally find them on the dining room table, hidden by some envelopes.

I start to head out when I remember that my car is still busted. I'm not even sure I brought the battery and fuses home from Sam's house. In a panic, I run upstairs to my bedroom. No battery. No fuses. I retrace what my drunken steps must have been, all the way back to the kitchen. I discover that the coat closet is slightly ajar and, amazingly, the auto parts bag is inside of it, resting alongside an empty beer can. A coat is wadded up in the back, like maybe I knocked it off its hanger. I lift it, intending on putting it back where it goes, when I hear a metallic thunk.

A gun rests on the linoleum. It's silver and black with the Smith & Wesson stamp on the side. I stare at it, and stare, like I'm seeing it wrong. Like it's going to turn out to be a toy. After a moment I hold up the wide-collared coat. Black. Big. Like the one on the video.

Which makes that gun the one that killed my brother.

I put both the coat and the gun back, carefully, thrusting the evidence as far into the closet as it will go.

I wonder when she decided to shoot Philip. It must have been after she came back from Atlantic City. I can't believe that she knew about his deal with the Feds before then. Maybe she went to Philip's house and saw some of the papers—but, no, he wouldn't be that stupid. Maybe she spotted Agent Jones or Hunt talking to Philip. It would take only a single look at either one of them to know they were law enforcement.

But even that doesn't seem like enough. I don't know why she did it.

I only know that this is my mother's house, and my mother's closet, making that my mother's coat.

Making that my mother's gun.

AT SCHOOL MONDAY

morning I catch up with Lila on my way to French class. I touch her shoulder, and she spins around, her smile tinged with longing. I hate having so much power over her, but there is a sinister creeping pleasure in knowing I am so much in her thoughts. A pleasure I have to guard against.

"Did you go to Philip's house?" I ask.

She opens her mouth uncertainly.

"I found one of your cigarettes," I say before she can lie.

"Where?" she asks. Her arms wrap around her chest protectively. She grips her shoulder tightly with one gloved hand.

"Where do you think? In his ashtray." I see her expression darken, and I abruptly change my mind about what's going to make her talk. She looks utterly closed to me, a house locked against burglars, even ones she likes. "Tell me it wasn't yours and I'll believe you."

I don't mean that for a second, though. I know the cigarette was hers. I just also know the best way to get into a locked house is to be let in the front door.

"I have to go to class," she says. "I'll meet you outside at lunch."

I lope on to French. We translate a passage from Balzac: *La puissance ne consiste pas à frapper fort ou souvent, mais à frapper juste.*

Power does not consist in striking hard or often, but in striking true.

She's waiting for me by the side of the cafeteria. Her short blond hair looks white in the sunlight, like a halo around her face. She's got on white stockings that stop at her thighs, so that when she swishes her rolled-up skirt, I can almost see skin.

"Hey," I say, determined not to look.

"Hey yourself." She smiles that crazy, hungry smile she has. She's had time to pull her act together, and it shows. She's decided what to tell and what to hide.

"So . . . ," I say, gloved hands in my pockets. "I didn't know you still smoked."

"So, let's take a walk." She pushes off the wall, and we start down the path toward the library. "I started again this summer. Smoking. I didn't really mean to, but everyone around my father smokes. And besides, it was something to do with my hands."

"Okay," I say.

"It's hard to quit. Even here at Wallingford, I take a paper towel tube, stuff it with fabric softener sheets, and exhale into that. Then I brush my teeth a million times."

"Rots your lungs," I say.

"I only do it when I'm really nervous," she says.

"Like when you're in a dead man's apartment?"

She nods quickly, gloves rubbing against her skirt. "Like that. Philip had something that I wanted to make sure no one found." Her gaze darts to my face. "One of the bodies."

"Bodies?" I echo.

"One of the people that you . . . changed. I've heard there's ways to tell if an amulet is real and, well, maybe someone—the cops or the Feds—could use that to tell if an object has been worked. I was worried for you."

"So why didn't you tell me?" I ask.

She turns to me, eyes blazing. "I want you to *love* me, you idiot. I thought that if I did something for you, something huge, then you would. I wanted to save you, Cassel, so that you'd have to love me. Get it now? It's horrible."

For a moment I don't know why she's so angry. Then I realize that it's because she's embarrassed. "Gratitude isn't love," I say finally.

"I should know that," she says. "I'm grateful to you and I hate it."

"You didn't do me any other favors you haven't mentioned,

right?" I ask, not relenting. "Like murdering my brother?"

"No," she says sharply.

"You had every reason to want him dead," I say, thinking of Sam and Daneca's accusations in the kitchen of Daneca's fancy house.

"Just because I'm glad he's dead doesn't mean I killed him," she says. "I didn't order him killed either, if that's what you're going to ask next. Is that what those agents wanted? To tell you I murdered your brother?"

I must look blank, because she laughs. "I go to this school too. Everyone knows you got cuffed and thrown into the back of a black car by guys in suits."

"So, what do most people think?"

"There's a rumor going around that you're a narc," she says, and I groan. "But I think the jury's still out."

"I don't know what the suits want with me any more than the school does," I say. "I'm sorry I asked you about the cigarette. I just had to know."

"You're getting very popular," she says. "Not enough Cassel to go around."

I look up. We've walked past the library. We're almost to the woods. I swing around, and she does the same. We walk back together quietly, lost in separate thoughts.

I want to reach out for her hand, but I don't. It's not fair. She'd have to take it.

I'm heading toward Physics when Sam stops me in the hall.

"Did you hear?" he asks. "Greg Harmsford went crazy and trashed his own laptop."

"When?" I ask, frowning. "At lunch?"

"Last night. Apparently everyone on his hall woke up to him drowning it in a sink. The screen was already cracked like he'd been punching it." At that, Sam can no longer contain his laughter. "Serious anger management problem."

I grin.

"He says that he did it in his sleep. Way to steal your excuse," says Sam. "Besides, everyone could see that his eyes were open."

"Oh," I say, the grin sliding off my face. "He was sleepwalking?"

"He was *faking*," Sam says.

I wonder where Lila was while I drove around with her father. I wonder if she visited Greg's room, if he asked her to come in, if she slowly removed her gloves before she ran her hands through his hair.

Sam turns to me to say something else.

Then, thankfully, the bell rings and I have to run to class. I sit down and listen to Dr. Jonahdab. Today she's talking about the principal of momentum and how hard it is to stop something once it has been set in motion.

Daneca rushes past me out of the room at the end of Physics. She heads for Sam's class and stands near the door, waiting for him. The expression she's wearing makes it clear that Sam hasn't started talking to her yet.

"Please," she says to him, hugging her books to her chest, but he walks past her without even hesitating. The skin around her eyes is red and swollen with recent tears.

"Everything's going to be okay," I say, although I'm not sure I believe it. It's just something people say.

"I guess I should have expected it," she says, pushing back a lock of purple-tipped hair and sighing. "My mom said lots of people want to know workers but would never date one. I thought Sam was different."

My stomach growls, and I remember that I skipped lunch. "No, you didn't," I say. "That's why you lied to him."

"Well, I was right, wasn't I?" she asks plaintively. She wants to be contradicted.

"I don't know," I say.

My next class—ceramics—is held across the quad at the Rawlings Fine Arts Center. I'm surprised when Daneca follows me onto the green; I really doubt her next class is there too.

"What do you mean?" she asks. "Why do you think he's like this?"

"Maybe he's mad you didn't trust him. Maybe he's mad you didn't tell him the real reason you didn't want to be tested. Maybe he's just happy to be in the right for once—you know, enjoying having the upper hand."

"He's not like that," she says.

"You mean he's not like me?" I ask. In the nearby parking lot a tow truck is starting to pull out with a car attached.

She blinks, as if startled. I have no idea why; it's not like she doesn't keep assuming terrible things about me. "I didn't say that."

"Well, you're right. I *would* like it, even if I didn't want to admit it. Everyone likes a little power, especially people who feel powerless." I think of Sam at the start of the semester, feeling like he could never measure up to Daneca, but I doubt she has any idea about that.

"Is that how you are with Lila?" If she wasn't judging me before, she's judging me now.

I shake my head, trying to keep the annoyance out of my voice. "You know it's not the same—not real. Haven't you ever worked—"

I stop speaking as I realize the car being towed is mine. "What the hell?" I say, and take off running.

"Hey!" I shout as I see the bumper of my car smack against the last speed bump before the road. All I can see of the guy driving is that he's got a cap on, pulled low enough to shade his eyes. I can't even see the license on the tow truck, since my own car is obscuring it. I can see the name airbrushed on the side of the truck, though. Tallington Towing.

"What just happened?" Daneca asks. She's standing in the empty parking spot where my Benz used to be.

"He stole my car!" I say, utterly baffled. I turn and sweep my hand to indicate all the other vehicles in the parking lot. "Why not one of these? These are nice cars! Why my crappy broken down piece of—"

"Cassel," Daneca says sternly, interrupting me. She points to the ground in front of her. "You better take a look at this."

I walk over and spot a small black jewelry box with a black bow sitting in the middle of the empty space. I squat down and touch the small tag, flip it over. There on the black paper, in even blacker ink, is a crude drawing of the crenellations of a castle. Frowning at it, I feel the familiar pull of the shadow world of crime and cons. This is a gift from that world.

Castle.

Cassel.

I pull the ribbon, and it comes free easily. Before I lift the lid, I briefly consider that there's going to be something unpleasant—a bomb or a finger—but if there's really a body part inside, waiting's only going to make everything worse. I open the box. Inside, nestled in cut black foam, is a square Benz key. Shiny. Silver edged and so newfangled that it looks more like a flash drive than anything to do with a car.

I lift it up and click the unlock button. Headlights flicker in a car across from where I'm standing. A black Roadster with chrome trim.

"Are you kidding me?" I say.

Daneca walks over and presses her face against the window. Her breath fogs the glass. "There's a letter inside."

I hear the bell ring faintly from inside the academic center. We're officially late for class.

Daneca seems not to hear it. She opens the door and takes out the envelope. Her gloved fingers make quick work of it, ripping open the flap before I can stop her.

"Hey," I say. "That's mine."

"Do you know who it's from?" she asks, unfolding the paper.

Sure. There's only one person it could be from. Zacharov. But I'd rather she didn't know that.

I make a grab for the letter, but she laughs and holds it out of reach.

"Come on," I say, but she's already reading.

"Iiiiinteresting," Daneca says, her gaze rising to meet mine. She holds out the note:

A taste of your future.
—Z

I snatch it out of her hand and crumple it. "Let's take a drive," I say, holding the key up in front of her. "We're already cutting class—at least we can have some fun."

Daneca slides into the passenger seat without protest, shocking me. She waits until I've buckled myself in before she asks, "So, what's that note about?"

"Nothing," I say. "Just that Zacharov wants me to join his merry band of thieves."

"Are you going to keep this?" she asks, brushing gloved fingers over the dashboard. "It's a pretty expensive bribe."

The car is beautiful. Its engine hums and the gas pedal responds to even the lightest touch.

"If you keep it," Daneca says, "he'll have his claws in you."

Everyone has their claws in me. Everyone.

I pull out onto the street and head for the highway. We ride in silence for a few moments.

"Before—when we were heading to class—you asked me if I ever worked anyone." Daneca looks out the window.

"Please know that I am seriously the last person in the world to judge you."

She laughs. "Where are we going anyway?"

"I thought we'd get coffee and a doughnut. Brain food."

"I'm more of an herbal tea girl," Daneca says.

"I'm shocked," I say, taking one hand off the wheel and placing it over my heart. "But you were about to tell me all your secrets. Please, continue."

She rolls her eyes, leans forward, and fiddles with the radio. The speakers are just as fantastic as the rest of the car. No hiss. No distortion. Just full, clear sound. "There's not much to tell," she says, adjusting the volume down. "There was this guy I liked when I was twelve, right before I came to Wallingford. His name was Justin. We were both at this arts-focused middle school and he was a kid actor. He'd done some commercials and everything. I was just on the edge of his friends circle, you know."

I nod. I survive at the edge of friends circles.

"And I followed him around like a puppy dog. Every time he talked to me, I felt like my heart was in my throat. I wrote a haiku about him."

I look over at her, eyebrows raised. "Seriously? A haiku?"

"Oh, yeah—want to hear it? 'Golden blond hair and eyes like blue laser beams. Why won't you notice me?'"

I laugh, snorting. She laughs too.

"I can't believe you remember that," I say.

"Well, I remember it because he *read it*. The teacher hung up all of our haikus without telling us she was going to, and a girl in class told him about mine. It was horrible. Humiliating. All his friends would tease me about it and he would just look at me with this smug smirk. Ugh."

"He sounds like a jerk."

"He was a jerk," Daneca says. "But I still liked him. I think in some weird way I liked him more."

"So, did you work him?"

"No," Daneca said. "I worked *me*. To stop feeling the way I did. To feel nothing."

I didn't expect that. "You're a good person," I say, humbled. "I give you a hard time about it, but I really do admire you. You care so much about doing the right thing."

She shakes her head as I pull into a coffee shop. "It was weird. Every time I looked at him afterward, I had that tip-of-the-tongue feeling, like I couldn't quite remember a word I ought to have known. It felt wrong, Cassel."

We get out of the car. "I'm not saying that working yourself is a great idea . . ."

The coffee place has tin ceilings and a counter full of fresh-baked cookies. Its tables are filled with students and the self-employed, tapping away on laptops and clutching cups with a reverence that suggests they just crawled out of bed.

Daneca orders a maté chai latte, and I get a regular cup of coffee. Her drink comes out a vivid grass green.

I make a face. We head to the only free table, one next to the door and the racks of newspapers. As I sit down, one of the headlines catches my eye.

"Don't look like that," Daneca says. "It's good. Want a sip?"

I shake my head. There is a photograph of a man I know beside the words "Bronx Hitman Jumps Bail." The type under the picture says "Death worker Emil Lombardo, also known as the Hunter, missing after being indicted for double homicide." They didn't even bother to lie to me about his name.

"Do you have a quarter?" I ask, fishing around in my pockets.

Daneca reaches into her messenger bag and feels around until she finds one. She slaps it down on the table. "You know what the weirdest thing about me working myself over that boy was?"

I find fifty cents and feed our combined change into the machine. "No, what?"

I lift out the paper. The double homicide was of a thirty-four-year-old woman and her mother. Two witnesses to another crime—something about the Zacharovs and real estate. There are smaller pictures of the dead women beneath the fold. They both look like nice people.

Nice people. Good people. Like Daneca.

"The weirdest thing," Daneca says, "is that after I stopped liking him, he asked me out. When I turned him down, he was really hurt. He didn't know what he'd done wrong."

I touch my gloved finger to the murdered women's faces, letting the leather smear the ink. Last night I helped their killer get away. "That is weird," I say hollowly.

When we get back to school, it's just in time for my computer class. I walk in as the bell stops ringing.

"Mr. Sharpe," says Ms. Takano without looking up.

"They're looking for you in the office." She hands me her official hall pass, a large plastic dinosaur.

I take my time walking across the green. I think about my new car, gleaming in the sun. I think of the sophomore-year production of *Macbeth*, and Amanda Kerwick as Lady Macbeth, holding up her bare hands, looking for blood.

But there is no mere spot on me. As her husband says, "I am in blood/Stepp'd in so far that, should I wade no more,/ Returning were as tedious as go o'er."

I shake my head. I'm just looking for excuses to keep the car.

When I walk into the office, Ms. Logan frowns. "I didn't think you'd be back so soon. Cassel—you know you're supposed to sign out when you leave campus."

"I know," I say contritely. I'm hoping that Northcutt gives me only a single demerit for cutting class. Not a week ago I was bragging to Lila about my strategies to get off campus without trouble. Then I drove off without implementing a single one.

But Ms. Logan just shoves the sign-in folder at me. "Put the time you left here," she says, brushing her gloved finger over the line. "And when you came back, here."

I write them down faithfully.

"Good," she says. "The lawyer said you were a bit dazed when he called to remind you about the meeting. Northcutt wants you to know that you don't have to go back to class if you're not ready."

"I'm okay," I say slowly. Something's going on. I better figure out what before I screw it up.

"We just want you to know that we're very sorry for your loss, Cassel. And I hope everything went as well as it could today."

"Thank you," I say, trying to look somber.

I head for the door, thinking over what just happened. One of Zacharov's people must have called and pretended to be the family lawyer—maybe it was even the fellow driving the tow truck—to give me not only the car, but time to tool around in it. Being courted by a mobster sure is sweet. Hard for the offers of the federal agents to compare.

I am crossing back toward my computer class when I see Daneca come out of the office.

"Hey," I say. "I didn't see you in there."

"I was in Northcutt's office," she says dejectedly. Then she kicks a clod of dirt off the quad. "I can't believe I let you talk me into that."

Looks like Daneca just got her first demerit for cutting class.

"Sorry," I say.

She makes a face like she knows I'm not that sorry. "So, what's Lila up to?"

"Lila?" I am feeling very stupid lately.

"You know, your *girlfriend*? Blonde? Cursed to love you? Ringing any bells yet?" Daneca holds out her phone to show me a text from Lila: *Come to Spanish classroom. Third floor. Urgent.*

"No idea," I say, looking at the words. I pull out my phone, but there are no messages.

Daneca laughs. Her voice is teasing. "So, wait, you *don't* know who Lila is?"

I realize my mistake and laugh. But it makes me think. The Lila I remember was fourteen. She hadn't spent three years as an animal in a cage and hadn't been forced to feel anything, and even then she was a mystery to me. I wonder if I have any idea who Lila is after all.

We find Lila sitting on one of the desks in the empty class-room, swinging her legs, when we walk in. Propped in another is Greg Harmsford. He's wearing sunglasses, but his head is tilted all the way back and it's clear he's uncon-scious. At least I hope he's unconscious. In front of him are two cans of Coke, both open.

"What did you do?" I ask.

"Oh, hi, Cassel." A faint blush has started at the tips of her ears. She holds out a piece of paper. It's a printout of an e-mail. I take it from her but don't really look.

Daneca clears her throat and points to Greg's prone body, widening her eyes to emphasize that she wants me to *do something*.

"Is he dead?" I ask. Someone's got to.

"I roofied him," Lila says matter-of-factly. The late after-noon light has turned her blond hair to gold. She's wear-ing a crisp white shirt and tiny blue stones in her ears that match one of her eyes. She looks like the last girl in the world who would drug a boy in the middle of the day. *Like butter wouldn't melt in her mouth*, the old folks in Carney would say.

"Look what I found on his computer," Lila says.

I finally look at the page in my hand. It's from Greg and is addressed to a bunch of e-mail addresses I don't know. The text informs parents that "Wallingford supports a club encouraging criminal activities" and that "worker kids are allowed to openly brag about their illegal exploits." I look at the e-mail addresses again. I guess they're the addresses of our parents. There are photos attached, and although Lila has printed out only the first page, the two there make it pretty obvious that he attached stills of everyone at the HEX meeting. "Wow," I say, and pass the paper to Daneca.

I don't mention that to get that off his computer before he tried to drown it in his dorm sink, she must have been working him. I don't mention that Greg's passed out now, asleep, vulnerable to any invasion of his dreams.

"I'm going to *kill* him," Daneca says. She looks angrier than I have ever seen her.

Lila takes a deep breath, then lets it out slowly. "This is all my fault."

"What do you mean?"

She shakes her head, avoiding my gaze. "It's not important. What matters is that I'm going to make it right. We're going to get him back. For Ramirez and the video. For that e-mail. I have a plan."

"Which is . . . ?" I ask.

Lila hops off the desk.

"Greg Harmsford is about to join HEX," she says. "He's going to attend his first meeting today. Right now, hopefully. Before he wakes up." Her eyes are brimming with manic glee, and I realize how much I've missed her like this, ferocious. Missed the fearless girl who used to beat me at races and order me around.

I laugh. "You are *evil*," I tell Lila.

"Flatterer," she says, but she seems pleased.

"I don't know if I can get anyone to come out for a meeting," Daneca says. She walks to the door and checks the hallway, then looks back at us. "Do you think people would believe it? Could we pull it off?"

Lila reaches into her bag and pulls out a tiny silver camera. "Well, we'll have pictures. Besides, stuff like this is in the news all the time. Government officials who are all anti-worker turn out to be workers themselves. It's totally believable. The fact that he got the footage the first time will make him seem guiltier."

I grin. "I guess we better make some calls if we want to convene an entire HEX meeting."

It takes Daneca a lot of begging to get even a small group together. No one wants to be associated with HEX right now. They've all got stories about being hassled. Some even have stories about classmates' parents trying to hire them to do shady things. They're freaked, and I don't blame them.

Daneca gives each one the same song and dance about how important it is that we stick together. Lila gets on the line and swears up and down that it'll be funny. I try to prop up Greg Harmsford.

Posing an unconscious body isn't easy. Greg's not comatose, just sleeping. He still moves when I put him in an uncomfortable position, still makes a face and pushes away my hands when I try to make him sit up. I search around in the desk until I find some tape and pencils. I use those to build a kind of splint on the back of Greg's head. From the front he might look like he's slouching, but at least he'll seem awake since his head will be upright. He makes a protesting sound as I attach the tape, but after a minute, he seems to get used to it.

"Nice work," Lila says absently. She's busy writing "HEX MEETING" in chalk on the board.

"How long will he be like that?" Daneca asks, poking Greg's shoulder. He twitches a little, almost shifting enough to ruin the effect of my pose, but not quite. Daneca smothers a shriek with both her hands.

"I'm not really sure, but when he wakes up, he'll probably be sick. Side effect." Lila says distractedly. "Cassel, can you put Greg's arm up on the chair or something? I don't think he looks very natural."

"We should get Sam," I say with a sigh. "Special effects are his area of expertise. I have no idea what I'm doing."

"No," says Daneca, taking my phone out of my hand and setting it down on a desk. "We're not calling him."

"But he's—," I start.

"No," she says.

Lila looks at us in confusion.

"They're having a fight," I explain.

"Oh," she says, then tilts her head and squints at Greg. "There's something still off. Maybe if we had some junk food? We've always got stuff at real meetings. Daneca, can you go to the vending machine before people start showing up? Cassel, maybe you can look and see if there are empty chip bags in the trash? They'd just be props. I could run to the store—"

"I'll go if Cassel promises not to call Sam," Daneca says.

I groan. "I'll pinky swear if you want."

Daneca gives me a dark look and heads into the hallway. Instead of following, I turn toward Lila, who's rifling through her bag.

"Why do you think this is your fault?" I ask.

Her gaze darts from me to Greg. "There's not a lot of time. We should . . ."

I wait, but she doesn't say anything else. Her cheeks pink and she turns her gaze to the floor.

"Whatever happened," I say, "you can tell me."

"It's nothing you don't already know. I was jealous and stupid. After I saw you and Audrey together, I went and talked to Greg. Flirted with him, I guess. I knew he had a girlfriend and it was a mean, bad thing to do, but I didn't think things would get—I didn't think it would be as bad as it was. Then he asked about you, wanted to know if we were together. I told him 'sorta.'"

"Sorta," I echo.

She rubs her hand over her eyes. "Everything was so complicated between us. I didn't know *what* to say. Once he heard that we were—whatever—he started really hitting on me. And I just wanted to feel something—something other than the way I felt."

"I'm not—," I start to say. *I'm not worth that.* I reach out and tuck a loose strand of hair behind her ear.

She shakes her head, almost angrily. "The next day, I

can tell he was bragging about me. One of his friends even asks me about it. So I go over to Greg and think of the worst possible thing I can say. I tell him that if he doesn't shut up about me, I will swear up and down that he's awful in bed. That he's hung like a worm."

I give a snort of incredulous laughter.

She's still not looking at me, though. And her cheeks are, if anything, redder. "He's all, 'You know you liked it.' And I say—"

She stops. I can hear people in the hallway. In a few moments, they'll be inside.

"What?" I ask.

"You have to understand," she says, quickly. "He got really mad. Really, really mad. And I think that's why he went after HEX."

"Lila, what did you *say*?"

She closes her eyes tightly. Her voice is almost a whisper. "I said I was thinking about you the whole time."

I'm glad her eyes are closed. I'm glad she can't see my face.

People start filing in. Nadja, Rachel, and Chad are the first to arrive and Lila, still blushing, doesn't waste any time directing them. Soon, everyone is arranging chairs.

I fake my way through seeming calm and collected. Daneca comes in a few moments later with snacks.

It's not your fault, I want to tell Lila. But I don't say that. I don't say anything.

We take picture after picture with the backdrop of the blackboard and the scrawled "HEX MEETING" on it. Ones with someone standing in the center of a circle of chairs, talking earnestly. Ones with everyone laughing and a girl on Greg's lap. Halfway through our photo shoot, he wakes up enough to pull the pencils off the back of his neck and push up his sunglasses. He looks at all of us in confusion, but not with any real alarm.

"What's going on?" Greg slurs.

I want to snap his neck. I want to make him sorry he was ever born.

"Smile," says Daneca. He gives a lopsided grin. A girl throws her arm over his shoulder.

Lila keeps clicking away.

Eventually Greg goes back to sleep, head cradled in his arms on a desk. Lila, Daneca, and I go to the corner store and use the booth there to print out all the photos from the SIM card.

They look great. So good that it would be a crime not to share them with everyone at Wallingford.

Most people never report being conned, for three reasons. The first reason is that con artists don't usually leave a lot of evidence. If you don't really know who did this to you, there's no point in reporting them. The second reason is that usually you, the mark, agreed to do something shady. If you report the con artist, you have to report yourself along with him. But the third reason is the simplest and most compelling. Shame. You're the dummy who got conned.

No one wants to look stupid. No one wants to be thought of as gullible. So they hide how dumb and gullible they were. Con artists barely have to cover up at all, with marks so eager to cover up for them.

Greg Harmsford insists he was Photoshopped into the pictures, loudly and to anyone who will listen. He's furious when his story gets questioned. Eventually the teasing gets to him and he punches Gavin Perry in the face.

He's suspended for two days. All that because he doesn't want to admit that he got had.

I'm sitting in my room for study hall, working on my world ethics homework, when my phone rings. I don't know the number, but I pick it up.

"We have to meet," says the voice on the other end. It takes me a moment to realize I'm talking to Barron. His voice sounds colder than usual.

"I'm at school," I say. I'm not in the mood for more sneaking around. "I can't get out of here before the weekend."

"What a coincidence," Barron says. "I'm at Wallingford too."

The fire alarm sounds. Sam jumps up and starts shoving his feet into sneakers.

"Grab the PlayStation," he says to me.

I shake my head, covering the phone. "It's a prank. Someone pulled it." Then I nearly spit into the phone, "You idiot. Even if you wanted me to leave, there's no way I can now. They will take a head count. They will make absolutely sure we're all back in our rooms."

Sam ignores me and starts unhooking his game system.

"I already made your hall master forget you," Barron says. The words send a chill up my spine.

I file out with Sam and all the other kids to stand on the grass. Everyone's looking up at the building, waiting for wisps of smoke to unfurl or flames to light the windows. It's easy to back away until I'm near trees and shadows.

No one's looking for me. No one but Barron.

His gloved hand comes down on my shoulder heavily. We walk away from the school, along the sidewalk, toward houses bathed in the flickering blue light of televisions. It's only around nine, but it feels much later.

It feels too late.

"I've been thinking about the Zacharovs," says Barron too casually. "They're not the only game in town."

I should never have let my guard down.

"What do you mean?" It's hard to look at Barron now, but I do. He's smirking. His black hair and black suit make him into a shadow, as if I conjured some dark mirror of myself.

"I know what you did to me," he says, and although he's trying to keep his tone even, I can hear rage bleeding through. "How you took advantage of the holes in my memory. How for all your bellyaching about doing the right thing, you're no different from me or Philip. I met two nice men from the FBI—Agent Jones and Agent Hunt. They had a lot to tell me about my big brother—and about my little one. Philip told them how you turned me against him. How somehow you'd messed up my head so that I didn't remember that I'd been in on his plan to make Anton head of the

Zacharov family. At first I didn't believe them, but I went back and looked at my notebooks again."

Oh, crap.

There are master forgers in the world, folks who know exactly what chemicals ink had in it in the sixteenth century versus the eighteenth. They have sources for paper and canvases that will carbon date correctly; they can create perfect craquelure. They practice the loops and flourishes of another hand until it is more familiar than their own.

It probably goes without saying that I am not a master forger. Most forgeries get by because they are good enough that no one checks them. When I sign my mother's name to a permission slip, so long as it looks like her handwriting, no one brings in a specialist.

But if Barron compared the notebook I hastily forged to his older ones, the fake would be obvious. We are all specialists in our own handwriting

"If you know what I did to you," I say, trying not to seem rattled, "then you know what you did to me, too."

That brings out his lopsided grin. "The difference is that I'm willing to forgive you."

That's so unexpected that I have no reply. Barron doesn't seem to need one. "I want to start over, Cassel," he says, "and I want to start at the top. I'm going to the Brennan family. And for that I need you. We'll be an unstoppable team of assassins."

"No," I say.

"*Ouch.*" He doesn't sound all that put out by my refusal. "Think you're too good for such a dirty job?"

"Yeah," I say. "That's me. Too good."

I wonder if he really could rationalize what I did to him, really treat betrayal like the slight transgression of a recalcitrant business partner. I wonder if I hurt him.

If he can rationalize what I did to him, it's easy to imagine how he rationalized what he did to me.

"Do you know why you agreed to change all those people into inanimate objects? Why you agreed to kill them?"

I take a deep breath. It sucks to hear the words out loud. "Of course I don't. I don't remember anything. You *stole all my memories.*"

"You would follow Philip and me around like a little puppy," Barron says. I can hear the violence in his voice. "Begging to do a job with us. Hoping we'd see your black heart and give you a chance." He pokes me in the chest.

I take a step back. Rage flashes through me, sudden and nearly overwhelming.

I was their baby brother. Sure, I idolized them. And they kicked me in the teeth.

Barron grins. "It's pretty clever, really. I made you believe you'd killed before. That's all! I made you believe that you were what I wanted you to become. You loved it, Cassel. You loved being a goddamn assassin."

"That's not true," I say, shaking my head, willing myself to shut out his words. "You're a liar. You're the prince of liars. And since I don't remember, you know you can say anything. I would be stupid to believe you."

"Oh, come on," Barron says. "You know your own nature. You know if something *feels* true."

"I'm not going to do it," I say. "You and the Brennans can go to hell together."

He laughs. "You will do it. You already have. People don't change."

"No," I say.

"Like I said, those federal agents came to see me," Barron says. I start to interrupt him, but Barron just raises his voice. "I didn't give them anything important. Nothing like I could have. If I told them what you are, it would just be a matter of time before they connected the dots and figured out you're the murderer they're looking for."

"They'd never believe you," I say, but I feel unsteady. The world has already tilted. I can feel myself falling.

"Of course they would," Barron says. "I can show them a body. The one you left in the freezer in Mom's house."

"Oh," I say faintly. "That."

"Sloppy," Barron says. "I was the one who told you about him, after all. Didn't you think I would look?"

"I don't know what I thought." Truly, I don't.

"Then they can make you that same crap offer they made Philip, get what they want, and lock you away for a thousand years."

"Philip had immunity," I say. "I saw the contract."

Barron laughs. "I saw it too. Too bad Philip didn't show it to me before he sold them his soul. I was pre-law, remember? That contract's worthless. Agents can't offer immunity; it wasn't worth the paper it was printed on. It was for show. They could have taken Philip in whenever they wanted."

"Did you tell him that?" I ask.

"Why bother?" Barron says. "Philip didn't want to hear it. He just wanted to say good-bye before they shipped him off to witness protection land."

I can't tell if Barron's lying or not. I have a sinking feeling that this time he's telling the truth.

Which means I can't trust the Feds.

But Barron's going to go to the Feds if I don't throw in my lot with the Brennans.

And Zacharov will have me killed in a heartbeat if I do work for the Brennans.

There's no way out.

I think about what Zacharov said at Philip's funeral. *There are people close to you that you will have to deal with eventually.*

You will do it, Barron said. *You already have. People don't change.*

I look over at him. He smirks. "Not a tough choice when I lay it all out for you, is it, Cassel?"

It's not.

BARRON WALKS ME BACK

to my dorm. I get there before lights-out at eleven. The hall master looks surprised to find someone occupying the other half of Sam's room when he comes in for the final hall check, but he doesn't say anything. He must figure that he's getting old, to be forgetting things like which students he's supposed to be responsible for. He must worry about dementia, Alzheimer's, getting enough sleep. It's a trick that wouldn't have worked at any other time but the beginning of the year.

It did work, though. Barron's clever.

"What happened to you during the fire drill?" Sam asks, pulling on a ratty Dracula T-shirt. His sweatpants have a hole on the knee.

"Went for a walk," I say, peeling off my gloves. "Fresh air."

"With Daneca?" Sam asks.

I frown. "What?"

"I know you took her out in that new, fancy car of yours. You got her in trouble, man."

"Yeah, I'm sorry about that." Then I grin. "But it was kind of funny. I mean, she never does anything bad, and now she's cutting class, getting thrown in jail . . ."

Sam isn't smiling. "You're going to treat her the same way you treated Audrey, aren't you? Barely noticing if you hurt her. I always knew Daneca liked you. Girls *like* you, Cassel. And you ignore them. And then they like you more."

"Hey," I say. "Wait a minute. She skipped class because she was miserable over *you*. We talked about *you*."

"What did she say?" I can't tell if he believes me, but at least I've distracted his focus.

I sigh. "That you're a bigot who doesn't want to date a worker girl."

"I'm not!" Sam says. "That's not even why I'm mad at her."

"I told her that." I chuck a pillow at him. "Just before we leaped into each other's arms and made out passionately, like weasels on Valentine's Day, like those really magnetic magnets, like greased-up eels—"

"Why am I your friend?" Sam moans, flopping back onto the bed. "Why?

A knock on the door startles us just before our hall master jerks it open. "Is there a problem? Lights-out was fifteen minutes ago. Keep it down in here and go to sleep or I'm giving you both a Saturday detention."

"Sorry," we both mumble.

The door closes.

Sam snickers and pitches his voice low. "Okay, fine. I get it. I'm insecure. But look, girls aren't exactly getting in line, you know? And then there's Daneca, and I figure she's too good for me so there has to be some kind of catch, and then there *is*. She's hiding that she's a worker. She doesn't trust me. She's not taking me seriously."

"You ignoring Daneca is making you both insane," I say. "She made a mistake. I've made plenty of mistakes. It doesn't mean she doesn't like you. It means she wants you to like her and she thought she had to lie to make that happen. Which makes her less perfect, sure. But isn't that a relief?"

"Yeah," he says quietly, his pillow half-covering his mouth. "I guess. Maybe I should talk to her."

"Good," I say. "I need you to be happy. I need one of us to be happy."

It's a dream. I'm pretty sure it's a dream, but I am back in my grandfather's basement in Carney, lying on top of Lila, and my hands are tightening on her arms, and it's really hard to concentrate on anything but the smell of her hair and the feel of her skin. Except then I look down at her and she's staring up at the ceiling, her face slack and pale.

And in the dream I lean down to kiss her anyway, even though I can see that her neck is slit with the worker's smile, cut too deep, running with blood. Even though she's dead.

Then I'm teetering on the roof of my old dorm, slate tiles biting into the pads of my feet. Leaves rustle overhead. I look down at the empty quad, just like I did last spring.

This time I jump.

I'm awake, sweating through the sheets, hating myself for the hot shudder that's running through my body. On the other side of the room, Sam is snoring gently.

I reach for my cell phone before I think better of it.

Stop it, I type to Lila.

What? she texts back a moment later. She's awake.

And then I'm pushing open the window and sneaking out to the quad in the middle of the night, in just a T-shirt and boxers. It's stupid, stupid like driving off campus with no plan. I'm acting like I want to get caught, like I want someone to stop me before I have to make the decisions I am careening toward.

Once, a year ago, I would never have believed how easy it was to just walk out of one building and into another. The front doors of the dorms aren't even locked. Each floor door *is* locked, but not with anything challenging. No bolt. Just a quick twist and swipe, and I'm walking across her floor and into her room, like getting caught is the last thing on my mind.

"*You*," I say, my voice low but not low enough. She's huddled in blankets and peering up at me owlishly.

"I can't keep having these dreams," I whisper. "You have to stop giving them to me."

"Are you crazy?" She rolls onto her back, kicking off

the blanket and sitting up. She's only got on a tank top and underwear. "You're going to get us both thrown out of school."

I open my mouth to bargain with her, but I feel suddenly undone by despair. I am like a clockwork automaton whose gears just locked.

She touches my arm, bare skin on bare skin. "I'm not giving you any dreams. I'm not working you. Can't you believe there's one person in your life who's not out to get you?"

"No," I say, too honest by half. I sit down on the bed and put my head in my hands.

She puts her hand on my cheek. "There's something really wrong, isn't there?"

I shake my head. "It's just dreams."

I don't want Lila to see that I hoped the dreams were from her, wanted them to be clues that added up to something, wished for them to be something that could just stop. I didn't want more evidence that the inside of my head is an ugly place.

She drops her hand and looks at me, head tilted to one side. For a moment I am flooded with nostalgia for us being kids, for my own uncomplicated and completely impossible yearning.

"Tell me," she says.

"I can't," I say, shaking my head again.

There is a sound in the hallway, a door shutting and then footsteps. Lila looks toward her closet, and I start to pad my way toward it. Then I hear the flush of a toilet.

I sigh and lean against the wall.

"Come here," she whispers recklessly, opening the covers. "Get under. You'll be hidden if someone comes in."

"I don't know if that's such a—," I begin.

"*Shhhh.*" She cuts me off, smiling in a way that suggests that she's mocking her own motivations before I get the chance. "Come on. Quick."

It's not that I don't know that it's a bad idea. It's that, lately, bad ideas have a particular hold over me. I get under the covers. They're warm from being against her skin, and they carry her smell—soap and the faint trace of ash. When she throws an arm over my torso, urging me to press against her, I do.

Her skin is soft and scorchingly hot after the cool night air. Her leg twines around mine. It feels so good, I have to choke back a gasp.

It's so easy. Wrong, but easy. There are so many things I want to say to her, and they're all unfair. I kiss her instead, smothering the unutterable *I love you. I have always loved you* against her tongue. Her mouth opens under mine with a whimper.

When she pulls her tank top over her head and throws it onto the floor, I am hollowed out, empty of everything but gnawing self-hate. When her bare fingers thread through my hair, even that fades away. There is nothing but her.

"I'm a good pretend girlfriend," she says, like she's telling a joke that's just between us.

We should really stop.

Everything slows to her skin, the swell of her lip

between my teeth, the arch of her bare back. My hands slide to her hip bones and the edge of her cotton underpants.

"The best," I say. My voice sounds unfamiliar, like I've been screaming.

Lila's mouth moves against my shoulder. I can feel her smile.

I push her hair gently back from her cheek. I can feel her heartbeat throbbing in the pulse at her throat, measuring out the moments before she's gone.

The moment she was cursed, I lost her. Once it wears off—soon—she will be embarrassed to remember things that she said, things she did, things like this. No matter how solid she feels in my arms, she is made of smoke.

I should stop, but there's no point in stopping. Because I'm not strong enough—eventually, I won't stop.

I thought the question was "Will I or won't I?"

But that's not the question at all.

It's "When?"

Because I will.

It's just a matter of time. It's now.

Lila kisses me again, and even that thought spirals away. I close my eyes.

"We can do whatever you want," I say, voice ragged. "But you have to tell me—"

The sound of shattering glass seems impossibly loud. I am up on my knees in the bed, cold air from outside sobering me before I really understand what's happening. But then I see the tableau: the jagged outline of what's left of the window, a rock lying in the glittering fragments on the floor, and a girl turning to run.

For a moment my gaze locks with Audrey's. Then she's halfway across the quad, rain boots sinking in the dirt.

Lila's bent over the stone, looking dazed, a crumpled piece of paper in her hand. "There was a note taped to it. It says 'Die, curse worker.'" She looks out the window. Too late. Audrey's gone.

I hear footsteps in the hall, the banging of doors. Voices.

"You have to hide," Lila whispers. She's still bare to the waist. It's really distracting.

I look around the room instead of looking at her. There's nowhere to go—under the bed and in the closet might work for a quick room check, but not something like this.

All I can think to do is change myself.

I have never transformed myself beyond a slight changing of my hands, and only the terror of getting both of us thrown out of school is enough to make me concentrate. I jerk my body into shifting. It happens fast; I'm getting better. I fall forward onto the pads of four feet. I want to shout, but what comes out of my mouth is a yowl.

"A black cat?" Lila snorts, leaning down. Her fingers sink into my fur as she lifts me up. I'm glad she's holding me, because the shift in perspective is dizzying. I'm not sure how to manage my feet.

Someone, probably her hall master, bangs on the door. "What's going on in there? Ms. Zacharov, you better open up."

Lila leans out the remains of the window, swinging my new body over the quad. My tail lashes back and forth without my knowing how I'm making that happen. It's a long way down.

"Too far," she says suddenly. "You're going to hurt your—"

She's forgotten that I'm not going to look like a normal cat in a moment. I squirm, twisting until I can bite her hand.

"Ow!" she yells, and lets go.

The air rushes past me, too fast for me to make any sound. I try to keep my limbs loose, not to brace myself for impact, but hitting the ground feels like a punch in the chest. My breath goes out of me.

I barely manage to crawl into the bushes before the blowback hits.

Everything aches. I lift my head to see a pink light glowing behind the stretch of trees near the track. Morning.

I'm still a cat.

Blowback as something smaller than yourself is even more bizarre than usual. Nothing feels real or right. No part of your body is your own. Even perspective is all wrong.

Waking up in an unfamiliar body is stranger still.

My senses are heightened to a surreal degree. I can hear insects moving through blades of grass. I can smell mice burrowing into the soft wood. I feel very small and very scared.

I'm not sure I can walk. I push myself up, leg by leg, and wobble until I'm sure I've got my balance. Then I shift one front paw and one back one, moving in a staggered limp across the quad in the early morning light.

It feels like it takes hours. By the time I make it to beneath my own window, I'm exhausted. The window is just as I left it, slightly lifted from the sill, but not so wide that Sam would be woken by the breeze.

I yowl hopefully. Sam, predictably, hears nothing.

Closing my eyes against the pain, I force the transformation. It *hurts*, like my skin was still raw from shifting the first time. I push open the window and hop inside, falling onto the floor with a thump.

"Hrm," Sam says muzzily, turning over.

"Help me," I say, lifting my arm to touch the metal edge of his bed. "Please. The blowback. You've got to keep me from being loud."

He's staring at me with wide eyes. They only get wider when my fingers start to curl like vines. My leg starts shaking.

"It hurts," I say, shamed by the whine in my voice.

Sam is getting up, throwing his comforter over me. Two pillows come down on either side of my head so I can't thrash it around too badly. He's totally awake now, looking at me with true adrenaline-pumping horror.

"I'm sorry," I manage to get out before my tongue turns to wood.

I feel a sharp nudge on my side. I turn stiffly and blink up at Mr. Pascoli.

"Get up, Mr. Sharpe," our hall master says. "You're going to be late for class."

"He's sick," I hear Sam say.

I am cocooned in blankets. Just moving is hard, like the air has turned semi-solid. I groan and then close my eyes again. I have never felt so worn out. I had no idea that back-to-back blowback could do this to me.

"What is he doing on the floor?" I hear Pascoli say. "Are you hungover, Mr. Sharpe?"

"I'm sick," I slur, borrowing Sam's excuse. My mind isn't working fast enough to come up with one of my own. "I think I have a fever."

"You better get down to the nurse, then. Breakfast is almost over."

"I'll take him," Sam says.

"I want to see a copy of that slip, Mr. Sharpe. And you better get one. If I find out you've been drinking or using, I don't care what's going on with your family, you're going to be off my hall. Understand?"

"Yeah." I nod. Right now I am willing to say whatever I think will make Pascoli go away faster.

"Come on," Sam says, picking me up under my arms and dumping me onto my bed.

I struggle to stay sitting up. My head swims. I'm not really sure how I pull on jeans, gloves, and boots, which I fumble over and finally decide not to lace.

"Maybe we should call someone," he whispers once Pascoli is out of the room. "Mrs. Wasserman?"

I frown, trying to concentrate on his words. "What do you mean?"

"Last night you seemed way screwed-up. And today? You look pretty bad."

"Just tired," I say.

He shakes his head. "I've never seen anything like—"

"Blowback," I say quickly, reluctant to hear his description of what it looks like. "Don't worry about it."

He narrows his eyes but waits for me to get up. He follows as I shuffle dazedly across campus.

"I need one more thing," I say, "when we get to the nurse's office."

"Sure, man," he says, but I don't think he's decided yet. I'm freaking him out.

"When we go in there, I am going to have a coughing fit, and you are going to volunteer to get me a glass of water. But you're going to get me *hot* water—as hot as you can get it out of the tap. Okay?"

"Why?" asks Sam.

I force a grin. "Easiest way to fake a fever."

Even semiconscious I can still manage a minor con.

Hours later I wake up in the nurse's office, drooling on a pillow. I'm ravenously hungry. I get up and realize I'm still wearing my boots. I lace them and pad out to the front room.

The school nurse is gray-haired, short, and round. She moves around her white room, with its anatomical posters, with purpose born of the fact that she believes that all student problems can be cured with (a) rest on one of her cots,

(b) two aspirin, or (c) Neosporin and a bandage. Luckily, there's nothing else I need.

"Hey," I say. "I'm feeling better. I'm going to go back to my room now if that's okay?"

Nurse Kozel's in the middle of giving pills to Willow Davis. "Cassel, why don't you sit down and let me check your temperature. It was pretty high before."

"Okay," I say, slouching in a chair.

Willow swallows her medicine with a sip from a paper cup as Nurse Kozel crosses to the other side for the thermometer.

"You might as well lie down in the back until the pills start working," Kozel calls. "I'll come in a little while to check on you."

"I'm so hungover," Willow says to me under her breath.

I smile the conspiratorial smile of people who have used the nurse's office to sleep off the night before.

She heads for the back, and I get a thermometer stuck under my tongue. While I wait, I consider for the first time what happened—and didn't happen—with Lila.

It's just a matter of time.

Even in the light of day, the thought feels no less true.

Temptation is tempting. I like my shiny new Mercedes-Benz; I like getting fancy dinners with the head of a crime family; I like the Feds off my back and my mom safe. I like having Lila kiss me as if we could have some kind of future. I like it when she says my name as though I'm the only other person in the world.

I like it so much that I'll probably do anything to get it.

Ignore that Lila doesn't really love me. Kill my own brother. Become a hired assassin. Anything.

I thought that I could never betray my family, never work someone I loved, never kill anyone, never be like Philip, but I get more like him every day. Life's full of opportunities to make crappy decisions that feel good. And after the first one, the rest get a whole lot easier.

THE GREAT THING ABOUT

a sick day is that it's not hard to walk out of school. I do. I could drive, but I worry they'd notice my car missing. I can't afford to take any more chances.

Besides, right now I'm not sure I should be trusted with nice things.

I have woken with a new resolution. No more stupid risks. No more trying to get caught. No more leaving things up to fate. No more waiting for the other shoe to drop. I walk until I get far enough off campus to be safe. Then I call a cab with my cell phone.

Barron doesn't want to go to the Feds. If he tells them everything, then he gets nothing from the Brennans. But if he really believes I'm not going to cave to his demands, he might turn me in, and I need to tidy things up before he gets the chance. Especially because I know something that he can't—there isn't evidence just of what I've done at the old house. There's evidence of Mom's crime too.

First things first, I have to get rid of that.

I'm her son. It's my job to keep her safe.

I wait on the tree-lined sidewalk in front of a bunch of nice-looking houses. Ones with backyards and swings. A white-haired lady smiles at me when she ducks out to get her mail from a polished brass box.

I smile back automatically. I bet those fat pearls she's got in her ears are real. If I asked politely, she'd probably let me wait on her porch. Maybe even make me a sandwich.

My stomach grumbles. I ignore it. After another moment she goes back inside, the screen door slamming on my chances for lunch.

The trees shake with a sudden gust of wind, and a few still-green maple leaves fall around me. I toe one with my booted foot. It doesn't look it, but it's already dead.

The cab pulls up, the driver frowning when he sees me. I slide into the back and give him directions to the garbage house. Happily, he doesn't ask any questions about picking up a kid three blocks away from a high school. Probably he's seen a lot worse.

He drops me off, and I hand him the cash from a few recent wagers. I'm low on funds and I'm spending money that I don't really have. An unexpected dark horse bet coming in could clean me out.

I head up the hill toward the old place. It looks ominous, even in the day. Its shingles are gray with neglect, and one of the windows in the upper story—the one to Mom's old room—is broken with a bag taped over it.

Barron had to know I might come here. He had to think I might hide the body, now that he warned me that he knows where it is. But whatever surprises he left for me must be in the basement, because the kitchen looks identical to the way I left it on Sunday. My half cup of coffee is still sitting in the sink, the liquid inside looking ominously close to mold.

The coat is right where I left it too, in the back of the closet, gun still rolled inside. I kneel down and pull the bundle out just to be sure.

I picture my mother, pressing the barrel against Philip's chest. He couldn't have believed she'd shoot—he was her firstborn. Maybe he laughed. Or maybe he knew her better than I did. Maybe he saw in her expression that no amount of love was worth her freedom.

But the more I try to imagine it, the more I see myself in his place, feel the cold barrel of the gun, see my mother's smeary lipsticked mouth pull into a grimace. A shudder runs down my back.

I force myself up, grab a knife from the block and a plastic bag from under the sink. I need to stop *thinking*. I start chopping the buttons off the coat instead. I'm going to burn the cloth, so I want to make sure any hooks or solid parts go into the plastic bag with the gun. After that I plan on weighting it with bricks and sinking it in the Round Valley

Reservoir up near Clinton. Grandad once told me that half of New Jersey's criminals have dropped something down there—it's the deepest lake in the state.

I turn the pockets inside out, checking for coins.

Red leather gloves tumble onto the linoleum floor. And something else, something solid.

A familiar amulet, cracked in half. At the sight of it I know who killed Philip. Everything snaps into place. The plan changes.

Oh, man, I am an *idiot*.

I call her from a pay phone, just like Mom taught me.

"You should have told me," I say, but I understand why she didn't.

On the cab ride back to school, I get a text from Audrey.

I remember how there was a time when that would have thrilled me. Now I open my phone with a sigh.

mutually assured destruction
meet me @ the library tomorrow @ lunch

I have been too busy worrying about my immediate problems to really consider who to tell—or even *whether* to tell anyone—that Audrey threw a rock through Lila's window, but Audrey raises an interesting point. If I report Audrey, then Audrey reports seeing me in Lila's room. I'm not sure which crime they'll think is worse and neither of us has any proof, but I don't want to get tossed out of Wallingford in our senior year, even if I get tossed out with someone else.

And I do know which one of us Northcutt thinks is more trustworthy.

I text her back: *i'll be there*

I'm exhausted. Too tired to do anything more than drag myself back to the dorm and eat the rest of Sam's Pop-Tarts. I fall asleep on top of my blankets, still in my clothes. For the second time that day, I don't even remember to take my boots off.

Wednesday afternoon, Audrey is waiting for me on the library steps, red hair tossed by the wind. She's sitting with her hands in bright kelly green gloves, clasped in the lap of her Wallingford pleated skirt.

Seeing her makes me think ugly thoughts. Zacharov's story about Jenny. The words scrawled on the paper. Shards of glass shining at Lila's feet.

"How could you?" Audrey spits when I get close, like she's the one with a reason to be angry.

I'm taken aback. "What? You *threw a rock*—"

"So what? Lila took everything from me. Everything. From the first time she saw me with you, she hated me." Her neck has gone red and blotchy, like it always does when she's upset. "And then you're there, in her room, in the middle of the night like you don't care if you get caught. How could you do that after what she—what she—"

Tears stream down her cheeks.

"What?" I ask. "What did she do?"

She just shakes her head, incoherent with weeping.

I sigh and sit beside her on the steps. After a moment I put my arm around her shoulders, drawing her shaking body against me. She tucks her head into my neck, and I inhale the familiar floral scent of her shampoo. I know that she'd probably hate me if she knew what I was really like or what I could really do, but she was my girlfriend once. I can't help caring.

"Hey," I say softly, meaninglessly. "It's okay. Whatever it is."

"No, it's not," Audrey says. "I hate her. I hate her! I wish the rock smashed her face in."

"You don't mean that," I say.

"She got Greg suspended, and then his parents wouldn't let him come home." She gives a wet gasp. "They saw those stupid pictures your friends took. He had to beg for his mother to—to even listen through the door." She's crying so hard that her breaths are more like big hiccupping gulps of air. She fights to get words out between sobs. "So they finally took him to get tested. And when they found out he wasn't a worker, they decided to enroll him at Southwick Academy."

Audrey stops trying to talk at that point. It's as though she's possessed by grief, as if something other than herself has hold of her body.

Southwick Academy is famously anti-worker. It's in Florida, close to the Georgia border, and requires all student applications to come with a copy of their hyperbathygammic test. A test with clear negative results. If the student is accepted, then he or she is retested by the on-staff physician.

Sending Greg to Southwick means that his reputation, and presumably the reputation of his parents, is saved. I'd feel bad, if I didn't think he'd enjoy being at a school where everyone feels the way he does about workers.

"We'll all be out of high school in less than a year," I say. "You'll see him again."

After a few moments Audrey pulls away and looks up at me with red-rimmed eyes. Then she shakes her head. "He told me about Lila before he left. How he cheated on me. That she worked him to make him want—"

"That's not true," I say.

She takes a long, shuddering breath. Then she wipes her cheeks with her kelly green gloves. "That just makes it worse. That you want her and he wants her and no one was forced and she's not even nice."

"Greg's not nice," I say.

"He was," she says. "To me. When we were alone. But I guess it didn't mean anything. Lila made it not mean anything."

I get up. "No, she didn't. Look, I get why you're pissed. I even get why you smashed her window, but this has to stop. No more rocks. No more slurs."

"She cheated on you, too," Audrey says.

I just shake my head.

"Fine," she says, standing and dusting off her skirt. "If you don't tell anyone what I did, I won't say that you were in her room."

"And you'll leave Lila alone?"

"I'll keep your secret. This time. I'm not promising anything else." Audrey stalks down the steps and across the quad without looking back once.

My shirt is still wet with her tears.

Classes go about as well as usual. Lately, I can't seem to get it together. Emma Bovary and her basket of apricots blur together with information asymmetries and incomplete markets. I close my eyes in one class and when I open them, I'm in another.

I walk into the cafeteria for dinner and pile food onto my plate. Tonight's main course is chicken enchiladas with salsa verde. My stomach is so empty that even the smell of the food makes it churn. I'm early, so I have a few minutes at the table alone. I use them to shovel food into my face.

Eventually, Sam sits down across from me. He grins. "You look slightly less close to death."

I snort, but most of my attention is on watching Lila walk in and pick up a tray of food. Looking at her brings a hot flush of memory to my skin. I'm ashamed of myself and I want to touch her again, all at once.

She and Daneca come to the table and take seats. Daneca looks over toward Sam, but he's staring at his plate.

"Hey," I say as neutrally as I can.

Lila points her fork at me. "I heard a rumor about you."

"Oh?" I can't tell if she's teasing or not, but she's not smiling.

"I heard that you were taking bets about me." Lila rubs her gloved hand across her forehead, pushing back her bangs. She seems tired. I'm guessing she didn't get any sleep last night. "Me and Greg. Me being crazy. Me being in a prison in Moscow."

I glance quickly at Sam, who is wearing an expression of almost comical surprise. He's been helping me keep the books for bets, since his stint running the business, so he knows what's come in and what's gone out. He knows we're busted.

"Not because I wanted to," I say. "If I didn't, I was afraid people would make too much of it. I mean, I take bets on *everything*."

"Like who's a worker?" she asks. "You're making money off those bets too, aren't you?"

Daneca narrows her eyes at me. "Cassel, is that true?"

"You don't understand," I say, turning to her. "If I suddenly pick and choose what bets to take, then it would seem like I knew something—like I was protecting someone. I sit with you three; everyone would assume I was protecting one of you. Plus people would stop telling me what's going on—what rumors are being spread. And I couldn't spread any rumors of my own. I wouldn't be any help."

"Yeah, and you'd have to take a stand, too," Lila says. "People might even think *you're* a worker. I know how much you would hate that."

"Lila—," I say. "I swear to you, there's a stupid rumor about every new kid that comes to Wallingford. No one believes them. If I didn't take those bets, I would basically confirm that you and Greg—" I stumble over the words and start over, not wanting to piss her off any worse than

I already have. "It would make everyone think the rumor was true."

"I don't care," Lila says. "You're the one that's making me into a joke."

"I'm sorry—," I start, but she cuts me off.

"Don't con me." She reaches into her pocket and slaps five twenty-dollar bills down on the table. The glasses rattle, liquid sloshing. "A hundred bucks says that Lila Zacharov and Greg Harmsford did it. What are my odds?"

She doesn't know that Greg's never coming back to Wallingford. She doesn't know just how much Audrey hates her. I look automatically toward his old table, hoping that Audrey can't overhear any of this.

"Good," I force out. "Your odds are good."

"At least I'll make a profit," she says. Then she gets up and stalks out of the dining hall.

I rest my forehead against the table and fold my arms on top of my head. I really can't win today.

"You gave back that money," Sam says. "Why didn't you tell her?"

"It doesn't matter," I say. "I *did* take bets on who was a worker. I thought I was doing the right thing. Maybe she's right. Maybe I was just covering my ass."

"I took those bets about who was a worker too," says Sam. "It was the only thing we could do to have any leverage." He sounds more sure than I feel.

"Cassel?" Daneca says. "Wait a second."

"What?" Her voice sounds so odd—tentative—that I look up.

"She shouldn't have been able to do that," Daneca says. "Lila just *told you off.*"

"You can love someone and still argue with—," I start to say, and stop myself. Because that's the difference between real love and cursed love. When you really love someone, you can still see them for who they are. But the curse makes love sickly and simple.

I look in amazement toward the doors Lila walked through. "Do you think she could be—better? Not cursed?"

The hope that blooms inside of me is terrifying.

Maybe. Maybe she could come out of this and not hate me. Maybe she could even forgive me. Maybe.

I cross the quad, heading back to my dorm room, Sam next to me. I'm smiling, despite knowing better. Despite knowing my own luck. I'm dreaming dreams where I'm clever enough to weasel my way out of all my problems. Sucker dreams. The kind of dreams con artists love to exploit.

"So," Sam says slowly, his voice low. "It's always like that? When you transform?"

Yesterday morning seems so long ago. I remember Sam's look of terror as he stared down at me, sprawled on the floor. I can still feel the blowback creeping up my spine. I want to deny any of it happened; in those moments I felt more naked than I ever have in my life. So naked I was turned inside out.

"Yeah," I say, watching moths circling the dim lights along the path. The moon overhead is just a sliver. "Pretty much. That was worse than usual because I worked myself twice in one night."

"Where were you?" Sam asks. "What *happened*?"

I hesitate.

"Cassel," Sam says. "Just tell me if it's bad."

"I was in Lila's room."

"Did you break her window?" he asks. I should have realized the story was all over campus. Everyone knows about the rock, about the threat.

"No," I say. "The person who did that couldn't have known I was there."

He looks over sharply, a line appearing over the bridge of his nose, between his eyebrows, as he frowns. "So you know who it was? Who broke the window?"

I nod my head, but I don't volunteer Audrey's name. Telling Sam isn't like telling Northcutt, but I still feel bound to keep the secret.

"When it rains, it pours," Sam says.

As we head into the building, my phone buzzes in my pocket. I open it against my chin and put it to my ear. "Yeah?"

"Cassel?" Lila says softly.

"Hey," I say. Sam turns and gives me a knowing look, then keeps walking, leaving me to sit on the steps to the second floor.

"I'm sorry I yelled at you," she says.

My heart sinks. "You are?"

"I am. I get why you took those bets. I'm not sure I like it, but I get it. I'm not mad."

"Oh," I say.

"I guess I just freaked out," she says. "After last night. I don't want this to be just pretend." She's speaking so quietly now that I can barely make out the words.

"It's not," I say. The words feel ripped out of my chest. "It never was."

"Oh." She's quiet for a long moment. Then, when she does speak, I can hear the smile in her voice. "I still expect my winnings, Cassel. You can't sweet-talk me out of those."

"Whatever you say," I tell her, grinning down at the stair. Someone dropped their gum, someone else stepped on it. Now it's a streak of grimy pink.

I'm such a fool.

"I love you," I say, because I might as well now, when it no longer matters what I do. I've made up my mind. Before she can reply, I close my phone, hanging up on her.

Then I rest my head on the cold iron railing. Maybe the curse would fade eventually, but I'd never be sure it was completely gone. I'd never know if the way she felt about me was real. Curses are subtle. Sure, emotion work is supposed to wear off, but how can anyone *know*? Love shouldn't be about possessing and caging and keeping. It shouldn't be stolen.

There never were any good choices.

I call Agent Jones. I've lost his card, so I just call the main number for the agency in Trenton. After a couple of transfers, I get an answering machine. I tell him that I need more time, just a couple more days, just until Monday, and then I'll give him his murderer.

Once you decide you have to do something, it's almost a relief. Waiting is harder than doing, even when you hate what you're about to do.

The longer I look for alternatives, the darker those alternatives get.

I have to accept what is.

I am a bad person.

I've done bad things.

And I'm going to keep on doing them until somebody stops me. And who's going to do that? Lila can't. Zacharov won't. There's only one person who can, and he's shown himself to be pretty unreliable.

Yeah, I'm talking about myself.

Sam's up in our room, paging through *Othello* when I come in. His iPod is plugged into our speakers, and the sound of Deathwërk rattles the windows.

"You okay?" he shouts over the guttural vocals.

"Sam," I say, "remember how at the beginning of the semester you said you went to that special effects warehouse and cleaned it out? How you were ready for anything."

"Yeah . . . ," he says, suspicious.

"I want to frame someone for my brother's murder."

"Who?" he asks, turning down the sound. He must be used to me saying crazy things, because he's totally serious. "Also, why?"

I take a deep breath.

Framing someone requires several things.

First you have to find a person who makes a believable villain. It helps if she's already done something bad; it helps even more if some part of what you're setting her up for is true.

And since she's done something bad, you don't have to feel so terrible about picking her to take the fall.

But the final thing you need is for your story to make sense. Lies work when they're simple. They usually work a lot better than the truth does. The truth is messy. It's raw and uncomfortable. You can't blame people for preferring lies.

You especially can't blame people when that preference benefits you.

"Bethenny Thomas," I say.

Sam frowns at me. "Wait, what? Who's that?"

"Dead mobster's girlfriend. Two big poodles. Runner." I think of Janssen in the freezer. I hope he'd approve of my choice. "She put out a hit on her boyfriend, so it's not like she hasn't murdered *someone*."

"And you know that how?" Sam asks.

I'm trying really hard to be honest, but telling the whole thing to Sam seems beyond me. Still, the fragments sound ridiculous on their own. "She said so. In the park."

He rolls his eyes. "Because the two of you were so friendly."

"I guess she mistook me for someone else." I sound so much like Philip that it scares me. I can hear the menace in my tone.

"Who?" Sam asks, not flinching.

I force my voice back to normal. "Uh, the person who killed him."

"*Cassel.*" He groans, shaking his head. "No, don't worry, I'm not going to ask why she would think that. I don't want to know. Just tell me your plan."

I sit down on my bed, relieved. I'm not sure I can endure another of my confessions, despite the fact that I have so much yet to confess.

I used to stake out joints for robberies with my dad sometimes, back when I was a kid. See what people's patterns were. When they left for work. When they returned. If they ate at the same place each night. If they went to bed at the same time. The more tight a schedule, the more tidy a robbery.

What I remember most, though, are the long stretches of sitting in the car with the radio on. The air would get stuffy, but I wasn't allowed to roll down the windows far enough to get a good breeze. The soda would get stale, and eventually I'd have to piss into a bottle because I wasn't supposed to get out of the car. There were only two good things about stakeouts. The first thing was that Dad let me pick out anything at the gas station mart that I wanted snack-wise. The second was that Dad taught me how to play cards. Poker. Three-card monte. Slap. Crazy eights.

Sam's pretty good at games. We spend Friday night watching Bethenny's apartment building and gambling for cheese curls. We learn that the doorman takes a couple of smoking breaks when no one's around. He's a beefy dude who tells off a homeless guy harassing residents for change out front. Bethenny takes her dogs for a run in the evening and walks them twice more before she goes out for the night. At dawn the doormen change shifts. The guy who comes in is skinny. He eats two doughnuts and reads the newspaper before residents start coming downstairs. It's late Saturday morning by then, and Bethenny's still not back, so we bag it and go home.

I drop Sam off at his place around eleven and crash for a few hours at the garbage house. I wake up when the cordless phone rings next to my head. I'd forgotten that I brought it into the room days ago. It's tangled in the sheets.

"Yeah?" I grunt.

"May I speak with Cassel Sharpe?" my mother asks in her chirpiest voice.

"Mom, it's me."

"Oh, sweetheart, your voice sounded so funny." She seems happier than I've heard her in a long time. I shove myself into a sitting position.

"I was sleeping. Is everything okay?" My automatic fear is that she's in trouble. That the Feds have gotten tired of waiting and have picked her up. "Where are you?"

"Everything's perfect. I missed you, baby." She laughs. "I've just been swept up in so many new things. I met so many nice people."

"Oh." I cradle the phone against my shoulder. I should probably feel bad that I suspected her of murder. Instead I feel guilty for not feeling guilty. "Have you seen Barron recently?" I ask. I hope not. I hope she has no idea he's blackmailing me.

I hear the familiar hiss of a cigarette being lit. She inhales. "Not in a week or two. He said he had a big job coming up. But I want to talk about *you*. Come see me and meet the governor. There's a brunch on Sunday that I think you'd just love. You should see the rocks some of the women wear, plus the silverware's *reeeal.*" She draws the last part out long, like she's tempting a dog to a bone.

"Governor Patton? No, thanks. I'd rather eat glass than eat with him." I carry the phone downstairs and pour out the old coffee in the pot. I dump in new water and fresh grounds. The clock says its three in the afternoon. I have to get moving.

"Oh, don't be like that," says Mom.

"How can you sit there while he goes on and on about Proposition 2? Okay, fine. He's a really tempting mark. I'd love to see him get conned, but it's not worth it. Mom, things could get really bad. One mistake and—"

"Your mother doesn't make mistakes." I hear her blow out the smoke. "Baby, I know what I'm doing."

The coffee is dripping, steam rising from the pot. I sit down at the kitchen table. I try not to think about her the way she was when I was a kid, sitting right where I am now, laughing at something Philip said or ruffling my hair. I can almost see my dad, sitting at the table, showing Barron how to flip a quarter over his knuckles while she makes breakfast. I can smell my dad's cigarillos and the blackening bacon. The back of my eyes hurt.

"I don't know what *I'm* doing anymore," I say. You might think I'm crazy, telling her that. But she's still my mother.

"What's wrong, sweetheart?" The concern in her voice is real enough to break my heart.

I can't tell her. I really can't. Not about Barron or the Feds or how I thought she was a murderer. Certainly not about Lila. "School," I say, resting my head in my hands. "I guess I'm getting a little overwhelmed."

"Baby," she says in a harsh whisper, "in this world, lots of people will try to grind you down. They need you to be small so they can be big. You let them think whatever they want, but you make sure you get yours. *You get yours.*"

I hear a man's voice in the background. I wonder if she's talking about me at all. "Is someone there?"

"Yes," she says sweetly. "I hope you'll think about coming on Sunday. How about I give you the address and you can think about it?"

I pretend to copy down the location of Patton's stupid brunch. Really I'm just pouring myself a cup of coffee.

WAKING UP IN THE MIDDLE

of the day always leaves you with a slightly dazed feeling, as though you've stepped out of time. The light outside the windows is wrong. My body feels heavy as I force it up and into clothing.

I stop at the store for more coffee and a prop, then head over to Daneca's house. I walk across the green lawn, up to the freshly painted door between two manicured bushes. Everything is as pretty as a picture.

When I ring the bell, Chris answers. "What?" he says. He's got on a pair of shorts and flip flops with an oversize shirt. It makes him look even younger than he is. There's a smudge of something blue in his hair.

"Can I come in?"

He pushes the door wide. "I don't care."

I sigh and walk past him. The scent of lemon polish fills the hallway, and there's a girl in the living room running a vacuum. For some reason it never occurred to me that Daneca grew up with maids, but of course she did.

"Is Mrs. Wasserman here?" I ask the girl.

She takes headphones out of her ears and smiles at me. "What was that?"

"Sorry," I say. "I was just wondering if you know where Mrs. Wasserman is."

The girl points. "In her office, I think."

I walk through the house, past the artwork and the antique silver. I knock on the frame of a glass-paneled door. Mrs. Wasserman opens it, hair pulled up into a makeshift bun with a pencil shoved through her mass of curls. "Cassel?" she says. She's got on paint-stained sweatpants and is holding a mug of tea.

I hold out the violets I bought at the garden supply store. I don't know much about flowers, but I liked how velvety they looked. "I wanted to say thanks for the other day. For the advice."

Gifts are very useful to con men. Gifts create a feeling of debt, an itchy anxiety that the recipient is eager to be rid of by repaying. So eager, in fact, that people will often overpay just to be relieved of it. A single spontaneously given cup of coffee can make a person feel obligated to sit through a lecture on a religion they don't care about. The gift of a tiny, wilted flower can make the recipient give to a charity they dislike. Gifts place such a heavy burden that even throwing away the gift doesn't remove the debt. Even if you hate coffee, even if you didn't want that flower, once you take it, you want to give something back. Most of all, you want to dismiss that obligation.

"Oh, thank you," Daneca's mother says. She looks surprised, but pleased. "It was no trouble at all, Cassel. I'm always here if you want to talk."

"You mean that?" I ask, which is maybe laying it on really thick, but I need to push her a little. This is her chance to repay me. It doesn't hurt that I know she's a sucker for hard-luck cases.

"Of course," she says. "Anything you need, Cassel."

Bingo.

I like to think it's the gratitude that makes her overgenerous, but I guess I'll never know. That's the problem with not trusting people—you never find out if they'd have helped you on their own.

Daneca is on her computer when I come into her room. She looks up at me in surprise.

"Hey," I say. "Your little brother let me in." I'm already not being entirely honest by failing to mention I talked with her mother, but I'm determined to do nothing more dishonest than that. I hate myself enough already without conning one of my only friends.

"Chris is not my brother," Daneca says automatically. "I don't even think it's legal for him to live here." Her room looks exactly like I would have expected. Her bedspread is batik, studded with silver discs. Fringed scarves drape over the tops of the linen curtains. The walls are covered in posters of folk singers, in poems, and with a big worker rights flag. On her bookshelf, next to copies of Ginsberg and Kerouac and *The Activist's Handbook,* is a line of horses. White and brown, speckled and black, they're arranged like a chorus line.

I lean against the doorjamb. "Okay. Some kid who's always hanging around at this address let me in. He was pretty rude about it too."

She half-smiles. I can see past her to the paper she's writing, the letters like black ants on the screen. "Why are you here, Cassel?"

I sit down on her bed and take a deep breath. If I can do this, then I can do everything else.

"I need you to work Lila," I say. The words come easily to my lips, but my chest hurts as I speak them aloud. "I need you to make her not love me anymore."

"Get out," Daneca says.

I shake my head. "I need you to do it. Please. Please just listen." I'm afraid my voice is going to break. I am afraid she is going to hear how much this hurts.

"Cassel, I don't *care* what reason you have. There is *no* reason good enough to take away someone's free will."

"It's already been taken! Remember when I said that I tried to stay away from Lila?" I say. "I've stopped trying. How's that for a good reason?"

She doesn't trust me. Surely she can understand if I don't trust myself either.

The look Daneca gives me is full of disgust. "There's

nothing I can do anyway. You know that. I *can't* take the curse off her."

"Work her so that she feels nothing for me," I say. My vision blurs. I wipe the dampness away from my eyes angrily. "Let her just feel nothing. Please."

She looks at me in an odd, stunned way. When she speaks, her voice is soft. "I thought the curse was fading. It might already be gone."

I shake my head. "She still likes me."

"Maybe she likes you, Cassel," Daneca says carefully. "Without the curse."

"No."

She waits for a long moment. "What about you? How are you going to feel when she—"

"It doesn't matter about me," I say. "The only way that Lila could be sure—that anyone could be sure—the curse was over is if she didn't love me."

"But—," Daneca begins.

If I can just get through this, then nothing else can hurt me. I will be capable of anything. "It has to be this way. Otherwise I'll create reasons to believe that she wants me, because I'd like that to be true. I can't be trusted."

"I know that you're really upset—," Daneca says.

"*I can't be trusted.* Do you understand me?"

She nods, once. "Okay. Okay, I'll do it."

I exhale all at once, a dizzy rush of breath.

"But this is a onetime thing. I will never do this again. I will never do anything like this again. Do you understand me?"

"Yes," I say.

"And I'm not even sure how to do it, so there are no guarantees. Plus the blowback is going to make me act all weird and emotional, so you are responsible for baby-sitting me until I am stable. Okay?"

"Yes," I say again.

"She won't care about you." Daneca tilts her head to one side, like she's seeing me for the first time. "You'll just be some guy she once knew. Everything she feels about you—everything she felt about you—it will all be gone."

I close my eyes and nod my head.

The first thing I do when I get back home is go down into the cellar. I open the cooler. Janssen is right where I left him—milk pale, with sunken eyelids and frosty hair. He looks like a demented marble sculpture—portrait of a killer, killed. All the blood must have made its sluggish way to his back before it froze. I bet if I turned him over, he'd be purple.

I strip off my right-hand glove and place my hand on his chest, pushing aside the stiffened fabric of his undershirt, letting my fingers rest against his icy skin.

I turn his heart to glass.

The change takes only a moment, but recovering from it takes longer. Once the blowback wears off, I rub my head where I smacked it against the floor. Everything aches, but I'm getting used to that.

Then I go upstairs, take the gun out of the plastic bag, close my eyes, and shoot two bullets into the ceiling of the parlor. Dust rains down on me, covering the room in a powdery cloud. A single chunk of plaster nearly brains me.

Cons aren't glamorous. They're hauling out the ancient vacuum from the closet, changing the bag, and making sure you get up most of the dust. They're sweeping in the basement to hide that you were recently rolling around after a transformation. They're fieldstripping the gun according to instructions on the Internet and carefully buffing off any fingerprints with a lightly oiled cloth, then wrapping the whole thing in paper towels. They're driving a mile to an abandoned stretch of road and soaking the murderess's coat and gloves with enough lighter fluid that they burn to ash. They're waiting to make *sure* they burn to ash and then scattering that ash. They're smashing any remaining buttons from the coat with a hammer, then tossing them along with the vacuum bag and any hooks or metal parts in different Dumpsters far from where you burned the clothes. Cons are all in the details.

By the time I'm done, it's late enough to call Sam and get the next part of the plan under way.

My mother's a purist when it comes to scamming people. She's got her thing, and it's pretty effective. Glamorous clothes, a touch of her hand, and most people are willing to do what she wants. But I'd never really thought about costumes or props until I met Sam. I have my computer open to Cyprus View's website. They have examples of the layout of their apartments for prospective renters. Very helpful.

Sam's expectantly holding up a fake wound on a thin rubbery piece of silicone. "Look, you said yourself that guard wanted to be a hero," Sam is telling me.

It might be true that I said that. I don't remember. I said a lot of things on the stakeout, mostly boring observations about the place or completely exaggerated claims about how I was going to beat Sam at cards. "But then we need another person," I say. "That's a three-person job."

"Ask Lila," he says.

"She's all the way in the city," I say, but it's a halfhearted objection. The thought of seeing her one last time before I lose her is poisonously compelling.

"Daneca and I are still . . . I don't know. Besides, she's not the best actress."

"She did fine at Zacharov's fund-raiser," I say, thinking of the way she smiled in my brother's face moments after she slipped me a fake blood packet.

"I had to give her a pep talk on the way," he says. "How about if I'm the one who calls Lila?"

Mutely I hand him my phone. I want her to come. If I resist this, I don't think I will have any resistance left.

We pick Lila up at the train station in Sam's hearse. He works on her in the back while I fiddle with the radio nervously in the front seat and eat a slice of pizza.

"Almost done?" I call, looking at the clock on the dashboard.

"Don't rush the artist," Lila says. Her voice goes through me like a knife, leaving a wound so clean I know it won't even hurt until the knife's pulled out.

"Yeah," I say. "Sorry, Sam."

Finally she climbs into the front seat. She's got a bruise painted on her cheek. It looks real, partially hidden by curls of a long blond wig.

I reach out automatically to touch her face, and then jerk my hand back.

"Don't mess me up," she says with a lopsided grin.

"We ready to go?" I call into the back.

"One second," Sam says. "I just have to get this scrape on my mouth, and it's not sticking."

Lila leans toward me, nervous and determined. "That thing you said before you hung up the phone," she half-whispers. "Did you mean it?"

I nod.

"But I thought it was all fake—" She stops and bites her lip, like she can't quite bring herself to ask the rest of the question, for fear of my answer.

"I faked faking," I say softly. "I lied about lying. I couldn't think of another way to make you believe we couldn't be together."

She frowns. "Wait. Then why tell me now?"

Crap. "Because I am about to be devoured by poodles," I quip. "Remember me always, my love."

Mercifully Sam picks that moment to lean into the front. "Okay, all done," he says.

"Here's what you asked me for," Lila says, pulling a green glass bottle out of her backpack. It's wrapped in a T-shirt. "Is this what you're going to plant in her house?"

I take it, careful not to touch the neck of the bottle. It's bizarre to think that this small thing is what Lila took from

Philip's house. It's even more bizarre to know it used to be a living person. "Nope," I say. "My plan is even more secret than that."

She rolls her eyes.

I pull my pizza delivery boy cap low and start the engine.

The plan is pretty simple. First we wait until Bethenny Thomas leaves the building without her dogs. This is the twitchiest part, because she might decide to spend her Saturday night at home, curled up in front of the television.

At ten, she gets into a cab, and we're on.

I go into the building with three boxes of pizza. I'm wearing the cap—which was pretty easy to lift from the busy shop where we ordered the pizzas—and regular clothes. Keep my head down in front of the security cameras. I say I have a delivery for the Goldblatts. We picked them because, of all the people we were able to identify as living in the building—thanks to the white pages online—they were the first not to answer when we called.

The big guy behind the desk looks up at me and grunts. He lifts the phone, pressing a button. I try very hard to act like I am bored, instead of nearly jumping out of my skin with adrenaline.

Sam comes roaring out of the darkness, hitting the glass wall of the lobby like he barely notices it. He starts screaming, pointing at the bushes. "Stay away from me. Stay the hell away!"

The guard stands up, still holding the phone but no longer paying any attention to it.

"What the hell?" I say.

Lila runs up the path toward Sam. She slaps him so hard that all the way inside the lobby, I can hear the crack of leather glove against skin. I sincerely hope that he taught her some kind of stage trick, because otherwise that had to hurt.

"I saw you looking at her," Lila shrieks. "I'm going to scratch out your eyes!"

If he was a different person, the front desk guy might just call the cops. But when I saw him toss that homeless guy off the property Friday night, I realized that he's not the type to call anyone if he thinks he can handle it.

Now I just have to hope I read him right.

When he puts down the receiver, I let out a breath I shouldn't have been holding. That's no way to look casual.

"Wait a sec," he says to me. "I got to get these kids out of here."

"Man," I groan, trying to sound as exasperated as possible. "I need to deliver these pizzas. There's a fifteen-minute guarantee."

He barely even looks at me as he heads for the door. "Whatever. Go on up."

As I step into the elevator, I hear Lila yell about how the front desk guy better mind his own business. I grin as I hit the button.

The door to Bethenny's apartment is identical to all the others. White doors in a white hallway. But when I slip my pick into the keyhole, I hear the dogs start barking.

The lock is easy, but there's a dead bolt on top that takes longer. I can smell someone frying fish across the hallway and hear someone else playing classical music with the sound turned way up. No one comes out into the hallway. If they had, I would have asked them for a number that's on a different floor and headed for the elevators. Lucky for me, I make it inside Bethenny's apartment without a lot of detours.

The minute I'm inside, the dogs run toward me. I close the front door and sprint for the bedroom, slamming the door in their snouts. They scratch against the wood, whining, and all I can hope is that they aren't scarring the door too deeply. I silently thank the building again for putting the layout of their apartments online.

Inside I dump the boxes onto the wood floor and open them up. The first has the remains of an actual pizza in it. The few slices we didn't eat are covered in pepperoni and sausage—in a pinch that might effectively distract the dogs.

The second contains the gun, wrapped in paper towels; baggies to put over my feet; bleach-soaked wipes; and disposable gloves.

The third pizza box has my getting-out-of-the-building outfit. A suit jacket and pants, glasses, and a soft leather briefcase. I change clothes quickly and then gear up.

As I tie the plastic over my feet, I glance around the room. The walls are a sea blue, hung with framed photographs of Bethenny in various tropical settings. She smiles at me, cocktail in hand, from a hundred pictures, reflected a thousandfold in the mirrors on her closet doors. I can't help seeing myself too, dirty hair hanging in my face. I look like I haven't slept in weeks.

The dogs stop whining and start barking. Over and over, a chorus of sound.

Dresses are strewn around the opening of her closet in frothy, glittering profusion, and shoes are scattered all over the room. On top of a white dresser, a tangle of gold chains droops into a drawer overstuffed with satiny bras.

I touch nothing except for the mattress. Lifting up one end, I get ready to shove my gun on top of the box spring.

Another gun's already there.

I stare at the large silver revolver. It makes the pistol in my hand look dainty.

I am so thrown that I momentarily have no idea what to do. *She already has a gun under her mattress.*

I start to laugh, the hysteria bubbling up out of my throat. All of a sudden it overwhelms me. I can't help it. I am crouched down in front of the bed, sucking in deep breaths, tears starting to run out of my eyes.

It feels as helpless as blowback, as helpless as grief.

Finally I get it together enough to put the Smith & Wesson between the mattress and box spring near the foot of the bed. I figure no one grabs for a gun there, and no one lifts up their mattress really high when they're grabbing for a different gun.

Then I break down the pizza boxes, shoving them into the briefcase along with the jeans and jacket I was wearing when I came in. I dump the extra pizza, paper towels, and wipes in too. I change my gloves. Then I run a bleach-soaked wipe over the floor to get rid of any crumbs, grease, or hairs. I toe it along to the door just to be safe.

Outside the room the poodles' barking has reached a fever pitch. I tuck the wipe into my pocket.

I hear one of the dogs thump against the knob, and suddenly, horribly, it turns. One of them must have caught it with a paw. A moment later they rush in, barking furiously. I barely jump up onto the bed in time to avoid getting bitten.

Okay, I know what you're thinking. They're poodles, right? But these things aren't little fuzzy toy poodles. They're *standard* poodles, huge and snapping at me, white teeth bared and a growl rumbling up their throats when I make a move toward the edge of the mattress. I look at the chandelier hanging above me and contemplate trying to swing from it.

"Hey," I hear a voice call. "Beth? How many times do I got to tell you to keep those dogs of yours quiet?"

Oh, *come on*. This cannot be happening.

Of course, it wouldn't be happening if I'd thought to lock the apartment door after I picked the lock. Cons are all in the details. They're about the little things that you either remember or you don't.

"If you don't shut them up, I'm gonna call the police," the guy yells. "This time I mean it—Hey, what the—"

He stands in the doorway, looking at me, astonishment silencing him. In a moment he's going to yell. In a moment he's going to rush into his apartment and dial 911.

"Oh, thank God," I say, trying to give him my most grateful look. I clear my throat. "We got a report—one of the neighbors complained. I had an appointment with—"

"Who the hell are you? What are you doing in Bethenny's apartment?" The neighbor is a guy, balding and probably in his early forties. He's sporting a pretty heavy beard and mustache. His worn T-shirt has the faded logo of a construction company.

"The apartment manager sent me to evaluate the situation with these dogs," I shout over the din of barking. "The door was open, and I thought that perhaps Ms. Thomas was in. She's been avoiding my calls, but I finally got her to agree to a meeting. I didn't expect them to attack."

"Yeah," the guy shouts. "They're high strung. And spoiled all to hell. If you want to get down from there, you better give them a treat or something."

"I don't have a treat." I decide I better move, if I want to be convincing. I jump down from the bed, grab my briefcase, and run for the neighbor. I feel teeth close on my leg.

"Augh," I yell, nearly falling.

"You *stay*," the neighbor shouts at the poodles, which miraculously seems to make them pause long enough for us to slam the bedroom door.

I lean down and pull up the hem of my pants. My left ankle is bleeding sluggishly, soaking my sock. I have only a couple of minutes before my blood spills over the plastic covering my feet and hits the floor.

"This is ridiculous!" I say. "She told me this was the only

time that she could meet, even though it was extremely inconvenient for me. And she's not even here—"

The guy looks back toward the door of the apartment. "Do you want a bandage or something?"

I shake my head. "I'm going immediately to a hospital so that the wound can be photographed and entered into evidence. It's extremely important right now that Ms. Thomas not know the building is trying to put together a case against her. Can I rely on your discretion?"

"Are you trying to get Bethenny kicked out?" he asks. I adjust my answer when I see his expression.

"Our first step is going to be suggesting that Ms. Thomas enroll her dogs in intensive obedience classes. If that doesn't work, we may have to ask her to place them elsewhere."

"I'm tired of all their noise," he says. "I'm not going to say anything to her, so long as you're not trying to mess with her lease."

"Thank you." I glance down at the floor, but I don't see any blood. Good. I head for the hallway.

"Aren't you kind of young to work for the management?" the neighbor says, but he seems more amused than suspicious.

I push the glasses up the bridge of my nose the way Sam does. "Everyone says that. Lucky me, I've got a baby face."

I limp through the lobby. The change in the way I walk probably helps my disguise—the desk guy barely looks up. I walk out the door, going over all the things I could have done wrong. I make my way stiffly down to the street and then over to the supermarket parking lot, where the hearse is idling.

Lila hops out of one side and comes running toward me. The wig's gone, bruise makeup is smeared across her nose, and she's laughing.

"Did you see our performance? I think you missed the part where we convinced Larry that he'd accidentally punched me. He wound up begging us not to press charges." She throws her arms around my neck, and all of a sudden her legs are around my waist and I'm holding her up.

I spin around to hear her giggling shriek, ignoring the pain in my ankle. Sam is getting out of the car, grinning too.

"She's such a con artist," he says. "Better than you, I think."

"Don't sass me," I say. I stop spinning, walking over to Sam's car and setting her down so she's sitting on the hood. "I know she's better."

Lila grins and doesn't unlock her legs from my waist. Instead she pulls me toward her for a kiss that tastes of greasepaint and regret.

Sam rolls his eyes. "How about we hit a diner? Larry paid us fifty bucks to go away."

"Sure," I say. "Absolutely."

I know I will never be this happy again.

MONDAY MORNING I PULL

into the parking lot of the FBI office in my shiny mob-bought Benz. I feel pretty good with the built-in GPS reassuring me that I've arrived at my destination, the leather seats heating my ass, and the surround-sound speakers blasting music from my iPod loudly enough that I can feel it in my bones.

I get out, throw my backpack over my shoulder, hit the button so that the alarm sets, and walk into the building.

Agent Jones and Agent Hunt are waiting for me inside the lobby. I follow them into the elevator.

"Nice car," Agent Hunt says.

"Yeah," I say. "I like it."

Agent Jones snorts. "Let's go upstairs, kid, and see what you've got to say. You better have something this time."

We get to the fourth floor, and they march me into a different room. No mirror this time. I'm sure it's bugged, though. Simple furniture. Table, metal chairs. The kind of room someone could lock you in for a long time.

"I want immunity," I tell them, sitting down at the table. "For any and all past crimes."

"Sure," Agent Jones says. "Look, here's my verbal agreement. You're just a kid, Cassel. We're not interested in busting you for whatever little—"

"No," I say. "I want it in writing."

Agent Hunt clears his throat. "We can do that. Not a problem. Whatever makes you feel the most comfortable. Give us a little while and we'll get something put together for you. Whatever you say to us, we can guarantee that no prosecutor will ever file charges against you. You'll have your deal. We want you on board."

I reach into my backpack and take out three copies of a contract.

"What's this?" Agent Jones says. He doesn't sound happy.

I swallow. My fingers dampen the paper with sweat. I hope they don't notice. "These are my terms. And, unlike the deal you made with my brother, I need this to be authorized by an attorney in the Justice Department."

The two agents exchange a look. "Philip was a special case," Agent Hunt says. "He had some information we needed. If you're proposing a trade, you have to give us something."

"I'm a special case too. Philip told you—or at least he strongly implied—that he knew the identity of a transformation worker, right? So do I. But I'm not a sucker like him, okay? I don't want a bunch of empty promises. I want this contract signed by *an attorney from the Justice Department.* Not by you two jokers. Then I fax it to my lawyer. When I get her okay, I'll tell you everything."

Agent Hunt looks a little stunned. I don't know if they guessed the killer was a transformation worker or not, but I can't take chances. Besides, I have only a few cards to play.

"And if we can't do that?" Agent Jones asks. He doesn't seem so friendly right at the moment.

I shrug my shoulders. "I guess neither of us gets what we want."

"We could pick up your mother. You think we don't know what she's been up to?" Agent Hunt says.

"I don't know what she's been up to," I say, keeping my voice as mild as I can. "But if she's done something wrong, then I guess she's going to have to pay for it."

Agent Jones leans in across the table. "You're a death worker, right, kid? You strongly implied that the last time you were here. Maybe something went wrong before you knew how to control your work? It happens, but you think we aren't going to find out about a missing kid somewhere in your past? Then it's going to be too late for deals."

It's going to be too late for deals much sooner than that, I think.

I wonder what it would be like working for the Brennan

family. I wonder what it's like to kill someone when you have to remember it.

"Look," I say, "I have outlined my conditions in the document in front of you. In exchange for immunity I will give you the full name and location of the transformation worker and proof of one or more crimes committed by that person."

"It's Lila Zacharov, isn't it?" Agent Hunt says. "We already know that. Not much of a secret you've got there. She disappears, and her father suddenly gets a new assassin."

I touch the top of the paper, tracing the words, willing myself not to react. Finally I look up at them both. "Every minute you spend talking to me is a minute you're not talking to the Justice Department. And in a couple of minutes I am going to get up and walk out of here and take my offer with me."

"What if we don't let that happen?" Agent Hunt says.

"Unless you plan on bringing in a memory worker to . actually go through my brain like it's a deck of cards, you can't force me into a deal—and, let's face it, if you were going to do that, you would have already done it. I guess you could physically keep me here, but you can't keep me interested."

"You better really have the goods," Agent Jones says, standing up. "I can't make any promises, but I'll make the call."

They leave me alone in the room. I figure I'm going to be there a while. I brought my homework.

When they bring me back the first contract, I call my lawyer. Unfortunately, she doesn't know she's my lawyer quite yet.

"Hello?" Mrs. Wasserman says.

"Hi, it's Cassel," I say, letting all the fear I actually feel creep into my voice. The agents have left me alone in the room, but I have no doubt that they are recording everything I say. "Remember when you told me I should ask you if I needed anything?"

I hear the hesitation in her voice. "Did something happen?"

"I really need a lawyer. I need you to be my lawyer." I have no doubt that right now she's wishing she never took those violets from me.

"I don't know," she says, which isn't no. "Why don't you tell me what happened?"

"I can't really explain." Knowing people is important to conning them. I know Mrs. Wasserman wants to help worker kids, but she also likes to know things. It doesn't hurt to add a little incentive. "I mean, I want to tell you, but if you're not my lawyer . . . I shouldn't put you in that position."

"Okay," she says quickly. "Consider me your lawyer. Now explain what's going on. My caller ID has you calling from an unlisted number. Where are you?"

"Trenton. The federal agents here are putting together a contract to try to get me immunity if I give up the identity of a transformation worker—a *murderer*," I say, in case she starts feeling protective of the unnamed worker. "But I need you to make sure the immunity deal is airtight. Plus, they want me to work for them. I need to make sure I can finish out the year at Wallingford before I start. And there's one other thing—"

"Cassel, this is very serious. You never should have tried to work out a deal like this on your own."

"I know," I say, happy to be chastised.

It takes hours and I wind up having to call Daneca's mother four times with changes before she approves the paperwork. Finally I sign. The Justice Department signs. And since I am still a minor, Mrs. Wasserman sends over the page with my mother's forged signature—the one I prepared in advance and left on Mrs. Wasserman's desk on Saturday, flipped over so it looked like just another piece of blank paper. She doesn't, of course, know that it's forged although I imagine she must *guess*.

Then I tell the Feds who the transformation worker is.

That really doesn't go well.

Agent Jones taps his fingers irritably against the press-board top of the table. The bottle rests in front of him, light making the green glass glow softly. "Let's go through your story one more time."

"We've gone through it twice already," I say, pointing to the paper he's making notes on. "I've given you a written statement."

"One more time," says Agent Hunt.

I take a deep breath. "My brother Barron is a memory

worker. My other brother—my dead brother—Philip—was a physical worker. He was employed by a guy named Anton. Anton was the one who ordered the hits. No one else knew what he was doing. We were his private execution squad. I'd transform someone, and then Barron would make me forget about it."

"Because he didn't think you'd go along with this whole deal?" Agent Jones asks.

"I think—I think that Philip thought he was doing right by me. That I was just a kid. That if I didn't know, then it was no big deal." My voice cracks, which I hate.

"Would you have killed those people?" Agent Hunt asks. "Without magical coercion?"

I imagine my brothers coming to me and telling me that I was important, needed. That I would be in on the jokes, be a real part of the family, no longer an outsider. I could have everything I wanted, if I would just do this one thing for them. Maybe Barron was right about me. "I don't know," I say. "I don't even know if I thought they were dead."

"Okay," says Agent Jones. "When did you discover that you were a transformation worker?"

"I figured out there was something wrong with my memory, so I bought a couple of charms and kept them on me. I figured out what I was. I even changed something and Barron couldn't make me forget, because of the charms. Philip told me the rest." It's weird to tell it so blandly, without all the horror or the betrayal. Just the facts.

"So you knew that we were talking about people you killed that first time you were in this office?"

I shake my head. "But I figured it out when I looked at the files. And I was able to remember enough to find that bottle."

"But you don't know where any of the other bodies are? And you don't know whose body that is?"

"True. I really don't know. I wish I did."

"Is there any special significance to the bottle? Why did you pick that?"

I shake my head again. "I have no idea. Probably it just came to mind."

"Why don't you tell us about Philip's murder again. You're saying you did not shoot your brother, correct? Are you sure? Maybe you don't remember it."

"I don't know how to use a gun," I say. "Anyway, I know who shot my brother. It was Henry Janssen. He broke into my mom's house and tried to kill me, too. I wasn't wearing gloves, so I just . . . I reacted."

"And what day was this?" asks Hunt.

"Monday the thirteenth."

"What did you do exactly?" Jones asks.

It's like remembering lines for a play, Sam said.

"Mom had signed me out of Wallingford to go to a doctor's appointment and get lunch. After, I figured I had some time to kill, so I went home."

"Alone?" asks Agent Hunt.

"*Yes.* Like I said twice before, *alone.*" I yawn. "The front door was kicked in."

I think of Sam, with an oversize shoe on his foot, slamming the sole against the door. The wood splintered around the lock. He looked satisfied and also startled, like he'd never allowed himself to do anything so violent.

"But you weren't worried?"

I shrug. "I guess I was, a little. But the house is pretty busted up. I assumed that Barron and Mom had a fight. There's not much worth stealing. It made me a little more alert, maybe, but I honestly didn't think there was anyone inside."

"Then what?" Agent Jones crosses his arms over his chest.

"I took off my jacket and my gloves."

"You always take off your gloves at home?" asks Agent Hunt.

"Yeah," I say, looking Hunt in the eye. "Don't you?"

"Okay, go on," says Agent Jones.

"I turned on the television. I was going to watch some TV, eat a sandwich, and then go back to school. I figured I had about an hour to hang."

Agent Hunt scowls. "Why go home at all? None of that sounds very exciting."

"Because if I went back to school, I'd have to do after-school stuff. I'm lazy."

They share another look, not a very friendly one.

"This guy comes out, pointing a gun at me. I hold up my hands, but he comes right up to me. He starts telling me this story about how Philip was supposed to kill him and he had to take off in the middle of the night, leave everything behind. I was with Philip, although I don't remember it, and he blamed me, too. Which, I guess, is fair. He goes on, saying that he and his girlfriend capped Philip and that I'm next."

"And he told you all this?"

I nod my head. "I guess he wanted to be sure I was afraid."

"Were you afraid?" asks Agent Jones.

"Yeah," I say, nodding. "Of course I was scared."

Agent Hunt scowls. "Was he alone?"

"The girlfriend was there. Beth, I think. Her picture was in those files you gave me. I don't think she's a professional. She didn't act like one. I guess that's how she wound up walking in front of a camera."

"How come he came back now, after all this time?"

"He said that Philip no longer had Zacharov's protection."

"Is that true?"

"I don't know," I say. "I'm no laborer. At the time I didn't really care. I had to do something, so I rushed him."

"Did the gun go off?"

"Yeah," I say. "Two in the ceiling. Plaster everywhere. My hand hit his skin and I changed his heart to glass."

"Then what?" Agent Jones asks.

"The woman screamed and grabbed for the gun," I say. My hands feel clammy. I concentrate on minimizing my tells. Thinking of the last time I told this story, I make sure not to use the same language, so it doesn't seem like a memorized speech. "She ran."

"Did she shoot at you?"

I shake my head. "Like I said, she ran."

"Now, why do you think that is? Why not take a shot at you? You were right there. Blowback was going to knock you out in a minute. She probably could have carved you up slow." It doesn't comfort me that Agent Hunt knows so much about the way transformation blowback works, but the delight in his voice when he talks about what she could have done to me worries me even more.

"I have no idea," I say. "I guess she freaked out. Maybe she didn't know. I'm not telling you anything new here. I don't know, and no matter how many times you ask me, all I can do is guess."

"So you put him in the freezer? Sounds like you've disposed of a body before." Agent Jones says it like he's joking, but he's not.

"I watch a lot of television," I say with a meaningless wave of my hand. "Turns out bodies are heavier in real life."

"Then what? You went back to school like nothing happened?"

"Yeah, kind of," I say. "I mean, I went back to school like I'd just killed a guy and put him in my freezer. But I'm not sure you can tell the difference from the outside."

"You're a pretty cool customer, huh?" says Agent Hunt.

"I hide my inner pain under my stoic visage."

Agent Hunt looks like he would like to put his fist through my stoic visage. Then Agent Jones's phone rings and he gets up, walking out of the room. Agent Hunt follows him. His last look in my direction is some combination of suspicion and alarm, like he suddenly thinks I might be telling the truth.

I go back to my homework. My stomach growls. According to my watch it's nearly seven.

It takes them twenty minutes to come back.

"Okay, kid," Agent Hunt says when they do. "We found the body in the freezer, just like you said. Just one last question. Where are his clothes?"

"Oh," I say. For a moment my mind goes blank. I knew I forgot something. "Oh, yeah." I force a shrug. "I dropped them into the river. I thought maybe it would suggest he'd drowned, if someone found them. No one did, though."

Hunt gives me a long look, then nods once. "We also visited Bethenny Thomas and recovered two guns, although ballistics will still need to match the bullets. Now let's see you transform something."

"Oh, right. The show," I say, standing up.

I strip off my gloves slowly and press my hands down onto the cool, dry surface of the table.

At eleven that night I call Barron from my car.

"Okay," I say. "I made my decision."

"You really had no choice," he says, smug. He sounds very big-brotherly, like he already warned me not to cross the street by myself and there I am on the other side, cars whizzing by and no way back. Just as casual as that. I wonder if Barron really doesn't feel violated, if he's so steeped in magic and violence that he believes cursing and blackmailing one another is just what brothers do.

"No," I say. "No choice at all."

"Okay," he says, laughter in his voice. He sounds relaxed now, no longer wary. "I'll let them know."

"I'm not doing it," I say. "*That's* my decision. I'm not working for the Brennans. I'm not going to be an assassin."

"I could go to the Feds, you know," he says stiffly. "Don't be an idiot, Cassel."

"Go, then," I say. "Go ahead. But if you do, then they'll know what I am. You'll lose the ability to control me. I'll be common property." It's easy to bluff now, when the Feds already know what I am.

There is a long pause on the other end of the line. Finally he says, "Can we talk about this in person?"

"Sure," I say. "I can sneak out of Wallingford. Pick me up."

"I don't know," he says sourly. "I don't want to encourage your delinquency."

"There's a store near the school," I say. "Be there or be square."

"It'll take me fifteen minutes."

When we hang up, I look out the window of the car. My chest feels tight, cramped, the way my legs would sometimes get after running—a pain so sudden that it would wake me from a sound sleep.

There's only one thing to do when that happens. You wait for it to pass.

I figure that the Benz will make Barron nervous about my loyalties, so I wait for him on foot, leaning against the concrete wall. Mr. Gazonas, who owns the corner store, looked at me sadly from behind the counter when I came in and bought a coffee.

"You should be in school," he said, then looked at the clock. "You should be asleep."

"I know," I said, putting my money on the counter. "I've got family troubles."

"No trouble ever got fixed late at night," he said. "Midnight is for regrets."

I don't like to think about that as I sip coffee and twiddle my thumbs, but everything else I've got to think about, I like even less.

Barron's only a half hour late. He pulls up and rolls down his window. "Okay," he says. "Where do you want to go?"

"Somewhere private," I say, getting into the car.

We drive a couple of blocks until we come to an old cemetery. He pulls onto the pebbled road, past a NO TRESPASSING sign.

"Look," I say. "I get that you have something on me. You could run your mouth. Tell people what I am and what I've done. Hell, you could scream it from every rooftop. I would be screwed. My life would be over."

He frowns. I can't tell if he's considering what I said or just scheming.

"The thing is," I say, "I could change my face and start a totally different life. All I'd need is a name and a Social Security number. I'm pretty confident that Mom raised me well enough to commit a little identity theft."

He looks startled, like he'd never even considered that.

"I don't want to be a murderer," I say.

"Don't think of it like that," he says, leaning over and picking up my coffee from the cup holder. He takes a long swallow. "The people we'd be taking out aren't good guys. Let me explain how this would work. The Brennans don't even have to meet you. They'll just get to see your work. I'm your agent and accomplice and fall guy. I help you set up the crimes, and I hide your identity."

"What about school?"

"What about it?" he asks.

"I'm not leaving Wallingford."

He nods, lip curling up. "Now that Lila's at Wallingford, I just bet you don't want to leave. It always comes back to her, doesn't it?"

I frown. "So why couldn't I do this on my own? Cut you out?"

"Because you need me to do the research," he says, clearly relieved to be asked a question he can easily answer. "I'll make sure we find the right person on the right night. And, of course, I'll make sure the witnesses don't remember anything."

"Of course," I echo.

"So?" he says. "Come on. We could make a lot of money. And I could even make you forget—"

"No," I say, cutting him off. "I don't think so. I don't want to do it."

"Cassel," he says desperately. "Please. Look, you've *got* to. *Please*, Cassel."

For a moment I am uncertain about everything.

"I don't," I say finally. The inside of the car feels stuffy, cramped. I want to get out. "Just take me back to Walling-ford."

"I already took a job," he says. "I was so sure that you'd say yes."

I freeze. "Barron, come on. You can't manipulate me like this. I'm not going to—"

"Just this once," he says. "One time. If you hate it, if it goes to hell, we never have to do it again."

I hesitate. After I changed Barron's notebooks, he became the brother I always wanted. There's always a price. "So instead of pizza night, we're supposed to bond over murder?"

"So you'll do it?" he asks.

I feel sick. For a moment I really think I am going to throw up. He looks so genuinely pleased by the idea that I might agree. "Who?" I ask, leaning my head against the cool glass of the window. "Who's this victim?"

He waves his hand in the air dismissively. "His name's Emil Lombardo. No one you know. Total psycho."

I am glad my face is turned, so he can't see my expression. "Okay," I say. "Just this once."

He claps me on the shoulder just as a car pulls between the pillars behind us. Red and blue lights whirl, sending the gravestones into bizarre strobing relief.

Barron punches the dashboard. "*Cops.*"

"It does say no trespassing," I remind him, pointing toward the sign.

He leans down and peels off one of his gloves.

"What are you doing?" I ask.

He raises his eyebrows, his lip quirking on one side. "Getting out of a ticket."

The floodlight on the cop car turns on suddenly, making spots dance behind my eyes.

I look nervously through the rear window. One of the officers has gotten out and is walking toward us. I take a deep breath.

Barron rolls down the window, a grin splitting his face. "Good evening, sir."

I grab Barron's wrist in my gloved hand before he can strike. He looks at me, too shocked to register that he ought to be angry, as Agent Hunt lowers the barrel of a gun to his face.

"Barron Sharpe, step out of the car," Hunt says.

"What?" he demands.

"I'm Agent Hunt, remember?" Agent Hunt looks pleased for the first time since I've met him. "We had a nice conversation about your brother. You told us a bunch of things that didn't quite check out."

Barron nods his head, glances at me. "I remember you."

"We just heard your very interesting proposition," Agent Hunt says. In the side mirror, I see Agent Jones get out of the car.

He walks around to my side and opens the door. Barron turns toward me.

I do the only thing I can think of. I lift up my shirt to show him the wire.

"Sorry," I say. "But I figured that if you could force me to work for someone, then you couldn't be too mad if I did the same to you. I enrolled us in a program."

He looks like he doesn't quite agree with my logic.

I think of Grandad sitting in his backyard, looking up at the sky, wishing things could have been different for us kids. I'm sure this wasn't what he was picturing.

So what if I led the horse directly to water, I tell myself. *It's not like I made him drink.*

They slap the cuffs on Barron. Good thing I've already negotiated his deal, because Hunt and Jones look like they'd much rather lock him in a deep dark hole than work with him. I recognize the look. It's the same one they give me.

THE HARDEST THING IS

making sure that I don't have a tail. Agent Hunt gave me a lift back to my car at Wallingford, which made me nervous. I drive around aimlessly for about an hour, until I'm sure there's no one behind me.

The streets are nearly empty. This late at night, there are few good reasons to be on the road.

Finally I head to the hotel. I park in the far back, near the Dumpsters. The night air is like a slap in the face. It seems too early in the season for the temperature to have dropped so abruptly. Maybe it's just colder at three in the morning.

The hotel she picked is brick, with a central building and then a couple of other buildings that form a C-shape around a greenish pool. All the rooms open onto the outdoors, so there's no need to walk through a lobby.

She's in room 411. Upstairs. I knock three times. I hear the chain slide, and then the door opens.

My brother's widow looks less gaunt than she did the last time I saw her, but her eyes are as bruised as ever. Her hair is a silky brown tangle, and she's wearing a tight black dress that I in no way deserve.

"You're late." She motions me inside and locks the door. Then she leans against it. Her hands and feet are bare, and I have to remind myself that she's not a worker.

Her suitcase is open in one corner, and her clothes are spread across the floor. I move a slip off the one chair in the room and sit down. "Sorry," I say. "Everything takes longer than you think it will."

"You want a drink?" Maura asks me, indicating a bottle of Cuervo and a couple of plastic cups.

I shake my head.

"I knew you'd figure it out." She drops a couple of cubes into the cup and gives herself a generous pour. "You want to hear the story?"

"Let me tell it," I say. "I want to see how much I actually figured out."

She takes her glass and goes over to the bed, where she lies down on her stomach. I'm pretty sure this isn't her first drink.

"Philip and you had one of those relationships that was all ups and downs, right? Highs and lows. Lots of screaming. Passionate."

"Yeah," she says, looking at me oddly.

"Oh, come on," I say. "He was my brother. I know what *all* his relationships were like. Anyway, maybe the fighting got to be too much for you, or maybe it was different after you had the baby, but at some point Barron got involved. Started making you forget fights you'd had with Philip. Made you forget you'd decided to leave him."

"That's when you gave me the amulet," she says. I think of handing it to her in the kitchen of the apartment, my nephew howling in the background, Grandad snoring on a chair in the living room.

I nod. "He made me forget a lot too."

She throws back a good portion of the liquid in her cup.

"And you'd already started to get some pretty bad side effects." I think of her sitting at the top of the stairs, legs dangling off the edge, her whole body moving in time with a song I couldn't hear.

"You mean the music," she says. "I miss it, you know?"

"You said it was beautiful."

"I used to play the clarinet in middle school—did you know that? I wasn't very good, but I can still read music." She laughs. "I tried to write down snatches of it—a few notes, even—but it's all gone. I may never hear it again."

"It was an auditory hallucination. I get headaches. Be glad it's gone."

Maura makes a face. "That is a very unromantic explanation."

"Yeah." I sigh. "So anyway. You realized what Barron and Philip were doing to you and you split. Took your son."

"Your nephew has a name," she says. "It's Aaron. You never say it. Aaron."

I flinch. For some reason I never connected the kid with me. He was always Philip's son, Maura's son, not someone with a name who'll grow up to be another screwed-up member of my screwed-up family.

"You took Aaron," I say. "Philip guessed that I had something to do with you two leaving, by the way."

She nods. There's a story there, one about the slow realization of how betrayed she really was, one where she jumped a little as she felt the amulet pinned under her shirt splitting. One where she had to think fast and not gasp, and keep pretending even when she must have felt drowned by horror. But she doesn't move to tell it, and it's her story to keep. My brothers did this to her. She doesn't owe me anything.

"So you've got a big family, right? Or a best friend who moved to the South. Someone you thought you'd be safe staying with in Arkansas. You get in your car and just go. Maybe trade it in for another vehicle. You're using your maiden name, and even though you figure Philip is going to freak out about you taking his son, you know that you've got lots on him. You're sure that he's going to be afraid of you going to the police, so you never even consider that *he* will.

"You're careful, but not careful enough. Maybe it's hard to find you, but far from impossible. So when the Feds call, looking for you, with stories about your husband going into witness protection and wanting you with him, you freak out. The Feds need you—Philip wouldn't give them what they wanted until he saw you—so I'm sure they didn't care about your feelings. Your country needed you."

Maura nods.

"You realize you'll never get away from him. Legally, with the Feds helping him out, he might be able to get joint custody of your son. You might even be forced to live nearby—and then maybe a couple of his friends would come over. Either they'd work you or they'd work you over, but you knew he could get you back. You knew that you were in danger."

She's watching me like I'm a snake, coiling back and ready to strike.

"You know where Philip keeps his guns. You drive up from Arkansas, you take one, and you shoot him."

At the word "shoot" she flinches. Then she swallows the rest of her tequila.

"You wear a big coat and those very lovely red gloves. Security had put in cameras outside the condos recently. Luckily for you, all they could tell was that the person who entered Philip's apartment that night was a woman."

"What?" She sits up and stares at me like I've finally surprised her. She presses both her hands to her mouth. "No. There was a camera?"

"Don't worry," I say. "After, you toss the clothes and the gun someplace where you figure they'll be safe. My house. Mom's out of jail, after all. You figure she'll be hoarding again in no time. A garbage house really would be a great place to hide evidence—under so much crap that even cops aren't going to have the patience to sort through it all."

"I guess I'm no criminal genius, though," she says. "You found them. And I had no idea about being taped."

"There's just one thing I didn't figure out," I say. "When I talked to the Feds, they said they spoke to you in Arkansas the morning after Philip's murder. That's at least a twenty-hour drive. There's no way you shot him and got back in time to take that call. How did you do it?"

She smiles. "You and your mother taught me. The agents called my house. Then my brother called me on a prepaid cell phone with an Arkansas area code. He conference-called me and then called back the federal agents. Simple. It looked like I was returning their call from home. Just like how I had to help your mother make all those calls from jail."

"I am all admiration," I say. "I actually thought the coat and gloves and gun belonged to Mom, until I saw the amulet I gave you. The one you left in the pocket."

"I made a lot of mistakes. I see that now," she says, pulling a gun from underneath the covers and leveling it at me. "You understand I can't afford to make any more."

"Oh, absolutely," I say. "So you sure don't want to kill the guy who just framed someone for his own brother's murder."

The gun wavers in her hand.

"You didn't," she says. "Why would you?"

"I tried to protect Philip when he was alive." I'm sincere, although I'm sure she's used to sincere liars. "I don't think he believed that, but I did. Now that he's dead, I'm trying to protect you."

"So you're really not going to tell anyone," she says.

I stand, and the gun comes up.

"I'll take it to my grave," I say, and grin. She's not smiling.

Then I turn and walk out of the hotel room.

For a moment I think I hear a click, and my muscles stiffen, anticipating the bullet. Then the moment's past and I keep moving—out of the room, down the stairs, and into my car. There's this old Greek myth about this guy named Orpheus. He goes down to Hades to get his wife back, but he loses her again because on the way out of hell, he looks behind him to see if she's really there.

That's how I feel. Like if I look back, the spell will be broken. I'll be dead.

It's only when I pull out of the parking lot that I can breathe again.

I don't want to go back to Wallingford. I just can't face it. Instead I drive down to Carney and bang on Grandad's door. It's well past the middle of the night, but eventually he answers, wrapped in a bathrobe.

"Cassel?" he says. "Did something happen?"

I shake my head.

He waves to me with his good hand. "Well, get in here. You're letting in all the cold air, standing in the doorway."

I walk into his dining room. There's some mail on the table, along with a bunch of wilted flowers from the funeral. It seems like it happened so long ago, but really it's just been a few weeks since Philip died.

On the sideboard are a bunch of photos, most of them

of the three of us kids when we were little, doing a lot of running through sprinklers and posing awkwardly, our arms around one another, on lawns. There are other photos too, older ones of Grandad with Mom in her wedding dress, Grandma, and one of Grandad and Zacharov at what looks like Lila's parents' wedding. The thick wedding band on Zacharov's finger is one I haven't seen him wear before, but it looks familiar.

"I'm going to put on the kettle," he says.

"That's okay," I say. "I'm not thirsty."

"Did I ask you?" Grandad looks at me sternly. "You take a cup, you drink it, and then I'll make up a bed for you in the spare room. Don't you have school tomorrow?"

"Yeah," I say, chastened.

"I'll call them in the morning. Tell them you're going to be a little late."

"I've been late a lot," I say. "Missed a lot of classes. I think I'm failing physics."

"Death messes you up. Even a fancy school like yours knows that." He goes into the kitchen.

I sit down at the table in the dark. Now that I'm here, I feel a calm settle over me that I can't explain. I just want to be here, sitting at this table, forever. I don't want to move.

Eventually there is a metallic whistle from the kitchen. Grandad comes back, setting down two mugs. He flicks a switch on the wall, and the electric lights of the chandelier glow so brightly that I shade my eyes.

The tea is black and sweet, and I'm surprised that I've finished half of it in a single gulp.

"You want to tell me what's going on?" he asks finally. "Why you're here in the middle of the night?"

"Not really," I say as forthrightly as I can manage. I don't want to lose this. I wonder if he'd even let me into his house if he knew I was working for the government, no less that I blackmailed my brother into joining me. I'm not even sure they allow federal agents into the worker town of Carney.

He takes a slug from his cup and then winces, like maybe his doesn't have tea in it. "Are you in some kind of trouble?"

"I don't think so," I say. "Not anymore."

"I see." He stands and shuffles over to put his ruined hand on my shoulder. "Come on, kid. I think it's time for you to get to bed."

"Thanks," I say, getting up.

We go into the back room, the same room where I slept when I spent the summers in Carney. Grandad brings in some blankets and a pair of pajamas for me to sleep in. I think they might be an old pair of Barron's.

"Whatever's eating you," he says, "it's never worse in the morning."

I sit down on the corner of the mattress and smile wearily. "G'night, Grandad."

He pauses in the doorway. "You know Elsie Cooper's oldest son? Born crazy. He can't help it. No one knows how come he turned out like that—he just did."

"Yeah," I say vaguely. I remember people in Carney talking about how he never left the house, but I can't recall much else. I look over at the folded pajamas. My limbs feel so heavy that even thinking about putting them on is an effort. I have no idea where Grandad's story is supposed to be going.

"You were always good, Cassel," he says as he closes the door. "No idea how you turned out that way—you just did. Like the crazy Cooper kid. You can't help it."

"I'm not good," I say. "I play everybody. *Everybody*. All the time."

He snorts. "Goodness don't come for free."

I'm too tired to argue. He switches off the light, and I'm asleep before I even crawl underneath the covers.

Grandad calls school to tell them I won't be there for classes today, and I basically just sit around his house all morning. We watch *Band of the Banned* reruns and he makes some kind of turmeric beef stew in the Crock-Pot. It comes out pretty good.

He lets me stretch out on the couch with an afghan, like I'm sick. We even eat in front of the television.

When it's time to go, he packs up some of the stew into a clean Cool Whip container and hands it to me along with a bottle of orange soda. "You better go study that physics," he says.

"Yeah," I say.

He pauses when he sees the shiny new Benz. We look at each other silently over the hood for a moment, but all he says is, "Tell that mother of yours to give me a call."

"I will, Grandad. Thanks for letting me spend the night."

His brows furrow. "You better not say anything stupid like that to me again."

"All right." I grin, holding up my hands in a gesture of surrender. Then I get into the car.

He slaps the hood. "Bye, kid."

I drive off. I get twenty minutes out of Carney before I drink the orange soda. By the time I arrive at Wallingford, I've missed most of the day. I roll into the break period after study hall and before lights-out.

Sam is sitting on the striped couch of the common lounge, next to Jeremy Fletcher-Fiske. A newscaster is on the television, talking about football. Some guys are playing cards on a folding table. Another senior, Jace, is watching a carrot on a plate rotate in the microwave.

"Hey," I say, waving.

"Dude," says Sam. "Long time, no see. Where have you been?"

"Just family stuff," I say, sitting down on the arm of the couch.

Tomorrow I am going to have to get my homework from teachers. I'm going to have to start buckling down if I want to pass everything this semester, but I figure that tonight I might as well just relax.

On the screen another announcer starts in on the local news. He says that on Sunday, Governor Patton held a brunch where his unexpected and controversial announcement had his constituents up in arms.

They show a clip of a big ballroom covered in tables and Patton up on a podium with a blue curtain behind him and my mother standing nearby, along with another guy in a suit. Her hair is pulled back and she's wearing a yellow dress with short white gloves. She looks like a costumer's idea of a politician's wife. I am so busy trying to make out her expression that for a moment I don't realize what Patton's saying on the clip.

"*—and furthermore, after consideration, I have come to realize that my stance was an unrealistic one. While having access to information regarding who is or is not hyperbathygammic would be convenient for law enforcement, I now see that the price for that convenience is too high. Worker rights groups have made the point that it's unlikely the information would remain confidential. As governor, I cannot countenance any risk to the privacy of New Jersey citizens, especially when that privacy may protect their lives and livelihoods. Even though I have been in the past a strong supporter of Proposition 2, I am withdrawing that support as of this moment. I no longer believe that mandatory testing for workers is something this government should tolerate, no less dictate.*"

I must be staring at the screen in horror.

"Crazy, right?" asks Jeremy. "Everyone's saying that the guy got paid off. Or worked."

Sam flinches. "Oh, come on. Maybe he just grew a conscience."

That's the brunch my mother invited me to, the one she said I'd love. *Baby, I know what I'm doing.*

A shiver runs down my back. The news has moved on to coverage of an earthquake, but I am still stuck with the memory of my mother's face on that clip. If you didn't know her, you wouldn't notice it, but she was fighting back a smile.

She worked him. There is no doubt in my mind.

I want to scream. There's no way to get her out of this. There's no way it won't be discovered.

Sam is speaking, but the buzzing in my head is so loud, it drowns out all other sounds.

I call my mother dozens of times that night, but she never picks up. I fall asleep with the phone still in my hand and wake up when its alarm goes off the next morning. I drag myself through my classes. I'm behind in everything. I stumble through answers, fail a quiz in statistics, and botch a French translation to great hilarity.

When I get up to my room, I find Daneca waiting for me. She's sitting on Sam's bed, her clunky brown shoes kicking the bed frame absently. Her eyes are red-rimmed.

"Hey," I say. "I don't know where Sam is. I haven't seen him since I passed him in the hall on the way to Physics."

She pushes a thick braid off her shoulder and straightens up like she's steeling herself to do something unpleasant. "He already went to play practice. He's still acting weird, and I'm not here to see him, anyway. I have to talk to you."

I nod, although I'm not in the frame of mind to say anything remotely sensible. "Sure. Fine."

"It's about Lila."

She couldn't go through with it, I realize. "That's okay,"

I say lightly. "Maybe it was a terrible idea anyway."

"No, Cassel," Daneca says. "You don't understand. I really screwed up."

"What?" My heart is a drum, beating out of time. I toss my backpack onto my bed and sit down beside it. "What do you mean—'screwed up'?"

Daneca looks relieved that I finally seem to understand her. She scoots forward, leaning in toward me. "Lila caught me. I'm an idiot. It must have been obvious what I was trying."

I picture Daneca trying to get off her glove without Lila noticing. It didn't occur to me until now how hard it must have been. Daneca doesn't know how to brush someone accidentally, the way you need to for a working or to lift a wallet. She's no expert at sleight of hand.

"So you didn't—," I say. "So you didn't work her?" All I feel is relief so intense that I almost laugh.

I'm glad. Horribly, shockingly glad.

I can learn to live with guilt. I don't care about being good. I can learn to live with anything if it means being with Lila too.

Daneca shakes her head. "She made me tell her everything. She can be really frightening, you know."

"Oh," I say. "Yeah, she can be."

"She made me promise not to say anything to you," Daneca says, voice low.

I look out the window. There are so many thoughts running through my head, it's like I'm not thinking at all. But still I force myself to give her a quick smile. "She didn't think you would break a *promise*? We've got to do something about that reputation of yours, Goody Two-shoes."

"I'm sorry," Daneca says, ignoring my attempt at humor.

"It's not your fault," I say. "I shouldn't have asked you. It wasn't fair."

She stands up and starts toward the door.

"See you at dinner," she says, looking at me with surprising fondness.

As the door closes behind Daneca, I feel a terrible wave of emotion sweep through me, reckless joy and horror so mixed up that I don't know what to feel first.

I tried to make myself do the right thing. Maybe I didn't try hard enough. All I know right now is that I love Lila, and for a little while she'll love me back.

When I find Lila, she's heading toward the library. The collar of her shirt is open and the white silk scarf around her throat flutters in the wind. She looks like she's about to go for a drive in a car with the top down.

"Hey," I say, jogging up alongside her. "Can we talk for a minute?"

"Cassel," she says, like my name tastes sour on her tongue. She doesn't slow.

"I know you're probably furious about Daneca," I say, walking backward so I can look at her while I'm talking. "And you have every right to be. But let me explain."

"Can you?" Lila says, stopping abruptly. "I'm not a toy you can just turn off."

"I know that," I say.

"How could you think that it would be okay to work me? How would it be any different from what your mother did?" She looks like she feels a little bit sorry for me and a little bit disgusted. "The curse is over. We're over."

"Oh." Of course. I grit my teeth against the reflexive flinch. All I can hear is my mother's words in Atlantic City: *She wouldn't have given you the time of day, Cassel.*

"It wasn't enough for you to have your joke, pretending to love me, pretending you weren't pretending—" She stops herself, closing her eyes for a moment. When she opens them again, they're bright with fury. "I'm not cursed anymore. I'm not going to grovel for your attention. It must have been thrilling to have me sigh over *every one* of your thoughtless smiles, but that's never going to happen again."

"That's not what it was like," I say. I'm stunned, all of my months of pain and panic reduced, in her eyes, to gloating.

"I'm not weak, Cassel. I'm not the kind of girl who cries over you." Her voice shakes. "I'm not the girl who does whatever you want whenever you want it."

"That's why I asked Daneca—," I say, but I can't finish. It's not even true. I asked Daneca to work her because I was starting to believe the illusion. Daneca was trying to save me from myself.

"You wanted to make me feel nothing for you?" Lila says. "Well, let me do you one better. I *hate* you. How about that? I hate you, and you didn't have to do a thing to make me."

"Come on, now," I say. I can hear the self-loathing in my voice. "I did plenty." I lost Lila the moment my mother cursed her. Everything else was just a pathetic game of pretend. None of it real.

Her expression wavers, then smoothes out into a mask of blandness. "Good-bye, Cassel," she says, and turns to go. Her head is bent and her scarf must have shifted, because I glimpse redness along her throat. From this angle it looks like the edge of a burn.

"What is that?" I say, walking after her, pointing to my own collar.

"*Don't*," she says warningly, holding up her gloved hand. But there is something in her face that wasn't there a moment ago—fear.

I grab one end of her scarf. It comes unknotted with a single pull.

Her pale throat is cut, one side to the other, newly scabbed and dark with ash. The criminal's second smile. A glittering choker of dried blood.

"You're—," I start. But of course, she always was. A crime boss's daughter. Mobster royalty.

Talking with someone who just signed up to be a federal agent.

"The ceremony was on Sunday," she says. "I told you I was going to be the head of the Zacharov family someday. No one starts at the top, though. I have a long way to go. First I have to prove my loyalty. Even me."

"Ah." Lila has always known who she was and what she wanted. There is something horrifyingly final about her scar, like a shut door. She's not afraid of her future. "Brave," I say, and I mean it.

For a moment she looks like she wants to tell me more. Her mouth opens, and then I see her swallow those words, whatever they were. She takes a deep breath and says, "If you don't stay away from me, I'll make you sorry you were ever born."

There's nothing to say to that, so I say nothing. I can already feel numbness creeping into my heart.

She continues her walk across the quad.

I watch her go. Watch the shadow of her steps and her straight back and the gleam of her hair.

I remind myself that this is what I wanted. When that doesn't work, I tell myself that I can survive on memories. The smell of Lila's skin, the way her eyes shine with mischief, the low rasp of her voice. It hurts to think of her, but I can't stop. It ought to hurt.

After all, hell is supposed to be hot.

ACKNOWLEDGMENTS

Several books were really helpful in creating the world of the curse workers. In particular, David W. Maurer's *The Big Con*; Sam Lovell's *How to Cheat at Everything*; Kent Walker and Mark Schone's *Son of a Grifter*; and Karl Taro Greenfeld's *Speed Tribes*.

I am deeply indebted to many people for their insight into this book. Thanks to Cassandra Clare, Robin Wasserman, Sarah Rees Brennan, and Delia Sherman, who were always kind enough to stop what they were doing and help me work through problems during our Mexican writing retreat. Thanks to Libba Bray and Jo Knowles for helping me enormously with the push to the end. I am grateful to Justine Larbalestier for talking with me about liars and to Scott Westerfeld for his detailed notes. Thanks to Joe Monti for his enthusiasm and book recommendations. Thanks to Elka Cloke for her medical expertise. Thanks to Kathleen Duey for pushing me to think about the larger world issues. Thanks to Kelly Link, Ellen Kushner, Gavin Grant, Sarah Smith, and Joshua Lewis for looking at very rough drafts. Thanks to Steve Berman for his help working out many, many details, especially in that last draft.

Most of all, I have to thank my agent, Barry Goldblatt, for his encouragement; my editor, Karen Wojtyla, who pushed me to make the book far better than I thought it could be; and my husband, Theo, who gave me lots of advice about private school and scams, and who let me read the whole thing to him out loud.

BLACK HEART

To Fizzgig, my long-haired gray moppet of a cat,
who was patient and friendly
despite always appearing enraged.

MY BROTHER BARRON

sits next to me, sucking the last dregs of milk tea slush noisily through a wide yellow straw. He's got the seat of my Benz pushed all the way back and his feet up on the dash, the heels of his pointy black shoes scratching the plastic. With his hair slicked back and his mirrored sunglasses covering his eyes, he looks like a study in villainy.

He's actually a junior federal agent, still in training, sure, but with a key card and an ID badge and everything.

To be fair, he's also a villain.

I tap my gloved fingers impatiently against the curve of the wheel and bring a pair of binoculars to my eyes for about the millionth time. All I see is a boarded-up building on the wrong side of Queens. "What is she *doing* in there? It's been forty minutes."

"What do you think?" he asks me. "Bad things. That's her after-school job now. Taking care of shady business so Zacharov's gloves stay clean."

"Her dad won't put her in any real danger," I say, but the tone of my voice makes it pretty obvious I'm trying to convince myself more than I'm trying to convince my brother.

Barron snorts. "She's a new soldier. Got to prove herself. Zacharov couldn't keep her out of danger if he tried—and he's not going to be trying real hard. The other laborers are watching, waiting for her to be weak. Waiting for her to screw up. He knows that. So should you."

I think of her at twelve, a skinny girl with eyes too large for her face and a nimbus of tangled blond hair. In my memory she's sitting on the branch of a tree, eating a rope of red licorice. Her lips are sticky with it. Her flip-flops are hanging off her toes. She's cutting her initials into the bark, high up, so her cousin can't claim she's lying when she tells him she got higher than he ever will.

Boys never believe I can beat them, she told me back then. *But I always win in the end.*

"Maybe she spotted the car and went out the back," I say finally.

"No way she made us." He sucks on the straw again. It makes that rattling empty-cup sound, echoing through the car. "We're like ninjas."

"Somebody's cocky," I say. After all, tailing someone isn't easy, and Barron and I aren't that good at it yet, no matter what he says. My handler at the agency, Yulikova, has been encouraging me to shadow Barron, so I can learn second-hand and can keep myself safe until she figures out how to tell her bosses that she's got hold of a teenage transformation worker with a bad attitude and a criminal record. And since Yulikova's in charge, Barron's stuck teaching me. It's supposed to be just for a few months, until I graduate from Wallingford. Let's see if we can stand each other that long.

Of course, I'm pretty sure this isn't the kind of lesson Yulikova's been imagining.

Barron grins, white teeth flashing like dropped dice. "What do you think Lila Zacharov would do if she knew you were tailing her?"

I grin back. "Probably she'd kill me."

He nods. "Probably she would. Probably she'd kill me twice for helping you."

"Probably you deserve it," I say. He snorts.

Over the last few months I got every last thing I ever wanted—and then I threw it all away. Everything I thought I could never have was offered up on a silver platter—the girl, the power, a job at the right hand of Zacharov, the most formidable man I know. It wouldn't even have been that hard to work for him. It probably would have been fun. And if I didn't care who I hurt, it would still all be mine.

I lift the binoculars and study the door again—the worn paint striping the boards and crumbling like bread crumbs, the chewed-up bottom edge as ragged as if it had been gnawed on by rats.

Lila would still be mine.

Mine. The language of love is like that, possessive. That should be the first warning that it's not going to encourage anyone's betterment.

Barron groans and throws his cup into the backseat. "I can't believe that you blackmailed me into becoming Johnny Law and now I have to sweat it out five days a week with the other recruits while you use my experience to stalk your girlfriend. How is that fair?"

"*One*, I think you mean the extremely dubious benefit of your experience. *Two*, Lila's not my girlfriend. *Three*, I just wanted to make sure she was okay." I count off these points on my leather-covered fingers. "And *four*, the last thing you should want is *fairness.*"

"Stalk her at school," Barron says, ignoring every-thing I've just said. "Come on. I have to make a phone call. Let's pack in this lesson and get a couple of slices. I'll even buy."

I sigh. The car is stuffy and smells like old coffee. I'd like to stretch my legs. And Barron is probably right—we should give this up. Not for the reason he's saying but for the one that's implied. The one about it not being okay to lurk around outside buildings, spying on girls you like.

My fingers are reaching reluctantly for my keys when she walks out of the worn door, as though my giving up summoned her. She's got on tall black riding boots and a steel gray trench. I study the quicksilver gestures of her gloved hands, the sway of her earrings, the slap of her heels on the steps, and the lash of her hair. She's so beauti-ful, I can barely breathe. Behind her follows a boy with his hair braided into the shape of two antelope horns. His skin is darker than mine. He's got on baggy jeans and a hoodie. He's shoving a folded-up wad of something that looks like cash into an inside pocket.

Outside of school Lila doesn't bother wearing a scarf. I can see the grim necklace of marks on her throat, scars black where ash was rubbed into them. That's part of the ceremony when you join her father's crime family, slicing your skin and swearing that you're dead to your old life and reborn into wickedness. Not even Zacharov's daughter was spared it.

She's one of them now. No turning back.

"Well, now," says Barron, gleeful. "I bet you're thinking we just observed the end of a very naughty transaction. But let's consider the possibility that actually we caught her doing something totally innocent yet embarrassing."

I look at him absently. "Embarrassing?"

"Like meeting up to play one of those card games where you have to collect everything. Pokémon. Magic the Gathering. Maybe they're training for a tournament. With all that money she just handed him, I'm guessing he won."

"Funny."

"Maybe he's tutoring her in Latin. Or they were painting miniatures together. Or he's teaching her shadow puppetry." He makes a duck-like gesture with one gloved hand.

I punch Barron's shoulder, but not really hard. Just hard enough to make him shut up. He laughs and adjusts his sunglasses, pushing them higher on his nose.

The boy with the braids crosses the street, head down,

hood pulled up to shadow his face. Lila walks to the corner and raises her hand to hail a cab. The wind whips at her hair, making it a nimbus of blown gold.

I wonder if she's done her homework for Monday.

I wonder if she could ever love me again.

I wonder just how mad she'd be if she knew I was here, watching her. Probably really, really mad.

Cold October air floods into the car suddenly, tossing around the empty cup in the backseat.

"Come on," Barron says, leaning on the door, grinning down at me. I didn't even notice him getting out. "Grab some quarters for the meter, and your stuff." He jerks his head in the direction of the boy with the braids. "We're going to follow him."

"What about that phone call?" I shiver in my thin green T-shirt. My leather jacket is wadded up in the backseat of my car. I reach for it and shrug it on.

"I was bored," Barron says. "Now I'm not."

This morning when he told me we were going to practice tailing people, I picked Lila as my target half as a joke, half because there's something wrong with me. I didn't think that Barron would agree. I didn't think that we'd actually see her leaving her apartment building and getting into a town car. I for sure didn't think that I would wind up here, close to actually finding out what she's been doing when she's not in school.

I get out of the car and slam the door behind me.

That's the problem with temptation. It's so damn tempting.

"Feels almost like real agent work, doesn't it?" Barron says as we walk down the street, heads bowed against the wind. "You know, if we caught your girlfriend committing a crime, I bet Yulikova would give us a bonus or something for being prize pupils."

"Except that we're not going to do that," I say.

"I thought you wanted us to be good guys." He grins a too-wide grin. He's enjoying needling me, and my reacting only makes it worse, but I can't stop.

"Not if it means hurting her," I say, my voice as deadly as I can make it. "Never her."

"Got it. Hurting, bad. But how do you excuse stalking her and her friends, little brother?"

"I'm not excusing it," I say. "I'm just doing it."

Following—*stalking*—someone isn't easy. You try not to stare too hard at the back of his head, keep your distance, and act like you're just another person freezing your ass off in late October on the streets of Queens. Above all you try not to seem like a badly trained federal agent wannabe.

"Stop worrying," Barron says, strolling along beside me. "Even if we get made, this guy will probably be flattered. He'd think he was moving up in the world if he had a government tail."

Barron is better at acting casual than I am. I guess he should be. He's got nothing to lose if we're spotted. Lila couldn't possibly hate him more than she does. Plus, he probably trains for this all day, while I'm at Wallingford studying to get into the kind of college there is no way I am ever going to attend.

It still annoys me. Since I was a kid, we've competed over lots of things. Mostly, all those competitions were ones I lost.

We were the two youngest, and when Philip would be off with his friends on the weekends, Barron and I would be stuck doing whatever errands Dad needed doing, or practicing whatever skill he thought we needed to learn.

He particularly wanted us to be better at pickpocketing and lock-picking than we were.

Two kids are the perfect pickpocket team, he'd say. *One to do the lift, the other one to distract or to take the handoff.*

We both practiced dips. First identifying where Dad kept his wallet by looking for a bulge in a back pocket or the way one side of his coat swung heavily because something was inside. Then the lift. I was pretty good; Barron was better.

Then we practiced distraction. Crying. Asking for directions. Giving the mark a quarter that you claim they dropped.

It's like stage magic, Dad said. *You've got to make me look over there so I won't notice what's happening right in front of my face.*

When Dad didn't feel like fending off our clumsy attempts at lifts, he'd bring us to the barn and show us his collection: He had an old metal tackle box with locks on all the sides, so you had to run the gauntlet of seven different locks to get into it. Neither Barron nor I ever managed.

Once we learned how to open a lock with a tool, we'd have to learn to pick it with a bobby pin, with a hanger, then with a stick or some other found object. I kept hoping that I'd be naturally great at locks, since I was pretty sure I wasn't a worker back then, and since I already felt like an outsider in my family. I thought that if there was one thing I was better at than all of them, that would make up for everything else.

It sucks to be the youngest.

If you get into the supersecure box, we'll sneak into the movie of your choice, Dad would say. Or, *I put candy in there.* Or, *If you really want that video game, just open the box and I'll get it for you.* But it didn't matter what he promised. What did matter was that I only ever managed to pick three locks; Barron managed five.

And here we are again, learning a bunch of new skills. I can't help feeling a little bit competitive and a little bit disappointed in myself that I'm already so far behind. After all, Yulikova thinks Barron has a real future with the Bureau. She told me so. I told her that sociopaths are relentlessly charming.

I think she figured I was joking.

"What other stuff do they teach you at federal agent school?" I ask. It shouldn't bother me that he's fitting in so well. So what if he's faking it? Good for him.

I guess what bothers me is him faking it better than I am.

He rolls his eyes. "Nothing much. Obvious stuff— getting people to trust you with mirroring behavior. You know, doing whatever the other person's doing." He laughs. "Honestly, undercover's just like being a con man. Same techniques. Identify the target. Befriend. Then betray."

Mirroring behavior. When a mark takes a drink from his water glass, so should you. When he smiles, so should you. Keep it subtle, rather than creepy, and it's a good technique.

Mom taught it to me when I was ten. *Cassel,* she said, *you want to know how to be the most charming guy anyone's ever met? Remind them of their favorite person. Everyone's favorite person is their own damn self.*

"Except now you're the good guy," I say, and laugh.

He laughs with me, like we both know that's a joke.

But now that I'm thinking about Mom, I can't help worrying about her. She's been missing since she got caught using her worker talent—emotion—to manipulate Governor Patton, a guy who hated curse workers to begin with and now is on national news every night with a vein popping out of his forehead, calling for her blood. I hope she stays hidden. I just wish I knew where she was.

"Barron," I say, about to start up a conversation we've already had about a million times, the one where we tell each other that she's fine and she'll contact us soon. "Do you think—"

Up ahead the boy with the braids steps into a pool hall.

"In here," Barron says, with a jerk of his head. We duck into a deli across the street. I'm grateful for the warmth. Barron orders us two coffees, and we stand near the window, waiting.

"You ever going to get over this thing with Lila?" he asks me, breaking the silence, making me wish I'd been the one to do it, so that I could have picked another subject. Any other subject. "It's like some kind of illness with you. How long have you been into her? Since you were what, eleven?"

I don't say anything.

"That's why you really wanted to follow her and her new hire, right? Because you're hoping that if she does something awful enough, maybe you'll deserve each other after all."

"That's not how it works," I say, under my breath. "That's not how love works."

He snorts. "You sure?"

I bite my tongue, swallowing every obnoxious taunt that comes into my mind. If he doesn't get a rise out of me, maybe he'll stop, and then maybe I can distract him. We stand like that for several minutes, until he sighs.

"Bored again. I'm going to make that phone call."

"What if he comes out?" I ask, annoyed. "How am I going to—"

He widens his eyes in mock distress. "Improvise."

The bell rings as he steps out the door, and the guy at the counter shouts his customary "Thanksforcomingcome-again."

On the sidewalk in front of the deli, Barron is flirting like crazy as he paces back and forth, dropping the names of French restaurants like he eats off a tablecloth every night. He's got his phone cradled against his cheek, smiling like he's buying the line of romantic nonsense he's selling. I feel sorry for the girl, whoever she is, but I am gleeful.

When he gets off the phone I will never stop making fun of him. Biting my tongue won't be enough to keep me from it. I would have to bite off my whole face.

He notices me grinning out the window at him, turns his back and stalks to the entranceway of a closed pawnshop half a block away. I made sure to waggle my eyebrows while he was looking in my direction.

With nothing else to do, I stay put. I drink more coffee. I play a game on my phone that involves shooting pixelated zombies.

Even though I've been waiting, I'm not really prepared when the boy with the braids walks out of the pool hall. He's got a man with him, a tall guy with hollow cheekbones and greasy hair. The boy lights a cigarette inside his cupped palm, leaning against the wall. This is one of those moments when a little more training would help. Obviously running out of the deli and waving my arms at Barron is the wrong move, but I don't know the right one if the boy starts moving again. I have no idea how to signal my brother.

Improvise, he said.

I walk out of the deli as nonchalantly as I can manage. Maybe the kid's just hit the street for a smoke. Maybe Barron will notice me and come back over on his own.

I spot a bus stop bench and lean against it, trying to get a better look at the boy.

This isn't a real assignment, I remind myself. It doesn't matter if he gets away. There's probably nothing to see. Whatever he's doing for Lila, there's no reason to think that he's doing it now.

That's when I notice the way that the boy is gesturing grandly, his cigarette trailing smoke. Misdirection, a classic of magic tricks and cons. *Look over here,* one hand says. He must be telling a joke too, because the man is laughing. But I can see his other hand, worming out of his glove.

I jump up, but I'm too late. I see a flash of bare wrist and thumb.

I start toward him, not thinking—crossing the street, barely noticing the screech of a car's brakes until I'm past it. People turn toward me, but no one is watching the boy. Even the idiot guy from the pool hall is looking in my direction.

"Run," I yell.

The hollow-cheeked man is still staring at me when the boy's hand clamps around the front of his throat.

I grab for the boy's shoulder, too late. The man, whoever he was, collapses like a sack of flour. The boy spins toward me, bare fingers reaching for skin. I catch his wrist and twist his arm as hard as I can.

He groans and punches me in the face with his gloved hand.

I stumble back. For a moment we just regard each other. I see his face up close for the first time and am surprised to notice that his eyebrows are carefully tweezed into perfect arches. His eyes are wide and brown beneath them. He narrows those eyes at me. Then he turns and runs.

I chase after him. It's automatic—instinct—and I'm wondering what I think I'm doing as I race down the sidewalk. I risk a look back at Barron, but he's turned away, bent over the phone, so that all I see is his back.

Figures.

The boy is fast, but I've been running track for the last three years. I know how to pace myself, allowing him to get ahead of me at first when he starts sprinting, but catching up once he's winded. We go down block after block, me getting closer and closer.

This is what I'm supposed to do once I'm a federal agent, right? Chase bad guys.

But that's not why I'm after him. I feel like I am hunting my own shadow. I feel like I can't stop.

He glances back at me, and I guess he sees that I'm gaining on him, because he tries a new strategy. He veers abruptly into an alley.

I take the corner in time to see him reaching for something under his hoodie. I go for the nearest weapon I can find. A plank of wood, lying near a stack of garbage.

Swinging it, I catch him just as he gets out the gun. I feel the burn of my muscles and hear the crack as wood hits metal. I knock the pistol against the brick wall like it's a baseball and I'm in the World Series.

I think I'm as surprised as he is.

Taking slow steps, I hold up the plank, which is split now, a big chunk of the top hanging off by a splinter, the remainder jagged and pointed like a spear. He watches me, every part of him tense. He doesn't look much older than I am. He might even be younger.

"Who the hell are you?" When he speaks, I can see that some of his teeth are gold, flashing in the fading sun. Three on the bottom. One on top. He's breathing hard. We both are.

I bend down and lift the gun in one shaking hand. My thumb flicks off the safety. I drop the plank.

I have no idea who I am right now.

"Why?" I say, between breaths. "Why did she pay you to kill him?"

"Hey," he says, holding up both his hands, the gloved and ungloved one, in a gesture of surrender. Despite that, he seems more stunned than scared. "If he was your friend, then—"

"He wasn't my friend."

He lowers his hands slowly until they rest at his sides, like he has made a decision about me. Maybe that I'm not a cop. Maybe that it's okay to relax. "I don't ask why anyone wants anything. I don't know, okay? It was just a job."

I nod. "Let me see your throat."

"No marks." He pulls the neck of his shirt wide, but there's no scarring there. "I freelance. I'm too pretty for all that bullshit. No one puts a collar on Gage."

"Okay," I say.

"That girl—if you know her, you know what she's about." He reaches into his mouth, pulling out a loose tooth—a real one—black with rot at the top. It sits like a flawed pearl in the palm of his glove. Then he grins. "Good thing murder pays so well, right? Gold's expensive."

I try to hide my surprise. A death worker who loses only a single tooth with each hit is a very dangerous guy. Every curse—physical, luck, memory, emotion, dream, death, and even transformation—causes some kind of blowback. As my grandfather says, all work works the worker. Blowback can be crippling, even lethal. Death curses rot a part of the worker's body, anything from a lung to a finger. Or, apparently, something as minor as a tooth.

"What's a death worker need a gun for anyway?" I ask.

"That gun's real sentimental. Belonged to my gran." Gage clears his throat. "Look, you're not going to shoot. You would have done it already. So can we just—"

"You sure you want to double-dog-dare me?" I say. "You sure?"

That seems to rattle him. He sucks on his teeth. "Okay, all I know is what I heard—and not from . . . *her*. She never said anything, except where I could find him. But there's rumors that the guy—he goes by Charlie West—bungled a job. Killed a family in what was supposed to be a simple smash and grab. He's a drunk coward—"

My phone starts to ring.

I reach down and tug it out of my pocket with one hand, then glance down. It's Barron, probably just having realized that I ditched him. At that moment Gage vaults himself at the chain-link fence.

I look at him go, and my vision blurs. I don't know who I'm seeing. My grandfather. My brother. Myself. Any of us could be him, could have been him, coming from a hit, scrambling to get over a fence before getting shot in the back.

I don't yell for him to get down. I don't fire a warning shot or any of the stuff that I could do—that a federal agent trainee watching a murderer escape should do. I just let him go. But if he's got the role that I was supposed to have, then I have no idea how to be the person left in the alley. The good guy.

I wipe off the gun on my green shirt, then tuck it in the

waistband of my jeans, against the small of my back, where my jacket will cover it. After I'm done, I walk to the mouth of the alley and call Barron.

When he arrives, he's with a bunch of guys in suits.

He grabs me by the shoulders. "What the hell were you doing?" his voice is low, but he sounds honestly shaken. "I had no idea where you were! You didn't answer your phone."

Except for that last time, I hadn't even heard it ring.

"I was *improvising*," I say smugly. "And you would have seen me if you hadn't been busy hitting on some girl."

If his expression is any indication, only the presence of other people keeps him from strangling me. "These guys showed up at the murder scene right after the cops," he says, giving me a loaded look. As mad as he is, I understand what he's trying to communicate. *I didn't call them,* his expression says. *I didn't tell them anything about Lila. I didn't betray you. I didn't betray you yet.*

The agents take down my statement. I tell them that I followed the hit man, but he got ahead of me and over the fence. I didn't see where he went from there. I didn't get that good of a look at him. His hood was up. No, he didn't say anything. No, he didn't have a weapon—or at least nothing other than his bare hand. Yes, I shouldn't have followed him. Yes, I know Agent Yulikova. Yes, she will vouch for me.

She does. They let me go without patting me down. The gun remains tucked in the back of my jeans, rubbing against the base of my spine as Barron and I walk back to the car.

"What really happened?" Barron asks me.

I shake my head.

"So, what are you going to do?" he asks, like he's challenging me. Like there's even a question. "Lila ordered that hit."

"Nothing," I say. "What do you think? And you're not doing anything either."

Girls like her, my grandfather once warned me, girls like her turn into women with eyes like bullet holes and mouths made of knives. They are always restless. They are always hungry. They are bad news. They will drink you down like a shot of whisky. Falling in love with them is like falling down a flight of stairs.

What no one told me, with all those warnings, is that even after you've fallen, even after you know how painful it is, you'd still get in line to do it again.

WALLINGFORD PREPARATORY

on a Sunday night is full of exhausted students trying to do the homework we were sure would be easy, back on Friday when the weekend stretched before us, full of lazy hours. I yawn as I walk in, as guilty as anyone. I still have a paper to write and a big chunk of *Les Misérables* to translate.

My roommate, Sam Yu, is lying on his stomach on his bed, headphones covering his ears, head nodding in time with music I can't hear. He's a big guy, and the springs of his bed groan when he turns over to look at me. The dorms are full of cheap cots with frames threatening to break every time we sit on them, chipboard dressers, and cracked walls.

It's not like the Wallingford campus doesn't have beautiful wood-paneled chambers with soaring ceilings and leaded glass windows. It's just that those spaces are for professors and donors. We might be allowed in them, but they're not for us.

I shoulder my way into our closet and step up onto a sagging box. Then, reaching under my jacket, I pull out the gun, and tape it with a roll of duct tape high on the back wall, above my clothes. I arrange a jumble of old books on the shelf just below it to block it from view.

"You've got to be kidding me," Sam says.

He clearly watched the whole thing. I didn't even hear him get up. I must be losing my touch.

"It's not mine," I say. "I didn't know what to do with it."

"How about *getting rid of it?*" he says, his voice dropping to a harsh whisper. "That's a *gun*. A gun, Cassel. A guuuuuuuun."

"Yeah." I climb down, hopping off the box and landing with a thud. "I know. I will. I just didn't have time. Tomorrow, I promise."

"How much time does it take to throw a *gun* in a *dumpster?*"

"I really wish you would stop saying the word 'gun,'" I say, low, flopping down onto my own bed and reaching for my laptop. "There's nothing I can do about it now, unless I want to chuck it out the window. I'll deal with it tomorrow."

He groans and goes back to his side of the room, picking up his headphones. He looks annoyed, but nothing worse. I guess he's used to me acting like a criminal.

"Whose?" he asks finally, nodding toward the closet.

"Some guy. He dropped it."

Sam frowns. "That sounds likely—and by 'likely' I mean *'not at all likely.'* And by the way, did you know that if someone found that thing in here, not only would you be thrown out of school, you would be, like, stricken from school memory. They would burn your face out of the Wallingford yearbooks. They would get a team of memory workers to come in and make it so that no one even recalled they'd ever gone to school with you. This is exactly the kind of thing they promise parents will never happen at Wallingford Preparatory."

A shudder runs across my shoulders at the mention of memory workers. Barron is one. He used his power to make me forget a lot of things—that I am a transformation worker, that he pushed me into becoming a disturbingly efficient assassin, even that I transformed Lila into an animal and he kept her in a cage for years. My sociopathic big brother, who stole chunks of my life. The only brother I have left. The one who's training me.

That's family for you. Can't live with them; can't murder them. Unless Barron rats me out to Yulikova. Then I really might.

"Yeah," I say, trying to regain the thread of the conversation. "I'll get rid of it. I promise. No, wait, I already promised. How about I pinkie swear?"

"Unbelievable," Sam says, but I can tell he's not really mad. As I am busy determining this, watching the play of emotions cross his face, I notice he's got about a dozen pens piled on the navy blanket next to him and he's marking a pad with each one.

"What are you doing over there?"

He grins. "I got these on eBay. A whole case of disappearing-ink pens. Nice, right? They were used by the KGB. These are serious spy tools."

"What are you going to do with them?"

"Two choices, really. Awesome prank or potentially actually useful for our bookmaking operation."

"Sam, we've already talked about this. It's yours now, if you want it, but I'm out." I've been the bookie for ridiculous school stuff for as long as I've been at Wallingford. If you wanted to put money down on the football game, you came to me. If you wanted to put down money on whether or not there was Salisbury steak for lunch three times a week or whether Headmistress Northcutt and Dean Wharton were having an affair or whether Harvey Silverman would die of alcohol poisoning before he graduated, you also came to me. I would calculate the odds, hold the cash, and charge a commission for my trouble. In a school with lots of bored rich kids, it was a good way to line my pockets. It was pretty harmless, until it wasn't. Until kids started taking bets on which students were curse workers. Until those students were targets.

Then it felt a lot like I was taking blood money.

Sam sighs. "Well, there are still endless pranks we could pull. Imagine a whole room full of test takers, and then *nothing* on any of the tests twenty-four to forty-eight hours later. Or what if you slipped one of these into a teacher's grade book? Chaos."

I grin. Chaos, beautiful chaos. "So, which one will you choose? My pickpocketing skills are at your service."

He chucks a pen in my direction. "Be careful you don't do your homework with that," he says.

I snatch it out of the air a moment before it crashes into my lamp. "Hey!" I say, turning back to him. "Watch it. What's with the wild pitch?"

He's looking at me with a strange expression on his face. "Cassel." His voice has gone low and earnest. "Do you think you could talk to Daneca for me?"

I hesitate, glancing down at the pen in my hands, turning it over in my gloved fingers, then looking back up at him. "About what?"

"I apologized," he says. "I keep apologizing. I don't know what she wants."

"Did something happen?"

"We met up for coffee, but then it turned into the same old argument." He shakes his head. "I don't understand. She's the one who lied. She's the one who never told me she was a worker. She probably never would have told me either, if her brother hadn't blurted it out. How come I'm the one who has to keep apologizing?"

In all relationships there's a balance of power. Some relationships are a constant fight for the upper hand. In others one person is in charge—although not always the person who thinks they are. Then, I guess there are relationships so equal that no one has to think about it. I don't know anything about those. What I do know is that power can shift in a moment. Way back at the beginning of their relationship, Sam was always deferring to Daneca. But once he got mad, he couldn't seem to stop being angry.

By the time he was ready to hear her apology, she no longer wanted to give it. And so they've somersaulted back and forth these past few weeks, neither one sorry enough to placate the other, neither of them sorry at the right time, both sure the other is in the wrong.

I can't tell if that means they're broken up or not. Neither can Sam.

"If you don't know why you're apologizing, your apology probably sucks," I say.

He shakes his head. "I know. But I just want things to go back to the way they were."

I know that feeling all too well. "What do you want me to say to her?"

"Just find out what I can do to fix things."

There's so much desperation in his voice that I agree. I'll try. He's got to know he's already in a pretty bad way if he's coming to me for help in matters of the heart. There's no point rubbing it in.

———

In the morning I am crossing the quad, hoping the coffee I drank in the common room will kick in soon, when I pass my ex-girlfriend, Audrey Dolan, in a clump of her friends. Her copper hair gleams like a new penny in the sunlight, and her eyes follow me reproachfully. One of her friends says something just low enough for me not to hear, and the rest laugh.

"Hey, Cassel," one of them calls, so that I have to turn around. "Still taking bets?"

"Nope," I say.

See, I'm *trying* to go legit. I'm trying.

"Too bad," the girl shouts, "because I want to put down a hundred bucks that you'll die alone."

Sometimes I don't know why I am fighting so hard to stay here at Wallingford. My grades, always determinedly and consistently mediocre, have really taken a dive in the last year. It's not like I'm going to college. I think about Yulikova and the training my brother is getting. All I would have to do is drop out. I'm just delaying the inevitable.

The girl laughs again, and Audrey and the others laugh with her.

I just keep walking.

In Developing World Ethics we talk a little bit about journalistic bias in reporting and how it influences what we think. When asked to give an example, Kevin Brown brings up an article about my mother. He thinks that too many reporters blame Patton for being an easy dupe.

"She's a criminal," says Kevin. "Why try to act like Governor Patton was supposed to be prepared for his girlfriend to try to curse him? It's an obvious example of a reporter trying to discredit the victim. I wouldn't be surprised if that Shandra Singer had gotten to him, too."

Someone snickers.

I stare at my desk, focusing on the pen in my hand, and the sound of chalk scraping across the board as Mr. Lewis quickly launches into an example from a recent news story about Bosnia. I feel that strange hyper-focus that occurs when everything narrows to the present. The past and the future fade away. There is only now and the ticking moments, until the bell rings and we hustle out into the hall.

"Kevin?" I say softly.

He turns, smirking. People rush around us, clutching bags and books. They look like streaks of color in my peripheral vision.

I hit Kevin's jaw so hard that I feel the impact right down to my bones.

"Fight!" a couple of kids yell, but teachers come and drag me back from Kevin before he can get up.

I let them pull me away. I feel numb all over, the adrenaline still coursing through my veins, nerves sparking with the desire to do something more. To do something to someone.

They take me to the dean's office and leave me with a slip of paper pressed into my hand. I crumple it up and throw it against the wall as I am shown inside.

Dean Wharton's room is stacked with papers. He looks surprised to see me, getting up and lifting a pile of folders and crossword puzzles out of the chair in front of his desk and indicating that I should sit. Usually whatever trouble I'm in is so bad I get sent straight to the headmistress.

"Fighting?" he says, looking at the slip. "That's two demerits if you're the one who started it."

I nod. I don't trust myself to speak.

"Do you want to tell me what happened?"

"Not really, sir," I say. "I hit him. I just—I wasn't thinking straight."

He nods like he's considering what I said. "Do you

understand that if you get one more demerit for any reason, you'll get expelled? You won't graduate from high school, Mr. Sharpe."

"Yes, sir."

"Mr. Brown will be here in a moment. He's going to be telling me his side of the story. Are you sure you don't have anything more to say?"

"No, sir."

"Fine," Dean Wharton says, pushing up his glasses so that he can massage the bridge of his nose with brown-gloved fingers. "Go wait outside."

I go and sit in one of the chairs in front of the school secretary. Kevin walks past me with a grunt, on his way into Wharton's office. The skin along Kevin's cheek is turning an interesting greenish color. He's going to have a hell of a bruise.

He's going to tell Wharton, *I don't know what came over Cassel. He just went nuts. I didn't provoke him.*

A few minutes later Kevin leaves. He smirks at me as he walks out into the hall. I smirk right back.

"Mr. Sharpe, can you come in here, please?"

I do. I sit back in the chair, looking at the piles of paper. Just one push would send a stack crashing into all the others.

"You angry about something?" Dean Wharton asks me, as though he can read my thoughts.

I open my mouth to deny it, but I can't. It's like I have been carrying this feeling around with me for so long that I didn't even know what it was. Wharton, of all people, has put his finger on what's wrong with me.

I'm *furious.*

I think of not knowing what compelled me to strike a gun out of the hand of a killer. Of how satisfying it was to hit Kevin. Of how I want to do it again and again, want to feel bones snap and blood smear. Of how it felt to stand over him, my skin on fire with rage.

"No, sir," I manage to get out. I swallow hard because I don't know when I became so distanced from myself. I knew Sam was angry when he talked about Daneca. How come I didn't know that I was mad too?

Wharton clears his throat. "You've been through a lot, between the death of your brother Philip and your mother's current . . . legal woes."

Legal woes. Nice. I nod.

"I don't want to see you head down a path you can't come back from, Cassel."

"Understood," I say. "Can I go back to class now?"

"Go on. But remember, you have two demerits and the year isn't even half over. One more and you're out. Dismissed."

I get up, sling my backpack over my shoulder, and slink back to the Academic Center in time for the next bell. I don't see Lila in the halls, although my gaze pauses on any blond-haired girl who passes me. I have no idea what I will say to her if I do see her. *So, I hear you ordered your first murder. How was that?* seems a little on the nose.

Besides, who says it was her first?

I duck into the bathroom, turn on the faucets, and splash my face with cold water.

It's a shock, liquid streaming over my cheeks and col-
lecting in the hollow of my throat, splashing my white shirt.
Darkening my gloves. Stupidly, I forgot to take them off.

Wake up, I tell myself. *Snap out of it.*

Reflected in the mirror, my dark eyes look more shadowed than ever. My cheekbones stand out, like my skin is
too tight.

Really fitting in, I tell myself. *Dad would be so proud.
You're a real charmer, Cassel Sharpe.*

I still make it to physics before Daneca does, which
is good. Theoretically she and I are still friends, but she's
been avoiding me since she started fighting with Sam. If I
want to talk to her, I'm going to have to corner her.

We don't have assigned seats, which means it's easy
for me to find a desk near where Daneca usually sits and
dump my stuff on the chair. Then I get up and talk to someone on the other side of the room. Willow Davis. She seems
suspicious when I ask her a question about the homework,
but answers without too much hesitation. She's telling me
something about how there are ten different dimensions of
space and one of time, all curled around one another, when
Daneca comes in.

"Understand?" Willow asks. "So there could be other
versions of us living in other worlds—like maybe there's a
world where ghosts and monsters are real. Or where no one
is hyperbathygammic. Or where we all have snake heads."

I shake my head. "That can't be real. That *cannot* be real
science. It's too awesome."

"You didn't do the reading, did you?" she asks, and I

decide that this is the moment to retreat to my new desk.

When I walk back, I see my plan has worked. Daneca is sitting where she always does. I move my backpack and flop into its place. She looks up, surprised. It's too late for her to get up without it being really obvious that she doesn't want to sit next to me. She scans the room like she's racking her brain for some excuse to move, but the seats are mostly full.

"Hey," I say, forcing a smile. "Long time, no see."

She sighs, like she's resigned herself to something. "I heard you got into a fight." Daneca's wearing her Walling-ford blazer and pleated skirt with neon purple tights and even brighter purple gloves. The color of them more or less matches the faded purple streaks in her wooly brown hair. She kicks clunky Mary Janes against the brace of the desk.

"So you're still mad at Sam, huh?" I realize this proba-bly isn't how he'd want me to broach the subject, but I want information and class is about to start.

She makes a face. "He told you that?"

"I'm his roommate. His moping told me that."

She sighs again. "I don't want to hurt him."

"So don't," I say.

Daneca leans toward me and lowers her voice. "Let me ask you something."

"Yes, he's really, really sorry," I say. "He knows he overre-acted. How about you guys forgive each other and start—"

"Not about Sam," she says, just as Dr. Jonahdab walks into the room. The teacher picks up a piece of chalk and starts sketching Ohm's law on the board. I know what it is because of the words "Ohm's law" above it.

I open my notebook. "What, then?" I write, and turn the pad so that Daneca can see it.

She shakes her head and doesn't say anything else.

I am not really sure I understand the relationship between current and resistance and distance any better by the end of class, but it turns out Willow Davis was right about the whole snake-head dimension thing being possible.

When the bell rings, Daneca takes my arm, her gloved fingers digging in just above my elbow.

"Who killed Philip?" she asks suddenly.

"I—," I start. I can't answer without lying, and I don't want to lie to her.

Daneca's voice is low, an urgent whisper. "My mother was your lawyer. She did your immunity deal for you, the one that got the Feds off your back, right? You made a deal to tell them who killed those people in the files. And Philip. For *immunity*. Why did you need immunity? What did you do?"

When the Feds dumped a bunch of files onto my lap and told me Philip had promised to name the killer, I didn't really stop Daneca from looking at them. I knew that was a mistake, even before I realized the files were all of people I'd transformed, a list of bodies that were never found— and haven't been found since. More missing memories.

"We've got to get going," I say. The classroom has emptied out, and a few students are starting to come in for the next class. "We're going to be late."

She reluctantly lets go of my arm and follows me out the door. It's funny how our positions are reversed. Now she's the one trying to corner me.

"We were working on that case together," Daneca says. Which is sort of true. *"What did you do?"* she whispers.

I look down at her face, searching for what she thinks the answer is. "I never hurt Philip. I never hurt my brother."

"What about Barron? What did you do to him?"

I frown, so confused that for a moment I can't think of what to say. I have no idea where she got that from. "Nothing!" I say, throwing my hands wide for emphasis. "Barron? Are you crazy?"

A faint flush colors her cheeks. "I don't know," she says. "You did something to *someone*. You needed immunity. Good people don't need immunity, Cassel."

She's right, of course. I'm not a good person. The funny thing about good people—people like Daneca—is that they really honestly don't *get* the impulse toward evil. They have an incredibly hard time reconciling with the idea that a person who makes them smile can still be capable of terrible things. Which is why, although she's accusing me of being a murderer, she seems more annoyed than actually worried about getting murdered. Daneca seems to persist in a belief that if I would just *listen* and understand how bad my bad choices are, I'd stop making them.

I pause near the stairs. "Look, how about I meet you after dinner and you can ask me whatever you want? And we can talk about Sam." I can't tell her everything, but she's my friend and I could tell her more than I have. She deserves as much truth as I can afford to give. And who knows, maybe if I just *listen* for once, I will make some better choices.

I couldn't make much worse ones.

Daneca brushes a brown curl behind her ear. Her purple glove is smeared with ink. "Will you tell me *what* you are? Will you tell me that?"

I suck in my breath in honest surprise. Then I laugh. I've never told her my biggest secret—that I'm a transformation worker. I guess it's time. She must have worked out something or she wouldn't have asked.

"You got me," I say. "You got me there. Yeah, I'll tell you that. I'll tell you everything I can."

She nods slowly. "Okay. I'll be in the library after dinner. I have a paper to start."

"Great." I jog down the stairs, running full tilt when I hit the quad so I can make it to ceramics before the final bell. I already have two demerits. I've been in enough trouble for a single day.

My pot comes out totally misshapen. It must have had an air bubble in it too, because when I put it into the kiln, it explodes, taking out three other people's cups and vases along with it.

On my way to track practice, my phone rings. I flip it open and cradle it against my cheek.

"Cassel," Agent Yulikova says. "I'd like you to stop by my office. Now. I understand your classes are over for the day, and I've arranged for you to be excused. The office understands that you have a doctor's appointment."

"I'm on my way to track," I say, hoping that she'll hear

the hesitation in my voice. I have a gym bag slung over my shoulder, bouncing off my leg. Overhead the trees are blowing in the wind, covering the campus in a drifting carpet of leaves with the colors of a sunrise. "I've missed a lot of meets."

"Then they won't notice if you miss another one. Honestly, Cassel. You almost got yourself killed yesterday. I would like to discuss the incident."

I think of the gun, taped in the closet of my dorm room. "It wasn't any big thing," I say.

"Glad to hear it." With that, she hangs up.

I head toward my car, kicking leaves as I go.

A FEW MINUTES LATER

Agent Yulikova is gathering up piles of paper and shifting them out of the way so that she can get a better look at me. She's got straight gray hair, chopped to hang just beneath her jawline, and a face like a bird's—delicate and long nosed. Masses of chunky beaded necklaces hang around her throat. Despite holding a steaming cup of tea and wearing a sweater under her navy corduroy jacket, her lips have a bluish tint, like she's cold. Or maybe like she *has* a cold. Either way she more closely resembles a professor from Wallingford than the head of a federal program to train worker kids. I know she probably dresses the way she does on purpose, to lure trainees into feeling comfortable. She probably does everything on purpose.

It still works.

She's my handler, the one who's responsible for ushering me into the program as soon as I am eighteen, per the deal I made with the Feds. Until then, well, I don't know what she's supposed to do with me. I suspect she doesn't know either.

"How are you doing, Cassel?" she asks me, smiling. She acts like she really wants to know.

"Good, I guess." Which is a huge, ridiculous lie. I'm barely sleeping. I'm plagued with regrets. I'm obsessed with a girl who hates me. I stole a gun. But it's what you say to people like her, people who are evaluating your mental state.

She takes a sip from her mug. "What's it been like shadowing your brother?"

"Fine."

"Philip's death must make you feel more protective of Barron," she says. Her gaze is kind, nonthreatening. Her tone is neutral. "It's just the two of you now. And even though you're the younger brother, you've had a lot of responsibility placed on you. . . ." She lets her words trail off.

I shrug my shoulders.

"But if he put you in any danger yesterday, then we need to put a stop to things immediately."

"No, it wasn't like that," I say. "We were just following someone—a random person—and then Barron got a call. So I was on my own for a couple minutes, and I saw the murder. I chased after the kid—the killer—which was stupid, I guess. But he got away, so that's that."

"Did you talk to him?" she asks.

"No," I lie.

"But you cornered him in the alley, correct?"

I nod, then think better of it. "Well, for a second he was cornered. Then he went for the fence."

"We found a broken plank near the scene. Did he swing it at you?"

"No," I say. "No, nothing like that happened. Maybe he stepped on it as he was running. It all happened so fast."

"Could you describe him?" She leans forward in her seat, peering at me, like she can see my every fleeting thought in the involuntary flinches and flushes of my body. I really hope that's not true. I'm a good liar, but I'm not world class. My experience has been mostly with two different kinds of adults—criminals, who act in ways I can anticipate, and marks, who can be manipulated. But with Yulikova I'm out of my depth. I have no idea what she's capable of.

"Not really," I say with a shrug.

She nods a few times, like she's taking that in. "Is there anything else you want to tell me about what happened?"

I know I should admit to taking the gun. If I confess now, though, she'll ask me why I took it. Or maybe she'll just ask Barron what we were doing. Who we were tailing. If he's in the right mood, he might even tell her. Or worse, he'll make up a story so fanciful that it leads her straight to Lila faster even than the truth would.

It's not that I want to be this person, doing the wrong thing again, lying to Yulikova. I want to learn how to do the right thing, even if I hate it. Even if I hate her for it. I just *can't* this time.

But next time—next time I'll do better. I'll tell her everything. Next time.

"No," I say. "It really was no big thing. I was just stupid. I'll be more careful."

She picks up a clipped packet of papers from her desk and drops them in front of me with a significant look. I know what they say. Once I sign them, I'm no longer a regular citizen. I will be agreeing to a private set of regulations and laws. If I screw up, I will have agreed to be tried in a private court. No more jury of my peers. "Maybe it's time for you to leave Wallingford early and train with Barron and all the other students full-time."

"You've said that before."

"And you've said no before." She smiles. Then, opening up one of the drawers of the desk, she pulls out a tissue. She coughs into it. I see something dark stain the paper before she wads it up. "I'm guessing you're going to say no again now."

"I want to be a federal agent and work for the LMD. I want—" I stop. *I want to be better. I want you to make me better.* I can't say that, though, because it's crazy. Instead I say, "Becoming a high school dropout isn't exactly a dream of mine. And anyway, my immunity agreement—"

She cuts me off. "We might be able to scare up a diploma for you."

I imagine not having to see Lila, her white-gold hair long enough to curl at the nape of her neck, her smoky voice distracting enough that I can barely pay attention to whatever it is that I'm doing when she speaks. I imagine not having to grit my teeth to avoid calling her name every time I pass her in the hall. "Soon. I just want to finish out the year."

Yulikova nods, like she's disappointed but not surprised. I wonder about her coughing and the tissue—was that blood on it? I don't feel right asking. None of this feels right.

"How are you doing with the charms?" she asks.

I reach into my pocket and pull them out. Five perfect circles of stone with holes bored in the middle. Five transformation amulets to stop a curse from a worker like me, not that there are many workers like me. Making the charms was draining, but at least there was no blowback involved. They'd been sitting in my glove compartment for a week, waiting for me to deliver them.

"Very rare," she says. "Have you ever worn one of these amulets and cast a curse?"

I shake my head. "What would happen if I did?"

Yulikova smiles. "A lot of nothing. The stone would crack and you would be exhausted."

"Oh," I say, oddly disappointed. I don't know what I was expecting. Shaking my head at myself, I drop the amulets onto the desk in front of her. They roll and spin and clatter like coins. She looks at them for a long moment, then raises her eyes to me.

"It's personally important that you stay safe." She takes another sip of her tea and smiles again.

I know that she probably says that to dozens of potential recruits, but I still like it when she says it to me.

On the way out her gloved hand touches my arm briefly. "Have you heard from your mother?"

Yulikova's voice is soft, like she's really concerned about a seventeen-year-old boy on his own and scared for his mother. But I bet she's fishing for information. Information I wish I had.

"No," I say. "She could be dead for all I know." For once I'm not lying.

"I'd like to help her, Cassel," she says. "Both you and Barron are important to us here in the program. We'd like to keep your family together."

I nod noncommittally.

Criminals get caught eventually—it's a tenet of being in the life. But maybe things are different for government agents. Maybe their mothers stay out of prison forever. I guess I ought to hope so.

———————⌇

From the outside the building is nondescript, a dull medium-size concrete structure in the middle of a parking lot, its mirrored windows gleaming with reflected light from the setting sun. No one would guess that a federal agency occupies the upper floors, especially since the sign out front promises RICHARDSON & CO., ADHESIVES AND SEALANTS and almost everyone coming in and out is wearing a sharp-looking suit.

Above me the trees are mostly brown and bare, the reds and golds of early autumn faded by the cold October wind. My Benz is right where I left it, reminding me of the life I could have had if I'd accepted Lila's father's offer and become his secret weapon.

More and more I feel like the boy who cut off his nose to spite his face.

I drive back to Wallingford, arriving with just enough time to dump off my gym bag and grab a granola bar before I have to meet Daneca at the library. I jog up the stairs and am about to unlock the door to my room when I realize it's already open.

"Hello?" I say as I go in.

Sitting on my bed is a girl. I've seen her around campus, but I don't think we've ever spoken. She's a sophomore, Asian—Korean, I think, with long black hair that hangs to her waist like a waterfall, and thick white socks that come almost to her knees. Her eyes are lined with glittering blue pencil. She looks up at me from under long lashes and smiles shyly.

I'm a little flustered, I have to admit. This doesn't happen a lot. "Are you waiting for Sam?"

"I was hoping to talk to you." She stands, lifting her pink book bag and biting her bottom lip. Then, hesitating, she adds, "I'm Mina. Mina Lange."

"You're really not supposed to be in my room," I say, dropping my gym bag.

She grins. "I know."

"I was just about to head out," I say, glancing toward the door. I have no idea what kind of game she's playing, but the last time a girl turned up on my bed, everything went directly to hell sans handbasket. I'm not exactly optimistic. "I don't mean to be rude, Mina, but if there's something you want to tell me, you should probably do it now."

"Can't you stay?" she asks, taking a step toward where I'm standing. "I have a really big favor to ask, and there's no one else who can help."

"I find that hard to believe." My voice comes out a little strained-sounding. I think of Daneca and all of the explaining I have ahead of me. The last thing I need is to be late and have one more thing to explain. "But I guess I could wait a few minutes if it's important."

"Maybe we could go somewhere else," she says. Her lips are glossy pink, soft-looking. Her white-gloved finger wraps around a strand of her long black hair, twirling it nervously. "Please."

"Mina, just tell me," I say, but the tone of my voice isn't very commanding. I don't mind indulging in the illusion that there's something absolutely vital that I can do for a beautiful girl, even if I don't believe it myself. I don't mind lingering a little while longer, pretending.

"You're busy," she says. "I shouldn't keep you. I know that we're not—I know you don't know me that well or anything. And this is all my fault. But please, please can we talk sometime?"

"Yeah," I say. "Of course. But didn't you want—"

She cuts me off. "No, I'll come back. I'll find you. I knew you'd be nice, Cassel. I just knew it."

She brushes past me, close enough that I can feel the warmth of her body. Moments later I hear her light step in the hall. I stand alone in the middle of my room for a long moment, trying to figure out what just happened.

⸺⸺⸺⬩〜

The air has turned from chilly to the kind of cold that seeps into your bones and lives in your marrow. The kind of cold that keeps you shivering after you've come into a warm room, as if you have to shudder ice from your veins. I am almost to the library.

"Hey," someone calls from behind me. I know the voice. I turn.

Lila's standing at the edge of the grass, looking up. She's wearing a long black coat, and when she speaks, her breath condenses in the air like the ghosts of unspoken words. She looks like a ghost herself, all black and white in the shadow of leafless trees. "My father wants to see you," she says.

"Okay," I say, and follow her. Just like that. I'd probably follow her off a cliff.

She leads me to a silver Jaguar XK in the parking lot. I don't know when she got the car—or her license—and I want to say something about that, offer her some kind of congratulations, but when I open my mouth, she gives me a look that makes me swallow the words.

I get in quietly on the passenger side and take out my phone. The inside smells like spearmint bubble gum and perfume and cigarette smoke. A half-empty bottle of diet soda is resting in the cup holder.

I take out my phone and text Daneca: *Can't make it 2nite.*

A few seconds later the phone starts ringing, but I set it to vibrate and then ignore it. I feel guilty for standing her up after making a promise to be more honest, but explaining where I am going—no less why—seems impossible.

Lila looks over at me, half her face lit by a streetlight, blond lashes and the arch of her brow turned to gold. She's

so beautiful that my teeth hurt. In psychology class freshman year our teacher talked about the theory that we all
have a "death instinct"—a part of us that urges us toward
oblivion, toward the underworld, toward Thanatos. It feels
exhilarating, like taking a step off the edge of a skyscraper.
That's how I feel now.

"Where's your dad?" I ask her.

"With your mom," Lila says.

"She's alive?" I am so surprised that I don't have time
to be relieved. My mother is with Zacharov? I don't know
what to think.

Lila's gaze finds mine but her smile gives me no comfort. "For now."

The engine starts, and we pull out of the parking lot. I
see my own face reflected back in the curve of the tinted
window. I might be going to my own execution, but I don't
look all that torn up about it.

WE DRIVE INTO THE

basement garage, and Lila parks in a numbered spot next to a Lincoln Town Car and two BMWs. It's a car thief's dream lot, except for the fact that anyone who steals from Zacharov will probably get dropped off a pier with cement boots on.

As Lila kills the engine, I realize that this will be the first time I've ever seen the apartment where she lives when she's with her father. She was quiet on the drive, leaving me with plenty of time to wonder if she knows that I followed her yesterday, if she knows that I'm being recruited for the Licensed Minority Division, if she knows that I saw her order a hit or that I have Gage's gun.

To wonder if I'm about to die.

"Lila," I say, turning in my seat and putting my gloved hand on the dashboard. "What happened with us—"

"Don't." She looks directly into my eyes. After a month of being forced to avoid her, I feel stripped bare by her gaze. "You can be as much of a charming bastard as you want, but you're never going to bullshit your way into my heart again."

"I don't want that," I say. "I never wanted that."

She gets out of the car. "Come on. We have to get back to Wallingford before curfew."

I follow her into the elevator, trying to behave myself, trying to puzzle through her words. She pushes the P3 button. I guess the *P* stands for "penthouse," because soon we are whirring up the floors so fast that my ears pop. She lets her messenger bag drop off her shoulder and hunches forward in her long black coat. For a moment she looks frail and tired, like a bird huddling against a storm.

"How did my mother wind up here?" I ask.

Lila sighs. "She did a bad thing."

I don't know if that means working Patton or something else. I think about the reddish stone my mother was wearing on her finger the last time I saw her. I think too of a picture I found in the old house, of a much younger Mom decked out in lingerie and looking like Bettie Page— a picture obviously taken by a man who wasn't my father and who might have been Zacharov. I have a lot of reasons to worry.

The elevator doors open into a massive room with white

walls, a black and white marble floor, and what looks like a Moroccan style wood ceiling at least eighteen feet above us. There's no carpet, so the tap of our shoes echoes as we walk toward the lit fireplace on the opposite wall, flanked with sofas, and with two people mostly hidden by shadows. Three huge windows show Central Park at night, a patch of near blackness in the shimmering city surrounding it.

My mother sits on one of the couches. She has an amber-colored drink in her hand and is wearing a filmy white dress I've never seen on her before. It looks expensive. I expect her to jump up, to be her usual exuberant self, but the smile she gives me is subdued, almost fearful.

Despite that I nearly collapse with relief. "You're okay."

"Welcome, Cassel," Zacharov says. He's standing by the fire, and when we get close, he crosses to where Lila is and gives her a kiss on the forehead. He looks like the lord of some baronial manor, rather than a seedy crime boss in a big Manhattan apartment.

I incline my head in what I hope is a respectful nod. "Nice place."

Zacharov smiles like a shark. His white hair looks gold in the firelight. Even his teeth look golden, which reminds me uncomfortably of Gage and the gun taped to the wall of my closet. "Lila, you can go do your homework."

She touches her throat lightly—gloved fingers tracing the marks she took, the marks that make her an official member of his crime family, not just his daughter—rage in every line of her face. He barely notices. I'm sure he doesn't realize that he just dismissed her like a child.

My mother clears her throat. "I'd like to talk to Cassel alone for a moment, if that's all right, Ivan?"

Zacharov nods.

She gets up and walks to me. Linking her arm with mine, she marches me down a hallway to a massive kitchen with ebony wood floors and a center island of a bright green stone that looks like it might be malachite. While I sit down on a stool, she puts a clear glass kettle on one of the burners. It's eerie, the way she seems to know Zacharov's apartment.

I want to grab her arm to reassure myself that she's real, but she's moving restlessly, not seeming to notice me.

"Mom," I say. "I'm so glad that you—but how come you didn't call us or—"

"I made a big mistake," Mom says. "Huge." She takes a cigarette from a silver case, but instead of lighting it she sets it down on the counter. I've never seen her so agitated before. "I need your help, sweetheart."

I am uncomfortably reminded of Mina Lange. "We were really worried," I say. "We didn't hear from you for weeks, and you're all over the news, you know? Patton wants your head."

"*We?*" she asks, smiling.

"Me. Barron. Grandad."

"It's nice to see you and your brother so close again," she says. "My boys."

"Mom, you are on every news channel. Seriously. The cops are looking everywhere for you."

She shakes her head, waving away my words. "When I

got out of prison, I wanted to make some quick money. It was hard, sweetheart, inside. I spent all the time when I wasn't planning that appeal planning what I would do when I got out. I had a few favors to call in and a few things put away for a rainy day."

"Like?" I say.

Her voice goes low. "The Resurrection Diamond."

I saw it on her finger. She wore it once, out to lunch, after Philip died. The stone's a pretty distinctive color, like a drop of blood spilled into a pool of water. But even when I saw it, I thought I must have been mistaken, because even though I knew Zacharov wore a fake diamond on his tie pin, that didn't mean he'd lost the original. And it certainly didn't mean *my mother* had taken it.

"You stole it?" I mouth, pointing to the other room. "From *him*?"

"A long time ago," she says.

I can't believe that she's treating this so lightly. I keep my voice low. "Back when you were screwing him?"

After all these years I think I've finally shocked her. "I—," she starts.

"I found a photo," I say. "When I was cleaning out the house. The guy who took it was wearing the same ring that I saw Zacharov wearing in a picture at Grandad's place. I wasn't sure, but now I am."

Her gaze goes toward the other room, then back to me. She bites her lower lip, smearing lipstick on her teeth. "Yes, fine, back then," she says. "One of those times. Anyway, I stole it and got a copy made of it—but I knew he would want the real one back, even after all this time. It doesn't make him look good not to have the real one."

The understatement of the year. If you're the head of a crime family, then, no, you don't want people to find out that your most valuable possession was stolen. You certainly don't want people to know that it was stolen years ago and you've been wearing a fake ever since. Especially if your most valuable possession is the Resurrection Diamond, which, according to legend, makes its wearer invulnerable; the loss of it is going to make you seem suddenly vulnerable. "Yeah," I say.

"So I thought I would sell it back to him," Mom says.

I forget to keep my voice down. "You *what*? Are you *crazy*?"

"It was all going to be fine." Now she puts the cigarette to her lips and leans into the burner on the stove to catch the edge of the flame. She inhales deeply, and embers flare. She blows smoke.

The tea water is starting to boil. Her hand is shaking.

"He doesn't care if you smoke in the house?"

She goes on without answering me. "I had a good plan. Worked through a middleman, everything. But it turned out that I didn't have the real thing. The stone's gone."

I just stare at her for a long moment. "So someone found yours and switched it out?"

She nods quickly. "That must have been it."

This is turning into one of those stories where each new piece of information is so much worse than the thing before that I don't want to ask for more details, but I am pretty sure there's no way around it. *"And?"*

"Well, Ivan might not have minded paying a little bit

to get his property back, especially since he'd probably given up on getting the real thing returned to him. I think he would have just made the exchange. But when he found out the stone was a *fake*, well, he killed the middleman and found out I was behind it."

"How'd he find that out?"

"Well, the *way* he killed the middleman was—"

I hold up my hand. "That's okay. Let's skip that part."

She takes a deep drag from her cigarette and blows three perfect rings of smoke. When I was a kid, I loved those. I would try to pass my hand through them without the breeze from the movement blowing them apart, but it never worked. "So, Ivan—he was angry. Well, but he knows me, so he didn't want to kill me right out. We have history. He told me I had to do a job for him."

"A job?"

"The Patton job," she says. "Ivan has always been interested in the government. He said that it was important to stop Proposition 2 from passing in New Jersey, because if it passed in one state then it could pass elsewhere. All I had to do was make Patton renounce it, and Ivan thought the whole thing would just collapse. . . ."

I put a hand to my forehead. "Stop. Wait. It doesn't make any sense! When did all this happen? Before Philip died?"

The kettle starts to wail.

"Oh, yes," Mom says. "But you see, I blew it. The job. I didn't manage to discredit Patton at all. In fact, I think I made the chance of Proposition 2 passing better than ever. But you know, sweetie, it's never really been my thing—

politics. I know how to make men give me things, and I know how to get away before things get too hot. Patton's nosy aides were always asking questions and looking up things about me. That's just not the way I work."

I nod numbly.

"So now Ivan says I have to get the stone back. Only, I have no idea where it is! And he says he won't let me leave until I give it back—but how can I give it back when I can't even look for it?"

"So that's why I'm here."

She laughs, and for a moment she's almost like herself. "Exactly, sweetheart. You'll find the stone for Mommy, and then I'll be able to come home."

Sure. She'll be able to waltz right out of Zacharov's apartment and into the waiting arms of every cop in New Jersey. But I nod again, trying to work through everything she's said. "Wait. When I met you and Barron for sushi— the last time I *saw* you—you were *wearing* the ring. Had Zacharov already put you on the Patton job?"

"Yes. I already told you. But I figured that since the diamond was a fake, I might as well wear it."

"Mom!" I groan.

Zacharov appears in the doorway, a silver-haired shadow. He walks past both of us to the stove, where he clicks off the burner. Only when the kettle stops its screaming do I realize how loud it had became.

"Are you two finished?" he asks. "Lila says it's time for her to go back to Wallingford. If you'd like to go with her, I suggest you go now."

"One more minute," I say. My palms are sweating inside my gloves. I have no idea where to even start looking for the real Resurrection Diamond. And if I don't find it before Zacharov runs out of patience, my mother could wind up dead.

Zacharov takes a long look at my mother and then me. "Quickly," he tells us, heading back down the hallway.

"Okay," I say to my mother. "Where was the stone last? Where did you keep it?"

She nods. "I hid it wrapped up in a slip in the back of a drawer of my dresser."

"Was it still there when you got out of prison? In the same exact place?"

She nods again.

My mother has two dressers, both of them blocked by huge piles of shoes and coats and dresses, many rotted through, most moth-eaten. The idea that someone went through all that and then her drawers seems unlikely— especially if they didn't know to target the bedroom.

"And no one else knew it was there? You didn't tell anyone? Not in prison, not at any time? No one?"

She shakes her head. The ash on her cigarette is burning long. It's going to fall on her glove. "No one."

I think for a long moment. "You said you switched the stone with a fake. Who made the fake?"

"A forger your father knew up in Paterson. Still in business, with a reputation for discretion."

"Maybe the guy made two forgeries and kept the real one for himself," I say.

She doesn't look convinced.

"Can you just write down his address?" I say, looking toward the hall. "I'll go talk to him."

She opens a few drawers near the stove. Knives in a wooden block. Tea towels. Finally she finds a pen in a drawer full of duct tape and plastic garbage bags. She writes "Bob—Central Fine Jewelry" and the word "Paterson" on my arm.

"I'll see what I can find out," I say, giving her a quick hug.

Her arms wrap around me, bone-achingly tight. Then she lets me go, turns her back, and throws her cigarette into the sink.

"It's going to be all right," I say. Mom doesn't reply.

I head into the other room. Lila is waiting for me, bag slung over her shoulder and coat on. Zacharov stands beside her. Both their expressions are remote.

"You understand what you have to do?" he asks me.

I nod.

He walks us to the elevator. It's right where other people would have front doors to their apartments. The outside of it is golden, etched with a swirling pattern.

When the doors open, I look back at him. His blue eyes are as pale as ice.

"Touch my mother, and I'll kill you," I say.

Zacharov grins. "That's the spirit, kid."

The doors close, and Lila and I are alone. The light overhead flickers as the elevator begins its descent.

We pull out of the garage and start toward the tunnel out of the city. The bright lights of bars and restaurants and clubs streak by, patrons spilling out onto the sidewalk. Cabs honk. In Manhattan the night is just starting in all its smoky glory.

"Can we talk?" I ask Lila.

She shakes her head. "I don't think so, Cassel. I think I've been humiliated enough."

"Please," I say. "I just want to tell you how sorry—"

"Don't." She flips on the radio, adjusting it past the news, where the host is discussing Governor Patton's terminating the employment of all hyperbathygammic individuals in government positions, whether or not they've been convicted of a crime. She leaves it on a channel blasting pop music. A girl is singing about dancing inside someone else's mind, coloring their dreams. Lila cranks it up.

"I never meant to hurt you," I yell over the music.

"I'm going to hurt *you* if you don't shut up," she shouts back. "Look, I know. I know it was awful for you to have me crying and begging you to be my boyfriend and throwing myself at you. I remember the way you flinched. I remember all the lies. I'm sure it was embarrassing. It was embarrassing for both of us."

I press the radio button, and the car goes abruptly silent. When I speak, my voice sounds rough. "No. That's not how it was. You don't understand. I wanted you. *I love you*—more than I have ever loved anyone. More than I ever will love anyone. And even if you hate me, it's still a relief to be able to tell you. I wanted to protect you—from me and the way I felt—because I didn't trust myself to keep remembering that it wasn't really—that you didn't feel like I— Anyway, I'm sorry. I'm sorry you're embarrassed. I'm sorry I embarrassed you. I hope I didn't— I'm sorry I let things go as far as they did."

For a long moment we are both quiet. Then she jerks the wheel to the left, tires screeching as she veers off the road, making a turn that takes us back into the city.

"Okay, I'm done," I say. "I'll shut up now."

She slams her hand down on the radio, turning it on and up so that it drowns the car in sound. Her head is turned away from me, but her eyes are shining, as if wet.

We careen around another block, and she pulls up to the curb abruptly. We're in front of the bus station.

"Lila—," I say.

"Get out," she tells me. Her head is turned away from me and her voice shakes.

"Come on. I can't take the bus. Seriously. I'll miss curfew and I'll get expelled. I already have two demerits."

"That's not my problem." She fumbles around in her bag and lifts out a large pair of sunglasses. She pushes them on, hiding half her face. Her mouth is curved down at the corners, but it's not nearly as expressive as her eyes.

I can still tell that she's crying.

"Please, Lil," I say, using a name I haven't called her since we were kids. "I won't say a thing for the whole way back. I swear. And I'm sorry."

"God, I hate you," she says. "So much. Why do boys think that it will be better to lie and tell a girl how much they loved her and how they only dumped her for her own good? That they only tried to rearrange her brain for her own good? Does it make you feel better, Cassel?

Does it? Because from my perspective, it really sucks."

I open my mouth to deny it but then remember I promised not to talk. I just shake my head.

She pulls away from the curb suddenly, the force of acceleration enough to throw me back against the seat. I keep my eyes on the road. We're quiet all the way back to Wallingford.

I go to sleep tired and get up exhausted.

As I pull on my uniform, I can't stop thinking about Zacharov's cold vast apartment where my mother is now imprisoned. I wonder what it's like for Lila to wake up there on a Saturday morning and wander into that kitchen for coffee.

I wonder how long she's going to be able to look at my mother before she tells Zacharov what Mom did to her. I wonder if each time Lila sees her, she remembers what it was like to be forced to love me. I wonder if each time, she hates me just a little bit more.

I think of her in the car, her head turned away from me, her eyes filled with tears.

I don't know how to even start to make Lila forgive me. And I have no idea how to help Mom. The only thing I can think of—aside from finding the diamond—that might keep Zacharov pacified is if I agree to work for him. Which means betraying the Feds. Which means giving up on trying to be good. And once I start working for the Zacharovs— Well, everyone knows that paying off a debt to the mob is impossible. They just keep piling on interest.

"Come on," Sam says, scratching his head and making his hair stand straight up. "We're going to miss breakfast again."

I grunt and head to the bathroom to brush my teeth. I shave. When I sweep back my hair from my face, I grimace at the redness of my eyes.

In the cafeteria I make a mocha with coffee and a packet of hot chocolate. The sugar and caffeine wake me up enough to finish up a couple of problems due for Probability & Statistics. Kevin Brown glowers at me from across the room. There's a bruise darkening his cheekbone. I can't help it; I grin at him.

"You know, if you did your homework at night, you wouldn't have to do it in your other classes," Sam says.

"That would also be true if someone would let me copy their answers," I tell him.

"No way. You're on the straight and narrow now. No cheating allowed."

I groan and get up, shoving aside my chair. "See you at lunch."

I sit through morning announcements, resting my head on my arms. I turn in my hastily done homework and copy down new problems from the board. As I come out of third-period English and trudge through the hallway, a girl falls into step beside me.

"Hi," Mina says. "Can I walk with you?"

"Uh, sure." I frown. No one's asked me before. "Are you okay?"

She hesitates and then says the words all in a rush. "Someone's blackmailing me, Cassel."

I stop walking and stare at her for a long moment as students rush around us. "Who?"

She shakes her head. "I don't know. It doesn't matter, does it?"

"I guess not," I say. "But what can I do?"

"Something," she says. "You got Greg Harmsford kicked out of school."

"I didn't," I say.

She looks up at me through lowered lashes. "Please. I need your help. I know you can fix things."

"I really don't think that I can do as much as—"

"I know you made rumors go away. Even when they were true." She looks down when she says it, like she's afraid I'm going to be mad.

I sigh. There were some perks to being the school bookie. "I never said I wouldn't *try*. Just that you shouldn't expect too much."

She smiles at me and tosses that gleaming mane of hair over her shoulders. It falls down her back like a cloak.

"And," I say, holding up one hand, cautioning her against being so thrilled by my answer, "you're going to have to tell me what's going on. All of it."

She nods, her smile fading a little.

"Now would be good. Or you can keep putting it off and—"

"I took photos." She blurts it out, then presses her lips together nervously. "Photos of me—naked ones. I was going to send them to my boyfriend. I never did, but I kept them on my camera. Stupid, right?"

Some questions have no good answer. "Who's this boy-friend?"

She looks down and reaches across her body to adjust the shoulder strap of her bag, making her seem smaller and more vulnerable. "We broke up. He didn't even know. He couldn't have anything to do with this."

She's lying.

I'm not sure which part is the lie, but now that we're getting to the details, she's exhibiting tells. Avoiding eye contact. Fidgeting.

"So I guess someone got a hold of them," I say, prompting her to continue.

She nods. "My camera got taken two weeks ago. Then this past Sunday someone slipped a note under my door. It said that I have a week to get five thousand dollars. I have to bring that to the baseball pitch at six in the morning next Tuesday or the person's going to show the photos to everyone."

"The baseball pitch?" I frown. "Let me see the note."

She reaches into her book bag and gives me a folded piece of white printer paper, probably from one of the computer labs on campus. The note says exactly what she told me.

I frown. Something doesn't add up.

She swallows. "I don't have that kind of money—not like the note wants—but I could pay you. I could find *some* way to pay you."

The way she says it, with her lashes fluttering and her bruised voice, I know what she's implying. And while I don't think she'd actually follow through, she must be panicked to try that angle.

Plenty of people get conned because they don't know any better. They're just gullible. But lots of people *are* suspicious at the start of a con. Maybe the initial investment is small enough that they can afford to lose it. Maybe they're bored. Maybe they're hopeful. But you'd be surprised how many people start a con knowing there's a good chance they're being conned. All the signals are there. They just keep ignoring them. Because they want to believe in the possibility of something. And so, even though they know better, they just let it happen.

"So you'll find a way to help me?" she asks. "You'll try?"

Mina's lack of skill at lying touches my heart. I know I'm being conned—just like all those other suckers—but somehow, in the face of her enormously obvious attempt at manipulation, I can't turn her down.

"I'll try," I say.

I don't understand much about this situation, except there's a pretty girl and she's looking at me like I can solve all her problems. I want to. Of course, it would help if she told me the truth about what they were.

I could really use a win.

She throws her arms around my neck as she thanks me. I inhale the scent of her coconut body wash.

I STALK INTO PHYSICS

and slide into my new spot, next to Daneca. She's opening her notebook and smoothing down the pleats of her black skirt. She turns to give me a poisonous look. I glance away from her eyes and notice that the gold thread on the Wallingford patch over the pocket of her blazer is fraying.

"I'm really sorry I didn't make it to the library yesterday," I say, putting my gloved hand to my heart. "I really meant to be there."

She doesn't reply. She tugs back a mass of her purple-tipped hair and rolls it into a loose bun, then slips an elastic band off her wrist and around the whole thing. It doesn't seem like it should hold, but it does.

"I saw Lila," I say. "She had to tell me something about my family. It really couldn't wait."

Daneca snorts.

"Ask her, if you don't believe me."

She takes a chewed-on pencil out of her bag and points it in my direction. "If I asked *you* one question, would you answer it honestly?"

"I don't know," I say. There are some things I can't talk about and other things I'm not sure I want to. But at least I can be honest with her about my uncertainty. I'm not sure she sees that as the same step forward I do, though.

"What happened to that cat we saved from the animal shelter?"

I hesitate.

Here's the problem with telling the truth—smart people figure out the parts you don't say. A lie can be airtight, easy. The truth is a mess. When I told Daneca the story about my brothers changing my memory, about how they wanted me to kill Zacharov and how they'd held Lila captive, I left out one essential detail. I never told her that I was a transformation worker.

I was too scared. I was already trusting her so much that I couldn't bring myself to give up that last secret. And I was scared of the secret itself, scared to say the words out loud. But now Daneca's put the whole thing together and found the gap. The cat that she saw me hold—the one that she never saw again.

"I can explain," I start.

Daneca shakes her head. "I thought you'd say that." She turns away from me.

"Come on," I say. "I really can explain. Give me a chance."

"I already did," she whispers as Dr. Jonahdab starts taking attendance. "You blew it."

No matter how angry Daneca is with me, I know she always wants answers. But maybe she feels like she already has them.

Something prompted her to start thinking about stuff that happened seven months ago. Lila must have said something—maybe even told her that I was a transformation worker, that it was because of me she spent years trapped in a body that wasn't hers, that she was the cat we stole. She and Daneca have been hanging out a lot. Maybe Lila needed to talk to someone. It's as much Lila's secret as it is mine.

Now I guess it's Daneca's secret as well.

I skip track practice, flop down on the sofa in the common room of my dorm, and Google Central Fine Jewelry in Paterson. There's a crappy website that promises to pay cash for gold and claims to accept consignments. It's open only until six, so there's no way I can make it there before closing time.

I dial the number listed. I pretend to be a regular, checking when Bob works, claiming he's the only one I'll trust with some estate pieces. The grouchy woman on the other end of the line says he'll be in on Sunday. I thank her and hang up. I guess I have plans for the weekend.

Central Fine Jewelry doesn't seem like the kind of place where you keep working after you make a mint reselling the Resurrection Diamond, though, so I'm not feeling optimistic.

They do have a page on the site featuring amulets. It looks pretty legit. They don't claim to have any transformation amulets. Claiming to have one is a sure sign of a scam, since no one but a transformation worker can make them. Most of the stones in stock are for luck magic. They list a few more unusual amulets, ones to prevent memory work and death work—well, prevent it once, before the amulet snaps and you're left buying a new one—but nothing too good to be true. I figure that since he knew my dad, Bob used to have ties to curse workers. His inventory is proof that he still does.

It figures that a forger would be in with workers. The thing about curse magic being illegal is that it turns everyone who uses it into a criminal. And criminals stick together.

That thought makes my mind turn inevitably toward Lila.

As much as she hates me now, she will hate me that much more once I sign the papers and become a federal agent. Down in Carney, where we spent our summers growing up, if a curse worker joined the government, that person was considered a traitor, the lowest of the low, someone not worth spitting on if he was on fire.

There's some part of me that takes a perverse delight in doing the one thing that is going to make a bunch of murderers, con men, and liars all gasp and clutch their pearls.

I bet they didn't think I had it in me.

But I never wanted to hurt Lila—at least not hurt her worse than I already have. And no matter what any of them think of me, I will never let the government get its claws in her.

Another senior, Jace, comes into the common room and turns on the television. He flips the channel to some reality show about beauty queens stranded on a desert island. I'm not really watching. My mind is skipping to Mina Lange and blackmail.

I don't want to even consider how thinking about Lila brought me to Mina.

Still, I turn her story over and over in my head, trying to see if there is some clue I can glean from the little she told me. Why did it take the thief two weeks after stealing the camera to start blackmailing Mina? Don't people who steal cameras usually want the *camera* more than what's on it, anyway? Who bothers flipping through another person's pictures? But then, it's not like most kids at Wallingford can't afford to buy a camera, and it's weird how many rich kids steal for fun. They'll shoplift from the convenience store down on the corner, break into each other's rooms to grab boxes of cookies, and clumsily jimmy open doors so that they can grab iPods.

Which, unfortunately, only widens the suspect pool, instead of shrinking it. The blackmailer could be anyone. And, more than probably, the person is joking about the five grand and the baseball field, trying to scare Mina. The remote cruelty points to a girl or a bunch of girls. Whoever she is, she probably just wants to make Mina squirm.

If I'm right, it's a pretty good con. Even if Mina calls their bluff, she can't do much about it, because she won't want the pictures to get out. But the girls probably can't resist giggling when Mina comes into the cafeteria or teasing her in class, even if they don't say anything about the pictures.

I just wish I was sure Mina was telling me the truth.

Assignments like these are what FBI agents do, right? On a grander scale but still, using the same techniques. This might be like one of the exercises that Barron is given, except that this one is mine. A little investigation for me to practice on in secret. So that when I finally join up, I'll be better than him at something.

A little investigation to prove to myself that I am making the right decision.

I'm still running through ways to draw out the blackmailer when the beauty queen program is interrupted by news footage of Governor Patton. He's on the steps of the courthouse, surrounded by microphones, railing loudly.

"Did you know that government bodies exist staffed entirely by curse workers—curse workers with access to your confidential files? Did you know that no one requires testing of applicants to government jobs to determine who among us are potentially dangerous criminals?" he says. "We must root all workers out of our government! How can we expect our legislators to be safe when their staffers, their aides, even their security team could be seeking to undermine policies directed at bringing these sinister predators to light, because those policies would inconvenience them."

Then we cut to the reporter's serious, perfectly made-up face and are told that a senator from New York, Senator James Raeburn, has made a statement denouncing Patton's position. When they show Senator Raeburn, he appears in front of a blue curtain, at a lectern with the state insignia on it.

"I am deeply disappointed by the recent words and actions of Governor Patton." He's young for a senator, with a smile like he's used to talking people into and out of things, but he doesn't look slick. I want to like him. He reminds me of my dad. "Are we not taught that those who have confronted temptation and triumphed over it are more virtuous than those who have yet to face their own demons? Are not those who are born hyperbathygammic and tempted into a life of crime—tempted to use their power for their own benefit—are not those people just like us, who resist temptation and choose instead to work to shield us from their less moral kind, are they not to be celebrated rather than treated to Governor Patton's witch hunt?"

The newscaster tells us that more details will be forthcoming and more statements are expected from other members of government.

I fumble for the remote and switch the channel to a game show. Jace has his laptop open and doesn't seem to notice, for which I am grateful. I guess anything that distracts Patton from talking about my mother is a good thing, but I still hate the sight of him.

──────●──●∼∼──

Before dinner I head up to my room to drop off my schoolbooks. As I get to the top of the stairs, I see Sam storming down the hall. His hair is a mess and his neck and cheeks are flushed. His eyes look too bright, the way they do in people who are in love, people who are enraged, and people who are completely bonkers.

"What's wrong?" I ask.

"She wants all her stuff back." He slams his hand into the wall, cracking the plaster, a move so uncharacteristic that I just stare. He's a big guy, but this is the first time I've ever seen him use his size for violence.

"Daneca?" I ask, like an idiot, because *of course* he's talking about Daneca. It's just that the whole thing doesn't make sense. They've been fighting, sure, but the fight is over something stupid. They both care about each other—surely more than they care about an exaggerated misunderstanding. "What happened?"

"She called me and told me it was over. That it had been over for weeks." He sags now, arm bent against the wall, his forehead resting on his arm. "Didn't even want to see me to get her things. I told her that I was sorry—over and over I told her—and that I would do anything to get her back. What else am I supposed to do?"

"Maybe she just needs some time," I say.

He shakes his head pitifully. "She's seeing somebody else."

"No way," I say. "Come on. You're just being—"

"She is," he says. "She said she was."

"Who?" I try to think of anyone I saw Daneca talking to—anyone who she looked at lingeringly or walked down the halls with more than once. I try to think of any guy who

stayed behind after HEX meetings to talk with her. But I come up blank. I can't picture her with anyone.

He shakes his head. "She wouldn't tell me."

"Look," I say, "I'm really sorry, man. Let me dump my bag and we can go off campus—get some pizza or something. Ditch this place for a couple of hours." I was planning on meeting Mina tonight in the dining hall, but I push that thought aside.

Sam shakes his head. "Nah. I just want to be by myself for a little while."

"You sure?"

He nods and lurches away from the wall to thud down the stairs.

I go into our room and toss my bag of books onto my bed. I'm about to go out again, when I see Lila, on her knees, peering under Sam's dresser. Her short gold hair is hanging in her face, the sleeves of her dress shirt rolled up. I notice that she's not wearing tights, just ankle socks.

"Hey," I say, stunned.

She sits up. I can't read her expression, but her cheeks look a little pink. "I didn't think you were going to be here."

"I live here."

She turns so that she's sitting on the floor with her legs crossed, pleated skirt riding high over her thighs. I try not to look, not to recall what her skin felt like against mine, but it's impossible. "Do you know where Daneca's stuffed owl is? She swears she left it here, but Sam says he never saw it."

"I never saw it either."

She sighs. "How about her copy of Abbie Hoffman's *Steal This Book*?"

"My bad," I say, and take it out from one of my drawers. She gives me a look. "What? I thought it was Sam's when I borrowed it."

She gets up in a single fluid movement and snatches the book from my gloved hand. "It's not that. I don't know. I don't know how I got talked into this. Daneca was just so upset."

"She was upset? She's the one who just broke his heart."

I expect Lila to say something cruel about Sam or me or about love in general, but she just nods. "Yeah."

"Last night—," I start.

She crosses the room, shaking her head. "How about a T-shirt with the words 'NERD HERD' on it? Have you seen one of those?"

I shake my head as she starts picking up laundry off the floor. "So I guess you guys got really close? You and Daneca?" I ask.

Lila shrugs. "She's been trying to help me."

I frown. "With what?"

"School. I'm a little behind. I might not be here for that much longer." Lila straightens, a wadded-up shirt in her hand. When she looks at me, she looks more sad than angry.

"What? Why?" I take a step toward her. I remember something Daneca said about Lila having to do remedial work. She hasn't been taking classes since she was fourteen; that's a lot to catch up on. Still, I figured she could handle it. I figured she could handle anything.

"I only came here for you. I'm no good at this school stuff." She unsticks a postcard from the wall over Sam's bed, which involves her climbing onto the mattress in a way that ignites every filthy thought I've ever had. "Okay. I think that's it," she says.

"Lila," I say as she walks toward the door. "You're one of the smartest people I know—"

"She doesn't want to see you, either," Lila says, cutting me off. "I have no idea what you did to Daneca, but I think she's madder at you than she is at Sam."

"Me?" I drop my voice to a whisper so that we won't be overheard. "I didn't do anything. You're the one who told her I turned you into a cat."

"What?" Lila's mouth parts slightly. "You're crazy. I never said that!"

"Oh," I say, honestly puzzled. "I thought you must have. Daneca was asking me all these questions—weird questions. Sorry. I didn't mean anything. It's your story to tell if you want to tell it. I've got no right—"

She shakes her head. "You better hope she doesn't figure it out. With her mother's crazy worker advocacy stuff, she'd probably go straight to the government. You'd wind up press-ganged into one of those federal brainwashing programs."

I smile guiltily. "Yeah, well, I'm glad you didn't say anything to her."

Lila rolls her eyes. "I know how to keep a secret."

As she leaves with Daneca's stuff, I am shamed into realizing how many secrets Lila *has* kept. She's had the means to ruin my life pretty much since she became human again. One word to her father, and I would be dead. Since my mother worked her, Lila has even more means and a better motive. The fact that she hasn't done it is a miracle. And I have not even the slightest idea why she hasn't, when she has every reason, now that the curse has worn off.

I lean back on my bed.

My whole life I've been trained as a con artist, trained to read what people mean underneath what they say. But right now I can't read her.

At dinner Mina denies knowing anyone who would blackmail her for spite. No one has ever teased her at Wallingford, no one has ever laughed behind her back. She gets along with absolutely everybody.

We sit together, slowly eating roast chicken and potatoes off our trays while she answers my questions. I wait for Sam to show up, but he never does. Lila doesn't come into the dining hall either.

When I press Mina, she tells me that her ex-boyfriend doesn't go to school at Wallingford. His name is Jay Smith, apparently, and he goes to public school, but she isn't sure which one. She met him at the mall, but she's a little fuzzy on where. His parents are very strict, so she was never allowed to go to his house. She deleted his number when they broke up.

Everything is a dead end.

Like she doesn't want me to suspect anyone. Like she doesn't want me to be investigating the very thing she asked me to fix.

Like she *already knows who's blackmailing her*. But that makes no sense. If she did, she'd have no reason to involve me.

When I get up from the table, Mina hugs me and tells me that I'm the sweetest boy in the world. Even though she doesn't mean it and she's probably saying it for all the wrong reasons, it's still nice.

I find Sam lying in bed when I get back to the room, headphones over his ears. He stays that way all through study hall, snuffling quietly into his covers. He sleeps in his clothes.

Wednesday he barely speaks and barely eats. In the cafeteria he picks at his food and responds to my most outrageous jokes with a grunt. When I see him in the halls, he looks haunted.

On Thursday he tries to talk to Daneca, abruptly chasing her out onto the school green after breakfast. I follow them, dread in the pit of my stomach. The skies are overcast and it's cold enough that I won't be surprised if we get sleet instead of rain. Wallingford looks bleached out, gray. For a moment Sam and Daneca are standing close together, and I think he's got a chance. Then she lurches back and starts off in the direction of the Academic Center, braids whipping behind her.

"Who?" he yells after her. "Just tell me who he is. Just tell me why he's better than me."

"I should never have told you anything," she shrieks back.

People want to lay bets on the identity of this mysterious guy, but no one's willing to go to Sam with their guesses. He looks wild-eyed, stalking around the campus like a madman. When they come to me, I am glad that I already gave up the business.

By Friday I'm worried enough that I make Sam come home with me. I leave my Benz at Wallingford and we drive over to my mom's old house in his grease-powered hearse. As we pull in, I notice there's already another car parked in the driveway. Grandad's come to visit.

I WALK IN THE FRONT

door to the house, Sam right behind me. It's unlocked and I can hear the chug of the dishwasher. My grandfather is standing at the counter, chopping potatoes and onions. His gloves are off and the blackened stubs where his fingers used to be are clearly visible. Four fingers; four kills. He's a death worker.

One of those kills saved my life.

Grandad looks up. "Sam Yu, right?" he says. "The roommate."

Sam nods.

"You drove up from Carney," I say. "And you're making dinner. What's going on? How'd you even know I was going to come home this weekend?"

"Didn't. You heard from that mother of yours?" Grandad asks.

I hesitate.

He grunts. "That's what I thought. I don't want you to get caught up with her bullshit." He nods toward Sam. "Kid can keep a secret?"

"He's currently keeping almost all of mine," I say.

"Almost all?" Sam says, the corner of his mouth lifting. That's the closest he's been to smiling in days.

"Then both of you listen up. Cassel, I know that she's your mother, but there's nothing you can do for her. Shandra got herself in over her head. She's got to get her own self out. You understand?"

I nod.

"Don't be yessing me to death when you mean no," Grandad says.

"I'm not doing anything crazy. I'm just seeing if I can find something she lost," I say, glancing toward Sam.

"What she *stole*," says Grandad.

"She stole from Governor Patton?" Sam asks, clearly bewildered.

"I wish it was just that idiot she had to worry about," says Grandad, and he goes back to his chopping. "You two go sit down awhile. I'm making steaks. There's plenty for three."

I shake my head and walk into the living room, drop my backpack near the couch. Sam follows.

"What's going on?" he asks. "Who's your grandfather talking about?"

"My mother stole something and then tried to sell a fake back to the original owner." That seems like the simplest explanation. The details only make the whole thing more confusing. Sam knows that Lila's father is a crime boss, but I'm not sure he really thinks of anyone's parent as potentially lethal. "The guy wants the real version, but Mom doesn't remember where she put it."

Sam nods slowly. "At least she's okay. In hiding, I guess, but okay."

"Yeah," I say, not even convincing myself.

I smell the onions hit a hot pan of grease in the kitchen. My mouth waters.

"Your family is badass," Sam says. "They set a high bar of badassery."

That makes me laugh. "My family are *lunatics* who set a high bar for *lunacy*. Speaking of which, don't mind my grandfather. Tonight we can do whatever you want. Sneak into a strip club. Watch bad movies. Crank call girls from school. Drive down to Atlantic City and lose all our cash at gin rummy. Just say the word."

"Is there really gin rummy in Atlantic City?"

"Probably not," I admit. "But I bet there are some old folks who'd be willing to sit in on a game and take your money."

"I want to get drunk—so drunk," he says wistfully. "So drunk that I forget not just tonight but, like, the last six months of my life."

That makes me think uncomfortably of Barron and his memory curses. I wonder how much, right now, Sam would pay to be able to do just that. To forget Daneca. To forget he ever loved her.

Or to make her forget that she stopped loving him.

Like Philip got Barron to make Maura—Philip's wife—forget she was going to leave him. It didn't work. They just had the same fights over and over again as she fell out of love with him exactly the same way she had before. Over and over. Until she shot him in the chest.

"Cassel?" Sam says, shoving my shoulder with a gloved hand. "Anyone home in there?"

"Sorry," I say, shaking my head. "Drunk. Right. Let me survey the booze situation."

There's always been a liquor cabinet in the dining room. I don't think anyone's been in it since before Dad died and Mom went to prison. There was so much clutter in front of it that it wasn't exactly easy to get into. I find a couple of bottles of wine in the back, along with some bottles of brown liquor with labels I don't recognize, and a few newer-looking things in the front. The necks are coated in dust. I take everything out and pile it on the dining room table.

"What's Armagnac?" I call to Sam.

"It's fancy brandy," my grandfather says from the kitchen. A few moments later he sticks his head into the room. "What's all that?"

"Mom's liquor," I say.

He picks up one of the bottles of wine and looks at the label. Then he turns it upside down. "Lot of sediment. This is either going to be the best thing you ever drank or vinegar."

The inventory turns out to be three bottles of possibly sour wine; the Armagnac; a bottle of rye that's mostly full; pear brandy with a pale globe of fruit floating in it; and a container of Campari, which is bright red and smells like cough medicine.

Grandad opens all three bottles of wine when we sit down to dinner. He pours the first into a glass. It's a dark amber, almost the same color as the rye.

He shakes his head. "Dead. Toss it."

"Shouldn't we at least try it?" I ask.

Sam looks at my grandfather nervously, like he's expecting to get in trouble for our liquor cabinet raid. I don't point out that among most people I know, legal drinking age isn't going to exactly be a sticking point. Sam should cast his mind back to Philip's wake.

Grandad laughs. "Go ahead if you want, but you're going to be sorry. It'll probably do better in your gas tank than in your stomach."

I take his word for it.

The next one is nearly as black as ink. Grandad takes a sip and grins. "Here we go. You kids are in for a treat. Don't just glug this stuff."

In the kind of fancy magazines my mother reads when she's shopping for men, they rate wines, praising them for tasting like things that don't sound good to drink—butter and fresh cut grass and oak. The descriptions used to make me laugh, but this wine really does taste like plums and black pepper, with a delicious sourness that fills my whole mouth.

"Wow," says Sam.

We finish off the rest of the wine and start on the rye. Sam pours his into a water glass.

"So what's the matter?" Grandad asks him.

Sam bangs his head against the table lightly and then downs his drink in three long swallows. I'm pretty sure he's forgotten to be worried about getting in trouble with anyone. "My girlfriend dumped me."

"Huh," Grandad says, nodding. "The young lady with you at Philip's funeral? I remember her. Seemed nice enough. That's too bad. I'm sorry, kid."

"I really—I loved her," Sam says. Then he refills his glass.

Grandad goes into the other room for the Armagnac. "What happened?"

"She hid something big—and when I found out, I was really pissed. And she was sorry. But by the time I was ready to forgive her, she was the one who was pissed. And then I had to be sorry. But I wasn't. And by the time I was, she had a different boyfriend."

My grandfather shakes his head. "Sometimes a girl's got to walk away before she knows what she wants."

Sam pours some of the Armagnac into his glass, along with the dregs of the rye. He tops off the concoction with a shot of Campari.

"Don't drink that!" I say.

He toasts to us and then tosses the whole thing back.

Even Grandad winces. "No girl's worth the hangover you're going to have come morning."

"Daneca is," Sam says, words slurring.

"You got a lot of ladies to get through. You're still young. First love's the sweetest, but it doesn't last."

"Not ever?" I ask.

Grandad looks at me with a seriousness he reserves for moments when he wants me to really pay attention. "When we fall that first time, we're not really in love with the girl. We're in love with being in love. We've got no idea what she's really about—or what she's capable of. We're in love with our idea of her and of who we become around her. We're idiots."

I get up and start stacking dishes in the sink. I'm not too steady on my feet right now, but I manage it.

When I was a kid, I guess I loved Lila like that. Even when I thought I'd killed her, I still saw her as the ideal girl—the pinnacle of girlhood that nobody else was ever going to be able to get close to. But when she came back, I had to see her the way she was—complicated, angry, and a lot more like me than I'd ever guessed. I might not know what Lila is capable of, but I know her.

Love changes us, but we change how we love too.

"Come on," Sam says from the table, pouring bright red liquor into teacups he's found somewhere. "Let's do shots."

I wake up with the horrible taste of cough medicine in my mouth.

Someone is pounding on the front door. I turn over and cover my head with a pillow. I don't care who it is. I'm not going downstairs.

"Cassel!" My grandfather's voice booms through the house.

"What?" I shout back.

"There's somebody to see you. He says he's from the government."

I groan and roll out of bed. So much for my avoiding answering the door. I pull on jeans over my boxers, rub sleep out of my eyes, and grab for a shirt and a pair of clean gloves. Stubble itches along my cheeks.

As I brush my teeth, trying to scrub the taste of the night before out of my mouth, dread finally catches up with me. If my grandfather guesses that I'm thinking about working for Yulikova, I have no idea what he will do. There's no worse kind of traitor to guys like Grandad. And as much as I know he loves me, he's also somebody who believes in putting his duty before feelings.

I shuffle down the stairs.

It's Agent Jones. I'm surprised. I haven't seen him or Agent Hunt since they turned me and Barron over to the Licensed Minority Division. He looks unchanged—dark suit, mirrored sunglasses. The only difference I detect is that his pasty skin looks red across his cheeks, like sunburn or maybe windburn. He's standing in the doorway, shoulder against the frame like he's going to push his way in. Grandad obviously hasn't invited him over the threshold.

"Oh, hey," I say, coming to the door.

"Can I talk to you . . ." He gives my grandfather a dark look. "Outside?"

I nod, but Grandad puts a bare hand on my shoulder. "You don't have to go anywhere with him, kid."

Agent Jones is staring at my grandfather's hand like it's a snake.

"It's okay," I say. "He was working Philip's murder."

"Fat lot of good that did," says Grandad, but he lets go of me. He walks to the counter and pours coffee into two mugs. "You take anything in your coffee, government leech?"

"No, thanks," Jones says, and points at Grandad's hand. "You hurt yourself there?"

"Wasn't me that got hurt." Grandad hands me one of the cups.

I take a swig and follow Jones out through the sagging porch and into the front yard.

"What do you want?" I ask under my breath. We're standing near his shiny black car with the dark tinted windows. The cold breeze cuts through the thin fabric of my T-shirt. I cup the mug closer to me for warmth, but the coffee is cooling fast.

"Something the matter? Afraid the old man's going to find out what you've been up to?" His smile is gloating.

I suppose it's too much to expect that just because Jones and I are on the same side now, he's going to start acting like it.

"If you've got something to say to me, spit it out," I tell him.

He folds his arms over his chest. I can see the bulge of his gun. He reminds me of every mobster I've ever met, except less polite. "Yulikova needs to see you. She said to tell you that she's sorry for bothering you on a weekend, but something really big has come up. She says that you'll want to hear it."

"Too big for them to tell you what it is?" I don't know why I'm taunting him. I guess I'm scared, what with him flaunting my connection to the Feds right in front of Grandad. And I'm angry—the kind of anger that burns you up from the inside. The kind of anger that makes you stupid.

His lip curls. "Come on. Get in the car."

I shake my head. "No way. I can't. Tell her I'll come later today. I just have to come up with an excuse."

"You have exactly ten minutes to square this with your grandfather, or I'll tell him that you framed your own brother. That you ratted him out to us."

"Yulikova didn't tell you to do that," I say. A shiver runs through me that's only partially from the cold. "She'd be pissed off if she knew you were threatening me."

"Maybe. Maybe not. Either way, you're the one who's screwed. Now, are you coming with me?"

I swallow roughly. "Okay. Let me get my coat."

Agent Jones is still grinning when I go back into the house. I swallow the rest of the coffee, even though it's like ice.

"Grandad," I shout. "They want to ask me some questions about Mom. I'll be right back."

My grandfather comes halfway down the stairs. He's wearing gloves. "You don't have to go."

"It'll be fine." I tug on a long black coat and grab for my phone and wallet.

I feel like a terrible person.

Whatever else I'm shaky on, I'm pretty sure you're not supposed to con the people you love.

Grandad gives me a long look. "Do you want me to come along?"

"I think someone better stay with Sam," I say.

At the mention of his name, Sam looks up from where he's draped on the couch. A strange expression passes over his face, and a moment later, he lunges for the wastebasket.

Hard to believe it, but someone's about to have a worse morning than I'm having.

⚬━━━━⟡

I don't say anything while Agent Jones drives. I play a game on my phone and look out the window from time to time, checking on our progress. At some point I realize we're not taking the right roads to get to Yulikova's office, but I still don't speak. What I do is start planning.

A couple more minutes and I am going to tell him I need a rest stop. Then I'm going to lose him. If I can scope out an old enough car nearby, I can hot-wire it, but it would be better if I could con a ride. I go over various stories in my head and settle on looking for a middle-aged couple— a husband who's big enough not to be intimidated by my height or my skin, and a wife to argue on my behalf, ideally a couple who might have kids about my age. I'm planning on giving them a story about a drunk friend who wouldn't give me his keys and stranded me without a way home.

I'll have to work fast.

As I am thinking it through, we pull into the parking lot of a hospital, three huge brick towers linked at the base, with an ambulance blinking its red lights in front of the emergency room entrance. I let out my breath. Escaping from a hospital is a piece of cake.

"We're meeting Yulikova here?" I ask incredulously. Then I think better of it. "Is she all right?"

"As all right as she ever is," he says.

I don't know what that means, but I don't want to admit it. Instead of responding, I try the handle, and when I can get it open, I jump out of the car. We walk together to one of the side doors. The hallway is antiseptic, typical. No one questions us.

Jones seems to know where we're going. We pass a nurse's station, and Jones nods to an elderly woman behind the desk. Then we walk down another long corridor. I glance inside an open doorway to see a man with a big grizzly beard and balloons around his wrists, so that he can't bring his own hands to his face. He turns to me with a haunted look.

We stop at the next door—this one closed—and Agent Jones knocks once before heading inside.

It's a regular hospital room but clearly both larger and better-furnished than some others we passed. There is a multicolored afghan thrown over the foot of the hospital bed and several jade plants along the window. There are also two comfortable- but generic-looking chairs sitting across from the bed.

Yulikova is in a batik-print robe and slippers. She's got a plastic cup and is watering the plants when we come in. She's not wearing makeup, and her hair looks not so much wild as uncombed, but she doesn't otherwise look unwell.

"Hello, Cassel. Agent Jones."

"Hi," I say, lingering in the doorway like I might with a sick relative that I haven't seen in a long while. "What's going on?"

She looks at her surroundings and laughs. "Oh, this. Yes, it must seem a little bit dramatic."

"Yeah—and Agent Jones hustled me over here like a house was on fire and I was the only bucket of water in town." I sound only half as annoyed as I am, which is plenty. "I didn't even get to shower. I'm hungover and probably stink like I've been using booze as aftershave—except that I also didn't get to shave. What's the deal?"

Jones glowers.

She laughs a little and shakes her head at him. "I'm sorry to hear that, Cassel. There's a bathroom through there that you are welcome to use, if you'd like. The hospital has little packets of toiletries."

"Yeah," I say. "I might."

"And Agent Jones can go down to the commissary and get us something to eat. The hospital doesn't have much, but it's not as terrible as hospital food used to be. They have decent burgers and snacks." She walks over to the other side of her bed and opens one of the drawers in the side table, taking out a brown leather pocketbook. "Ed, why don't you get a bunch of different sandwiches and cups of coffee. The egg salad isn't bad. And a couple of bags of chips, some fruit, and something for dessert. Get some extra packets of mustard for Cassel. I know he likes them. We'll sit down and have a nice lunch."

"Very civilized," I say.

Agent Jones ignores her looking for her wallet and goes to the door. "Fine. I'll be right back." He looks from me to her. "Don't believe everything that little weasel tells you. I know him from before."

When he walks out, she gives me an apologetic look. "I'm sorry if he was difficult. I needed to get an agent on this, and I wanted someone who'd worked with you before. The last thing we need is lots of people knowing you're a transformation worker. Even here, I can't count on total discretion."

"You worried about a leak?"

"We want to be sure that when and if people find out about you, they receive that information directly from us. You know there's a rumor that there's a transformation worker in China? Many people in our government feel that that information was carefully planted."

"If they have one at all, you mean?"

She nods, a smile pulling at one corner of her mouth. "Exactly. Now go freshen up."

In the bathroom I manage to slick my hair back with water and take a safety razor to my stubble. Then I gargle with mouthwash. When I emerge, I do so in a cloud of mint.

Yulikova's gotten a third chair from somewhere and is arranging them near the window. "Much better," she says.

It's something that a mother would say. Not *my* mother, but *a* mother.

"You need help with anything?" I ask her. It doesn't seem like she should be moving furniture.

"No, no. Sit down, Cassel. I'm fine."

I grab a chair. "I don't mean to pry," I say, "but we're in a hospital. You sure you're fine?"

She sighs heavily. "No getting anything past you, huh?"

"I also often notice when water is wet. I have a keen detective's mind like that."

She has the good grace to smile. "I'm a physical worker. Which means I can alter people's bodies—not to the extent that you can, but brutal basic things. I can break legs and heal them again. I can remove some tumors—or at least reduce them in size. I can draw out an infection in the blood. I can make children's lungs work." I try not to show how surprised I am. I didn't know physical workers could do that. I thought it was just pain—sliced skin, burns, and boils. Philip was a physical worker; I never saw him use it to help anyone.

"And sometimes I do all those things. But it makes me very sick. All of it, any of it, hurting and healing. And over time it has made me sicker. Permanently sicker."

I don't ask her about the legality of what she's doing. I don't care, and if she doesn't care either, well, then, maybe we have something in common after all. "Can't you heal yourself?"

"Ah, the old cry of 'Physician, heal thyself!'" she says. "A perfectly logical question, but I am afraid I can't. The blow-back negates any and all positive effects. So occasionally I have to come here for a while."

I hesitate before I ask my next question, because it's so awful. Still, I need to know, if I'm about to sign my free will away on the strength of her promises. "Are you dying?"

"We're all dying, Cassel. It's just that some of us are dying faster than others."

I nod. That's going to have to do, because Agent Jones walks back into the room with an orange cafeteria tray, the whole thing piled with sandwiches, muffins, fruit, and coffee.

"Put it on my bed. We can buffet off of that," she tells him.

I retrieve a ham sandwich, a cup of coffee, and an orange and sit back down while Jones and Yulikova choose their food.

"Good," she says, pulling the wrapper off what looks like a lemon poppy seed muffin. "Now, Cassel, I'm sure you're familiar with Governor Patton."

I snort. "Patton? Oh, yeah. I love that guy!"

Jones looks like he wants to choke the sarcasm out of me, but Yulikova just laughs.

"I thought you'd say something like that," she says. "But you should understand—what your mother did to him and then what was done to fix him—he's become more and more unstable."

I open my mouth to object, but she holds up her hand.

"No. I understand your impulse to defend your mother, and it's very noble, but right now that's irrelevant. It doesn't matter who's to blame. I need to tell you something confidential, and I need your assurance that it won't leave this room."

"Okay," I say.

"If you've seen him on the news recently," Yulikova says, "you can almost see Patton losing control. He says and does things that are extreme, even for anti-worker radicals.

But what you can't tell is how paranoid and secretive he's become. People very high up in the government are worried. Once Proposition 2 passes, I'm afraid that he's going to try to lock down the state of New Jersey, then round up and jail workers. I believe—and I'm not the only one—that he wants to bring back the work camps."

"That's not possible," I say. It's not that I can't believe Patton might want that; it's that I can't believe he'd actually try to *do* it. Or that Yulikova would admit suspecting all of this, especially to me.

"He has a lot of allies in Washington," she continues. "And he's been putting more in place. The state police are behind him, and so are more than a few folks at Fort Dix. We know he's been having meetings."

I think of Lila pressing her hands to the bars as Sam, Daneca, and I sat in the jail cell after the protest rally in Newark. No phone calls, no charges, no nothing. And then I think of the other people, the ones that were reported as held there for days.

I look over at Agent Jones. He doesn't look like he much cares either way, but he should. Even if he doesn't want to admit it, the fact that he's working in this division of the federal government means that he's a worker too. If Patton is really that crazy, a badge isn't going to save Jones.

I nod, encouraging her to go on.

She does. "I've been in conference with my superiors, and we agree that we have to stop him before he does something even worse. There are rumors of murders—rumors of terrible things, but no hard evidence. If we arrest him now, he could use that to his political advantage. A very public trial, where we don't have enough evidence, would play right into his hands."

I nod again.

"I've gotten permission for a small operation to remove Patton from power. But I need your help, Cassel. I can promise that your safety will be our first priority. You can abort the mission at any time if you don't feel completely secure. We'll handle all the planning and manage the risks."

"What are we talking about here?" I ask.

"We want you to transform Patton." She looks at me with her kind eyes, as if any answer I give will be the right one. She takes a sip of her coffee.

"Oh," I say. For a moment I'm so shocked that her words just ring in my head.

But then I realize that of course this moment was going to come. Being a transformation worker is the most valuable thing about me—the reason they want me in the program, the reason that they let me get away with murder.

They let me get away with murder so that I can murder for them.

"Sorry," I say. "I'm just surprised."

"It's a lot to take in," Yulikova says. "I know that you're uncomfortable with what you can do."

Agent Jones snorts, and she gives him a dark look.

When she turns back to me, there is still some of that anger in her eyes. "And I know what I'm asking isn't easy. But we need for there to be no trace of him. This can't seem to be an assassination."

"Even though it is?" I say.

That seems to take her by surprise. "We'd like you to change him into a living creature. I understand that it would be possible for him to survive like that indefinitely. He won't be dead. He'll just be *contained*."

Being caged, trapped like Lila was in her cat body, forever, seems as awful as death. But maybe it will let Yulikova sleep better at night.

She leans toward me. "I have gotten approval to make you an offer, in light of the huge service you'll be doing for us. We'll make the charges against your mother go away."

Jones brings his hand down hard on the arm of his chair. "You're making *another* deal with him? That family of his is slipperier than black ice on a highway."

"Do I have to ask you to wait outside?" Her voice is steely. "This is a dangerous operation, and he isn't even a part of the program yet. He's seventeen years old, Ed. Let him have one less thing to worry about."

Agent Jones looks from me to her and then away from both of us. "Fine," he says.

"Here at the LMD we often say that heroes are the people who dirty their hands so other hands get to stay clean. We're terrible so you don't have to be. But in this case you do have to be—or at least we're asking you to be."

"What happens if I don't agree—I mean to my mother?"

Yulikova picks off a piece of her muffin. "I don't know. I'm authorized by my boss to offer you this, but he's the one who would be making it happen. I suppose your mother could continue to evade justice or she could be picked up and extradited—if she's out of the state. I'd be afraid for her safety if she were locked up in any place Patton could get to."

I am suddenly gripped with certainty that Yulikova knows exactly where my mother is.

They're manipulating me. Yulikova letting me see how sick she is, saying nice things, making us sit down to lunch. Jones being such an asshole. It's classic good cop–bad cop. Which isn't to say that it's not working.

Patton's a bad guy and he's out to get my mother. I want him stopped and I want her safe. I'm very tempted by anything that lets me have both. Plus there's the fact that I'm backed into a corner. Mom needs a pardon.

And if I don't trust my own instincts toward right and wrong, I have to trust someone's. That's why I wanted to join the government, right? So that if I was going to do bad things, it would at least be in the service of good people.

I am a weapon. And I have put myself in Yulikova's hands.

Now I have to let myself be used as she sees fit.

I take a deep breath. "Sure. I can do that. I can work him."

"Cassel," says Yulikova. "I want you to understand that you can decline this job. You can tell us no."

But I can't. She's seen to it that I really can't.

Jones doesn't say a single snarky thing.

"I understand." I nod to show that I really do. "I understand, and I'm telling you yes."

"This is going to be a very discreet mission," Yulikova says. "A very small team operating with the tacit support of my superiors—providing we can pull it off. Otherwise, they will disavow all knowledge. I will be running this—any questions should come directly to me. No one else needs to know. I trust I can count on both of your discretion."

"You mean if something goes wrong, it could be our careers," Jones says.

Yulikova takes another sip of her coffee. "Cassel isn't the only one with a choice. You don't need to be a part of this."

Agent Jones doesn't say anything. I wonder if it will hurt his career either way. I wonder if he even knows he's playing the bad cop. I kind of suspect he doesn't.

I eat my sandwich. A nurse pokes her head in and says that she'll be bringing medicine in about ten minutes. Yulikova stands and starts gathering empty cups and tossing them into the wastebasket.

"I can do that," I say, getting up and grabbing a sandwich wrapper.

She puts her gloved hands on my arms and looks into my eyes, like she's trying to see the answer to a question she hasn't asked. "It's okay to change your mind, Cassel. At any time."

"I'm not going to change my mind," I tell her.

Her fingers tighten. "I believe you. I do. I'll be in touch in a few days with more details."

"Let's not tire her out," Jones says, frowning. "We should go."

I feel bad leaving Yulikova with the mess, but now they're both looking at me with the expectation that our interview is over. Jones walks to the door, and I follow him.

"Just for the record, I don't like any of this," Agent Jones says, his gloved hand on the door frame.

She nods once, like she's acknowledging his words, but the ghost of a smile is on her mouth.

Their exchange makes me even more sure I made the right choice. If Agent Jones approved of what I was doing, that's when I'd be worried.

I FOLLOW AGENT JONES

through the corridors of the hospital, but when I get to the parking lot, I'm done. The guy hates me. There's no way I'm letting him take me back to the old house. I don't want him talking to my grandfather again.

"I'm going to take off," I tell him. "See you around."

Agent Jones looks at me incredulously, then snorts. "You planning on walking?"

"I'll call a friend."

"Get in the car," he growls, switching from amused to impatient in a single breath. There is something in his face that makes me even more certain that going with him is a bad idea.

"Make me," I say. "I dare you."

When he doesn't actually lunge at me, I take out my cell phone and call Barron.

"Little brother," he drawls, picking up on the first ring. "You *need* to leave school and join up with the Feds. Last night we raided a worker strip club, and I was knee-deep in naughty gloves. Did you know no one uses Velcro on tear-away gloves anymore? The new kind are held together by magnets so they just *slide* right off the hand—"

"That's, uh, interesting," I say. "But what I really need right now is a ride."

"Where are you?" he asks.

I tell him the name of the hospital while Agent Jones watches me with a cold, furious look in his eyes. We don't like each other. He should be *relieved* that he isn't getting forced to spend any more time with me, but he's obviously brimming with rage instead. The more I study his expression, the more unnerved I am. He's not looking at me the way an adult looks at an obnoxious kid. He's studying me the way a man studies his opponent.

———————

I sit on the cold stoop and wait, letting the chill seep into my skin. It takes a while for Barron to show—long enough that I start wondering if I should call someone else. But just as I decide that I'm going to have to go inside and get something warm to drink or con a blanket from one of the nurses, Barron pulls up in a red Ferrari. He rolls down a dark tinted window and flashes me a grin.

"You stole that," I say.

"Even better. This beautiful car was seized during a raid. Can you believe it? There's a whole warehouse of stuff that gets confiscated and then just sits around until the paperwork is sorted out. Best warehouse ever. Come on, get in."

I don't need to be told twice.

Barron is looking very pleased with himself. "Not only did I manage to get myself some new wheels, but I filled up the trunk with a bunch of tins of caviar and bottles of Krug that were just sitting around. Oh, and some cell phones I am pretty sure I can resell. Altogether a pretty good Saturday. How about yourself?"

I roll my eyes, but I'm already relaxing in the warmth of the heater, leaning back against the seat. "I've got to tell you some stuff. Can we go somewhere?"

"Anywhere you like, kid," Barron says.

Despite his extravagant offer, we wind up getting takeout Chinese and heading to his place in Trenton. He's fixed it up some, replacing the broken windows he'd previously just covered in cardboard. He even bought some furniture. We sit on his new black leather sofa and put our feet up on the trunk he's using for a coffee table. He passes me the tub of lo mein.

On the surface his place looks more normal than it used to, but when I go to the cabinet to get a glass, I see the familiar pattern of sticky notes on the fridge, reminding him of his phone number, his address, his name. Whenever he changes someone's memories, blowback strips out some of his—and he can't be sure which ones will go. He could lose something small, like his memory of eating dinner the night before, or something big, like the memory of our father's funeral.

It makes you a different person, to not have a past. It eats away at who you are, until what's left is all construct, all artifice.

I'd like to believe that Barron has stopped working people, the way he promised he would, that all these little reminders are here because of habit or in case of an emergency—but I'm not an idiot. That warehouse wasn't unguarded. I'm sure someone had to be made to "remember" paperwork that let Barron load up a car with whatever he wanted and drive it out of a government building. And then that same person had to be made to forget.

When I come back to the living room, Barron is mixing a concoction of duck sauce and hot mustard on his plate. "So what's up?" he asks.

I explain about Mom and her failed attempt to sell Zacharov back his own diamond, and the long-standing affair she appears to have had with him.

Barron looks at me like he's considering accusing me of lying. "Mom and Zacharov?"

I shrug. "I know. It's weird, right? I'm trying really hard not to think about it."

"You mean about the part that if Zacharov and Mom got married, that would make you and Lila brother and sister?" He starts laughing, falling back on the cushions.

I chuck a handful of white rice at him. A few of the grains stick to his shirt. More stick to my glove.

He keeps on laughing.

"I'm going to go talk to the forger tomorrow. Some guy up in Paterson."

"Sure, we could do that," he says, still giggling a little.

"You want to come?"

"Of course." He opens the chicken with black bean sauce and dumps it over his mustard and duck sauce concoction. "She's my mother too."

"There's something else I should tell you," I say.

He pauses with his hand on a packet of soy.

"Yulikova asked me if I would be willing to do something. A job."

He goes back to pouring out the sauce and taking a first bite. "I thought you couldn't get put to work, since you haven't officially joined up."

"She wants me to take out Patton."

Barron's brows draw together. "*Take out?* As in transform him?"

"No," I say. "As in *take out to dinner*. She thinks we'd make a good couple."

"So you're going to kill him?" He regards me carefully. Then he mimes a gun with his fingers. "Boom?"

"She didn't tell me much about the plan, but—," I start.

He throws back his head and laughs. "You should have joined the Brennans if you were just going to become an assassin anyway. We could have made a lot of money."

"This is different," I say.

Barron laughs and laughs. Now that he's off again, there's no stopping him.

I stab at the lo mein with my plastic fork. "Shut up. It is different."

"Please at least tell me that you're going to get paid," he says when he manages to catch a breath.

"They said they'd get the charges against Mom dropped."

"Good." He nods. "Any cold hard cash going along with that?"

I hesitate, then have to admit, "I didn't ask."

"You have a skill. You can do something *no one else* can," Barron says. "Seriously. You know what's good about that? It's *valuable*. As in you can trade it for goods or services. Or *money*. Remember when I said it was wasted on you? I was so right."

I groan and shove rice into my mouth so that I don't decide to dump the whole carton over his head.

After we finish eating Barron calls Grandad. He tells a long and complicated series of lies about the questions the federal agents asked and how we weaseled out of answering all of them through our inherent charm and wit. Grandad cackles down the line.

When I get on, Grandad asks me if any of what Barron said was true.

"Some," I tell him.

He stays quiet.

"Okay, very little," I finally admit. "But everything's okay."

"Remember what I said. This is your mother's trouble, not yours. Not Barron's, either. Both of you need to stay out of it."

"Yeah," I say. "Is Sam still there? Can I talk to him?"

Grandad gives the phone to Sam, who still sounds groggy but not all that upset to be abandoned for most of the day and the rest of tonight.

"It's okay," he informs me. "Your grandfather is teaching me how to play poker."

If I know Grandad, that means what he'll really be teaching Sam is how to cheat.

Barron offers to let me take his bed, saying that he can sleep anywhere. I'm not sure if he's suggesting that there are beds all over town for him to slip into or just that he's not picky about sleeping on furniture, but I take the sofa so I don't have to find out.

He digs up a couple of blankets that used to be at the old house. They smell like home, a somewhat dusty stale odor that's not entirely pleasant but that I inhale greedily. It reminds me of being a kid, of being safe, of sleeping late on Sundays and watching cartoons in my pajamas.

I forget where I am and try to straighten out my legs. My feet kick against the armrest, and I remember that I'm not a kid anymore.

I'm too tall to be comfortable, but I curl on the couch and manage to doze off eventually.

I wake up to the sounds of Barron making coffee. He pushes a box of cereal at me. He's terrible in the morning. It takes him three cups of coffee before he can reliably put together a whole sentence.

I take a shower. When I come out, he's wearing a dark

gray pin-striped suit with a white T-shirt under it. His wavy hair is gelled back, and he's got a new gold watch on his wrist. I wonder if that was in the FBI warehouse too. Either way, he looks like he made an impressive effort for a Sunday afternoon.

"What are you all dressed up for?"

Barron grins. "Clothes make the man. You want to borrow something clean?"

"I'll muck through," I tell him, pulling on my T-shirt from yesterday. "You look like a mobster, you know."

"That's another thing I'm good at that most trainees aren't," he says, getting out a comb and running it through his hair one last time. "No one would ever guess that I'm a federal agent."

By the time we're ready to leave, it's early afternoon. We get into Barron's ridiculous Ferrari and head upstate, toward Paterson.

"So how's Lila?" Barron asks once we're on the highway. "You still hung up on her?"

I give him a look. "Considering you locked her in a cage for several years, I guess she's okay. Comparatively speaking."

He shrugs, glancing in my direction with a sly look. "My choices were limited. Anton wanted her dead. And you surprised the hell out of us by transforming her into a living thing. After we got over the shock, it was a relief—although she made a terrible pet cat."

"She was *your girlfriend*," I say. "How could you have agreed to kill her?"

"Oh, come on," he says. "We were never that serious about each other."

I slam my hand down on the dashboard. "Are you crazy?"

He grins. "You're the one who changed her into a cat. And you were *in love* with her."

I look out the window. The highway is flanked by towering soundproofing walls, vines snaking through the gaps. "Maybe you made me forget almost everything, but I know I wanted to save her back then. And I almost did."

His gloved hand touches my shoulder unexpectedly. "I'm sorry," he says. "I really did start messing with your memories because Mom said it would be better for you not to know what you were. Then, when we got the idea to go into the killing business, I guess I thought that so long as you didn't remember, nothing we made you do counted."

I have no idea what to say in return. I settle for not saying anything at all. Instead I lean my cheek against the cool glass of the window. I look at the stretch of asphalt highway snaking in front of us, and I wonder what it would be like to leave all of this behind. No Feds. No brother. No Lila. No Mom. No mob. With just a little magic I could change my face. I could walk out of my life entirely.

Just a few fake documents and I'd be in Paris. Or Prague. Or Bangkok.

There I wouldn't have to try to be good. There I could lie and cheat and steal. I wouldn't really be me so it wouldn't really count.

Change my identity. Change my name. Let Barron take care of Mom.

Next year Sam and Daneca are going to be away at college. Lila will be doing whatever bootleg business her father tells her to do. And where will I be? Killing people for Yulikova. Everything's arranged, all for the best, and as bleak as a desert road.

Barron knocks on the side of my head. "Hey, anyone in there? You've been quiet for, like, fifteen minutes. You don't have to tell me that you forgive me or anything like that— but you could say *something*. 'Good talk.' 'Shut up.' Whatever."

I rub my face. "You want me to say something? Okay. Sometimes I think I am what you made me. And sometimes I don't know who I am at all. And either way I'm not happy."

He swallows. "Okay . . ."

I take a deep breath. "But if you want forgiveness, fine. You've got it. I'm not mad. Not anymore. Not at you."

"Yeah, *right*. You're pissed off at someone," he says. "Any idiot can see that."

"I'm just angry," I say. "Eventually it will burn off of me or something. It has to."

"You know, this might be your cue to say that you're sorry about forcing me to go into this whole federal agent training program—"

"You never had it so good," I say.

"But you didn't know that," he says. "I could be miserable right now, and it would be all your fault. And then you'd feel bad. Then you'd be sorry."

"Then I might. Now I'm not," I say. "Oh, and—good talk."

Really, it *was* a pretty good talk. About the best I could

expect from my sociopathic amnesiac jerk of an older brother.

We park on the street. Paterson is an odd collection of old buildings and bright awnings with neon signs advertising cheap cell phones, tarot card readings, and beauty salons.

I get out and feed a few quarters into the meter.

Barron's phone chirps. He takes it from his pocket and looks at the screen.

I raise my eyebrows, but he just shakes his head, like it's nothing important. His gloved fingers tap the keys. He looks up. "Lead on, Cassel."

I head toward the address of Central Fine Jewelry. It looks like all the other stores on the street—dirty and poorly lit. The front window is filled with a variety of hoop earrings and long chains. A sign in one corner reads WE'LL PAY CASH FOR YOUR GOLD TODAY. There's nothing special about it, nothing that makes the place stand out as the location of a master forger.

Barron pushes open the door. A bell rings as we walk in, and a man behind the counter looks up. He's short and balding, with huge horn-rimmed glasses and a jeweler's loupe on a long chain around his neck. He's dressed tidily in a black button-up shirt. Fat rings sparkle over his gloves on each of his fingers.

"Are you Bob?" I say, walking up to the counter.

"Who's asking?" he says.

"I'm Cassel Sharpe," I tell him. "This is my brother Barron. You knew our father. I don't know if you remember him, but—"

He breaks into a huge grin. "Look at you! All grown up. I saw pictures of the three of you Sharpe boys in your daddy's wallet, God rest his soul." He claps me on the shoulder. "Getting into the business? Whatever it is you need, Bob can make it."

I glance around the shop. A woman and her daughter are looking at a case of crosses. They don't seem to be paying attention to us, but we are probably the kind of people you try a little harder not to notice.

I lower my voice. "We want to talk to you about a custom piece you already made—for our mother. Can we go somewhere in the back?"

"Sure, sure. Come into my office."

We follow him past a curtain made from a blanket stapled to the top of a plastic door frame. The office is a mess, with a computer in the center of a sagging wooden rolltop desk, the surface covered completely in papers. One of the drawers is open, and inside are watch parts and tiny glassine bags with stones in them.

I pick up an envelope. The name on it is Robert Peck. Bob.

"We want to know about the Resurrection Diamond," Barron says.

"Whoa." Bob holds up his hands. "I don't know how you heard anything about that, but—"

"We saw the fake you made," I say. "Now we want to know about the real thing. We need to know what happened to it. Did you sell it?"

Barron walks intimidatingly close to Bob. "You know, I work memories. Maybe I could help you recall something."

"Look," Bob says, his voice quavering slightly, rising a little too high. "I don't know what's made the two of you take this unfriendly tone with me. I was a good friend to your father. And I never told nobody that I'd copied the Resurrection Diamond—that I knew who'd stolen it. How many people would do that, huh, when there was so much money on the line? If you think I know where your father kept it or if he sold it, I don't. We were close, but not close like that. All I did was make the fakes."

"Wait. I thought you made the stone for my *mother*," I say. "And what do you mean, *fakes*? How many?"

"Two. That's what your dad asked for. And there was no way I switched anything. He didn't let me keep the original diamond for longer than it took to take the measurements and some photographs. He was no fool, you know. You think he'd let something that valuable out of his sight?"

I exchange a look with Barron. Dad was a lot of things, but he wasn't lazy about a con.

"So what happened?" I ask.

Bob takes a few steps away from us and opens a drawer in his desk, pulls out a bottle of bourbon. He screws off the cap and takes a long pull.

Then he shakes his head, like he's trying to shake off the burn in his throat.

"Nothing," he says finally. "Your father came in here with that damn stone. Said he needed the two copies."

I frown. "Why two?"

"How the hell should I know? One fake I set on the gold tie pin where the original had been. The other I put in a ring. But the original, the real one? I kept that loose, just the way your father wanted it."

"Are they good fakes?" Barron asks.

Bob shakes his head again. "Not the one on the pin. Phil came in here, wanting it fast, you know? Within the day. But the second one, he gave me some more time. That was a fine piece of work. Now, are you two going to tell me what this is about?"

I glance at Barron. A muscle in his jaw is jumping, but I can't tell if he believes Bob or not. I'm trying to think, to play this thing through. So maybe Mom gives Dad the stone and says she needs a fake really fast, before Zacharov notices that the piece is gone. Dad goes straight to Bob, but he asks for *two* stones, because he already knows that he's going to steal the diamond for himself— maybe out of spite, since he discovered that Mom was screwing around with Zacharov? Anyway, Dad brings her one of the fakes, and she slips it back to Zacharov before he notices that it's gone. Then Dad tells her he has a present for her—a ring with the Resurrection Diamond set in it, which is actually the second fake. If that's what happened, the original could be anywhere. Dad could have sold it years ago.

But why put the diamond in a ring that Mom can't wear outside the house without drawing attention? That, I'm not sure about. Maybe he was so pissed off that he liked seeing it on her hand and knowing he'd gotten one over on her.

"What would something like that be worth on the black market?" I ask.

"The real thing?" Bob asks. "Depends if you really believe it'll keep you from getting killed. As a stone with historical value, sure, it's something, but the kind of people who buy rocks like that don't want something they can't show off. But if you believe— Well, what's the price on invulnerability?"

Barron gets a glint in his eye that tells me he's considering the question seriously rather than rhetorically, pricing the thing out in dollars and cents. "Millions," he says finally.

Bob pokes Barron's chest with his gloved finger. "Next time, before you come in here acting heavy, you get your story straight. I'm a businessman. I don't cheat the families, I don't cheat other workers, and I don't cheat my friends, no matter what your mother told you. Now, before you go, you better be buying something nice. Something expensive— you get me? Otherwise I'm going to tell a couple of my friends how rude you boys were to Bob."

We go out to the counter. Bob pulls out a couple of pieces that are in the right price range for our transgression. Barron picks out a diamond heart set in white gold for nearly a grand. I manage to seem convincingly broke— something that isn't hard, since it's true—and am allowed to buy a much cheaper ruby pendant.

"Girls like presents," Bob tells us as he lets us out of the store, adjusting his glasses. "You want to be a charming guy like me, you got to shower your girl with gifts. Give my best to your mother, boys. She looks good on the news. That woman always knew how to take care of herself!"

He winks, and I'm ready to slug him, but Barron grabs my arm. "Come on. I don't want to have to buy the matching earrings."

We march back to the car. Our first mission together, and it was pretty much a bust. I rest my head against the frame while Barron takes out the keys.

"Well, that was . . . interesting," he says, unlocking the doors with a click. "For a dead end."

I get in, sliding into the passenger seat with a groan. "How the hell are we going to find this thing? The stone's gone. There's just no way."

He nods. "Maybe we should try to think if there's something else we can give Zacharov?"

"There's me," I say. "I could—"

The car starts, and he pulls away from the curb, veering into traffic like he's daring the other cars to a game of chicken. "Nah. You're already mortgaged to the hilt. But hey, maybe we're looking at this the wrong way. Mom has a nice apartment to stay in and an older gentleman to keep her company. Three square meals. Patton can't get to her. What exactly are we trying to save her from? Given what we know about her history with Zacharov, she might even be getting—"

I hold up a hand to ward off whatever he's about to say next. "LALALA. I can't hear you."

He laughs. "I'm just figuring that *maybe* she *might* be better off unsaved—safer, happier—which is excellent, because, as you said, our chances of finding that stone are pretty much zero."

I tip my head back against the seat, looking up at the Ferrari's tinted sunroof. "Just drop me at Wallingford."

He pulls out his phone and texts while he drives, making him nearly pull into another lane by accident. A moment later his phone buzzes and he glances at the screen. "Yeah, okay. That's perfect, then."

"What do you mean?"

"Hot date," he says, grinning. "I need you gone."

"I knew it," I say. "I so knew you weren't dressed up like that to go to Paterson with me and meet Bob."

Barron takes his hands away from the wheel to straighten his lapels and to tuck his phone into the inside pocket of his jacket. "I think Bob appreciated my outfit. He made me buy the more expensive pendant. You might think that was to my disadvantage, but I accept that status comes with a price."

"Not usually so immediately." I shake my head. "You better not be hitting on federal agent ladies. They'll arrest you."

His grin widens. "I like handcuffs."

I groan. "There is something seriously wrong with you."

"Nothing that a night being worked over by a hot representative of justice couldn't fix."

I study the clouds through the sunroof. I think I see one in the shape of a bazooka. "Hey, so do you think Dad lied to Mom about the second fake diamond? Or do you think Mom lied to us?"

"To *you*," he says. "She didn't even try to tell me." The smile has curled off his mouth.

"Yeah." I sigh. "Either way it's a hell of a dead end."

Barron nods. His foot presses the accelerator harder, and he veers into the fast lane. I don't protest. At least he has something good to race back to.

Barron drops me in front of Strong House. I slide out of the car and stretch. Then I yawn slowly. It's just barely night-fall. The last of the sun is still blazing on the horizon, making all the buildings look like they're catching fire.

"Thanks for the ride," I say.

"Okay, well," he says, his voice full of impatience. "Sorry, but you've gotta scram. Call me when you talk to Mom—so long as it's not tonight."

I smirk and slam the car door. "Have fun on your date."

"*Byeee,*" he says, and waves. As I head toward the dorm, I glance back at the parking lot. I keep expecting a sweep of headlights as he pulls out, but the Ferrari's still there. He's only rolled it forward a little. Is he seriously waiting until I get to the door of my dorm, like I'm a little kid who can't be trusted to make it home after dark? Am I in some danger I don't know about? I can't think of a good reason for him to keep idling near the curb when he so obviously wanted to get going.

I walk into the building, my scheming brain still rear-ranging the puzzle pieces. It takes me until I get to the hallway, fishing for my dorm key in the back pocket of my jeans, before I stop abruptly.

He wanted *me* to get going.

I run into the common room, ignoring Chaiyawat

Terweil's cry of protest when I jump over the cords connecting his PlayStation to the television. Then I drop to
my knees in front of the window. Peering out, half-hidden
behind a dusty curtain, I watch as a figure steps out of
shadow, walks to where Barron is waiting, and opens the
passenger side door.

She's not wearing her uniform, but I know her just
the same.

Daneca.

Purple-tipped braids glowing under the streetlight.
Heels a lot higher than anything I've ever seen her in—
high enough for her to wobble as she bends down. There's
no reason on earth why she should glance back at the
Wallingford campus like she's afraid of someone seeing
her, no reason for her to be getting into my brother's car,
no reason for her to be dressed like that, no reason that
makes sense. No reason but one.

The boy she's been dating is my brother.

THERE IS NO WAY I CAN

tell Sam.

He's in our dorm room, still looking pretty hung over, sipping on a can of coconut water. "Hey," he says, rolling toward me on his cot. "Your grandfather is a madman, you know that? After we finished with the poker, he showed me a bunch of old photos. I thought they were going to be pictures of you as a kid, but no. They were vintage snapshots of burlesque ladies with no gloves. From back in the day."

I force a grin. I'm still thinking about Daneca and my brother, wondering how many times she's been out with Barron, wondering *why* she ever went out with him even once. It's hard to concentrate. "You looked at porn with my grandfather?"

"It wasn't porn! Your *grandmother* was one of the ladies."

Of course she was.

"The costumes were amazing," he says dreamily. "Feathers and masks and sets like you wouldn't believe. Crescent moon thrones and a massive rose with petals that swung like doors."

"You were looking at the *sets*?" Now I'm laughing for real.

"I didn't want to stare at the women. I wasn't sure which ones were your relatives! And your grandfather was *right there*!"

I laugh some more. Mom told me about theaters back then, with curtained balcony seating where curse workers could conduct business while the show provided a legitimate front. Then came the raids. Now no one risks that kind of setup. "Imagine you in a place like that. You would be agitating them to do zombie burlesque in no time."

"Untried market," he says. Then he taps his gloved finger against the side of his head. "Always thinking. That's me."

He doesn't look happy, but he doesn't look crushed and miserable, the way he did all last week. If he's still thinking about Daneca, at least she isn't all he can think about. But if he knew about Barron—if he knew that my brother was the one she was seeing—that would change.

I know that if I'm going to be a better person, that includes being less of a liar. But sometimes a lie of omission is what you need until the world starts being fair on its own.

When Lila finds someone else, I hope they all lie to me.

I wake up with the alarm on my phone vibrating against my skull. Yawning, I glance over at Sam. He's still asleep, his comforter half-kicked to the floor. I get up quietly, grab some clothes, and pad into the bathroom.

I set my alarm to wake me up silently, so I could go find Daneca before Sam's up and noticing little things like me yelling at his ex-girlfriend. Before Daneca has a chance to see my good-for-nothing brother again. Before this situation gets even worse.

I shower and shave—so fast that I cut my neck right along my jawline. I wash the blood away, splash with stinging aftershave, and hurry to the cafeteria.

I'm early, which is rare. To celebrate I get myself two cups of black coffee and a piece of toast covered in crisp bacon. By the time Daneca comes in, I am considering a third cup.

Her hair is pulled back by a sandalwood hair band, and she's got on brown herringbone stockings with brown leather Mary Janes. She looks like she always does, which for some reason surprises me. My idea of who she is has changed completely. She's been seeing my brother secretly for days—maybe weeks. All that stuff she said, all the questions she suddenly had for me, now it makes sense. But the answer tilts my world on its axis.

I wait until she gets through the line, and then follow her back to her table.

"What do you want?" she asks me, setting her tray down.

"He's not who you think he is," I say. "Barron. Whatever he told you, it's not true."

Surprise makes her take a step back. Gotcha. Then she recovers herself, looking even more furious than she did before. Nothing makes people angrier than getting caught.

Trust me, I know.

"Yeah, I saw you last night," I say. "You suck at sneaking."

"Only you would think I should be ashamed of that," she snaps.

I take a deep breath, trying to control my anger. It's not her fault she got tricked. "Okay, look. Say whatever you want about me. *Think* whatever you want about me. But my brother is a *compulsive liar*. He can't even help it. Half the time I don't think he remembers the real story, so he just fills in whatever he dreams up."

"He's *trying*," Daneca says. "That's more than I can say about you. He told me what you did. To Lila. To Philip. To him."

"Are you kidding me?" I ask her. "Did he tell you what *he* did to Lila?"

"Stay away from me, Cassel."

Girls say that to me a lot lately. I'm starting to think I'm not as charming as I like to believe.

"Just please tell me he didn't take off his gloves," I say. "No, actually, I'd rather you said he did. Because there is no way the Daneca that I know would fall for my brother's crooked smile and his crooked patter."

"He told me you'd say that. He practically told me the

exact words you'd use. And he wasn't lying about that, was he?"

I sigh. My brother can be a smart guy when he wants to be.

"Daneca, look. There are two ways he could know what I'd say. One, he knows me really well. And two, he knows the truth. The actual truth. Which is what I'm telling you—"

"*You're* going to tell me the truth? That's a joke." She turns her back on me, picks up her toast, and starts toward the door.

"*Daneca,*" I call after her.

My voice is loud enough that people look up from their breakfasts. I see Sam in the entranceway to the cafeteria. Daneca brushes by him on her way out. He glances at her. Then he rounds on me. There is so much anger in his face that I stand, frozen, until he swivels on his heel and walks back out.

I call Barron before I walk into statistics, but I get his voice mail. The class is a blur. As soon as I walk out the door, I try him again.

This time he picks up. The connection is bad, staticky. "How's my favorite and only living brother?" he asks.

"Stay away from her." My hand shakes with the urge to deck him. I will bet anything that she was the girl he was talking to when I ran down that death worker. I will bet anything that he loved getting away with talking to Daneca right in front of me. Texting her from the car. Bragging about his date.

He laughs. "Don't be so dramatic."

I remember what he said long ago when I accused him of dating Lila just because she was Zacharov's daughter. *Maybe I'm dating her just to mess with you.*

"Whatever you're trying to pull . . . ," I say, keeping my voice level. "Whatever it is, it's not going to work."

"Me and her—it bothers you, doesn't it? I saw the way it got under your skin when I talked to her, first at Zacharov's little fund-raiser—where you got Anton killed—and then at Philip's funeral. It bothered you, but it made her blush. Guess you shouldn't have brought her around if you wanted her for yourself."

"Daneca is my friend. That's all. I don't want her to get hurt. I don't want you to hurt her. And I know it's impossible for you to date a girl and not hurt her, so I want you to leave her alone."

"You're only trying to convince me because you already failed to convince her. Nice try, Cassel, but are you really betting on my backing down?" His voice is smug.

The problem with cell phones is that you can't slam them down into a cradle when you hang up. Your only option is to throw them, and if you do, they just skitter across the floor and crack their case. It's not satisfying at all.

I close my eyes and bend down to pick up the pieces.

There is only one person I can think of with the power to convince Daneca to stay away from Barron. Lila.

I text Lila that I will meet her anywhere she wants, that I need to tell her something, that it's not about her or me, that it's important. She doesn't respond. I don't see her in the halls or the lunch room.

Sam grabs my arm the minute I walk into the cafeteria, though, so even if she was, there wouldn't be much I could say to her. He's got bed-head and is looking at me with the gaze of someone who's hanging on to their sanity by a very thin thread.

"Why didn't you wake me up?" he demands in a tone that suggests false calm. "You snuck out. You wanted me not to see you with her."

"Whoa." I hold up both of my hands in a sign of sur-render. "You grunted and opened your eyes. I thought you were awake already." It's a lie, but hopefully a believable one. Lots of times I've said a few things, rolled over, and gone immediately back to sleep. It's just that Sam usually kicks my bed frame again before he heads out.

He blinks a couple times, rapidly, like he's restraining himself.

"What were you and Daneca arguing about this morn-ing?" he asks finally.

"I said she was being a jerk," I tell him, frowning. "That you didn't deserve the way she was treating you."

"Yeah?" He slouches a little. I feel like the lout that I am. He wants to believe me, I can tell. "You sure? It seemed worse. She looked really mad."

"I guess maybe I didn't say it in a nice way," I say.

He sighs, but the fury has gone out of him. "You shouldn't talk to her like that. She's your friend too."

"Not anymore," I say, and shrug.

Then he looks grateful and I feel even worse, because I sound like a loyal friend who is declaring how firmly I'm on his side, when actually she's the one who's done with me.

"Cassel," a girl's voice says from just behind us. I turn to find Mina Lange looking up at me. She smiles, but she looks tired, which makes me feel suddenly protective. "Can we talk about tomorrow?"

Sam glances at her, then back at me. Then he looks up toward heaven, like that's the only possible explanation for luck like mine with women.

I can guarantee that's not where it comes from.

"Uh," I say. "Sure. I've been considering things, and—" I'm improvising, since I honestly haven't thought much about Mina's problem since our last conversation. The weekend came and swept everything away with it.

"Not here," she says, interrupting me.

I jerk my head toward the door. "Sure. We'll go to the library. There won't be that many people there, and we can find a quiet place in the back."

"What's going on?" Sam asks.

"Ah," I say. "Sam, Mina. Mina, Sam."

"We have a film studies class together," Sam says. "I know who she is."

"I'm just helping her out with something." It occurs to me that this is a perfect opportunity to distract Sam from all things Daneca-related. "But you should come to the library with us. Be the Watson to my Sherlock, the Hawk to my Spenser, the Mouse to my Easy, the Bunter to my Wimsey."

Sam snorts. "The fat Sancho Panza to your delusional

Quixote." Then he looks at Mina and his neck colors, as if he has realized that he just made both of us sound pretty bad.

"I really don't think—," Mina starts.

"Sam is completely trustworthy, if overly modest," I say. "Anything you can tell me, you can tell him."

She gives him a suspicious once-over. "Okay. But it's happening tomorrow. We need to get the camera back before then or find some way to pay them or—"

"The *library*," I say, reminding her.

"Okay." Mina nods, looking relieved.

I grab a few pieces of fruit from the bowl near the card swipe and we cross the quad together. A few students are sitting at library tables, studying through lunch. I navigate through and head for the far back, picking a spot near the stacks marked SOCIETIES, SECRET, BENEVOLENT, ETC. and sit down on the carpet.

I pass out the apples and take a bite of mine. "Let's start by going over the facts of the case one more time. This will get Sam up to speed and help us see the whole thing with fresh eyes."

Sam is looking a bit bewildered, possibly because I am talking like we really are playing detective here.

Mina looks at Sam. "Someone's blackmailing me. I'm supposed to pay that person five thousand dollars. Which I don't have. And I'm supposed to give it to them tomorrow morning." Then she looks back at me. "Please tell me that you know what I should do, Cassel."

"What do they have on you?" Sam asks. "Did you cheat on a test or something?"

Mina hesitates.

"Pictures," I say. "The naughty kind."

She flashes me a hurt look.

"Hey," Sam says. "Nothing to be ashamed of. We have all taken them. I mean, not me personally, but Cassel's *grandmother*, you should really see—"

"Okay," I say. "The point is, she had them on a camera. Then the camera got stolen. Mina, the more I think about it, the more I think that someone on your hall must have done it. One of the girls. Maybe she broke in to steal a packet of hot chocolate, saw the camera, and took it. Then a week later she started flipping through the images, found the naked pictures, and during one long night of giggling and eating too much junk food, she and her friends dreamed up a funny prank."

"You said you would help me." This time when she looks at me, her eyes are wet. She isn't crying exactly, but tears cling to her lashes, making her look lush and terribly vulnerable. Her misery makes me doubt myself.

"I am trying to help you," I say. "Honestly, it fits. But look, tomorrow morning Sam and I are going to get up early, go out to the baseball field, and watch. There's no way whoever is setting you up like this is going to be able to resist seeing if you bought it."

"You're upsetting her," Sam says.

Mina turns to him. "He doesn't believe me."

I sigh. I do think she's hiding something, but since I don't know what, it's no help. Telling her that I don't entirely believe her won't be any help either. "Look, if the blackmailer shows to get the money, we'll know who it is."

"But what about the money?" Mina says. "I won't have it."

"Just bring a big enough bag that it looks possible for you to have the cash."

Mina looks disconsolately out the window and takes a shaky breath.

"It's going to be fine," I tell her, curling my gloved hand around her arm in what I hope is a sympathetic way. She looks tired.

The bell rings, loud enough to startle us. Mina jumps up and brushes off her skirt. When she tosses her hair, it moves like a wave. It moves the way hair does only in movies.

No real hair moves like that.

I take another look at her as she pushes a lock of it behind her ear. "You seem really nice," she tells Sam. "Thanks for trying to help."

There are no split ends, I realize. And while her bangs make it hard to see, the part on top of her head shows a color that's subtly different from the rest of her skin.

Sam nods, expression grave. "Anything I can do."

"We'll figure this out," I say.

She gives me one of those almost-smiles that some girls seem to be able to summon up, the kind where her lip trembles and she looks so vulnerable that you find yourself desperate for a way to turn it into a real smile. Her lashes are still wet from tears that never fell. I wonder what it would feel like to wipe those tears with my thumb. I imagine the softness of her cheek against my bare skin. Then she picks up a messenger bag covered in pictures of singing anthropomorphic strawberries and marches out of the library.

Her wig swings behind her.

—————

The rest of the day is a blur of hastily composed texts that don't get returned. Lila isn't in the common room of her building, and I had to promise Sharone Nagel a copy of my statistics homework to get her to look. Lila's car is not even in the lot. By the time I discover that she's not at dinner, I am practically crawling out of my skin with my desire to find her.

Daneca doesn't come to dinner either.

Sam at least is there, flipping through a catalog of masks, barely paying attention to the cooling mound of shepherd's pie piled on his plate. "So," he says, "are you going to tell me what this thing with Mina is really about?"

"Nothing to tell. We're going to save a maiden in distress like old-timey knights. I just wish I knew exactly what distress we were saving her from. The whole thing is fishy."

"You don't believe what she said about the pictures?" he asks, pausing on a page with a rubbery werewolf snout that is supposed to be attached with spirit gum.

"I don't know. All I'm sure of is that she's lying about *something*. But maybe it's nothing important. We all lie, right?"

That makes him snort. "So what's the plan, Sir Bonehead?"

"Pretty much what I said. We see who shows up to blackmail Mina or who shows up to laugh at how gullible she is."

I gaze across at where Mina is sitting with her friends, playing with a lock of her wig and drinking a diet soda. Even being nearly sure her hair isn't real, I wonder at it. It *looks* real, better than real, rippling down her back in a glossy sheet.

Was she sick? If so, it must have been long enough ago that no one at Wallingford remembers her absence from school, but not so long ago that her hair has grown back. Or I guess it could be something else. Maybe she just likes the convenience of not worrying about styling it in the morning.

I wonder what would make someone want to blackmail a girl like her. Anyone could tell that her family isn't flush if they just *looked*. Her watch is nice, but she always wears it. The leather band is worn. And her shoes are black ballet flats. Cute but cheap. It's not that she can't afford nice things. She has last year's cell phone and a two-year-old laptop covered in pink crystals. That's more than lots of people have. Plus she goes to Wallingford. It's just that she wouldn't be the person I'd target if I wanted to grift an easy five large. It has to be a prank.

Unless the blackmailer knows something I don't.

After dinner I go back out to the parking lot, but Lila's car still isn't there. I consider that maybe she and Daneca are together, since neither of them were at dinner. Maybe Daneca listened to what I said about Barron, no matter what she pretended. Maybe she even started to doubt him. If she ran into Lila, then maybe that's why Lila hasn't called me back. Daneca's house is close by; it would have been a small thing to go there for dinner. I imagine them in Daneca's kitchen, eating pizza and talking about what jerks those Sharpe boys are. I don't mind the thought. It is, in fact, a huge relief, compared to all the other possibilities. I have a couple of hours before in-room check and no better ideas, so I decide to drive by Daneca's house.

I know what you're thinking. You're thinking that it's ironic that Barron, who's wrong about so many things, is right about me being a stalker.

After parking on her leaf-lined street in Princeton, I walk down the block, past stately brick dwellings, each one with a manicured lawn, sculpted bushes, and a shining door knocker. Each yard is full of fall decorations—dried corn and gourds or planters with stacked pyramids of pumpkins, even the occasional leftover scarecrow.

As I walk up the path to her house, I realize that I figured wrong. Neither car is in the driveway, and I've just come this way for nothing.

I turn around and am about to walk away when the front door opens and the porch light flickers on.

"Hello?" Daneca's mother calls into the darkness. She's got a gloved hand up, shadowing her eyes. The porch light does the useless thing that porch lights often do, nearly blinding her and rendering me just a shadow.

I walk closer. "It's me, Mrs. Wasserman. Cassel. I didn't mean to scare you."

"Cassel?" she says, as though she's still nervous. Maybe more nervous. "Aren't you supposed to be at school?"

"I was looking for Daneca. We're seniors, so we can

go off campus as long as we're back on time. But, yeah, I should probably be at Wallingford. I'm going back there right now." I make a vague gesture in the direction of where I parked.

She's quiet for a long moment. Then she says, "I think you'd better come inside."

I walk over the worn marble threshold and step onto the gleaming wooden floors. I smell the remainder of whatever they had for dinner—something with tomato sauce—and hear the television from the living room. Daneca's father and her not-a-brother, Chris, are sitting on the couches, staring at the screen. Chris turns to glance in my direction as I pass, eyes bright with reflected light.

Mrs. Wasserman beckons me toward the kitchen, and I follow her.

"Do you want something to drink?" she asks, walking to the stove and filling the kettle. It reminds me uncomfortably of my mother in Zacharov's house.

"I'm okay."

She points to a chair. "Sit down at least."

"Thanks," I say, sitting awkwardly. "Look, I'm really sorry to bother you—"

"Why is it that you thought Daneca would be here instead of at Wallingford?"

I shake my head. "I don't know where she is. All I want to do is talk to her about her boyfriend. She's dating my brother. If you met him, you'd understand why I am—"

"I have met him," Mrs. Wasserman says. "He came to dinner."

"Oh," I say slowly, because I bet he told her something bad enough to explain her discomfort around me. "Barron came here? To dinner. Here?"

"I just want you to remember, Cassel, I know how hard things can be for worker kids. For every kid like Chris who finds a place to call home, there are lots of other kids who are kicked out onto the streets, taken in by crime families and then sold off to the rich—forced to endure continual blowback so that other people can line their pockets, or forced to become criminals themselves. And it must be even worse to be raised to believe you had to do those things. I don't know what you've done or what your brother's done, but—"

"What is it you think we did?"

She glances at my face, like she's searching for something. Finally she says, "Daneca called here earlier today. She said that you didn't approve of her going out with your brother. I know you're worried about Daneca. You're Sam's roommate, and I can see that you want to protect her. Maybe you want to protect both of them. But if you expect to be forgiven for your past mistakes, then you have to see that your brother deserves a second chance too."

"What the hell did he say about me?"

"That's not important," she says. "It's in the past. I am sure you want it to stay there."

I open my mouth and close it again. Because I want to defend myself, but it's true that I've done bad things. Things that I want to stay in the past. But I also want to know what he told her, because I really doubt he told her the whole story.

The problem with people like Mrs. Wasserman is exactly this. She's *kind*. She's *good*. She wants to help people, even people that she shouldn't. Like Barron. Like me. It's easy to take advantage of her optimism, her faith in how the world should work.

I should know. I've already done it.

When I look into Mrs. Wasserman's face, I know that she's a born mark for this particular kind of con.

IF YOU ARE A CRAZY

person who needs to have clandestine meetings, then, just like in real estate, what matters most is location, location, location.

You want to control the situation, so you better control the terrain. No surprises. No buildings, no trees, no shadowy corners where your enemies can hide. You want only those hidden spots that will be occupied by your people. But the place can't be *so* open that a passerby would have a clear sight line. Clandestine meetings have to stay clandestine.

The baseball field isn't a terrible choice. Far from other buildings. A nearby wooded area is the only place to hide, and it's not *that* close by. The time's good too. Six in the morning is too early for most students to be up, but there's no rule against it. Mina won't have to sneak out. And there's enough time for an exchange of goods before classes start. The blackmailer could get the money, take their sweet time stashing it, and still make it to breakfast.

On the other hand, six in the morning seems way too early for girls pulling a prank to be anywhere but in bed. I figure they'll be in their pajamas, leaning out of the windows of their dorm, jeering, when Mina returns from the baseball field after no one shows to the meeting. If I'm right, that's what's going to happen. Then the real negotiation starts, because I still have to somehow convince them to give up the camera and its contents. That's when we'll find out what's actually going on.

———————

Sam's alarm goes off like a siren at four thirty in the morning, an hour I hope I never see from this end again. I knock my phone onto the floor trying to turn it off, before I realize the sound is coming from a totally different part of the room.

"Get up," I say, and throw a pillow in his direction.

"Your plan sucks," Sam mumbles as he lurches out of bed and heads for the showers.

"Yeah," I say softly to myself. "Tell me one thing that doesn't suck right now."

It's too early for there to be any coffee. I stare dully at the empty pot in the common room, while Sam picks up a jar of instant grounds.

"Don't," I warn him.

He scoops up a heaping spoonful and, heedlessly, shoves it into his mouth. It crunches horribly. Then his eyes go wide.

"Dry," he croaks. "Tongue . . . shriveling."

I shake my head, picking up the jar. "It's dehydrated. You're supposed to add water. Good thing you're mostly made of water."

He tries to say something. Brown powder dusts his shirt.

"Also," I tell him, "that's decaf."

He runs to the sink to spit it out. I grin. There's nothing quite as funny as someone else's misery.

By the time we're outside, I feel a little more awake. It's so early that the hazy fog of morning is still settling over the grass. Dew has crystallized on the bare branches of trees and on piles of fallen leaves, turning them pale with frost.

We trek over to the baseball field, the dampness wetting our shoes. No one is there yet, which is the idea. You never want to be the last person to a clandestine meeting.

"Now what?" Sam asks me.

I point toward the woods. It's not ideal but will be close enough to see if anyone shows up, and after chasing down a death worker, I am confident that I can catch up to a student if I really have to.

The ground is frozen. The grass crunches as we sit. I get up to check from a few angles until I'm sure we're pretty well hidden.

Mina arrives about fifteen minutes later, just at the point when I think that Sam is about to fidget himself to death. She's clutching a paper bag nervously.

"Um, hello?" she calls from the edge of the trees.

"Here," I say. "Don't worry. Just go to the middle of the field—to the right, by first base—and make sure to turn so that we see you."

"Okay," Mina says, her voice shaking. "I'm sorry to have dragged you into this, but—"

"Not right now. Just go stand over there and wait."

Sam lets out a long-suffering sigh as she walks off. "She's *scared*."

"I know," I say. "I just didn't know how to— We don't have time for that."

"You must be the worst boyfriend in the whole world," Sam whispers.

"My track record isn't great," I whisper back.

Waiting is hard. It's boring, and the more bored you get, the more you want to close your eyes and take a cat-nap. Or pull out your phone and play a game on it. Or talk. Your muscles get stiff. Your skin gets that pins-and-needles warning that your foot is falling asleep. Maybe no one's coming. Maybe you were spotted. Maybe you made one of a million other miscalculations. All you want is an excuse to leave your post and get a cup of coffee or take a nap in your own bed. Time slows to a jagged crawl, like the passage of an ant along your spine.

Getting through it once makes it easier to believe that it can be gotten through again. Sam shifts uncomfortably. Mina looks pale and anguished, pacing back and forth. I alternate between watching her face for some sign that the blackmailer has arrived, and planning what I will say to Lila.

Daneca won't believe me. Please just tell her what Barron did.

I get as far as that, and my mind stalls. I can't picture what she says back. I can't imagine the expression on her face. I keep thinking of how she wouldn't look at me after I told her that I loved her. The way she wouldn't believe me. And then I remember her mouth on mine and the way she looked up at me when we were lying on the same grass I am looking at now, except the grass was warm and she was warm and she said my name like nothing else in the world mattered.

I press the tips of my gloved fingers against my eyes, to force away the images.

Sam jerks next to me, and I take away my hands slowly. Mina's posture has stiffened, and she's looking across the grass at someone we can't quite see. Adrenaline floods my veins, making my heart pound. The risk at this point is that we'll be too eager. We need to wait until the blackmailer has his back to us, and then we need to move as quietly as we can.

Mina turns slightly as the figure approaches her. She does exactly what I told her, except for a glance in our direction. Our gazes lock, and I try to silently communicate that she needs to *never look over here again*.

Then the figure comes into view.

I don't know exactly what I was picturing, but it wasn't a freshman, tall and gangly and so twitchy that I relax at the sight of him. Maybe he found the camera and decided he'd make some fast cash. Maybe he thinks blackmail is the high school equivalent of shoving a girl you like into a mud puddle. I don't know. All I do know is that he is playing way out of his league.

It seems cruel to jump him, so instead I pull the lamest trick ever. Making sure his back is to me, I stuff my hand into the pocket of my jacket, point my first and middle fingers so that I'm making the little-kid gun shape.

I cross the lawn quickly, fast enough that by the time he hears me coming, I am pretty close.

"Freeze," I tell him.

It's comical, the sound that the kid makes when he sees me. A scream so high pitched, I can't hear half of it. Even Mina looks rattled.

Sam walks up until he's looming over the freshman. "That's Alex DeCarlo," he says, looking down. "We're in chess club together. What's he doing here?"

I raise my fake pocket gun. "Yeah. What exactly did you want with five grand?"

"No," Alex says, his face gone bright red with misery. "I didn't want to—" He looks over at Mina and takes a nervous breath. "I don't know about the five thousand dollars. I was just supposed to bring the envelope that, uh, *he* gave me. Mina's my friend, and I would never—"

Lying, lying. Everyone is *lying*. I can hear it in their voices. I can tell in the way their expressions don't quite match the words, in a dozen small tells.

Well, I can lie too. "If you don't tell me the truth, I am going to *blow your brains out.*"

"I'm sorry," he squeaks. "I'm sorry. Mina, you didn't say

that he would have a gun." The kid looks like he's about to puke on his own shoes.

"Alex," she says sharply, like a warning.

Sam takes a step closer to her. "Hey, it's going to be—"

Alex takes a trembling breath. "She said that all I had to do was come here and tell you this story, but I don't want to die. Please don't shoot. I won't tell anyone—"

"Mina?" I say incredulously. Dropping the pretense of the gun, I take my hand out of my pocket and snatch the envelope out of Alex's hand. "Let me see that."

"Hey!" says Alex. And then, as I start ripping open the package, he says, "Wait. That wasn't real? You don't have a gun?"

"Oh, he has a gun all right," Sam says.

"Don't!" Mina says. She reaches out to snatch the package from me. "Please."

I give her a dark look. There are printed-out pictures inside the envelope, not negatives or a SIM card or a missing camera.

But it's too late. I'm already looking.

There are three pictures, Mina standing in profile in all of the shots, her long black wig spilling over her shoulders. She's not naked. In fact, she's wearing her Wallingford uniform. The only thing naked about her is her right hand.

Her bare fingers touch the collarbone of the man beside her, Dean Wharton. His white dress shirt is open at the neck. His eyes are closed, perhaps with dread or with pleasure.

I let the photos fall. They scatter on the ground like dead leaves.

"You're ruining everything," Mina says, her voice almost feral. "I did this to make you believe me. I had to convince you."

Sam reaches down and picks up one of the photos. He stares at it, probably, like me, puzzling through what it could mean.

I roll my eyes. "Let me get this straight. You lied to us so that we'd believe you?"

"If you knew what was happening from the start, if you knew a dean was involved, you wouldn't have agreed to help me." Mina looks from me to Sam to Alex, like she's trying to figure out which one of us might still be vulnerable to her pleading. Her eyes are welling with tears.

"I guess we'll never know," I tell her.

"Please," she says. "You can see why I didn't want to— you can see why I was afraid."

"I have no idea," I say. "You've lied so much that I have no goddamn idea why you would be afraid."

"Please," she says tragically. Despite myself there is a part of me that really feels bad for her. I've been where she is, trying to manipulate people because I was too afraid to do anything else. Too convinced that they would never help me if I didn't con that help out of them.

"Liars don't get the benefit of being trusted twice," I tell her, trying to keep my voice firm.

She covers her face with one slender gloved hand. "You hate me now, I bet. You hate me."

"No," I say, relenting with a sigh. "Of course not. Just, this time, let's have the whole story okay?"

She nods quickly, wiping her eyes. "I promise. I'll tell you everything."

"You can start with your hair," I say.

She touches it self-consciously, gloved fingers threading through the black mass. "What?"

I lean forward and give a lock of it a hard tug. Her whole hairline slips to one side, and she gasps, her hands flying to try to correct it.

Alex gasps too.

"That's a wig?" Sam says, not really asking, but in that way when you haven't gotten your head around something yet.

She stumbles away from me, her face red. "I asked you to help me. All I wanted was your help!" Her voice is ragged and guttural. She sobs suddenly, and this time I am sure her reaction is entirely real. Her nose starts to run. "I just wanted—"

She turns and legs it back toward the dorms.

"Mina!" I call after her, but she doesn't turn.

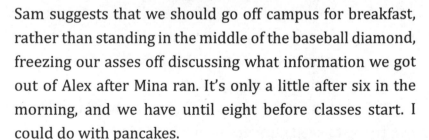

Sam suggests that we should go off campus for breakfast, rather than standing in the middle of the baseball diamond, freezing our asses off discussing what information we got out of Alex after Mina ran. It's only a little after six in the morning, and we have until eight before classes start. I could do with pancakes.

I get into the passenger side of Sam's hearse. I lean back against the headrest and close my eyes. It's just for a moment, but the next thing I know Sam is shaking me awake. We're parked in back of the Bluebird Diner.

"Get up," Sam says. "No one gets to sleep in my car unless they're already dead."

I yawn and scramble out. "Sorry."

I wonder if this morning was any kind of useful training for being a federal agent. After I graduate from Wallingford in the spring and enroll in the official training program with Yulikova, I'll learn how to catch real blackmailers. Blackmailers who aren't like Alex DeCarlo and don't believe I'm holding a real gun when I push two fingers against my jacket pocket.

Blackmailers who are actually blackmailing someone.

We go inside. A waitress who has got to be at least seventy, her cheeks rouged like a doll's, seats us and passes out menus. Sam orders us a round of coffee.

"Refills are free," the waitress tells us with a frown, like she's hoping we're not the kind of people who ask for endless refills. I am already sure we are exactly those people.

With a sigh Sam opens his menu and starts ordering food.

A few minutes later I am drinking my third cup of coffee and poking at a stack of silver dollar pancakes. Sam spreads cream cheese on half a bagel and tops it with salmon and capers.

"I should have spotted that wig," he says, pointing the dull knife toward his chest. "I'm the special effects guy. I should have noticed."

I shake my head. "Nah. I don't even know how I noticed. And besides, I have no idea what it means. Why do girls wear wigs, Sam?"

He shrugs and finishes off another cup of coffee. "My gran wears them to keep her head warm. Think it's that?"

I grin. "Maybe. Who knows, right? I mean, you'd think we could find out if she was being treated for a serious illness. She'd miss class."

"Doesn't hair fall out from stress? Maybe all this lying has really gotten to Mina. She's not the pro that you are."

I smirk. "Or sometimes people have a condition where they pull out all their hair. I saw it on some late-night reality TV show. They eat their follicles too. And they can get this giant deadly hair ball called a bezoar."

"Trichotillomania," he says, clearly proud to have summoned that word from somewhere. Then he pauses. "Or it could be blowback."

I guess we were both thinking it. "You mean those could be photos of Mina working Dean Wharton? If that's true, the first question is, who took them? And then the other question is, why give them to us? And the most important question is, if she's working him, what's she *doing* to him?"

"'Why give them to us?' But she didn't. You grabbed them out of Alex's hands," Sam says, raising his cup, signaling to the waitress that we need another round of free refills. "There's no way she wanted us to see the photos."

"Nah. She must have," I say. "Or why even send Alex with them? And why take them in the first place? I think she got upset because we saw the pictures without hearing what she wanted us to hear."

"Wait. You think she *took* the pictures of herself? So

there's *no* blackmailer?" Sam is staring at me like he's waiting for me to tell him that Mina is a robot from the future come to doom our world.

"I think she's the blackmailer," I say.

After Mina left, we got Alex to explain the story he was supposed to give. Mina told him to say that the blackmailer was Dr. Stewart and that Stewart wanted five grand or he was going to ruin Wharton's career and Mina's reputation. Dr. Stewart was sending word through Alex for Mina to get the money and bring it to him. Or else.

I had Stewart last year. He's a hard-ass. The kind of teacher who seems delighted when you fail a quiz. I always figured him as a guy who loved rules—and who thought that if you didn't stick to the rules, then you deserved what you got.

Not exactly the criminal type.

There are several other problems with the story, besides the unlikely villain. One, involving Alex is just stupid. If Stewart was actually trying to cover his tracks by using Mina as a buffer between his identity and Wharton, then there's no way that he would be stupid enough to enlist a student with nothing to lose by telling everyone.

"I don't get it," Sam says.

"Neither do I," I say. "Not really. Is she a scholarship student?"

He shrugs. "Could be."

"We need to know if she's doing something to Wharton or for Wharton. Is he paying her, or is she making him—I don't know—do something that benefits her?"

"He's paying her," Sam says. "Because if he wasn't the one who was paying, then she wouldn't want there to be any documentation of what's going on, right? She wouldn't let us see the photos. Wouldn't have given them to Alex. Wouldn't rock the boat. If you're right about that part, then Wharton's hiring Mina."

I take out one of the photos and set it down in the center of the table. Sam moves mugs and plates so there's room.

We stare at Mina's bare fingers and the way that Wharton's head is turned away, like he's ashamed of what he's doing. We stare at the composition—the figures not centered, like maybe the photos were taken without anyone to aim. There's ways to do that, even with a cell phone. It can be programmed to take pictures every couple of minutes. The only hard part for Mina would be making sure that Wharton was standing in the right spot.

"Do you like her?" Sam asks.

I look up at him sharply. "What?"

"Nothing. Luck work, maybe. She could be a luck worker. He could have a gambling problem," Sam says.

"Or she could be a physical worker like Philip, although his hair didn't fall out." I try not to think about what Sam just asked me, but now I can't help wondering if he's interested in Mina. There's something about a lady in distress— we all want to save her. And there's nothing like getting dumped to make anybody eager for a rebound.

"Maybe she's a physical worker curing Wharton's *baldness*," Sam says, and we both laugh. "But seriously, what do you think? What was Mina trying to do?"

I shrug. "I guess she wanted the money, right? So she must have thought we could help her get it? Maybe she thought we'd find some way to squeeze Stewart for it or help her blackmail Wharton and blame Stewart."

The waitress sets the bill at the end of the table and clears our plates. We pause the conversation until she goes.

I wonder where Lila is now.

"But what does Mina need five grand for?" Sam asks, fumbling for his wallet with one hand and reaching for his refilled mug with the other. I drag my attention back to the present.

"It's money. Could be for anything—maybe just to have it. But if Wharton's been paying her to get himself worked, then I guess it's possible the payments are coming to an end. All grifters dream of the big score."

"The big score?" Sam grins, teasing.

"Sure," I say. "The one that you can live on forever. The legendary one. The one that your name becomes synonymous with. I admit that five large isn't *that* large, but it's pretty big for high school. And if she thinks that she's not going to be making money off him regularly anymore, maybe there's no reason not to go for it."

I throw ten bucks down onto the table. He does the same, and we slide out of the booth.

"No reason except getting caught," Sam says.

I nod. "That's why the big score is a myth. A fairy tale. Because no one ever quits after a successful job. They get stupid and cocky and think they're invulnerable. They convince themselves to do just one more, just this last time.

And then the time after that, because if a job goes sideways, then you want to do another to get the taste of failure out of your mouth. And if it goes well, you do another to chase that feeling."

"Even you?" Sam asks.

I look over at him, surprised. "Not me," I say. "I'm already on the hook with the Feds."

"My grandfather took me fishing a couple of times," Sam says as he unlocks the hearse. "I wasn't very good at it. I always had trouble reeling them in. Maybe it'll be like that."

I want to say something funny back, but the words stick in my throat.

———————

Instead of going to class I head to Lila's dorm. I have some idea that I'm going to talk to her about Daneca, but it's become so jumbled up with a sheer, mad desire to see Lila that it doesn't make any real sense.

I thought I was getting better at this. I thought I was starting to make peace with being in love with a girl who despises me, but I don't think I'm so okay with it after all. Somewhere along the line I made a dark bargain with the universe without really being aware of it—a bargain that if I was allowed to see her, even if we never spoke, then I could live with that. And now a week without her has swallowed up all of my rational thinking.

I feel like a junkie, sick for my next fix and not sure if it will come.

Maybe she's eating breakfast in her room, I tell myself.

That's a reasonable thought, a normal one. I can just catch her before she leaves. I won't let her see how much it matters.

I race up the stairs of Gilbert House, past a couple of freshmen girls, who giggle.

"You're not supposed to be here," one says, mock-scolding. "This is the girls' dorm."

I pause and give her my best smile, my coconspirator smile. The one that I practice in front of the mirror. The one that's supposed to promise all kinds of evil delights. "Good thing I have you to cover for me."

She smiles back, her cheeks going pink.

At the top of the steps I catch the door to Lila's hall as Jill Pearson-White comes out. She's got her backpack thrown over one shoulder and an energy bar in her mouth. She barely pays attention to me, taking the stairs two at a time.

I cross the corridor, fast, because if Lila's hall mistress sees me, I am totally screwed. I try Lila's door, but it's locked. I don't have time for anything fancy. I pull out a bank card from my wallet and slide it down the seam. That trick has worked on my own door before, and I'm lucky, because it works now.

I expect Lila to be sitting on her bed, maybe lacing her shoes. Or pulling on a pair of gloves. Or printing out a paper at the last possible minute. But she's not.

For a moment I think I'm in the wrong room.

There are no posters on the walls. There is no book-case, no trunk, or vanity or illicit electric kettle. The bed has been stripped down to the mattress, and there's nothing else there.

She's gone.

The door swings shut behind me as I cross the empty room. Everything feels like it has slowed down, the edges a little dim. The awfulness of it, the loss of her, hits me in the gut. Gone. Gone and there's nothing I can do about it.

My eyes are drawn to the window, where light's streaming in, casting an odd shadow. There on the sill, resting against one of the panes of glass, is a single envelope.

My name is written on it in her handwriting. I wonder how long it's been sitting there. I imagine her loading all her stuff into boxes and carrying it down the stairs, Zacharov himself helping her, like all the other dads did. With two goons, guns tucked into their waistbands, helping him.

The thought should make me smile, but it doesn't.

I sink to the floor, the paper clutched to my chest. I rest my head on the bare wood. Somewhere in the distance I hear a bell ring.

I've got no reason to get up, so I don't.

WHEN I FINALLY OPEN

the letter, it makes me smile, despite everything. And for some reason, that makes it even more awful that she's gone.

4/ 8\6/5/3\ 9/6/8| 4/ 9\2\7// 6|6/ 4\6/6/3\ 2\8\
7//2/4|6/6/5/ - 9\3|5/5/ 4/6\ 6|6/8\ 4\6/6/3\
2\8\ 7//2\9/4/6|4\ 4\6/6/3\2|9/3| 3|4/8\4|3|7/
- 4/ 2\5/9\2\9/7// 5|6|3|9\ 9\4|2\8\ 4/ 9\2\7//
4\6/4/6|4\ 8\6/ 2|3| 9\4|3|6| 4/ 4\7/3|9\ 8|7\ -
4/ 2\5/9\2\9/7// 5|6|3|9\ 9\4|6/7//3| 7//4|6/3|7//
4/ 4|2\3\ 8\6/ 3/4/5/5/ - 2\6|3\ 4/ 6|3|8/3|7/
7//2\4/3\ 4/8\ 2|8|8\ 4/ 3|6|8/4/3|3\ 9/6/8| 3/6/7/
6|6/8\ 4|2\8/4/6|4\ 3|8/3|7/9/8\4|4/6|4\ 2\5/5/
7\5/2\6|6|3|3\ 6/8|8\ - 4/ 5|6|6/9\ 4/8\ 9\2\7//6|8\

2\5/9\2\9/7// 3|2\7//9/ - 7\3|6/7\5/3| 3\4/3\6|8\
8\7/3|2\8\ 9/6/8| 5/4/5|3| 9/6/8| 9\3|7/3|
4/6\7\6/7/8\2\6|8\ 2|8|8\ 9/6/8| 9\3|7/3| 3/7/3|3|

9/6/8| 7//8\4/5/5/ 2/2\6| 2|3| 2|8|8\ 9/6/8|7/3|
4\6/4/6|4\ 8\6/ 4|2\8/3| 8\6/ 8\7/9/ 4|2\7/3\3|7/
4/3/ 9/6/8| 9\2\6|8\ 8\6/ 7//8\2\9/ 8\4|2\8\ 9\2\9/

—5/4/5/2\

It's a code. One I recognize immediately, because Lila and I used it to leave notes for each other when we were kids. It's a simple one. Nobody with a real secret and any knowledge of cryptography would use this. You just take a phone and copy down the number that goes with each letter. Like *L* would become "5" and *A* would become "2." But since there's more than one letter for each number on a keypad, the code has a second symbol. A slash or straight line indicates the letter's position on the phone button, like this: \|/. So the final code for *L* is "5/" because *L* is to the far right on the key. And *A* is "2\" because *A* is to the far left. And if it's one of those numbers with four letters, then you add an extra slash, so that "9/" is *Y* and "9//" is *Z* and so on. It's time consuming to translate back, but easy, especially if there's a phone in front of you.

The existence of the letter—that she knew I would come here and find it, that she remembered our old code and believed I'd remember it too—makes my throat hurt. Nobody at Wallingford sees me the way I am, underneath everything. But she did. She does.

I smooth the paper out on the floor, find the receipt from the diner and a spare pen, and start translating:

> *I told you I was no good at school. Well, I'm not good at saying good-bye either. I always knew what I was going to be when I grew up. I always knew whose shoes I had to fill. And I never said it, but I envied you for not having everything all planned out. I know it wasn't always easy. People didn't treat you like you were important, but you were free.*
>
> *You still can be, but you're going to have to try harder if you want to stay that way.*
> *—Lila*

I'm tracing my fingers over the coded paper, thinking about how long it must have taken her, picturing her lying on her bed, making mark after laborious mark, when my phone rings.

I fumble to answer, startled, suddenly reminded that I shouldn't be on the girls' hall—and that if someone hears a sound, they're going to investigate. The actual students who bunk here are all in class.

"Hello?" I say, keeping my voice low.

"Cassel?" It's Yulikova. "Is that you?"

I get up and cross the room, lean my arm against the closet door frame. "Yeah, I'm here. Sorry."

"The operation is moving forward. We're going to pick you up next Wednesday, okay? I need you not to tell anyone, but it looks like you're going to be gone for a few days. You'll need a story. Family member in the hospital, something like that. And pack a bag."

"A few days? When is the actual event—"

"I'm sorry. I'm not authorized to tell you that, although obviously I wish I could."

"Can you at least tell me what the plan is?"

Yulikova laughs. "We will, Cassel. Of course. We want you to be as involved as possible. But not over the phone."

Obviously. Of course.

The language of someone who's trying very hard to convince me. Too hard.

"Okay," I say. "So next week?"

"We want you to be safe, so please, just act normal. Spend time with your friends and plan out how you're going to get away for a while without anyone noticing. Start laying the groundwork for whatever excuse you think would work best. And if you need us to come up with something—"

"No," I say, "I've got it."

They don't trust me. She needs me, but she doesn't trust me. Not completely. Not enough. I wonder if Jones said something to her, but I guess it doesn't matter.

I've got it, but I don't have to like it.

I make it through my afternoon classes and try not to think about the morning ones I missed. About how close I am to getting chucked out of Wallingford. About how little I care. I try not to think about Lila.

At track practice I run in circles.

As soon as I can make an excuse, I change into normal clothes and head to my car, skipping dinner. I feel oddly distant, my gloved hands turning the wheel. There is a kind of dark hope in my heart—the kind that I don't want to examine too carefully. It's fragile. Just looking at it straight on could crush it dead.

I drive to Lila's apartment building. I don't even bother trying to get into the lot with its closed gates and coded lock. I find a space a couple blocks down, hope I won't get towed, and walk into the building.

At the desk a gray-haired man sitting in front of a bunch of monitors asks for my identification. Once I hand over my driver's license, he buzzes the Zacharov apartment. He picks up a battered gray headset, waits a few moments, and then mispronounces my name into it.

I hear static and a voice on the other end, so distorted that I don't recognize it. The front desk guy nods once, then pulls off the headset and hands me back my license.

"Go right up," he says with his slight Eastern European accent.

The elevator is just as shiny and cold as I remember.

When the doors open, Zacharov is there, pacing the floor in suit pants and a half-buttoned white shirt, staring at the television.

"I'm going to rip his head off," he yells. "With my bare hands."

"Mr. Zacharov," I say. My voice echoes. "Sorry—I—the doorman told me I could come up."

He turns around. "You know what that prick has done now?"

"What?" I ask, not sure who we're talking about.

"Look." He points at the flat screen.

Patton is shaking hands with a gray-haired man that I don't know. I look at the screen, and underneath the image are the words "Patton Proposes Joint Venture to Test Government Employees at Summit with Governor Grant."

"That's the governor of New York. Do you know how much money I've donated to his reelection campaign? And now he's acting like that lunatic has anything worthwhile to say."

Don't worry about Patton. He'll be gone soon. That's what I want to say, but I can't. "Maybe Grant's just humoring him."

Zacharov turns toward me, seeming to actually be aware of me for the first time. He blinks. "Are you looking for your mother? She's resting."

"I was hoping I could talk to Lila."

He frowns at me for a drawn-out moment, then points toward the sweeping staircase that leads to a rounded archway on the second floor. I don't know if he remembers that I don't know my way around or if he just doesn't care.

I jog up the steps.

When I'm halfway there, Zacharov calls, "I heard that useless brother of yours is working for the Feds. That's not true, is it?"

I turn back, keeping my face carefully blank, a little puzzled. My heart is beating so fast that my chest hurts. "No," I say, and force a laugh. "Barron's no good with authority."

"Who is, right?" asks Zacharov, and laughs too. "Tell him

to keep his nose clean. I'd hate having to break his neck."

I lean against the railing. "You promised me—"

"Some betrayals even I can't afford, Cassel. He wouldn't just be turning his back on me. He'd be turning his back on you and your mother. He'd be putting you in danger. And Lila."

I nod numbly, but my heart is skipping along, like a stone on the surface of a lake right before it drops under. If he knew what I'd done, if he knew about Yulikova and the Licensed Minority Division, he would shoot me as soon as look at me. He would kill me six times over. But he *doesn't know*. At least I don't think he knows. His expression, the slight lift of one side of his mouth, tells me nothing.

I resume my walk up the steps, each footfall heavier than it was.

There's a hallway.

"Lila?" I call softly as I pass several glossy wooden doors with heavy metal trim on the hinges and knobs.

I open a door at random and see a bedroom, an empty one. It's too tidy to be anything but a guest room, which means that they have enough bedrooms to have my mother in one and at least another spare. The place is even bigger than I realized.

I knock on the next. No one answers, but down near the end another door opens. Lila steps into the hall.

"That's a linen closet," she says. "There's a washing machine and dryer in there."

"I bet you don't even need exact change to use them," I say, thinking of the dorms.

She grins, leaning against the door frame, looking like

she just got out of the shower. She's got on a white tank and black skinny jeans. Her feet are bare, her toenails painted silver. A few locks of pale wet hair stick to her cheek; a few more stick to her neck where her scar is.

"You got my letter," she says, walking closer. Her voice is soft. "Or maybe—"

I touch the pocket of my jacket self-consciously and give her a lopsided grin. "Took me a while to translate."

She pushes the hair out of her face. "You shouldn't have come. I put everything in the letter, so that we wouldn't have to—" She stops speaking, as if the rest of the sentence has deserted her. Despite the words, she doesn't sound angry. She takes another half step toward me. We're close enough that if she whispered I'd hear it.

I look at her, and I think of how it felt when I saw her in my bedroom in the old house, before I knew that she'd been cursed, when everything still seemed possible. I see the soft line of her mouth, and the clear brightness of her eyes, and I remember dreaming about those features when it still seemed like she could be mine.

She was the epic crush of my childhood. She was the tragedy that made me look inside myself and see my corrupt heart. She was my sin and my salvation, come back from the grave to change me forever. Again. Back then, when she sat on my bed and told me she loved me, I wanted her as much as I have ever wanted anything.

But that was before we'd scammed our way into a high-rise and laughed ourselves sick and talked in the funeral parlor the way I've never talked to anyone and might never talk to anyone again. That was before she stopped being a memory and started being the only person who made me feel like myself. That was before she hated me.

I wanted her then. I wanted her a lot. Now I barely want anything else.

I sway toward Lila, waiting for her to pull back, but she doesn't. My hands come up, gloved fingers closing around her upper arms, crushing her to me as my mouth catches hers. I'm braced for her to stop me, but her body folds against mine instead. Her lips are warm and soft, parting in a single sigh.

That's all it takes.

I push her back against the wall, kissing her the way I've never let myself. I want to swallow her up. I want her to feel my regret in the slide of my mouth and taste devotion on my tongue. She makes a sound that's half gasp and half a moan and pulls me closer against her. Her eyes close, and everything is teeth and breath and skin.

"We've got to—," she says against my mouth, her voice seeming to come from a great distance. "We've got to stop. We've got to—"

I stagger back.

The hallway seems very bright. Lila is still leaning against the wall, one hand against the plaster, like it's holding her. Her lips are red, her face flushed. She's looking at me with wide eyes.

I feel drunk. I am breathing so hard that I feel like I've been running.

"You should probably go," she says unsteadily.

I nod, agreeing, even though leaving is the last thing I want. "But I have to talk to you. It's about Daneca. That's why I came. I didn't mean—"

She gives me a nervous look. "Okay. Talk."

"She went out with my brother. She's *been* going out with him, I think."

"Barron?" She pushes off from the wall, paces the carpet.

"Remember when I thought that *you'd* told her about my being a transformation worker? Well, that was him. I don't know exactly what he told her, but he mixed up enough truth with the lies that I can't convince her to stay away from him. I can't convince her of anything."

"That's not possible. He's not the kind of boy she would like. Daneca's too smart for that."

"You went out with him," I say before I think better of it.

She gives me a scorching look. "I never said I was too smart." Her tone makes it clear that if she *were* smart, she wouldn't have just been up against the wall with my tongue in her mouth. "And I was a kid."

"Please," I say, "just talk to her."

Lila sighs. "I will. Of course I will. Not for your sake either. Daneca deserves better."

"She should have stayed with Sam."

"We all want things that aren't good for us." She shakes her head. "Or things that aren't what they seem."

"I don't," I say.

She laughs. "If you say so."

Down the hall a door opens, and we both jump. A man in jeans and a sweatshirt emerges, a stethoscope around his neck. He starts stripping off plastic gloves as he comes toward us.

"She's doing well," he says. "Rest is really the best thing for her now, but in another week I'd like to test her mobility with that arm. She's going to have to move it as soon as she's able to do so without pain."

Lila looks at me, her eyes slightly too wide. Like she's trying to gauge my reaction. Like there's something for me to be reacting about.

I take a chance. "Your patient is my mother," I say.

"Oh—I didn't realize. You can go see her now, of course." He reaches into his pocket and comes out with a card. He smiles, revealing a mouth full of crooked teeth. "Call me if you have any questions. Or if Shandra does. Gunshot wounds can be tricky, but this was a clean one. Through and through."

I take the card and shove it into my pocket as I start down the hallway. I'm walking fast enough that Lila would have to run to catch up.

"Cassel," she calls, but I don't even slow.

I push open the door. It's a regular guest room, like the other one. Big four-poster bed, but this one has my mother in it, propped up and watching a television that's on one of the dressers. She's got a bandage around her arm. Her face looks pale without her usual makeup. Her hair is a mess of curls. I have never seen her like this. She looks old and frail and nothing like my indomitable mother.

"I'll kill him," I say. "I'll murder Zacharov."

Shock distorts her features. "Cassel?" she says, fear in her voice.

"We're getting out of here." I come around to the side of the bed, ready to help her up. My eyes search the room for a weapon, any weapon. There's a heavy-looking brass cross over the bed. It's primitive-looking, with jagged sides.

"No," she says. "You don't understand. Calm down, sweetheart."

"You're kidding, right?"

The door opens and Lila's standing there, looking almost afraid. She pushes past me and gives my mother a quick glare.

"I'm sorry," she says, turning back to me. "I would have told you, but your mother made us promise not to. And she's okay. If she wasn't okay, I would have told you. No matter what. Honest, Cassel."

I look between them. It's hard to even imagine them being in the same room together. Maybe Lila's the one who shot her.

"Come here, baby," my mother says. "Sit on the bed."

I do. Lila stands by the wall.

"Ivan has been very good to me. This past Sunday he said I could go to church, so long as I went with some of his people. Isn't that nice?"

"You got shot in *church*?" I wonder which particular religion she's claiming to belong to, but I keep that question to myself.

"On the way back. If it wasn't for dear Lars, that would have been it. The car pulled up and I didn't even see it, but he did. I guess that's what he does, as a bodyguard and all. He pushed me and I fell, which made me mad when it was happening, but he saved my life. The first bullet hit me in the shoulder, but the rest missed and the car went screeching off." She sounds like she's reciting the plot of a particularly exciting episode of a soap opera, not telling me about something that actually happened to her.

"You think they were gunning for you? As in, you specifically? It wasn't some enemy of—" I glance at Lila. "You don't think it was a misunderstanding?"

"They had government plates," my mother says. "I didn't notice, but you can bet that Lars did. Amazing instincts."

Government plates. Patton. No wonder Zacharov was livid.

"Why didn't you call me right away? Or Barron? Either one of us. Or Grandad, for hell's sake. Mom, you're hurt."

She tilts her head and smiles at Lila. "Could you give the two of us a couple minutes alone?"

"Yeah," Lila says. "Of course." She heads out the door, closing it behind her.

Mom reaches out and pulls my face close to hers. She's not wearing gloves, and her bare nails sink into the skin of my throat. "What the hell have you boys been up to? Messing around with federal agents?" she hisses, low and vicious.

I push away, my neck stinging.

"I raised you better than this," she says. "Smarter. You know what they'll do to you if they find out what you are? They'll use you to hurt other workers. They'll use you. Against your grandfather. Against everyone you love. And Barron—that boy thinks he can wriggle out of anything, but if you got him into this, he's in over his head. The government put us in camps. And they'll do it again if they figure out a legal way to manage it."

I am left with the uncomfortable echo of Lila's words about Daneca being too smart to get involved with Barron. I guess we're all smart about some things and dumb about others. But the federal government isn't just some bad boyfriend. If Mom knew what they wanted me to do, I think she'd have a different opinion of them. If anything, looking at her, pale and furious in her pile of blankets, I am more committed than ever to getting rid of Patton.

"Barron can take care of himself."

"You're not denying it," she says.

"What's wrong with wanting to do something good with my life?"

She laughs. "You wouldn't know good if it bit you on the ass."

I look at the door. "Does Lila—does she know?"

"No one *knows*," Mom says. "They suspect. That's why I didn't want you to hear about my little accident. I didn't want you coming here—you or your brother. It's not safe. There was a boy who described you in connection with some agents."

"Fine," I say. "I'm going now. I'm glad you're okay. Oh, and I went to the jewelry store. It was a dead end, but I did learn one thing. Dad had two forgeries made. And by the way, it would have really helped if you'd mentioned that he was the one who met with Bob."

"*Two?* But why would he do—" She stops speaking as the obvious answer sinks in. She got conned by her own husband. "Phil would never do that. Never. Your father wasn't greedy. He didn't even want to sell the stone. He just wanted to keep it as insurance, in case we needed money. Our retirement fund, that's what he called it."

I shrug. "Maybe he was pissed off about your affair. Maybe he didn't think you deserved nice things."

She laughs again, this time without any malice. For a moment she seems like herself. "You ever hear of a sweetheart scheme, Cassel? You think your father didn't know?"

Sweetheart schemes have been Mom's bread and butter since Dad died. Find a rich guy. Curse him so he falls in love with her. Get his cash. She even went to jail for one of her less successful cons, although the conviction was overturned on appeal. But I never thought she'd done anything like that when Dad was alive.

I stare at her, my mouth parted. "So Dad knew about you and Zacharov?"

She snorts. "You really are such a prude, Cassel. Of course he did. And we got the stone, didn't we?"

"Okay," I say, trying to push away all thoughts of what she's done. "So, then, what *would* he do with it?"

"I don't know." Her gaze slides away from me as she contemplates the grooves of the plaster wall. "I guess a man is entitled to a few secrets."

I give her a long look.

"Just not very many," she says, and smiles. "Now come and give your mother a kiss."

Lila's in the hallway when I leave. She's leaning against the wall, near a modernist painting that's probably worth more than my mother's house and everything in it. Lila's arms are folded against her chest.

I take out my phone and make a show of typing in the doctor's information from the card he gave me. It was just a number with no name attached, so I call him Dr. Doctor.

"I should have told you," she says finally.

"Yes, you should have told me," I say. "But my mother can be very convincing. And she made you promise."

"Some promises aren't worth keeping." Her voice drops low. "I guess it was stupid to think that I could just drop out and be gone from your life. We're all tangled up together, aren't we?"

"You're not *sentenced* to me," I say stiffly. "This thing with my mother will be resolved, you'll talk to Daneca, and then . . ." I make a vague gesture with my hand.

Then I'll be out of her life, more or less.

She laughs abruptly. "That's how it must have felt—me following you everywhere, begging for attention, obsessing over you—like you were sentenced to me. I even screwed up that on-again, off-again thing you had with Audrey, didn't I?"

"I think I screwed that one up all on my own."

Lila frowns. I can tell she doesn't believe me. "So *why*, Cassel? Why tell me that you loved me, then have Daneca work me so I couldn't feel anything for you, then tell me you love me all over again? Why come here and kiss me up against a wall? Do you just like messing with my head?"

"I— No!" I start to say more, to give her some explanation, but she keeps on going.

"You used to be my best friend in the world, and then, suddenly, you're the reason I'm a caged animal and you're acting like you don't even care. I know they took your memories, but I didn't know it then. I hated you. I wanted you dead. Then you were the one who freed me from my prison, and before I could come to terms with any of that, I was forced to be desperately in love with you. And now, when I see you, I feel everything, all those things, all at once. I can't afford to feel like that. Maybe you were right. Maybe I would be better off if I couldn't feel anything at all."

I don't know what to say. "I'm sorry," is all I manage.

"No, don't be. I don't mean it," Lila whispers. "I wish I wished that, but I don't. I'm just kind of a mess right now."

"You're not," I say.

She smiles. "Don't con me."

I want to reach for her, but her crossed arms keep me from it. I walk toward the stairs instead. At the top I look back at her. "No matter what happens, no matter what else I feel, no matter what else you believe, I hope you believe that I'll always be your friend."

One side of her mouth lifts. "I want to."

As I descend, I see Zacharov standing near the mantel talking to a boy. I recognize his braids, pulled back from his head like horns, and the flash of gold teeth. He looks up at me with dark unfathomable eyes and raises a perfectly manicured eyebrow.

I freeze.

Today he's dressed differently from the hoodie and jeans I saw him in when I chased him through the streets of

Queens. He's got on a purple motorcycle jacket over jeans, and has tapered gold plugs in his ears. He's wearing eyeliner.

Gage. That's the name he gave me.

Zacharov must see the look that passes between us. "Do you two know each other?"

"No," I say quickly.

I expect Gage to contradict me, but he doesn't. "No, I don't think it was him." He circles me, lifting a gloved hand to my chin, tilting my face toward him. He's a little shorter than I am. I pull back, jerking free of his grip.

He laughs. "Hard to believe I'd forget a face like that."

"Tell Cassel that story you told me," Zacharov says. "Cassel, take a seat."

I hesitate, glancing toward the elevator. If I ran, I think I could make it, but who knows how long it would take for the doors to open. And even if I got to the ground floor, I'd probably never get out of the building.

"*Sit down,*" Zacharov says. "I asked Gage to come over because the more I thought about your brother working for the Feds, the more I was sure that if it was true, you'd try to cover it up. Especially since I threatened his life. I take that back. But after Philip turned out to be a rat, I think we both understand that we have a lot to lose if your other brother started squealing."

I suck in a breath and sink onto one of the sofas. Flames flicker in the fireplace, filling the massive room with eerie shifting shadows. I can feel my palms start to sweat.

Lila looks over the edge of the railing. "Dad? What's

going on?" Her words echo through the big room, bouncing off the wooden ceiling and stone floors.

"Gage stopped by," Zacharov says. "I understand he ran into some complications the other day."

Gage looks up at her and grins. I wonder how long they've known each other. "I did that job like you wanted. It was quick. He was in the first place I looked."

Lila's face is shadowed. I can't read her expression.

"Charlie West didn't give you any trouble?" Zacharov asks.

Lila starts down the stairs.

Gage sucks his teeth, making a dismissive sound. "I didn't give him a chance for trouble."

Lila walks onto the black and white marble. Her bare feet make almost no sound as she pads across the floor. "Should Cassel be hearing this?"

It strikes me that once upon a time I thought of her as part of the class of people with magic. I knew that there were regular people and there were workers, and workers were better than regular people. That's what everyone in Carney believed, or it's at least what they told me. When I was a kid, Lila's cousin, my own brother's best friend, didn't even want me to be around her, because he thought I wasn't a worker.

But even among workers there are different roles. Lila is inheriting Zacharov's position, where you order murders but don't actually have to carry them out. She doesn't hold the gun, she just calls the shots.

"Let Gage tell his story," Zacharov says. "We trust Cassel, don't we?"

She turns her head toward me. The fire highlights the curve of her jawline, the point of her chin. "Of course we do."

Zacharov once asked me whether I would mind taking orders from his daughter. At the time, I said I wouldn't. Now I wonder what it would really be like. I wonder if I would resent it.

Gage clears his throat. "After I tap him, some psycho do-gooder decides to chase me through the streets and nearly breaks my arm." He laughs. "Guy picks up a plank and knocks my gun right out of my hand. If I was a couple of seconds faster, he would have got himself shot."

I concentrate on not reacting. I try to keep a vaguely interested expression on my face.

"You described him looking a lot like Cassel, didn't you?" Zacharov asks.

Gage nods, his gaze on me. He's laughing with his eyes. "Sure. Black hair, tan skin, tall. Cute. Stole my gun."

Zacharov crosses to where Lila is standing and puts his gloved hands on her shoulders. "Could it have been his brother? They look pretty alike."

"Barron is no do-gooder," I say.

Gage shakes his head. "Without a picture I'm not sure, but I don't think so."

Zacharov nods. "Tell him the rest."

"I have to climb a fence to get away," Gage says. "Three blocks later I get grabbed by guys in black suits. They hustle me into a car, and I think I'm done for, but they tell me that if I tell them what happened, they aren't going to investigate the hit."

"And did you tell them?" Zacharov asks, although I can tell he's already heard the story and knows the answer.

Lila pulls away from her father to perch on the edge of the couch.

"Well, at first I tell them no, I'm no snitch, but it turns out that they don't really care about who ordered me to do the job or even what I did. All they want to know about is the psycho do-gooder. They let me go, just for telling them about some guy I talked to for a couple of seconds. I said he took my gun."

I feel an odd sense of dizziness. It's almost like falling.

"They wanted to know if we knew each other. They wanted to know if he identified himself as a federal agent. I said no to both. Then, when they turned me loose, I came to Mr. Z, because I thought maybe he'd know what was going on."

"That sounds nothing like my brother," I say, giving them the steadiest look I can manage.

"A man can't be too careful," says Zacharov.

"Sorry I couldn't be more help," Gage says. "If you need anything else, let me know."

"I've got to get going," I say, standing up. "That is, if we're done here?"

Zacharov nods.

I start toward the elevator. My shoes tap a sharp rhythm on the stone tiles. I hear sudden footsteps following mine.

"Wait up," Gage says. "I'll ride down with you."

I look back to see Zacharov and Lila, across the room, watching us. Lila raises a hand in a half wave.

I get into the elevator and close my eyes as the doors shut.

"You going to kill me?" I ask in the silence that follows. "I hate waiting."

"What?" When I look at him, Gage is frowning. "You're the psycho who attacked me."

"You're a *death worker*. I figured you lied back there because you wanted some kind of personal revenge." I sigh. "Why did you do it? Why not tell Zacharov it was me?"

"No big thing. You let me go; I pay my debts." He's got sharp, almost delicate features, but he's muscled under his coat. I can tell from his shoulders. "All I want is my gun. It's a 1943 Beretta. A family heirloom. It belonged to my grandmother. She got it from some Italian boyfriend after the war—and she gave it to me when my parents kicked me out. I slept the whole bus ride to New York with that thing under what I was using for a pillow. It kept me safe."

I nod. "I'll get it to you."

"Just give the gun to Lila and she'll pass it along," he says. "Look, whatever those agents wanted you for, I figure it's none of my business. It didn't sound to me like you were one of them, and Lila wouldn't thank me for getting you in trouble with her father."

I frown. "What do you mean?"

"You're the youngest Sharpe brother, right? Cassel. Lila's been talking about you for *forever*." He grins appraisingly, raising both his eyebrows. "I didn't think you could possibly measure up, but it's the rare boy who can catch me."

I laugh. "How long have you known her?"

"I did a job for her father when I was thirteen. I guess

she was about twelve at the time. We got along like a house on fire. Used to go into her mother's room and try on her clothes and sing in front of her big double mirror. We were going to start a band called the Skies over Tokyo, but neither of us could play an instrument and neither of us could sing."

It takes me a moment to put it together that he means he killed someone for Zacharov when he was just a kid. I'm shocked before I remember that I was doing the same thing for Anton.

Then I realize that I'm going to do it again, for Yulikova this time. Yulikova, who knows I've already lied to her once.

My stomach sinks as the elevator doors open. I feel like I am still going down.

THE NEXT MORNING I AM

called into Dean Wharton's office right after morning announcements.

I stand in front of his burnished wooden desk and try not to think of the pictures I saw of him, with Mina's bare hand parting the collar of his starched white shirt. I guess everyone has a dark side, but I don't think I was prepared for that to extend to elderly Wallingford faculty.

Wharton's not a guy that I've thought a lot about. He's the dean of students, probably close to retirement age, with tufts of carefully combed-over silver hair on his head. He's never much liked me, but I've always given him plenty of reasons to feel that way, what with my bookmaking operation, the sleepwalking, and my mother being a convicted criminal.

I feel like I'm looking at him with fresh eyes now, though. I see today's newspaper, half-hidden in a stack of files, open to the crossword, a few shaky blue pen marks in the margins. I see the cap of a pill case under the desk and a single yellow pill. And perhaps most telling of all, I see the tremble in his left hand, which might be a nervous tic but shows how close he's playing to the edge. But then maybe I am reading him backward—seeing what I want to see. I know he's doing something bad, so I expect him to be nervous.

I just wish I knew exactly what he was doing.

"Mr. Sharpe, being in my office twice in as many weeks does not bode well for any student." His tone is as sternly exasperated as ever.

"I know that, sir," I say, as contritely as possible.

"You cut your morning classes yesterday, young man. Did you think there wouldn't be any consequences?"

"I'm sorry, sir. I wasn't feeling well, sir."

"Oh, is that right? And do you have a note from the nurse's office?"

"I just went back to sleep. Then, when I was feeling better, I went to class."

"So, no note?" he asks, raising both silver brows.

Okay, so say Mina's a luck worker. Say he has a gambling problem. Maybe he's coming up on retirement and realizes—for whatever reason—that he doesn't have enough socked away. I figure he's a guy who, at least mostly, stuck to the straight and narrow. But honest people get screwed too. The bottom falls out of the market. A family member gets sick and insurance doesn't even begin to cover it. For whatever reason, maybe he veers off the path.

My eye is drawn to the single yellow pill on the carpet.

Hiring a luck worker is pretty easy. He wouldn't need to target a student, although I guess maybe, being so straightlaced, he didn't know where else to go. But using luck work to win at gambling is a pretty uncertain proposition. Although sometimes people can get around it, most racetracks and casinos have ways to control for luck work.

Of course, he might need luck for some other reason. Maybe Northcutt is leaving and he wants to be the new headmaster.

"No note," I say.

"You're going to serve a Saturday detention with me, right here in this office, Cassel. I want you here at ten in the morning. No excuses. Or you're going to get that third demerit you're flirting with."

I nod. "Yes, sir."

The pill under his desk might be nothing. It could be aspirin or allergy medicine. But I don't have many clues, and I want this one. I should drop something, but all the little stuff that it would make sense to be holding is in my bag. I don't have keys or a pen or anything.

"You can go," he tells me, handing over a hall pass without really looking. I think about dropping that, but I imagine it fluttering to the floor far from where I need it to be. It's impossible to aim paper.

I stand and take a few steps toward the door before I have an idea. It's not a very good one. "Uh, excuse me, Dean Wharton?"

He glances up, brows knitted.

"Sorry. I dropped my pen." I walk over to his desk and bend down, grabbing for the pill. He pushes back his chair so he can look, but I'm up again fast.

"Thanks," I say, walking to the door before he can think too much about it.

As I start down the stairs, I look at the pill in my hand. There are ways to search online to find out about medication. You can put in details—like the color and shape and markings—and get a whole gallery of pills to compare against. I don't have to do any of that, because this pill has ARICEPT stamped into the top and 10 on the other side.

I know what it is; I've seen the commercials on late-night television.

It's medication to control Alzheimer's.

Daneca is waiting for me outside the cafeteria at lunch. She's sitting on one of the benches, her mass of brown and purple hair hanging in her face. She waves me over and shifts aside her hemp book bag so that I can sit down.

I lean back and stretch my legs. It's cold and a storm is rolling in, but there's still enough sun that it's nice to sit in a patch of it. "Hey," I say.

She shifts, and I can see what her hair hid before—red eyes and puffy skin around them. Streaks of salt on her cheeks marking the map of tears.

"Lila called you, huh?" I don't mean to sound callous, but the words come out that way.

She wipes her eyes and nods.

"I'm sorry." I reach into my pocket, hoping I have a tissue. "Honest."

She snorts and touches her cell phone where it's resting in the lap of her pleated Wallingford skirt. "I broke things off with Barron about ten minutes ago. I hope you're happy."

"I am," I say. "Barron is a sleaze bag. He's my brother—I should know. Sam is a much better guy."

"I know that. I always knew *that*." She sighs. "I'm sorry. I'm mad at you for being right, and I shouldn't be. It's not fair."

"Barron's a sociopath. They're very convincing. Especially if you're one of those girls who thinks she can fix a boy."

"Yeah," she says. "I guess I was. I *wanted* to believe him."

"You've got a real taste for darkness," I say.

She looks away from me, out at the overcast sky, the formless shifting mass of clouds. "I wanted to think there was a part of him that only I could see. A secret part that wanted kindness and love but didn't know how to ask for it. I'm stupid, right?"

"Oh, yeah. The taste for darkness, but not the stomach for it."

She flinches. "I guess I deserve that. I'm sorry I believed what he said about you, Cassel. I know you haven't told me everything, but—"

"No." I sigh. "I'm being a jerk. I'm mad because I wanted you to be the person that I could count on to always know right from wrong. That's not fair to expect from anyone. And I guess . . . I thought that we were better friends, despite all our sniping at each other."

"Friends screw up sometimes," she says.

"Maybe it'd help if I put my cards on the table. Tell me what Barron said, and I'll tell you the honest truth. This is a onetime offer."

"Because tomorrow you'll go back to lying?" she asks.

"I don't know what I'll do tomorrow. That's the problem." Which is one of the truest things I have ever said.

"You never told me what kind of worker you are, but Lila and Barron both did. I don't blame you for not telling me. That's a pretty big secret. And you really just found out last spring?"

"Yeah," I say. "I didn't think that I was a worker at all. When I was a kid, I used to pretend I was a transformation worker. I imagined that I could do anything, if I was one. That turns out to be almost true."

She nods, considering. "Barron said you told the federal agents . . . what you are, in exchange for immunity for all past crimes."

"I did," I say.

"Immunity for murdering Philip, for instance."

"*That's* what Barron thinks?" I shake my head and laugh without actually being amused. "That I killed Philip?"

She nods, braced. I'm not sure whether she's braced for me to tell her what an idiot she is or because she thinks

I'm about to confess to the whole thing. "He says the guy they're blaming for Philip's murder was dead way before Philip was."

"That part's true," I say.

She swallows.

"Oh, come on. I didn't kill Philip! I know who did, that's all. And, no, I'm not going to tell you, even if you ask, because it's got nothing to do with either one of us. Let's just say that the dead guy could afford to carry a murder charge in addition to his many other crimes. He was no angel."

"Barron said that you killed him—and that you kept him in the freezer of your house. That you were some kind of assassin. That you're the one who killed the people in those files you showed me after Philip's funeral."

"I'm no angel either," I say.

She hesitates. There's fear in her eyes, but at least she's not leaving. "Lila explained. She said that they—that Barron—messed with your memories. You didn't know what you'd done. You didn't know what you were or what happened to her."

Selfishly I wonder if Lila said anything else. I have no idea how I could persuade Daneca to tell me.

"He really kept her in a cage?" Daneca asks in a small voice.

"Yeah," I say. "Memory work—it erases part of who you are. If we're who we remember ourselves to be, then what's it like to have huge chunks of your identity missing? How you met the girl sitting next to you. What you had for dinner the night before. A family vacation. The law book you studied all last week. Barron's replaced all that with whatever he makes up in the moment. I have no idea if he really remembered who Lila was or even that he had a cat in the first place."

She nods slowly and pushes back a mass of curls. "I told him that it was contemptible, what he did. I told him that I would never forgive him for lying to me. And I told him he was an ass."

"That sounds like quite a lecture," I say, laughing. "I hope he was properly chastened."

"Don't make fun of me." She stands up, grabbing her bag. "He really sounded sad, Cassel."

I bite back everything I want to say to her. How he's an excellent liar. How he's the prince of liars. How Lucifer Morningstar himself could learn a thing or two from the conviction with which Barron lies.

"Lunch is almost over," I say instead. "Let's grab a sandwich while we can."

Afternoon classes slide by in a flurry of diligent note-taking and quizzes. A cup I made in ceramics comes out of the kiln in one piece, and I spend the better part of forty minutes painting it a muddy red, with the words RISE AND WHINE across it in big black letters.

Dr. Stewart is in his office when I swing by before track. He frowns at the sight of me.

"You're not in any of my classes this semester, Mr. Sharpe." His tone makes it clear that he considers that to be better for both of us. He adjusts his thick black-framed glasses. "Surely you aren't here trying to beg me to change a past grade? I maintain that anyone who misses as much school as you have shouldn't even be—"

"Mina Lange asked me to come by and drop something off for her," I say, pulling a paper bag out of my backpack.

It's not that I believe that Dr. Stewart has anything to do with blackmail or Wharton or Mina. It's that I want to be as sure as possible.

He crosses his arms. I can tell he's annoyed that I interrupted him before he could tell me once again how students suspended for almost falling off a roof should have to go to summer school, at the very least. "Mina Lange is not in any of my classes either, Mr. Sharpe."

"So this isn't for you?"

"Well, what is it?" he asks. "I can't imagine what she would be handing in to me."

"You want me to look?" I try to seem as unaware as possible. Just the stupid messenger.

He throws up both gloved hands in obvious disgust. "Yes, please do, and stop wasting my time."

I make a show of opening up the bag. "Looks like a research paper and a book. Oh, and it's for Mr. *Knight*. Sorry, Dr. Stewart. I really thought she said your name."

"Yes, well, I'm sure she's glad she trusted you to courier it over."

"She's not feeling well. That's why she couldn't bring it herself."

He sighs as though wondering why he is constantly

being punished by the presence of inferior intellects. "Good-bye, Mr. Sharpe."

He might not be a nice guy, but Stewart's never blackmailed anyone in his life.

I love running. I love the way that, even in a marathon, I only have to worry about my feet hitting the pavement and my muscles burning. No guilt and no fear. It's just me hurtling forward, as fast as I can, with no one to stop me. I love the cold wind against my back and the sweat heating my face.

Some days my mind is blank when I run. Other days I can't stop thinking, turning everything over and over again in my head.

Today I come to a couple of different conclusions.

One: No one is blackmailing Mina Lange.

Two: Mina Lange is a physical worker, fixing Wharton's Alzheimer's.

Three: Since Alzheimer's can never be cured, she can never stop working him, which means she just gets sicker and sicker, while he stays the same.

Four: Despite all her lies, Mina is probably actually in trouble.

Sam looks up from his bed when I walk into our dorm room. I've got a towel wrapped around my waist and am fresh from the shower.

He's got a bunch of brochures scattered beside him, colleges his parents want him to consider. None of them have a department that teaches visual effects. None of them will let him make his own rubber masks. All of them are Ivy League. Brown. Yale. Dartmouth. Harvard.

"Hey," he says. "Look, I was talking to Mina over lunch yesterday. She said she was sorry. She basically admitted what you said. That she wanted us to blackmail Wharton for her."

"Yeah?" I start rooting around for sweatpants, and put them on when I finally locate them under a pile of other clothes at the bottom of my closet. "Did she say why she needed the money?"

"Said she wanted to leave town. I didn't really understand it, but it seems like someone's brokering the deal between Wharton and her. That person won't let her leave, so she's got to run. Do you think it's her parents?"

"No," I say, thinking of Gage and myself and Lila and of what Mrs. Wasserman said when I was sitting in her kitchen. *Lots of kids are kicked out onto the streets, taken in by crime families and then sold off to the rich.* "Probably not her parents."

"Don't you think we can help her?" he asks.

"There's too much that's fishy about this situation, Sam. If she needs the money, then she should blackmail Wharton for it herself."

"But she can't. She's afraid of him."

I sigh. "Sam—"

"You nearly yanked her wig off in public. Don't you think you should make it up to her? Besides, I told her that the investigative firm of Sharpe & Yu was still on the case."

He grins, and I'm glad to see him distracted. I wonder again if he likes Mina. I really, really hope not.

"I think she's sick, Sam," I say. "I think that she's curing Wharton and it's making her sick."

"Even more reason to do something. Tell him he's got to give her the money. Explain the situation. You know, make it clear she's not alone. Wharton's the one who got her into this. We've got pictures."

"She's a player," I say. "She could still be playing us."

"Come on, Cassel. She's a lady in trouble."

"She *is* trouble." I scratch my neck, where I cut myself shaving. "Look, I have a Saturday detention with Wharton. He'll be alone in his office. Maybe we can talk to him then."

"What if she can't wait until the weekend?"

"We'll burn that bridge when we come to it." I open my laptop. "What's with the brochures?"

"Oh," he says. "I've got college applications to write. How about you?"

"I've got to plan an assassination," I say, logging into the school's wireless and bringing up the search engine. "I know. Weird, right?"

"Cassel Sharpe: boy assassin." He shakes his head. "You should have your own comic book."

I grin. "Only if you'll be my runty spandex-wearing sidekick."

"Runty? I'm taller than you are!" He sits up, and the springs of the bed groan, echoing his point.

I grin at him. "Not in my comic, you're not."

Killing someone is a lot like conning someone. You need to know a lot of the same things.

Maybe the Feds have to keep me in the dark, but I have to follow my own instincts. If something goes wrong with their plan, I'll need to improvise. And to do that I need to study my victim.

Patton's a public figure. Learning about him isn't hard— every detail of his life has been analyzed by the press, all his faults enumerated by his opponents. I look at photos until I know every detail of his face, until I can spot the lines of pancake makeup at the edges of his neck when he's camera-ready, until I see how he combs the few white hairs he's got and how he dresses to match the tone of his speeches. I look at pictures of him in his home, at rallies, kissing babies. I pore over news reports and gossip columns and restaurant guides to see who he meets with (many, many people), his favorite food (spaghetti Bolognese), what he orders at the diner he frequents (eggs over easy, buttered white toast, turkey sausage), and even how he takes his coffee (cream and sugar).

I study his security, too. He always has two bodyguards who follow him everywhere. They aren't always the same two guys, but they all have broken noses and smirking smiles. There are a few articles about Patton using funds to hire ex-cons to round out his security staff, men he personally pardoned. He never goes anywhere without them.

I watch several YouTube videos of him ranting about conspiracy theories, workers, and big government. I listen to the faint traces of his accent, the way he enunciates, and the way he pauses just before he says something he thinks is really important. I watch the way he gestures, reaching out to the audience like he's hoping to wrap them in his arms.

I call my mother and get a few more particulars while pretending to be interested in how she edged herself into his life. I find out where he buys his suits (Bergdorf; they have his measurements so he can just call and have a suit tailored and overnighted to a speaking engagement). What languages he speaks (French and Spanish). The medicine he takes for his heart (Capoten and a single baby aspirin). The way he walks, heel to toe, so that the backs of his shoes always wear down first.

I watch and look and listen and read until I feel like Governor Patton is standing over my shoulder and whispering into my ear. It's not a good feeling.

FRIDAY AFTERNOON, AS

I'm coming back from classes, my phone buzzes in the pocket of my uniform pants. I take it out, but the number is blocked.

"Hello?" I say into the mouthpiece.

"We're coming to get you tomorrow night," says Yulikova. "Clear your schedule. We want to be moving by six p.m."

Something's wrong. Really, really wrong. "You said everything was happening *next* Wednesday, not this Saturday."

"I'm sorry, Cassel," she says. "Plans change. We have to be flexible right now."

I lower my voice. "Look, that thing with the death worker and me tailing him—I'm sorry I didn't tell you about the gun. I know you know. I just panicked. I still have it. I didn't do anything with it. I could bring it to you."

I shouldn't bring it to her. I promised it to Gage.

I should bring it to her. I should have given it to her in the first place.

She doesn't speak for a long moment. "That wasn't your smartest move."

"I know," I say.

"Why don't you turn the gun in tomorrow night and we'll just call the whole thing a misunderstanding."

"Right." My feeling of disquiet grows, although I can't say why. There's just something not right about her tone. Something that makes me feel like she's already distanced herself from this situation.

I'm surprised she's letting me off so easy about the gun. Nothing about this sits right.

"I was reading about Patton," I say, to keep her talking.

"We can talk about this when we pick you up." She says it kindly, but I can hear the dismissal in her voice.

"He has private security with him at all times. Tough guys. I was just wondering how we were getting around that."

"I promise you, Cassel, we've got good people handling this. Your part is significant but small. We're going to take care of you."

"Humor me," I say, putting some of the anger I feel into my voice.

She sighs. "I'm sorry. Of course you're concerned. We understand the risk you're taking, and we appreciate it."

I wait.

"We have one of them on the payroll. He's going to stall the other guard for long enough that you can take care of things. And he's going to watch your back."

"Okay," I say. "I'll meet you at Wallingford. Call me when you get here."

"Try not to worry," Yulikova says. "Good-bye, Cassel."

My heart's racing and my stomach is in knots as I close my phone. There is nothing worse than the creeping formless sense of dread—until that moment when it becomes clear what you should have been dreading all along. When you know it's not just all in your head. When you see the danger.

The Feds don't need me to bring in Patton. They don't need me at all. If they've really got one of his bodyguards on their payroll, they could disappear him anytime they wanted.

I sit down on the library steps and call Barron.

I can hear traffic in the background when he picks up. "You want something?" He sounds annoyed.

"Oh, come on," I say. I'm not exactly pleased with him, either. "You can't really be pissed off—just because you thought that I couldn't convince her you were lying when you were *actually lying.*"

"So you called to gloat?" he asks.

"Yulikova moved up the date for the thing, and she has

an inside man already. Someone positioned to do this job a lot better than me. Does that sound fishy to you?"

"Maybe," he says.

"And that death worker I chased down. Her people picked him up after to see if I lied about anything."

"Did you?"

"Yeah. I took something from him and I . . . I kind of let him go. She knew that and never said anything."

"That does seem weird. I guess you're screwed. Sucks to be you, Cassel. Looks like the Feds aren't your friends after all."

He hangs up, leaving me with silence.

I don't know why I expected anything else.

I sit on the steps for a long time. I don't go to track practice. I don't go to dinner. I just turn the phone over and over in my hands until I realize I have to get up and go somewhere eventually.

I dial Lila's number. I don't expect her to answer, but she does.

"I need your help," I say.

Her voice is low. "We've helped each other enough, don't you think?"

"I just need to talk through some things with someone."

"It shouldn't be me."

I take a deep breath. "I'm working with the Feds, Lila. And I'm in trouble. A lot of trouble."

"I'm getting my coat," she says. "Tell me where you are."

We arrange to meet at the old house. I get my keys and head to my car.

I'm sitting in the kitchen in the dark when she opens the door. I'm thinking about the smell of my father's cigarillos and what it was like when we were very young and nothing really mattered.

She flips on the lights, and I blink up at her.

"Are you okay?" She comes over to the table and puts one gloved hand on my shoulder. She's wearing tight black jeans and a scarred leather jacket. Her blond hair is as bright as a gold coin.

I shake my head.

Then I tell her everything—about Patton, about Maura, about wanting to be good and falling short, about following her that day when I chased down Gage without knowing why, about Yulikova and the gun. Everything.

By the time I'm done, she's sitting backward in one of the chairs, resting her chin on her arms. She has shouldered off the jacket.

"How mad at me are you?" I ask. "I mean, exactly how mad—like on a scale of one to ten, where one is kicking my ass and ten is a shark tank?"

She shakes her head at my scale. "You mean because you watched me put out a contract on someone and then watched Gage kill him? That you're cooperating with the law, maybe even working for them? That you never told me any of this? I'm not *happy*. Does it bother you—what you saw me do?"

"I don't know," I say.

"You think I have ice in my blood?" She asks it lightly, but I know the answer matters.

I wonder what it would be like, being raised to be a crime lord. "You are what you always were going to be."

"Remember when we were kids?" she says. There's a slight smile on her mouth, but the way she's looking at me doesn't quite match up. "You thought I would be the one making deals and enemies, backstabbing and lying. You said you were going to get out, travel the world. Not get swept up in the life."

"Shows what I know."

"That's one long game you've been playing, Cassel. One long, dangerous game."

"I didn't mean for everything to get so crazy. It was one thing after another. I had to fix things. *Someone* had to fix things for Maura, and I was the only one who knew, so there just wasn't anyone else. And I had to keep Barron from going to the Brennans. And I had to stop myself—" I do stop myself there, because I can't say the rest. I can't explain how I needed to stop myself from being with her. I can't explain how I nearly didn't manage it.

"Okay, well, quit." She makes a wild gesture with her hands, as though stating something so obvious that it shouldn't have to be said. "You did what you thought you had to do, but you still have a way out, so take it. Get away from the Feds. And if they don't want to let you off easy, then go into hiding. I'll help. I'll talk to my dad. I'll try to see if he can take some of the pressure off the thing with your mother, at least until you can solve this. Don't let them play you."

"I can't quit." I look away, at the peeling wallpaper above the sink. "I can't. It's too important."

"What makes you so eager to throw away your life on whatever cause comes along?"

"That's not true. That's not what I was doing—"

"*None of it is your fault.* What is it that you feel so damn guilty about that makes you act like *you* don't matter?" Her voice rises, and she rises with it, coming around the table to push against my shoulder. "What makes you think that you've got to solve everyone's problems, even mine?"

"Nothing." I shake my head, turning away from her.

"Is it Jimmy Greco and Antanas Kalvis and the rest? Because I knew them, and they were really bad men. The world's a better place without them in it."

"Stop trying to make me feel better," I say. "You know I don't deserve it."

"*Why don't you deserve it?*" she yells, her voice sounding like the words are being ripped out of her gut. Her hand is on my upper arm; she's trying to get me to look at her.

I won't.

"You," I say, standing. "Because of *you.*"

For a moment neither of us speaks.

"What I did—," I start, but I can't make that sentence go anywhere good. I start over. "I can't forgive myself—I don't *want* to forgive myself."

I sink down to the linoleum tiles and say what I have never said before. "I killed you. I remember killing you. I killed you." The words, over and over and over, rolling out of me. My voice is catching. My voice is breaking.

"I'm alive," Lila says, sliding to her knees so that I have to look at her, have to see her. "I'm right here."

I take a deep, shuddering breath.

"We're alive," she says. "We made it."

I feel like I'm about to shake apart. "I've screwed up everything, haven't I?"

Now it's her turn not to meet my gaze. "I wouldn't let Daneca work me," she says, slowly and carefully, putting every word together as if having one out of place will make everything fall apart. "But I didn't stop loving you. Because I always have, Cassel. Since we were kids. You have to remember: I paraded around in my underwear at my own birthday party."

That startles a laugh out of me. I touch the ear she pierced that night, the hole closed now, and try to imagine a world where I wasn't the only one who felt something. "I didn't think that meant—"

"Because you're an idiot," she says. "An *idiot*. When the curse wore off, I couldn't let you see that I still had feelings. I thought I was the only one who'd ever had them."

She has woven her fingers together and is clenching them tight, the leather taut over her knuckles. "You were kind. You're always kind. I figured you pretended to love me until you couldn't pretend anymore. And I couldn't let you think you still had to. So I'd jab myself in the hand with scissors, or pens—with anything sharp in reach— whenever I thought of you. Until when I saw you I could concentrate on that moment of pain. . . . And despite that, I still wanted to see you."

"I haven't been pretending, Lila," I say. "I never was. I know how it looked, me asking Daneca to make you not feel anything. But I kissed you before I knew what my mother had done, remember? I kissed you because I had wanted to for a very long time."

She shakes her head. "I don't know."

"That night, in your dorm room— Lila, *you were cursed*," I say. "And I almost didn't care. It was awful, because you acted like you really felt all these things, and I had to constantly remind myself that it wasn't real—and sometimes I was overwhelmed by the awfulness. I wanted to blot out how bad I felt. I knew it wasn't right and I still didn't stop myself."

"Okay," she says. "It's okay."

"But I would never want—"

"I know that, Cassel," she says. "You could have explained."

"And said what? That I did want to be with you?" I demand. "That I just couldn't trust myself enough? That I—"

She leans forward and brings her mouth to mine. I have never been so profoundly glad to be forced to shut up.

I close my eyes, because even seeing her is too much right now.

I feel like a man who's been living on bread and water and is now overwhelmed by a feast. I feel like someone chained in the dark for so long that the light has become terrifying.

Her lips are soft, sliding against mine. I am lost in kiss after drowning kiss. My gloved fingers trace the skin of her cheek and the hollow of her throat until she moans into my mouth. My blood is boiling, pooling low in my gut.

She unknots my tie with quick fingers. When I pull back

to look at her, she grins and tugs the cloth free from my collar in a single motion.

I raise both eyebrows.

With a laugh Lila pushes herself off the floor and reaches out her gloved hand to haul me to my feet. "Come on," she says.

I stand up. Somehow my shirt has gotten untucked. Then we're kissing again, staggering up the stairs. She stops to kick off her boots, bracing herself against me and the wall. I shrug out of my jacket.

"Lila," I say, but that's all I can manage as she begins to unbutton my white dress shirt.

It falls to the floor of the hallway.

We lurch into my bedroom, where I imagined her a thousand times, where I thought I had lost her forever. Those memories seem blurred now, hard to count as important beside the vividness of her cool leather-clad hand brushing over the hard, tensed planes of my stomach and the corded muscles of my arms. I suck in my breath.

She steps away to bite the end of her glove, pulling it off her hand that way. When she drops it, my gaze tracks its fall.

I catch her bare hand and kiss her fingers, which makes her stare at me, wide-eyed. I bite down on the heel of her hand, and she groans.

When I pull off my own gloves, my hands are shaking. The taste of her skin is on my tongue. I feel feverish.

If I have to die tomorrow when the Feds come for me, then this is the last request of my heart. This. The sight of lashes brushing her cheek as her eyes flutter closed. The pulse in her throat. Her breath in my mouth. This.

I have been with girls I cared about and girls I didn't. But I have never been with a girl I loved more than anything else in all the world. I am staggered by it, overwhelmed with the desire to get everything right.

My mouth dips low to trace the scar on her neck. Her nails dig into my back.

Lila breaks away to yank her shirt over her head, and throws it onto the floor. Her bra is blue and covered in lace butterflies. Then she comes back into my arms again, her lips opening, her skin impossibly soft and warm. When I run my bare hands over it, her body arches against me.

She starts to unbuckle my belt with fumbling fingers.

"Are you sure?" I say, pulling away.

In answer she steps back, reaches around, and unclasps her bra, tosses it in the direction of her shirt.

"*Lila,*" I say helplessly.

"Cassel, if you make me talk about this, I will kill you. I will literally kill you. I will strangle you with your own tie."

"I think that tie's downstairs," I say, fighting to remember why in the world I wanted to talk as she comes forward to kiss me again. Her fingers thread through my hair, tugging my mouth down to hers.

A few short steps and we sprawl backward onto the bed, knocking pillows to the floor.

"Do you have anything?" She's speaking against my shoulder, her bare chest against mine. I shudder with each word and force myself to focus.

It still takes me a moment to realize what she means. "In my wallet."

"You know I haven't done this a lot." There's a tremble in her voice, as if she's suddenly nervous. "Like, once before."

"We can stop," I say, stilling my hands. I take an unsteady breath. "We should—"

"If you stop," she says, "I will also kill you."

So we don't.

I WAKE UP WITH SUNLIGHT

streaming in through the dirty windowpane. I reach out my bare fingers, expecting them to brush warm skin, but they close on a tangle of bedsheets instead. She's already gone.

I didn't stop loving you, Cassel.

My skin is alive with the memory of her hands. I stretch, bones all down my spine popping languorously. My head feels clearer than I can ever remember.

I grin up at the cracked plaster of my ceiling and picture her creeping out of the room while I'm sleeping, hesitating to kiss me good-bye, not leaving a note or any other normal-person thing. Of course not. She wouldn't want to seem sentimental. She'd dress in the bathroom and splash water on her face. Carry her boots and run across the lawn in stocking feet. Sneak back into that fancy penthouse apartment before her criminal mastermind of a father could realize that his daughter spent the night at a boy's house. At my house.

I can't stop grinning.

She loves me.

I guess I can die happy.

I head into my parents' room and dig around, find a beat-up leather duffel bag into which I stuff a couple of T-shirts and my least favorite pair of jeans. No point in packing anything I like, since I have no idea where Yulikova is taking me or whether I'll ever see any of this stuff again. I stash my wallet and identification under my mattress.

My objectives are simple—figure out if Yulikova's going to double-cross me, do the job so Patton can't hurt my mother, and come home.

After that I guess we'll see. I didn't sign any papers, so I'm not an official member of the LMD. I can still get out if I want. At least I think I can. This is the federal government we're talking about, not some crime family with blood oaths and slashed throats.

Of course, even if I'm not an agent, I'll still have to deal with everyone else who's looking for someone with my particular talents.

I imagine for a moment being on my own after high school, living in New York, waiting tables and meeting Lila for espressos late at night. No one would need to know what I am. No one would need to know what I can do. We'd go back to my tiny apartment, drink cheap wine, watch black-and-white movies, and complain about our jobs. She could tell me about gang wars and all the new things that fell off trucks, and I could—

I shake my head at myself.

Before I get too involved in fantasies about an impossible future, I better show up for detention. Otherwise I'm not even going to graduate from Wallingford.

Glancing at the clock on my phone, I see that I have about a half hour. That gives me time to go back to my dorm, pick up Sam, and figure out what we're going to say on Mina's behalf. Barely enough time, but still.

I'm walking out to my car, duffel bag over one shoulder, when my phone rings.

It's Barron. I flip it open. "Hey," I say, surprised.

His voice is carefully neutral. "I did some digging."

I stop, leaning against the front of my Benz, keys still in my hand. "What kind of digging?"

"After what you said about the Patton job, I persuaded one of my friends to let me use her ID card and rifle through some files. You were right. It's a setup, Cassel. You're supposed to get pinched."

I feel cold all over. "They want to arrest me?"

He laughs. "The really hysterical part is that they're getting you to turn Patton into a toaster or whatever to cover their own screwup. They could go in, guns blazing, if they weren't the reason Patton's so unstable in the first place. This is their mess."

I look out at the lawn. The leaves have almost all fallen,

leaving behind barren trunks of trees, their black branches reaching for the sky like the long fingers of endless hands. "What do you mean?"

"Patton's aides called the Feds once they realized Mom had worked him. If she hadn't been so sloppy, you wouldn't be in the lurch."

"She didn't have time to do a better job," I say. "Anyway, politics isn't exactly her thing."

"Yeah, well, my point is that I read the reports and they tell a fabulous tale of fuckupitude. After the aides call the Feds, they bring in a state-sanctioned emotion worker to "fix" Patton. But, see, the government is full of hyperbathygammic idiots who have been taught not to use their powers unless they really have to, so the emotion worker agent they sent in didn't exactly have a deft touch.

"He works Patton to hate and fear Mom, thinking that strong emotions are the only way to negate what she did. But instead Patton gets completely unhinged. Like, no hinge in sight. All violent outbursts and crying jags."

I shudder, thinking about what it would be like to be made to feel two contradictory things at the same time. It's worse when I realize that's what I was asking Daneca to do to Lila. Love and indifference warring together. I don't know what might have happened. Thinking about it is like looking down into the deep ravine you somehow missed stepping into in the dark.

Barron goes on. "Now, the backbone of getting Proposition 2 passed is having workers who are also upstanding citizens endorse it. Prominent members of the community coming forward and submitting themselves for voluntary testing makes the rest of us look bad, but it makes the program look good. Safe. Humane. Problem was, Patton decided that now was the time to be crazy. He got everyone with a positive HBG test fired.

"Then he started asking federal employees to get tested. He managed to put a lot of pressure on them. He wanted the federal units with hyperbathygammic agents disbanded."

"Like the LMD," I say, thinking of Yulikova and Agent Jones. "But he's got no authority over them."

"I told you this was a comedy of errors," says Barron. "Sure, he can't do a thing to make that happen. But he can threaten to embarrass them by telling the press how they worked him against his will. So, in all their wisdom, what do you think Team Good does?"

"I have no idea," I say. Another call makes my phone buzz, but I ignore it.

"They send *another* worker so that he can fix the first botched job on Patton's brain."

I laugh. "I bet that went real well."

"Oh, yeah. Patton *killed him*. That's how well it went."

"Killed him?" Since this is Barron, it's possible he's embellishing the truth, if not outright lying. But the story he's telling adds up in a way that the story Yulikova told me doesn't. Barron's story is messy, full of coincidences and mistakes. As a liar myself, I know that the hallmark of lies is that they are simple and straightforward. They are reality the way we wish it was.

"Yeah," Barron says. "The agent's name was Eric Lawrence.

Married. Two kids. Patton strangled him when he figured out that Agent Lawrence was trying to work him. Amazing, right? So they have a homicidal governor on their hands and the higher-ups tell them they need to clean up the mess before there's a huge scandal."

I take a deep breath and let it out slowly. "So after I transform Patton, what? They arrest me, I guess. I have a motive, because of Mom. Then I'd get put in jail. What's the use of that if they want me to work for them? I can't work for them in prison—or at least whatever I could do would be pretty limited. Transform other inmates. Make cigarettes into bars of gold."

"That's the brilliant part, Cassel," Barron says. "You're not getting it. Not only would they have a scapegoat, but once you become a criminal who is no longer protected by an immunity deal, you'd have a lot fewer civil liberties. They could control you. Totally. They'd have exactly the weapon they want."

"Did you find out where this is going to take place?" I ask, and open the car door. I feel numb.

"Monday speech out near Carney, on the site of a former internment camp. They'll pitch tents by the memorial. The Feds have got the security sewn up, but who cares, Cassel? You're obviously not going."

I have to go, though. If I don't go, Patton gets away with it and Mom doesn't. I might not think my mother is a good person, but she's better than him.

And I don't want the Feds to get away with it either.

"Yes, I am," I say. "Look, thanks for doing this. I know

you didn't have to, and it really helps, knowing exactly what I'm getting into."

"Fine, go. But just show up and screw it up. What are they going to do, give you a good scolding? Mistakes happen. You screw up everything anyway."

"They'll just set me up again," I say.

"Now you'll be looking for it."

"I was *already* looking for it," I say. "I still didn't see what was going on. Besides, someone *should* stop Patton. I have a chance."

"Sure," he says. "Someone should. Someone who's not being *set up*. Someone who's *not you*."

"If I don't go along with this, the Feds are threatening to go after Mom. And that's the best we can hope for— because Patton will kill her. He's already tried once."

"He did what? What do you mean?"

"She got shot and she didn't want us to know. I would have told you, but the last time we talked, you hung up on me abruptly."

He ignores the rest of what I've said. "Is she okay?"

"I think so." I belt myself into the driver's seat. Then, sighing, I turn on the ignition. "But look, we have to do something."

"*We* aren't doing anything. I've done all I'm going to do, looking through those files. I'm looking out for myself. Try it sometime."

"I have a plan." The vent floods the car with cold air. I crank up the heat and rest my head against the wheel. "Or, well, not a *plan* exactly, but the beginnings of one. All

I need you to do is stall Patton. Find out where he's going to be on Monday and keep him there so he's late to his speech. For Mom's sake. You don't even have to visit me in jail."

"Do something for me, then," he says, after a pause.

The chances of me pulling this off and getting away with it are so bad that I'm actually not that concerned about whatever evil scheme my brother will try to involve me in next.

It's kind of freeing.

"Fine. I'll owe you a favor. But after. I don't have time right now." I look at the clock on the dashboard. "In fact, I don't have any time. I have to get to Wallingford. I'm already late."

"Call me after your school thing," Barron says, and hangs up. I toss the phone onto the passenger seat and pull out of the driveway, wishing that the only plan I've got didn't depend on putting my faith in two of the people I trust least in the world—Barron and myself.

It's ten after ten when I pull into the Wallingford parking lot. There's no time to go to my room, so I grab for my phone as I'm crossing the lawn, figuring I'll call Sam and get him to bring the photos of Wharton. But as I start thinking about the pictures, I have that awful feeling that there's something I've overlooked. In the diner I said that I thought Mina must have intended for us to *see* the pictures, but she didn't just let us see them. She made sure that we had copies.

Cold dread works its way up my spine. She wanted

someone else to blackmail Wharton. Someone to claim they took photographs and they want money. But we don't have to really do it. We just have to *seem like we're doing it.*

Stupid, stupid. I am so stupid. As I am thinking that, the phone rings in my hands. It's Daneca.

"Hey," I say. "I can't really talk. I'm so late to detention, and if I get another demerit—"

She sobs, liquid and awful, and I bite off whatever I was planning to say next. "What happened?" I ask.

"Sam found out," she says, choking out the words. "That I was seeing your brother. We were in the library together this morning, studying. Everything was just normal. I don't know, I wanted to see him—and figure out if there was still anything between us, if I felt—"

"Uh-huh," I say, crossing the green, hoping that Wharton is still in his office. Hoping that I'm wrong about Mina's plans. Hoping that Sam is somewhere burning those photos, even though I'm pretty sure he's too busy being devastated, and even if he wasn't, he has no reason to think we're in trouble. "Maybe he'll get over it."

It's pointless to think about the fact that neither of them getting over things is what broke them up in the first place. He's going to be furious with her and doubly furious at me for not telling him about Barron. Which, predictably, I deserve.

"No, *listen.* I left the room for a minute, and when I got back— Well, Barron must have texted me. And Sam read it—and read the other ones too. He started screaming at me. It was really ugly."

I pause. "Are you okay?"

"I don't know." She sounds like she's trying to fight back more tears. "Sam's always been so gentle—sweet. I just never thought he could be that angry. He scared me."

"Did he hurt you?" I am pushing open the doors of the administrative building, trying to think.

"No—nothing like that."

I head for the steps. No one's in any of the offices. My footfalls are loud in the hallways. The only sounds I can hear are the ones I'm making. Everyone's home for the weekend. My heart starts to race. Wharton's gone, and Mina has probably already told him that Sam and I are blackmailing him. He'll toss our room, and if he does, he's going to *find the pictures* . . . and, oh God, the gun. He's going to find the gun.

"Sam threw his books across the room, and then he got really cold, really distant," Daneca is saying, although it's hard to focus on her words. "It was like something just switched off inside him. He told me that he was supposed to meet you and he didn't care if you didn't show. He said that he'd take care of things, for once. He said he had a—"

"Wait. What?" I ask, snapping to attention. *"What did he say he had?"*

A shot rings through the stairwell from the floor above me, echoing through the empty building.

I don't know what I expect to see when I burst into Wharton's office, but it's not Sam and the Headmaster grappling on the antique oriental rug. Wharton is crawling across the floor, toward a gun that seems to have skittered away from both of them, while Sam's trying to pin him down.

I go for the gun.

Wharton looks at me dazedly when I swing the barrel in his direction. His white hair is sticking up all over the place. Sam slumps bonelessly, with a moan. That's when I realize that the red stain surrounding Sam isn't part of the pattern of the carpet.

"You shot him," I say to Wharton, in disbelief.

"I'm sorry," Sam gets out between locked teeth. "I screwed up, Cassel. I really screwed up."

"You're going to be fine, Sam," I say.

"Mr. Sharpe, you are *twenty minutes late* for your detention," Dean Wharton says from the floor. I wonder if he's in shock. "If you don't want to be in more trouble than you already are, I suggest that you give me that gun."

"You're kidding me, right? I'm calling an ambulance." I cross to Wharton's burled wood desk. The photos of Mina are there, on top of the other papers.

"No!" Wharton says, pushing himself to his feet. He lunges for the phone cord and pulls it out of the wall with a violent jerk. He's breathing hard, looking at me with glazed eyes. "I forbid it. I absolutely forbid it. You don't understand. If the board finds out about this— Well, you just don't understand the difficult position that will put me in."

"I can imagine," I say, pulling out my cell with one hand. I can't quite work out how to dial and keep the gun trained on him at the same time.

Wharton staggers toward me. "You can't call anyone. Put that phone down."

"You shot him!" I yell. "Stay back or I'll shoot you!"

Sam moans again. "It really hurts, Cassel. It really hurts."

"This can't be happening," Wharton says. Then he looks at me again. "I'll tell them that you did it! I'll say that you both came here to rob me and you two got into an argument, and then you shot him."

"I should know who shot me," says Sam. He winces as he puts pressure on his leg. "I'm not going to say it was Cassel."

"That won't matter. Whose gun is that, Mr. Sharpe?" Wharton says. "Yours, I'll wager."

"Nope," I say. "I stole it."

He gives me a sudden blank look. He is used to good boys in tidy uniforms who only play at being trouble-makers before doing what they're told, and the sudden suspicion that I'm nothing like that seems to disorient him. Then his mouth twists. "That's right. Everyone knows your background. Who are they going to believe—you or me? I am a respectable member of the community."

"Not when they see the pictures of you and Mina Lange. That's pretty sketchy stuff. You're not going to look good. You're sick, right? Brain starting to go. First you forget small things, then bigger ones, and the doctor gives you the news that it only gets worse from here. Time to resign from Wallingford. Not much you can do legally—but *illegally*— Well, now we're talking. You can buy children, little girls like Mina, and she can't cure you because it's degenerative, but she can give you the next best thing.

"So you don't get any worse and she starts getting sick. At first you rationalize it. She's young. She'll get better. So she misses some classes? That's nothing for her to be upset about. After all, you've gotten her a scholarship to Wallingford, a prestigious prep school, so that you could have her on hand whenever you needed her.

"When she told you we had the pictures, you probably were willing to pay. But then when Sam comes in here, he says something that makes you realize the money is for Mina. And that puts you in a tough spot. If she goes, you get sick again. And if anyone sees the pictures, you lose your job. You can't have that, so you go for the gun."

Wharton looks toward the desk as though he wants to make a mad grab for the photos. Sweat is beading on his forehead. "She was in on it?"

"She *orchestrated* this. She took those pictures. The only thing she didn't expect was someone to actually try to help her. Sam did, because he's a good guy. See what it got him. Now I am making this call and you're not going to stop me."

"No," Wharton says.

I glance at Sam. He looks very pale. I wonder how much blood he's already lost.

"Look, I don't care about Mina or the money or you losing your mind," I say. "Take the photos. Keep your secret. Tell the ambulance people whatever you want when they come. But he's really hurt."

"Okay. Let me think. You must know someone," the dean says in a low, pleading voice. "The kind of doctor who won't report a shooting."

"You want me to call a *mob doctor*?"

The eagerness on his face is exaggerated, manic. "Please. Please. I'll give you anything. You can both graduate with a 4.0. You can blow off all your classes. If you make this go away, as far as I'm concerned, you can do whatever you want."

"And no more demerits," says Sam weakly.

"Are you sure?" I ask Sam. "This doctor's not going to have all the stuff that a real hospital—"

"Cassel, *think about it*," Sam says. "If an ambulance comes, we're all in trouble. We all lose."

I hesitate.

"My parents," he says. "I can't—they can't find out." I look at him for a long moment and then remember that Sam was the one who brought a gun into the dean's office and threatened him with it. Normal parents probably frown on that kind of thing. I bet judges don't like it either. This isn't a zero-sum game for the dean, Sam, and me. There's plenty of trouble to go around.

With a sigh I flick the safety on, shove the gun into my pocket, and make the call.

The doctor with the crooked teeth arrives a half hour later. His answering service never asked for a name from me and never gave one for him, either. In my head I am still calling him Dr. Doctor.

He's wearing a similar outfit to the one I saw him in the last time—sweatshirt and jeans. I notice he's got on sneakers with no socks and there's a scab of some kind on his ankle. His cheeks look more sunken than I remember, and he's smoking a cigarette. I wonder how old he is. He looks like he's maybe in his thirties with a full head of unruly curls and the scruff of a man who can't be bothered to shave every day. The only thing that indicates he's a doctor at all is the black bag he's carrying.

I've elevated Sam's leg and padded it with my T-shirt. I am sitting on the floor, applying pressure. Dean Wharton wrapped Sam in my coat to stop him from shivering. We've done our awful best, and I am feeling like the worst friend in the world for not insisting we take him immediately to the hospital, whatever the consequences.

"You got a bathroom?" the doctor says, glancing around.

"Through those doors and down the hall," says Dean Wharton, frowning at the doctor's cigarette disapprovingly, still apparently trying to stay in control of the situation. "This is a no smoking building."

The doctor gives him an incredulous look. "I've got to scrub in. Clear off the desk while I'm gone. We're going to have to get the patient up there. And get some more lights. I need to see what I'm doing."

"Do you trust that man?" Dean Wharton asks me as he lifts stacks of papers and shoves them into his filing cabinet haphazardly.

"No," I say.

Sam makes a choked sound.

"I didn't mean it that way," I say. "You're going to be fine. I'm just pissed off. Mostly at myself—no, scratch that, mostly at Wharton."

The dean drags a floor lamp to his now clear desk and flips it on. He manages to position a couple of other lights on the bookshelves, tilting their flexible necks to point bulbs at the table, like faces all turned toward a performance.

"Help me get him up," I say.

"Don't lift me," Sam says, slurring the words slightly. "I can hop."

This seems like a terrible idea, but I am not arguing with a wounded man. Putting his arm around my neck, I haul him up. He makes a low sound in the back of his throat, like he's biting back a scream. His gloved fingers dig into my bare arm. His face contorts with pain and concentration, his eyes closing tightly.

"Don't put any weight on it," I remind him.

"Screw you," he says through gritted teeth, which I take to mean that he's doing okay.

We move across the room, his body half-slumped on mine. My T-shirt slides off his leg, and blood seeps sluggishly from the hole as he climbs up onto the desk.

"Lie down," I say, reaching for the shirt. I have no idea how clean anything is, but I try to mop up the worst of the blood and reapply pressure.

Wharton stands back, watching us with what looks like a mixture of distaste and terror. Possibly he's mourning the ruination of his desk.

The doctor comes back into the room, his cigarette gone. He's got on what looks like a plastic poncho and gloves. His hair has been pulled back with a bandana.

Sam moans. "What—what is he going to do?"

"I am going to need an assistant for this," the doctor says, looking at me. "You okay with blood?"

I nod.

"You're lucky. My last job wasn't too far from here. Sometimes I can get pretty backed up."

"I bet," I say. I wish he would stop talking.

He nods. "So . . . I need the money. It's going to be five hundred up front, like my answering service said. Maybe more, depending on how things go, but I'll need to have that now."

I look over at Wharton, and he fusses around with one of the drawers in his desk. He must be used to paying other people in cash, because he unlocks some section inside a lower part and counts out a wad of bills.

"Here's a grand," the dean says, his hand shaking as he holds out the cash. "Let's make sure things go well. No complications, do you understand?"

"Money soaks up germs. It's dirty stuff. You take it, kid," Dr. Doctor says. "Put it in my bag. And take out the bottle of iodine. Then, before you do anything else, I want you to go wash your hands."

"My gloves?" I ask.

"Your *hands*," he tells me. "You're going to wear a pair of plastic gloves. Those are ruined."

In the bathroom I scrub furiously. My hands. My arms. He's right about my leather gloves. They are so sodden with blood that my hands were stained red underneath. I splash water onto my face for good measure. Bare to the waist, I feel like I should try to cover up somehow, but there's nothing to cover up with. My T-shirt is a disgusting mess. My coat is still on the floor of the other room.

I return to the dean's office to find the doctor has his bag open. It's a mess of bottles, cloths, and clamps. He's taking out sharp, scary metal instruments and laying them out on a side table he's dragged over. I put on a pair of thin plastic gloves and get out the iodine.

"Cassel," Sam says faintly. "I'm going to be okay, right?"

I nod. "I swear."

"Tell Daneca I'm sorry." Tears are welling up in the corners of his eyes. "Tell my mom—"

"Shut up, Sam," I say fiercely. "I said you were going to be fine."

The doctor grunts. "Get me one of the swabs, soak it in the iodine, and wipe off the bullet hole."

"But—," I say, not sure how to proceed.

"Cut off his pants." He sounds exasperated, and I can see that he's taking out a brown vial and a large needle.

I try to keep my hand steady as I take out the scissors from the kit and slice open Sam's cargo pants. The material rips wide, to his thigh, and I see the actual wound, just above his knee, small and welling with blood.

When my fingers touch his skin, brushing it with brown medicine, he twitches.

"It's fine, Sam," I say.

Across the room Wharton sits down heavily in a chair and puts his head in his hands.

The doctor walks over to Sam, holding up a syringe.

He taps it, like he's trying to get the air out. "This is morphine. It should help with the pain."

Sam's eyes go wide.

"You're going to need to be sedated for this," the doctor says.

Sam swallows and, visibly steeling himself, nods.

The doctor sticks the needle into a vein in Sam's arm. He makes a sound that's half moan and half swallow.

"Do you think she really likes him?" Sam asks. I know who he means. Barron. And I don't know the answer, not really.

The doctor looks at me, then back at Sam.

"No," I say. "But maybe you shouldn't worry about that now."

"Distracting—" Sam's eyes roll back in his head, his body going limp. I wonder if he's dreaming.

"Now you've got to hold him down," the doctor says. "While I dig out the bullet."

"What?" I say. "Hold him how?"

"Just keep him from moving too much. I need his leg to stay steady." He looks across the room at Dean Wharton. "You. Come over here. I need someone to hand me forceps and a scalpel when I ask for them. Put on these gloves."

The dean stands and crosses the room dazedly.

I move to the other side of the desk and put one hand on Sam's stomach and the other on his thigh, leaning my weight against them. He turns his head and groans, although he remains out of it. I let go immediately, stepping back.

"*Hold him.* He won't remember this," the doctor says,

870

which doesn't comfort me even a little. There's lots of stuff I don't remember, but that doesn't mean it didn't happen.

I put my hands back in place.

Dr. Doctor leans in and presses around the wound. Sam moans again and tries to shift position. I don't let him. "He's going to stay semiconscious. It's safer that way, but it means you've really got to stop him from moving. I think the bullet's still in there."

"What does that mean?" Dean Wharton asks.

"It means we've got to get it out," says the doctor. "Give me the scalpel."

I turn my head at the moment the point of the knife sinks into Sam's skin. He writhes under my hands, squirming blindly, forcing me to put my full weight against him. When I look again, the doctor has cut a deep slice. Blood is welling up out of it.

"Retractor," the doctor says, and Wharton hands it over.

"Hemostat," the doctor says.

"What's that?" Wharton asks.

"The silver thing with the curved tip. Take your time. It's not my emergency."

I shoot the doctor my filthiest glare, but he isn't looking. He's pushing an instrument into Sam's leg. Sam moans, low, and jerks slightly.

"Shhh," I say. "It's almost over. It's almost over."

Blood sprays out of the leg suddenly, hitting my chest and face. I stagger back, shocked, and Sam nearly jerks off the table.

"Hold him, you idiot!" the doctor shouts.

I grab Sam's leg, slamming myself down onto it. The blood pulses along with the beat of his heart, rising and falling. There is so much blood. It's in my eyelashes, smeared over my stomach. It's all I can smell and all I can taste.

"When I say hold him, I'm not joking! Do you want your friend to die? *Hold him.* I have to find the vessel I nicked. Where is that hemostat?"

Sam's skin looks clammy. His mouth looks bluish. I turn my head away from the surgery, my fingers digging into his muscles, holding him down as firmly as I can. I grit my teeth and try not to watch the doctor tie off the artery or watch him root out the bullet or start stitching up the wound with black string. I hang on and watch the rise and fall of Sam's chest, reminding myself that so long as he's breathing and moaning and shifting, so long as he's in pain, he's alive.

After, I slump on the floor and listen to the doctor give Dean Wharton instructions. My whole body hurts, my muscles sore from fighting Sam's.

"He's going to have to take antibiotics for two weeks. Otherwise he's at serious risk for infection," the doctor says, taping the gauze in place and wadding up his bloody poncho. "I can't write him a prescription, but this is enough for the first week. My answering service will contact whichever one of you called about getting more antibiotics."

"I understand," the dean is saying.

I understand too. Dr. Doctor can't write a prescription because he's had his license revoked. That's why he's acting as a concierge doctor for Zacharov and for us.

872

"And if you need a cleanup service for in here, I know some very discreet people."

"That would be very much appreciated."

They sound like two civilized men, discussing civilized things. They are two men of the world, a man of medicine and a man of letters. They probably don't think of themselves as criminals, no matter what they've done.

As the doctor walks out the door, I take my phone out of my pocket.

"What are you doing?" Dean Wharton demands.

"I'm calling his girlfriend," I say. "Someone's going to have to stay with him tonight. It can't be me, and he wouldn't want it to be you."

"You have somewhere more important to be?"

I look up at Wharton. I'm exhausted. And I hate that I can't stay, when this is all my fault in the first place. My gun. My dumb joke with Mina, the finger in my pocket that made it seem like bringing a gun was the right move. *It can't be me.*

"I absolutely forbid you to call another student, Mr. Sharpe. This situation is chaotic enough as it is."

"Bite me," I say, my gloved fingers leaving sticky brown marks behind when I tap the keys.

"Did you find him?" Daneca says, instead of "hello." "Is he all right?"

The connection isn't very good. She seems scratchy and far away.

"Can you come to Dean Wharton's office?" I ask. "Because if you can, I think you should come now. Sam could really use you. It would really help if you came right now. But don't panic. Please just don't panic and please come now."

She says she will in a bewildered tone that makes me think I must sound very strange. Everything feels empty.

"You should go," I tell Dean Wharton.

By the time Daneca arrives, he's already gone.

She looks around the room, at the blood-soaked carpet, and the lamps on the bookshelves, at Sam lying on Wharton's massive desk, unconscious. She looks at his leg and at me, sitting on the floor without a shirt on.

"What happened?" she asks, walking over to Sam and touching his cheek lightly with her glove.

"Sam got—he got shot." She looks scared. "A doctor came and fixed him. When he wakes up, I know he'll want you there."

"Are you okay?" she asks. I have no idea what she means. Of course I'm all right. I'm not the one lying on a desk.

I stagger to my feet and pick up my coat.

I nod. "But I have to go, okay? Dean Wharton knows about this." I gesture vaguely, mostly toward his carpet. "I don't think we can move Sam until he wakes up. It's what— about noon now?"

"It's two in the afternoon."

"Right," I say, glancing toward the windows. Dean Wharton drew the blinds, I remember. Not that I would be able to tell the time by the amount of sunlight. "I can't—"

"Cassel, what's going on? What happened? Does where you're going have to do with Sam?"

I start to laugh, and Daneca looks even more worried. "Actually," I say, "it's totally unrelated."

"Cassel—," she says.

I look at Sam, lying on the desk, and think of my mother in Zacharov's house, nursing her own gunshot wound. I close my eyes.

At the end of a criminal's life, it's always the small mistake, the coincidence, the lark. The time we got too comfortable, the time we slipped up, the time someone aimed a little to the left.

I've heard Grandad's war stories a thousand times. How they finally got Mo. How Mandy almost got away. How Charlie fell.

Birth to grave, we know it'll be us one day. Our tragedy is that we forget it might be someone else first.

I AM SHAKING WHEN I

walk out of Wharton's office, trembling with such force that I'm afraid I'll stumble as I make my way down the stairs. Sam's blood is staining my skin, soaking through my pants. I force myself to walk across the quad, hunched over so that my coat hides the worst of it. Most students are gone on the weekends, and I am careful not to take any of the paths, and to veer away if I see anyone. I stick to the shadows of trees and darkness.

Once I make it to my dorm hall, I head straight for the communal bathroom. I see myself in the mirror. There is a smear of red across my jaw, and for a moment, as I try to wipe it and only smear it wider, I feel like I am looking at a stranger, someone older with hollow cheekbones and lips curled in a mean scowl. A madman fresh from a murder. A sicko. A killer.

I don't think he likes me much.

Despite the scowl on his face, his eyes are black and wet, as if he's about to start crying.

I don't like him much either.

My stomach lurches. I have barely enough time to make it into one of the stalls before I start to retch. I haven't eaten anything, so it's mostly sour bile. On my knees on the cold tile, choking, the wave of anger and self-loathing that sweeps over me is so towering and vast, I cannot imagine how there will be anything of me that's not carried away with it. I feel like there's nothing left. No fight in me.

I have to focus. Yulikova will be here in a couple more hours, and there's stuff I need to take care of, things that need to happen before I can go with her. Arrangements. Last details and instructions.

But I'm frozen with horror at everything that has happened and everything in front of me. All I can think of is blood and the guttural, raw sound of Sam moaning in agony.

I better get used to it.

I take a shower so hot that my skin feels sunburned when I get out. Then I dress for my date with the Feds—crappy T-shirt that got chewed up by one of the dryers, my leather jacket, and a new pair of gloves. The bloody clothes I run under the tap until they're less foul, then wrap them in a plastic bag. Even though it's a risk, I keep my phone, turning off the ringer and tucking it into my sock.

I shove a bunch of other things into my jacket—things I plan on transferring to the duffel I left in the car. Index cards and a pen. Styling gel and a comb. A few pictures of Patton that I print out with Sam's crappy ink-jet and then fold. A beaten-up detective paperback.

Then I walk to the corner store, dumping the plastic bag of bloody clothes into the garbage can outside. Mr. Gazonas smiles at me, like he always does.

"How's your little blond girlfriend?" he asks. "I hope you're taking her someplace nice on a Saturday night."

I grin and get myself a cup of coffee and a ham and cheese sandwich. "I'll tell her it was your idea."

"You do that," he says as he gives me my change.

I hope I get to take Lila out some Saturday night. I hope I get a chance to see her again.

Trying not to think about that, I go back to the parking lot and force down my food, sitting in my parked car. Everything tastes like ashes and dust.

I listen to the radio, flipping through channels. I can't concentrate on what I'm listening to, and after a while I can't keep my eyes open either.

I wake to a tapping on the window. Agent Yulikova is standing beside the car, with Agent Jones and another woman I don't recognize beside them.

For a moment I wonder what would happen if I refused to get out. I wonder if they'd have to leave eventually. I wonder if they'd get one of those jaws of life and pop the top off my Benz like it was a tin can.

I open the car door and grab for my duffel.

"Have a nice rest?" Yulikova asks me. She's smiling sweetly, like she's the den mother of my Boy Scout troop instead of the lady who wants to send me up the river. She looks healthier than she did in the hospital. The cold has made her cheeks rosy.

I force a yawn. "You know me," I say. "Lazy as a bedbug."

"Well, come on. You can sleep in our car if you want."

"Sure," I say, locking the Benz.

Their car is predictably black—one of those huge Lincolns that you can spread out in. I do. And while I'm getting comfortable, I lean down to put my key into my bag and surreptitiously lift out my cell. Then, leaning back, I palm my phone into the pocket of the car door.

The last place anyone is going to look for contraband is in their own vehicle.

"So, you have something to turn in?" Yulikova says. She's in the back with me. The other two agents are up front.

The gun. Oh, no, the gun. I left it in Wharton's office, under the desk.

She must see it in my face, the flash of horror.

"Did something happen?" she asks.

"I forgot it," I say. "I'm so sorry. If you let me out, I'll go get it."

"No," she says, exchanging a look with the other female agent. "No, that's all right, Cassel. We can get it when we bring you back. Why don't you tell us where it is."

"If you want me to get it—," I say.

She sighs. "No, that's fine."

"Are you going to tell me what's going on now?" I ask. "I'd really feel a lot more comfortable if I was in on the plan."

"We're going to tell you everything. Honest," she says. "It's very simple and straightforward. Governor Patton is going to give a press conference, and when it's over, we'd like you to use your gift to change him into—well, into a living thing that can be contained."

"Do you have a preference?"

She gives me a look, like she's trying to gauge whether or not I'm testing her. "We'll leave that up to you and whatever is going to be easier, but it's imperative that he doesn't get away."

"If it's all the same, I'll turn him into a big dog, I guess. Maybe one of those fancy hounds with the pointy faces— salukis, right? No, *borzois*. Some guy my mother used to know had those." His name was Clyde Austin. He hit me in the head with a bottle. I leave those details out. "Or maybe a big beetle. You could keep him in a jar. Just remember to put in the airholes."

There is a sudden flicker of fear in Yulikova's eyes.

"You're upset. I can see that," she says, reaching out and touching her gloved hand to mine. It's an intimate, motherly gesture, and I have to force myself not to flinch. "You're always sarcastic when you're nervous. And I know this isn't easy for you, not knowing details, but you have to trust us. Being a government operative means always feeling a little bit in the dark. It's how we keep one another safe."

Her face is so kind. What she's saying is reasonable. She seems truthful, too—she's got no obvious tells that would indicate otherwise. The thought nags me that Barron could have made up everything he told me about the content of the files. That would be profoundly awful and totally plausible.

I nod. "I guess I'm used to relying on myself."

"When you first came to us, I knew you were going to be a special case. Not just because of your power but because of where you were from. We seldom have significant contact with boys like you and Barron. The average LMD recruit is a kid who's been living on the street, either because they left home or because they were forced out. Sometimes a family contacts us with a child who they think might be a worker, and we bring them into the program."

"Nonworker families, you mean?" I ask. "Are they scared—the parents?"

"Usually," she says. "Sometimes the situation is so potentially violent that we have to remove the child. We have two schools in the country for worker children under the age of ten."

"Military schools," I say.

She nods. "There are worse things, Cassel. Do you know how many worker children are murdered by their own parents? The statistics are one thing, but I've seen the bones, heard the terrified excuses. We'll get a report of a kid who might be a worker, but when we get to the town, the girl will be staying with "relatives," whom no one has any reliable contact information for and who don't have a phone. The boy will have transferred to another school, only there's no record of where that might be. They're usually dead."

I don't have anything to say to that.

"And then there are the neglected children, the abused children, the kids who are raised to think their only choice is becoming a criminal." She sighs. "You're wondering why I'm telling you all this."

"Because that's what you're used to—not kids like me, with mothers like mine and brothers like mine."

She nods, glancing toward the front of the car, where Agent Jones is sitting. "I'm not used to being thought of as the enemy."

I blink at her. "That's not what I think."

She laughs. "Oh, I so wish for a lie detector test right now, Cassel! And the worst part is that I realize it's at least partially our fault. We only know about you because you had no other choice but to turn yourself in—and now with your mother being in a lot of potential trouble, well, let's just say that our loyalties are not in alignment. We've had to make deals, you and I, which isn't how I want us to proceed. I want us to be on the same page, especially going into such an important mission."

She lets me chew that over for a while. Eventually the car stops in front of a Marriott. It's one of the innocuous massive box hotels that are perfect for keeping track of someone in, because every floor leads to one central lobby. Pick a high enough floor, and all you need is someone posted outside the room and maybe another person by the stairs and another by the elevator. That's three people—exactly the number in the car with me right now.

"Okay," I say as Agent Jones kills the engine. "After all, I am entirely in your hands."

Yulikova smiles. "And we're in yours."

I grab my duffel, they take navy overnight bags and briefcases out of the trunk, and we head for the main entrance. I feel like I am going to a very dull sleepover.

"Wait here," Yulikova says, and leaves me standing in the lobby with the nameless female agent while Yalikova and Jones check us in.

I sit on the arm of a beige chair and stick out my free hand. "Cassel Sharpe."

She regards me with all the suspicion that Jones usually does. Her short ginger hair is pulled back into a low pony-tail, and her navy suit matches her overnight bag. Sensible beige pumps. Panty hose, for God's sake. Tiny gold hoops in her ears complete the effect of a person with no tells and no inner life. I can't even tell her age; it could be anywhere between late twenties and late thirties.

"Cassandra Brennan."

I blink several times, but when she reaches out her hand, I take it and we shake.

"I see why they gave you this job," I say finally. "Brennan family, huh? Yulikova said she hadn't worked with *many* people who come from worker families. She didn't say she'd worked with *none*."

"It's a common enough name," she says.

Then Yulikova comes back and we head to the elevators.

My room is part of a suite, attached to the rooms where

Yulikova, Jones, and Brennan will be sleeping. Of course, I'm not given my own key. My door, predictably, does not exit into the hallway but opens onto the main room, where there's a crappy couch, a television, and a mini fridge.

I dump my duffel in my bedroom and head back out into the central room. Agent Jones is watching me, as if I'm about to pull some kind of ninja move and escape through the air vent.

"You want something from the vending machine, you ask one of us to accompany you. Otherwise you won't be able to reenter the room—the doors lock automatically," he says, like I've never been in a hotel before. Jones is about as subtle as a two-by-four to the face.

"Hey," I say. "Where's that partner of yours? Hunt, wasn't it?"

"Promoted up the chain," he says tersely.

I grin. "Give him my felicitations."

Jones looks like he wants to slug me, which is only subtly different from his usual way of looking at me like I'm a slug.

"Are you hungry?" Yulikova asks me, interrupting our little conversation. "Did you have dinner?"

I think of the remains of the sandwich moldering in my car. The thought of eating still fills me with a vague queasiness, but I don't want them to notice.

"I didn't," I say. "But I am eager to hear some specifics about what happens next."

"Perfect," Yulikova says. "Why don't you wash up, and Agent Brennan can go out and get us some food. There has to be a Chinese place around here. Then we'll talk. Cassel, is there anything you don't like?"

"I like everything," I say, and walk into my room.

Jones follows. "Can I have a look at that bag?"

"Go right ahead." I sit down on the bed.

He smiles thinly. "It's just procedure."

My duffel seems to bore him after he feels around the lining and looks at my pictures and blank index cards. "Have to pat you down too," he says.

I stand up and think of my cell phone in the pocket of their car door. It's hard not to smile, but I remind myself that congratulating myself on my own cleverness is a good way to get caught.

He leaves, and I waste some time reading my paperback. It contains the unlikely reveal that the detective and the murderer he's been tracking are actually the same person. I am incredulous at how long it took him to figure that out. I got it a lot faster when it was me.

A little while later I hear the far door to the suite open and some conversation. Then someone knocks on my door.

By the time I emerge, Brennan is passing out paper plates. The smell of grease makes my mouth water. I thought I wasn't hungry, but I am suddenly ravenous.

"Did we get hot mustard?" I ask, and Jones passes a couple of packets in my direction.

As we eat, Yulikova puts a map on the table. It's of an open area, a park. "Like I said in the car, this is a very straightforward plan. Complications are to be avoided. We wouldn't allow you to be part of an operation we weren't very confident in, Cassel. We understand that you're inexperienced.

"Governor Patton is giving a press conference on the site of one of the former worker internment camps. He'd like to position Proposition 2 as helping workers, but he'd also like to subtly remind everyone to be afraid."

She takes out a ballpoint pen from her jacket and marks an *X* on a clearing. "You'll be here the whole time, in one of the trailers. The only real danger is that you're going to be bored."

I smile and take another bite of my kung pao chicken. I get a hot pepper and try to ignore my burning tongue.

"They're going to build a stage there." She touches the page. "And a trailer for Patton to get dressed in will go here. Over this way are a few other trailers for his staff to work out of. We've managed to get one that we're assured can be kept secure."

"So I'm going to be by myself?"

She smiles. "We'll have people everywhere outside, posing as local police. We also have a few people in Patton's security detail. You'll be in good hands."

Which makes sense, sort of. But it also makes sense that if I'm alone in the room and I come out and attack Patton, I'll look like I was acting alone. The Feds will be off the hook.

"What about security cameras?" I ask.

Agent Brennan raises her eyebrows.

"Because it's outdoors, there aren't any," Yulikova says, "but what we need to worry about are press cameras." She makes a blue dot in front of where she marked the stage.

"The press pit is here, but there will be vans parked in the lot over there, where our vehicles will be too. If you stay in the trailer, you should be out of sight."

I nod.

Agent Jones serves himself another pile of sesame chicken and rice, squirting soy sauce over the whole thing.

"Governor Patton is going to make a brief speech, and then he's going to answer questions from reporters," Yulikova says. "You're going to slip into one of the trailers and stay there until Governor Patton takes the stage. We have a monitor set up so that you can watch the local news. They're broadcasting the event live."

"What's the speech supposed to be about?"

Yulikova coughs discreetly. "Senator Raeburn has attacked Patton in the press. This is supposed to be his chance to redirect the conversation—and to reach out to the rest of the country. If Proposition 2 passes in New Jersey, other states will start drafting similar legislation."

"Okay, so I wait until Patton leaves the stage. Then what? Do I count to three and jump out at him?"

"We have a uniform for you. You'll have a clipboard and headset mic. You'll look like one of the crew backstage. And we have a specially formulated black ink that covers your hand. It looks like you're wearing a glove, but your fingers will remain bare."

"Clever." I am eager to see that stuff. My grandfather would be happy to know that the government really has been holding out on us in terms of secret cool toys. Too bad I can't tell him.

"While Patton is giving his speech, you will move to his dressing room and wait for him there. When he comes in, well, it's a pretty tight space. It shouldn't be too difficult to get your hands on him. We'll be able to communicate with you through the headset, so if you have any questions or want to know the position of the governor, we will be able to give you all the support you need."

I nod again. It's not a terrible plan. It's a lot less complicated than Philip's whole lurk-around-the-bathroom-all-night scheme for killing Zacharov. It's also eerily similar. I guess transformation work assassinations all have a certain pattern.

"So, okay. Governor Patton's a borzoi. Everyone's freaking out. Now what? What's my exit strategy? I have a minute or two—maybe less—before the blowback hits. His bodyguards are right outside."

She makes a circle on the paper where the trailer is. "Figure the confrontation happens here."

Agent Brennan leans forward to see the mark.

"The bodyguard who's in our employ—the man who's going to be on the left—will explain that Patton doesn't want to be disturbed. Patton will doubtless be in great distress, but—"

"Doubtless," I say.

No one ever laughs at this stuff.

"We believe his erratic behavior makes it likely that our agent will be able to explain away the scuffle and the sounds that follow. When you're ready, let us know through the headset and we'll get you both out of there."

"I won't be able to go right away," I say. Agent Jones starts to speak, and I hold up a gloved hand, shaking my head. "No, I mean I *can't*. The blowback makes it so that I will be shifting shape. You might be able to move me a short distance, but it's going to be complicated, and I won't be able to help."

They look at one another.

"I've seen him do it before," Jones says. "As much as I hate to say it, he's right. We're going to have to stall for time."

Yulikova and Agent Brennan are both eyeing me speculatively.

"It's that bad?" Agent Brennan asks. "I mean—"

I shrug. "I don't know. I'm not really looking. Sometimes I don't really have anything to look *with*, if you know what I'm saying."

She blanches. I think I may have successfully freaked out my first FBI agent.

Go me.

"All right," Yulikova says, "we'll change the plan. We'll wait out Cassel's blowback and *then* get him out. We'll have a car standing by."

I grin. "I'll need a leash."

Agent Jones gives me an evaluating look.

"For Patton. And a collar. Can we get a really embarrassing one?"

His nostrils flare.

"That's very practical thinking." Yulikova seems sincere and calm, but Jones's jumpiness is getting on my nerves. It might just be that he gets like this before missions, but it is driving me up the wall.

"And that's it," Yulikova says, reaching for another egg roll. "The whole thing. Any questions, Cassel? Any questions, anyone?"

"Where will you all be?" I touch the map, pushing it a little toward her.

"Back here," she says, her gloved finger tapping against the table, indicating a vague place distantly in front of the stage. "There's a van we can use as a command center where Patton won't be threatened by our presence. He's requested all his own security, so we can't be too obvious. But we will be there, Cassel. Very close by."

Very close by, but not anywhere I'll know about. Great.

"What if I need to find you?" I ask. "What if the monitor isn't working or the headset shorts out?"

"Let me give you some very good advice that was once given to me. Sometimes on missions things go wrong. When that happens, you have two choices: Keep going because the thing that went wrong wasn't important, or abort the mission. You've got to go with your gut. If the monitor goes out, just stay in the room and do nothing. If it doesn't feel right, do nothing."

That is good advice—and it's not the kind that seems useful to give someone that you want to get caught. I look at Yulikova, drinking her diet soda and chewing her food. I think of my brother. Am I really trying to decide which of them is more worthy of my trust?

"Okay," I say, and pick up the map. "Can I keep this? I want to make sure I know the layout."

"You act like you've done this before," Agent Brennan says.

"I come from a long line of grifters," I say. "I've pulled a con or two."

She snorts, shaking her head. Jones glowers at both of us. Yulikova cracks open her fortune cookie and holds up the fortune. Printed across the ribbon of paper in block letters are the words: "You will be invited to an exciting event."

I turn in shortly after that.

Looking at the hotel phone by my bed, I itch to call Daneca and find out how Sam's doing. Even knowing that it's probably bugged, I am tempted. But he should be resting, and I don't even know if he'll want to talk to me.

Any mention of him being shot would have the Feds making all the wrong guesses and asking too many questions. One more thing no one can afford.

I shouldn't call Lila, either, even though last night seems more dream than real. Just thinking of her as I sit on the scratchy hotel comforter, remembering the slide of her skin on mine, the way she laughed, the curve of her mouth—it feels risky. As though even the memory of her will give the Feds something they can use against me.

Now that she knows I'm working with the agency, I wonder what she'll do with that information. I wonder what she'll expect me to do.

I get into bed and try to sleep, my thoughts careening between Lila and Sam. I hear her laugh and see his blood, feel her bare hands and hear his scream. On and on until everyone's laughing and everyone's screaming all the way down into my dreams.

The next morning I stumble out into the main room.

Agent Jones is there, sitting on the couch and drinking a mug of room service coffee. He glowers in my direction in the manner of a man who has taken a shift that started many hours ago. I bet the three of them traded off all night, to make sure I didn't skip out.

I find another cup and pour myself some coffee. It's terrible.

"Hey," I say, thinking suddenly of my mother and a hotel nothing like this one. "Can you really cook meth in a hotel coffeepot?"

"Sure," he says, looking into his cup thoughtfully.

Guess Mom was right about one thing.

After I take a shower and get dressed, the rest of them are there, ordering breakfast. The whole day stretches in front of us with very little to do. Jones wants to watch a basketball game on the big plasma television, so I spend the afternoon playing cards with Yulikova and Brennan at the table. First we gamble for candy from the vending machine, then for spare change, then for choice of which film we rent.

I pick *The Thin Man*. I need a laugh.

MONDAY MORNING I WAKE

up not remembering where I am. Then it all comes rushing back—the hotel, the Feds, the assassination.

Adrenaline hits my bloodstream with such force that I kick off the covers and stand, pace the room with no idea where I am going. Corralling myself into the bathroom, I avoid my own gaze in the mirror. I am nearly sick with nerves, doubled over by them.

I don't know whether to believe Barron or not. I don't know if I'm being set up. I don't know who the good guys are anymore.

I thought that the people I grew up around—mostly criminals—were different from regular people. Certainly different from cops, from federal agents with their shiny badges. I thought grifters and con men were just born bad. I thought there was some inner flaw in us. Something corrupt that meant that we'd never be like other people—that the best we could do is ape them.

But now I wonder—what if everyone is pretty much the same and it's just a thousand small choices that add up to the person you are? No good or evil, no black and white, no inner demons or angels whispering the right answers in our ears like it's some cosmic SAT test. Just us, hour by hour, minute by minute, day by day, making the best choices we can.

The thought is horrifying. If that's true, then there's no right choice. There's just choice.

I stand there in front of the mirror, trying to figure out what to do. I stand there for a long time.

When I get it together enough to go out into the main room, I find Yulikova and Jones already dressed. Brennan isn't with them.

I drink crappy gray room service coffee and eat some eggs.

"I've got your props," Yulikova says, disappearing into her room. She comes back with a paintbrush, a small tube of what looks like oil paint, a brown hoodie, a lanyard with an ID tag hanging from it, and a headset.

"Huh." I turn the ID tag over in my hands. The name George Parker is on it, underneath a blurred picture that could pass for me. It's a good piece of identification. The photo is forgettable and would be useless on a wanted poster or blasted across the Internet. "Nice."

"This is *our job*," she says wryly.

"Sorry." She's right. I have been thinking of them as amateurs, honest and upright government employees trying to pull off a scam they're unused to—but I keep forgetting, this is what they do. They con criminals, and maybe they're conning me.

"I'll need you to take off your gloves," she says. "This stuff takes a long time to dry, so if you need to do any last preparations, do them now."

"She means go take a piss," Agent Jones says.

I shoulder on the hoodie and zip it up, then go into the bedroom, where I fold the pictures of Patton up and shove them into the back pocket of my jeans. I put the comb in the other pocket, with the index cards. The pen and hair gel I stick into the front pocket of the hoodie, along with my car keys.

I walk back out to the table and take off my gloves, spreading my fingers out on the pressed wood of the table as I sit.

Yulikova glances at my face and then back at my hands. She picks up my right hand with her gloved fingers and draws it closer to her, turning it palm up.

Jones is watching us, readiness in every line of his body. If I grabbed for the bare skin of her throat, he'd be out of his chair and on us in seconds.

If I grabbed for her throat, he'd be too late. I bet he knows it too.

She uncaps the tube and squirts cold black gel onto the back of my hand. She doesn't look flustered at all, just calm

and efficient. If she thinks of me as anything more dangerous than just another worker kid she's training, she doesn't
show it.

The bristles of the brush tickle—I'm not used to anything touching my hands so directly—but the paint covers my skin thoroughly, drying to a dull leathery sheen.
Yulikova is careful to ink everything, even the pads of my
fingers, and I am careful not to move, no matter how much
I want to laugh.

"Okay," she says, capping the tube. "As soon as that
dries, we'll be ready to go. You can relax now."

I study her face. "You promise that the charges against
my mother will be dropped after this, right?"

"It's the least we can do," she says. There is nothing in
her expression that gives me any reason not to believe her,
but her words aren't exactly a guarantee.

If she's lying, I know what I have to do. But if she's not,
then I will have thrown away everything for nothing. It's an
impossible choice. The only chance I have is to rattle her
into revealing something. "What if I don't want to join the
LMD? I mean, after this operation. What if I decide I'm not
cut out for federal agenting?"

That makes her stop in the process of cleaning off the
brush in a cup of water. "That would be very difficult for
me. My superiors are interested in you. I'm sure you can
imagine. A transformation worker is very rare. In fact . . ."

She brings out a stack of familiar papers. The con-
tracts. "I was going to wait to do this later, when we had a
few minutes alone, but I think now is the time. My bosses

would feel a lot more comfortable if you would go ahead and sign."

"I thought we agreed to wait until I graduated."

"This operation has forced my hand."

I nod. "I see."

She leans back and pushes her gloved fingers through her mop of gray hair. She must not have gotten all the paint off her glove, because some of it smears like soot over her bangs. "I can understand if you have doubts. Go ahead and think about them, but remember why you first talked about joining us. We can keep you from becoming a prize to be fought over by rival crime families. We can protect you."

"Who's going to protect me from you, though?"

"From *us*? Your family are some of the worst—," Jones starts, but Yulikova stops his words with a wave of her hand.

"Cassel, this is a real step forward for you. I'm glad you're asking me this—I'm glad you're being honest."

I don't say anything. I am holding my breath, without really knowing why.

"Of course you feel this way. Listen, I know you're conflicted. And I know you want to do the right thing. So we'll keep talking and keep being honest. For my part, I am telling you honestly that if you walk away from the LMD now, my bosses won't be happy with your decision and they won't be happy with me."

I stand up, flexing my fingers, looking for cracks in the faux gloves. They move like a second skin.

"Is this about Lila Zacharov?" Yulikova asks. "The reason you're hesitating?"

"No!" I say, and then close my eyes for a long moment, counting my breaths. I didn't rattle Yulikova. She rattled me.

"We always knew you two had a close relationship." She has tilted her head and is studying my reaction. "She seems like a nice girl."

I snort.

"Okay, Cassel. She seems like a very ruthless girl whom you like very much. And she also seems like she wouldn't want you working for the government. But this decision is yours, and you should make it. You and your brother are a lot safer here. She'll come around if she really cares about you."

"I don't want to talk about her," I say.

Yulikova sighs. "All right. We don't have to, but you need to tell me whether you're going to sign."

There is something reassuring about the stack of paperwork. If they were just going to throw me in prison, they wouldn't need me to agree to anything. They'd have all the bargaining power once I was behind bars.

I pick up the lanyard and hang it around my neck. Then I grab the headset off the table. I'm not going to be able to figure anything out this way—we could talk forever and Yulikova would never slip up, never reveal anything by mistake.

"The Zacharovs are a crime family, Cassel. They'll use you up and spit you out if you let them. And her, too. She's going to have to do things for them that will change her."

"I said I didn't want to talk about it."

Agent Jones stands up and looks at his watch. "It's almost time to go."

I glance toward the bedroom. "Should I pack up my things?"

Jones shakes his head. "We'll come back here tonight before we drop you off at Wallingford. Let you sleep off the blowback and wash off that paint."

"Thanks," I say.

He grunts.

All of that sounds possible. I might really be coming back to this room, Yulikova and Jones might really be federal agents trying to figure out how to deal with a kid whose criminal past and valuable skill make him both an asset and a liability. They might really not be planning on double-crossing me.

Time to go all in, one way or the other. Time to decide what I want to believe.

You pays your money and you takes your chance.

"Okay," I say, sighing. "Give me the papers." I take the pen out of my hoodie and sign on the dotted line, with a flourish.

Agent Jones's eyebrows go up. I grin.

Yulikova walks over and looks at the papers, tracing one gloved finger just under my name. She puts the other hand on my shoulder. "We're going to take good care of you, Cassel. I promise. Welcome to the Licensed Minority Division."

Promises, promises. I put away the pen. Now that the final decision is made, I feel better. Lighter. The burden of it is removed from my shoulders.

We head out. In the elevator I ask, "Where's Agent Brennan?"

"Already there," is Jones's response. "Setting things up for us."

We cut through the lobby and go out to the car. When I get in, I make sure to take the same side that I rode in on the way here. As I fumble with my seat belt, I grab my cell phone out of the side well in the door and shove it into my pocket.

"You want to stop for a breakfast burrito or something?" Jones asks.

Last meal. I think it but don't say the words aloud.

"Not hungry," I say.

I look out the tinted window at the highway and silently go over all the things I am going to have to do once we arrive at the press conference. I list them all to myself and then list them all again.

"It's going to be over soon," Yulikova says.

That's true. It's all going to be over soon.

They let me out into the memorial park by myself. I squint against the bright sunlight. I keep my head down as I pass through security, holding up my ID tag. A woman with a clipboard tells me that there's a courtesy table with coffee and doughnuts for volunteers.

There is a big stage with a blue curtain covering the back. Someone is rigging a mic up to an impressive-looking lectern with the seal of New Jersey on it. A roped VIP section is being set up to one side of the press pit. A couple other people are stacking speakers under the stage, which is fronted by a shorter curtain, this one white.

Behind that is the area where the trailers are, arranged in a semicircle around several tables where volunteers arrange stacks of leaflets, signage, and T-shirts. Then there's the far table, with the food on it. People are milling around, talking and laughing. Most of them are wearing headsets like mine.

Yulikova did her homework. The layout is just like the map. I pass by the trailer that Governor Patton's supposed to use and head into the one that Yulikova marked for me. Inside is a gray sofa, a dressing table, a small bathroom, and a television mounted high on the wall, tuned to a news channel that's promising a live broadcast of the speech. Two newscasters are talking to each other. Below them is the closed-captioning of what they're saying, slightly off and on a delay, based on my limited lipreading skills.

I check my phone. It's seven forty in the morning. Patton's speech isn't until nine. I have a little time.

I depress the flimsy lock on the doorknob, then rattle the door a little. It seems to hold, but I don't trust the lock. I could probably pick it blindfolded.

There's a crackle in the headphones, and then Agent Brennan's voice. "Cassel? Are you in?"

"Yeah, everything's perfect here," I say into the mouthpiece. "Never better. How about you?"

She laughs. "Don't get cocky, kid."

"Duly noted. I guess I just watch TV and wait."

"You do that. I'll check with you in fifteen minutes."

I take off the headset and rest it on the table. It's hell to just sit here and do nothing, especially when I have so much to do. I want to get started, but I also know that they're going to be paying attention now. Later they'll get bored. For now I take out the index cards and pen and amuse myself by figuring out where in the room a camera could be hidden. Not that I am sure there is one. But I figure that if I stick to being as paranoid as possible, I can't go wrong.

Finally I hear the headset crackle again. "Anything to report?"

"Nada," I say, picking it up and speaking into the mic. "All good."

It's nearly eight. An hour isn't a lot of time.

"I'll check in with you in another fifteen," she says.

"Make it twenty," I say, hopefully just as casually. Then I find the switch on the headset and turn it off. Since they didn't specifically tell me not to do that, I figure that even though they probably won't be happy, they probably won't come looking for me either.

If they've got some kind of GPS tracking thing on me, it's in the ID tag, the hoodie, or the headset. I'm betting it's not the ID tag, since it has to be scanned. I take off the hoodie and leave it on the table. Then I go into the bathroom and turn on the taps to muffle any sounds.

I strip off my clothes. I fold them and rest them on the small table with the towels and antibacterial glove soap. I take out and unfold my pictures. Then, naked, I crouch down on my knees and rest my bare hands on my thighs. The floor is cold. I dig my fingers into my skin.

I concentrate on everything I learned over the past week, every detail I know. I concentrate on the photos in front of me and the videos I saw. I bring Governor Patton into my mind's eye. Then I become him.

It hurts. I can feel everything shift, bones crack, sinews pull, flesh reshape itself. I try very hard not to scream. I mostly succeed.

Just as I'm starting to stand up, the blowback hits.

My skin feels like it's cracking open, my legs melting. My head feels like it's the wrong shape and my eyes are at first closed, then wide, seeing everything through a thousand different lenses, as though I am covered in unblinking eyes. Everything is so bright, and all the different textures of pain unfold around me, pulling me under.

It's so much worse than I remembered.

I don't know how much time passes before I'm able to move again. It feels like a while. The sink's flooded, splashing over onto the floor. I wobble to my feet and turn the taps, grabbing for my clothes. The T-shirt and boxers fit badly. I can't get into the jeans at all.

I look at myself in the mirror, at my bald head and lined face. It's jarring. It's him. With my comb and gel I groom the few silver hairs on my head to be just like in the photos.

My hands are shaking.

When I was a kid, I wanted to be a transformation worker because it was rare. It was special. If you were one, *you* were special. That's all I knew. I never really thought about the actual power much. And then, when I figured out that I *was one*, I still didn't really understand. I mean, I knew it was unique and powerful and cool. I knew it was dangerous. I knew it was rare. But I still didn't really comprehend why it scared powerful people so deeply. Why they wanted me on their side so much.

Now I know why people are afraid of transformation workers. Now I know why they want to control me. Now I get it.

I can walk into someone's house, kiss their wife, sit down at their table, and eat their dinner. I can lift a passport at an airport, and in twenty minutes it will seem like it's mine. I can be a blackbird staring in the window. I can be a cat creeping along a ledge. I can go anywhere I want and do the worst things I can imagine, with nothing to ever connect me to those crimes. Today I might look like me, but tomorrow I could look like you. I could *be* you.

Hell, I'm scared of myself right now.

Holding my phone in one hand and my index cards in the other, edging past where I guess cameras might be so as not to be caught on film, I walk out of the trailer.

People turn their heads, wide-eyed, at Governor Patton in his underwear, standing in the open air. "Wrong damn trailer," I growl, and push open the door to Patton's.

There, just like I hoped, hangs the suit I ordered from Bergdorf Goodman, zipped up in a cloth storage bag and tailored to his measurements. A new pair of shoes and socks and a fresh white shirt, still in plastic. A silk tie is wrapped around the hanger holding the suit.

Other than that the trailer looks a lot like mine. Couch, dressing area. Television monitor.

Seconds later an assistant comes in the door without knocking. She looks panicked. "I'm so sorry. We didn't realize you had arrived. They're ready for you in makeup, Governor. No one saw you come in, and I didn't— Well, I'll let you finish getting ready."

I glance at my phone. It's eight thirty. I lost about half an hour being unconscious and missed checking in with Agent Brennan on top of it. "Come back and get me in ten minutes," I say, trying to keep my voice inflections as like his as I can. I watched all those videos and I practiced, but it's not easy to sound entirely unlike yourself. "I have to finish getting dressed."

When she leaves, I call Barron.

Please, I say to the universe, to whatever's listening. *Please pick up the phone. I'm trusting you. Pick up the phone.*

"Hey, little brother," Barron says, and I slump onto the couch with relief. Until that moment I wasn't sure he would come through. "One government drone to another, how are you doing?"

"Just tell me you're actually—," I start.

"Oh, I am. Oh, *definitely*. I'm here with him now. I was just explaining how our mother's a federal agent and how this was all a government conspiracy."

"Oh," I say. "Uh, good."

"He already knew most of it." I can hear the grin in his voice. "I'm just filling in details. But go ahead and let everyone know that Governor Patton is going to need to delay that press conference by a half hour, okay?"

I guess that if you tell a compulsive liar to stall a guy who's completely paranoid, then wild conspiracy theories are the way he's going to do it. I should be glad that Barron isn't explaining how the governor of Virginia is aiming a laser at the moon and they all need to proceed to underground bunkers immediately. I grin too. "I can definitely do that."

Hanging up, I grab the suit pants and shove my foot into the leg hole. They're nicer clothes than I've ever worn before. Everything about them feels expensive.

By the time the assistant comes back, I'm tying my tie and ready to go to makeup.

━━━━━◆～～

You might wonder what I'm doing. I kind of wonder that myself. But someone has to stop Patton, and this is my chance.

There are tons of people on the governor's support staff, but luckily, most of them are still at his mansion, waiting for the real Patton to leave. I only have to deal with the ones who came ahead. I sit on a director's chair outside and let a girl with short, spiky hair spray foundation on my borrowed face. People ask me a lot of questions about interviews and meetings that I can't answer. Someone brings me a coffee with cream and sugar that I don't drink. Once, a judge calls, asking to talk to me. I shake my head.

"After the speech," I say, and study my mostly blank index cards.

"There's a federal agent here," one of my aides tells me. "She says there could be a security breach."

"I'd expect them to try to pull a trick like that. No—I'm going on. They can't stop me," I say. "I want one of our security officers to make sure she doesn't disrupt me when I'm onstage. We're going out live, right?"

The aide nods.

"Perfect." I don't know what Yulikova and the rest of them suspect or don't, but in a few minutes it won't matter.

That's when Agent Brennan comes around the side of the trailer I'm supposed to be in, holding up her badge.

"Governor," she says.

I stand and do the only thing I can think of. I walk up onto the stage, in front of the small crowd of supporters waving signs and the larger crowd of press correspondents with video cameras pointed at me. It might not be that many people, but it's enough. I freeze.

My heart thumps in my chest. I can't believe I am really doing this.

It's too late to stop.

I clear my throat and reshuffle my index cards, walking until I'm standing behind the lectern. I can see Yulikova, talking frantically into a radio.

"Fellow citizens, distinguished guests, members of the press, thank you all for extending me the courtesy of your attendance today. We stand on the very spot where hundreds of New Jersey citizens were detained after the ban passed, during a dark period in our nation's history—and we stand here looking ahead to legislation that, if it passes, may again take us in directions we don't anticipate."

There is applause, but it's cautious. This isn't the tone that the real Patton would take. He'd probably say some crap about how testing workers will keep them safe. He'd talk about what a glorious day we are at the dawn of.

But today I'm the one with the microphone. I toss my

index cards over my shoulder and smile at my audience. I clear my throat. "It was my plan to read a short prepared statement and take questions, but I am going to diverge from my usual procedure. Today is not a day for politics as usual. Today I plan to speak to you from the heart."

I lean against the lectern and take a deep breath. "I've killed *a lot of people*. And when I say 'a lot,' I mean—really— a lot. I've lied, too, but honestly, after hearing about the killing, I doubt you care about a little lying. I know what you're asking yourself. Does he mean he killed people directly or merely that he ordered their deaths? Ladies and gentlemen, I'm here to tell you—I mean both."

I look out at the reporters. They're whispering back and forth. Cameras flash. Signs sag.

"For example, I killed Eric Lawrence, of Toms River, New Jersey, with my own hands. Gloved hands, mind you. I'm not some kind of pervert. But I did strangle him. You can read the police report—well, you could have if I hadn't suppressed it.

"Now you might ask yourself, why would I do such a thing? And what does this have to do with my crusade against workers? And what in the world made me say any of this out loud, no less in public? Well, let me tell you about a very special lady in my life. You know how sometimes you meet a girl and you go a little crazy?"

I point at a tall guy in the front. "*You* know what I mean, don't you? Well, I want to come clean with regard to Shandra Singer. I might have exaggerated some things there. If your girlfriend breaks up with you, sometimes you get upset— and you might be tempted to phone her up twelve times in a row to beg her to take you back . . . or maybe spray paint something obscene on her car . . . or *maybe* you frame her for a massive conspiracy . . . and try to have her gunned down in the middle of the street. . . . And if you're really upset, maybe you try to wipe out all workers in the state.

"The more you love her, the crazier you get. My love was great. My crimes were greater.

"I'm not here asking for forgiveness. I don't expect forgiveness. In fact, I expect a media circus of a trial followed by a lengthy incarceration.

"But I tell you this today because you, my fellow citizens, deserve my honesty. Hey, better late than never—and I've got to say, it does feel really good to get it all off my chest. So in summary, I killed people. You probably shouldn't put too much stock in other stuff I said before right now, and— oh, yeah. Proposition 2 is a terrible idea that I supported mostly to distract you from my other crimes.

"So, any questions?"

For a long moment there is only silence.

"Okay, then," I say. "Thank you. God bless America, and God bless the great state of New Jersey."

I stumble off the stage. There are people with clipboards and aides in suits all staring at me as if they're afraid to approach me. I smile and give them the thumbs-up sign.

"Good speech, huh?" I say.

"Governor," one of them says, heading in my direction. "We have to discuss—"

"Not now," I tell him, still smiling. "Have my car brought around, please."

He opens his mouth to say something—maybe that he has no idea where my car *is*, since it's probably still with the real Patton—when my arm is jerked behind me and I nearly lose my balance. I yelp as metal comes down on my wrist. Handcuffs.

"You're under arrest." It's Jones in his sharp black federal agent suit. *"Governor."*

Cameras flash. Reporters are streaming toward us.

I can't help it. I start to laugh. I think about what I just did, and I laugh even harder.

Agent Jones marches me away from the crowd of shouting people, to a cleared spot of street where police cars and television vans are parked. A few of the cops come over to try to push back the rush of news cameras and paparazzi.

"You really dug your own grave," he mutters. "And I'm going to bury you in it."

"Say that louder," I tell him, under my breath. "I dare you."

He gets me to a car, opens the door, and pushes me inside. Then I feel something go over my head, and I look down. Three of the amulets I made—the ones that prevent transformation, the ones I gave to Yulikova—are hanging around my neck.

Before I can say anything, the door slams.

Agent Jones gets into the driver's seat and guns the engine. Flashes go off through the window as we start to pull away from the crowd.

I lean back, letting my muscles relax as much as possible. The cuffs are too tight to get out of, but I'm not worried. Not anymore. They can't arrest me—not for this, not when now they can arrest Patton without difficulty. Simple lies are always better than a complicated truth.

Explaining that the Patton on television, the one that confessed, wasn't really Patton, but the real Patton *had* actually committed those crimes, is too confusing.

They might scream at me, they might not want me to be a member of the LMD anymore, but they'll eventually have to admit that I solved the problem. I took down Patton. Not the way that they wanted, but no one got hurt, and that has to be worth something.

"Where's Yulikova?" I ask. "Are we going back to the hotel?"

"No hotel," Jones says.

"Want to tell me where we are going?" I ask.

He doesn't say anything, just keeps driving for a few more moments.

"Come on," I say. "I'm *sorry*. But I had some information that there was a plan to set me up for working Patton. You can deny it if you want to—and maybe my information was wrong—but I got cold feet. Look, I know I shouldn't have done what I did, but—"

He pulls abruptly onto the shoulder of the road. Cars are whizzing by us on one side, and there is a dark patch of trees on the other.

I stop talking.

He gets out and comes around to open my door. When he does, he's pointing a gun at me.

"Get out," he says. "Slowly."

I don't move. "What's going on?"

"Right now!" he yells.

I'm cuffed; I don't have a lot of choices. I slide out of the car. He pushes me around to the back and pops the trunk.

"Uh," I say.

Then he undoes the top two buttons on my shirt, so that he can push the amulets against my skin. When he buttons everything up and tightens my tie, the charms are trapped underneath. Now I have no chance of shaking them off.

"Get in," he says, indicating the trunk. There's not much in there. A spare tire and a first aid kit. A length of rope.

I don't even bother to tell him no, I just run. Even with my hands cuffed behind me, I think I can maybe make it.

I crash down the hill, sliding more than anything else. The dress shoes are awful, and my body is heavy and unfamiliar. I'm not used to the way it moves. I keep losing my balance, expecting my legs to be longer. I slip, and my suit pants slide on the muddy grass. Then I'm up again and heading for the trees.

I'm moving way too slow.

Jones comes down hard against my back, tackling me to the ground. I struggle, but it's no use. I feel the cold muzzle of the gun against my temple and his knee against the hollow of my back.

"You're as cowardly as a goddamn weasel. You know that? A *weasel*. That's what you are."

"You don't know me," I say, spitting blood onto the dirt. I can't help it. I start to laugh. "And you obviously don't know much about weasels, either."

His fist slams into my side, and I nearly black out from the pain. Someday I am going to learn to keep my mouth shut.

"Get up."

I do. We walk back to the car like that. I don't crack any more jokes.

When we get there, he shoves me against the trunk.

"In," he says. "Now."

"I'm sorry," I say. "Patton's fine. He's alive. Whatever you think I did—"

The gun clicks once, ominously close to my ear.

I let him shove me into the trunk. He takes rope and knots it around my legs, connecting that to the chain of the handcuffs in back—tight, so that I can barely move. No more running for me.

Then I hear the rip of duct tape and feel it wrap my hands in two separate sticky cocoons. He's taping something against my palms, something heavy—stones. When he's done, he rolls me over, so that I'm looking at him and the highway beyond. Every time a car barrels past, I think that maybe someone will stop, but no one does.

"I knew you were too much of a wild card when we brought you in. You're too dangerous. You'll never be loyal. I tried to tell Yulikova, but she wouldn't listen."

"I'm sorry," I say, a little desperate. "I'll tell her. I'll tell her you're right. Just let her know where we are."

He laughs. "Nope. But, then, you're not Cassel Sharpe anymore, are you? You're Governor Patton."

"Okay," I say, fear making me babble. "Agent Jones, you're one of the good guys. You're supposed to be better than this. You're a *federal agent*. Look, I'll go back. I'll confess. You can lock me up."

"You should have just let us frame you," Jones says, cutting off a length of silvery duct tape with an army knife. "If no one has any control—if you're out there, free to make deals with anyone—how's that going to be? It's only a matter of time before some foreign government or some corporation makes you a deal. And then you will be the dangerous weapon we let slip through our fingers. Better to just take you out of the equation."

It barely registers that I was right, that they were setting me up.

"But I signed the—"

He brings the tape down over my mouth. I try to spit and turn my head, but he gets it on, tight across my lips. For a moment I forget I can breathe through my nose and I panic, trying to suck in air.

"And while you were making your little speech, I had an idea. I called up some very bad people who are real eager to meet you. I think you know Ivan Zacharov, don't you? Turns out he's willing to pay a lot of money for the pleasure of personally murdering a certain governor." He grins. "Bad luck for you, Cassel."

As the trunk lid comes down, plunging me into darkness, and then the car starts to move, I wonder if I've ever had any other kind.

THE AIR GETS WARM FAST

in the trunk, and the oil and gasoline fumes make me want to gag. Worse, every bump in the road sends me sliding around, banging against metal. I try to brace with my feet, but as soon as we turn a corner or hit a pothole, my head or arms or back smacks into one of the sides. The way I'm tied, I can't even curl against the blow.

All told, this is a pretty bad way to spend the last hours of my life.

I try to think through my options, but they're dismal. I can't transform, not with three amulets around my neck. And since I can't touch my own skin with my hands, even if I somehow managed to rip the amulets off, I'm not sure I could change myself anyway.

One thing I have to say for Agent Jones—he is thorough.

I hear the moment that we pull off the highway. The noise of traffic dims. Gravel under the tires sounds almost like heavy rain.

A few minutes later the engine gutters out and a car door slams. I hear voices, too distant and low to be recognized.

By the time Agent Jones opens up the trunk, I am wild-eyed with panic. The cold air rushes in, and I start struggling against my bonds, even though there's no way that I am going to do anything but hurt myself.

He just watches me squirm.

Then he pulls out his knife and saws through the rope. I can finally extend my legs. I do so slowly, my knees hurting from being bent too long.

"Out," he says. I struggle to sit up. He has to help me onto my feet.

We are outside, underneath a massive industrial structure, with huge iron framing pieces holding up a tower that looms above us, spewing fire into the cloudy late morning sky. Plumes of smoke rise to blot out the shining steel bridges leading to New York. It looks like it's about to rain.

I turn my head and see that maybe ten feet away from me is another sleek black car, this one with Zacharov leaning against it, smoking a cigar. Stanley is standing next to him, screwing a silencer onto a very large black gun.

Then, just as I am sure nothing about this can get worse, the passenger door opens and Lila steps out.

She's got on a black pencil skirt with a gray belted coat and calf high leather boots. Sunglasses cover her eyes, and her mouth is painted the color of old blood. She's got a briefcase in her gray gloved hands.

I have no way to signal her. Her only glance in my direction is cold and perfunctory.

I shake my head *No, no, no.* Agent Jones just laughs dryly. "Here he is, just like I promised. But I never want to see his body again. Do you understand?"

Lila sets down the suitcase next to her father. "I have your money," she tells Jones.

"Good," says Agent Jones. "Let's get started."

Zacharov nods, blowing a cloud of smoke that spirals up and away from him, like the plumes from one of the buildings. "What guarantee do I have that you aren't going to try to pin it on my organization? Your offer came as a real surprise. We don't make so many deals with representatives of the government."

"This is just me. One man, doing what I think is right." Agent Jones shrugs his shoulders. "Your guarantee is that I'm here. I'm going to watch you gun him down. My hands might be clean, but we're both responsible for his death. Neither one of us wants an investigation. Forensics might find a way to place me at the scene. If I rat on you, I'll go down for kidnapping at the very least. I'll hold up my end of the bargain."

Zacharov nods slowly.

"You got cold feet?" Jones asks. "You get to be a worker hero, and eliminate a guy who has been gunning for you lately."

"That was a misunderstanding," Zacharov says.

"You mean that you haven't been sheltering Shandra Singer? My mistake." Agent Jones doesn't even attempt to disguise his sarcasm.

"We don't have *cold feet*," says Zacharov.

"I'll do it," Lila says. Then she looks at Stanley, pointing to the gun. "Give me that."

I widen my eyes, pleading silently. I move my foot in the dirt, hoping I can spell something out fast. *M*, I try to manage, upside down, so she can read it. *ME*, I want it to say.

Agent Jones clocks me on the side of the head with the butt of his gun, hard enough to make the world shift out of focus. I feel like my brain is actually rattling around in my skull. I fall onto my stomach, hands still cuffed behind my back. I didn't even see that he'd drawn a weapon.

I lie there, gasping.

"It's so unexpectedly nice to see him squirming in the dirt," Zacharov says, walking over to me and bending down to pat my cheek with one gloved hand. "Governor, did you really think that no one could touch you?"

I shake my head, not sure what that's supposed to convey. *Please*, I think. *Please ask me something you need answered. Please rip off the tape. Please.*

Lila steps forward with the gun held at her side. She looks at me for a long moment.

Please.

Zacharov rises to his feet. His black coat swirls around him like a cape.

"Get him up," he tells Agent Jones. "A man should be on his feet when he dies—even this man."

Lila's blond hair blows gently around her face, a halo of gold. She takes off her sunglasses. I'm glad. I want to look into her eyes one last time. Blue and green. The colors of the sea.

A girl like that, Grandad said, perfumes herself with ozone and metal filings. She wears trouble like a crown. If she ever falls in love, she'll fall like a comet, burning the sky as she goes.

At least it's you pulling the trigger. I wish I could say that, if nothing else.

"Are you sure?" Zacharov asks her.

She nods, touching a gloved finger to her throat, almost unconsciously. "I took my marks. I'll take the heat."

"You'll have to go into hiding until we're sure it won't be traced to you," Zacharov says.

Lila nods again. "It'll be worth it."

Ruthless. That's my girl.

Agent Jones pulls me to my feet. I stagger unsteadily, like a drunk. I want to cry out, but the tape smothers the sound.

The gun in her hand wavers.

I take one last look and then close my eyes so tightly that they're wet at the corners. So tightly that spots dance in the blackness of my vision.

I wish I could tell her good-bye.

I expect the gunshot to be the loudest thing in the world, but I forgot about the silencer. All I hear is a gasp.

Lila is leaning over me, pulling off her gloves so that she can get a fingernail under the corner of the duct tape. She rips it off my mouth. I am looking up at the late morning sky, so grateful to be alive that I am barely conscious of the pain.

"I'm me," I say, babbling. "Cassel. I swear it's me—"

I don't even remember falling, but I am lying on the gravel. Agent Jones is beside me, unmoving. Blood pools in the dirt. His blood, as bright as paint. I try to roll onto my side. Is he dead?

"I know." She touches the side of my face with bare fingers.

"How?" I say. "How did you— When?"

"You are such a jackass," she says. "Do you think I don't watch television? I heard your insane speech. Of course I knew it was you. You told me about Patton."

"Oh," I say. "That. Of course."

Stanley pats down Jones and unlocks my cuffs. As soon as they're off and the duct tape is pulled away, taking skin and stone and ink with it, I rip at my collar, pulling off the amulets and throwing them onto the ground.

All I want is to get out of this body.

For the first time the pain of the blowback feels like a release.

I wake up on an unfamiliar couch, with a blanket slung over me. I start to sit up, and realize that Zacharov's sitting on the other side of the room, in a shallow pool of light, reading.

The glare of the bulb is giving his face the hard lines of a sculpture. A study of a crime boss in repose.

He looks up and smiles. "Feeling better?"

"I guess so," I say, as formally as I can manage from a mostly prone position. My voice creaks. "Yeah."

I sit upright, smoothing out the wrinkled mess of my suit. It doesn't fit anymore, my arms and legs too long for the sleeves and pants, the body of it hanging off me like extra skin.

"Lila's upstairs," he says. "Helping your mother pack. You can take Shandra home."

"But I didn't find the diamond—"

He puts down the book. "I don't hand out compliments easily, but what you did—it was impressive." He chuckles. "You single-handedly torpedoed a piece of legislation I've been working toward ending for a long while, and you eliminated a political enemy of mine. We're square, Cassel."

"Square?" I echo, because I can't quite believe it. "But I—"

"Of course, if you do find the diamond, I would really appreciate your returning it to me. I can't believe your mother *lost* it."

"That's because you've never been to our house," I say, which isn't exactly true. He was in the kitchen once—and maybe he was there other times I didn't know about. "You and my mother have had quite a history." After the words come out of my mouth, I realize that whatever he says next isn't something I want to hear.

He looks faintly amused. "There's something about her— Cassel, I have met many evil men and women in my life. I have made deals with them, drank with them. I have done things that I myself have difficulty reconciling— terrible things. But I have never known anyone like your mother. She is a person without limits—or if she has any, she hasn't found them yet. She never needs to reconcile anything."

He says this thoughtfully, admiringly. I look at the glass on the side table next to him and wonder how much he's had to drink.

"She fascinated me when we were younger—I met her through your grandfather. We—she and I—never much liked each other, except when we did. But— Whatever she said to you about what was between her and me, I want you to know that I always respected your father. He was as honest as any criminal can hope to be."

I'm not sure I want to hear this, but suddenly it becomes clear why he's telling me: He doesn't want me to be angry on my father's behalf even though he knows I know he slept with my mother. I clear my throat. "Look, I don't pretend to understand—I don't *want* to understand. That's your business and her business."

He nods. "Good."

"I think my dad took it from her," I say. "I think that's why it's gone. He had it."

Zacharov looks at me oddly.

"The diamond," I say, realizing I wasn't making any sense. "I think my dad took the diamond from my mom and replaced it with a fake. So that she never knew it was gone."

"Cassel, stealing the Resurrection Diamond is like stealing the *Mona Lisa*. If you have a buyer lined up, then you might get something close to its real value, but otherwise you steal it because you're an art lover or just to show the world that you *can*. You can't fence it. There would be too much attention. You would have to cut it into pieces, and then it would only fetch a fraction of its worth. For that, you might as well steal a handful of white diamonds at any jewelry store in town."

"You could ransom it," I say, thinking of my mother and her crazy plan to get money.

"But your father didn't," Zacharov says. "If he had it. Although he would have had it for only a couple of months."

I give him a long look.

He snorts. "You aren't seriously asking yourself if I caused your father to have a car accident, are you? I think you know me better than that. If I'd killed a man who I knew had stolen from me, I would have made him an example. No one would have failed to know who was responsible for a death like that. But I never suspected your father. He was a small-time operator, not greedy. Your mother I considered, but dismissed. Wrongly, as it turns out."

"Maybe he knew he was going to die," I say. "Maybe he really believed the stone would keep him alive. Like Rasputin. Like you."

"I can't think of anyone who didn't like your father—and if he was really afraid, surely he would have gone to

Desi." Desi, my granddad. It jolts me to hear his first name; I forget he has one.

"I guess we'll never know," I say.

We regard each other for a long moment. I wonder whether he sees my father or my mother when he looks at me. Then his gaze seems to focus on something else.

I turn. Lila's on the stairs in her pencil skirt and boots, with a filmy white shirt. She smiles down at us, her mouth curved upward on one side, turning the expression wry.

"Can I have Cassel for a minute?"

I start toward the stairs.

"Bring him back in one piece," her father calls after her.

<hr/>

Lila's bedroom is at once exactly what I should have expected and nothing like I imagined. I was in her dorm room at Wallingford, and I guess I figured this room would be a somewhat nicer version of that one. I didn't take into account the wealth of her family and their love of imported furniture.

The room is huge. On one end a very long light green velvet daybed rests next to a mirrored dressing table. The shining surface is littered with lots of brushes and open pots of makeup. Several satiny ottomans sit on the floor nearby.

On the other end, beside the window, there's a massive ornate mirror, the silvering faded in some spots, showing its age. Near that is her bed. The headboard looks old and French, carved from some light wood. The whole thing is piled with more satin—a bedspread and pale yellow pillows. An overstuffed bookshelf works as her side table, covered in piles of books and a big golden lamp. A huge gilt chandelier swings from the ceiling, glittering with crystals.

It's an old-fashioned starlet's room. The only incongruous thing is the gun holster hanging from one side of her dressing table. Well, that and me.

I catch sight of myself in the mirror. My black hair is tangled, like I just got out of bed. There's a bruise on the side of my mouth and a lump at my temple.

She leads me in and then stops, like she's not sure what to do next.

"Are you okay?" I ask, moving to sit on the daybed. I feel ridiculous in the remains of Patton's suit, but I don't have any other clothes here. I shrug off the jacket.

She raises her brows. "You want to know if *I'm* okay?"

"You shot someone," I say. "And you ran out on me before that, when we— I don't know. I thought maybe you were upset."

"I *am* upset." She doesn't speak for a long moment. Then she starts pacing the floor. "I can't believe you made that speech. I can't believe you almost died."

"You saved my life."

"I did! *I absolutely did!*" she says, pointing at me accusingly with a gloved finger. "And what if I hadn't? What if I wasn't there—if I hadn't figured out it was you? What if that federal agent thought there was someone with a bigger grudge against Patton than my dad?"

"I—" I suck in a breath and let it out slowly. "I guess I'd be . . . dead."

"Exactly. You can't go around making plans that have

you getting killed as a by-product. Eventually one of them is going to *work*."

"Lila, I swear I didn't know. I thought I would get in trouble, but I didn't have any idea about Agent Jones. He just snapped." I don't talk about how scared I was. I don't tell her that I thought I was going to die. "None of that was part of my plan."

"You keep talking, but you're not making any sense. Of course you upset someone in the government. You *pretended to be the governor of New Jersey* and *confessed to a bunch of crimes*."

I can't help the small smile that's playing at the corners of my mouth. "So," I say, "how did it go over?"

She shakes her head, but she's smiling too. "Big. It's being broadcast on all the channels. They say Proposition 2 will never pass now. Happy?"

I am struck by a sudden thought. "If he'd been assassinated, though . . ."

She frowns. "I guess you're right. It would have passed easily."

"Look," I say, standing and walking to her. "*You're* right. No more crazy schemes or lunatic plans. Really, really. I'll be good."

She's studying me, clearly trying to decide if I'm telling the truth. I curl my fingers around her small shoulders and hope she doesn't push me away when I bring my mouth down to hers.

She makes a soft sound and reaches up to fist her hand in my hair, pulling it roughly. The kiss is frantic, bruising. I can taste her lipstick, feel her teeth, am drinking down the panting sobs of her breath.

"I'm okay," I tell her, speaking against her mouth, echoing her own words, my arms coming around her to hold her tightly against me. "I'm right here."

She tucks her head against my neck. Her voice is so soft that I can barely make out the words. "I shot a federal agent, Cassel. I'm going to have to go away for a while. Until things cool down."

"What do you mean?" I ask, dread making me stupid. I want to pretend I misheard her.

"It's not going to be forever. Six months, maybe a year. By the time you graduate, probably things will have blown over and I'll be able to come back. But it means that—well, I don't know where that leaves us. I don't need any promises. It's not like we're even—"

"But you shouldn't have to go," I say. "It was because of me. It's *my* fault."

She slides out of my arms, walks to the dressing table and dabs at her eyes with a tissue. "You're not the only one who can make sacrifices, Cassel."

When she turns around, I can see the shadows of the mascara she's wiped away.

"I'll say good-bye before I go," she tells me, looking at the floor, at the ornate pattern of what is probably a ridiculously expensive rug. Then she glances at me.

I ought to say something about how I'll miss her or about how a couple of months is nothing, but I am silenced by rage so terrible that it locks my throat. *It's not fair*, I want to scream at the universe. I just found out she loves me. Everything was just beginning, everything was perfect, and now it's snatched away again.

It hurts too much, I want to shout. I'm tired of hurting.

Since I know that those are not okay things to say, I manage to say nothing.

The silence is broken by a knock on the door. After a moment my mother comes in and tells me that it's time to go.

Stanley drives us home.

WHEN I GET UP THE NEXT

morning, Barron is downstairs frying eggs. Mom is sitting in her dressing gown, drinking coffee out of a chipped porcelain mug. Her mass of black hair is twisted up into ringlets and clipped like that, with a bright scarf to keep it all in place.

She's smoking a cigarette, tapping the ashes into a blue glass tray.

"There are some things I will definitely miss," she's saying. "I mean, no one likes being held prisoner, but if you are going to be locked up, you might as well— Oh, hello, dear. Good morning."

I yawn and stretch, reaching my arms toward the ceiling.

It feels truly wonderful to be back in my own clothes, back in my own body. My jeans are comfortable, old and worn. I can't face putting on a uniform right now.

Barron hands me a cup of coffee.

"Black, like your soul," he says with a grin. He's got on dark slacks and wing-tip shoes. His hair is rakishly disheveled. He appears not to have a care in the world.

"We're out of milk," Mom informs me.

I take a deep and grateful gulp. "I can run out and get some."

"Would you?" Mom smiles and touches my hair, pushing it back from my forehead. I let her, but I grit my teeth. Her bare fingers brush my skin. I am thankful when none of my amulets crack. "Do you know what the Turkish say about coffee? It should be black as hell, strong as death, and sweet as love. Isn't that beautiful? My grandfather told me that when I was a little girl, and I never forgot it. Unfortunately, I still like my milk."

"Maybe he was from there," Barron says, turning back to the eggs. Which is possible. Our grandfather has passed down lots of different stories to explain our ancestry, from the one about being descended from an Indian maharaja to the one about runaway slaves to something about Julius Caesar. Turkish, I never heard. Yet.

"Or maybe he read it in a book," I say. "Or maybe he just ate a box of Turkish delight and that's what it said on the back."

"Such a cynic," my mother says, picking up her plate, scraping the toast crusts into the trash, and putting it in the sink. "You boys play nice. I'm going to go get dressed."

She brushes by us, and I hear her footfalls on the stairs. I take another sip of coffee. "Thanks," I say. "For delaying Patton. Just—thanks."

Barron nods. "Heard on the radio that they arrested him. He had a lot to say about conspiracies that I take credit for personally. It was good stuff. Of course, after that speech, everyone has to realize that he's bonkers. I don't know where you got all that—"

I grin. "Oh, come on. It was some fine rhetoric."

"Yeah, you're like a modern day Abraham Lincoln." He sets a plate of eggs and toast in front of me. "'Let my people go.'"

"That's *Moses*." I grab for the pepper mill. "Well, my years on the debate team finally paid off, I guess."

"Yeah," he says. "You're the hero of the hour."

I shrug.

"So what happens now?" he asks.

I shake my head. I can't tell Barron what happened after I got off the stage, how Agent Jones tried to kill me and is now dead, how Lila is leaving town. To him it must seem like a large-scale prank, a joke I played on Yulikova.

"I think I'm done with the Feds. Hopefully they're done with me, too," I say. "How about you?"

"Are you kidding? I love being a G-man. I'm in for the long haul. I'm going to be so corrupt that I'll be a legend down in Carney." He grins, sitting across from me at the table and stealing a piece of toast off my plate. "Also, you owe me one."

I nod. "Sure," I say, with a feeling of dread. "And I fully intend to pay up. Just tell me."

He looks toward the door and then back at me. "I want you to tell Daneca what I did for you. That I helped. That I did something good."

"Okay," I say, frowning. There must be a catch. "That's it?"

He nods. "Yeah, just tell her. Make her understand that I didn't have to do it, but I did it anyway."

I snort. "Whatever, Barron."

"I'm serious. You owe me a favor, and that's what I want." His expression is one I don't often see him wear. He looks oddly diffident, as though he's waiting for me to say something really cruel.

I shake my head. "No problem. That's easily done."

He smiles, his usual easy, careless grin, and grabs for the marmalade. I toss back the rest of my cup.

"I'm going to get Mom's milk," I say. "Can I take your car?"

"Sure," he says, pointing to the closet near the door. "Keys are in the pocket of my coat."

I pat down my jeans and realize my wallet is upstairs, under the mattress, where I left it for safekeeping before I went off with the Feds. "Can I borrow five bucks, too?"

He rolls his eyes. "Go ahead."

I find his leather jacket and root around in the inside pocket, eventually coming up with both keys and wallet. I flip open the wallet and am in the process of taking out money, when I see Daneca's picture in one of the plastic sleeves.

I slide it out with the cash and then leave quickly, slamming the door in my haste.

After I get to the store, I sit in the parking lot, staring at the picture. Daneca's sitting on a park bench, her hair blowing in a light wind. She's smiling at the camera in a way that I've never seen her smile before—not at me and not at Sam. She looks lit up from the inside, shining with a happiness so vast that it's impossible to ignore.

On the back is the distinctive scrawl of my brother's handwriting: "This is Daneca Wasserman. She is your girlfriend and you love her."

I look at it and look at it, trying to decipher some meaning behind it other than the obvious—that it's true. I never knew Barron could feel that way about anyone.

But she isn't his girlfriend anymore. She dumped him.

Leaning against the hood of the car, I take one last glance at the photo before I rip it into pieces. I throw those into the trash can outside the store, nothing more than colored confetti on top of discarded wrappers and soda bottles. Then I go inside and buy a pint of milk.

I tell myself that he meant to throw out Daneca's picture, that he just forgot. I tell myself I got rid of it for his own good. His memory is full of holes, and an outdated reminder would just be confusing. He might forget that they broke up, and embarrass himself. I tell myself that they would have never worked out, not in the long run, and he'll be happier if he forgets her.

I tell myself that I did it for him, but I know that's not true.

I want Sam and Daneca to be happy together, like they were before. I did it for myself. I did it to get what I want. Maybe I should regret that, but I can't. Sometimes you do the bad thing and hope for the good result.

There is a black car idling next to the driveway when I return.

I pull past it, park, and get out. As I start toward the house, the passenger-side door opens and Yulikova steps onto the grass. She's got on a tan suit with her signature chunky necklaces. I wonder how many of the stones are charms.

I walk a little ways toward her but stop, so that she has to close the distance on her own.

"Hello, Cassel," she says. "We've got some things to talk about. Why don't you get into the car?"

I hold up the milk. "Sorry," I say. "But I'm a little busy right now."

"What you did—you can't think there are no consequences." I'm not sure if she means the speech or something worse, but I don't much care.

"You set me up," I say. "One big con. You can't blame me because I turned out not to be gullible enough. You can't blame the mark. That's not how it works. Have some respect for the nature of the game."

She's quiet for a long moment. "How did you find out?"

"Does it really matter?"

"I never meant to betray your trust. It was for your safety as much as anything else that I agreed we should implement—"

I hold up one gloved hand. "Just spare me the justifications. I thought you were the good guys, but there are no good guys."

"That's not true." She looks honestly upset, but then, I've learned that I can't read her. The problem with a really excellent liar is that you have to just assume they're always lying. "You would never have spent a single night in jail. We weren't going to lock you up, Cassel. My superiors felt that we needed a little leverage over you, that's all. You haven't exactly been trustworthy yourself."

"You were supposed to be better than me," I say. "Anyway, that's done."

"You think you know the truth, but there are more factors in play than you're aware of. You don't understand the larger picture. You can't. You don't know what chaos you've created."

"Because you wanted to get rid of Patton, but you also wanted Proposition 2 to pass. So you decided to make a martyr out of him. Two birds, one stone."

"It's not about what I want," she says. "It's bigger than that."

"I think we're done here."

"You know that's not possible. More people are aware of you now, people high up in the government. And everyone is very eager to meet you. Especially my boss."

"That and a dollar will almost buy me a cup of coffee."

"You signed a contract, Cassel. That's binding."

"Did I?" I say, smirking. "I think you should check again. I'm pretty sure you're going to find out that I never signed anything. My name is nowhere. My name is gone." *Thank you, Sam*, I think. I would have never thought a disappearing-ink pen could come in so handy.

Her irritation shows on her face for once. I feel oddly triumphant. She clears her throat. "Where's Agent Jones?"

She says it like that's her trump card.

I shrug. "Beats me. Did you lose him? I hope you find him, even though— Let's face it, he and I were never close."

"You're not this person," she says, waving her hand in the air to indicate me. I don't know what she was expecting. Clearly she's frustrated by my reaction. "You're not this— this *cold*. You care about making the world a better place. Snap out of it, Cassel, before it's too late."

"I've got to go," I say, jerking my head toward the house.

"Your mother could be brought up on charges," she says.

Fury makes my mouth curl. I don't care if she sees it. "So could you. I hear you used a worker kid to frame a governor. You can ruin my life, but you'll have to destroy your own to do it. I promise you that."

"Cassel," she says, her voice rising several decibels. "I am the least of your worries. Do you think that if you were in China you would be free?"

"Oh, give me a break," I say.

"Right now you're a bigger problem than Patton was, and you saw how my superiors handled that problem. The only way this can be over is if you—"

"*This is never going to be over,*" I shout. "Someone will always be after me. There's always consequences. Well, *BRING IT.* I am done with being afraid, and I am done with you."

With that, I stalk back to the house. But on the porch I hesitate. I look back at Yulikova. I wait until she walks back to the gleaming black car, gets in, and is driven away. Then I sit down on the stoop.

I stare out at the yard for a long time, not really thinking about anything, mostly just shaking with anger and adrenaline.

The government is big, bigger than any one person can game. They can come after the people I care about, they can come for me, they can do something that I haven't thought of yet. They could make their move now or a year from now. And I'm going to have to be ready. Always and forever ready, unless I want to give up everything I have and everyone I love.

Like, they could go after Lila, who shot and killed someone in cold blood. If they ever managed to figure that out, to charge her with Agent Jones's murder, I would do anything to keep her free.

Or they could go after Barron, who works for them.

Or—

As I'm thinking, I realize I am looking out at our old barn. No one's gone in there in years. It's full of old furniture, rusted tools, and a bunch of stuff my parents stole and then didn't want.

It's where my dad taught me how to pick locks. He kept all his equipment out there, including the supersecure box. I vividly recall my father, cigarillo resting in one corner of his mouth as he worked, oiling the gears of a lock. My memory adds in the spool pins, the mortis sets, and the bolts.

I remember that no one could get into that box. Even knowing there was candy inside, we were still hopeless.

The barn is the one place that Grandad and I didn't clean out.

I leave the milk on the stoop and walk over to the big, worn double doors, then lift the latch. The last time I was inside was in a dream. It feels dreamlike now, dust rising up with my footfalls, the only light coming through gaps in the planks, and windowpanes shaded gray with cobwebs and dirt.

It smells like rotten wood and animal habitation. Most of the furniture is covered with moth-eaten blankets, giving everything a ghostly appearance. I spot a garbage bag filled with plastic bags, and several worn cardboard boxes overstuffed with milk glass. There's an old safe—so rusted that the door is ossified open. Inside I find only a pile of pennies, greenish and stuck together.

Dad's worktable is covered with a cloth too. Pulling it back with a single sweep of my hand, I see the piled mess of his tools—a vise, cylinder remover, sesame decoder, hammer with interchangeable heads, the supersecure box, a bundle of twine, and a bunch of rusted picks.

If my father had the Resurrection Diamond, if he wanted to keep it, if he *couldn't* sell it, then I can picture him tucking it away where no outsider would think to look and no family member was skilled enough to get into. I cast about for a few minutes and then do what I never would have thought to do as a kid.

I clamp the box in the vise. Then I plug in a reciprocating saw and slice it open.

Metal filings are scattered across the floor, curled in glittering piles, by the time I'm done. The box is destroyed, the top cut completely off.

There's no diamond inside, just a bunch of papers and a

very old half-melted lollipop. I would have been extremely disappointed, had I ever managed to open it as a kid.

I'm disappointed now.

I unfold the papers, and a photo falls out into my hands. A bunch of very blond boys standing in front of a huge house—one of those old-money Cape Cod mansions with a widow's walk and columns, looking right onto the ocean. I turn it over and see three names in a spidery hand I don't recognize: "Charles, Philip, Anne." Guess one of them wasn't a boy after all.

For a moment I wonder if I'm looking at the research for an old con. Then I unfold another piece of paper. It's a birth certificate for a Philip Raeburn.

Not Sharpe, a name I always knew was as fake as the prize in a Cracker Jack box. Raeburn. My dad's real last name. The one he gave up, the one he hid from us.

Cassel Raeburn. I try it out in my head, but it sounds ridiculous.

There's a newspaper clipping too, one about how Philip Raeburn died in a boating accident off the shore of the Hamptons at the age of seventeen. A ridiculously expensive way to die.

The Raeburns could afford to buy anything. Certainly they could afford to buy a stolen diamond.

The door creaks open, and I turn around, startled.

"I found the milk by the door. What are you doing out here?" Barron asks. "And—what did you do to Dad's lockbox?"

"Look," I say, holding up the lollipop. "There really was candy in there. Go figure, right?"

Barron gapes at me with the horrified expression of someone realizing that he might be the stable brother after all.

———————

I am back at Wallingford just after dinner. My hall master, Mr. Pascoli, gives me an odd look when I try to hand him the note my mother wrote me.

"You're fine, Cassel. The dean already explained that you might be out for a few days."

"Oh," I say. "Right." I'd nearly forgotten about the deal Dean Wharton made with Sam and me. There was so much about to happen back then that taking advantage of it was a dim hope. Now that I am at Wallingford again, though, I wonder what I can really get away with.

I wonder if I could stay in bed and just sleep until I wasn't tired anymore, for instance.

Probably not.

I don't know what I expect when I walk into my room, but it's not Sam, lying on the bed, his left leg wrapped with gauze. Daneca is sitting beside him and they're playing what appears to be a very intense game of gin rummy.

Clearly Sam is already getting away with having a girl in our dorm room. I admire his gumption.

"Hey," I say, leaning against the door frame.

"What happened to you?" Daneca asks. "We were worried."

"*I* was worried," I say, looking at Sam. "Are you okay? I mean—your leg."

"It still hurts." He lowers it gingerly to the floor. "I have a cane for right now, but I might have a limp, the doctor said. It might not go away."

"That quack? I hope you got a second opinion." The wash of guilt I feel makes the words come out harsher than I intend.

"We did the right thing," Sam says, taking a deep breath. There is a seriousness in his face that I don't remember being there before. Pain shows. "I don't regret it. I almost ruined my whole future. I guess I took it for granted before—everything. The good college, the good job. I thought what you were doing seemed so exciting."

"I'm sorry," I say, and I am. I am very, very sorry if that's what he thought.

"No," he says. "Don't be. I was stupid. And you saved me from getting into a lot of trouble."

I look over at Daneca. Sam is always too generous, but I can trust her to tell me if she thinks I've done something wrong. "I never wanted you—I never wanted either of you to get hurt because of me."

"Cassel," Daneca says, in the exasperated affectionate tone she reserves for us when we're being complete idiots. "You can't blame yourself for Mina Lange. She's not someone you brought into our lives. She goes to school here, remember? You didn't make this happen. And you can't blame yourself for—for whatever else you're thinking of. We're your friends."

"That might be your first mistake," I say, half under my breath.

Sam laughs. "In a good mood, are we?"

"Did you see?" Daneca asks me. "Proposition 2 isn't going to pass. And Patton resigned. Well, he was arrested, so I guess he had to. You must have seen it. He even admitted that your mother hadn't done anything wrong."

I think about telling Daneca the truth. Of all the people I know, she's the one who would be the most proud of me. But it feels unfair to get them involved—no matter what they say, especially since this is something far bigger and more dangerous than anything I've been in the middle of before.

"You know me," I say, shaking my head. "I'm not much for politics."

She looks at me slyly. "Too bad you didn't see it, because if I am made valedictorian of our class, I'd love to have help writing my speech, and Patton's is the perfect model. It sets the exact right tone. But I guess if you really don't care about that kind of thing—"

"You want to tell everyone that today's the day you speak from your heart and confess all your crimes? Because I didn't think you had all that much to confess."

"So you did see it!" Sam says.

"You're a liar, Cassel Sharpe," Daneca says, but there's no heat in it. "A lying liar who lies."

"I guess I heard someone talking about it somewhere." I smile up at the ceiling. "What do you want? A leopard can't change his spots."

"If the leopard was a *transformation worker*, he could," Sam says.

I get the sense that maybe I don't have to say anything.

They appear to have put a theory together on their own.

Daneca grins at Sam.

I try not to think of the photo in Barron's wallet or of the way she was smiling at my brother in the picture. I especially try not to compare it to her smile now.

"Deal me in next go-around," I say. "What are we playing for?"

"The sheer joy of victory," Sam tells me. "What else?"

"Oh," Daneca says, and gets up. "Before I forget." She walks over to her bag and pulls out a bundled T-shirt. She unknots it and pushes back the cloth. Gage's gun is there, oiled and gleaming. "I got this out of Wharton's office before the cleaners came."

I stare at the old Beretta. It's small, and as silvery as the scales of a fish. It shines under the light of the desk lamp.

"Get rid of it," Sam says. "For real, this time."

The next day it starts to snow. The flakes float down, coating the trees in a thin powder, making the grass sparkle with ice.

I walk from statistics to Developing World Ethics to English. Everything seems bizarrely normal.

Then I see Mina Lange, hurrying to class, wearing a black beret dusted white.

"You," I say, stepping in front of her. "You got Sam shot."

She looks at me with wide eyes.

"You're a terrible con artist. And you aren't a very nice person. I almost feel sorry for you. I have no idea what happened to your parents. I have no idea how you wound up stuck curing Wharton, with no end in sight and no way out and no friends you trust enough to let help you. I can't even say that I wouldn't have done what you did. But Sam almost died because of you, and for that I will never forgive you."

Her eyes fill with tears. "I didn't mean—"

"Don't even try it." I reach into my jacket and give her Yulikova's business card and the wrapped T-shirt bundle. "I can't promise you anything, but if you really want to get out, take this. There's a death worker, a kid named Gage, who wants his gun back. You give it to him, and I bet he'd be willing to help you out. Teach you how to be on your own, get work, and not be beholden to anyone. Or you can call the number on the card. Yulikova will make you a trainee in her program. She's looking for the gun too. She'll help you too, more or less."

Mina stares at the card, turning it over in her hand, holding the bundle against her chest, and I walk away before she can thank me. The last thing I want is her gratitude.

Giving her that choice is my own personal revenge.

The rest of the day goes about as well as any day. I make another mug in ceramics that doesn't blow up. Track is canceled because of the weather. Dinner is a somewhat gummy mushroom risotto, haricots verts, and a brownie.

Sam and I do our homework, flopped on our beds, throwing wadded-up pieces of paper at each other.

It snows even harder while we sleep, and in the morning we have to fight our way to class through a volley of snowballs. Everyone arrives with ice melting in their hair.

The debate club has a meeting in the afternoon, so I go

to that and doodle in my notebook. Through sheer lack of attention I wind up stuck with the topic Why Violent Video Games Are Bad for America's Youth. I try to argue my way out of it, but it's impossible to debate the whole debate team.

I am crossing the quad, heading back to my room, when my phone rings. It's Lila.

"I'm in the parking lot," she says and hangs up.

I trudge through the snow. The landscape is hushed, quiet. In the distance there is only the sound of cars moving through slush.

Her Jaguar is idling near the pile of snow the plow built at one end of the lot. She's sitting on the hood, in her gray coat. The black hat she's wearing has an incongruously cute pom-pom at the top. Strands of gold hair blow in the wind.

"Hey," I say, walking closer. My voice sounds rough, like I haven't spoken in years.

Lila slides off the car and comes sweetly into my arms. She smells like cordite and some kind of flowery perfume. She's not wearing makeup and her eyes have a slight puffy redness that makes me think of tears. "I told you I'd say good-bye." Her voice is almost a whisper.

"I don't want you to go," I murmur into her hair.

She pulls back a little and twines her arms around my neck, drawing my mouth down to hers. "Tell me you'll miss me."

I kiss her instead of speaking, my hands sliding up to knot in her hair. Everything is quiet. There is only the taste of her tongue and the swell of her lower lip, the curve of her jaw. There is only the sharp shuddering gasp of her breath.

There are no words for how much I will miss her, but I try to kiss her so that she'll know. I try to kiss her to tell her the whole story of my love, the way that I dreamed of her when she was dead, the way that every other girl seemed like a mirror that showed me her face. The way my skin ached for her. The way that kissing her made me feel like I was drowning and like I was being saved all at the same time. I hope she can taste all that, bittersweet, on my tongue.

It's thrilling to realize that I'm allowed this at last, that for this moment she's mine.

Then she takes an unsteady step back. Her eyes shine with unsaid things; her mouth is ruddy from being pressed against mine. She bends down and picks up her hat. "I've got to—"

She's got to go and I've got to let her.

"Yeah," I say, curling my hands at my sides to keep from grabbing for her. "Sorry." I shouldn't already feel the loss of her so acutely, when she's not yet gone. I have had to let her go so many times, surely practice ought to make this easier.

We walk to her car together. The snow crunches under my feet. I look back at the bleak brick dorms.

"I'll be here," I say. "When you get back."

She nods, smiling a little, like she's humoring me. I don't think she realizes just how long I've been waiting, how long I will wait for her still. Finally she meets my gaze and smiles. "Just don't forget me, Cassel."

"Never," I say.

I couldn't if I tried.

Believe me, once upon a time, I tried.

She gets into the car and closes the driver's side door

with a slam. I can tell it costs her something to act casual, to give me that last little wave and grin, to put her car into gear and start to pull out of the lot.

That's when it hits me. In a single moment everything becomes suddenly, gloriously clear. I have a choice other than this one.

"Wait!" I yell, legging it over and knocking on the window.

She hits the brakes.

"I'm coming with you," I say as she rolls the window down. I'm grinning like a fool. "Take me with you."

"What?" Her face looks blank, like she's not sure she's hearing me right. "You can't. What about graduating? And your family? And your whole life?"

For years Wallingford has been my refuge, proof that I could be a regular guy—or that I could pretend well enough that no one could tell the difference. But I don't need that anymore. I'm okay with being a con artist and a grifter. With being a worker. With having friends who will hopefully forgive me for taking off on a mad road trip. With being in love.

"I don't care." I get in on the passenger side, slamming the door on everything else. "I want to be with you."

I can't stop smiling.

She looks at me for a long moment, and then starts to laugh. "You're running away with me with your book bag and the clothes on your back? I could wait for you to go to your dorm—or we could stop by your house. Don't you need to get anything?"

I shake my head. "Nope. Nothing I can't steal."

"What about telling someone? Sam?"

"I'll call from the road." I hit the knob on the radio, filling the car with music.

"Don't you even want to know where we're going?" She's looking at me like I'm a painting she's managed to steal but will never be allowed to keep. She sounds exasperated and oddly fragile.

I look out the window at the snow-covered landscape as the car starts to move. Maybe we'll go north and see my father's family, maybe we'll try to find her father's diamond. It doesn't matter.

"Nah," I say.

"You're crazy." She's laughing again. "You know that, right, Cassel? Crazy."

"We've spent a lot of time doing what we're supposed to do," I say. "I think we should start doing what we want. And this is what I want. You're what I want. You're what I've always wanted."

"Well, good," she says, tucking a lock of spun-gold hair behind her ear and leaning back in her seat. Her smile is all teeth. "Because there's no turning back now."

Her gloved hand turns the wheel sharply, and I feel the giddy rush that comes only at the end of things, that comes when, despite everything, I realize that we actually got away with it.

Every con artist's fairy tale.

The big score.

ACKNOWLEDGMENTS

Several books were really helpful in creating the world of the curse workers. In particular, David W. Maurer's *The Big Con*; Robert B. Cialdini's *Influence: The Psychology of Persuasion*; Kent Walker and Mark Schone's *Son of a Grifter*; and Karl Taro Greenfeld's *Speed Tribes*.

I am deeply indebted to many people for their insight into this book. Thanks to Cassandra Clare, Sarah Rees Brennan, Josh Lewis, and Robin Wasserman for looking at many, many permutations of scenes and for their suggestions on two scenes in particular. Thanks to Delia Sherman, Ellen Kushner, Maureen Johnson, and Paolo Bacigalupi for the many helpful suggestions and general cheerleading while we were in Mexico. Thank you to Justine Larbalestier and Steve Berman for their detailed notes and focus on getting the details just right. Thank you to Libba Bray for letting me talk the whole end through with her. Thanks to Dr. Elka Cloke and Dr. Eric Churchill for their medical expertise and generosity. Thanks to Sarah Smith, Gavin Grant, and Kelly Link for helping me polish the whole book to a shine.

Most of all I have to thank my agent, Barry Goldblatt, for all his sincere support; my editor, Karen Wojtyla, for pushing me to make these books far better and for the care she took with all aspects of the series; and my husband, Theo, who gave me lots of insight into private schools and scams and who once again let me read the whole book to him out loud.

LILA ZACHAROV IN 13 PIECES

THE SUMMER LILA CAME

back from Europe, everything was different. She was used to drinking her coffee with a croissant dipped in it and taking the Metro by herself. She liked shopping in Le Marais. She had been to Rome and to Madrid and Marrakesh. Before her return, her father had even let her go to a salon and have her hair chopped to chin length and dyed bright pink. She knew she'd changed—but she figured everyone else would be the same.

They weren't.

Cassel was taller, for one thing. He went from about her height to probably near six feet. It made him look alarmingly adult with the new hard angles of his face and a slight roughness to the skin of his jaw. He must have started shaving.

Her mother was angrier. They fought constantly—over Lila's hair, over how independent she was, and the music she listened to and the books she read. And boys. Every time a boy tried to chat her up on the beach, her mother interrogated her about every detail of what he'd said, warning her in dire terms about diseases and pregnancy.

Her mother grew so paranoid that she actually relented about Lila hanging out with Cassel, since he was a known quantity and his grandfather was always home.

So Lila and Cassel spent a lot of time sprawled on an old leather couch in the basement of his grandad's house, renting black-and-white films where smoky-eyed starlets drank cocktails and laughed in the face of danger. They once even convinced his oldest brother, Philip, to drive them to a vintage store at an indoor flea market a half hour away. There Cassel got a fedora with a red feather in it while Lila bought a pair of huge sunglasses and a scarf to tie back her hair like an old-time movie star.

Afterward they walked around, looking at the other stalls.

"Did you see that knife in the shape of a snake?" Cassel asked. "Isn't a knife-shaped knife scary enough? Why disguise it? I mean, how is a snake scarier than a knife?"

Lila grinned. "I thought the rhinestone eyes were a very frightening touch."

"Look at this!" He grabbed a beret off a hat rack and plopped it down on her head. "I bet you wore one of these all the time in Paris."

She laughed, trying to yank it away from him. They spun around and she was suddenly very aware of him, of how close she was to being in his arms.

"That's how I pictured you, anyway," he said, grinning, looking down at her, shockingly handsome with his sooty lashes and square jaw. He had the face of a pirate or a Romani prince.

"Oh, you pictured me, did you?" she asked. "A lot?"

His arms rested on her shoulders as he tilted the hat with gloved hands. He shook his head. "Barely ever." Then, with a yank, he pulled the beret down over her eyes.

She howled, pulling it off and chasing him through the aisles as shopkeepers yelled after them. It was only after they'd stopped in the parking lot, still laughing and gasping for breath, that she realized what it meant that her heart was still slamming against her rib cage, that she was still looking for an excuse to touch him, that her whole body seemed to thrum with joy at his happiness.

But she had no idea what to do about it.

It's not that Lila didn't like weddings. It's just that, by thirteen, she had gone to lots of them. Her father's business was full of bad young men who planned on dying young and rich, with a wife and children to weep over their graves. Criminals were, as a rule, disgustingly sentimental.

Her father had to preside over all the weddings, as necessary as the luck curse and the pair of rings. He had to give out envelopes of money to the brides, just like he gave envelopes to the widows at the funerals that would follow. And since her parents' divorce, Lila had become the woman on his arm.

She had acquired a closet full of dresses to go with her new role. Half of them were black.

That day, she was in light gray. As the bride and groom danced, she played gin rummy with her cousin Anton for silver candied almonds. He mostly won.

"Lila," her father said, interrupting a game. His black silk suit looked perfectly pressed, red diamond tie pin stabbing through his ivory tie, keeping even that in place. "Do me a favor." He'd been drinking steadily since they arrived, but he didn't slur his words.

"Sure," she said.

He reached into his inside breast pocket and took out an envelope. "Hand this to the new Mrs. Consenza. Tell her it's from the family." Ice cubes clinked as he swished them around his highball glass. He took a swallow of amber liquor.

"Okay," she said.

His gloved hand patted her shoulder. "There's my good girl."

She rolled her eyes as he walked off.

"Give me that," Anton said, reaching for the envelope. "I'll do it."

She pulled her hand off the table, shifting the envelope to her lap. "No."

"How about I play you for it? We finish out the hand." He was smiling, but it looked forced.

She stood up. "What's wrong with you?"

His eyes flashed with the promise of violence. "You're too young to represent the family. That's all. Look, in a couple of years, things will be different."

"You don't get to decide that," she said. It was a little thing, an errand. She wouldn't have thought twice about it if Anton hadn't been so weird. But now, stubbornly, she stood up and walked to the head table.

The couple was still spinning around the dance floor.

They looked happy, entirely focused on each other, eyes bright with joy.

Lila waited until the bride came back from dancing, flushed and giddy.

"From the family," Lila told her, putting the envelope into her hand.

The bride's hand trembled as she took it. She gave a quick, nervous grin. "Thank you. Tell your father thank you."

"We both wish you the best," Lila improvised.

The bride and groom thanked her again, sincerely. They seemed to accept without question that she spoke for her father.

And if she told them something else some other time—even gave them an order—she bet they'd accept that without question too.

She could see why Anton wanted people to believe that he spoke for her father. Why he wanted her to get used to letting him boss her around. Why she couldn't let him.

Instead, she walked over to the bar, grinning in Anton's direction as she did. There, she ordered the only drink she could think of, one from an old movie, *The Thin Man*, she'd seen the summer before—a martini.

The bartender gave it to her.

She took a sip and nearly spat it out. It smelled like rubbing alcohol and burnt the inside of her mouth.

Determined, she went to the bathroom and dumped it in the sink, refilling the glass with water. No one questioned her as she sipped it. The bartender even gave her a toothpick with extra olives.

Lila wondered how many other things she could make people give her.

If she wanted to be more than the girl on her father's arm, his good little girl, she'd better start making an impression.

When Lila was twelve, she flew to Paris with her father. They sat in first class, which meant big seats, comfortable headphones, and a little television with dozens and dozens of movies her mother would have said she was too young for. The flight attendants brought out dinner with three separate courses plus a dessert of cookies before they folded the seats into beds.

Lying in her seat-bed, though, she couldn't sleep. She was too excited to be on the plane. Too excited about Paris.

So she'd watched a movie—the one about cheerleaders who are murdered one by one by the nerdy boy whose feelings they hurt. Then, because she still wasn't tired, she'd watched another movie—the one where three teenage werewolves make a pact to lose their virginity on the same night. And after that, they were so close to landing that there was no reason not to watch the period drama about a lady in fancy dresses who went to masked balls but was really in love with a highwayman.

The exhaustion didn't hit her until they landed. She dragged herself through the airport, barely awake enough to pull her luggage in a straight line. She fell asleep in the cab and had to be shaken awake by her father.

"It's the middle of the day," he said as they shuffled up

the stairs to their flat in the Latin Quarter. "I told you to sleep on the plane."

Her only answer was a yawn.

The apartment was huge and beautiful with dark wood floors and soaring ceilings covered in beautiful moldings. Her father didn't seem to notice any of it. He took off his perfectly pressed coat and tossed it onto a slipcovered white sofa. "If you stay up today, you'll get over the jet lag. Otherwise, your body's going to have a hell of a time adjusting to the time zone shift."

"Okay," she said. "Can I just take a nap then?"

"I have to make some calls," he said. "I'll get you up in an hour."

He went off to do whatever business mob bosses can do in foreign countries over a phone, but when he tried to rouse her, she didn't budge. She slept through the whole day, getting up sometime after midnight.

She woke ravenously hungry and disoriented at the darkness outside the big picture window. Padding into the kitchen of the apartment, she opened the refrigerator, but it was empty.

"Lila?" her father said, coming into the dim room from his bedroom. He looked unusually rumpled, like maybe he'd been sleeping too.

"Sorry I totally zonked out," she said, yawning and stretching. Her fingers reached up for the ceiling and curled. She'd slept in her gloves.

He gave her a slight smile, a corner of his mouth lifting. "You hungry?"

"Starving," she said.

"Go get dressed, then," he told her. "Paris is beautiful at night."

She walked back to her room and opened her suitcase. Her mother had helped her pack it, explaining that she'd better bring only nice things because people in Europe dressed differently. They weren't slobs like Lila and her friends. They would never wear dresses layered over jeans or big clunky boots. "Don't embarrass your father," Mom had said, as if he cared what she wore. *Don't embarrass me* was what she meant.

Lila put on a heavy camel-colored dress. With her pale skin, it made her look completely washed out. She sighed and went into the bathroom to wash her face, brush her teeth, and comb her scraggly shoulder-length blond hair. Then she put on her knee-high black boots—the ones she'd snuck into the front zipped compartment of the suitcase before leaving—and tied the laces.

Clomping out to the sitting room, she found her father waiting, reading a French paper. He put it down absently and twirled the keys to the flat around his finger. Outside, Paris was lit up and beautiful. Everything seemed familiar—reminding her of some parts of New York—but the details were wrong. It reminded her, too, of the lady in the period drama, rattling past buildings like these in her carriage. Lila looked into the darkened windows of all the shops to see displays of dresses on headless mannequins, paintings, and costume jewelry.

Each store they passed was closed.

Finally, Lila saw a cafe with its lights still on. A couple was even sitting at one of the tables, sipping espresso.

"Dad," she said, pointing.

When they got there, the front door was locked and the closing time was listed as midnight. A clock on the door in the lobby showed that it was nearly one.

Lila's father knocked on the door. A waiter came over and opened it halfway, speaking with slightly bored irritation. Lila couldn't understand everything he said—just enough. The restaurant was closed.

Her father reached into his coat pocket and took out his wallet. As he did, she saw the strap under his arm and the butt of a silvery gun.

The waiter saw it too.

Her father grinned like a shark, said a few words she didn't know, and took five hundred euros from his billfold. The door opened wide.

The money was exchanged as they were escorted inside.

"And how old is the lady?" the waiter asked her in accented English as he pulled out her chair.

"Âgé de douze ans," she said.

Her father laughed and the waiter smiled, but stiffly, as though they were performing parts in a play.

"Very good," said the waiter, although she knew it wasn't. She wasn't even sure if it was right.

As he walked off, she opened the menu. Her father leaned across the table.

"Money will buy you anything in the world," he said in a low, satisfied voice. "It's all for sale. People's time. Their dignity. Whatever. Whenever. And most people's price is shockingly low."

That's the lesson he thought he taught Lila, but the lesson she learned was different. It wasn't money that opened that door. It was fear.

Lila's winter friends were different from her summer friends. Her winter friends were real friends—the ones who came to her apartment after school, who went shopping with her and celebrated her birthdays with candles and sleepovers.

Jennifer and Lorraine and Margot. They all went to the small exclusive academy for rich curse worker children— where they fought to be the prettiest, the smartest, and the cruelest. They stole boyfriends back and forth. They shared books and clothes and told one another secrets. They danced to music and lied to their parents so they could stay out late.

Once, Lila tried to explain about her summer friends, about Cassel and his brothers. Jennifer laughed and said they were made up. Lorraine wanted to meet them. Margot looked at the one picture Lila had—a grainy and faded one with a sprinkler in the background where Cassel had his arm thrown over her shoulders and his shirt off—and said that he looked stupid but hot.

"He's not a worker," Lila said, and they all laughed, because a boy who wasn't a worker couldn't be anything but a plaything to a girl like Lila.

Sometimes Cassel felt made-up. If Margot was angry

with her and Lorraine was busy or Jennifer was taking Margot's side, Lila would call him. He could make her laugh. And she didn't need to be afraid to tell him all the true things that she couldn't tell anyone else.

He was her summer friend. He wasn't part of her real life. Telling him didn't count.

Three weeks before Lila's fourteenth birthday, her mother took her shopping. They walked around the upper levels of Saks, where all the grown-up dresses were.

"Just look around," her mother told her. "Try on anything you like. It's your day!"

Lila didn't mention that she hated parties. She already knew that her mother only remembered facts she liked. Anything else she instantly forgot and would keep forgetting no matter how many times she was reminded.

Instead, Lila brushed her gloved fingers over the rack of gowns until she came to one that looked like something heroines wore at the end of movies. It was sacrificial and beautiful.

"Not white," her mother said. "You're not a little girl anymore and this isn't your wedding."

Lila moved her fingers to the straps of a red dress and raised her eyebrows.

Her mother laughed. "Your father would kill me, but go ahead, try it on."

They pulled more—gold dresses and pink dresses, black dresses and dresses as silver as the moon.

"There's a language of clothing," Lila's mother said as

Lila came out of the dressing room and twirled around in midnight blue velvet. "Like the language of flowers . . . or jewelry. For instance, that makes you look older, but not in a good way. You're saying 'I'm stuffy before my time.'"

Lila ran her gloved hand down the bodice. She wondered what it would be like to touch the little beads glittering there like stars, but she knew that if she took off her glove it would upset the sales lady.

She made a face at her mother and went back into the stall to put on the red dress with the deep vee neck. It clung to her waist, to her breasts—already grown too big for the training bra she'd been wearing, and what a relief to have taken it off—and to the newly formed curve of her hip. She looked like a starlet.

"Jailbait prostitute," her mother said, and Lila blushed hotly.

"I like it," she said, narrowing her eyes.

"I just bet you do," her mother said, waving her back into the dressing room. "Now tell me what you want your party dress to say, because it won't be that."

Since the divorce, her mother and father had fought over Lila by buying her things—the trip to Paris with her father, the party, this dress. And they both wanted not just her love, but her promise of loyalty.

She wanted the people at the party to see her as her father's heir. Instead, she was afraid they'd see her as his spoiled daughter. She didn't know how a dress could change that, when the whole party was one big indulgence she never asked for and still had to act gleeful about. And even if a dress could make people see her that way, she couldn't tell her mother what she wanted, when her mother would only see it as a betrayal.

"A force to be reckoned with," Lila said finally, hoping that was vague enough. "That's what I'd like."

Her mother laughed. "Well, it's accurate!"

She sounded so condescending that Lila ground her teeth. She went back to the rack of garments and picked one at random. Then she stood in front of the mirror, looking at her hair: shorter and nearly white after her mother insisted the stylist bleach it back from pink. Everything about her was so pale that she felt like a ghost.

While she slipped on the silver dress and smoothed the shining paillettes of it over her hips, she imagined turning fourteen. She hoped that it would transform her somehow, change her in some way that would give her the kind of knowledge older girls at her school seemed to have. She hoped it would make her brave. There was a boy—a boy she had no idea what to do about.

The silver looked darker on her—more iron than the bright tinsel she'd initially thought it was—and the paillettes looked almost like scales. The color made her blue and green eyes stand out against her skin like jewels.

"This is the one I want," Lila said, stepping out of the dressing room.

Her mother looked at her and sighed. "It's a little short," she said. "And shiny. Shiny can be vulgar. Maybe you should try on the light pink. Pink is youthful and very elegant when it's on the beige side."

"No," Lila said. "This is perfect."

Lila loved the dress. It said just what she wanted to say. It was the precise color of her father's favorite gun.

Barron slung his arm over her shoulders casually as they walked down the concrete steps.

Lila stopped to take her shoes off before she stepped onto the wet sand. He had to let go of her, and she spun away from him, inhaling deeply. The crash of the waves sent up a faint salt spray that dusted her skin.

"You look really nice tonight," he said, coming close again. His gloved hand rested at the curve of her back, the swell of her hip.

She froze for a second, then forced herself to relax. Being nervous was silly.

"Thanks," she said. "You do too."

She'd known Barron for years, after all. He'd spent his summers in the same little town that she did. She'd even had a hopeless crush on his younger brother, Cassel, but Cassel never asked her out, not even after she'd paraded around in front of him in nothing but a big baggy shirt and underwear, with glittery, smoky eye makeup.

So there she was with Barron, who had asked her and who had his license. Who was charming. Who was clearly, technically, the better boyfriend. The one her friends would be jealous about.

And they'd eaten pizza and joked around on the first part of the date, which was fun. And now they were taking a romantic walk on the beach. The moon was hidden behind clouds, but there was enough light to make the breaking waves shimmer as they crashed on the shore.

"You want to sit on the jetty?" he asked her.

This was the exact kind of thing people were supposed to do on dates.

"Okay," she said and followed him onto the rocks. As she walked out, waves broke higher and higher, in plumes of foam. The surf raged all around them, trickling out through flooded tide pools.

She turned to say something when he took her chin and kissed her. His lips were soft and for a moment, everything seemed perfect. She wound her arms around his neck. But then he was drawing her down to the rock, his hands running over the sides of her legs. And she felt thrilled and scared all at the same time.

It happened so fast. His tongue was inside her mouth and their bodies were pressed together, his legs between hers. Her head rocked back against cold stone.

"Uh," she said, pulling away slightly.

He looked at her in bafflement and she felt the shame of not knowing what she was supposed to do, of being so much younger than him, crash over her like one of the waves.

"What's wrong?" he asked.

"Nothing," she said, scrambling to sit up. She tried to think of something else to say, something casual and sophisticated.

He looked at her for a long moment, then sighed. "We should go back." Standing, he offered her his hand, helping her to her feet.

"We don't have to stop," she said uncertainly.

He shook his head. "It's getting late anyway."

Lila was quiet on the way to the car and then on the drive home. He talked the whole way, cheerily, but she couldn't focus on what he was saying.

She was wondering if this was what love felt like. She was wondering if he would ask her out again and what they would do on that date. She hoped he would ask her, but she was already dreading it.

Once, Lila Zacharov was in love with a boy with hair as black as spilled ink and eyes as dark as coffee. She would trace his name on her skin, over and over, write it in the condensation of her breath on panes of glass, scrawl it on the bottoms of her feet with the tip of her nail, like she was casting a spell.

He would come to her mother's house, and they would lie on the wooden floor of her room, making up games. Once, Lila took out her old book of fairy tales to show him a picture of a dragon that she wanted to draw on his arm like a tattoo.

"Wouldn't it be great if bears and foxes could really talk?" he said, half kidding, pushing a lock of hair back from his eyes.

"I could give you a dream where they did," she said.

He looked away from her quickly, like he didn't want her to see his face. His family was full of workers, but he wasn't one.

"Thanks," he said. "But no thanks."

There was a silence between them, a silence that hadn't been there when they were younger. She wondered if he was afraid. She wondered if he was jealous that she had magic and he didn't. She wondered if he wanted to kiss her.

"If you had a million dollars, what would you do with it?" he asked her.

She leaned back. "I don't know. Maybe get a car. A really fast red one."

He laughed. "You couldn't drive it."

"I could buy a fake ID too! I'd have a bajillion dollars. I could bribe everyone."

He shrugged his shoulders, but he was still grinning. There was something about the curve of his mouth, something lurking behind his eyes that made her want to touch him, made her want to strip off her glove and feel the warmth of his skin against hers.

"I'd get out of here," he said. "Go someplace where no one knew me. Start over. Go to Paris like you did or go to—I don't know—Prague. Somewhere." He looked toward the window, like he could already see himself gone.

"Oh," she said, because it hurt that he was thinking about that when she was thinking about him. She narrowed her eyes. "What's stopping you?"

The boy looked down at the book of fairy tales. "Nothing," he said.

Lila wanted to be the one to stop him.

He reached between them and tucked a strand of her long blond hair behind her ear with one gloved finger. The shiver that started at the base of her spine felt like a warning.

When Lila Zacharov was eight, she dressed up in one of her mother's long beaded dresses and clasped a diamond necklace around her forehead, like it was a crown. Then she stood in front of the huge gilt mirror in her parents' bedroom to look at herself. Her hair was a tangle of pale curls, and the dress was so long that it trailed behind her like a train, but if she squinted, she could almost see someone else—a mysterious shadow self—reflected back at her.

"I'm a princess," she told her grandmother, whom she called Babchi. Babchi had lived in the apartment with Lila and Father and Mother ever since Grandpa died. Each night Babchi sat at the end of Lila's bed, telling her stories about firebirds and white bears, while Mother went out to plays or fancy dinners and Father did business.

"Yes," said Babchi, coming to stand behind Lila. "My princess. The princess of a land of ice and snow. With icicles as sharp as knives."

"I'm a fairy," Lila said, spinning in circles until she tripped on the edge of her mother's dress and fell.

"Yes," said Babchi. "My fairy. You aren't like other girls. You will laugh when others weep. Your heart will be a riddle."

"Someday, I will fall in love with a boy," Lila said, pursing her lips. "And he will be a prince."

"If you fall in love, little one, there is a cure for that," Babchi told her. "You—and you must do this yourself—you cut out his heart and eat it. Then you won't love him anymore."

Lila made a face and stuck out her tongue. Babchi laughed.

"I won't want to be cured," Lila insisted. It was her story and she wanted Babchi to understand, to get it right. The fairy princess met a prince and then they were happy. That's how the story went. Lila had a book to prove it—a book so covered in glitter that flecks of it came off on her hands when she read about their wedding. Her mother had bought it for Lila's birthday.

"That is very true and that is exactly what makes it so hard," Babchi said, nodding. "If you wanted to, it would be easy. But you'll do it anyway. You're my princess, and when the time comes, you'll know what you have to do."

Lila nodded too, because Babchi had that tone in her voice that said that she would be sad if Lila didn't agree, and if Babchi was sad, she might not want to play anymore. She might go in the other room and watch television.

Lila had lots of other costumes to try on. She wanted Babchi to stay and see them all.

When Lila was nine, she chopped off all of her hair with nail scissors and let it stick up in tufts as if it were wild grass in a meadow.

"It isn't your fault we're getting a divorce," her mother told her.

The day after, Lila and her mother drove down to Carney, even though it wasn't summer yet. Lila sat at the kitchen table of her grandmother's house, drawing black swirls on her hand with a Sharpie. The whorls went up her arm, curling in on themselves.

"Your father is very selfish," her mother said, drinking

her third cup of coffee. After each sip, she set the cup back down on the saucer with a *clink*. "Always out somewhere with someone. And the women! He never understood what it takes to be married—no less to have a daughter."

"Mmmmm-hmmm," Lila said. She was used to making encouraging noises. If she didn't, her mother would get upset.

"He expects me to be like his mother was—never complaining, working my fingers to the bone in the kitchen, never asking any questions. But that's just what he saw of his mother—what she showed him! How does he know what happened behind closed doors? Or how miserable she was—just look at the lines on her face! I used to walk the runways of Milan! I order takeout!"

The back door opened and Lila's grandmother walked in with a grocery bag in each arm. She set them down on the counter. "I could hear you all the way to the driveway, Irina. Tell me your troubles; leave her out of it. What's the best cure for heartbreak?"

"His heart," Lila said distractedly. She got to a tricky part by her elbow and wasn't sure if she could bend her arm quite as far as she needed to draw the snaking circles just right.

Her mother gasped. "What did you say?"

Lila's grandmother smiled and ruffled Lila's shorn head with a gloved hand. "I was thinking of a big chocolate cake with chocolate icing and that's just what I am going to bake."

"Do you like my tattoos, Babchi?" Lila asked, holding out her arm.

"No she does not," her mother said, voice rising with

irritation. "And you are going to have to scrub yourself raw to get them off. With that hair—you just look ridiculous. Did you draw on your gloves, too? Give me those!"

Lila took off her gloves and set them down in a crumpled pile. Her tattoos didn't look right anymore. They stopped abruptly at her wrist.

"She looks like a child," Lila's grandmother said. "Lila, why don't you go play and leave us old folks to talk?"

Lila obediently set down the black pen and went outside. It was only when she got there that she realized she didn't have her gloves on—they were back on the kitchen table. But she didn't want to go inside again, and the air was cool on the skin of her palms.

She walked around town, kicking a squashed tin can and catching a toad near the stump of a tree. It had golden eyes and smelled like rich, wet earth, and she could hardly believe her luck when her fingers closed around it like the bars of a cage. She liked the way it wriggled in her hand.

She walked over to Mr. Singer's house. The screen door was open, but she didn't hear anyone inside. She tapped at the metal with her foot.

"Cassel?" she called. "I caught something." Even though she and Cassel didn't see each other during the rest of the year, every summer they were instantly best friends again. But the beginning was always like an indrawn breath, with both of them not sure when they were allowed to let it out.

No one answered. She waited a few more minutes and then walked to the side yard. Mr. Singer—Cassel's grandfather—was raking in the back. He looked older than she remembered, his hair grayer. Lila tried to wave, but her hands were full with the toad.

He walked over. "Lila Zacharov? I almost didn't recognize you."

"Yeah," she said, braced for him to tell her how bad it looked. "My hair's different."

"The boys aren't here yet—won't be down for a couple weeks."

"Oh," she said, pain stinging the backs of her eyes. She remembered that it wasn't summer, but she forgot Cassel wasn't just always there, waiting for her.

Mr. Singer pointed to her hands. "What's that you've got?"

She bent to let go of the toad, smiling with sudden pride. "I never caught one before by myself."

Mr. Singer grinned. "He's a real handsome fellow."

For a moment, the toad stayed very still in the grass, then exploded into motion, hopping toward the hedges in three flashes of brown and green.

Mr. Singer laughed. "Fast, too. When the boys come down, they'll be real impressed. I'll tell 'em."

"Yeah?" she asked hopefully.

"No doubt." He gave her a considering look. "I like what you've done. Short hair's good for the summer. Keeps you cool. Maybe you want to get some clippers and even it out, though."

She touched the tufts of it with her bare fingers. "Do you have some?"

"Sure." He took her inside the house and showed her

where they were and how they worked. Then he made her a cup of tea, and they watched *Ban of the Banned* on the television until her mother came looking for her.

"Is my daughter here?" Lila's mother asked from the doorway while Lila pretended to be asleep on the couch.

"Sure is," Mr. Singer said.

"I'm so sorry," her mother said. Her voice was a little unsteady, like she was afraid. Lila cracked open her eyes.

Mr. Singer was shrugging. "No trouble. Kids are always in and out in the summer."

Lila got up, and she and her mother walked home together in the early dark. For a long time, they didn't speak. Lila was braced for shouting.

"You can't go over there anymore," Lila's mother said softly, instead, as they got to the edge of their lawn. She didn't comment on Lila's hair or the fact that she was going around gloveless.

"Why not?" Lila asked. "I always play over there."

"That man works for your father," her mother said. "None of them are good people and they're beneath you besides."

"Cassel's my friend."

"He's not even a worker. He's nothing. Listen to me— you stay away from Mr. Singer and those Sharpe boys. Things are different now. I don't want you winding up like your father."

When Lila got back to her grandmother's, she took the pen into her bedroom and finished drawing the swirls, covering her fingers in black ink. In the mirror of her room, she could see her hair, military-short and gold with reflected light from her desk lamp.

Things were different now.

She was different.

She was alone.

After what felt like hours of sitting in silence, someone finally took the hood from over Lila's head. Cool air started drying the sweat on her brow. She swept back her bangs with one bare hand and tried very hard not to tremble. Tried to seem like the kind of girl who was never afraid.

Three men were standing in front of her—three men she'd known for a long time. Fat Jimmy, Big Louie, Nat the Knife. They were like uncles to her. Wicked uncles who had tutored her in wickedness.

The room was dark, but the shadows seemed to cling to the dusty boards of the wall. The only light in the room came from a candle on a table. Next to it was a cloth, a knife, and a fifth of cheap vodka. She could hear traffic, but distantly. She would bet the building she was in was abandoned. It would be an excellent place to leave a body. She just hoped that body wasn't going to be hers.

"This is my initiation, right?" she asked.

Nat grinned, but none of them answered.

"Where are my gloves?" she asked.

"Take a shot," Fat Jimmy said. "And toast to your old life. Say good-bye."

The scent of old blood rose up, maybe from the floorboards, maybe from the cloth or the knife. Sometimes, when Lila was a little girl, her father would come home smelling like this. She wondered what it would be like to smell the scent on her own skin.

She went to the table, found a small glass hidden behind the wadded-up cloth, and poured vodka in it. Despite feeling nauseous and a little dizzy, she downed the drink. It seared her throat.

Fat Jimmy said something else, something about honor or respect or silence, but Lila couldn't quite pay attention. She wasn't done saying good-bye.

Once upon a time there was a girl with golden hair and no fear. She burned her hands on stoves because she wanted to touch the pretty red coils, she stuck her fingers in sockets and ran with knives. She told her cousins that when she grew up, she would be the boss of them all, and she meant it. There was a girl whose heart was as hard as diamonds.

Until someone locked her in a cage and hid the key.

That was the story Lila told herself, the one that might not have been true, but that she repeated over and over anyway. That was the way she kept herself eating and drinking and pushing at the bars, looking for a way out. That was the fairy tale that sent her off to sleep each night and woke her every morning.

Once upon a time there was a girl with golden hair and no fear. Someone locked her in a cage and hid the key. But the girl would have her revenge.

"There are dog people and cat people."

That's what Anton, Lila's cousin, told her one afternoon while they sat near the lake in Carney. She was wearing her first ever bikini—a white one that her mother told her wasn't supposed to get wet. Annoyed, she was sitting on the hot planks of the dock and dipping her feet in the water while the boys swam.

Philip, Anton's best friend, pulled a cooler out of his car, dumping it on the bank. He was just turning twenty, and the scars on his neck showed his loyalty to her father. A shallow cut, packed with ash so that it darkened, marking him as dead to his old life and born anew as part of the Zacharov family. Sometimes when she looked at his neck, she felt guilty. Other times she felt nothing at all.

"You want a sandwich or something?" Philip asked her. "My grandfather packed up some stuff. There's peanut butter. And some soda."

Anton grabbed for a beer.

"Can I have a soda?" Lila asked. When he gave it to her, she pressed it against her forehead and neck, letting its coolness push back some of the muggy heat.

"Guys like you," Anton told Philip. "Dog people. Dependable. Friendly."

"Will bite the hand that feeds me," said Philip.

She looked out at the lake where his youngest brother, Cassel, floated in the middle of the lake, his skin bronzed by the sun. Anton and Lila both had the kind of skin that never tanned. It just turned lobster red and faded back to pale. Already, Anton's shoulders had gone pink.

Cassel waved to her. His black hair was a messy halo of floating curls. His eyes were as dark as the water.

"You coming in?" he called.

She wanted to explain about her swimsuit, although she wasn't sure why her mother bought her a suit she couldn't actually swim in. But if she said that, she was afraid he'd laugh at her. She shook her head instead.

"Which one am I?" she asked, turning back to her cousin.

"Oh come on," he said. "You know you're a cat person. Fickle. Finicky. Don't listen to anyone." He laughed.

"Lazy."

Lila kicked the surface of the lake, sending up a spray. "So what are you?"

"We're family," he said. "Two of a kind."

"But cats hate water," she said and jumped in.

It was a cold shock after the oppressive heat, but it was the feeling of recklessness that made her giddy. She ribboned through the lake, swimming toward Cassel.

"Um," he said as she bobbed beside him. He had a very strange expression on his face. She couldn't be sure, but he seemed to be blushing.

"Anton says there's cat people and dog people," she said. "What do you think?"

"Right now, I think I'm more of a rat," he said, glancing down then back up to her eyes. He looked like he was about to start laughing, but there was a joke he was just waiting for her to get, so she could laugh too.

She followed his gaze and finally figured out why her

mother told her not to get the suit wet. The white fabric had gone translucent.

A hot flush crept up her neck.

"Get me your T-shirt," she said. "Go."

"This is me not saying all the things I could say." His eyes danced with mirth. "This is me being your knight in shining armor."

She looked toward the bank, where Anton was watching her, still drinking his beer. She kept treading water.

Being a dream worker sounded silly. It sounded like crystals and clouds and rainbows. Only babies were afraid of nightmares, after all.

Lila remembered one of her father's friends, Fat Jimmy, laughing when her father told him what her talent was.

"A cute kinda curse for a kinda cute gal," he said, chuckling.

She took off her glove and poked him in the arm. That night he had the dream she'd seen wandering around in her father's head—one of being shot over and over and over again by each one of his friends. The next time she saw Fat Jimmy, he couldn't quite meet her eyes.

Cursing people was something that you shouldn't do. It was illegal, for one thing, but since she was a member of the Zacharov family, no one she knew thought breaking the law was a big deal. It was rude though, as her mother reminded her.

But it was also easy. If she could touch someone without them noticing, then she could crawl around in their dreams, learn their fears and their desires. She could give them dreams suggesting things. She could even, she discovered, make people move while they were asleep. Once, she convinced her mother to go to the kitchen and make a cup of cocoa without ever waking.

The bad thing was that it ate away at her sleep. No matter if she gave people nightmares or watched their dreams like television or made them dance around the living room with their eyes closed, the price was insomnia.

She would lie awake for days at a time, until she finally cursed herself to resting. Then, when she woke, she had to pay for that, too.

Once, she made a boy come out of his house and kiss her under the streetlight. It was her first kiss. She thinks it was probably his, too.

She never told him and she never, ever will.

HOLLY BLACK is the author of bestselling contemporary fantasy books for kids and teens. Some of her titles include The Spiderwick Chronicles (with Tony DiTerlizzi), the Modern Faerie Tales series, the Curse Workers series, *Doll Bones*, *The Coldest Girl in Coldtown*, *The Darkest Part of the Forest*, the Magisterium series (with Cassandra Clare), and the Folk of the Air series. She has been a finalist for the Mythopoeic Award, a finalist for an Eisner Award, and the recipient of both an Andre Norton Award and a Newbery Honor. She lives in New England with her husband and son in a house with a secret door. Visit her at BlackHolly.com.